WASHOE COUNTY LIBRARY

3 1235 00586 7366

P9-DVY-243

SPARKS BRANCH
WASHOE COUNTY LIBRARY

NOV 2 6 1990

Elizabeth Gage

By the same author
A Glimpse of Stocking

3 1235 00586 7366 SP

WASHOE COUNTY LIBRARY
RENO, NEVADA

PANDORA'S BOX

F-6a
1990

SIMON AND SCHUSTER
New York London Toronto Sydney Tokyo Singapore

SIMON AND SCHUSTER
Simon & Schuster Building
Rockefeller Center
1230 Avenue of the Americas
New York, New York 10020

This book is a work of fiction. Names, characters, places
and incidents are either the product of the author's
imagination or are used fictitiously. Any resemblance to
actual events or locales or person, living or dead, is
entirely coincidental.

Copyright © 1990 by Gage Productions Ltd.

All rights reserved
including the right of reproduction
in whole or in part in any form.

SIMON AND SCHUSTER and colophon are registered trademarks
of Simon & Schuster Inc.

Designed by Levavi & Levavi/Carla Weise
Manufactured in the United States of America

1   3   5   7   9   10   8   6   4   2

ISBN 0-671-70304-8

ACKNOWLEDGMENTS

I would like to extend my sincere thanks to the following for their cooperation and advice in the preparation of this novel:

The U.S. Capitol Historical Society
The Historical Society of Washington, D.C.
International Association of Clothing Designers
Coty
The New York Historical Society
The Brooklyn/Long Island Historical Society
Photographic Society of America
Professional Photographers of America
CW3 Glen A. Bender, U.S. Army (Ret.)
Master Sgt. Henry Natad, U.S. Army (Ret.)
Ernst H. Huneck, M.D.

Special thanks also to Ms. Tina Gerrard and Mr. Jon Kirsh for their indispensable help in my research on the early years of network television, the American fashion industry, and the international political situation between 1950 and 1964. And my heartfelt appreciation to those, both actors and witnesses, who have generously shared their reminiscences about this era without wishing to be named here.

Though the turbulent years of the Kennedy and Eisenhower administrations are evoked as a background for the events of this novel, I would like to caution the reader that this background is used fictionally, and is not intended as an exposé. Powers such as those wielded by certain characters in this story are not attainable, or should not be, in a free society.

Finally I wish to thank Mr. Michael Korda, Ms. Trish Lande, and Mr. Bill Grose, my editors at Simon and Schuster/Pocket Books, for their help and advice; and Mr. Jay Garon for his patience, support, and friendship, at every stage of my work.

Elizabeth Gage

To Maile and the B's—
Where home is

CONTENTS

Pandora was the first woman on earth. Zeus was angry because Prometheus had stolen fire from the gods to give to men. He ordered Vulcan to create a being out of earth and water. It would be an evil creature that all men would desire. Vulcan made a woman.

Aphrodite gave her beauty. Athena gave her mastery of the arts. The Graces gave her attractive garments, and Hermes gave her flattery and cunning. Zeus named her Pandora.

Pandora had brought with her a box that the gods had warned her never to open. But her curiosity was too strong, and at last she raised the lid. All the sins and evils, cares and troubles in the world sprang out of the box.

Pandora shut the lid as quickly as she could, but everything escaped except one thing. That thing was Hope, which alone remained to console mankind.

PANDORA'S BOX

PROLOGUE

1964

HISTORY SELDOM BOTHERS to praise the dubious heroes who were the first to discover its great calamities.

Later that week, when it was all over, and when nearly everyone inside and outside Washington could feel the fate of the nation veering in a direction that could only be evil, a handful of newspapers would take the trouble to report that it had been Dan Aguirre, alert despite the monumental confusion surrounding Haydon Lancaster, who had thought of Bess and gone in search of her.

And found her.

Understandably, the law enforcement agencies were in chaos that night. Dozens of hand-picked agents had been sent out in force to protect all the candidates, Republican, Democrat, and third-party, from harm, in the wake of what had happened.

Of course, no one believed it was really necessary, for the danger was past. The show of proud police power was in the nature of a memorial rather than a true act of protection. The worst had happened already, and could not be undone.

But Dan Aguirre, wandering the unfamiliar FBI headquarters on Pennsylvania Avenue, and idly comparing its spic-and-span orderliness with the musty squalor of his detective squad room back in New York, had begun wondering about Lancaster's wife, and had called the agent in charge of the Georgetown house to check on her.

"She's asleep," he was told. "Under sedation since eleven-thirty. They gave her Seconal. She's out like a light."

Dan looked at his watch. It was two-thirty in the morning. He thought for a moment.

"When was the last time you saw her?" he asked.

"One of our people is posted outside her door. I don't know how long it's been now. Probably an hour, half-hour. They said not to disturb her. Christ, after what she saw tonight. . ."

"Would you mind looking in for me?" Aguirre asked.

There was a silence. Aguirre could feel the resentment of the FBI at being asked a favor by an outsider. The Bureau could not bear to be told its job by anyone, least of all a New York cop.

"Look, Officer—what did you say your name was?"

"Aguirre, Dan Aguirre."

"Look, Dan. I follow my orders. We were told to sedate her, lock her up, and sit outside the door. Now, if you want to change those orders . . ."

"All right," Dan interrupted curtly. "Jim Cipriani is around here somewhere. Shall I have him ask you himself, or will you do me this courtesy?"

The agent stopped short at the name of his superior.

"No, that's okay. Hang on a second and I'll check."

Aguirre heard the phone being placed unceremoniously on the table in the Georgetown house, a house he himself had never seen. He could only imagine the life the Lancasters had led there over the past several years, years that had brought Lancaster from a junior senator's seat to the threshold of the White House.

Who could have imagined that it was all leading to tonight? Aguirre shook his head. There was too much mystery in the simplest human story, too much enigma. One could only glimpse a narrow corridor of people's lives, seen as through a keyhole. The rest remained in shadow.

Yet, to a trained eye, the little that one could see bristled with meanings too dark to be ignored. The events of this evening, part of history now, had occurred because no trained eye—his own included—had bothered to look in the right direction.

But what was past was past. Dan Aguirre had the present to think about now. He had to be sure that Bess Lancaster was safely sequestered in her house on this night. For if she was not, if she was free, then everything was changed. The story that was over in the eyes of the already grief-stricken nation might not be finished yet.

A nameless tension built inside Aguirre as the pause lengthened at the other end of the line.

Then, at last, the phone was picked up. A commotion was audible in the background, highlighted by urgent voices calling back and forth.

"Jesus," the agent said into the phone. "I don't understand it. She must have faked being asleep. She was so out of it . . . . She looked like a wounded deer."

"She got away, then?" Aguirre asked.

"Sometime in the last hour. The window is closed. That's why none of our people on the outside got suspicious. Christ, I don't understand it."

"All right," Aguirre said, suppressing the curse on his lips. "Thank you."

He hung up and rushed into the crowded room next door. Cipriani, an overweight agent whose quick humor and rumpled look differentiated him from the stereotyped G-men he commanded, turned red when he heard the news.

"Get some people out to every one of the Lancaster residences right away," he told his assistant. "And send somebody back to Lancaster's offices, and to all the campaign headquarters. God damn it . . ."

The office, a scene of hushed preoccupation a moment ago as the agents waited out the long night, burst into movement. Phones were being picked up, doors slamming as operatives hurried to carry out their orders.

Dan Aguirre leaned against Cipriani's desk, oblivious to the flurry around him.

I should have known.

He had never met Elizabeth Lancaster. But he knew enough about her to realize that this display of desperate guile was to be expected of her. She would not take the destruction of her world lying down, sedated by indifferent government agents in her own bedroom.

She would take action.

And Dan Aguirre, alone among the men here tonight, had some idea of what that action might be.

He looked at Cipriani, a good man but limited by the organization for which he worked. The FBI did a certain type of job very well. But the challenge facing them now was far outside their accustomed alleys. For they had never really known Haydon Lancaster, Senator and candidate for President of the United States. And, obviously, they did not know his wife.

But Dan Aguirre did.

What had come to find Lancaster tonight, and what was coiled about his wife now as she hurried toward her unseen destination, was the past. For a long time, without realizing it, Dan Aguirre had held the key to that past. But he had understood its significance only a few hours ago.

Well, better late than never. He knew now where Bess was going.

He picked up the phone and dialed long distance.

"Aguirre here," he said when the phone was answered. "Listen, I have to come home right away. I'll need a quick hop to New York."

He looked at his watch. He wondered how much time he had. If she had left in the last hour, surely he must arrive ahead of her. After all, she had to move covertly, while he only had to jump on a police plane or chopper.

Flipping a mental coin, he decided not to tell New York any more of the story. They probably would not believe it anyway.

As he hurried out of the headquarters, he tried to suppress the sinking feeling inside him. It seemed as though fate were working out its unfinished business tonight. Perhaps no human mind could have foreseen what had happened. Perhaps no human hand could stay what was still to come.

The seeds had been sown so long ago. . . . Now that the terrible fruits were ripe, they would take what human lives they wished, and perhaps—perhaps—spare others.

Laura's?

That was the question.

So Dan Aguirre left the floundering FBI behind him, and set off alone into the night to do what he could for Laura.

Even if it was too late.

. . .

The office was illuminated by only the old green-shaded Federal lamp on the desk top. Outside the windows the cityscape of Albany was visible, a nondescript backdrop for the seat of government of a great state.

The Senator was seated in his large desk chair, in his shirtsleeves and suspenders. His jacket hung on the coatrack that had once stood in his office in Washington. A souvenir of the First Senate Chamber, which had been used until 1859, it had, according to legend, supported the hats of Webster and Clay, and of the framers of the Louisiana Purchase.

The sight of it filled him with regret. Like so many of his other things, it was a relic of a time when his surroundings matched his great power. A power that had been taken away by Haydon Lancaster.

The building was silent. No one was working tonight. The attention of both lawmakers and public was fixed for the moment on the campaign that would determine the immediate future of the nation. Laws, after all, could be made and unmade any old time. The election of a president was a different matter.

He glanced down at the naked girl kneeling on the carpet before him. She was looking at him through upturned eyes, curious and knowing. Her hands flirted lightly across his knees. Her hair flowed down her back, which was very slim. He could see the pert globes of her buttocks as a creamy outline behind her head.

Her perfume pervaded the smoke-dulled air of the office. The clothes she had arrived in—a clinging silk dress, sheer stockings, a tiny black bra and panties—were strewn on the floor where they had fallen during the languid strip she had performed moments ago. She had worn spike heels, no doubt in order to be ready for anything, but had taken them off when she realized they were irrelevant to what he wanted.

She was so young! Underneath the ageless mask of her vocation she must be no more than twenty-two or twenty-three. At that age his daughter had been a struggling college student, still addicted to chocolate, worried about her complexion, and touchingly uncertain as to whether her history major had been the right decision after all. A mere girl . . .

But the creature on her knees before him was separated from human years by a gulf even deeper than the promise of money on which she thrived. That was why her eyes, behind their look of coy domination, were so empty.

She lived up to the advance billing, he had to admit. By all accounts she was the best in the business. From the moment she had arrived, a tall, sensual presence almost too beautiful to be believed, she had seen how dark his mood was, and had modulated her seduction accordingly.

Her posture, standing or sitting, was suggestive. Every movement of her hands seemed somehow lewd, as she touched at the old Senate quill pen on the desk top, brushed a finger along the back of the couch, brought her glass of sherry to her lips. When she picked up the gavel he had been given by the Majority Leader in Washington a decade ago —one of the handful still surviving from Calhoun's own collection—it seemed for all the world an instrument of perversion.

She understood that he had been an important man once. Her sidelong look was on him every second, even when she studied the pictures of him with Eisenhower, Roosevelt, Truman, and others on the wall behind the desk. And all her movements were like sketches of the more triumphant dance she would do when she knew what his private needs were.

But he wasn't telling. Perhaps it was part of his cautious politician's nature. Or perhaps in the wake of the catastrophe of recent days he simply did not know what he wanted. Indeed, he was not sure why he had invited her. Sex seemed the last thing he could focus on tonight.

But, in a way, he had wanted to be close to someone. He had never felt so alone.

So she was here.

She had begun to talk dirty almost before she got comfortable on the couch. A girl like her had no time to lose.

"Why do you look at me that way?" she had asked, giving him a long, slow stare that must have been one of the strongest weapons in her arsenal. "I think you have a little bit of a dirty mind. I can feel it all the way from here, so don't try to deny it."

She had put down her drink and stood up before him, her long body swaying subtly, hands on hips.

"Which part of a girl do you like best?" she asked, unzipping the dress so that it slipped gently to the floor, revealing creamy limbs touched by the black bra and panties like dark flowers.

"What about here?" She unhooked the bra and ran her finger around a firm, shapely breast. Her eyes bored into him with sharp inquiry.

"Or do you like it down here?" Slim hands were reaching beneath the elastic of the panties to pull them down to her knees. "Do you like to play with girls down here?"

Then a smooth pirouette to show him her backside, the pretty buttocks poised ripe and sensual before him.

"Or is it this part you like best?" she murmured, eyes watchful over her shoulder. "Do you like it where you're not supposed to? Shame on you . . ."

She came forward, dropped to her knees before him, and smiled. "My, my," she purred as she unzipped his fly. "You're a mighty big fellow, aren't you?"

She began to play with him. The mastery of her lips and fingers astonished him. Being caressed by her was like being examined by a competent nurse whose movements were automatic, quick and fluid so as to get the job done in the smallest possible amount of time.

It felt good. The almost medicinal impersonality of her performance found a perverse echo in his own emptiness. Her trade was the oldest and coldest in the world. This common bond with himself, perhaps more than her brute skill, was bringing orgasm up from his loins quicker than he had expected.

Sensing the last wave, she murmured encouragement and worked faster at him.

At that instant the phone rang.

"Damn."

It was too late. The final spasm had come, but the shock of the sudden noise had ruined his pleasure. He cursed himself for not having unplugged the phone. He had not expected it to ring tonight. Now he would have to answer it.

"What is it?" he said irritably into the receiver, looking down at the girl.

He listened for a moment, through the halting breaths of his wasted orgasm.

Then all at once he reddened.

"Are you sure of this?" he asked. "When did it happen?"

The girl was looking up at him now with a rather unpleasant expression of perplexity and impatience. He listened some more, breathed in to ask a question, but remained silent. He could not believe what he was hearing.

"Lancaster," he sighed at last. "Jesus Christ."

Then he listened to a question from the caller.

"No," he said firmly. "Nothing now. No comment until tomorrow morning at the earliest. For Christ's sake . . . All right. Keep me informed at this number, unless you hear otherwise from me."

He hung up the phone. For a moment he seemed lost in thought, his eyes on the night sky outside the window.

Then he glanced down at the girl. She looked at once resigned and reproachful. She knew her performance was forgotten now. Business had eclipsed pleasure.

"Put your clothes on," Amory Bose said. "Go now." The command in his voice was not without its note of sympathy. She had done her best, after all.

He found hundred-dollar bills in his wallet and threw three on the desk as she pulled her underthings on. He did not see her pick up the money before she put on her coat to leave.

He had forgotten her existence. The news he had heard obliterated everything but itself.

Lancaster, he thought savagely. *You son of a bitch.*

Even in this absurd, final way, Lancaster had managed to frustrate him. For now he would be a hero forever. He would own the public's heart for good. That, more than any other victory, was what Bose had wished to avoid.

Lancaster out of the picture—the very dénouement Bose had fought for all this time—but as a winner. An eternal victor in the eyes of the world.

Amory Bose shook his head, pondering an irony too fine for even his astute political mind to measure. He was accustomed to the vicissitudes of day-to-day political reality, but what had happened tonight belonged more to the mysteries of fate than to mere human doings.

So this is how history is made, Amory Bose mused as the office door closed and he was left alone with himself and the image of Lancaster's smile.

. . .

Chicago's Union Station was nearly deserted. The clock above the portal leading to the trains said 4:08 A.M.

A scattered handful of somnolent travelers were waiting out the night. There was a sailor asleep with his head against his duffel bag, his closely shaved crew cut making him look very young and vulnerable. Nearby a snoring drunk seemed to try to look as respectable as he could, even in his sleep, so as to avoid being rousted by the station cop before morning.

A woman with two heavy canvas traveling bags, a huge straw purse, and two sleeping children was sitting numbly on one of the heavy benches, staring at nothing. It was clear she was an immigrant, no doubt on her way to join her husband somewhere. She gazed out at the promised land of America through eyes dulled by the assault of the alien, and perhaps by the grim parade of a dozen dingy waiting rooms before this one.

The only ticket seller on duty sat sleepily behind his barred window, ignoring the girlie magazine on his desk as he rested his chin on his hand. Music could be heard from a radio somewhere.

All at once a quiet step awakened the ticket master. He gulped despite himself as he saw an amazingly pretty young woman appear before him. She wore a light raincoat that hugged the outline of sweet young breasts. He sensed the stirring of her hips under the crisp fabric. He saw that she was carrying a purse and a single small suitcase.

"Yes, ma'am," he blurted out with a bit too much gallantry. "What can I do for you?"

She glanced behind her at the deserted station.

"When does the next train leave?" she asked.

"Where to?" His eyes were caught by the curve of her lips and the ghost of a smile in her eyes as she looked through the bars at him.

"That depends," she said.

He fumbled through his schedule.

"Got an express to Albuquerque in ten minutes," he said. "That will get in around eight tomorrow night. Or, let me see, the special to Los Angeles. That will get you in Wednesday morning. Then there's the regular train to New York, Philadelphia, or Washington . . ."

She shook her head. "Not that one," she said.

Again her beauty arrested him. She had chestnut hair, fresh and wavy. Her eyes were a sort of aquamarine, glinting with girlish candor and a hint of playful sensuality.

"Or," he went on, taking his eyes off her with difficulty, "there's the 4:30 to Las Vegas and points west. You'll get in by nightfall. Hot out there this time of year, I imagine . . ."

"Las Vegas," she repeated. "That sounds like a nice place. First class, please."

"Yes, ma'am." He reached to pull out a ticket for her, feasting a sidelong glance on her soft cheeks and glowing eyes as he did so.

She glanced around the station as he made out the ticket. The voice singing on the radio, a clear baritone, echoed hollowly off the marble floor and walls. The song was about love, she noticed, and about loss. She listened for a second before turning back to the ticket seller.

"Twenty-three fifty," he was saying.

She reached into her purse and produced a fifty-dollar bill.

"Hear about the big news in Washington?" he asked as he opened the change drawer.

"Big news?" She raised an eyebrow inquiringly.

"That Lancaster business." He shook his head. "Quite a story. Terrible thing. Such a handsome young fellow. Why, I thought he'd be our next president. I was all set to register and everything. But you never know, miss. You just never know."

She nodded, a trace of caution darkening her expression of polite interest.

"The early *Trib* has the story," he added, pointing to the newsstand across the waiting room. Her eyes followed the direction of his gnarled finger as she put away her change.

"Thank you," she said.

"You never know," he repeated with a sigh. "That's all I can say about this world we live in. By golly, you just never know."

He watched her cross the room. Her stride was easy, graceful. She was very composed and feminine in her movements. He noticed that she was heading straight for the newsstand.

She approached the old woman who sold candy bars, cigarettes, and papers. She bought a *Tribune* and sat down on one of the empty benches.

She studied the front page for a long time. The headline was enormous, but the story was sketchy, an extra that was too late to be included in the body of the paper. Only the bare bones of what had happened were given.

She closed her eyes for a long moment. The voice on the radio sang of parting and of a love that could not die. The paper remained in her hands. She could not see the ticket seller, whose fascinated gaze remained fixed on her from behind the barred window of his cubbyhole.

He did not try to divine her thoughts, for his attention was riveted to the pretty legs emerging from the raincoat, and the lush hair falling to her shoulders.

Lancaster, she was thinking. *How in the world . . . ?*

The story had shocked her. It was the last thing she would have expected. She, of all people, had known where Haydon Lancaster stood as of a day ago, and what was going to happen for him and the country. She had made it happen. Almost at the cost of her own life.

And now it was all for nothing.

She thought of Amory Bose. Her sharp mind worked quickly, trying to put two and two together. What had happened to Lancaster must have come from left field. Bose could hardly have had a hand in it. After all, Bose's own plans for Lancaster were a thing of the past now.

Thanks to her. Thanks to Leslie.

Yet it had happened. At this late hour, when all the battles had been won and lost, and the dust was settling around the next president of the United States, the man all but nominated, all but elected—it had happened anyway.

Leslie folded the paper and put it on the seat beside her. Again she closed her eyes, as much out of lingering amazement as from the fatigue of her long journey.

All at once she thought of Bess. How must Bess feel tonight? Was she bitter? Devastated? Or was she perhaps relieved, in some private way, that the war was finally over, the last battle fought to the finish?

Leslie could not imagine. After all, she barely knew Bess. Their paths had crossed only for the briefest of moments, thanks to Amory Bose.

Yet it was Leslie who had done the one thing that could have saved everything for Bess—and for her husband.

Oh, well.

The world is a kaleidoscope, someone had once said. One little turn of the wheel, and everything is in a different place. All the fragments of shape and color thrown into new positions, the patterns unrecognizable. Even the rules of the game changed forever.

And the desperate plans and dreams of those who had played the game, all forgotten now.

She looked down at the ticket in her hand. Las Vegas. The place where a throw of the dice or the whim of a dancing roulette ball decided the fates of human beings. Why not? It would be a good place for her to wait things out.

She glanced at the bench where the immigrant woman sat motionless, her arms curled protectively around the shoulders of her sleeping children. America must seem a harsh and indifferent land to her, turning a cold shoulder to her anxieties as it left her to forget home and adjust to strange new challenges all by herself. While for her children, so tiny now, the old home would soon be just a memory. Less than a memory, indeed: a forgotten dream borne inside them without their knowledge as they hurried eagerly toward their own future—a future that would reveal its trumps too late, as well. An instant too late, like the coy roulette ball.

The handsome face of Haydon Lancaster, glimpsed a moment ago on the cover of the newspaper, lingered before her mind's eye like the smile of the Cheshire Cat, full of whimsy and complex charm. Even as it faded, the spell it cast seemed to grow deeper.

All the bets were off, all promises broken. What was left?

Leslie smiled. Life was left. A poor joke, perhaps, but one that might as well be told to the end. The gods were nothing if not cruel. Yet they had a peculiar sense of humor that too often went unappreciated by those who were their pawns.

Las Vegas, then.

Why not?

. . .

Dan Aguirre brought his unmarked car to a screeching halt in the puddle-filled street before the old factory building where the loft was located.

He left the car double-parked and flung open the door. He bounded across the sidewalk, his steps echoing weirdly in the humid night air. The entryway was in front of him, with its battered mailboxes and list of tenants.

He pushed all the buzzers at once. For an instant that seemed an eternity there was no answer. Then the speaker squawked interrogation at him from one of the apartments.

"Police emergency," he said loudly. "This is Detective Aguirre speaking. Open the door, please."

To his relief, after another brief pause the buzzer sounded, and he pulled the door open. The familiar elevator was waiting, but he remembered how slow it was, and took the stairway, bounding up the steps three at a time.

He was out of breath when he reached the top floor. As he paused on the landing he saw that Laura's door was closed.

He knocked once, twice, his free hand on the butt of the gun in his shoulder holster. There was no answer. He tried the door. It was not locked.

Slowly, knocking once more, he turned the knob and watched the door swing open.

He tensed as he peered into the living room.

They were there together.

He knew at once that he was too late.

Blood was everywhere. It was hard to distinguish the two women from one another, for both were covered in an obscene welter of crimson that shone dark and sticky under the glow of the small living room lamp.

An ancient instinct told him one of them was dead.

She was lying with her head in the lap of the other, who sat emptily against the heavy couch.

Aguirre felt his hand clutch pointlessly at the .44 under his jacket.

He sighed. There was nothing to do but question the one who remained alive. This part of his job, the saddest, was all that was left.

He came to her side, knelt, and cleared his throat.

"What happened?" he asked.

She did not seem to hear. She was absolutely still, staring at nothing.

"I'm sorry," he said. "I have to know." He touched the neck of the dead body, feeling for a pulse. There was none. Shot through the heart, he decided. Point blank range, probably.

The living woman was still gazing into space, her hands buried almost possessively in the hair of the dead one.

The emptiness in her eyes sent a chill down his spine. She looked as though she had taken leave of the planet. He wondered if he would be able to bring her back.

Then, suddenly, he recalled the boy.

"What about . . . ?" He gestured toward the bedroom.

She shook her head. It was the barest sketch of a movement, the first sign that she even realized he was there.

He got up, walked to the bedroom door, and opened it soundlessly. Inside, on the bed, was a tiny figure covered by a blanket. There was no blood. Dan Aguirre, a father, knew in a second by instinct that the boy was alive, and sleeping soundly. To be on the safe side, he approached the bed, pulled back the covers, and replaced them when he saw the little face resting on the pillow.

He closed the door and returned to the living room.

She was still sitting there on the floor, holding the dead body to her breast.

"I have to know what happened," he said, crouching beside her, "before I call anyone else. Please . . ."

Her eyes turned to him at last. But they did not focus. They seemed to look past him at something beyond this room, beyond this night.

At length her small voice came, a whisper repeating his question. "What happened?"

"Tell me." He touched her blood-soaked arm. She did not recoil. Her flesh seemed indifferent, almost as cold as that of the dead one. Grief, he knew, could do that. The living were capable of putting one foot in the grave behind those who had meant the most to them.

Her brow furrowed in concentration. Then she looked at him.

"We all got what was coming to us," she said.

He waited, looking into her eyes.

"But we didn't see it coming," she added. "It was coming all along . . ." She seemed calm, as though measuring a theorem. "If only we'd seen it."

"I don't understand," he said.

Her eyes were dimming now. "Neither do I," she said. The words seemed to close a door on him. He could feel her slipping further away.

Now she rocked the dead woman in her arms, murmuring softly into the unhearing ears. He could not make out her words, for they came in a fluttering whisper too weak to be intelligible.

It was an uncanny sound. Though the meaning slipped incomprehensibly through the grasp of his reason, the words sapped his courage to stand up, to go to the phone, to do his job.

We all got what was coming to us . . .

He rose to his feet. He looked down at the two women, one dead, one alive. The dead one looked oddly at peace, the living one inhumanly empty.

Dan Aguirre sighed. He had seen many murder scenes in his time, but the reality of death had never hit him in quite this way before. It seemed to devour the room, the hour, the whole world.

With an effort he turned toward the phone. The pictures on the walls wheeled before him, faces whose haunting expressions drew a dark new luster from their proximity to death.

But we didn't see it coming.

If only we'd seen it. . . .

So be it, he decided. There was nothing left to say or think. Her own anthem was as good as any.

Too late, Dan Aguirre thought.

Too late.

BOOK ONE

Rainy Day Thoughts

I

April 22, 1933

THEY WERE BORN the same night, in hospitals four hundred miles apart.

It was late when the Damerons came into Holy Family Hospital, located in the farm country east of Cleveland. They were en route to St. Louis, and so had no local obstetrician of their own. There was no one to handle the delivery except the house staff. The physician in charge was Dr. Firmin, a young graduate of the University of Toledo Medical School who was doing his residency here.

Mrs. Dameron was a tiny, pinched-looking woman whose humorless manner was in stark contrast to that of her husband Robert—"Call me Bob," he told the nurses with a twinkle in his eye, his charm belying his worry over his wife's condition. There was some concern about the ability of Mrs. Dameron's skinny hips to accommodate a normal birth, so she was watched carefully during her four hours of labor.

Meanwhile, in the early hours of the morning on the South Side of Chicago, an immigrant couple had entered the emergency ward at Michael Reese Hospital. Their name was Bělohlávek, and, as very recent newcomers to America, they also had no physician of their own. Mrs. Bělohlávek's water had broken at midnight, and she was dilating fast.

This couple was a reversed mirror image of the Damerons. Mrs. Bělohlávek—the unpronounceable Czech came across as a whisper on her lips—was a pretty, gentle woman who managed smiles to the nurses despite her pain. She had wispy brown hair, a rich complexion, and a sweet manner that seemed to apologize for the fuss occasioned by her condition. Her husband was a dour, intense man whose black eyes expressed suspicion and disapproval of everything and everyone around him, including the wife who was causing him the embarrassment of being the center of so much attention.

Dr. Eunice Diehl, an experienced staff physician, took charge of the case. The contractions were steady. The nurses stood by, expecting an imminent delivery. Mr. Bělohlávek sat moodily in the waiting room, awaiting the birth of his first child.

As it turned out, the Damerons' baby was born first. Young Dr. Firmin, busy with other emergency patients during the long wait for Mrs. Dameron to dilate, had to be called at the last minute from an accident case at the other end of the corridor. By the time he returned, his forceps ready in case of a problem delivery, the child was already coming into the world. It was a girl.

It was easy to see she would be a redhead, with the light complexion of the classic colleen. As he cleared her breathing passage, the doctor experienced an odd feeling. It was almost as though the pretty child were trying to tell him something, in an urgent and curiously adult way.

"I was waiting for you," she seemed to say as her eyes opened for the first time—luminous cloudy orbs already tinged by the brilliant emerald green they would become later—"and you were not there."

The doctor dismissed the feeling as he made sure that both the mother and the child were doing well, then hurried back to his accident case.

Meanwhile, in Chicago, Dr. Diehl oversaw the entirely normal birth of the little Bělohlávek girl. This baby was very calm, not even crying. Though her skin was fair, it was clear that she would be dark in hair and eyes. She seemed absorbed in herself, unfazed by the comings and goings in the delivery room around her.

Yet something about her was remarkable, the doctor noticed. Her eyes were very large, and unsettlingly deep. Though she was of course too little to be able to focus them, they looked out upon the new world with a sort of haunted acquiescence, as though they saw too much, far too much, and already possessed an inner knowledge that should not belong to so tiny a being.

Dr. Diehl was disappointed to see that the unfriendly Czech father, when shown his new baby girl, did not seem at all pleased. It was clear that he had hoped his wife would present him with a son and heir. His murmured words to her as she lay in her bed were full of ill-concealed reproach. One could hear it even through the foreign language he spoke.

The doctor was shocked by this male insensitivity. For herself, she not only thought the newborn girl extremely beautiful, but could not help admiring her as a person. She felt a brief wistful yearning to know what would happen to her when she grew up.

But such impulses were common for a physician who brought new lives into the world. By the end of her shift Dr. Diehl had forgotten her impression of the little Bĕlohlávek girl—and, indeed, her ridiculously complex name. She went home at 6:00 A.M. and gave the matter no more thought.

In Ohio, meanwhile, Dr. Firmin saw to the postnatal needs of Mrs. Dameron's new baby. He was pleased to see that the father, whose Irish charm was undiminished by his night-long ordeal of waiting, seemed not at all disappointed to have been given a girl instead of a boy by his wife. Though the joyous occasion of birth did not seem to have brought much happiness to dour Mrs. Dameron, her husband was passing out cigars to everyone in sight. He was thrilled with his little girl.

The Damerons left the Ohio hospital after one more day to continue their journey to their new home in St. Louis. The Bĕlohlávek family went home from Michael Reese Hospital to their South Side bungalow on the very day of their daughter's birth—at the father's insistence.

By the next day both births were mere notations in hospital records, with birth certificates for both babies duly registered in the state records of Ohio and Illinois respectively. The official world took no more notice of either child.

No one concerned thought to reflect that since all the great figures of history must have been helpless babies on some long-ago day—villains as well as heroes—they themselves might have played a small part in changing the future course of a nation by bringing these two tiny girls into the world on this chilly April night. After all, countless other babies had preceded these, and countless others would follow.

Thus the routine adventure of one night ended, and was consigned to the past.

And the future began.

. . .

Laura—for that was the name chosen by the Bĕlohláveks for their little girl—was to remember the first seven years of her life as an uncertain balance of her childish soul between two conflicting centers of gravity, her mother and her father.

Josef Bĕlohlávek was a tailor. He had brought his skill with him, along with his bitterness, from Czechoslovakia. He hated America, despite its vaunted opportunities, and spent all his spare time in moody ruminations about his past in the old country.

He had had a sweetheart there—though this was a fact his daughter was never to learn—a girl whose well-to-do parents would not allow her to marry him, for he was landless and of a family with no prospects. Under ambiguous circumstances in which his stormy character played no small part, he renounced his intended bride and took up with the girl he later married, a penniless but attractive and gentle creature named Maryna, with whom he emigrated a short time later.

Though he sensed on some level that he had got the better of the deal on both sides—the girl he married was far wiser and more loving than the rather shallow prize he had set his cap for back home, and America held a far better future for him than the old country—Josef Bělohlávek could not control his resentment.

During her first years little Laura quickly got used to the fact that her father was not really part of the family. He worked from dawn until after dark in the cramped sewing shed behind their bungalow. And when he was not sewing he was out shopping for fabric at the downtown wholesale markets.

At dinnertime he would enter the kitchen without a word, respond with a barely audible sigh to his wife's news of the neighborhood as he ate, and retire quickly to his sewing shed for more work. He neither spoke to his daughter during the meal nor kissed her goodnight.

His only acknowledgment of her existence was a grudging sidelong look that was full of regret. The little girl was too young to understand his embitterment over not having a son to carry on his name. Nor was she aware of the subsequent miscarriages that ended her mother's hopes of bringing a second baby to term.

But she was a sensitive child, and easily understood that her father was disappointed in her very existence. So she clung by instinct to her mother, whose warmth and understanding became the bulwark of the everyday world for her. The two of them faced life in a large American city hand in hand. Laura, for whom this was the only land she knew, learned to live with the paradox of having the sights and dangers of the South Side explained to her by a mother who could still not speak English properly, and whose comprehension of the New World was based more on rumor and fantasy than on real knowledge.

Meanwhile Father remained a moody, forbidding presence whom Laura avoided by skulking into corners at his approach and saying nothing in his presence. She never realized that in his eyes her birth had completed the process of exile and alienation that had begun with his marriage. His dream was to have become a landed proprietor in the old country, admired by his friends and relatives, with a son to inherit his name and his possessions. Instead he was an anonymous immigrant adrift in the tumult of an alien country where neither names nor people lasted, for all were washed away by the impersonal river of commerce and progress.

So in Laura's eyes Father took on the very coldness and indifference of the city outside her four walls, rather than forming a warm rampart against the unknown. She feared him more than anything else.

That is, until the day he began to teach her how to sew.

It was winter. She had been sent out to the shed by her mother to fetch him for an errand. She found him working at a piece of fabric on the old Singer machine that had cost him all his savings.

"*Pojd'te sem*," he said suddenly in Czech, "sit on my lap and learn something."

She watched the needle dance over a dull-looking piece of fabric, speeding up and slowing down according to some mysterious command emanating from her father's tense, cautious body. She shrunk deeper into his lap, frightened by the sharp little weapon which stabbed into the soft cloth.

Then, to her astonishment, Father cut off the thread, turned the fabric inside-out, and she saw that it was a gaily colored blouse, perfectly sewn, crystallizing with a flourish like a rabbit pulled from a magician's hat.

Josef Bělohlávek saw his daughter's enthusiasm for his trade, and he began to teach her. She took to the challenge like a natural, despite her tender age. She delighted in the painstaking process of sewing formless fragments into patterns until the finished garment emerged all at once in the beauty of its final shape and color.

From that first day forward Laura found that she had at last forged a relationship with her father. It never occurred to her that through her talent for sewing she was allowing Father to imagine that she was, by inclination at least, the son his wife could not give him. Nevertheless she gloried in the feeling of acceptance she enjoyed when she sat on his lap in the shed and operated the machine.

And sometimes he would make her special dresses and little outfits out of spare fabric he had picked up in town. He would try them on her, his fingers oddly gentle as they smoothed the garments over her tiny limbs. At these moments there was a warmth just beneath the surface of his touch that made her glow.

But outside the shed he was the same Father as always: silent, preoccupied, absorbed in bitter memories and a hatred of the world so intense that Laura could not help feeling it included herself and her mother.

So it was that she led a double life now, clinging to Mama for the daily necessities of touch, kiss, smile, while secretly waiting for the stolen intervals when, in the cluttered privacy of the sewing shed, she could renew her strange but important closeness with Papa.

The apotheosis of that intimacy came one Halloween, when she was six years old. Her father had managed to find some fine satin in pastel colors on one of his shopping trips, and he surprised her on Halloween morning with a fully finished clown costume, in a fancy harlequin design, complete with handsomely detailed piping, a false nose, and a lovely conical hat.

It was the most beautiful costume Laura had ever seen or imagined. When she went out trick-or-treating on her mother's arm, she looked back and saw Papa standing in the light of the front step, watching her. He would not take part in the alien American ritual of wandering the neighborhood at her side, but he waved goodbye to her with a proud look that seemed to shine for once with all the affection that had been missing in him all these years.

She turned to wave at him, again and again, pulling at her mother's hand to make her pause as they went down the sidewalk. Papa receded little by little, still answering her wave, acknowledging his daughter's love with a look of brittle tenderness that seemed to say, "I know, little one, I know. I am a cold man, and a bitter one. But I do love you just the same, with all the heart I have to give."

The memory of that evening was to stand like a sentinel over the largely forgotten pageant of Laura's early years. And the stoop on which her father stood, the light in which his thin silhouette was limned, the cautious smile on his lips, were all to vanish sooner than she thought possible.

For the following spring Laura's parents died.

A Czech relative had spoken of opportunities in Milwaukee, and Laura's father, never enamored of Chicago, had impulsively decided to move the family. He filled a rickety rented truck with their possessions, and they started out on Route 21 on the nineteenth of March, a cold and blustery morning whose harsh lake winds brought unexpected snow and sleet.

They drove all day, hampered by heavy traffic and slippery roads. It was late afternoon, and Laura was asleep in her mother's lap, when an oncoming car went out of control and forced the unwieldy truck off the road. Laura went straight from sleep into unconsciousness as her head struck the dashboard. She awoke eighteen hours later in a Wisconsin hospital, the chair beside her bed occupied by an aunt she had never seen before.

The dazed child was told her parents had both gone to Heaven, but that she would be cared for by the family. Her injuries, miraculously, were slight, and within two weeks she was out of the hospital and on the train to Queens, in the city of New York, where by decision of the extended family council she was to be taken in by her Uncle Karel and his American wife Martha.

Equipped by nature with a child's talent for accepting fate, Laura took in her new surroundings with wide eyes and never for a moment reflected that in her own way she was now suffering an exile similar to that which had uprooted her parents from their homeland and made them into bewildered wanderers, cut off from each other as well as the world.

She simply began all over again. The first seven years of her life became a prehistory as opaque as that of primitive man, a shadowy time survived and forgotten.

It fell to the future to show her who she was.

. . .

The Damerons had named their daughter Elizabeth, after a long series of aunts, cousins, and grandmothers in Ireland.

She was a beautiful child. So beautiful, in fact, that almost overnight she became an integral part of the long battle that had pitted her mother and father against each other since the day they had married, five years before her birth.

Bob Dameron was a fine figure of a man, and a great charmer with the women. He was just over six feet tall, with thinning blond hair and a florid complexion. He had twinkling eyes and a courtly, humorous manner. He was quick with a panoply of Irish jokes suitable for every situation according to their degree of sexual innuendo.

Bob was a popular and relatively successful sales representative for a St. Louis firm that manufactured kitchenware and small appliances. And he was a well-known local politician in the city, a ward heeler who got out the vote for the Democratic ticket by doing a host of small favors for his constituents, everything from helping out a shopkeeper with a small loan to making sure the garbagemen cleaned up the alleys in his district without leaving stray bottles and cans behind them.

No one who knew Bob Dameron could understand how such a strapping, masculine lover of life could have married so shriveled and humorless a creature as his wife. Flora Dameron had neither personal charm nor interests of any kind. She spent all her time cleaning and recleaning the modest house Bob owned in a working-class neighborhood, and barricading herself behind the swinging door of a kitchen to which neither her husband nor her daughter was invited.

It was rumored that Flora had brought with her a dowry that Bob had desperately needed at the time of his marriage. This could not be confirmed. What was certain, however, if not provable, was that Bob had had many affairs before his marriage, and many since. He met dozens of women through his business activities and his political rounds. He bestowed his physical charms on as many of them as he could find time and energy for—confining himself, though, to the married ones, for they alone had the discretion to understand the limited nature of his commitment to them, and to honor it.

Bob did not flaunt his infidelity. On the contrary, he used his considerable tact and intelligence to conceal it brilliantly. Nevertheless his sharp-witted wife was not fooled. Though she did not accuse him to his face, for her heritage and inclination proscribed such behavior in a wife, she displayed a suspicious, complaining personality and a hatred of America behind which her jealousy over her husband was thinly veiled.

Bob made a great show of his husbandly affection for his wife. But those who spent evenings with the Damerons were accustomed to the familiar sight of Flora repulsing him with a little shrug of disapproval when he tried to give her a hug and a peck on the cheek. At these moments concern for the proprieties was much less in her mind than reproach for her husband's perennial unfaithfulness.

She had never forgiven him for his philandering. And, by a curious process of extension, she never forgave her daughter either.

For little Elizabeth—nicknamed Tess by her doting father, after the memory of a favorite aunt he had admired as a boy—was not only a great beauty almost before she could walk, but had soon developed a naughty, vixenish personality that set her mother's teeth on edge.

She had brilliant red hair, glowing green eyes, and a creamy complexion touched by freckles like spots of sunlight. She was perfectly formed and moved with a quick natural grace. From the start it was obvious that she knew how to twist her father around her little finger. He could deny her nothing. And there was a knowing look in her eyes when she played with him that hardly passed unnoticed by her resentful mother.

Flora Dameron found herself unable to discipline her daughter effectively, not only because of the child's headstrong nature but because she could not depend on her husband to take her side against Tess. So as time went by she began to identify the little girl subconsciously with the faceless recipients of Bob's extramarital passion, and thus to blame her for the tense atmosphere in the Dameron house.

The mother was never seen to bestow affection of any kind on her daughter. Instead she treated her as a hated rival, an enemy under her own roof, to be watched over with cautious distaste and subjected to harsh restrictions intended to curb her wayward character.

Bob paid no attention to his wife's disapproval. In his eyes little Tess was not only beautiful, but spirited and bright, as a true Irish girl should be. He took her on his rounds, introduced her to political cronies and constituents, and even—without of course letting on—presented her to some of his ladies, so they could admire her smile, her beautiful eyes, and her clever personality.

The child seemed not to mind her mother's stubborn enmity, and indeed took little note of her existence. She basked in the glow of her father's unstinting love, and took advantage of him as a gallant defender on those occasions when her precociousness got her into trouble with friends or at school. For his part Bob doted on little Tess, and seemed untroubled by the fact that his withered wife was unable to conceive further children after the first one. He felt no lack of a son. His daughter was good enough for him. He had a good livelihood, a fine future in politics, and a fulfilling love life. What more could he ask?

Then something went wrong.

In the summer of Tess's eighth year, Bob Dameron was unlucky enough to be in the arms of one of his paramours when the lady's husband returned unexpectedly from a business trip. Word of the incident reached the wrong ears, and a sexual scandal resulted. Aspersions were cast on Bob's character in the district. Political strings were pulled by ambitious rivals. The balance tipped against Bob, and he lost his post as ward committeeman. To complete the disaster, his bosses at the kitchenware firm became nervous and fired him.

Despondent, Bob retired to the little office he had long maintained on the third floor of his cavernous old house, and began to drown his empty hours in Bushmills Irish whisky. He no longer sported his handsome three-piece suits, but sat around in his undershirt reading the sporting news, going out only to place a bet on a horse or to pay a visit to a loyal lady friend.

As time went by, his depression deepened. He stopped eating with his wife and daughter, and drunkenly left the house at all hours to haunt one of the downtown taverns or even to spend his dwindling dollars on a prostitute. The charm was draining out of him, and only the irresponsibility remained.

One day young Tess was summoned from her second-grade classroom at the neighborhood elementary school and brought to the principal's office, where she was told terrible news. Her house had burned down. Both her parents were dead, for the blaze had engulfed the rickety frame structure long before firemen could arrive at the scene. It was assumed the fire had started in Bob Dameron's upstairs inner sanctum, where he had fallen into drunken sleep with a forgotten cigar in his hand and let it fall to the carpet, so sealing his fate and that of his wife.

The little girl looked into the principal's eyes without emotion. Her beauty had never been so astonishing as in this moment of grief, when she bravely kept her feelings inside.

A cousin of her mother's was sent for, and a family council held to decide her fate. There was no future for her in St. Louis. The only family members who had resources to take her in were located in California, in a poor suburb of San Diego.

The funeral was held before a large crowd of friends and relations, including the erstwhile business and political cronies who had so recently turned their backs on Bob, as well as more than a handful of the women who would miss Bob's courtly smiles and bedroom charms in the future. An hour after the burial little Elizabeth was on a train to California with a stiffly protective aunt who was anything but pleased by the prospect of having another mouth to feed.

The sojourn of Tess Dameron in the great heartland of the Midwest had ended—as had that of little Laura Bělohlávek six months before her.

II

BBC Newsreel, June 10, 1937

Britons had a special reason to cheer today when Reid Lancaster, President Roosevelt's special advisor on British-American Affairs, arrived at Southampton with his family for meetings with the King, Prime Minister Chamberlain, and members of Parliament on plans for a new initiative on behalf of Roosevelt's "New Deal" to inaugurate an exchange program providing jobs for British citizens as well as relief funds for the needy throughout Britain.

The famous Lancaster profile was on view as the American financier, himself descended through a legendary lineage from both the Stuart and Lancaster dynasties, disembarked with his family to the cheers of a large welcoming crowd. At his side were his wife Eleanor, *née* Brand, heiress to the famous American cosmetics fortune; his oldest son Stewart, a handsome twenty-year-old who is currently a student at Yale University; eleven-year-old Haydon; and five-year-old Sybil, a charming blonde imp who became the darling of reporters from the moment she set foot on English soil.

The Lancasters will be in London for over a fortnight as Reid Lancaster works to set up the program that has been called a new lease on life for Depression-ridden Britain. We welcome this illustrious family of transplanted Britons and wish them a happy and productive stay.

"HEY, SHORT STUFF. Snap it up. Mom wants you."

Stewart Lancaster stood in the doorway in his black tie and tails, an almost absurdly handsome figure at a precociously masculine twenty, with aquiline nose, jet back hair, and flashing dark eyes which smiled down at his younger brother. All he lacked to make the princely image complete was the top hat that he would soon put on for the gala evening planned at Buckingham Palace.

Somehow the trappings of British formality suited him, despite the casual athleticism of his demeanor. After all, his very name bespoke his family's age-old roots in English tradition. He was the most recent in a long line of Stewarts who had occupied privileged places in his family tree—the Lancasters having stubbornly altered the spelling some two hundred years ago to conceal their intermarriage with the rival Stuart clan.

Stewart seemed to incarnate the Lancaster spirit which combined willful rebellion and respect for tradition. He wore the immense past of his prestigious family as casually as he wore the suit that hugged his hard body tonight.

His brother looked up from the bed where he had been languidly reading a book. Hal was only eleven, but already his own face bore the unique stamp of the Lancaster men. Yet in Hal's case there was a dreaminess that did not quite fit with the famous look. He had the dark, radiant Lancaster eyes; but something tender and whimsical shone in them, which softened him and gave him a different luster.

Stewart himself was pure Lancaster stuff, cut from his father's cloth, with a natural swagger and a blithe humor that concealed a very real understanding of his mission in life. He was perfectly aware of what it meant to be the first-born son of Reid Lancaster in the middle of a great Depression which could not remotely dissipate the Lancaster wealth, no matter what its effect on the world outside the Lancaster castle keep of power and pride. And he knew exactly where his Yale education, and the Harvard law degree to follow, were taking him.

In a few short years Stewart would have an important place in his father's financial empire. That place would become more exalted, step by step, until, when Reid Lancaster decided it was time to step down, he would enter a gracious semi-retirement and leave the reins of the family's extended business and philanthropic interests in Stewart's hands. It would fall to Stewart to manage the indefatigable growth of the Lancaster wealth, to be named advisor to presidents, ambassador to nations dependent on American ambition and know-how—and finally to carry the dynasty forward by arranging marital matches between the Lancasters and other families of similar influence and breeding.

All these things Stewart knew with a certainty that was not intellectual, but instinctive. That knowledge was so much a part of his youthful exuberance, his manifest happiness in the world, that, in the eyes of his younger brother Hal, it gave him an almost godlike assurance.

So there was more than a hint of respect in the young boy's eyes as he looked up from his book and smiled.

"Come on, Hal," Stewart grinned, stepping into the room. "Show me how you wrestle."

And with complete indifference to the elegant costume he would rumple by his play, Stewart lunged forward and caught Hal in a bear hug. Hal laughed in delight and tried to wriggle from his brother's iron embrace—Stewart was very strong, a middleweight wrestler since prep school—but could not escape.

"You're not so tough," he laughed, pushing at Stewart's chest. Though he was clearly outclassed in size as well as muscle, the younger boy put up a brave struggle, refusing either to give in or to take his probable defeat too seriously. He jabbed at Stewart's ribs, grasped his arms ineffectually, and flung his own body this way and that in an effort to throw him off, giggling all the while. Stewart's clothes were awry now, and his hair tousled by the fight, but he held on harder than ever.

Then, as Hal felt his strength beginning to wane under his older brother's hard grip, inspiration came to his rescue. He raised his knee and cuffed Stewart between the legs, not hard enough to hurt him, but with sufficient authority to show him where he was vulnerable.

"Ooo!" Stewie howled, feigning agony. "You don't play fair. Hitting a fellow below the belt." He bent double and made a show of holding his crotch in his hands. "I'm castrated," he said. "Know what that means, Short Stuff?"

Hal was leaning on one hand, contemplating his brother with a whimsical smile.

"Yes, I know," he said. "It means you sing soprano."

Stew rumpled the boy's hair and stood up. "Well, don't damage the merchandise," he smiled, straightening his tie.

Hal watched in silence as Stewart quickly righted his garments with easy movements, gave a push to an errant lock of hair, and leaned against the door frame, looking for all the world as though he had just stepped off a wedding cake. How handsome he was! Nothing in the world seemed to disturb the perfect composure of his body.

Stewart's reference to "the merchandise" reminded Hal of gossip he had heard about his brother's precocious prowess with the opposite sex. It was common knowledge on both the Lancaster and Brand sides of the family that more than one debutante of the past few seasons had carried a hot torch for Stewart. Not only was he perhaps the most desirable young Lancaster male to have come along in several generations, but also one of the most hungry for women's charms.

This fact filled young Hal with a kind of awe, for he understood that Stewie's prestige as an older, stronger brother also had its darker and more sensual side. Stewart had desires, and had tasted pleasures, that Hal could not imagine. For Hal had always thought of relations with girls as sissyish and effeminate, somehow unworthy of a man's hard pride.

But now he was forced to accept that the two things went hand in hand in the erect, attractive body of his brother, and in his twinkling eyes. Stewart's offhand "don't damage the merchandise" bespoke a proud sensuality that made Hal ill at ease.

Their horseplay tonight was a bit more restrained than, say, two years ago. Since Stewart had gone off to Yale the two brothers were not as close as they had been. Stewart belonged evermore to his own future and its manifold obligations, which included longer and longer private discussions with his father in his library at home or in the office in Manhattan.

Hal was not jealous of Stewart's obscure intimacy with Reid Lancaster, for he understood that the two of them had something in common which Hal himself lacked. Besides, Father was so remote a figure to Hal that it was impossible to covet his time and attention.

Hal did not seem to mind his increased solitude, and devoted himself to absorption in books and many hours spent in dreamy introspection.

So it was that tonight, while Stewart would be presented to the King and a dozen of the Empire's highest councilors as his father's heir and right-hand man, Hal would stay home to be fed by the servants and pass the evening by himself.

"What you going to do tonight?" Stewart asked, still lounging in the doorway.

"There's a radio show on. 'The Fall of the House of Usher,' " Hal said. "Mom says I can listen to it after Syb goes to bed."

"Good man," Stewart smiled absently. "I wish I didn't have to go to this shindig."

His discontent seemed real. But Hal guessed that if Stewie were free tonight, it would not be an evening with Hal and Sybil that he would choose.

"Well," Stewart smiled, "got to go shine my shoes. Daddy will break my neck if I don't look good. You take it easy, Hal. And don't forget— Mom is waiting for you."

The last words were spoken with a seriousness born of an ancient Lancaster sanction: loyalty to Mother.

Eleanor Brand Lancaster was a handsome woman in her forties, neither short nor tall, neither slim nor plump, with pale skin, hazel eyes, and wispy brown hair touched attractively by gray.

Her two sons had inherited the lush black hair of the Lancasters, while her five-year-old daughter Sybil, whose blonde locks showed no sign of darkening, seemed to have tapped the lineage of the Creightons, the manufacturing dynasty from which Eleanor's mother had emerged.

As in most families with three children, two had paired off. The boys were like each other, dark and strong, while Sybil was small, fair, with a temperament all her own.

But all three siblings seemed to have bypassed Eleanor's own particular qualities. None had her oval face, her delicate brow, her pale skin. They all took their traits from the dashing Lancasters or, in Sybil's case, the blue-eyed Creightons.

Eleanor was happy enough with this result. She had no desire for immortality. Nevertheless she could not help feeling left out of the genetic recipe of her own offspring, and thus exiled somehow from the fruit of her own loins. The very beauty of her three children made her feel a bit lonely.

Eleanor Lancaster had a worried, almost haunted look that was only half-concealed by the mask of sophistication ingrained in her by the wealthy society from which she had sprung. It was an integral part of her, and had been for so long that no one thought to recall that it had not been visible when she was a schoolgirl or a Sarah Lawrence undergraduate, many years ago.

Yet it could be clearly seen in her wedding picture, which stood today on the mantel in the smaller salon at Newport. And it shone in her eyes in every family photograph taken of her with Reid Lancaster.

Why it was that Reid Lancaster frightened his own wife, even she did not know for certain. But the fact remained that within five minutes in the presence of Eleanor and Reid, a complete stranger could not fail to sense that she was terrified of her husband.

Perhaps, she sometimes mused, it was the way he emerged in flesh and blood from the great line of his ancestors. It was almost as though he were a dashing ancestor himself, a famed Lancaster rake of the eighteenth or nineteenth century who had bounded from his gilded frame in one of the family galleries and sprung uncannily to life at her feet.

The incredible photogenic masculinity of his smile—more Douglas Fairbanks than Douglas Fairbanks, the cousins used to say—shone always the same in every picture he had taken either with his family or with a thousand dignitaries from Roosevelt to Henry Ford to the Prince of Wales. It was the Lancaster smile, as seen in many an ancestor's portrait, but distilled and intensified to a peak of energy for this particular member of the line.

From Lancaster lore came Reid's daunting way of crossing a room on long legs to shake a guest's hand, the deftness of his gesture as he pointed out a picture or a view, or his way of holding a visitor's elbow as he showed him about the Newport or Manhattan house. Even his calm attentiveness when he helped Eleanor with her chair or affectionately touched her hand—it was all Lancaster, alarmingly male and somehow impersonal.

The only time that Reid Lancaster's flashing, terrible smile really softened was when he looked at Stewie.

His firstborn son and heir, already so much like him, brought out an unaccustomed tenderness in Reid, especially when he thought no one was looking. He would watch the young man ride, swim, sail, his eyes full of soft sadness, perhaps at his own decline, but also full of immense pride that this tall, strapping boy, this wonderful sunshine that was Stewart, would take over all his burdens when the time came for him to pass the torch.

There were pictures of them together on the beach at Newport that wrung the heart. They looked like incarnations of the same man, first as a youth, and then in middle age. Immortality was visible in the picture, as the blood of a great family created new life. Reid seemed to sense that death could never take him from himself, for there would always be Stewart to carry on for him.

But Eleanor was not part of this community of spirit. The Lancasters were above all a clan of men. Her husband's very courtliness toward her was part of the wall that kept her outside him, and outside the destiny of achievement that owned him as it had owned his forefathers. His welcoming of Stewart into this secret society only confirmed his wife's exile from it.

Besides, that familiar courtliness went hand in hand with another kind of betrayal.

It was common knowledge in social and financial circles that Reid Lancaster had had many mistresses. This was a Lancaster trait and trademark, the hearty appetite for sexual adventures, combined with an almost overprotective deference toward one's wife. The amalgam was so closely identified with the Lancasters that no one had thought in generations of blaming the Lancaster men for their peccadilloes.

Instead, one admired them. They were dashing, hungry young men, spirited in their youth as strong colts, and they grew into charismatic, startlingly masculine adults, quite irresistible to women, before turning at last into sharp-eyed old men whose cunning and instincts were not dulled by age. They died as patriarchs, nearly always of strokes or heart attacks, only after having made their mark on the world. Even in the coffin they seemed to wear a halo of unyielding male hardness.

They were a proud race of empire builders, their fate linked intimately to the burgeoning wealth of the nation. The women they married—usually chosen for their own fortunes—always lived in their shadow, and were proud to do so. For the Lancaster men had a calling. They were pillars of the land itself, and above all of the cities that had been built on it.

So the infidelity of Reid Lancaster, father to Stewart and young Hal, was news to no one. In his sexual behavior he had not deviated an inch from the pattern of his ancestors—except, perhaps, once.

There was a story in the family—mentioned only in whispers—to the effect that Reid had fallen in love with a girl not of his class, shortly before his betrothal and marriage to Eleanor Brand. A long private talk with his father had ended the affair and sealed the marriage to Eleanor —but Reid had continued to carry a torch for the mysterious young woman. There were rumors of letters kept, of secret trysts in later years, of a lifelong passion carried on behind the scenes of Reid's public life. But the rumors were impossible to confirm or deny, since he had had so many mistresses over the years, often two or three at a time. Besides, a great love was not part of the classic Lancaster pattern, as ambition and plain promiscuity were.

Whatever Eleanor knew or suspected of all this only increased her awe before her husband. She lived in a sort of permanent shocked trance at the sight of him, her expression somewhere between admiration and alarm as she watched him enter a room, mount a horse, pick up a phone, or play with his children.

Strangely enough, her attitude toward Stewart was hardly different. She seldom dared admonish or scold him as a mother might, to make him clean his room or wash his face or comb his hair. He was beyond her dominion, and always had been. Even as a boy he had anticipated her commands and acceded to them in advance. He was almost fatherly in sparing her the need to reproach or discipline him.

Early on he had known by instinct that as his father's heir he possessed a mystical authority. He was the leader, his mother the follower, by family tradition. So he behaved as a perfect son, always kissing his mother's cheek with a dutiful display of affection, and then going his own way without paying further attention to her.

Eleanor would watch him rush out of the house for a sailing afternoon, a polo practice, a date with a young woman, her eyes following him with the same awe and admiration she felt for her husband.

There was no doubt about it. The Lancasters were a man's family. Eleanor was little more than a necessary piece of furniture added to their lives.

But, to her everlasting gratitude, there was one exception.

Hal entered the salon to say goodnight to his mother.

"I'm going to my room now," he said, noticing the perfect view of Hyde Park outside the tall windows. He was dressed in slacks and a sweater that hugged his slender body, accentuating both his boyhood and the adolescence soon to follow.

Her face brightened as she looked up at him. "Stay with me a moment."

The boy approached, looking at her through dark eyes filled with the quiet inquisitiveness she doted on.

"Tell me," she asked, "what will you do tonight?"

"I'm going to read," he said, letting his hand rest in hers while she curled her other arm about his waist. "Then we'll have dinner. Then I'll listen to the radio. Then I'll go to bed."

"A wise plan," Eleanor said, her smile whimsical. "I'll miss you, though."

"I'll miss you, too."

In his erect bearing, with his clever eyes scanning his new surroundings, he was already a Lancaster man. His youthful body was growing like a plant, impossible to hold back for a second in its lunge toward manhood. Yet he was still boy enough to let her hold him that way, as though he belonged in her embrace and wanted to be near her.

When he let her touch him she seemed to tap directly into the special core of sweetness and vulnerability that set him apart from the other

Lancaster men, and that had won her heart for Hal almost from the day he was born.

After Stewart's birth Eleanor had had trouble carrying babies to term. There were three miscarriages before Hal came, and Hal himself kept her in bed for four months before delivery. But he had been worth waiting for.

She was so pleased with him that she had thought to have no more children until, unexpectedly, at age forty, she had conceived Sybil.

Hal was her pride and joy, her personal treasure. If Stewart was Reid's alter ego and successor, the rich stream into which his life's blood could flow, then Hal belonged to Eleanor.

Of course she knew she must take her backseat as always, and let him go to his Lancaster destiny of wealth and achievement and many, many women. She could feel that destiny quickening in him with each passing day. Yet she knew she possessed something precious of him right now. He gave it to her freely, in a way Stewart never would have dreamed to do; and because of it she felt calm and happy when she was with him.

There was a wonder about Hal, an openness, that belonged to him alone. It set him apart not only from the Lancasters, but from all ordinary boys his age. Eleanor knew that this gift of whimsical humor and grave, private wisdom had not come from her, for despite her worried nature she was not a deep woman. Nevertheless a chord sounded in her heart when Hal turned his handsome eyes to her, as though something about him recalled an opportunity she had once let pass her by, a sensitivity that her own fate had not allowed her to enjoy.

Perhaps, Eleanor sometimes mused, the trait he possessed had touched someone in the family before, and been transferred to him across the generations by a quirk of fate. Life can work in subtle ways. They called him Hal—none of the Haydons in the family had ever used the nickname before—in memory of a great-great-uncle who had cut a special figure in Lancaster history. The original Hal (whose given name was Harry) had written poetry and music, to the astonishment and disapproval of the Lancasters of his day, and, it was said, killed himself for love. His portrait now hung in the Park Avenue mansion.

Eleanor did not know the truth behind the stories, but she doubted that the ancestor could have possessed young Hal's unique mixture of tart Lancaster roguishness and tender inquiry, which made him somehow more complete as a male and more irresistible. Of one thing her heart was sure: Hal was the jewel of the family, its diamond. Stewart was merely another in the handsome Lancaster line, his every trait admirable but predictable.

Perhaps then, she sometimes thought, it was for the best that the great public destiny of power and obligation should be reserved for Stewart, so that Hal might be spared the empty rigors of the Lancaster life, and find for himself a private individuality that had always been denied to his forebears.

At least she hoped it would work out that way.

The boy was still holding her hand.

"Mother," he said, "where did the Depression come from?"

Her brow furrowed. "Well," she said slowly, "everybody is poor, Hal. All the money went out of the businesses and banks that make the world run. And so all the people who work for money had to lose their jobs, because there was no money."

"Where did the money go?"

She sighed. "I don't really understand it myself. The money just sort of—shrunk. Because people became afraid, and they didn't want to put what they had in banks, or invest it in business so it could grow."

"Must money either shrink or grow?" he asked. "Can't money just stay the same?"

"Silly as it sounds, I think it's something like that, dear." Eleanor smiled sadly. "Money is a very strange thing."

She let her gaze linger on his face. How clever he was! And how typical of him to have asked her the question, rather than to have gone to Reid. Yet she could not answer the question. It was a Lancaster question, full of hungry curiosity about the state of the world and the structures that underpin it.

But Hal had graced her with his confidence. Stewart would never have done that. Stewart would have found the answer in advance, through that mysterious grapevine in which the Lancaster men communicated with each other, sharing their secrets and their ambition.

Yet Hal had asked her.

And his little formula was so telling. Indeed, money could never stay the same, because the world could never stay the same. It all slipped through one's fingers like cold quicksilver, on its way to some dreadful impersonal accumulation, somewhere—and it was up to the predatory hunger of men to make it work for them or be destroyed by it.

Today the world lacked the courage for that battle. The wind had gone out of its sails. That was the Depression—the fear that made the human spirit shrink from the arena of risk and danger in which men had contended so happily only a few years ago. Eleanor Lancaster understood this, because fear was something she knew all about.

"But we're not poor," the boy was saying.

"No," she said. "We're very lucky. We have a lot of money. The Depression hurts us, too, but not the way it hurts other people."

"Why do we have so much money?"

She dared to stroke his hair as she considered her answer. The delight of having his waist within her embrace made it hard to think clearly.

She said, "People in our families—your father's and mine—invested their money wisely, many years ago, and worked to make it grow. It grew very large and they invested more. Then we became very wealthy. And we're still growing."

There was detachment in her voice, but also sadness as she spoke of the rapacious world of business and success that surrounded them both like walls with ears. She didn't like to think of Hal's future in that world —a future that would devour his soul if he let it. For he was, after all, a Lancaster, filled with a blood that must sooner or later quicken to the challenge of great ambition. Today she clung to a part of him that seemed the delicate blossom of his youth. How long it could battle against the other part, she did not know.

"Do we share our money with other people?" he asked, his brow knitted in concern.

"Of course we do. We give to charity, we endow things . . . We give away huge amounts of money every year."

"To which people? Do we know them?"

"No," she admitted. "I've never met them. They receive the money through agencies."

Hal looked pensive.

"I'd like to know them," he said. "I wish they could come here and get the money."

His words wrung her heart. He was sensing the loneliness of the very rich, the estrangement from the human race that was part of the obligation of great wealth.

"When I grow up," he said, "I'm going to be a doctor. That way I'll know all sorts of people, because when they get sick they'll have to come to see me."

What a doctor you'd make, my sweet one, she thought.

"Who's Hitler?" he asked, his eleven-year-old mind jumping to another subject. Perhaps he was thinking about Hitler because they were in Europe tonight.

"Hitler is the chancellor of Germany," she said. "He is a very angry man, and many people are afraid of him. But some people say he is good for Germany. I don't know the answer."

Hal was getting ready to leave her now. She could feel it.

"Can I have a hug?" she asked, her voice almost suppliant.

He hugged her and, with a gesture that was peculiar to him, let his fingers run along her arm to the palm of her hand as he took his leave of her.

"I love you," she said.

"I love you, too."

"Save a dream for me?"

He nodded. "I will."

A smile lingered about her lips as she watched him stride from the room.

As he went out the door the nanny came in with Sybil.

"Time to say goodnight to Mummy, now." The nurse's brisk English voice murmured as Sybil's blonde ringlets eclipsed the disappearing form of Hal.

With an effort Eleanor Lancaster changed emotional gears and smiled into the watchful eyes of her five-year-old daughter.

Hal paused in the hallway, overhearing his mother as she said goodnight to the little girl.

"Have a good rest, now," came the voice. "Kiss Mommy. I'll look in on you when I get home."

Never *I love you*. Always *I'll look in on you later*. Mother alluded to the future as though to cover up a void in the present when she said goodnight to Sybil. Hal had first overheard this a long time ago. It had disturbed him ever since.

He went upstairs to his room, an unfamiliar and intriguing new place whose pictures and tables and exotic British smells were so different from home. He would explore its corners tomorrow and in the days to come. He sat down on the bed and picked up the book on the history of England that he had brought with him on the ship. Though he had finished it, he began to flip through its pages in search of his favorite parts.

Already he was turning his young mind away from what he had just overheard. In a few minutes it would be his turn to go in and kiss Syb goodnight. He felt sorry for her, and perplexed by his parents' behavior toward her. He knew somehow that Mom didn't really like her, had never warmed up to her. Father, for his part, hardly knew she existed.

Hal was too young to understand how profoundly Sybil's conception and birth had upset the delicate mechanism of Eleanor Lancaster's own personality.

A woman approaching middle age, Eleanor had at last found her place among the Lancasters—not without considerable effort and cost to herself—when the unexpected pregnancy came along. She had already accepted the lonely side of her life with her husband, and she had given him two sons.

She had suffered the thousand natural shocks that go with bringing up two healthy and energetic boys. There was the time Stewie was thrown by his horse in Larchmont, and the time his sailboat was lost in a squall at Newport, the Coast Guard bringing news of his rescue after Eleanor had already prepared herself for the worst. And there was Hal's rheumatic fever, which kept him in bed for four and a half months, a pathetic brave little figure whose heart murmur had the doctors seriously worried about his ultimate survival until improvement finally came. That episode had taken something out of Eleanor that was never restored.

All those terrors were behind Eleanor, and she was preoccupied with living life from day to day and caring for her own dying mother, when out of nowhere came Sybil. Previous trials had already stripped away what remained of Eleanor's thin skin. She had nothing left.

Another mother, delighted to have a girl at last after the two strapping boys and their remote father, would have claimed the child as her own and devoted herself to her, perhaps looking forward to a deep female bond to succor her in her advancing age.

But Eleanor had given the best part of herself to Hal already. And besides, at forty she was just unsure enough of her own femininity to be loath to share it with a lovely little packet of blonde perfection who drew oohs and aahs from legions of Lancaster relatives.

Finally, she simply felt too tired to exert herself running after the child, to worry about burns and spills and bruises—Sybil, as it turned out, was in fact accident prone—not to mention the later, inevitable crises of boys and debutante dresses and broken hearts and the right college and the right husband. Eleanor had not had the easiest relationship with her own mother. She sought, but did not find, a resource within her to cope with her daughter.

Whether it was because of this failure on the part of Eleanor, or some other unseen cause, that things started to go awry with Sybil, no one knew.

But something was wrong. Though the signs were subtle, no one in the family could be blind to them. Even as a toddler there was a remoteness about Sybil, a brittle absorption in herself, an absence of the smiles and giggles and energy one expects in tiny children. The hard look in her little eyes put one off. The very relatives who had covered her with adoring glances when she was an infant were keeping their distance by the time she was two.

There were discussions about taking her to a child psychiatrist. But Reid was so busy, and Eleanor so preoccupied with the boys, and besides, the very thought of a mental illness was too embarrassing to ratify by medical consultation. A compromise was reached whereby the child was given a series of routine psychological tests. When it was determined that her IQ was a staggering 165, her parents hopefully assumed that her unnatural intelligence was making a normal adjustment difficult. With the passage of time improvement would surely come.

So nothing further was done.

But Sybil did not get better. The look in her eyes became more private, more withdrawn, and the pattern of her play more strange. She spent hours alone, neither making a sound nor emerging from her room. She never seemed to sleep. Ordinary children's amusements like toys, music, the radio, left her cold. She closeted herself with her crayons and a handful of picture books, or simply stared out the window.

Still her protective parents balked at the idea that their little daughter was sick. And there was a special reason for this. The Lancasters, like many families whose great wealth has spanned countless generations, and whose marriages have been chosen from within the limited spectrum of high society, had developed an inbred sort of clannishness. They were tolerant of peculiarities among their own that might have passed for eccentricity or downright insanity in outsiders.

Everyone remembered cousin Denys, the hypochondriac, who carried a briefcase full of pills wherever he went and telephoned his doctor at least six times a day. And there was Great-Uncle Montague Lancaster, who had been arrested hundreds of times for shoplifting. Grandmother Leonie had been a nymphomaniac in her youth. Reid's favorite cousin Georgia, a compulsive house-cleaner, had for several years cherished the belief that sinister enemies had placed a radio transmitter in one of her teeth.

To the famed sexual promiscuity of the Lancaster men seemed to correspond, on the part of their sisters, a tendency to neurotic illnesses, often involving palpitations, phobias, morbid anxieties, and, in the case of two and perhaps more aunts, suicide at a young age.

Yes, there were many odd ones among the Lancasters, and among Eleanor's family as well. So it was natural for Sybil's peculiar sadness of character to be taken for granted, forgiven in advance, and politely ignored. Besides, she was a girl, and the fate of girls in the clan was hardly to be considered on a par with the future of Stewart or Hal.

So the child went her way, spending most of her time with one or more nannies, playing quietly on her own, and looking from one member of her family to another at the dinner table—when she ate with them, that is—for all the world as though they were strangers entertaining her for only an evening.

Sybil was like a guest in her own house, and she seemed to know it. The Lancasters were prepared to allow her anything, and to forgive her anything. But they did not open their arms or their hearts to her, for she had not made it easy for them to do so when she had the chance. Her sex and her temperament were against her, and that was the end of it. The family's ranks were closed as solidly as the limestone walls of its Park Avenue mansion.

With one exception.

Hal waited until the nanny had left, and stole silently to Sybil's door. He peeked inside, saw the tiny figure almost obliterated by the bedcovers, and crept along the floor toward the bed. He made a low growl and smacked his lips as he did so, and heard a muffled giggle from under the covers. He saw his sister squirm with anticipation and feigned terror.

"I'm the Piccadilly monster," he muttered, doing his best to fashion a voice of doom. "And I'm going to get you."

The giggling increased as he approached, and the little form flailed this way and that under the covers.

"Gonna getcha," he repeated with baleful humor. "I haven't eaten a little girl in a whole week, and I'm famished."

He drew closer, licking his chops, until his face was separated from her only by the sheet, and he knew she could feel his breath. When she could stand it no longer, he drew the sheet back and kissed her on the neck.

"Mmm, that's good," he said. "What a tasty morsel."

She tried to draw her shoulder into her neck to stop him, but all at once he tickled her briskly in the ribs, saw the neck exposed by her involuntary reaction, and planted his lips upon the soft skin once more as her squeals erupted close to his ear.

She was struggling hard now, but enjoying the assault, and he muttered complaints against her neck.

"Hey," he said, "How can I get in there if you won't let me in? Here, wait." He tickled her again to make her move her head. "That's better. Yum, yum—that's the nicest little girl I've had in days."

Her legs were fluttering wildly, her little hands pushing at him, and the song of her hilarity and excitement thrilled him as it always did, so that he went on with the charade, even though Mother complained about him giving Sybil the hiccups from too much laughing just before she was to sleep.

"Delicious," he concluded, smelling her sweet breath as he tickled her tummy. "Wonderful snack . . ."

"Hal, stop!" she cried through the low, throaty laughter that always charmed him. "You'll make me wet my pants."

Now he sat up, the ritual overture completed, and looked down at her with an affectionate grin.

"Did you have a nice day?" he asked.

"Yes," she replied in the prim little voice that was peculiar to her. "I played with Nurse and drew in my coloring book."

He smiled. She always spoke in complete sentences, with every adverb and conjunction perfectly placed. Years ago the family had realized in astonishment that she did not learn the language like other children, with thousands of halting steps and repetitions of phrases and words heard from adults. She began speaking a trifle late, but when she did she spoke quite like an adult. It was as though language had come to her overnight in one piece.

"Can I see what you drew today?" Hal asked.

She jumped out of the bed, found the book on the table, and handed it to him. As he turned on the light to look at the pictures she sat beside him, her thigh pressed against his own with a touching possessiveness, as though she needed to be in physical contact with him as much as possible.

He opened the coloring book. The pictures were impressive, as always. She had a child's talent for color, but also an innate feeling for line, for plane and rhythm, that never ceased to amaze him—for Hal was a sketch artist himself.

But her forms were grotesque. They were massive, engulfing shapes, dark and menacing.

"What's this one?" he asked, pointing to a greenish abstraction.

"That's a caterpillar," she replied. "He's eating a leaf."

"And this one?" He turned the page.

"That's a dinosaur," she said. "He's caught in a tar pit. He can't move. See?" She pointed to a dark mass that looked like a pool of discolored blood.

Hal nodded slowly. The form was really frightening. Her imagination was full of predators, monstrous encroaching evils, gruesome events. Moreover, she described them with a cool equanimity that was itself somehow unnerving.

"Let's tell a story," he said, closing the book.

He turned out the light, and she got back under the covers. This was their nightly ritual. Hal would start a bedtime story, and Syb would help him tell it. They would alternate, each taking cues from the other.

Then, as she grew tired, Hal would take over and finish, watching her drift off to sleep as he talked.

It was a responsibility he loved, for the sadness of the little girl touched something deep inside him. He felt a bond with her that he could not quite fathom. He did not consider himself sad in any way; yet he recognized her hurt in himself. It sometimes seemed as though she had freed him from his own melancholy by taking it so painfully on herself.

He was protective of her, because he knew somehow that the rest of the family was not supporting her. But as he taught her and played with her and learned from her, he also realized that she was giving him something essential as well, something he needed but could not name.

"Well, what's our story?" he asked. "You start."

She looked up at him.

"Once there was a prince," she said.

He sighed and rolled his eyes.

"You always say that," he complained. "Every night it's a prince."

She nodded stubbornly. "You said I could start."

"Okay," he smiled. "Once there was a prince." He held her hand and looked at the outline of her limbs under the covers. Her legs were already lengthening. She was so far from her babyhood already, so much a pretty little girl . . . "There was a prince, and he went to a strange kingdom where there was a beautiful princess. He fell in love with her."

"But there was a dragon," Sybil chimed in, "in the kingdom. A terrible dragon who lived under the ground. He lived in a cave, where the ocean met the land. It was a dark watery cave."

"Right," Hal said. "And the king and his soldiers had tried to fight the dragon, but many had been killed, and no one could save the kingdom."

"There was also a witch," Sybil added. She always wanted witches in her stories.

"Yes, there was a witch," Hal agreed, rolling his eyes again. "And she was the real reason no one could defeat the dragon. Because every time a soldier would go down into the cave, the witch would cast a spell on him."

"And the dragon would pull him down under the water and eat him up," Sybil concluded gruesomely.

"Right," Hal said. "Well, our prince told the princess that he would kill the dragon. She told him about the witch, but he said he would defeat the witch by playing a trick on her."

Sybil furrowed her brow. She was trying to figure out what must come next. The working of her quick mind made her look prettier than ever.

"The prince went to a wise man . . . ," Hal prodded.

She brightened. "And the wise man told him how to stop the spell."

Hal looked down at her proudly. "That's right. All he had to do was wait until the witch lay down to sleep, and say three magic words into her ear. Then she wouldn't be able to wake up for twenty-four hours, and he could sneak into the cave past her guard. That way he could fight the dragon and save the city. And when the witch woke up the dragon would be gone and her power would no longer terrorize the kingdom."

"So he said the three magic words . . . ," Syb said.

"*Sybil kabibil kabob*," Hal intoned solemnly.

"And the witch went to sleep." She grinned at his magic words.

"Then," Hal said, "the prince got his sword and his lance and he journeyed deep into the watery cave to fight the dragon."

"But the witch woke up."

Sybil's voice was clear, almost too sharp. Hal had seen this many times. She had a way of destroying happy endings.

"She hurried down to the cave," Sybil continued. "She used a special spell to make herself look exactly like the princess. When she saw the prince in the water, she called out, '*I'm here, the dragon's got me, help me!*' And the prince turned around to look at her. He thought she was the princess. And while his back was turned, the dragon bit him and pulled him under the water and he died."

Hal felt his smile fade as he looked down at the little figure in the bed. She was so sure, so implacable in the tragedy she had wrought.

"But how did she wake up?" he asked.

"Because the three magic words weren't strong enough," Sybil said. "The witch slept for a while, but then she woke up. And she put a spell on herself so she would look just like the princess, and she put a spell on the prince to make him turn and look at her, and then the dragon pulled him down into the water and ate him."

Something uncanny took possession of Hal. Though Sybil's dark imagination had become familiar to him in the past, tonight seemed the first time she had trusted him enough to unburden herself of its entire, terrible weight.

She was looking up at him through clear pretty eyes, as calm as though she had just finished saying "Good morning" instead of assassinating their fancied prince.

He smiled.

"And they all lived happily ever after," he said. The words resounded between them like a challenge.

Sybil said nothing, but continued staring at him with an expression of whimsical skepticism.

"Really," he insisted. "The old sorcerer knew a spell that brought the prince back to life, and the prince stepped on the dragon's foot, and the dragon ran away crying. And the prince made a scary face at the witch, and she ran away crying, too. Then the prince married the princess and became king, and they had lots of children, and sugarplums rained from the sky, and no one ever got sticky fingers from eating them, and none of the little girls in the kingdom ever had to wash or clean up their rooms ever again. So they all lived happily ever after."

Sybil watched him go on, his words echoing somewhere between an exorcism and a plea, and a tenuous bond extended from brother to sister, as though without it she might slip away from him forever into a region beyond his reach.

"You're silly," she said.

"So are you," he replied a bit uneasily. "I love you. Now go to sleep."

He turned off the light and kissed her once more. Then she turned over on her stomach, facing away from him, her eyes still open as she gazed at the blank wall. There was no sound from the bed as he left the room.

. . .

The weeks that followed were busy ones, filled with new sights and sounds and people with lovely British accents who made a great fuss over all three Lancaster children. Then it was time for the trip home and school and friends and plans and worries. Hal gave no more thought to the story he had shared with Sybil on their first night in England in the summer of 1937.

It would be many years before he looked back and mused that his own sleep had never been quite as peaceful after that night with Syb as before it.

III

Los Angeles Times, December 19, 1941

AMERICA GOES TO WAR

Today both houses of Congress overwhelmingly passed the conference-approved draft bill making all American men from ages 20 to 44 subject to military service.

The new law was enacted in the wake of the Japanese attack on the American fleet at Pearl Harbor which took place on December 7th—"a date which will live in infamy," in the words of President Roosevelt. The attack severely weakened American naval forces in the Pacific and damaged American morale even as it instantly placed the nation on a war footing.

Hundreds of thousands of American men are not waiting for the new law to be administered by the Selective Service, and are already thronging enlistment centers throughout the nation . . .

"ALL RIGHT, LADS. Let's have a toast."

The tiny house was full of guests. Though a festive Christmas tree stood in a corner, the minds of the dozen or so young men assembled here were not on the holidays, but on the war raging overseas. They knew they were about to fight in that war, leaving their women and children to celebrate future holidays without them.

Most of them, like their host, were young, out-of-work men planning to enlist for the war immediately. A few had already enlisted, and were to leave for basic training within days or even hours.

This was the house of Dennis Linehan, an unemployed dock worker who, like his friends, had lived in San Diego since his family settled here a generation ago as part of the Irish expansion throughout California.

San Diego's Irish population, always closely knit, had become even more so when the Depression left most of its best men without work. Now that the war had come to change all that, it was with a fierce sense of community and pride that Dennis Linehan and his friends prepared to fight as Irishmen for their adopted land.

"A toast, Dennie!" someone cried.

All eyes turned to Dennis, the host, who was generally considered the most eloquent among them.

"All right, then." Dennis raised his glass of ale. "To the good old U.S. of A.—and to all the lads who are going to beat the Hun, and his new pal the filthy Jap. And," he added, "to the women who will wait for us."

"Hear, hear."

"Well done, Dennie."

The men raised their glasses with a cheer. They were acutely aware that Britain was the only bastion preventing the Germans from over-running the civilized world. Now that America, pricked by the mad Japs, was at last entering the war, its Irishmen would have the chance to fight for their homeland on the very soil of Europe.

"A song, Dennis," called a young man.

"A song!" echoed the others. "Come on, Dennie. Don't let us down tonight."

Dennis Linehan blushed slightly. He was a handsome man in his thirties, with ruddy cheeks, soft brown eyes, and a clever sense of humor. His sweet Irish tenor was admired by all his friends, so he could not let them down now.

Someone had sat down at the battered upright piano that was kept in the parlor. Dennis nodded to the accompanist and cleared his throat. Silence fell as he began to sing.

> *By Killarney's lakes and fells,*
> *Emerald isles and winding bays,*
> *Mountain paths, and woodland dells*
> *Memory ever fondly strays.*

Hushed nostalgia could be felt throughout the room as his voice caressed the lyrics. Dennis's singing had in recent painful years been a balm to his companions during idle times spent in the frustration of unemployment. Now it seemed as though he was reminding them all of the faraway home whose green freedom they would really be fighting for when they faced the enemy.

> *Wings of angels so might shine,*
> *Glancing back soft light divine,*

> Beauty's home, Killarney,
> Ever fair, Killarney.

When the song was finished there was a charged pause. Eire glimmered in the hearts of all those present, while their adopted homeland girded for battle around them.

"America the Beautiful," someone called out, having correctly sensed the general mood.

Dennis smiled to his wife and growing sons and began to sing. The words had never sounded so lovely as his voice made them now. His eyes took on a special glow, and he beckoned to a little girl sitting across the room. She came to his side and sat on his knee as he went on singing. His hand rested on her shoulder, fingers stroking the waves of her red hair.

They made a touching picture, the man in his prime about to go off to war, singing in honor of his adopted land as his little girl sat on his knee. Her Irish beauty seemed to sum up the feelings stirred by Dennis's voice. She was not his flesh and blood, they knew, though she seemed so natural with him. She was the orphaned daughter of his cousin Bob, who had tragically perished with his wife in a fire. The girl was named Elizabeth, and she had been living with the Linehans ever since.

Dennis, who had two sons but no girl child of his own, had taken her to his heart, and it was said he loved her as much as if she were his own daughter. He took her everywhere with him, scraped up meager sums to buy her small presents, and showed her off to his fellow unemployed pals when he went walking about the town with her.

He treated her like a princess, and indeed she looked like one. At eight she already had the lengthening limbs of a lovely colleen, and milky white skin touched by sunny freckles. Her fiery hair was highlighted by strands of gold, and her eyes glowed as green as the hills of the motherland. Her personality, at once impish and precociously feminine, charmed everyone.

It was obvious to those present that not the least of the pangs of separation facing popular Dennis Linehan as he left for the war would be for this little girl. His misty eyes bespoke that pain as he held her close to him, and his pure tenor communicated it so eloquently that many of his friends had tears running down their cheeks as he finished the song.

Applause rang out, somewhat subdued now, for they all realized how desperate was the war to come, and how many of them might not return. The little girl's beauty seemed to symbolize everything they were about to leave behind, perhaps forever. Their collective gaze lingered on her with love and admiration.

But there was one person in the room whose thoughts were on an entirely different plane tonight.

Kathleen Linehan looked at her husband, and at the little girl on his lap.

The girl's eyes bore a soft expression, full of affection for her adopted father and of respect for those present. And there was something faraway and faintly sad in their green depths, which made the secret of her charm.

But Kathleen knew that this look was put on especially for Dennis and his friends. It was a mask, as was everything else about the little girl.

And Kathleen alone knew how crucial it was that she get this child out of her family as soon as possible.

Two years ago, when Bob Dameron and his wife died and the family chose Dennis and Kathleen to take in little Elizabeth, Kathleen had welcomed the child with open arms. She was a good-hearted woman, and happy to help the family. Moreover, she thought her two older sons would enjoy pampering a little sister.

But almost immediately after the little girl arrived, still only a child of seven, Kathleen had noticed something strange. Elizabeth's manner, so sweet and charming with Dennis and the boys, was different when it came to Kathleen herself. The first time she was alone with Elizabeth, Kathleen felt a coldness emanating from her. And when the child would sit on Dennis's lap—for he had taken an immediate liking for her—she would look across the room at Kathleen in an odd way, an up-from-under look of quiet triumph in her cool green eyes.

Kathleen was sure of her husband's love, and reproached herself for the unsettling feelings of jealousy that stole over her during those first weeks and months after Elizabeth's arrival. Nevertheless, before long her woman's intuition told her that Dennis's feelings had changed toward his adopted daughter. The look in his eyes when he held her on his lap, walked with her, bespoke something deeper than the mere affection of a foster parent. It was the look a man bears for a woman, not a child.

From that day forward Kathleen found herself watching her husband, calculating how much time he spent alone with Elizabeth, wondering, worrying. And though she forced her suspicions beneath the surface of her maternal behavior toward the girl, she knew she had a genuine adversary under her roof, and a determined one. That little gleam of triumph in Elizabeth's eyes when she looked at Kathleen was unbearable.

And now, two years later, though Kathleen dared not avow it in her Christian heart, there could be no doubt that something was truly wrong between Dennis and Elizabeth. His silent preoccupation with the little girl was clouding his normally happy personality. Their intimacy was too obvious when they were in the presence of family and friends. And, no matter how alertly Kathleen kept her eye on them, she noticed that they found time to be alone together when she could not be with them, and when the boys were out.

The truth could no longer be avoided. There was a beautiful, inhumanly clever homewrecker under Kathleen's own roof. And that siren was only eight years old.

Kathleen wondered how the perversity of nature could have created a child such as this. She knew that Bob and Flora Dameron had had an unhealthy marriage, and that Bob had spoiled his daughter terribly before his death. Flora had been a severe mother, and an unloving one. But could such a set of circumstances produce a creature as dangerous as Elizabeth?

Kathleen seemed to recall an old bit of family lore to the effect that the Damerons, in the last century, had produced more than one female of dubious moral character. Among the skeletons in the family closet were, it was said, two or three seductive courtesans who had fleeced some of Dublin's gentry out of great amounts of money and broken their hearts. The story was unconfirmed, for none of the Dameron cousins liked to talk about it.

Could little Elizabeth be the carrier of that hereditary taint? Was this why Flora Dameron had turned against her daughter so soon after the child's birth?

Kathleen Linehan did not know the answer.

But she did not intend to see her family ruined as Bob Dameron's had been. Tonight she had a plan.

Within a few days Dennis would be gone to the war. Once he was out of the way Kathleen would get rid of Elizabeth. She had already laid the groundwork with the extended Linehan and Dameron families. She herself was already working in a textile factory that was producing uniforms for the armed services. With the two boys in school, it was too much for her to handle a little girl as well—or so she had convinced the relatives.

They had all agreed that a religious girls' boarding school was the only solution. Once Dennis was gone little Tess would be sent to Bakersfield, where she would attend the Sacred Heart School for Girls and spend holidays with her uncle Ned and his wife Diane.

Of course, Dennis would never have approved such a plan had he known about it. But Kathleen had had a long, serious talk with Diane and her sister Moira as well, and they understood that the child must be kept well away from Dennis until she was grown. Only by placing an interval of miles and a rampart of relatives between her and Dennis could everyone else rest easy, Kathleen most of all.

It was the only way.

As Kathleen gazed at the little girl—so innocent in appearance, and yet so dangerous—she thought of Hitler and Munich, and the shame of Chamberlain and the Allies, the appeasements and accommodations that had led to the disaster now facing the world. Had something been done sooner to nip the evil in the bud, this extremity might never have been reached, and the violence now consuming the world might have been avoided.

Kathleen did not intend to make the same mistake.

Armed with her secret knowledge, she studied the beautiful child on Dennis's knee. Somehow the little girl sensed her scrutiny, and turned her green eyes to her. How clear they were, and yet how complicated! To any observer in the room it was just a sweet, loving look from adopted daughter to mother. One had to see it through Kathleen's eyes to feel what was in it. The cool challenge, the hatred, the triumph—a private stare from woman to woman, invisible to a third party.

In a way, Kathleen realized, it was already too late. Too late to cleanse the guilt from Dennis's heart, and to undo the damage to their family and their love. But one had to banish the evil nonetheless, and then pick up the pieces.

Too late, yes. But better late than never, Kathleen Linehan mused, turning her eyes from the little girl to her husband.

IV

June 7, 1942

"A major air and sea battle is rumored to be taking place between American and Japanese task forces in the vicinity of Midway Island, a tiny atoll in the far Pacific that has great strategic importance as a potential base for future Japanese attacks against American Pacific installations. The Americans, according to sources, are vastly outmanned by the Japanese fleet, which may include as many as five aircraft carriers, three to five battleships, and countless cruisers and destroyers, but are determined to hold the island at all costs . . ."

HAL LAY ON THE BED in his room, listening to the radio and staring at the maps on his walls. Outside the window the vista of the Upper East Side made a gray background under the cloudy sky. The sound of the Park Avenue traffic beyond the courtyard was a distant murmur. It was a cool and somehow depressing day, with rain not far off.

"The aircraft carrier Yorktown, according to informed sources, is in the area, and may be involved in the battle against the Japanese fleet . . ."

The newscast continued on the big radio Hal's father had given him for Christmas so he could listen to the war news in the privacy of his room. The maps Hal had collected showed all the major theaters of war, from the Pacific to the Russian front. He had drawn arrows on them showing the Allied advances and retreats, and had penciled in numbers estimating troop strength and the balance of American and enemy losses.

Hal was a precocious expert on everything concerning the war, from equipment to strategy to weapons research. He had focused his sixteen-year-old brain on the intricacies of combat the way many of his peers did on automobiles or college football or the New York Yankees.

Though he realized that his maps showed a seesaw battle against a powerful and determined enemy, and a world on the razor's edge between totalitarianism and freedom, his youth protected him from the fear he might have felt at this uneasy balance. He saw only victory for his side, an inevitability made certain by right and honor, and by the crucial fact that Stewart was fighting for his country at this very moment.

That was why Hal sat up to listen to the broadcast with special alertness. Stewart, a navy pilot, had already seen action this year in the Marshall Islands and then the Coral Sea. He had miraculously escaped unharmed when his carrier, the *Lexington*, was lost in May. And now, though the Navy's censors had prevented him from stating his whereabouts in his last letters, Hal was sure he was with another carrier—perhaps the *Yorktown*—and no doubt engaged in the battle for Midway.

"Take my word for it, little brother," Stewart had written not two weeks ago. *"We're in for a hot fight in this part of the world. Be thankful you're home and well out of harm's way."*

The words came back to Hal now, frustratingly glib in their reassurance. He did not want to be safe and sound here at home, ensconced in prep school while his brother risked his life as a navy pilot against desperate Japanese fighters. He wanted to be where Stewart was.

He turned now to look at the picture of Stewart that was kept on his dresser. The handsome chiseled face looked out from under the lieutenant's cap with careless arrogance etched by a flashing smile. It was a face full of confidence, glowing with utter faith in the cause Stewart served and in his ability to serve it well and heroically.

Downstairs, on the walls of the library and salon, were other pictures. They showed Stew at his graduation from Naval ROTC, Stew the day he received his pilot's wings, Stew home on furlough after being promoted to full lieutenant. His smile was identical in all the pictures, so much so that it might almost have been transferred optically from one image to the next. He had that trait in common with his father. He wore the smile like an armor proving his ability to dominate the world.

As for Father himself, though, the face he wore in the pictures with Stew showed more than a trace of his relief at each return of his son from duty, and of the silent dread he lived with when Stewie was gone. Part of Father had shared Stewie's exultation when the Japs attacked Pearl Harbor and he was called up for immediate action. The rest of him was not so sanguine, however, and he had to conceal his anxiety from the rest of the family as he heard each day's war news and wondered about his son's safety.

Stewart's last furlough, after the May action in the Coral Sea, had been a holiday from worry for the whole family. Unlike so many combat veterans who find themselves unable to talk to loved ones about the war, Stewart had been excited and voluble in telling stories about his own exploits and those of his fellow pilots. The war did not seem to daunt him at all. On the contrary, it offered an outlet for his brash masculinity.

He found time to be alone with Hal, and to confide his worries about the Japanese victories in the Pacific to the younger brother whom he knew to be an expert on the war. Sensing Hal's frustration at being too young to see any action—for no one believed this war could last more than another year or two—Stewart spoke to him man to man about the enemy's strength, and even shared his feelings of loss about his buddies who had not come back.

This brotherly confession confirmed Hal's boundless admiration for Stewart, and made him feel less cut off from the challenge facing his country. A sort of magic spread through the Park Avenue house during that furlough, as Stewart's inextinguishable confidence dissipated his parents' strain and fueled everyone's optimism about the eventual outcome of the war.

And today, as he listened to the news about faraway Midway Island, he knew that in another five or six weeks Stewart would be back again, with more stories to tell, and more smiles to warm his family with.

"Hey, Prince Hal. What's new?"

Hal looked up in surprise. He had not heard the soft knock at his door. A pretty face framed by wispy chestnut hair was looking down at him, lips curled in a gentle smirk at his dreaminess.

"Not much," he said. "Just looking out the window."

"Well, now. There can't be much new out there."

Tall, slim Kirsten Shaw entered the room without ceremony, flopped on the bed beside Hal, crossed her legs, and rumpled his hair affectionately.

She was wearing slacks and a patterned blouse, with a light sweater tied around her neck by its arms. Hal always felt a bit tongue-tied when Kirsten was around, for she possessed an Ivy League assurance of speech combined with a sort of lissome tweedy grace of body that made him feel somehow inadequate.

Kirsten was in her early twenties, a good six years older than Hal. She had been an unofficial member of the Lancaster family for as long as Hal could remember. During her girlhood she had spent vacations with the Lancasters at Newport and Bar Harbor, and after her mother's last illness had joined the family in the city as well.

Her father had been a Yale classmate and World War I buddy of Reid Lancaster, and when he died in the war Dad had taken a personal interest in Kirsten. Her mother Dorothy, never a very strong person or even a sensible one, was a distant Lancaster cousin who was only too happy to see a strong father figure present himself for her daughter.

When Dorothy died, Reid had a heart-to-heart talk with the girl, then aged eighteen, and she told him she would prefer membership in the Lancaster clan to being farmed out to her Shaw relatives in Detroit. This made sense socially, since Dottie's marriage into the Shaw family had never really been approved of by the Lancasters in the first place.

So it came about that Kirsten joined the family. She quickly became an integral part of it, though she retained a stubborn individuality that set her apart from her new siblings as well as their parents.

She was inseparable from Stewart, but more as a competitor than as a sister. She matched her considerable skills with his in horsemanship, tennis, and swimming, not to mention golf, at which she could beat him in matched play. She was a determined athlete and a natural one, with her long, lithe arms and legs and perfect timing.

As Hal grew up he joined them in threesomes at Shinnecock Hills or Winged Foot, and in mixed-doubles tennis when they could find a fourth. It always seemed to him that Stewart tolerated Kirsten without having much real affection for her, while Kirsten, so close in age to Stewie, was a bit jealous of his status within the family, and concerned above all to prove herself equal to him.

Meanwhile she was very much the confident older sister to Hal, not terribly sympathetic, not very forthcoming, and Hal always felt she was closer to Stewart than to himself, in temperament as well as in age.

Nevertheless it was Kirsten, with her poetic sense, who had first dubbed him "Prince Hal" in homage to his famous bedtime stories with Sybil, and who persisted affectionately in teasing him with references to Shakespeare's Henry V plays throughout his youth.

"Good morrow, sweet Hal," she would call after him as he passed through a room or came down to dinner. "How agrees the devil and thee about thy soul?" Or again, when they went riding, just to tease him: "I prithee, good Prince Hal, help me to my horse, good king's son."

The "Prince Hal" nickname stuck, not only because Hal's generosity of spirit matched that of Shakespeare's favorite king, but because there was something quietly heroic and self-sacrificing about Hal that impressed all those around him.

Kirsten was ignored by Reid Lancaster from the moment he accepted her under the aegis of his name and his responsibility. But she rapidly became indispensable to Eleanor, for her social sense was unerring, and she always knew which invitations had to be answered, which parties attended, which gift to choose for which relative on a given occasion.

Kirsten was everybody's majordomo, general secretary, and Girl Friday as well as life of the party. Her intelligence and sharp wit made her a crucial presence at all the Lancaster gatherings, where levity was a commodity hard to come by. The relatives were always delighted to see her come along, brisk and ready for fun, when Reid's family attended an important function.

Pretty Kirsten Shaw was that most ambiguous of creatures, a homeless relative liked by all, beloved of no one in particular, and smiling through it all as though nothing in the world could touch her. She had just finished an undergraduate degree at Vassar, and would probably go on to a brilliant future in any field she chose, as well as the best marriage Reid Lancaster could arrange for her.

But for the moment she was here at home, and the most blithe of the war-wearied spirits waiting for Stewart's return from the Pacific.

She had the run of the house, of course, so Hal was not surprised to see her turn up at his door this way. The maids never set foot in this wing after early morning, for his parents deemed it his private domain now that Stewart no longer occupied the bedroom adjacent to his own. They believed their boys had a right to privacy, especially during their growing-up years.

But Kirsten respected only her own right to wander where she chose. Besides, she reserved for herself a sister's privilege of accosting her self-absorbed little brother whenever the spirit moved her.

So here she was.

"Still keeping track of our Stew, are you?" she asked, looking at the wall maps with their pushpins and arrows. "How are we doing?"

Hal warmed to the subject. "We've got Ethiopia back," he said, "and the Germans can't beat England in the air. After Coral Sea, the Japs know we can beat them. I think Midway will be the key to everything." He pointed to the tiny dot in the Pacific marked by large arrows on his map. "This is where the war is going to turn around."

"Good for us," Kirsten said. Her interest in the subtleties of warfare was obviously lukewarm. "How is Stew?"

"Fine." They both knew that Stewart wrote letters for Hal alone, which were deemed to be more sensitive and confidential than those addressed to the whole family. Kirsten had sometimes expressed interest in the private parts of these, her face bearing an odd look. It seemed for all the world as though she were somehow jealous of what Stewie might be up to overseas.

But for now she accepted Hal's laconic reply, leaning back on her elbows and crossing her legs.

"You're expected at seven for dinner tonight," she said with a yawn. "Mother says don't be late." For the hundredth time Hal noticed the curious way she used the word "Mother." It meant, very clearly, "*Your* mother." Something in Kirsten's voice made it understood that she herself was not a real member of the family. And though she seemed to relish the independence that went with this separateness, Hal often wondered how lonely she was underneath.

He said nothing. She had kicked off her sandals, and her slender toes wriggled in the June air as the breeze furled the curtains. She had a way of making herself at home in any room, draping those long limbs over furniture that seemed to welcome her, and gazing at nearby objects through dusky brown eyes that were calmly sovereign, as though she owned everything she could see.

"You miss Stewart, don't you?" she asked, looking at Hal from her reclining position.

Hal shrugged. The question disconcerted him.

"Never mind, silly," she said. "I just mean you're a good brother to him. Has he written this week?"

Hal nodded, crossing the room on long coltlike legs to reach for a letter on the bookshelf. He hesitated for a moment, going over the letter's contents in his mind, and then handed it to Kirsten.

"Can I read it? Really?" she asked, interested.

"Go ahead." It was the first time he had given her one of Stew's letters. Though he was violating his personal policy, something about the way she had spoken of Mother just now made him feel sorry for her, and he did not want her to feel shut out.

He watched her bite her lower lip in concentration as she read. Her hair was splayed over the bolster pillow. The white outline of her bra stirred softly under her blouse as she turned the letter over, quickly reading through the male confidences. Hal could see the crucifix about her neck—her father had been Catholic, and she had come out of her family disasters with religion—though its tip was invisible, hidden among the shadows of her cleavage.

One of her shapely knees moved back and forth gently as she read. From where he stood, Hal could smell the attractive perfume of her, a delicate but musky scent that befitted her athletic personality.

All at once Hal felt uncomfortable. He had caught himself noticing her femininity again. He could not recall when it had happened for the first time—last fall, perhaps, or during the summer, or even earlier—but he knew that her moments alone with him put him on edge in a new way nowadays. And her teasing made him blush as it had never done before.

Now that Stewart was gone to the war, Kirsten and Hal had somehow grown closer. She no longer seemed so much older. Nor did she seem, paradoxically, as familiar as she once had been. There was something exotic about her, something alluring. When she walked through a room, he felt his senses tense at her approach. His eyes followed her despite himself, traveling down the slim catlike back to the curved hips and long legs, his gaze alert to the hidden rhythm of her movements.

This shamed and upset him, for Kirsten, as long as he could remember, had been nothing but a playmate, a resented older sister. It felt positively unnatural to become aware of her as a woman.

He watched now as she finished the letter, obviously disappointed in its contents, and tossed it on the table.

"Men," she said, a smirk on her lips. "You really love war, don't you?"

Hal shrugged. "We want to win," he said.

"Well, if you don't mind demolishing three quarters of Europe while you're at it, I suppose it's all right," she said.

Hal could think of no rejoinder.

Now he noticed that she was looking at him more closely, a subtle glimmer spreading across her pretty features.

"You know something?" she asked.

Hal felt a surge of discomfort inside him. He suspected she was going to say something he did not want to hear.

"What?" he asked.

"You're growing up," she said, studying him with a slow smile. "You're a big boy now."

He turned his face from her eyes and said nothing.

"You're getting to be a handsome fellow," she said, leaning back once more so that the fabric of her blouse stretched over her breasts. To his shock Hal thought he glimpsed a shadow of nipple under the white sheen of her bra. "Like your famous brother," she continued, glancing at the picture of Stewart on the dresser. "Only more so."

"Come on," he reproached her, looking back to the maps on the walls. The subject she raised discomfited him, so he tried to diminish its significance. Fighting and dying seemed far more important to him than being handsome.

"Well, you are," she insisted, amused at his embarrassment.

"Who cares?" he said, moving uncertainly away from her toward the window.

"You'll care one of these days," she insisted, "when you and your buddies at Choate start sneaking into town to look for fast girls—if you haven't already."

"I haven't," he said.

"And don't be surprised if you start getting eyes for some of our sexier debutantes pretty soon," she added.

Hal blushed. He knew there was truth to her words. One day he would care about girls. But the idea seemed absurd. For as long as he could remember the notion of romance, of love, had filled him with revulsion and contempt, as though it were an effeminate and unworthy occupation for a real man.

But recently, as Kirsten seemed to guess, his mind had been caught by thoughts of women in a new way. He found himself daydreaming about the contours of their legs, the soft attraction of their voices, the hollow of their necks leading down to the creamy shadowed skin of their breasts. Often he would see a strange girl on the street and fantasize about her for hours or days afterward.

He wished he could talk to Stewart about these feelings. Stewart had had dozens of girlfriends, and was engaged to Marcia Stallworth, the most attractive and talented debutante of last year—a perfect match, Father said, for both families. There was nothing about women that Stewart didn't know.

But Stewart was not here. So Hal suffered his strange new feelings alone. For some reason he did not want to tell his peers at school about them. The feelings were too private, too unsettling to confide to the crude boys his own age.

Hal's nights were a torment now. Sleep was hard to find as he lay on his stomach, taunted by somnolent fantasies of girls' smiles, of smooth brown thighs disappearing under a skirt, of the colorful and mysterious lushness of female hair shrouding creamy cheeks and subtle eyes. Over and over again he had to change his position, for the touch of the bedclothes made his sex hard and alert, and thrust sleep further away. The effort took hours.

This thought was in his mind as he looked at Kirsten now. She was still leaning back, her bare toes stirring in the silence. She was looking at him with a sort of wanton penetration that amazed him. He blushed again as her eyes traveled down his body and back up to his face.

"You've been thinking about it, haven't you?" she asked slyly.

"About what?" he asked. "What are you talking about?"

"Don't give me that," she said. "I know men, buddy. I can tell when they've got the hots."

She laughed, a deep husky murmur in her throat as she watched her words take effect.

"Don't be shy about it," she said, her knee moving from side to side in a gentle rhythm. "It shows you're a real man. Like your brother. Just relax, Hal. Let it come. You've got a lot of fun ahead of you."

He turned away. To his horror he realized that the caressing note in her voice was making him hard. She frightened him, for she seemed able to read his mind—or, rather, to read something into his thoughts that had perhaps not been there before, but which leapt into life at the sound of her words, straining suddenly forward just so that she could put her finger on it.

"What's the matter?" Her voice came from behind him.

"Nothing." He shook his head. "You're crazy, that's all." His words were a weak denial of the story his body told so eloquently.

He heard her sigh. There was a murmur of the bedcovers as she stirred. He kept his eyes on the cityscape outside the window.

Then he thought he heard a step. Perhaps she was going. Perhaps she would leave him alone.

In fact, as he listened, the door closed, very slowly and quietly.

Something told him she was still in the room.

"Don't turn around," she said. "I almost forgot. I have a surprise for you."

Hal felt atrociously trapped by her. He was still hard under his pants. He could not turn around. And now she had closed the door. They were completely alone, for no one else would be on this floor all day. Why was she doing this to him? Why wouldn't she let him alone?

He heard a soft rustle of clothes, which sent a shudder through his senses. Was she tucking in her blouse? It would be a good idea—it had been showing too much.

At last she spoke. "It's all right now, Hal. You can turn around."

He turned and looked.

What he saw left him breathless. She was still in her blouse, but the slacks were folded on the bed beside her, and her sandals were discarded on the floor. Long brown legs emerged from a pair of pink silk panties, the creamy thighs giving way to slim calves above bare feet at ease on his carpet.

"God, Kirs!" He swore at her despite himself. "What are you doing? You're crazy."

"Unh-unh," she shook her head, drawing a finger across her lips as her eyes slid over his body. "Not from what I see. I think I'm right on target, slugger."

He had turned toward her, and she was staring between his legs with a fixity that paralyzed him. Her thighs stirred, and he sensed the sex behind her panties, a dark and mysterious presence.

"Someone will come," he said weakly.

She shook her pretty head. "No, Hal," she smiled. "The maids are downstairs, and Mother is out. It's just you and me."

As he watched, speechless with surprise, she arched her back and shrugged out of the blouse. A small bra clung to her breasts. How slim and beautiful she was, her nakedness touched by the two flimsy shreds of fabric at breasts and crotch! He had never seen how sensual that willowy form could look until now, and he was overwhelmed.

"Kirsten . . . You're crazy," he murmured.

Coolly she reclined on his bed again, and raised both thighs so he could see between her legs. The curve of a buttock peeked out at him from behind the silken fabric of the panties. Her hair flowed over her shoulders, and her toes stirred as though to beckon him.

"I think," she cooed, "that a certain person is getting just a little bit hot and bothered." She looked into his eyes, her nakedness seeming to reach out to him across the room.

"Kirs, why are you doing this?" he asked weakly.

"Because it's time," she replied. "Don't be bashful, Prince Hal. When it was Stewie's time, I did it with him, too. But he fooled me, the clever dog. He had been screwing some hot little piece of baggage from Rosemary Hall before I knew what he was up to."

The mention of Stewart filled Hal with uncanny feelings.

Kirsten looked harder at him, if that was possible.

"But that's not true with you, is it?" she asked. "You're fresh as a daisy, aren't you? The only girls you've had were inside that naughty mind of yours, weren't they, Hal? Oh, I know you. You're too much of a straight arrow to be fooling around at your age."

Again Hal saw the long thighs move, saw the panties hug the girl's sex with almost obscene invitation. Only now did he realize how chaste his fantasies about lovemaking had been—they had never gone even this far. He was entirely out of his element.

"Close the shades," she said softly.

Without knowing why, Hal did as he was told.

When he turned back to the darkened room, he saw that she was unhooking the bra. As he watched, the tiny covering fell away to reveal perfect, firm breasts with hard pink nipples. She leaned forward.

"Take off your pants," she said.

Hal was terrified, as much of himself and the boiling in his senses as of Kirsten's hungry domination. She seemed to have outthought him, played him into a corner, as she did so often with her sharp strategic sense in chess, tennis, and other games.

Still, he would have refused her, would have risked angering and upsetting her, had not her allusion to Stewart pricked his pride in some unknown way.

He loosened his belt with trembling fingers. The slacks fell to the floor. He could feel his sex distending the tight cotton underpants. He knew he was wet already, wet as he had found himself so many times in his bed when tormenting visions of girls stole his sleep from him.

Her eyes were fixed hungrily to his crotch. She moved toward him, crawling on the bed. And now a note of tenderness crept into her voice.

"It's all right, baby," she said, dropping to her knees before him. "You're going to be fine."

Her fingers brushed his hips before they slipped under the elastic band and began pulling the underpants slowly down.

"Mmm," she murmured. "You're a big boy. I could tell you'd be this way, Hal."

Soft hands were on his loins, patting and soothing, but always pulling him toward her. She helped him off with his shirt, and out of the underpants bunched at his feet. Then he felt female fingers stealing up his legs, slowly along his knees and the insides of his thighs, and finally finding the sex he had touched so few times himself.

She took hold of the shaft with a little sigh. To his surprise he saw that it took both her hands to enclose it.

"My royal Hal, my sweet boy." She taunted him with Shakespeare even now. But there was reverence in her as she kissed the penis, and then she rubbed her cheek against his loins with an almost maternal affection.

She seemed to know he was too young to let her take him in her mouth. She did not want to spoil things by shocking him. So it was with a sweet languor that she began to caress the organ, working clever thumbs at the tip until she felt him tremble.

Then she stood up and stepped back a pace, and he watched her slip the panties down her beautiful legs. The dark warm triangle winked at him, and she came forward to pull him down on the bed with her.

"Come on, handsome," she said, squirming under him so that her thighs could caress his own. "Here's something you'll like."

She kissed him deeply, her tongue inviting his own to taste and explore the fragrant inside of her mouth. Then she offered him a firm young breast, and he sucked at it tentatively, hearing her sigh with deep hunger as he did so.

Her thighs were spread now, brushing at his hips, and as he tasted the hard bud of her nipple and felt it tense against his lips and tongue, he realized that the tip of him had found its way between her legs. A wild hot rhythm seemed to be overtaking him, thrilling in irresistible waves down his stomach and through his loins, and for an instant he thought his body did not belong to him any longer.

But then he felt something strange inside him, something wise, a sort of knowledge in the hard penis that was even now poising itself at the center of her, cleverly caressing her with its tip until her sighs took on a sudden haste.

"Oh, baby, come on," she whispered, frantic from the sucking at her nipple and the hard thing toying with her sex. "Quick."

He let the slow straining rhythms inside him have their way, and the shaft worked its way into her, an inch more, then more, until at last it was buried to its hilt. To his surprise he felt her shudder, and heard a cry in her throat. He held himself back for an instant, but already the eager hands on his hips and the moan on her lips told him it was pleasure that had made her cry out.

"Oh, God, Hal. Oh, God, you're marvelous." Her voice was a helpless whimper, worlds away from any sound he had ever heard from Kirsten before.

He gazed down at her impassioned face. It jerked this way and that, nestled in the hair splayed across his pillow, and her hot little nipples danced as her breasts shook under his thrusts.

All at once an amazing sense of power came to mingle with the swirling delight in his loins. Ancient wisdom coming from nowhere told him what to do. He timed a slow stroke, and felt it draw a deep groan of delight from her. He slid himself in and out, up and down, tender and careful in his caressing of her sex, and watched her respond with cries of anticipation, of greedy wanting, of sudden ecstasy.

He began to realize that he was owning her, possessing her with his body. Despite all her mocking ways and her narcissism, she was his slave now, the plaything of his flesh.

"Oh," she sighed, and "Oh! Hal . . . more . . . more . . ." And he felt that the thing between his legs could go on this way all night, drawing power from its own excitement, teasing her with languid strokes, overpowering her with harder, quicker thrusts, triumphant in its domination as it forced endless cries of passion from her.

How long it went on he did not know, that sweet expanding moment in which the living doll in his arms gave him the husky song of her orgasms. But at length, abetted by the weird murmurs of the female flesh fondling him, the last wave began to come, and Hal's body was following a law all its own, grinding his back and hips into her faster and faster.

He heard pathetic cries of wonderment and surrender in his ear, and felt her thighs grip him hard as he pushed into her with a final spasm. His own coming was like a river, flowing through himself and through her in great deep waves, as her fingers fluttered at his shoulders and her cries surrounded him.

She was actually weeping when at last, exhausted, he slumped atop her, and she hugged him close and kissed his eyelids.

"Darling," she whispered. "You're incredible. It was never like this. Never with anybody. Jesus. Oh, Jesus."

They lay that way for a long time, her words caressing him as the taut penis lingered inside her. When he ebbed from her at last he heard a little sigh of regret from her lips, and she lay beside him, studying him through admiring eyes, her fingers straying over his young body, touching at the sex that had given her so much pleasure.

When she sat up he saw the crucifix, forgotten until now, dangling like a talisman between her breasts. She got up to dress, and he lay naked watching her. He saw the soft lissome form, still glowing with his possession of her, as it disappeared into the bra and panties, then the slacks and blouse. She was recovering her poise as the clothes hid her body, though she still seemed a bit shaken by what had happened.

She paused before his mirror, fixing her hair. And when she turned to him with a smile she was once again her pert, athletic self instead of the sobbing, moaning slave he had held in his arms moments ago.

In that transformation Hal discovered an enigma about women that he was never to forget. The mocking look on Kirsten's pretty face as she gazed down on him was, along with her clothes, the mask with which she had found her way through his defenses and forced him to possess her. But behind it was the other mask, the face distorted by desperate hunger and ecstasy that had jerked this way and that under his body, the eyes half-closed, perhaps unseeing, blinded by pleasure.

Which was real? The smiling siren or the hot female animal? Behind which of those faces did a woman's heart really lie? Or were they both masks, closed doors to a reality even his deepest strokes could never touch?

That was the question.

Though his young mind was not yet capable of clearly framing it, the puzzlement it made him feel lingered in his senses as Kirsten, fully clothed and very beautiful in the shadowed room, bent to kiss him.

Her lips brushed his own, then touched briefly at his cheek, his chest, and down his stomach, very tenderly, to his crotch.

Then, her cool composure having returned to her like an invisible armor, she moved to the door.

"See you for dinner—slugger," she grinned, cocking an imaginary pistol at him with her thumb and forefinger before slipping out the door.

When she had gone, Hal lay nude on his bed, staring at the mirror in which the window was reflected, and listening to the murmur of the city outside. The maps were still in their places on the walls, with their pictures of the world at war. Stewart's photo was on the dresser, along with the pictures of Mom and Dad and Sybil.

But something was changed. Hal felt as though a hidden dimension he had been seeking all these years had at last been revealed to him. The whole world—the family, the war, his own self—made a different sort of sense now, as though another piece of the puzzle had been added, and with it a new meaning that boys can never understand, but which men can begin to fathom.

And with that new meaning came a new person inside Hal.

He liked it. He felt he could turn the next corner more easily, with new confidence, now that he knew this secret thing.

And if something about it made him a bit sad—something in the enigma of Kirsten's two faces, and the impenetrable emptiness behind them—he had a new pride to go with that sadness.

It was never like this. Never with anybody. Jesus. Oh, Jesus.

Kirsten's words rang in his ear as the once-familiar walls of his room loomed around him, their own faces changed now.

Pensive, Hal lay on his bed for a very long time before getting up.

At dinner that night he looked across the table at Kirsten, studying the beauty of her cheeks, her tawny eyes, her brows, the silken hair that was now pinned back for the pretty dinner dress she wore. She was in good humor, chaffing Mother about a forgotten social obligation, poking fun at assorted Lancaster aunts behind their backs, and even aiming a gentle dart or two at Father as he sat at the head of the table. And she even asked Syb about her day at school, listening carefully to the child's response.

Only once did she steal an unobserved instant to flash Hal a hooded look that told him what he already knew to be true: She was his now, whenever he wanted her and as long as he wanted her.

The conversation was amicable and unusually witty on all sides. Hal listened in quiet appreciation, savoring the way the world looked through his new eyes.

Then, at seven-thirty, they were interrupted by the butler.

"A phone call, sir," he whispered into Reid Lancaster's ear. "Senator Thorensen. He says it's quite urgent."

Father excused himself and left the room. Five minutes passed. The table was overtaken by a hush as Eleanor Lancaster's dread silenced all conversation.

At last her husband returned. He was white as a ghost, and seemed to have shrunk inside his own skin.

He moved to Eleanor's side and took her hands.

"It's Stewart," he said. His voice was low, confidential, but the anguish in it echoed off the walls like cruel thunder. "He's—"

Then Mother was on her feet, gripping him with fingers as cold as death.

"What?" she cried. "What?"

He hugged her.

"Stewart is dead, my dear."

Hal looked away from them. His eyes came to rest on Kirsten. She was staring straight at him with an expression he was never to forget. It was not precisely guilt, nor grief, nor even pain. Instead, it was a sort of awe.

Then he stood up, fighting back his own tears as he moved to Mother's side.

V

Brooklyn, New York
June 11, 1951

"NEXT STOP, NEPTUNE AVENUE. Neptune Avenue's next."

The conductor's voice was a hollow squawk from the tiny speaker at the front of the train. The passengers listened absently, their minds on their destination.

The train, an old subway warhorse marked by all the signs of advanced age, was lumbering toward Coney Island. Many of the passengers were young people bound for an evening at the amusement park, perhaps to celebrate the advent of summer, or their graduation from high school.

Such was the case with the young couple who sat near the front. The boy was tall, handsome, a high school athlete to judge by the letter jacket he wore. The girl was perhaps his classmate, though her small size made her look younger. They sat gazing in separate directions, and though they were neither holding hands nor showing any other outward sign of affection, an odd closeness seemed to join them.

The boy's name was Rob Emmerich. He was a graduating senior at Martin Van Buren High School in Queens. The son of a successful construction entrepreneur, he was to begin a business curriculum at Brooklyn College in the fall, and spend his summers working for his father while pursuing his higher education. He had resisted his father's urgings that he forgo college and join the Emmerich Construction Company immediately. He wanted a chance to test his wings in the world before deciding whether to devote himself to the family business.

Rob Emmerich was the most popular boy in the Martin Van Buren senior class. He had fine dark hair and gray eyes that glimmered with youthful arrogance and a yearning sensitivity that charmed all the girls at school off their feet. He was the star forward of the varsity basketball team, and had letters in baseball and track as well. He worked hard for his high grades, and found time to distinguish himself on the debate team as well as in sports.

Rob was everybody's "most likely to." He was the quintessential high school star, privileged and confident, and perfectly equipped for whatever future he chose to pursue.

But tonight Rob Emmerich's future hung in a delicate balance that was outside his control.

An unexpected change in his fortunes had taken place nine months ago, at the start of his senior year. At that time he was going steady with Bonnie Corcoran, a bright and good-looking girl of his own class whose parents, owners of a well-known chain of drugstores in Queens and Brooklyn, considered Rob a perfect match for her.

Bonnie was a cheerleader, an A student, and the star of the most popular crowd at school, as her election to Homecoming Queen attested. She had been going with Rob, more or less seriously, since they were both freshmen. It was taken for granted that their engagement would be announced not long after high school graduation, with marriage and a successful life together to follow.

Then, during his first week of senior year, Rob had noticed Laura Bělohlávek, the self-effacing girl with the unpronounceable Czech name, for the first time.

Laura was not a popular girl. In fact, she was a social nonentity. Not only did she come from a family far outside the social mainstream, but she was an orphan to boot. Ever since her freshman year, her shy ways and odd delicacy of manner had been interpreted by the other girls as aloofness, and she had been pigeonholed as a "creep" by those who counted.

Had Rob been asked about Laura Bělohlávek before that first week of senior English, he would have sworn that he had never laid eyes on her in his past three years of high school. That was how invisible she had been.

But he did notice her in English class, and he was taken by her fragile, waiflike beauty, her dark eyes and porcelain skin, and the odd way she seemed hidden within herself.

As luck would have it, he bumped into her in the hall between classes and found himself striking up a conversation with her. She seemed a bit daunted by the attention of someone so important, but not, he thought, entirely surprised.

The next thing Rob knew he had intentionally crossed her path on the sidewalk after school and walked her home to her family's apartment house, insisting on carrying her books. He marveled at the tininess of her body as she walked beside him, and also at the perfection of the figure under the homemade clothes that fitted her so well.

Her shy nature seemed to draw him out to extraordinary confidences about himself. Yet even as he talked he felt clumsy and tongue-tied in her presence. There was a softness in her demeanor that, combined with those big, deep eyes, threw him off balance. She was sweet and vulnerable in her responses, and yet one sensed a private depth in her that no other girl at school possessed.

By the time that first walk was over, something nameless and disturbing had taken possession of Rob Emmerich. He struggled with it for a difficult week, and then screwed up his courage to call Laura at home for a date. To his relief, he was accepted. He hung up the phone with a trembling hand, still hearing the small voice in his ear, and wondering what he was getting himself into.

He took Laura to see a movie—*A Place in the Sun*—and afterward to a local soda shop where they were noticed by more than a few interested eyes as they sat for an hour in conversation. Again Rob found himself driven by a strange need to open his heart to Laura. The fragility of her surface still made him feel like a clod alongside her, but she listened to him with a quiet attentiveness that struck a chord deep inside him, making him feel as though he was understood in a way he had never been understood before, even by himself.

Bonnie Corcoran was not long in hearing from her catty girlfriends about Rob's evening with Laura. She was more astonished than hurt, at least at first. Though Laura had grown in her high school years from a wide-eyed child into a pretty and fascinating teenager, the other girls, blinded by the taint of unpopularity they attributed to her, could not see her unusual beauty. Nor could they see behind her self-effacing demeanor to the intriguing aura of melancholy and mystery that set her apart from them in the eyes of the opposite sex.

But by the time Rob had had his third and fourth date with Laura—calling Bonnie only often enough to break his regular dates with her—the whole school knew that something earthshaking was afoot. Bonnie managed to keep her dignity by saying nothing to Rob herself. But she cried her eyes out to her closest friends. Her parents, meanwhile, were so alarmed by the breakup of what had seemed a perfect relationship that they made bold to speak to the Emmerichs.

Rob soon found himself listening to lectures from his varsity teammates about the folly of his behavior. A serious talk with his father followed, in which the importance of the future was discussed, along with the social wisdom of a match with Bonnie Corcoran and the insanity of wasting time on a nobody with an unpronounceable name and no parents of her own.

It was all to no avail. Rob found himself calling Laura again, waiting for her after school, and taking her out on date after date. He studied himself nervously in the mirror before going to pick her up, and changed his clothes over and over again, cursing the tousled hair that he had once accepted as part of his male charm.

He dared not kiss her goodnight, but contented himself with holding her hand in the movies and, when he felt he could no longer bear her mysterious attraction, putting his arm around her as they walked.

One night he walked her home and stopped her in the darkness not far from the front stoop of her building. He looked down at her shadowed form in the moonlight of late fall. He could not see her eyes, but a glow came from her body, so endearing that he had to take her in his arms. He had never felt anything so magical as that tiny, fragile packet of warmth in his embrace.

"Laura," he began, completely unaware of what he intended to say to her. But the words came as though of themselves: "You're a princess."

She laughed at his overestimation of her, and tried to put him at his ease. But he could not shake off that odd dual emotion of excitement and diffidence, of exultation and unworthiness, which she kindled in him. Something about Laura made him wonder not only about himself, but about all the truths he had taken for granted all his life. About everything, in fact—except her.

It seemed as though all the girls he had ever dallied with in his carefree past were merely a shallow prelude to this strange experience, the first real romance of his life.

But was it a romance? He could not say. He could neither tear himself away from Laura, nor screw up his courage to tell her how he felt about her. They went everywhere together—to movies, to ball games, to ice cream parlors and cafés and diners and park benches—and every week Rob fell deeper under Laura's spell.

Laura walked the halls of school with him, watched him play on the basketball team, and helped him make out his application for college. He waited with her for NYU's decision on her scholarship in art, and silently dreaded the separation that their respective college careers would bring about.

For Christmas he gave her a sterling silver bracelet on which he had not dared to have his name inscribed alongside hers. She gave him a sweater that she had knitted for him. When he put it on he felt a subtle quiver, as though her own small hands were touching his skin through the fresh new wool.

As winter became spring, Rob was no longer himself. He was thinner, for his appetite had been affected by his obsession with Laura. He slept less now, and walked about as though in a dream. He received his acceptance to Brooklyn College, and the good news about the granting of Laura's work-study scholarship, like a death sentence. He knew it would allow her to leave her step-family and move to an apartment in Manhattan when she went off to college, and the idea of being separated from her tore at his heart.

Friends told him of poor Bonnie's desolation, now that the moment for their official engagement plans was slipping by. He listened as though bored. All he could think of was Laura, who seemed each day to occupy a more central place in his heart even as she escaped his grasp and tormented him with her mystery.

So the passing days brought this double-edged life closer to the brink, and increased the intensity of the indecision building inside Rob Emmerich.

Something had to give.

"Next stop, Coney Island. Coney Island's next."

At last they were here. The aroma of the ocean breeze and of approaching summer wafted over the grease of the tracks and the smells of cars and amusement park concessions. The change of seasons was electric in the night air, a glorious ferment that even the doldrums of Brooklyn could not dampen.

Rob turned to Laura. She was looking at him curiously.

"Penny for your thoughts," she said.

"It's getting warmer." He nodded to the trees outside the window, with their new leaves getting darker and thicker. "I was thinking about this summer. I'm not looking forward to it."

"Why not?" she asked. "Maybe it will be fun."

"Try roofing on a hot August day," he said, referring to the job his father had earmarked for him at Emmerich Construction this summer. "That tar gets so hot it will melt you."

Laura said nothing. If she knew the real reason for his sadness, she did not show it. Privately he told himself he would spend the rest of his life laying roof tiles under a blazing sun if he knew he had Laura to come home to.

"Tell me something," he asked. "What will you do after you get this art degree? For a living, I mean."

"I might become a teacher. Or a college professor, if I get that far." Laura nibbled thoughtfully at her lip. "Or I might find a job in a museum. Maybe I could help restore paintings, or plan exhibitions. I'd like that. I've always liked museums."

He felt a pang at her words, for they described a future in which he was not included. He knew how serious she was about art. He had gone with her to the Metropolitan Museum when she was preparing her essay for the scholarship application to NYU. One of the museum's Van Goghs, a picture of some haystacks and a barn, had reduced her to a sort of awe. When he had asked her why she was so fascinated by it, she had been unable to explain. "The color . . . the sun . . . ," she had said weakly.

But the depth of her involvement with the painting had not been lost on him, for he had never seen that expression in her eyes when she was looking into his own face.

"And what if you didn't do that?" he asked now.

She looked at him, puzzled.

"I mean," he said, "what if that didn't happen after all? Would you be disappointed?"

Laura smiled. "No one can tell the future," she replied.

He looked away, his eyes troubled. "That's the problem," he said.

Then he brightened suddenly.

"Hey," he said, taking her hand. "Maybe you'll be head curator at the Met some day. And you'll need somebody to construct all your big exhibitions. You'll call on me, of course. And I'll bring in my men and tear down walls and build new partitions and hang pictures for you. Of course, I'm a little clumsy, so I might knock a few arms or legs off some of your sculpture—but who cares? Most really good sculptures don't have noses anyway."

He warmed to his fantasy, still holding her hand in his. "I'll probably track a lot of sawdust and tar and creosote through your museum," he said. "But you won't mind. And when people call me clumsy, you'll say, 'No, he isn't. He just has an unusual sense of where to put things.' And all your high-toned Manhattan friends will take you at your word and find me very original and invite me to all their parties . . .''

Laura was laughing hard, her nose wrinkled, her eyes half-closed in merriment. He had never seen anything so beautiful as her face, or heard a more lovely, musical sound than the husky laugh in her throat.

"You're crazy," she said.

"Well, that's a good quality in a man, don't you think?" he asked. "All work and no play, you know. A little craziness can make all the difference."

"You're right," she said, smiling at him. "A man needs that."

He held her hand tighter as they got off the train. He seemed encouraged somehow. Yet a sort of sixth sense was telling Laura that the future he had described would not come to pass. She could see it in his face, though she knew he could not see it himself.

This sixth sense had been with her off and on since her earliest childhood. It was a strange mood or aura that cast its shadow over the people around Laura, filling her mind with unbidden thoughts about the secrets behind their everyday faces and the world they occupied.

She had learned to call these episodes "rainy day thoughts," for they had a melancholy and mysterious quality. The thoughts seemed to spring from a fourth dimension beneath the world, like the deep water underneath the shining surface of an ocean, where strange currents and unsuspected truths silently stirred, their movements rippling the surface without themselves ever being seen by the creatures who floated on top.

When she was a very small girl the thoughts had scared her, for there was something forbidden about them, something poetic and disturbing that found no echo in what other people—children or adults—seemed to believe about life in general and themselves in particular. The thoughts drew Laura deeper into herself, and made the world over in a new image.

Moreover, they presented a concrete danger when she let herself go to them too freely. The members of her foster family did not relish having to recall her irritably from her reverie to one or another house-hold duty, and began to make fun of her for her "absentmindedness," soon after she came to them.

Even in those early days, when Laura was only a wide-eyed little girl, she had understood on some level that Uncle Karel and Aunt Martha had no great affection for her, and had only taken her in after her parents' deaths because the request of the extended family had been accompanied by a stipend that made it worth their while to have her under their roof. Their daughter Ivy, who was close enough to Laura in age to perceive her as a threat, was more openly hostile, while brother Wayne, already in his teens at the time, was too remote a presence to have any effect on Laura's life.

Laura was a fish out of water in her foster family. Tolerated by its members as an unavoidable nuisance, she could only accept her lot and try to avoid the punishments and little insults that went with her position.

This position changed, however, when Laura's precocious talent for sewing was discovered by Aunt Martha, a woman who was always eager to save a penny. Laura was pressed into service as the family seamstress, first in mending worn garments, and then in actually making clothes not only for Martha and Ivy (who never forgave Laura for this), but for Uncle Karel and Wayne as well. So astonishing was Laura's ability to improvise patterns from measurements, and to fashion garments that seemed to capture a person's essence and bring it out through his or her clothes, that before long the family was saving a fortune on store-bought attire and distinguishing itself among admiring neighbors at the same time.

As a result of her unexpected achievement, Laura was granted a quantity of respect by the family which she had not enjoyed before. The jokes at her expense grew less, and she was allowed a greater degree of privacy, which included her own room, a former storage closet in which the sewing machine that had been her father's was kept, along with the fabric she used to make her clothes.

But this grudging acceptance did not make Laura any less shy or introspective. By now Laura's private thoughts had thrown up a per-manent veil between herself and the family around her. Before long that veil extended to the people in the neighborhood as well, and then to the teachers at school. Finally it seemed to encompass the entire race of human beings who lived in Queens, New York—a race that grew more familiar to Laura in proportion to her experience, yet remained permanently foreign.

She was not sure what she was gaining or losing by living at so great a distance from the outer world. On one hand, the veil of "rainy day thoughts" between herself and other people made her feel lonely, for it was clear that no one else shared her unusual way of looking at things. But on the other hand, it was only through this veil that she saw something special about those very people—something they themselves were unaware of, and which could apparently not be seen through any other instrument than the rainy day thoughts.

One such thought was upon her now with great power, and the tension in Rob as he held her hand seemed to respond to it without words.

Their evening was a happy one, touched by a wistful feeling of parting and nostalgia. High school was behind them now. What lay ahead was a brief summer of transition, followed by a new life that neither of them could clearly imagine. They would be adults now, and would no doubt experience things differently from before. This was perhaps the most distressing undercurrent of tonight's melancholy magic.

They shot at targets in the shooting gallery, and Rob won Laura a grotesque but amusing Kewpie doll. They strolled through the sideshow, and looked at the fat lady and the thin man and the hermaphrodite who was half man, half woman. They saw the freaks, the dwarves and pinheads, and the little man with no arms or legs who had three toes sticking out of his side.

Laura was fascinated by them, for they seemed down-to-earth and very natural as they smoked cigarettes, sipped at Cokes, and asked her in their Bronx accents what grade she was in at school. They must have thought she was younger than she was, for her smallness brought out a protective instinct in them. She was loath to leave them, and when it was time for her to move on, the little man with no arms or legs made Rob promise to take good care of her.

They went on the famous roller coaster, which left Laura numb and dizzy, and on the parachute jump. But the most scary ride of all for Laura was the giant Ferris wheel.

When the huge wheel paused with them suspended at the top while new passengers got on at the bottom, it seemed to Laura as though the whole world had screeched to a temporary halt, the better to show her how terribly fast it was in the habit of spinning, and how precarious the human creature's balance on its surface.

The landscape below, so urban as it reached its border with the untamed ocean, spread out beneath her as remote and abstract as a map, captured by this strange pause in the midst of eternity. Time and space conspired to separate Laura from the world of Brooklyn and Queens, for which nevertheless she cherished a strange affection. All these years she had felt as though she was walking on an earth to which she did not belong, feeling her way through a maze in which her feet were never completely on the ground, and in which she could never feel at home.

Tonight, as she stood on the threshold of her future, she wanted to look back on the life she had led here and embrace it in its wholeness, as the giant wheel allowed her to see it below her. But that very future was pulling her irresistibly away, so that her mind's eye, drawn already to adventures that waited around the next corner, had no leisure to linger on the land of her youth, which had been a land of exile.

They saved the Tunnel of Love for last. Only as they were approaching it did Laura realize that this had been Rob's unspoken wish.

They got into the little boat, and Rob rowed her out to the island, which was bathed in a pale moonlight. They sat down on the grass, and listened to the shouts of the barkers and the *bings* of the shooting gallery across the water. Now the Ferris wheel loomed above them, whirling and pausing and reversing its direction like a strange master of ceremonies to the night itself, its movements speaking to the pale distant stars of human aspirations far below.

Impatient with herself for always sensing something cosmic behind the most everyday things, Laura put aside her thoughts and turned to Rob. His eyes were upon her. He seemed in the grip of something that was torturing him.

"What's the matter?" she asked. "Rob, what is it? Tell me."

He shook his head. The pain in him seemed to engulf her. She reached out a small hand to touch his cheek.

Then, somehow, she was in his arms, and his kisses were moist all over her cheeks, her eyes, her brow, and in her hair, kisses that seemed to struggle in agony at the surface of her body while his arms held her closer and closer.

She sensed his desperation, heard the catch of his breath. Her body was pressed hard to his, her arms around him, her own lips touching his face. But an indescribable pain wrung her heart. He seemed to be hanging on to her for dear life. She had never felt closer to him, but also more bereft of him, than in this embrace. Their kisses were a bestowal of need and of longing, but not of oneness.

"Oh, Laura," he whispered in her ear, very softly, almost so as not to be overheard. "Don't go. Stay with me. Be my wife. Stay with me forever. I love you."

For a long moment she listened to the words echo in her mind.

Somehow she knew they had been coming all this time, that she had been destined to hear them from the beginning, and that tonight was the night when they must come.

She held him about the shoulder with one arm, and her other hand rested on his chest, as though immobilizing him, holding him in the one position where she could really feel and know him, share his pain and do what she must do.

The tiniest movement of her head in the hollow of his neck gave him his answer. Though he understood it immediately, he held her close while it penetrated the deepest recesses of his hopes. It was many minutes later, after that long embrace had held them tenderly at each other's surface and let them get used to the truth that had come between them, that they got up in silence and returned to the boat.

"You know," Rob said as he rowed back to the park, "I've been thinking, Laura. Maybe it wouldn't be a bad idea to take my father up on his offer. I could put off school, and work for him for the next year. I'd only be roofing through the summer. Then I'd be in the office, and learning about the business. I could take some time to compare things, think them over. Then I could make the decision about college. What do you think?"

She was smiling in the shadows, as the groan of the oars and the rippling water echoed around them.

"It sounds like a good plan to me," she said.

She saw him nod. He seemed more relaxed now, even relieved.

She looked into his eyes, and thought she saw the image of Bonnie Corcoran behind them.

The shore was coming closer, the huge silent wheel turning backward above the park.

Now it was Laura's turn to relax.

They noticed the fortune-teller as they were on their way out of the park.

It was a small booth. A woman of indeterminate age was sitting languidly outside it on a small folding chair. She stood up as they approached, and smiled. She was oddly attractive in her flowing dress and beads. The expression on her face was kindly.

"Going home?" she asked. "Don't you want to have your fortune told first?"

Rob turned to Laura, who shrugged and smiled. They looked at the price posted beside the booth. They had spent a lot of money tonight, and were undecided.

The woman easily read their thoughts.

"No charge, tonight only," she said holding back the curtain. "It will be my treat. Come on."

They entered the booth. The place was crudely decorated with zodiacal symbols, stars, and other arcane images. But the woman had a pleasant, maternal quality that inspired both confidence and curiosity.

"Who goes first?" she asked, pointing to a small table with a crystal ball and two chairs. There was a world-weary tolerance in her eyes, as though even by telling bogus fortunes she had looked into thousands of faces and learned a great deal about people.

Rob volunteered. The woman sat him down, took his hands, and studied the palms carefully, tracing the lines with her finger. She took out a deck of cards and turned them over one by one, ignoring the crystal ball.

Then, still holding Rob's hand, she looked up into his eyes.

"I see much happiness," she said. "A house made of brick. The upstairs window—an accident will happen there. Your child, a boy, will get hurt. But he will recover and be well. A wife, very kind . . . A little girl also. You are looking over a newspaper, watching her play. A second boy, perhaps, somewhat later." A tired look came over her eyes, and she released Rob's hand. "I see much happiness," she concluded. "You will be lucky."

Rob thanked her and stood up, offering the chair to Laura.

The woman studied Laura's eyes, then her hand. Almost immediately she hesitated. Then she looked up at Rob.

"Will you be so kind as to leave the ladies alone for a moment?" she asked, her humor masking something serious.

Rob obediently left, promising to meet Laura outside.

The woman studied both Laura's palms carefully. Then she turned over the cards, one by one. She seemed troubled. When she was done she sighed, and looked into Laura's eyes with a strange, sad smile.

"You wish to hear?" she asked.

"Of course," Laura replied.

The woman held both her hands. "I see a crossing. This crossing is of the highest kind. There will be much love, but much pain also. A greater love brings more pain than common love."

She paused.

"I see a sundering," she said. "I see a death. It will not be your fault, but it will come through you. Your fate wishes it so. When the time comes, it will be your challenge to understand this, and to accept it."

Her hands were cold around Laura's palms. Her eyes were half-closed, their expression haunted.

"But there is more," she said. "In that sundering, even beyond death, you will give him what he wants above all things. Because of you, eternity will be his. If you accept this pain . . ."

There was a pause. Then Laura heard the sound of her own voice.

"Who is he?"

The woman shook her head.

"That I cannot tell you," she said. "When the time comes, you will know he is for you. This I can promise."

The chill from the woman's hands seemed to steal through Laura's body. She sat transfixed, unable to break the spell.

At last the woman's eyes brightened, and she seemed to relax.

"But don't listen to me," she smiled. "I am nothing but a fake." She gestured to the curtained doorway. "Your young man is very handsome. Go to him now."

Laura moved to the doorway, but turned to look at the fortune-teller for a last time. Somehow she did not want to say goodbye yet.

The woman took pity on her. "It is a good future," she said. "You will never want to turn your back on it."

Laura smiled, "Goodbye," she said.

An instant later she was outside with Rob.

"Why did she send me away?" he asked. "What's the deep dark secret?"

Laura thought for a moment. Then she laughed and took his hand. "She said I would be in a museum, with a man who drops wood shavings all over the place."

"Ah-hah," Rob smiled. "I knew I was on the money."

They held hands all the way home on the subway. But Laura was pensive. The fortune-teller's words were already dim in her mind, but they had convinced her that it was time for the future to have its say. The handsome boy beside her, so easy to touch and to hold, was as fugitive as the delicate green leaves on these June trees. It was time for summer to burnish them with its hot breezes, and then for fall to chill them from the branches as time forced the planet into new revolutions.

Rob left her at her doorstep with a kiss that sent unseen flames of her new womanhood thrilling through her even as it brought a coda to the music she had been hearing all night.

It was the last kiss. She was sure of that. But this goodbye was sweeter somehow than any greeting, more touched by eternity.

When he was gone she went into her room and lay quietly in her bed. The walls around her were poised to fly away, taking with them the borough of Queens and the last ten years, making room for an unknowable new life far from this time and place.

Laura lay pondering what she knew and what she did not know, until dawn glowed through the curtains at her window.

Tomorrow was here.

With that thought, she fell asleep at last.

VI

North Korea, South of Unsan
October 31, 1950

IT WAS 1530 HOURS.

Rifle Company D, First Battalion, Fifth Cavalry, was on the bank of the Ch'ongyang River, preparing to cross. Orders from Battalion were to cover this terrain and reach the assembly point by 1800 at the latest.

Since late September the company had been part of the steady northward march of the Fifth and Eighth Cavalries toward the Yalu, accompanied by the ROK First and Eighth Divisions. In the wake of MacArthur's risky but successful Inch'on invasion and the capture of Seoul, the North Koreans had been on the run. Resistance had been spotty, but tough enough to inflict significant casualties on the battalion.

These had included Captain McBride, the company commander, who took a North Korean shell fragment in the ribs and had to be sent home.

His replacement, a former rifle platoon leader named Hal Lancaster, now stood at the head of the company, looking across the muddy river. Beside him was his sergeant, Chester Coats, a grizzled World War II veteran and career Army man.

A bright sun was beating down, blinding the eyes as it was reflected off the river. Thanks to the fast pace Lancaster had set, they were here an hour early. The men were tired, but looking forward to reaching camp position by nightfall and having a good rest before moving on tomorrow.

The river was shallow here, but wide. Fifty yards of chest-deep water. According to Battalion Headquarters, the NKPA were a couple of miles ahead, so there was nothing to be concerned about. The river was of no great strategic importance, and the only bridge was a half mile to the east.

Of course, as everybody knew, scattered ambushes were taking place every day, leaving pockets of heavy casualties wherever the North Koreans decided, as though by the flip of a coin, to turn on their pursuers just to draw blood. One had to watch one's step at all times.

So it was a case of "proceed with caution," like every other day of this ugly war, a day in which the boredom of forced march could at any time be interrupted by the pop of rifle fire, the thud of mortar, or the blast of a land mine that claimed a buddy's leg or arm or life.

Lancaster was conferring with the sergeant.

"I'll take the lead across the water," he said. "Keep the weapons platoon back to cover us. We'll bring them up last."

Chet Coats suddenly looked worried. His small brown eyes were scanning the hills, thick with gnarled trees and scrub, on the other side of the river. He stroked his unshaven chin in concern.

"Lieutenant," he spoke quietly to the handsome young face close to his own. "Something about this bothers me. These gooks know we're coming. There's no real reason to defend this stream—but there's no reason not to defend it, either. I don't like the feel of it."

Lancaster turned his dark eyes to the impenetrable ranks of willows shrouding the far bank. Sergeant Coats could feel his mind working. The two men knew each other well by now.

"Battalion recon said it was clear here," Lancaster said. "The artillery is miles away. We can't call in an air strike . . ."

Coats slowly crushed a column of ants crawling beneath his boot, step, step, step, the way a horse taps its hoof softly in its stall.

"Maybe," he said, "we should send a squad across to scout the position. Just to be on the safe side."

Lancaster thought for a moment. "Our orders are to join up with A Company by 1800," he said. "They told us to make all speed. Aerial recon has already been over this ground."

He scanned the hills across the river with clear, careful eyes. In the long northward march he had had to make decisions like this before. He had been both right and wrong. Men's lives had been saved and lost because of him. Such was the price of a sudden battlefield promotion from platoon leader to company commander.

Coats watched the lieutenant. He knew Lancaster well enough to understand that the mask of businesslike calm and calculation he was wearing now was just that, a mask. His natural personality was a friendly and even humorous one. He hated war, hated it with an inner revulsion that made him all the more determined to get through it without blanching. He did not want to be here, but his rigid sense of his own duty required that he do the job well.

In many ways Lancaster was a fish out of water among his own men. The heir to a legendary fortune, he was a graduate of Choate and Yale, and had just finished Harvard Law when this war began and he enlisted for it. He was engaged to Diana Stallworth, by all accounts the most gorgeous girl to have emerged from the ranks of high society in twenty years. It was rumored that he had ambitions for a political career after the war.

All this ought to have alienated him from the grunts in the company, who spoke with crude lower-class accents and could look forward only to paying for kitchen curtains on the installment plan if they got out of this grimy war alive. Lancaster appeared for all the world like a leading man in a Hollywood war movie as he led his men through the rice paddies and rocky hills of Korea.

Yet the men did not seem to mind his Ivy League accent, his family's wealth, or even his reputation as a great womanizer back home. They teased him about these things, but in tones that showed that they had come to like and respect him. He was a stern leader who always did things by the book, but he never condescended to his men.

Perhaps, Coats mused, that was why McBride had chosen Lancaster to succeed him as company commander.

Coats watched the young man's dark eyes narrow as he studied the river.

"All right," Lancaster said, pushing his helmet back to run a hand through his hair. "We'll proceed with caution. I'll take the lead."

"Yes, sir."

Coats fell back a step, reflecting on the complexity of combat. He thought Lancaster was wrong, but he did not dispute his logic, or doubt his concern for his men's safety. At this moment there were two ways of doing things by the book. Lancaster had made his choice.

Coats turned to the men. "All right, you assholes," he bellowed. "Keep your mouths shut and your eyes open. Squad leaders, spread your men out. We're going across."

With a general groan of fatigue and unwillingness the column got to its feet. The rifle squads spread out along the riverbank. The weapons platoon remained in the rear with its 60- and 81-millimeter mortars and 57-millimeter recoilless rifles, ready to provide cover in the event of an attack from across the water.

Over a hundred men moved forward in nearly total silence. Only the lapping of the water and the occasional tap of a rifle butt against an ammo belt was heard as they crossed the stream. The current was weak, the breeze negligible.

Lancaster had almost reached the far bank, with his contingent of riflemen, when something astonishing happened.

All at once a large and jumbled group of old people and children, perhaps sixty or seventy in all, emerged from the thick willows by the riverbank, rushing at the Americans as though toward saviors.

Lancaster signaled the entire company to halt in its tracks as he tried to communicate with the nearest of the civilians. They looked like refugees, dazed and hysterical. An old man was pulling at the arm of one of the enlisted men, shouting pathetic imprecations at him. He looked as though he had been beaten, and was terribly thin.

Hal called to Coats to help him interpret. As he did so he saw that the whole ragtag group of civilians was in awful shape. They were emaciated, covered with dirt and, in some cases, with what looked like dried blood over bad bruises. Many of the children were half-nude, their clothes mere rags. They looked more like prisoners of war, and maltreated ones at that, than mere refugees.

Despite their apparent exhaustion and malnutrition, the people were full of panicked energy. They gabbled at the troops and clung to them, pulling them this way and that.

Chester Coats had now arrived at Hal Lancaster's side.

"What shall we do, Lieutenant?" he asked.

"Try to organize this bunch, and find out what happened to them," Lancaster frowned. "Then call Battalion Headquarters and tell them we've got a bunch of refugees with us. It's a good thing we're ahead of schedule. They'll slow us down. If necessary, we can escort them to the assembly point and turn them over to the ROK liaison personnel."

As he spoke he noticed the bulk of the civilians rushing headlong into the water. An old woman was wading to her knees, filling her palms and drinking greedily. Many of the children were doing the same thing.

What the . . . ? The incongruity of their behavior struck Hal, sending a warning signal through his mind.

"Look, Sergeant," he said to Coats. "These people are dying of thirst. Where did they come from? Why haven't they had a drink before, if they've been in the area all along?"

Chester Coats had removed the helmet and was scratching his balding scalp ruminatively.

"Christ," he said. "Damned if I understand it. If it didn't sound crazy, I'd say someone pushed them out of those trees, right under our noses, just to . . ."

At that instant a hail of machine-gun fire rang out from the slope, not fifty yards from where they stood. Hal's eyes were still on his sergeant. Before he could turn in the direction of the fire, he saw Chester Coats's head explode in a sunshot mire of blood and brains. The hand that had been scratching his scalp hung for an absurd, ugly instant in midair, a lifeless pausing thing, before his thick body clumped headless into the muddy water and began to stain it dark red.

Hal stood transfixed for a fraction of a second. He could hear North Korean knee mortars thudding along with the heavy machine-gun fire. A grenade exploded in the midst of the old people and children, killing at least half a dozen of them.

Realizing that his most trusted subordinate was a corpse under the water at his feet, Hal turned to survey the situation. The civilians were rushing at the troops in the water and milling among them frantically, even as bullets from the shore mowed them all down together. Mortar fire was cutting off the column's retreat from the rear as the machine guns tore up the trapped GIs. D Company were sitting ducks, neatly ambushed in the middle of a muddy stream already red with their own blood and that of the civilians.

Maybe we should send a squad across to scout the position.

Coats's words echoed in Hal's memory. He listened to them for a split second, long enough to know that he had made a mistake, had needlessly endangered his men's lives, and was perhaps about to lose his own because of it.

But guilt did not slow his reaction time. He shouted the retreat to the column in the stream, waved the men nearest him to cover, and plunged toward the shore.

As he did so he saw more machine-gun fire mercilessly cutting down the screaming old women and children, some of whom were still drinking the water even as bullets popped into it. Dead bodies were everywhere. A child's severed arm floated lazily in the shallows.

Hal lurched through the chaos toward the willows, hearing fatal bullets scream all around him. As he did so he realized what was happening. These starved civilians must be NKPA prisoners, perhaps rounded up from the countryside. The North Koreans had known that the Allied forces would be crossing this stream on their way to the Yalu. So they had brought out their store of civilian hostages, obviously starved, dying of thirst, and having been beaten and terrorized for days, maybe weeks —and then sent them to the riverbank to distract the GIs long enough for a hidden nest of NKPA to attack.

Why? As Hal jerked his feet through the tangled rushes on the bank, he mused that the NKPA had done it merely in order to kill Americans, and perhaps as a reprisal against these villagers and farmers whom they deemed hostile in some way. He had heard about North Korean atrocities, and seen a few along the way. But it would never have occurred to him that the NKPA would sacrifice seventy-five helpless women and children just for the pleasure of massacring a company of GIs, when the NKPA army was pulling back to the Yalu anyway.

Perhaps their generals had decided that a few extra casualties would make the Americans more amenable at the bargaining table, and would remind them that the North meant business. This thought—all these innocent people dying before his eyes as mere bargaining chips, anonymous ciphers of war, along with the cursing men in his own company—struck Hal a blow more painful than the bullet that had caught his right arm a second ago without his noticing it.

But he had no leisure to think about the brutal equation of blood with diplomacy, for as he looked behind him from the cover of the brush he saw the monstrous pageant of his men flailing this way and that in the water, blinded by the harsh sun, half the column staggering back toward the far shore on which North Korean mortar fire was already exploding, while the rest bled and died as frantic civilians clung to them insanely for protection.

Hal thought quickly. He knew his weapons platoon could not set up the 60- and 81-millimeter mortars in time to help the column. Nor would the radio operator's calls for help bring artillery or air support before the whole company was annihilated. His men's defenses were useless as long as the enemy kept them in ambush this way.

He could expect help from no quarter. He was alone.

He looked up toward the crest of the nearest hill and saw the smoke of the NKPA machine-gun fire. It was brisk and heavy, but his practiced ear told him it was all coming from one position, with perhaps a few extra NKPA in the trees somewhere.

He began to climb toward the position, his M1 carbine slung over his back, his ammo clips stained now by the blood creeping from his wounded arm. Adrenaline gave unexpected strength to his pumping legs and grasping hands as he realized there was absolutely no time. Unless he stopped the NKPA fire, all his men and the civilians would be dead in a matter of minutes.

There was no complexity now, no fork in the road to confuse him and lead him to the wrong decision. An odd indifference thrilled inside him, for he knew that nothing was left but the flying bullets and his will to stop them.

He plunged up the hill like a madman, sparked by rage at the image of the children drowning in their own blood in the water. The carbine was in his hands now, switched to fully automatic and scattering bullets at the scrub on the hillside. The twenty-round ammo clips were used up almost immediately at this setting, but he was tearing them loose and reloading the gun without realizing it, his fingers working like the mechanism of an engine.

A second bullet struck him between the neck and shoulder. He did not pause to feel the impact. The brush and leaves clung to him maddeningly as he clawed his way upward.

He pulled one of the grenades from his belt, pulled the pin and threw it up the slope without slackening his pace. To his surprise, he felt the shock but did not hear the explosion. There was no sound around him anymore, except for a sort of inhuman throb inside his brain. He felt a surge of strength pushing him upward, and a curious inner emptiness that freed him from all fear.

He did not hear the weird panting cry in his throat, or feel the third bullet strike his thigh. The nest was coming closer now, and he was rushing toward it, legs pumping automatically, breath grinding, carbine firing, a roar inside his nerves beyond human caring, beyond anything but death. He was unaware of the scattered fire coming from behind him as his troops saw him moving up the hill and attempted to cover him.

As far as Hal was concerned he was alone.

Except for Stewart.

For Stewart had appeared from nowhere before his mind's eye, a smiling Stewart resplendent in his dress uniform, standing at the door to Hal's bedroom, beckoning him forward and upward.

Come on, Short Stuff. We've got places to go.

Or was it a younger Stewart? A Stewart in his teens, calling Hal to go out riding or to play tennis or to go sailing on a sunny Sunday morning?

It did not matter, for it was Stewie, smiling through his death with his old insouciance, beckoning, summoning Hal to him.

Hal was overtaken by an insane joy now, alloyed incomprehensibly with his rage, filling him like a buoyant, lethal gas. He charged upward, dead already, indifferent to the bullets flitting through the sparse foliage and finding his legs, his ribs, his shoulder.

He threw his last grenade as he reached the top of the hill. When it had exploded he leapt into the bunker. It was full of North Koreans.

He had killed only a few of them. The rest looked surprised. He saw the machine gunner turning to mow him down. Hal shot him in the chest with his carbine.

Another NKPA darted toward the unmanned machine gun. Hal shot him as coolly as if he were a target in a shooting gallery.

Then he took in the scene before him. There were ten or fifteen North Koreans moving, some of them wounded. Hal lunged toward the nearest of them, bayonet raised. The man took the knife in his neck, and lay still as Hal pulled it free.

At that instant a bullet caught Hal in the back. Something told him this one was serious, and he gritted his teeth as he turned to shoot. He saw bodies jump as he emptied his carbine. He reached for another ammo clip, but realized he had none. He raised the rifle like a javelin and threw it at a young soldier who was taking aim at him. It struck the boy in the face. Blood inundated his uniform as he tumbled to the ground.

Hal was on his knees now, felled by the bullet in his back but not out yet. He grabbed a fallen NKPA rifle and swung to fire at the two North Koreans who were struggling to man the machine gun. One of them went down with a sigh, blood pouring from his chest. The other grabbed for the pistol in his holster, looked at Hal as though he were an apparition, and tried to take aim. Hal shot him in the stomach and turned back into the bunker.

He had been wrong. There were more NKPA—or new ones had seen him and come running to their comrades' aid. His rifle empty now, Hal took out his .45 and shot at them. He felt himself hit again, this time in the wrist.

The bullets no longer mattered. He knew the hit in the back was going to kill him anyway, so whatever they threw at him now could not hurt him.

Perhaps, indeed, he was dead already. If that were true, he reasoned, he could go on firing as long as he liked. He was a ghost. No wonder they were staring at him in such dismay.

He heard shouts in English. Perhaps his men were coming up the hill. Well, it did not matter. He had killed his whole company, caused their deaths by his inexperience and his obedience to orders and his foolish confidence. If any of the men survived this ambush, they would remember Hal as the incompetent lieutenant who had got his buddies killed.

So be it, Hal thought, shooting at the NKPAs, who were oddly still, perhaps already dead themselves.

We're all dead, then, he mused. *So we'll go on fighting forever.*

No wonder he felt this hectic invigoration flowing through the very wounds in his body. Waves of death were breaking over the bunker, buoying him skyward. Today was the triumph of Death. And—a syllogism so simple he wondered why he had not thought of it before—Death can't die.

This irony sustained him, and he went on shooting, bleeding from his mouth and ears and a half-dozen wounds, his bullets popping out their impotent curses to the laughing gods of war.

He was pointing his gun at a last Korean youth who was either aiming at him or scuttling away, either dead or alive, when a last bullet threw him down. He pirouetted crazily as he fell, and lay staring up at the blue sky that winked through the smoke overhead, peaceful as the sky over a golf course on Long Island in June.

But he remembered that today was not a summer day. Instead, it was the thirty-first of October. Halloween, to be exact.

He smiled as he saw three more North Koreans approaching him, carbines in their arms. He knew he would be dead before they could shoot him. In this pathetic way, at least, he was the victor.

And now, as though on cue, a last image of Stewart flashed before him, rakish and handsome, smiling as always.

Come on, Prince Hal. We've got places to go.

Hal managed a smile, blood seeping from his mouth as his lips parted. Stewart stole behind the living men and grinned from between them as they prepared to kill Hal, smiling through their eyes, lighting the irises with an absurd and comical mirth.

Hal began to feel tired.

Well, Stewie, he mused quietly, *they got us both. Too bad for Mom.*

And he saw his mother's face, with her soft careworn eyes, and thought of her loneliness. Too bad. Too bad.

It was her face that faded last, banished by the waves flowing blue and clean over his head, leaving him nowhere.

He was unconscious before he could realize that the three figures storming the bunker were his own men.

Ramirez and Kastner were in the lead, with Dick Terrell bringing up the rear.

Ramirez looked at the pile of dead NKPA and whistled.

"Cabrón," he said, putting up his M1 and looking at Terrell. "Fuck, Terrell, look at this. The goddamn lieutenant got 'em all."

Kastner was rushing to Hal's side, alarmed by the blood all over his face.

"Is he alive, man?" Ramirez asked dubiously.

Kastner saw his own face reflected in Hal's glazed unseeing eyes. He took his pulse and nodded. "Just."

"Jesus Christ," Ramirez shook his head. "Man, the lieutenant saved our fuckin' lives."

Terrell said nothing. He was counting the bodies surrounding the inert form of Haydon Lancaster.

He stopped at seventeen, for Kastner was shouting at him to signal cease-fire to the men below.

VII

February 14, 1951

SILENCE REIGNED on the South Lawn of the White House. A military band and color guard stood at attention. Servicemen in dress uniforms, many in wheelchairs, were lined up before a small gallery of observers and journalists. A contingent of generals and military dignitaries was present, including the Joint Chiefs of Staff and a representative of Lieutenant General Matthew Ridgway, the commander of all ground forces in Korea.

The President, a familiar figure in his overcoat and glasses, stood at a bank of microphones, facing the assembled combat veterans. A wintry Washington breeze reddened his cheeks as he contemplated the scene before him.

Though the occasion was a joyous one, the President's thoughts were grave. He was about to award his nation's highest honor for an action that had taken place three months ago—on Halloween, as a matter of fact—at the very moment when Chinese forces had entered the Korean War and changed its course for all time.

Since that fateful week at the end of October the Eighth Army and X Corps had had to retreat in the face of enormous Chinese offensives. Lieutenant General Walker, Commander of Eighth Army, had been killed in a jeep accident. The U.S.-U.N. forces had had to evacuate Seoul, and cease-fire negotiations with the Chinese Communists had gotten nowhere.

Worse yet, General MacArthur, the Supreme U.N. Commander, had been making irresponsible and dangerous statements critical of his country's handling of the conflict. If MacArthur could not be made to see reason soon, it would be necessary to relieve him. And such an action would make the President's position as Commander in Chief all the more difficult, given MacArthur's popularity with the public.

So the President was a troubled man indeed this afternoon. His country was involved in a war it did not seem able to win, against an enemy considered inconsequential by Administration experts until recently, in a remote land few people had even heard of until bloody fighting broke out there less than a year ago. The magnificent, epoch-making victory of the Allies over Nazism and the Japanese empire was only a memory now. The world had changed overnight. Evil was harder to identify now, and even harder to fight.

But some values had not changed. The President felt heartened as he contemplated the prepared text before him. It described an act of bravery and self-sacrifice that was not only exalted in itself, but peculiarly American. It made him proud of his country, and confident that in the terrible, ambiguous months and years ahead, it would endure somehow, and perhaps become greater than ever.

Clearing his throat, the President spoke into the microphone.

"Lieutenant Haydon Lancaster," he began, "commander of Rifle Company D. First Battalion, U.S. Fifth Cavalry Division."

A young man in a wheelchair was brought to his side. Still incapacitated by his wounds, the soldier could not stand up, so the President looked down at him as he read.

"Lieutenant Lancaster's company," he said, "was brutally ambushed while crossing the Ch'ongyang River by an emplaced platoon of North Korean soldiers. A large crowd of starved and frightened Korean civilians, all of them children and elderly people, were callously and savagely used by the enemy as decoys to sow confusion among the ambushed Americans."

The President paused as the horror of the situation he described made itself felt among the military men present.

"Lieutenant Lancaster," he went on, "realizing that his entire company of 130 men, as well as the trapped and helpless civilians, was exposed and in danger of annihilation, singlehandedly fought his way to the enemy's central machine-gun emplacement, sustaining several serious wounds as he climbed. With complete disregard for his own safety, and in complete indifference to the even more serious wounds he suffered upon arriving at his destination, he attacked and neutralized the enemy, killing or incapacitating twenty-three North Korean soldiers before his own troops arrived at the scene.

"Observers estimate that Lieutenant Lancaster's desperate action on behalf of his own men and the trapped civilians on the riverbank may have saved as many as 150 lives, most of which would certainly have been lost had the enemy's machine-gun and mortar fire not been stopped within a matter of minutes.

"Lieutenant Lancaster suffered wounds that would have incapacitated any ordinary man during his struggle against the enemy. By the time his fellow infantrymen reached the bunker, he was unconscious, but surrounded by the bodies of the enemy whose superior force he had braved alone."

The President paused. An attentive stillness had fallen over the South Lawn as those present struggled to imagine the scene he had evoked.

"It is with deep personal gratitude and admiration," he said, "and thoughts of those whose lives he saved, and those who have been and will be inspired by his gallantry and self-sacrifice, that I today present our nation's highest military award, the Congressional Medal of Honor, to Lieutenant Haydon Lancaster."

The President bent to place the medal around Lancaster's neck. As he did so, he saw the pain distorting the young man's smile of gratitude. The doctors said Lancaster would lead a normal life again, but only after a lot of hard rehabilitation.

"Congratulations, Lieutenant," he murmured. "We owe you a lot."

"Thank you, Mr. President."

"And get well soon," the President said. "I think your country is going to need you in the future."

He noticed an odd look in the soldier's dark eyes, full of humility, and also of a whimsy on the edge of sadness. A bandaged wrist began to rise to salute the Commander in Chief.

The President stopped him, and raised his own hand to his forehead.

"Not today, Lieutenant," he said. "Let me do the saluting."

As he thought of the bullets still lodged inside the slender body before him, the President almost forgot his own cares. He had never felt so proud to be an American.

VIII

Sacramento, California
July 19, 1951

LOUIS BENEDICT WAS a contented man.

His midsized electronics firm, Benedict Products, Inc., was solidly in the black and growing fast, after a slow start that had kept him working nights for nearly a decade. The money he had borrowed from his well-to-do father-in-law to start the business was long since paid back in full. At forty-six, Lou was at last the master of his own destiny.

He looked back on his early career—the beginnings as an engineer for a large San Diego corporation, the first years of marriage to Barbara, the births of the children, the long struggle to get Benedict Products on its feet—as a necessary process that had happily landed him on the plateau where he now stood.

He had three handsome children—Paul was sixteen, Cindy thirteen, and Joyce eleven. He had a fine four-bedroom house in an attractive Sacramento subdivision. He had good neighbors, friends who admired Barbara and himself, and a place in the community. Lou was perhaps a bit weary from his exertions of the past fifteen years, but happy with the results.

Today he could look forward to solidifying his market in northern California and down the coast to L.A. and San Diego, and perhaps soon to opening some branch facilities elsewhere in the west, as his national contracts proliferated. Business was good. Almost too good, in fact. The postwar economy favored firms like Benedict, for electronics was part of the wave of the future that was sweeping over American industry and technology.

Lou dreaded the work of setting up more branches, finding managers —hiring and firing was the one thing about business that he really hated, and was not very good at—delegating crucial responsibilities to others, and then having to worry about problems he could not see within his own four walls.

So he hung back for the moment, watching the plant struggle to accommodate the backlog of orders, and listening to complaints from his sales reps who were proud of their new conquests in far-flung cities, and anxious for him to expand.

Lou was the sort of boss who needed to have everything under his own fingertips. He not only knew every employee at Benedict Products, but knew every materials order, every drawing-board product scheme, and every inch of the profit-and-loss before his own accountants did. He could do every employee's job for him or her, and often did when someone was sick. Many nights he returned home with dirty fingernails and a soiled shirt, smiling at his wife's complaints that he was doing the work of the whole plant by himself.

He was called a soft touch by his friends. He knew his employees' families, called them or visited personally in times of trouble, and even made them interest-free loans out of his own pocket. Ten years ago he had masterminded a profit-sharing scheme that not only made his workers love him, but even earned him a write-up in the California business press as "the ideal boss." None of Benedict Products' talented young managers was interested in bolting the company for a higher salary elsewhere. Benedict was that rarest of rarities: one big happy family.

Lou was about as overweight as any man his age who drank a few too many Sunday beers and weeknight martinis, and ate too many hamburgers and french fries when the press of work would not allow him a less caloric lunch. He was not a handsome man, but with his ruddy complexion, tanned by golf outings under the hot Sacramento sun, his well-cut suits, his graying sandy hair and somewhat dreamy eyes, he had an all-American air of burly prosperity that was nice to look at.

Besides, he reasoned when he paused before his image in the mirror, he didn't have to look like Cary Grant to be the man he was and to do the job he did.

Lou Benedict was, if not the most creative of men, a dependable and honest one. And if he was not the most happy of men, he was content with his life. The concept of profound personal fulfillment, rather vague to him during even his adolescent and college years, had long since been eclipsed by the comforting value of hard work.

His bedroom relationship with Barbara—a pleasant-looking chestnut-haired woman from an old southern California family whom he had considered a great plum when she accepted him nineteen years ago— was no longer what it had once been. The stress of business and raising a family had seen to that. But they were still a devoted couple, and the constancy of their affection made up for the lack of a more passionate bond between them.

On balance, Lou Benedict felt he had all he needed to see him through his life. His past and future joined in a warm, comforting nest of hopes and obligations that more than made up for the headier thrills he had missed along the way.

Or so he thought.

"There's a Miss Dameron here," came the call from the personnel manager. "She's applying for the vacancy in Materials. She has no experience, but she's got great test scores, and a college degree from the University of Wisconsin."

"What's she doing way out here?" Lou asked.

"She doesn't come from the Midwest. She grew up in California. She had a 3.5 average in college, according to her application. And—well, I think you should see her, sir."

Lou knew what that meant. The applicant must have made an excellent in-the-flesh impression on Personnel. They could find nothing wrong with her. The decision was his to make.

"All right, send her up," he said.

A few moments later there was a knock at the door. The secretary poked her head in to announce Miss Dameron. Having put on his jacket in order to appear presentable as president of the company, Lou stood up and moved around the desk.

A tall, very pretty redhead, astonishingly youthful for her twenty-two years, yet almost too poised to be so young, entered the office and held out her hand.

"How do you do, Miss Dameron," Lou said, motioning her to the visitors' chair. He watched her out of the corner of his eye as she sat down. Her business skirt hugged long, aristocratic legs. A leather purse settled to the carpet beside her with a tiny sigh.

She looked up at him through striking green eyes whose depths told a story far more complex than the attentive expression on their surface. Now he realized she was more than pretty.

"Well," he said. "I've been hearing some impressive things from Personnel about you, Miss Dameron. Tell me, what got you interested in electronics? We're kind of an out-of-the-way company for a young woman with a college education from—which school was that again?"

"The University of Wisconsin, Madison, sir," she said, folding her hands in her lap.

"What made you go all the way to Wisconsin?" Lou asked, forcing himself to meet her gaze though his eyes were tempted to travel over the curves easily visible under her skirt and blouse. "It gets pretty cold in that part of the country, doesn't it?"

She smiled. It was a soft, elegant smile that warmed him while putting some secret part of him ill at ease.

"Wisconsin had a good business program," she said, "and they gave me a scholarship, so I went there. But all that cold and snow were not for me. As soon as I graduated, I came right back to California. I've always wanted to make my career here."

Her application was open before Lou. He could see that her parents were not living. She had been orphaned quite young, he gathered. Though her demeanor was very controlled and even formal, he sensed behind it an inner ember so feminine that he felt a small piece of his heart go out to her.

"I started looking through the want ads in the trade journals," she was saying, "and saw yours right away. I'm interested in materials, buying, and management. And I know a few things about electronics from school. I love the community here, and—well, your company has quite a reputation, Mr. Benedict. It seemed worth a try." She smiled. "Of course, it depends on how you feel about me."

Lou began to go through the motions of explaining his company's products and markets. As he did so he watched the applicant cross her legs. She had the figure of a beauty queen, tall and almost amazonlike in its lean contours. The flaming auburn hair, tinged with streaks of gold, increased her attractiveness, as did the perfect milky complexion touched by freckles like drops of sunshine.

She asked a couple of pungent, probing questions as Lou went through his speech, questions that proved she had done her homework and knew what made his sort of business tick. This impressed him.

But not as much as her thighs, which stirred ever so faintly as she listened, or the slender calves showing their shape from behind the screen of her stockings. She had the most beautiful legs he had ever seen outside a fashion magazine.

Her posture in the chair was businesslike, yet oddly provocative. Even the long fingers crossed in her lap looked like creatures capable of untold sensual exploits. Her eyes never left his, and their subtle expression seemed to caress him even at a distance.

As he took in each detail of her physical presence, the totality of her appeal increased geometrically. He was falling under her spell despite himself.

Lou was not a worldly enough man to realize that he was witnessing one of the most calculated displays of body language ever deployed before a vulnerable employer. He only knew that the look in her eyes and the smile of her flesh, combined with her obvious qualifications, were going to make it well nigh impossible for him to refuse her a place with his company.

When he had finished his speech, she surprised him by pointing to the pictures of Barbara and the kids on the shelf behind his desk.

"You have a lovely family, sir," she said. "Your children take after their father."

"Thank you," he said, turning to glance at the pictures. "I'm not sure that's a good thing. Barbara is the one in the family with the real head on her shoulders."

As he spoke, the veiled implication behind her compliment found its way to the core of his male instincts. She was congratulating him on his manhood as well as his attractive family.

He had to force himself to meet her eyes as he went through a few more pro forma questions. Her answers were concise, correct. He was impressed by her quiet pride and her composure, and seduced by that whispered intimacy of her voice and bearing.

At last there was nothing left but to surrender.

"Well," he sighed, "I don't mind telling you, Miss Dameron . . ."

"Oh, call me Liz. Please."

"Liz, then," he smiled. "I don't mind telling you, Liz, that Benedict Products is as interested in you as you are in us. If your background and qualifications are any indication, you'll have a good future here. We have a strong little company, and we work hard together as a team. We're not General Motors, but we're proud of what we do. You may not become famous working here, but you'll be respected, and you'll learn your trade as well as you could learn it anywhere."

Her face had lit up at the good news, making her look prettier and more girlish than before.

"Thank you, Mr. Benedict," she said. "I'm grateful for your confidence. I won't let you down."

They stood up together. The straightening of her body before his eyes almost made him lightheaded. Firm breasts stood out from behind the soft silk of her blouse, and her hips moved magnificently under her skirt. She was so rare a beauty that it was impossible to take in all her facets in the short space of one interview.

But he had already remedied that problem. He would be seeing lots more of Liz Dameron at Benedict from now on.

"When would you like to start?" he asked.

"There's no time like the present." Her purse was in her hand.

"Well, then, I'll take you down to Materials myself and introduce you to Larry and Glen. They can start right in showing you the ropes."

As they walked to the elevator, he asked her if she had a place to live. She said she was staying with a friend until she could find an apartment of her own. He offered to give her a few days to look, but she refused with a smile. He did his best to keep his eyes off her body as she preceded him into the elevator, and wondered if anyone in the corridors was noticing him with her.

Five minutes later he had introduced her to the staff in Materials and was on his way back upstairs. He felt an odd pang when he took his leave of her, because a melancholy hint of regret seemed to show in her eyes as she bade him goodbye. She waved gently to him through the glass-paned door as she turned back to Larry Whitlow, the manager in Materials.

When he was back in the solitude of his office, Lou felt a private pleasure bordering on guilt as the new girl's image lingered in his memory. Despite himself he found that his concentration on work was disturbed by fantasies about when he would see her again.

That night at dinner he was preoccupied as Barabara and the kids talked about their day's activities. His wife noticed the wistful look in his eyes.

The next morning, though, it was business as usual as he got to the office early, his attention claimed by a dozen different responsibilities.

A busy man, Lou Benedict never thought to check with the University of Wisconsin's registrar for a record of the Dameron girl's B.A., or to ask her for a copy of her transcript. There was not time for such niceties in today's competitive business world. Besides, Lou was not a suspicious man.

So he never suspected that Liz Dameron's youthful freshness might be a result of the fact that she was in reality only eighteen years old.

Indeed, such a notion, after the sophistication of her performance in his office, was simply unthinkable.

IX

"YOUR ATTENTION, PLEASE."

Professor Nathaniel Clear stood calm as a statue before the podium. The two hundred students in the lecture hall instantly fell silent. The only sound was the hurried swish of notebook pages as they prepared to take notes on whatever he might choose to say.

The professor allowed his gaze to stray over the students. His eyes were black as coals. He had dark hair, with an infinitesimal hint of gray at the temples. His tanned skin gave him a somewhat roguish, piratical look that was accentuated by the lean, powerful body under his sport jacket and turtleneck sweater.

His effect on his students was complex, for on one hand he was a controlled man whose silences inspired terror and awe in all those who waited for his judgments to be pronounced. On the other hand, when he warmed to his subject, he would pace back and forth on the stage, his movements full of a crackling male energy that kept the spectators on the edge of their seats.

His fame matched his personal appeal. At thirty-eight he was the youngest full professor to have been assigned an honorary chair at NYU in modern pedagogical history. He was Director of Undergraduate Studies in the History of Art, a fellow of every significant scholarly organization in his field, and the author of three important books: a study of Caravaggio derived from his Johns Hopkins doctoral dissertation, a monograph on Van Gogh that had won the prestigious Prix d'Arras in France, and a recent study of the nude in classical and romantic art that had made his worldwide reputation.

Nathaniel Clear was a prodigy, and without question the key attraction of the University's art department, not to mention its entire undergraduate faculty. Despite his strict grading policy and the harsh demands he made on his students, his courses were invariably full by the end of the first day of registration, and attended by scores of fascinated auditors.

It was largely because of Nathaniel Clear that Laura had decided to try to get a scholarship here. And it was with his critical eye in mind that she had written the essay on Delacroix that had accompanied her application. Who could tell? Perhaps he had been one of the judges who read the essay and decided to admit her with a full scholarship. Even before beginning her curriculum, she had tentatively decided to write her senior thesis on the nude, so entranced had she been by Clear's brilliant work on that subject.

Nathaniel Clear was the reason Laura now sat in the tenth row of the lecture hall, her pen poised, her attention riveted to the man on the stage.

Clear was ready to speak. A deep silence filled the crowded lecture hall.

He pointed to a thick pile of stapled essays. "I have your papers," he said. "Under the circumstances, I'm rather disappointed in you. We discussed the nude as an approach to the human body that grew from a thematic, iconic statement to a formal and plastic one. This was the essence of our work on Michelangelo, on Giorgione, and on Rubens. I asked you to analyze specific paintings with a view to deepening our understanding of this change in perspective."

He placed the papers on the table beside him.

"What you have given me, for the most part," he said, running a hand through his rich hair, "is pabulum. Warmed-over formulas in language stolen from books you've read—mine included."

He paused to scan the ranks of students, who were visibly nervous.

"It may interest you to know," he said, "that I read your papers personally—all of them. I don't use graduate assistants to do this work for me. And when I read your papers I look for several things. Commitment to the material, of course. Effort. Sincerity. Naturally, I expect to see some uninspired work; we can't all be intellectuals. We can't all have an eye for art. But I do expect to see *your* work—not mine. I've read my books already, you know."

Brief laughter greeted his words.

"Needless to say," he added, "the commitment I'm after isn't always there. Some of us are only here in order to get a grade. We will—a bad one, of course. But a grade we will get."

The laughter, more tense now, died quickly.

"But what I really want to see," he said more seriously, "is the person who has intellectual ability, and an eye for art, who is committed to the effort at hand—*and*—who has a heart. For it may interest you to know, you jaded undergraduates, that a brain alone cannot give good results in this course, any more than it can in any of the humanities, or even the sciences. It is a heart—a vulnerability to the world, an ability to feel a reality exterior to the self—that alone can give the eyes a capacity to see art."

He paused for a moment, letting his words sink in. Then he picked a single paper off the top of the pile.

"I'm going to read you a couple of paragraphs," he said, "that were written by a student in this room who possesses the quality I describe. The paper, I might mention, is the only one to receive an A this week. So the rest of you can go back to your drawing boards. Now, please give me your full attention. The subject is Giorgione's *Fête champêtre*, which, as you know, or should know, was the model for *The Picnic* by Manet, which created such a stir in Paris about eighty years ago."

He held the paper open in his hands. "Now," he began, "our author says the following: *'I can't agree with Horszowski when he says that the link between the paintings is purely formal. I think that Manet began by imitating, in his own style, Giorgione's image of female beauty. But he went further. He saw that throughout history woman's body has been treated as something ideal rather than genuinely human, and therefore, more often than not, something to be admired rather than respected. Thus Manet noticed the way in which the two men in Giorgione's painting do not even look at the women present, but engage one another in conversation while being served wine and music by the women. Manet parodied this structure, so that the nude female in the foreground of his picture looks straight out at the viewer, bored and curious, while the men in the image ignore her.*

" 'Giorgione's statement is protected by the use of myth and the pastoral tradition. But Manet states the theme so baldly that he calls down upon himself the wrath of the artistic establishment. Manet is ironically aware that the once-innocent pastoral subject—two clothed men and two nude women—will now shock the most academic of critics. And so he presents it, showing us his feeling for the beauty of the female form as well as his sympathy for the predicament of women in the world.' "

The professor closed the paper and put it back on the pile.

"Here we have a student," he said, "who has a feeling for the *why* of form, and who doesn't merely parrot the old jingle that form is 'important' in art. She sees—whoops, I revealed her sex. Sorry, I didn't mean to, and I certainly won't reveal her identity. She sees that the use of form is embedded not only in a societal view of women as figures, but also in an artist's comment on that view."

The audience was listening intently.

Nathaniel Clear shrugged. "I don't think she went far enough in her analysis," he said. "She could have pushed her thoughts further, and extended them to Manet's *Olympia* and perhaps Giorgione's *Sleeping Venus*. She might have found that there was more to Giorgione to begin with than a societally ratified view of women. Yes, there are things here that she didn't quite see."

He smiled through dark eyes that scanned the room with a sort of challenge. "But she's young yet, isn't she?" he said. "And she has that quality—perhaps dubious, perhaps dangerous—which we might call the capacity to be changed by a painting. It is her, and people like her, who will make the statements about art that matter in this world. I congratulate her. And, though I know she can't get up and take a bow, I hope you will now add your congratulations to mine."

Applause rang out, somewhat cowed by the professor's authority, but genuinely appreciative.

"And now," he said, moving quickly away from the pile of papers, "let's get to the business at hand. We left off last time at the beginning of the Renaissance . . ."

As his voice filled the large room Laura sat glued to her seat, hoping no one would see she was red as a beet.

She had thought her paper was awful. It had been written in haste and in anticipatory terror of what Professor Clear would do to it with his redoubtable blue pencil. She had liked the picture she had chosen to write on—the dusky, sensual Giorgione, and the strange sadness of Manet—but had not for a moment felt she really understood them.

And now Nathaniel Clear had given the paper—and Laura herself—his highest praise!

For four weeks she had been so hard-pressed to take her eyes off him that she hardly had the presence of mind to take clear notes on his lectures. Not only was he handsome in a unique, daring way, but he was so alive, so full of energy and brilliance, that the very sight of him took her breath away.

When she first saw him she was amazed by his youth, and by the sharp, daunting humor that kept his students constantly off-balance. How different he was from the cool, reasoned tone of his books! Dressed in the dark slacks that hugged his long tensile thighs, and the inevitable turtleneck and jacket under which one sensed his deep chest, he walked around the stage like a jungle cat, lithe and dangerous.

As the weeks passed, Laura found that the calm voice of his writing began to harmonize with his brusque, incisive lectures. She realized that Nathaniel Clear's intellectuality was itself a virile, manly thing. He used his mind the way an athlete would use his body—with hard twistings of sinew, powerful effort, and prideful confidence in his ability to dominate the subject matter he surveyed. There was something heroic about him that left Laura limp with admiration.

She knew, from that first day in class, that she had not been wrong in coming to NYU for his sake. The lure of his books was borne out by the thrill of working under his tutelage. If there was something important to be learned about art, he must be in possession of it.

She planned to take every course Nathaniel Clear gave, if her faculty advisor would let her. She would move heaven and earth to expand her young mind so that it could take in and embrace his thoughts.

And today he had told the world she was worthy of him.

Today he had given her an A!

At the end of the class she joined the crowd of students gathered beneath the podium to pick up their papers. She found hers, and was on her way out of the lecture hall when a voice stopped her.

"So," it said, "now you have a face as well as a name."

She turned to see Nathaniel Clear standing behind her, his long arms crossed over his chest.

Laura blushed and stood tongue-tied, her paper clutched in her hand.

"Your work was brilliant," he said, moving a pace closer. "I'm glad I had this chance to tell you in person."

"Oh, thank you, Professor Clear," she said in a small voice. She was awed by his physical presence, which was astonishing this close up. He was taller than she had realized, and stronger-looking. A faint aroma of tobacco and after-shave lotion came from him, along with the natural freshness of a man's skin.

There was a moment's silence. He seemed to be appraising her, as though skeptical that this tiny creature, so callow and abashed, could have written the paper on which he had publicly placed so high a value.

"Come and have coffee with me sometime," he said peremptorily. "I'd like to know more about you. Where you came from, how you came to my class. That sort of thing." He smiled. "After all, I like to know who my best students are."

"Oh, thank you," she stammered, still holding her paper in one hand and her books in the other. "That would be—well, thank you."

He looked at his watch.

"It's four o'clock," he said. "Why don't we make it now?"

She stood stock still, not knowing what to say.

"You don't have another class today, do you?" he asked, raising an eyebrow.

Laura shook her head after a moment's hesitation. "I don't—I mean, no."

"On your way to the library, I'll bet?"

He had read her mind. She spent every afternoon from four to seven studying in one of the large reference rooms before going home to her apartment for supper.

"Come on," he laughed, taking her arm. "You've been working too hard, I can see that. Don't rush off to the library. You need a break."

The power of persuasion in his fingers was too much for Laura. With a weak smile she let him lead the way.

His office was small and lined with heavy art books. It was at the end of a paneled corridor, with a perfect view of Washington Square Park and the city skyline behind.

He left her alone for a moment, went down the hall, and poured two cups of coffee. When he came back he found her looking out the window. Leaves were flying in the cold air, with a scattering of lonely snowflakes as the students hurried to their dorms or to the subway.

"A gothic afternoon," he said, reading her thoughts. "Whistling wind, lowering sky, everyone's hair tousled, pretty girls with pink cheeks and scarves around their necks. A good university afternoon, don't you agree, Miss Bělohlávek?"

Laura looked up, astonished. He had pronounced her name perfectly, the Czech syllables coming off his lips with complete naturalness.

"I speak a little Czech," he smiled, handing her a cup of coffee. "In my line of work you pick up bits and pieces of a lot of languages."

He sat down in the swivel chair at his desk, an athletic leg thrown over the arm, and looked at her. More facets of him were coming into focus now: the aquiline nose, the strong wrists with crisp wiry hair disappearing under the sleeves of his sweater, the flecks of gold in his dark eyes.

"Tell me about yourself," he said in the same blunt tone that had jarred her in the lecture room.

Laura tried to collect her thoughts.

"Well," she said, "I grew up with an aunt and uncle here in Queens after my—after my parents died. I went to Martin Van Buren High. I used to draw a lot, and for a while I wanted to paint. But I gave that up, and decided I liked art history. I . . . heard about you. I applied here at the university, and managed to get a scholarship. That's about it, really. I'm not very interesting."

"Oh, yes, you are." He was looking at her intently. "More than you know. I can see that already. So: you're planning to major in art?"

"Oh, yes," Laura nodded.

"Graduate work?"

"If I can afford it. I'd like to . . ."

"On what? What specialty? What period?"

"Well," Laura blushed, "I'm not really sure yet—but I think the nude."

He was already pulling confidences from her that she had never shared with anyone. Her most private thoughts about art seemed bound up with the human body, and with a mystery about it that had long troubled her, but which she must plumb more deeply before she could understand it. Her vocation in art was inseparable from this very personal concern.

Professor Clear was smiling. "Trying to upstage me, are you?"

"Oh, Professor Clear," she said, thinking of his brilliant work on the nude. "I could never . . ."

"Nonsense," he cut her off. "Of course you'll upstage me. You'll be an original, you'll do good work, and you'll make your contribution. What are we in this field for, if not to lay the groundwork for others who will go beyond us?"

There was a pause. The combined force of his penetration and his magnanimity left her off-balance.

"The reason I shared you with our class today," he said, "was that I felt there was something of the real artist in the way you write about art. Something deeply felt, something that sets you apart from other people. Now, tell me: would I be entirely wrong if I said you told a white lie a moment ago, when you said you had given up sketching entirely?"

She blushed again. How easily he understood her!

"I still draw," she admitted. "In my spare time. But I throw them all away."

This was not quite true, for at that moment, in a portfolio in her tiny apartment, there were sketches of Nathaniel Clear himself, in his turtleneck and sport coat, done from memory as she let her thoughts stray over her image of him in the darkened lecture hall.

If he saw through this lie, he did not say so.

"I'm not sure that's wise," he said. "Your artwork is a document of you. When you destroy it, you're stepping on a little piece of yourself, saying it's not important. I'd prefer to see you pile it all away somewhere and save it, even if you never looked at it."

Laura said nothing. She dared not meet his eyes, which were coolly scrutinizing her, though she was hanging on his every word.

"On the other hand," he smiled, "it tells me something else about you. Gives me one more clue to the mystery. You wanted to be an artist, and decided against it. Yet you continue drawing—but you throw away your work. You never say a word in my class, never raise your hand—yet you write the most brilliant paper I've seen in a long time. Do you want to know what all that makes me think?"

Intrigued, Laura nodded slowly.

"It makes me think you're of two minds," he said. "And for a very good reason. You're different from other people. Better, no doubt—but first of all different. And that difference makes you feel separate, like an exile. You don't belong. As you grow and learn, you'll never have to live with the boredom of other people's workaday dreams; but neither will you have their sense of security or of belonging."

He paused to let the words sink in. They would have seemed presumptuous, since he knew her so little—had they not been so terribly true.

"Now," he went on, "that solitude frightens you. You don't want to be all alone. You wish you could blend in. Yet you suspect already that you're never going to. Well, that's a dilemma, isn't it? So, you think you've found yourself a compromise. You'll find yourself a niche, just on the margins of ordinary society. And that niche will be an advanced degree in art history and a teaching slot somewhere. A quiet little corner that allows some creativity without asking you to pay the price for that creativity. No starving artist's life for you, Laura—may I call you Laura? No roach-infested garret. Instead, a cozy book-lined office like this one. Right?"

Laura's blush had turned to embarrassed pallor. He had seen through her too well. All that was missing from his analysis was her rainy day thoughts, about which he could know nothing. Those thoughts were still with her after all these years, and kept their hold on the most private part of her imagination. She seemed to be in constant involuntary contact with a darker region underneath the sunny surface world of human effort and human optimism, a region that seemed at once tragic and oddly beautiful.

His eyes seemed to burn into her. Yet his smile softened.

"Well?" he asked. "Have I got you pegged?"

Laura smiled. "I don't know. I'll have to think about it."

Something musical in her voice charmed him.

"You know," he said, "you're very pretty. In fact, if you don't mind an observation from an esthete, you're beautiful. In your own special way, that is. Your *different* way. One of these days some young man is going to come along and try to take you away from all those dreams to make you a housewife and mother."

Laura looked down at her cold hands around the coffee cup.

"Or has he come along already?" he probed.

She shook her head.

"That's good, anyway," he said. "You should let your own dreams have a chance before you think about giving them up."

Laura met his eyes with an embarrassed smile.

"But it's a conundrum you face," he said, "and it draws a lot of unsuspecting people into academia. I'll give you a piece of free information, Laura—may I call you Laura? You still haven't said yes . . ."

She laughed softly. "Yes."

"The fact of the matter," he said, "is that when you actually get that advanced degree and get your little office and start preparing courses and grading papers, you'll find that the other people in the university aren't any more like you than the ones around you now."

Taken aback by this thought, Laura listened intently.

"They'll be business people, essentially," he said, "out for a buck, a raise, a promotion, out to walk over you if they can. Except in this business the raises are called grants and fellowships, and the promotions are called tenure. And the money of the profession isn't dollars—it's publications, books and articles. Don't think you're going to be around people like yourself when you get here. You won't. You'll be more on your own than ever. But, in a way, isn't that the best place for you anyway, Laura?"

Her brow furrowed. She felt very strange in his company. On one hand he dissected her pitilessly, but on the other he seemed to caress her with his humor, and to be truly on her side.

"I—I don't know what to say," she said quietly.

"You don't have to say anything." He smiled. "Just relax."

They sat talking while the coffee grew cold in her cup. After a while he asked her if she would like him to freshen it. She looked at her watch and realized it had become late. The light of his desk lamp was casting a yellow glow over the room, for it was dark outside.

"I'd better go," she said. "I don't know how to thank you, Professor Clear . . ."

He frowned. "Please don't call me that," he said. "I can't stand being called Mr. Clear. It sounds like a detergent or a window-washing fluid. Just between the two of us, away from class—call me Nate."

Her lips tried to say his nickname, but couldn't. So she just smiled.

"And I'm going to ask one more thing of you," he added, leaning forward. "I hope you'll do me the favor of saying yes, though you've already given me more than I deserve through your paper and your time."

She waited expectantly.

"Will you have dinner with me?"

Laura's eyes opened as wide as those of a child. She could not believe what she was hearing.

"Well?" he asked. "I'm not an ogre. I won't eat you."

"I—I mean—when did you have in mind?"

"There's no time like the present," he said brightly. "I've already kept you from your books this long. Another hour won't hurt."

"But—but I'm sure you're busy," she objected.

"If I were busy I wouldn't have asked you," he said. "I never spend time where I don't want to be, or with people I don't want to be with. And I owe you this, Laura. You've restored much of my tarnished faith in the student mind. Let me pay you back."

"You don't owe me anything."

The very idea of him being under obligation to her seemed insane.

"Well, then, do it to give me pleasure," he said. "You have a kind heart, I can see that. You won't refuse a lonely academician an hour of your company."

She wanted to laugh at his absurd characterization of himself. Why, one hour of his time was worth a year of her own!

But this very thought told her what her answer must be.

"All right," she said. "Thank you."

"Thank *you*, Laura."

They dined at a small Italian restaurant in Greenwich Village. Laura would never recall what she ate at that dinner, or what Nathaniel Clear said. She only knew that in the course of one hour she told him almost everything she knew about herself, and a lot she had not realized she knew. The words came out in an uncontrollable stream, so full of yearning and innocence that she would later marvel over the fact that he never once smiled at her naiveté, but listened to her in complete seriousness.

After dinner he asked her where she lived, and insisted on walking her home. On the way he paused to point out a tall, narrow apartment building not far from Washington Square Park.

"That's where I live," he said. "Seventeenth floor."

"You must have a wonderful view," Laura said.

"That's why I live there," he nodded. "See that corner window up there? That's my place. I can see all the way uptown on my left, and all the way out to the Statue of Liberty and the Narrows on my right. It's worth the rent I pay to see the city that way."

"I can imagine," Laura smiled.

"Want to see it?" he asked. "Come on up—just for a minute. I'll walk you home afterward."

"Really, you don't have to," Laura objected. "I've taken up much too much of your time already . . ."

"Ah-ah," He held up a warning finger. "Remember what I said about my time. I never waste it on people who don't matter to me. On the other hand," he frowned, looking at his watch, "I feel guilty about keeping you this way. I know you have lots of work to do. Say no if you have to. I'll understand."

She smiled, thinking how impossible it would be for her to say no to anything Nathaniel Clear asked of her.

Once more he read her mind, and returned her smile.

"Just for a moment, then?" he concluded, taking her arm. "You won't regret it."

"All right."

The building had no doorman. They got into a tiny elevator, and emerged on a small landing on the seventeenth floor. There were three doors. Nathaniel Clear opened one with his key and motioned Laura inside.

As he turned on the dim table lamp she looked out the windows. She could hardly believe her eyes. The view of the Village was breathtaking. The streets through which she hurried on her daily errands were spread out below her like tiny tortured paths in the shadow of midtown's skyscrapers. And, just as Nathaniel Clear had said, the dark water of New York Bay spread out to the horizon, with the Statue of Liberty illuminated in the foreground.

It was the most beautiful view of New York that she had ever seen or imagined. It seemed to catch the city from one privileged angle that restored its youth and sureness of spirit, banishing its sadness and cynicism by some logic of perspective as mysterious as that of a great painter.

"What do you think?" he asked from behind her.

"It's wonderful."

As she spoke she felt her wool coat slipped from her shoulders. He hung it in the closet as she looked at the bookcases covering the walls. There were hundreds of books, only about a third of them on art. The rest were philosophy, literature, even mathematics, in several languages including French, German, Italian, and Russian.

"Now, don't get me wrong," he said as he handed her a glass of a golden liquid that might be sherry. "There's something in the bedroom that I want you to see. I'll let you go in by yourself while I stay out here. I didn't get you up here to show you my etchings."

He turned on the bedroom light and moved back into the living room as she went in. She caught an embarrassed glimpse of a large bed, heavy curtains, and more bookcases as she turned to the wall he had pointed out. It bore a small but striking painting in a black frame.

She moved closer to examine it. At first glance it seemed to be an entirely abstract composition, designed to express a mood that could not be put into a figurative image. The colors were haunted, the lines bold and strange.

But bit by bit Laura realized that there was a recognizable form after all, concealed in the heavy, slashing planes of gray and black and mauve.

It was a girl. She was shown in profile. Her hair was dark, her skin oddly luminous, though the lines of her face were limned only by the intersecting blocks of color that tore through her.

Most striking of all, the entire composition of the painting centered on the dark iris of her eye, which looked off beyond the picture plane toward something the viewer could not see.

And it was a fascinating eye. Bright, clear, yet shrouded somehow by its own vision, it was full of character and a nameless complexity. Laura felt immediately that this girl, this model—if she were real—was the most interesting and unusual of people.

It was a brilliant painting, and a terribly confident one, combining the psychological penetration of the old masters with the aggressive formal abstraction of the modernists. It seemed almost too brash, too powerful for its small frame.

Suddenly Laura knew why Nathaniel Clear was showing it to her.

She turned to see him standing in the doorway.

"You did this, didn't you?" she asked.

He nodded. "It was my last one. I won't tell you how long ago I did it. I don't want to date myself any more than these gray hairs already do. But it was a long time ago."

"It's marvelous," Laura said, looking from the painting to its creator. "Why did you stop?"

He entered the bedroom and stood behind her, looking at the picture. She watched his eye dart over its surface. Somehow his look made the girl's presence inside the painting even more compelling.

"She was someone special to me," he said. "A long time ago, when I was much younger and more—optimistic. Not the way a woman would be important to me today, I suppose. I don't know whether that's a good thing or a bad thing. Anyway, she died. She got leukemia, in her twenties. I painted this just after she first learned she was sick. Then, when she was gone, I decided to make this my last canvas. As a gesture to her, in a way. In my own mind, that is."

He laughed. "She would have killed me if she had known I quit that way. But I knew something she didn't, Laura. I knew I had said all I had to say, all I *could* say, as an artist, by that time. I could see it in this painting, and feel it—the completion. In a way it felt good. It was rather exciting to cross that line, knowing you could never turn back."

"But you shouldn't have!" Laura exclaimed, turning to look at him. "This is wonderful, brilliant. You should have gone on . . ."

He shook his head, smiling wistfully.

"No," he said. "You're mistaking the sunset for sunrise. That's what's in the picture: an ending. I keep it to remind me of what's over, of what can't be recovered, but also to remind me that I have the future to think about. I genuinely admire what I see in it—the youth, the anger, the confidence—but that doesn't make me regret what I am today. Isn't that what every painting really is? A statement about the artist's past, and his future? A bit of time in its pure state . . . Who was it who said that? Well, it doesn't matter."

Laura shook her head. "I still think you were wrong. You should have gone on. You still can."

"Why is that?" he challenged her.

"Because—" Her brow furrowed in concentration. "Because the changes in you, the changes you're talking about—they also could have been made into paintings. Even the losses, the corners turned, the steps that couldn't be retraced . . ." She paused, because her words seemed to be running away with her. "All those things could have been paintings," she concluded, a bit confused.

He shook his head slowly. "When you know me better, you'll understand why it couldn't be that way."

She looked into his eyes, and back at the painting again.

"Don't you feel—lonely? Without it, I mean," she asked. "I know I would."

All at once it occurred to Laura that this ambiguous painting contained Nathaniel Clear's own rainy day thoughts. And she understood why he had wanted to put them behind him. But surely he must feel bereft without them, as she would if she ever thrust her deepest feelings from her for good and all.

"I derive a lot of peace from knowing who I was and what I could do," he said. "And today I know who I am and what matters most to me. Sometimes a thing is the most valuable to us when it's over. There's no shame in that, Laura. 'The only real paradises,' someone once said, 'are the paradises that are lost.' Whoops—there I go, quoting again."

He looked down at her, measuring her perplexity.

"Tell me something," he said. "Would you show me your work, if I asked you to? Now that I've shown you myself with no clothes on, would you do the same for me?" He was studying her intently.

Laura hesitated, thinking of her sketches and watercolors, all embedded in the deepest part of her private life, each one an uncanny thing not intended ever to see the light of day.

"Don't you remember?" she said carefully. "I throw them all away."

"For the sake of argument, then," he said, pretending to take her at her word. "If there was one that hadn't gone into the trash yet."

"I'd be embarrassed," she said simply, looking at the painting on the wall.

"So was I," he said.

There was a silence. Laura could think of no reply. She felt at a distinct disadvantage in close proximity to so brilliant a man. He was unlike anyone she had ever met. So wise, so knowing . . . and yet he was not afraid to admit his own fears, his own limitations.

She looked once more at the girl in the picture. She looked pretty, and happy, but there was something complicated and deep about her that made her charm the more haunting.

"What was she like?" Laura asked.

"She was very bright, very gay," he said. "She loved going places. She behaved as though the world was her oyster—even when she knew it wasn't. She was aware of the other side of herself, but she wouldn't give in to it. She made a crusade out of keeping it behind that smile of hers."

Laura nodded. Though there was no smile in the painting, one could feel what Nathaniel Clear was talking about.

"She was very brave," he said. "Even when she was dying, she wouldn't let the dark side have its say. She kept making plans . . ."

He stopped talking so abruptly that Laura knew a powerful emotion had silenced him. She felt an impulse to touch him, but she lacked the courage to do so. Nor could she find words to fill the silence left by his own.

"I'll tell you a secret," he said at length. "I really brought you up here to have you look at this picture. Not the view. Can you guess why?"

She shook her head. "No, I can't."

"Take another look at her."

She looked again at the face in the painting, the hooded eyes with their moody clarity. Something about the girl was terribly private, so much so that the picture itself seemed indiscreet in revealing her, even in profile.

Only now did Laura realize that the girl's hair was short, like her own.

"Do you feel as though you're looking into a mirror?" Nathaniel Clear asked.

Laura looked at the picture again. Indeed, the girl's dark eyes and hair, her pearly complexion, bore a certain resemblance to herself.

"She looks like you, doesn't she?" he said.

Laura could think of no response. The comparison seemed to diminish the girl somehow. She herself felt completely ordinary when measured against a creature so exotic.

"Of course, you're not like her," he said. "You've got the other side, the side she kept hidden. Maybe that's why I wanted you to see her, and her to see you."

"Her to see me?" Laura turned to him.

"Why not?" he asked. "Perhaps in a way you are looking into a mirror. At the part of you that she couldn't accept in herself. Maybe I saw you in her all along. Maybe I painted her because something in me knew that I would meet you one day. Anything is possible."

The thought coiled around Laura like a serpent, for it was similar to a hundred thoughts she had had about things that had happened to her, and people she had known, and feelings she had had since she was a little girl. How deeply he probed into her mind, after so few hours' acquaintance, touching ideas she had not wanted to recognize there. He frightened her and made her feel protected, at the same time.

He had not moved or spoken. He was still standing behind her, his shadow thrown over her by the bedroom lamp. And as the warmth of him stole over her, something inside her seemed to fall apart. All this talk of the picture, and this gentle teasing followed by observations of the most deep and serious kind, had made her feel that for the first time in her memory she was less alone. Someone capable of seeing through to the most intimate part of her was doing so in a very kind way, generous with his intuition, his experience, and his wisdom. His nearness opened a hungry void that unnerved Laura, for she had spent long years trying to hide it from herself.

He must have sensed that she was ready to tumble from the fragile perch to which she had clung so long on her own. For it was with the tenderest of touches that he placed a warm hand on her shoulder.

Her whole body shuddered at this featherlight caress of male fingers on her surface, but already so much deeper. For a moment they did not move. Then, slowly, he began to turn her toward him.

She trembled once again, at the edge of past and future, and she felt part of herself try to flee him, back into the world she knew. But he was one tiny step ahead of her, and the long arms that stopped her were also arms that told her she need not fear him. He drew her to his chest and whispered, "Ssshhh," gently as an indulgent father, petting her shoulder with a soft palm.

Ashamed of her own weakness, she let herself rest against him, afraid to touch him with her hands. "Ssshhh," the sibilant little murmur soothed her, and she felt herself on the edge of an abyss from which she had shrunk throughout her cautious life, the abyss of needing someone else.

His lips touched her hair, for he was far taller than she. The hands on her shoulders slid to her neck, and careful fingers rubbed at its nape, calming her.

And somehow those same fingers were tipping her head upward, slowly, inevitably, so that her eyes were full of the dark beauty of his face, and her lips were opened to him with a yielding all their own.

His kiss was so soft at first, so respectful, that she did not quite realize it was happening. The faintest brush of lips against lips, intoxicating as the dark glow in his eyes that came closer and closer, knowing her utterly without touching her . . .

What happened next was a blur. The kiss had deepened, grown more urgent. There was a crimson flare at the core of her. It shot through her legs and up her spine, a paroxysm so intense that it took her breath away. For an instant it seemed like something natural, a lovely heat in all her senses, and proof of the wonderful fact of being a woman. Then, in a flash, it became unbearable, the lips pressed to her own, the pressure of the hard male body against her, the hands at the small of her back suffocating her.

She did not know how she extricated herself from his embrace, how she tore herself away from what he was offering her. She only knew that she had transgressed a terrible law in opening herself this way, and tempted a fate that must surely be quick to punish her for her presumption.

The roaring of self-reproach inside her mind made her deaf to her own words as she made lame excuses, found her coat somehow, and fled the apartment, hurrying downstairs into the black cold light, coming to herself only as she was walking the last block to her own building.

Then embarrassment came to join her shame as she rushed upstairs, locked the door, and threw herself upon her bed, still in her coat. How could she have led him on that way? How could she have opened those prohibited doors to a part of herself she had denied for so many years?

What madness had made her abandon all her defenses with one girlish smile, as though no punishment on earth could daunt her?

For a long moment, in a daze, she mused over what had happened. Then, before she even thought to turn out the light, sleep came over her with a heavy throb, and troubled dreams emptied her mind of all thought and all hope.

X

THANK GOD FOR MIDTERMS, Laura thought to herself a dozen times in the days that followed her distressing dinner with Nathaniel Clear.

The only thing standing between her and the unbearable feelings inside her was the pressing immediacy of work. She went to classes, ate a hurried lunch in the cafeteria, studied longer hours than ever in the library, and prepared for her exams with numb desperation. She memorized masses of material, wondering if any of it would stay in her head, for her mind felt like a black ocean in which all floating matter might sink to the bottom.

Making pot after pot of coffee on the little stove in her apartment, she buried herself in European history, her two art courses, and the biology course that was the hardest of them all. She knew there would be long sections of objective questions on all the midterms, with dates, names, and biological nomenclature that was dizzying in its complexity.

She immersed herself in the facts almost as though they were a drug that could blind her to everything else. As the days passed she began to slip into a tense, jittery indifference that made her feel better. The center of her felt oddly warm, like a low oven, but her hands and feet were like ice all day long. The world seemed far away from her, and therefore easy to manage.

She forced herself to go to Nathaniel Clear's last lecture before mid-terms, but could not bring herself to sit in her regular seat, ten rows from the front on the left-hand side. Instead she sat high up in the shadows of the lecture hall, along with the students who were afraid to be called on or to have their absence noticed when they did not come to class.

She flung open her notebook, determined to take notes on the abstraction of Clear's lecture without noticing the man behind the thoughts. As she did so, she noticed the paper on Giorgione and Manet to which he had given such high praise. It fell out of her notebook, and she pushed it from her to the seat beside her.

She took absurdly detailed notes on his lecture. Matisse's *Pink Nude* was projected on the screen above his lectern, and out of the corner of her eye she saw his pointer scan the bold lines of the naked woman's upraised knee, the curve of her thigh, the beautiful structure sketched by her arms, and her small head, miniaturized by the artist for the sake of the composition, yet somehow all the more striking for that.

Word by word Laura scribbled down what Clear said without looking at him as he stood on the stage. Curiously, she began to feel as though the flow of his thoughts was coming through her pen of its own accord, and using her as an intermediary to spread its liquid essence across the pages of her notebook. Laura watched this process in wonder, admiring the penetrating force of his intellect even as she shunned her peripheral view of him prowling nervously back and forth before her.

During the intervals in her writing she heard whispers from the row behind her. They were girls' voices, and audibly tinged by female admiration for the distant figure of Professor Clear. Their laughing little exchanges were full of undisguised expressions of sexual curiosity about him.

Laura recognized them. They were a trio of girls she had noticed in the class before. They always sat here in the back, where they could whisper without being heard. They were upperclassmen, art majors, whom she had occasionally noticed in the corridor outside the department office.

They were auditing this course, but were really only here because they were admirers of Clear and virtual camp followers in all his classes. They were obsessed by his mystique—as was nearly everyone else, for that matter—and liked to trail in his shadow as much as possible.

Though he paid no apparent attention to them, and sometimes made sarcastic reference in class to "the female art major in pursuit of an MRS. degree upon graduation" and to the "nubile young woman student who soulfully tells her male professor she would do *anything* to get a good grade in his course," this did not discourage them from coming to class and exchanging their sensual little whispers about his looks and his supposed sexual prowess, devouring him with their eyes and only taking a rare note or two on his lecture.

The prettiest of them was a blonde named Sandra Richter. Laura knew her name because they were both taking Modern Painting 103, where Sandra had an irritating habit of continually raising her hand to ply Professor Zuckerman with intrusive and ridiculously shallow questions.

Laura turned her attention away from the girls behind her. But as she did so the echos of their murmurs distressed her, for the mystery of sex was much on her mind now.

As things turned out, Laura's blind absorption in her studies had the desired effect.

She knew all the answers on her European history exam, and wrote a concise and closely reasoned essay on the influence of Bismarck's Triple Alliance on the balance of European power until World War I. On her biology exam she threaded her way without a false step through the reproductive, digestive, and nervous systems of invertebrates, the photosynthetic properties of plants, the complexities of fecundation among flowers. She answered all the questions on her Modern Painting mid-term as she knew fussy Professor Zuckerman would want them answered, and poured every ounce of her energy and intelligence into the difficult exam given by Nathaniel Clear.

When it was all over, on Friday afternoon, she walked slowly from the campus through the city streets toward home. It was a dark, windy afternoon, and she thought the world had never looked so prettily chilled, so meditative.

She climbed the long flights to her apartment, not tired by the steps, despite the fact that she had eaten very little these past days. She was beyond fatigue, beyond everything but this bland detachment in which nothing could touch her.

She was sitting on the edge of her bed, too preoccupied to think about dinner, when the buzzer rang.

Laura came to herself with a start. It was the first time the buzzer had rung since school began. She had never heard it since the day Uncle Karel and cousin Wayne had helped her carry her few things up the stairs before receding into their own life back in Queens.

She pressed the intercom. "Who is it, please?"

The voice that came from the speaker was male, but incomprehensible. She had to ask again who it was.

"*It's Nate Clear.*" At last she understood. "*I have something for you.*"

Laura turned pale.

"I—what?" she asked clumsily.

"*Your paper on Giorgione,*" came the distorted voice, in which however she now caught the echo of the professor's deep tones. "*Someone found it in the lecture hall. You must have lost it.*"

Laura's breath caught in her throat. She had not consciously missed the paper until now. But the sound of the voice on the intercom pricked at a memory she had suppressed, and she instantly realized that, yes, the paper was lost, it was gone from her notebook. She must have left it somewhere, or let it fall out.

She had seconds to decide what to do. The professor's voice was crisp and businesslike, devoid of humor or warmth.

She glanced desperately behind her at the cramped little studio apartment. It looked particularly abject, with its ugly sink and stove, yellowed plaster, chipped old furniture, and the filthy window to the airshaft outside.

Then she turned back to the intercom. Her eyes closed, her mind a blank, she pushed the buzzer to open the downstairs door.

She stepped back as though in horror at what she had done. She caught a glimpse of herself in the mirror above the sink. She looked terrible. Her hair was windblown and unkempt. Her cheeks were hollow from her recent overwork. She seized the comb on the counter and ran it hurriedly through her hair. It was too late to add a touch of color to her cheeks. He would be here in a few seconds.

She picked up her coat from the chair and hung it on the hook by the door. She pushed her books from the bed, cast a final helpless glance at her four lonely walls, and stood numbly facing the door.

She heard steps on the stairs, quick and athletic. Perhaps he was taking them two at a time.

Then there was a silence on the landing, and a brisk knock at the door that made her jump.

She went forward, fiddled with the latch, which seemed remarkably uncooperative somehow, and at last turned the knob to open the door.

Involuntarily she recoiled a pace as the opening grew wider. Nathaniel Clear was standing before her, his dark hair shining in the light of the bare bulb over the landing. He was wearing a leather jacket that hugged his chest and shoulders. She caught a glimpse of fine-fitting dark slacks that showed off the catlike power of his legs.

A breath of the fresh air outside came from him, and she actually felt it touch the bare skin of her cheek.

Now she saw what he had in his hand.

"You lost this." He held up the paper. "Someone turned it in at the office, and they gave it to me. I thought I'd drop it off on my way home. I didn't think you'd want to let it get away, since it was so good."

She saw that he also had an exam booklet in his hand, which he now separated from the paper.

"I brought your midterm, too," he said. "I corrected it this morning. An A, of course. You did a fine job . . ."

The look in her eyes silenced him. He stood still for an instant, framed by the door. Then he came slowly forward, closing it behind him.

Her arms were at her sides, the palms of her hands turned to him, trembling. She could not see the look of pleading and surrender in her own eyes.

After a pause that seemed to her the longest ordeal she had ever endured, she was in his arms. His embrace was more familiar than the home around her. It was as though she had never left him, as though this foolish interval of work and cold sleeplessness and dull study had never separated them.

Relief flooded her senses as she understood that the storm inside her now could not be held back any longer. Her hands came with a will of their own to rest on his hips. His kisses touched her brow, her eyelids, her cheeks.

"I know, Laura," he murmured into her ear. "I know."

Her face was tipped upward to his, and she parted her lips to receive the smooth male tongue that found her own and caressed it slowly. The hot ferment that had terrified her a week ago came back, licking at her legs, making her knees tremble, and thrilling through the quick of her, even more lovely now that she had lost the strength to oppose it.

It was time for her to lay down her arms, and give herself over to what must come. She did so with a grateful sigh.

"My sweet Laura," Nathaniel Clear murmured, seeming to understand both her struggle and the delight of her capitulation. "It's all right now."

XI

LOU BENEDICT kept a close eye on Liz Dameron from a safe distance.

Larry Whitlow reported that her work in his department was nothing short of phenomenal for a beginner. She had an instinctive feel for the planning-ahead and monetary politics involved in materials acquisition and management.

What was more, she had somehow familiarized herself—neither Larry nor Lou could imagine when or how—with Benedict Products' past and present status in the marketplace, and had valuable suggestions to make as to what sort of production strategies would work best for the company's future.

She spent many hours on her own time in the Research and Product Development Division, doing her homework on the complex effects of the postwar economy and recent scientific advances on metals and electronics. Obviously, she took her new career very seriously.

She did all her work ahead of schedule, was well liked by her coworkers, and saved Larry more than a few headaches by taking some of the responsibility off his shoulders at busy times.

In short, she was a prize.

As head of the firm Lou had always taken a personal interest in materials, so it was natural for him to make regular visits to the department. Liz would look up and send him a cheery wave when he came in. Occasionally he would pass a word with her on his way to Larry's office.

"How are they treating you down here?"

"Couldn't be better, sir."

His gentle banter would almost catch in his throat, for at the door he would have been struck by the outfit she was wearing, and even as he spoke he would be trying to fix it in his memory so he could recall it later at his leisure.

She wore simple pleated skirts that looked sensational over her long legs, and sweaters that hugged her firm breasts and slim rib cage with a peculiar delicacy. Sometimes she wore pretty dresses in bright colors, or suits in which she looked especially resplendent, her femininity out-matching the conservative cut of the garment.

And she had one black outfit, skirt and sweater, which left Lou breathless when he first saw it and occupied his fantasies ever after. She let her flaming red hair flow down over the black expanse, and she positively glowed in it, her creamy complexion magical as a Technicolor creation in the midst of these gray office walls, her green eyes shining like jewels as she smiled at him.

Lou found himself passing her surprisingly often in the corridors. Or was it that he was always subconsciously on the lookout for her? There was no denying that he strayed somewhat from his normal routines in order to cross her path. She was always with friends, two or three girls from various departments. Her beauty made them look like mongrel dogs next to a Greek goddess. He almost stopped in his tracks when she came into view.

Sometimes her image kept him awake at night as he lay next to Barbara. This disturbed him and left him worried when he woke up, eyes burning, the next morning.

As he glanced at the sleeping form of his wife, Lou began to wonder about his married life. Barbara was heavier now, her flesh no longer firm, and he made love to her far less often than even a few years ago. Now that the kids were older, she was spending more time on her own interests, women's groups, lunches with friends, evenings with her bridge club. He had suspected for some time that she no longer harbored any serious sexual stirrings for him. Now he admitted to himself that the feeling was mutual.

Lou Benedict had never considered himself a very passionate man. Kids, school, vacations, and the business were enough for him—or had been. But now something seemed to be missing.

And that something had unexpectedly taken up residence behind the glass-paned doors of Materials, where Liz Dameron sat at her desk telephoning, making out reports and projections, looking up to smile at her coworkers, and going about her beautiful, beautiful business.

Lou struggled to shake off the obsession taking hold of him. Alarmed by the amount of his private time that was going to thoughts of Liz, he worked harder, stayed at the office a little later. Then he asked himself whether he had really stayed because he hoped Liz would also work late, cross his path in a somnolent corridor, pass a word with him, maybe even accept an invitation for a drink.

Cursing this fantasy, he tried to be strict with himself. He sought to understand the change of life he was going through in early middle age, and the inevitable little tremors and temptations that must accompany it.

But his efforts at self-examination led nowhere. Lou was not an introspective man. For over twenty years he had lived only for action and hard work. He was not a thinker. He acted out his dream of personal achievement and financial security, without analyzing his own motives or the forces at work inside him.

Thus he was unprepared for Liz Dameron and her effect on him.

Finally he invited her to lunch.

He had a good pretext. Larry Whitlow was to take over Vern Innis's job as company vice president temporarily, for Vern was bedridden with a mysterious hepatitis. Thus Materials would be leaderless.

Liz already knew the department nearly as well as Larry; her many memos and suggestions during meetings made that clear. She was the obvious choice for an interim manager, despite her youth and apparent inexperience. Besides, there was no one else in the department whom Lou felt he could trust with the responsibility.

He took her to a rather too intimate restaurant on Stockton Boulevard to tell her the news. She drank a glass of sherry while he nursed his martini. She accepted his tidings with a sincere smile, businesslike even in her happiness.

"It's wonderful news," she said. "I'm grateful for your confidence in me. I know you can count on me to do the job. I've been hoping I could take on some more responsibility. I'd like to be in a position to learn more about the company as a whole."

"It's only temporary, of course," he said. "We expect Vern to be back at his desk before too long. But we'll appreciate your hard work, Liz, and we'll remember it, I assure you."

"Thank you for the chance, Mr. Benedict," she said.

"Lou." The word escaped his lips before he quite realized what he was saying.

Her smile was shy as she looked up at him. "Lou."

They made small talk as they ate their lunch, and Lou found himself confiding more than he had intended about his personal feelings as head of the company and even as a man. Something about that smile of hers, with its private little glow of trust and welcome, seemed to draw him out. He took the chance of ordering another martini as they chatted. It was worth it to have this communion with her, even if she found him a talkative and slightly pixilated boss.

But she seemed not to mind at all, and encouraged him with her questions, though something ladylike and earnest remained firmly in place in her at all times, keeping their *tête-à-tête* strictly on the up and up.

She gave him a brisk handshake when they returned to work. It was only the second time he had touched her since they had met, but the contact seemed more intimate now.

After he left her she went back to Materials and set about moving into Larry's office.

When Lou spoke of Liz to Barbara, he was surprised to find that Barbara did not seem to share his pride in the new girl's work or his enthusiasm for the young blood she brought to management. Barbara had met her at the Labor Day picnic for employees, but had said nothing about her since.

Lou shrugged off this almost subliminal conflict with his wife, reasoning halfheartedly that she must have something else on her mind if she did not return his smiles or nod her approval when he spoke of Liz.

But he was seeing Liz more often now, and exchanging more memos and phone calls with her. And he found that, by some sort of inadvertent tactlessness, he kept mentioning her at dinner with his wife. Liz this, Liz that . . .

Barbara's indifference grew more stony. Lou began to suspect that she either had conceived a personal animosity toward the girl for some neurotic reason, or took offense at what she imagined to be his inordinate admiration for her.

Naturally Liz herself could have no inkling of this, since she never saw Barbara, and since Lou never spoke of home when he was with Liz, except for brief allusions to his children's problems and achievements at school, and the headaches occasioned by their adolescence.

How surprised he was, then, when out of the blue Liz invited him and Barbara to her small apartment for dinner.

He could hardly refuse. Liz was an important part of the company now.

The evening was subtly strained. Liz greeted them with a smile, sat them down on the couch, served Lou a martini fixed exactly the way he liked them—four to one—and a ginger ale for Barbara, who did not drink. She put attractive hors d'oeuvre on the coffee table and made easy conversation as she served them a modest but well-prepared dinner.

Liz was so sweetly hospitable in her demeanor that Lou was surprised when Barbara did not seem to warm up to her. Barbara remained distant throughout the evening, and was coldly polite in thanking Liz when they took their leave.

Lou made bold to reproach his wife in the car on the way home.

"Couldn't you have been a little more friendly?" he asked, glancing from the road to her pensive face. "The girl was just trying to be nice to us, for God's sake. Look at all the trouble she went to."

"Never mind," Barbara said evasively. "I'm not feeling too well. I'm sure she's a very nice girl."

But her eyes told a different story.

For the next four weeks Liz ran Materials brilliantly, keeping the department a tight ship while retaining friendly relations with her staff. Her reports to Lou at executive meetings were more organized and specific than Larry's, with all the facts calculated in percentages and compared rigorously to the figures from last year, the year before, and even the past five years. Her intellectual grasp of the cash flow in Materials as a function of the larger company picture seemed stronger even than Lou's own.

"She's a gem," he told Larry in private. "I'm glad she came along, with Vern sick this way."

Larry nodded, but his normally twinkling eyes were clouded. After all, this attractive newcomer to Benedict Products was upstaging him at the very job to which he must return as soon as Vern recovered.

Sensing this, Lou added, "I'll feel better when you're back in charge, Larry. But I'm glad to see her trying so hard."

The uneasy equilibrium caused by Vern's absence seemed to be working to the company's advantage, and Lou congratulated himself for having had good people to move around in the crisis.

And he was honest enough with himself to thank his lucky stars for Liz Dameron. She was Efficiency personified. Had she not come along so providentially, he would have far more worries nowadays.

But as he worked more closely with her, he found that his appreciation of her abilities was becoming indistinguishable from his admiration for her youth and beauty. It was all one concept now: the indefatigable energy and confidence of a lovely and talented girl.

He could no longer disguise from himself that his white nights at the side of his sleeping wife belonged to Liz. She owned his thoughts. Though the warning signals from Barbara told him to speak less of Liz, to downplay her when he chatted about the company, the time he spent thinking about her only grew in inverse proportion.

He recalled how Barbara had looked seated at the small dinner table in Liz's apartment. Seen together, the two women had been like embodiments of Youth and Age, Liz all fiery color and creamy beauty, Barbara sallow and frumpy despite her makeup and the costly dress she wore.

That dual image haunted Lou, because it was more than just a memory. It seemed to represent a turning point as well, a fork in the road between a yesterday he had already known too well and a tomorrow as forbidden as it was alluring.

It was a turning point he could not shrink from. Its very existence bade him move forward, choose his direction, take the first step.

Subtly, day by day, as his fantasies about Liz outweighed all other thoughts, it began to occur to him that the first step had already been taken.

The reports about Vern Innis were getting more ominous. The tests seemed to rule out infectious hepatitis, and he was getting weaker. He looked drawn and jaundiced when Lou visited him in the hospital.

One night, staying late at the office, Lou called Liz Dameron at home.

"I wonder if I might drop over for a moment," he asked. "There's something I'd like to talk to you about."

There was a brief silence on the line. All at once he felt a schoolboyish fear that she would refuse him.

"Of course," she said evenly. "Come on over."

When he arrived she was wearing the black outfit he so admired. In the dim light of her table lamp she glimmered like an apparition. She served him a drink, then sat down and looked at him expectantly.

"I'm worried about Vern," he said. "I have a feeling he's not going to be back with us any time soon. The doctors aren't encouraging. He seems to be a very sick man."

"I'm so sorry," she said sadly. "I had hoped the news would be good . . ."

Lou took a sip of his drink.

"Now, this could leave me in quite a quandary," he said. "If Vern has to retire, I have Larry to take over his spot. But that would leave me with no permanent Materials manager. I could go through Personnel, of course, and try to headhunt someone—there are lots of good people around—but I'm not sure I want to do that."

There was a silence. Lou took a deep inner breath.

"I wonder how you'd feel, Liz," he asked, "about taking over Larry's job on a permanent basis."

She looked surprised. "I'm sure it will never be necessary," she said. "Vern will snap out of his problem soon—don't you think?"

"Well, we ought to be prepared for anything," Lou insisted. "Do you think you could handle the job?"

She looked reflective. It was strange to see so beautiful a creature absorbed in serious thought, pondering a sad situation with a face made only for smiles and happiness. Once again Lou noticed an odd afterlight of melancholy, sensitive and even mournful, in the heart of her eyes. It seemed to deepen her infinitely, and to make her even more attractive than she had been before.

At last she brightened. "I appreciate your confidence in me," she said. "If it becomes necessary, I'll do my best. I hope I won't let you down."

"Good," Lou said, letting out a deep breath. "That's a load off my mind. You know, we all think you've been doing a bang-up job, Liz. It helps me a great deal to know I can count on you."

She smiled.

He hesitated before going on.

"There's one more thing," he said. "And please don't be offended if I seem too curious. I hope I'm not introducing a conflict into your private life by asking what I've asked. I get the feeling you're a career woman, Liz . . . But if you have some plans—marriage, children, whatever—that might stand in the way of your taking on additional responsibility with us, well, that could make a difference. I'd need a lot of commitment from you, in time and energy. I wouldn't want to force you to spread yourself too thin . . ."

"Don't worry about that," she laughed. "I have no plans that don't involve Benedict Products."

There was a silence as her words echoed between them. Lou glanced at the landscapes on her walls. The modesty of the apartment seemed only to set off the loveliness of this girl the more spectacularly.

The assurance she had given him relaxed his nerves, and he felt loath to break off this moment of trust and intimacy.

"Well," he sighed, "I guess I'd better be on my way."

She stood up with him and moved to the closet to get his coat.

"Thanks for seeing me on such short notice," he said.

"It was a pleasure," she smiled, holding out the coat as she stood by the door. "Any time."

Charmingly, she held the coat by the collar so he could slip into it with his back to her. He felt her palms smoothing the fabric over his shoulders. He could smell her fragrance close behind him, and almost feel the warmth of her body through the raincoat.

As he turned to face her, his knees felt weak. He thought he saw the ghost of a smile on her lips. Then, all at once, she looked quite serious.

"Liz . . ." The syllable slipped from his lips of its own accord. Something had taken possession of him in that last second, at the touch of her hands on his shoulders. He struggled vainly to hold it in. His worry about Vern, about the company, his private upset of the past couple of months, the drink he had had—it was all too much. The girl seemed to be beckoning him to lay his head upon her pretty shoulder and forget his troubles.

"Really," he repeated miserably. "I'm sorry . . ."

"Don't be." She touched his lips to silence him. "Any time. Really. I'm glad to have you."

Now her smile returned, gentle and reassuring. He felt drawn to her by a power beyond human resistance. She was watching him with interest; without moving she seemed to reach out and surround him.

All at once his hand darted out with a will of its own, and almost touched the slim arm under her black sweater before he could pull it back. She was like a magnet, irresistible and inviting.

He held out for a last second, a slave to the shadows and the silence and the lovely eyes looking at him so candidly. The flesh under his clothes was straining toward her with an inhuman urgency. He felt himself sway in the charged air. His lips approached her by an inch, three inches, the slowest and most agonizing surrender of his life.

Then, as though the fates had taken pity on him, the waiting ended. She was in his arms, her lips touching his own, her fingers grazing the back of his neck.

He felt the gentle pressure of her breasts and hips against him. Her kiss was shy, a brush of warm lips at the very surface of him. But something in his own body must have sent her a signal, overcome her natural restraint, for now she parted his lips, and a sweet catlike tongue caressed his own with tentative delicacy.

His arms were around her, and for the first time he felt her slim back and rib cage under his fingers. How soft she was! And how naturally these lovely limbs nestled in his embrace.

Her taste came to join the sensations suffusing him. He had never felt or imagined anything so marvelous as this kiss. But before he could savor it further, there arose a new hunger in it, a thrilling new intimacy in the messages coming from her body to join his. He could feel the heat of female wanting eclipsing her almost girlish acquiescence. She was a real woman, majestic, beautiful, ready for love.

The sex under his pants was alert and hard, straining to meet her pelvis, so that he had to contort himself to keep it from touching her. *She wants me*, he heard a voice exult from within him. *My God, she wants me.*

They swayed in the shadows. He could neither move nor let her go. Aghast at his own passion, he fought for a control which would not come.

And so it was that, beside himself, he let his own hands have their way, and they slipped down her back to the two smooth globes he had so long admired, closing over them at last, pulling her hard against the embarrassing hungry rod of his sex as a groan scalded his throat.

She stopped him.

"No," she whispered very low, pulling her face from his and pressing a hand to his chest. "Lou, no."

The sound of his own name on those soft lips was the most imperious of commands. Chastened by her modesty, but only too aware that it was entirely appropriate, he let her go.

"My God, I'm sorry, Liz. I don't know what got into me. Please don't think . . ."

But her smile had reappeared, disarming him.

"Don't be sorry," she said, looking at him calmly.

Then, with a sweetness that removed the last ballast holding his feet to the earth, she returned his embrace, just long enough to brush her lips against his once more. As she did so, he felt the shy touch of those breasts again, the whisper of her long thighs and pelvis against him, the caress of her fingers on his neck. He felt faint.

"You be a good boy, now," she said, touching his lips.

He stood back, awed by her beauty, trying to measure his own shame and recover some sort of balance. He struggled to find words, but none would come.

"You should go now," she said. "Your wife must be anxious about you."

"Liz, really, I'm so sorry," he blurted out.

She shook her head, and patted his shoulder as she opened the door for him.

It was closing on her pretty face, a glowing unreal thing lit by fiery green eyes, as her last words reached him.

"It's all right," she said. "Really. Any time. Any time at all."

XII

LAURA LIVED IN A DREAM for the next month.

It was a strange dream, full of heady intellectual stimulation and urgent growth as well as a burning sensual intoxication that Laura had never imagined possible.

She led a double life. She went to her classes, taking copious notes, and spent long hours studying at the library. She stayed a step ahead of her professors, who were adept at inserting little traps into their quizzes and exams so as to turn every hoped-for A into a B, every B into a C, keeping the freshmen off-balance and on edge at all times.

Laura studied her teachers' personalities, looking for weaknesses that might allow her to catch each of them off guard and wring an A from him by showing off a bit of extra work he had not anticipated, or by quoting a paper he had published, or by extolling a critical school to which he belonged.

All these things Laura did with the clearest head and the coolest determination in the world.

Yet, as half of her exerted itself with complete concentration on the objective of gleaning a perfect A average in her first semester at college, another half waited underneath, oblivious to this insignificant endeavor, and hungrily fixed on something entirely different.

When the phone rang, and Nate's deep voice slipped into her ear with its quiet invitation, her prohibited other half would steal over her like an outlaw, turning her in an instant into a creature who lived only for the pleasure that waited at the other end of the line.

Laura put away her work—finished early in anticipation of this call, which now came several times a week—and hurried through the wind-whipped streets to Nate's building, and up the long elevator shaft to the landing where she saw him opening his door to greet her.

He would gather her to his arms and kiss her cheek as he closed the door behind her. Then, with an odd formality, he would sit her on his living room couch and ask her about her day, her classes, her papers and exams. Her answers would be brief, almost as monosyllabic as those of a child, because her interest in school was so eclipsed by her need for him.

At last he would laugh, reading her mind, and take her in his arms. Now their kisses were serious, and so intimate that in an instant the electric charge of male desire was in the long arms pulling her closer and closer to him.

Passion made them almost insane in those first moments. They were in the bedroom and naked in an instant, their lips and hands finding pleasure points so intense that they had to come together and finish it right away.

It was only after that first hot tryst that they could catch their breath, lie back amid the soft bedclothes, and savor the novelty of being together through little caresses, hugs, and whispered endearments.

During that charmed twilight moment Laura lay limp in her lover's arms. She could not see his face, for night fell early at this season. But his body was like a stronghold protecting her from all the uncertainties of the outside world, and she allowed herself to lie numb in his shadow, a slave to the spell he put on her with his flesh and his personality. Her very blindness seemed a balm, for she did not want to see anything outside him.

But his slow fingers and knowing lips were like flames licking at the ember sleeping inside her, and already she was opening herself to him again. This time their lovemaking was slower, more deliberately intimate, and even more consuming for its languor. He probed the secret places, so recently awakened, that seemed to make her flesh go crazy with desire.

When he could stand his own excitement no longer, he covered her with himself, his body bearing down and pushing with a power that took her breath away. She felt herself arch and strain to bring him deeper inside her, so that when his passion burst she would be owned by him entirely, with no corner of her held back from him.

And when it was over, and she felt the lingering pulsations of her womb as it clung to his seed, it seemed for all the world as though this living, liquid male essence had catalyzed her, destroying her old self and replacing it with a new one capable of thoughts, of hungers, of ecstasies she had never glimpsed before in her guiltiest fantasies.

They listened to the city sounds outside the window, an occasional siren, a truck rumbling heavily through an alley, the laughter of a passing couple far below. Laura sensed the city heaving and breathing underneath her, sending its enormous vitality up through the slender building and then through her veins as the touch of her lover sent tremors through her heart.

Curiously, her rainy day thoughts came to hover around her even now. But they were transformed from their old sinking melancholy into something lyrical and happy. For they sang the wildness of change and of the new that took one unawares like a surprise delighting a child. They celebrated the secret metamorphosis that hides under the bland sameness of the routine and every day—a dangerous change perhaps, but one full of magic and high adventure.

She looked at the shadowed form of Nathaniel Clear in the bed beside her. She realized that in many ways he remained an enigma to her. Something about him kept apart, even in their intimacy. He spoke little about his past, never about his family. (It was only from a graduate student in the art department that Laura first learned Nate had a brother in Oregon.) He refused to talk about art during his private times with her, saying he did not want to bring his work home from the office.

The depth of his closeness with her seemed physical, wordless. When he talked to her it was with a knowing humor that seemed to read her mind while revealing less and less of his own thoughts, which he debunked as uninteresting when she asked about them.

Sometimes the look in his eyes seemed to betoken private cares that he did not mention. Laura suspected he was trying to protect her from the complexities of his own life, so as not to trouble her. She thought this was wrong, for she wanted to share everything with him, including pain as well as pleasure.

But she willingly allowed him his privacy, not only because she was still in awe of him, but because she thought it the adult and womanly thing to grant her lover his separate existence, to make no claim on his freedom. And somehow this grave, cool adult separateness only added to the mystery and romance of their affair.

Sometimes, when it was quite safe, she stayed with him overnight, and they made love in the morning, their caresses bringing each other from somnolence to sudden excitement in the space of a few charmed instants. Afterward he liked to sit her naked before him in the light from the window and tell her how he would paint her if he still painted. He spoke of Manet's pictures of his model Victorine, of Picasso's haunting Dora, and explained to Laura how her own unique beauty could engender masterpieces as great as those.

Often they would look together at the painting of the girl in his bedroom. He would stand behind Laura, his hands on her hips, his loins brushing against her so that her eyes half-closed in pleasure.

It seemed as though the girl in the picture looked more like her all the time. Or was it that she herself was coming to resemble the girl somehow? She could not tell. She felt as though she were living in the middle of a Dorian Gray dream, in which the spectral image in the painting communicated with the deepest part of her own being.

"Sometimes she looks so different," she said to Nate, gazing at the canvas.

"More like you?" He had read her mind.

She nodded.

"Well, perhaps you've changed her," he said. "In fact, I know you have. She's not the same to me as she once was, you know. That's because of you. I suppose that's one way the living can contact the dead. Nothing is sacred. Nothing stays the same."

Laura listened to his words, felt them cast their spell, and was happy.

When she went to his class nowadays the thrill of listening to him speak was greater than ever before. She felt she understood him better, because she knew the man behind the thoughts that flowed so dizzyingly from his deep voice through her pen. She could embrace his concepts with the same open arms that embraced his body. Her own intellectual growth was being spurred by him to new heights she had never hoped to scale when she first entered this lecture hall.

But at the same time, as she looked past the ranks of her classmates to the stage on which Nathaniel Clear walked back and forth, his hard legs and long arms alive with harsh energy, his deep chest stirring under his sweater, she could not help glorying privately in the fact that she knew what that body looked like with no clothes on. And those sensitive male hands that gestured on the stage knew every inch of her, as did the lips that intoned words that held this huge class in thrall.

How illusory, how laughable even were these seventy feet of human space, these rows of seats, these students separating her from her lover! Even now she was in his arms, seduced by his voice, adrift in the pleasure of belonging to him from afar. The effect he had on her was so total, so sensual, that she had to wonder whether the change he had wrought in her might be visible to an outside observer.

One day, in fact, she had an indication that it was.

She was sitting in the back of the lecture hall, where she sometimes came now for the pleasure of increasing the physical distance between herself and Nate so she could savor the secret that annihilated that distance. Not far from her she noticed the little group of predatory female admirers of Professor Clear, with pretty Sandra Richter at their center.

Laura thought she saw them looking at her, and suspected that she was the subject of their whispers.

At first this thought made her feel guilty, and embarrassed that she had slipped up somehow or given herself away. But then she felt a sort of pride, for she knew how avidly those girls coveted a closeness with Clear about which they could only fantasize, but which was for her a living and joyous reality.

Their whispers made her intimacy with the distant figure on the stage seem uncomfortably public. But inside she wanted to shout it from the rooftops anyway. So she allowed herself a private smile as they ogled her.

Laura had lost some of the old inwardness that would have made her shrink from such a bold expression of her feelings. The madness in her senses made her shameless. What did it matter what others thought, what others knew or suspected? The roller coaster she was on could not pause for such timid thoughts.

At Halloween she surprised Nate by appearing at his door in a witch's mask that she had impulsively bought that afternoon.

"Well, little girl," he asked, stepping back a pace. "And what are you?"

She moved forward menacingly. "I'm a witch," she said, her words muffled by the mask. "And I'm going to put a spell on you unless you give me what I want."

"You'd do that to me?" he asked in feigned terror. "But then I wouldn't have any free will anymore, would I? I'd be in your power."

"Yes," she smiled behind the mask, moving a pace closer. "And you'd be mine forever."

He looked down at her. She was almost small enough to pass for a child. He saw the outlines of the beautiful body under her clothes. She was far more bewitching than she realized.

"So it's trick or treat, then, is it?" he smiled.

She nodded.

"I'll have to see what I have in my cupboard," he said.

He saw her shake her head.

"Oh," he raised an eyebrow. "So that's not the kind of treat you had in mind, then?"

She came to his arms. As he slowly raised the mask from her face he saw heart-shaped lips, still cool from the evening air, offered to him against the background of her pearly cheeks and dark curly hair.

And as he tipped her face to his and tasted those lips, pulling her tiny body quickly against his, she seemed for all the world a supernatural creature caught somewhere between the adult world and the forgotten mystery of childhood, a feminine Peter Pan gifted with charms possessed neither by children nor adults.

The door was closed now, and she drew him subtly toward the bedroom, her wool coat coming off and falling to the floor in their passage. When they were beside the bed, her hands touched at his belt, delicate even in their naughtiness, her impish smile putting him in a holiday mood, for the sweet forwardness of so quiet a girl was itself a strange and Halloweenish thing.

He stripped her gently, watching a body worthy of Botticelli or Caravaggio emerge from the skirt and blouse she had worn. His breath came short despite himself, and he gathered her quickly to him.

They made love all evening, as the faint murmur of children's voices in the street below made itself felt in the silence of the apartment.

Laura found herself recalling the few Halloweens she had enjoyed back in Chicago, and the odd exhilaration of running headlong through the darkened adult world at night, and seeing the routine daytime objects touched by the glimmer of mischief and magic that was Halloween.

And she remembered the year her father had made her the clown costume, a garment of rare artistry in silken fabrics he could ill afford. He had enjoyed surprising her with it. But, a bitter man closed in upon himself, he could not leave his house to accompany her on her rounds. She still recalled his look of pride and shrugging affection as she turned around on the sidewalk to wave goodbye to him, once, then again and again, as she started out with her mother.

Something of that Halloween mystique was with her tonight. As she and Nate made love again and again, both insatiable for some unknown reason, it seemed that their power to give each other pleasure was as magical as the holiday itself, and infinite. The rhythm of their bodies' intimacy was a song that could go on forever, so high, so keen, so tempestuous that it could last until their bodies could stand it no longer.

If this new life was a roller coaster onto which Laura had stepped despite her cautious past, then it was a roller coaster that did not go in a mere circle. It went straight ahead, hurtling into the black shining future, so that there was no turning back, and no time to catch one's breath. And around each bend, at the bottom of each dizzying slope, was a new Laura, light-years different from the one of old. She felt herself thrust headlong into the unknown, and she did not look back. She was alive at last, alive with the joyous clamor of her newfound womanhood, and nothing could take this away from her, come what might.

XIII

ON NOVEMBER NINTH Vern Innis's ailment was officially diagnosed as pancreatic cancer that had already spread to the liver.

Vern was a doomed man.

Benedict Products was left with an imminent vacancy at the highest executive level, for Vern had been with the company as long as Lou himself, and knew every cranny of it.

Unless the vacancy was filled from outside the company, the obvious choice to succeed Vern was Larry Whitlow, Lou's close friend and golf partner, who had been with Benedict for a dozen years and whom Lou had long been grooming for advancement. Larry would take over Vern's position as Vice President in charge of Product Development, and someone would have to replace Larry in Materials.

This was the predictable course of events.

What happened came as a surprise to everyone.

Lou Benedict was in an agony of emotional ferment.

Since the day three weeks ago when he had first kissed Liz Dameron, she had not been out of his thoughts for a single moment. He dreamed of her all night long. At the office her image haunted him so thoroughly that he could not concentrate on his work. He fumbled and stuttered in the executive meetings she attended in her capacity as acting Materials Manager. When he visited her department he stood tongue-tied before her, abashed as a schoolboy.

She did not seem to notice. She was the same toward him as she had been all along. She greeted him with her bright welcoming smile, spoke to him in friendly but respectful tones, and was all business as she showed him her department's accounts and sent him memos outlining clever changes both for Materials and for surrounding sectors of the company.

Liz was unchanged—while Lou was devoured by emotions he could not control. Something in his male instincts, long dormant, had come alive that fateful night in Liz's apartment, and would not be denied. His whole being was turned inside-out, straining toward something he could not have.

And the change in him was more than physical. It touched every corner of him, sparking odd feelings of wonder, of impulsive joy, of crushing melancholy, of desperate longing. Not even the long-forgotten romantic yearnings of his adolescence had ever approached this head-over-heels madness.

But his moral sense would not let him give in to the spell that had taken possession of him. He fought against himself with every ounce of his willpower.

The battle was not an easy one. For he knew with absolute certainty, as each workday began, that he would see Liz again, in the office, in the corridors or at lunch. This knowledge calmed his need, but also stoked his inner fires hotter than ever. Part of him piously wished Liz would quit her job, disappear, simply cease to exist. But the rest of him waited furtively for the opportunity to speak to her again, perhaps to take her to lunch, even to dare to return to her apartment—to get her alone *somehow.*

The struggle between his scruples and his desire was reaching a fever pitch. And it was only a matter of time until the weaker force gave in.

Liz solved the problem for him.

The week after the bad news about Vern hit the company, Liz came to Lou's office.

He had her shown in, and stood up as she appeared in the doorway. She was wearing a clinging skirt and blouse he had never seen before. She looked amazingly sexy under her businesslike exterior.

"What can I do for you, Liz?" he asked.

"I've been thinking about Vern's wife," she said, accepting the chair he held for her. "It occurred to me that instead of just sending flowers and cards and so on, we could begin taking up a collection among the employees, and planning ahead for —well, the inevitable. Ursula is such a nice woman, and with all those hospital bills she's going to have some terrible financial problems. Wouldn't it be smarter if we got organized now, instead of trying to raise money in a slapdash manner after—well, after Vern is gone?"

Lou nodded, tight-lipped.

"You're absolutely right," he said. "I should have thought of that myself. I knew the company health plan would never cover what Vern is going through now. And the pension plan won't be any help. I just didn't connect it all up in my mind. Unless I miss my guess, Ursula is going to be in real trouble. And I don't think they have any close family to help them out."

He looked at Liz. "What do you suggest?"

"Well, I've had a few ideas," she said, crossing her legs. "I'd like to hear what you think of them, since this sort of situation is quite new to me. Naturally, this would all have to be very secret, with Vern in the hospital." She paused. "Why don't you come over to my place one of these evenings, when it's convenient for you, and I'll lay out what I have in mind?"

He looked at her beautiful face, avoiding the eyes that were gazing into his own.

"I'd like that," he said, suppressing the flutter inside him. "How about, say, tomorrow?"

"Tomorrow would be wonderful." Her smile was warm and inviting. "Eight o'clock?"

Lou hoped the sigh of his capitulation was inaudible.

"Eight o'clock."

She was waiting for him when he arrived at her apartment.

This time she was dressed in flowing white slacks and a matching tunic of silky fabric, her feet bare, her hair flowing luxuriantly over her shoulders. A marvelous fragrance emanated from her, heavy with feminine charm. He could hardly take his eyes off her as she motioned him to the couch.

Without his asking for it, she brought him a martini. Then she poured herself a glass of club soda and sat down on the couch beside him.

On the coffee table was a legal pad on which she had sketched her plan for the sending of private, confidential memos to the department heads, who would in turn hold secret meetings with their employees to collect money for Ursula Innis. Additional contacts would be made with friends of the company, who would have the opportunity to contribute as well.

The fund would be deposited in a special escrow account at the company's bank, and held until the inevitable day of Vern's death.

Lou was instantly convinced by the plan as Liz had laid it out. Her thoroughness and foresight were remarkable, as was her tact in the face of Ursula's imminent bereavement.

"I'm very impressed, Liz," he said, sipping his martini. "I'm only ashamed that I had to wait for you to make me think of all this."

"Don't feel that way," she said. "You have so much on your mind. You can't be expected to think of everything, Lou."

There was a pause.

"This is such a terrible thing," she said, locking her fingers about her joined knees. "Vern is one of the nicest men I've ever met."

"Yes—that he is," Lou agreed weakly.

He was intoxicated by the atmosphere she had created between them. Even as he entered the apartment the sight of her had taken his breath away. And now her behavior, so grave and sad, and yet so full of a comforting warmth and naturalness, was destroying what was left of his resistance to her.

They talked a while longer, their conversation positively morbid as they evoked Vern's death and Ursula's widowhood. But Lou's mood was sparked by a quickening excitement which made him feel doubly ashamed of himself, for the lovely girl beside him seemed genuinely upset by the circumstances.

At last, at his wits' end, he got up to leave.

"Well," he said, "I sure appreciate your thinking ahead on this, Liz. It should have been me, but it's nice to have someone take up the slack."

"Don't thank me," she smiled. "It's the least I could do."

This time she held the coat out to him folded. He thought of the last time he had been here, when she had slipped it over his shoulders. His heart sank.

He opened the door a few inches and turned to her, his hand still on the knob.

"It's going to be lonely without Vern," he said. "He's a good friend."

She was standing close to him, prepared to watch him down the corridor to the stairs. The look in her eyes had changed somehow. Her body seemed to be holding him back, even as her position urged him to go through the door. In her white outfit she was a gorgeous apparition in stark contrast to the dim hallway.

"Lonely," she murmured, a husky note in her voice. "I know what you mean."

Something wise in her words stopped him cold. The door closed an inch, then another.

"Life can be awfully cruel sometimes," Lou said. "It could be any of us."

Once again Lou was deep under the spell that had taken possession of him three weeks ago in this very spot. This time it was simply impossible to resist it. He did not know where he was going to find the strength to leave her.

"Liz," he said, his words shaking in his throat. "I . . . really . . ."

But the touch of her hand on his lips silenced him. And to his enormous relief he felt the door close slowly until the lock clicked shut, immuring him here with her.

"Ssshhh," she murmured. "No more words."

Her hands had slipped to the lapels of his suit jacket, and with the subtlest of movements she was receding into the apartment, drawing him after her. He moved like a sleepwalker, his gaze fixed on her perfectly shaped lips, which were curved in the shade of a smile.

He tried to reach out to kiss them, but since she was moving away, his pursuit was vain. He was following her deeper into the apartment. He saw her smile curl a bit more.

At last, in the middle of the carpet, he stopped her with two hands on her shoulders and kissed her deeply, hungrily. The smooth inquiring tongue whose feel he had not forgotten for an instant in three long weeks was back in his mouth now, caressing and inflaming. Her hands rested on his ribs, her hips grazing the hot bulge of his sex as she swayed with him in the shadows.

What happened next was the greatest culmination of ecstasy and frustration he had ever imagined possible. For she remained shy and delicate in her own movements, slowly letting him kiss her again, and then again, letting him touch more and more of her, so that he was always the aggressor, though his every move was ordained and orchestrated by this supreme temptress.

It was her little shrug of acquiescence that allowed his hands once more to enfold and caress her loins, pulling her hips forward onto his sex. And it was her sigh as he touched the buttons of her tunic that told him he might make bold to undo them. And it was the way she arched her back, once her breasts were exposed, perfect firm globes round as forbidden fruit, that told him he might bend in worship to kiss them, to taste the hard little nipples which drove him mad with excitement.

Each and every step of the way it was she who controlled, encouraging him with a tremor, a returned kiss, a moan, until, despite his fumbling, the fabrics covering her had fallen away, blouse and slacks and bra, and she was naked in her panties, and he still fully clothed, his shirt and tie in disarray, his sex on fire between his legs.

Finally he fell before her like a slave and, holding her by the backs of her perfect thighs, kissed her stomach, her navel, her hips, hypnotized by the waiting sex under those panties.

The last of his courage was gone. He lacked the will to pull the panties down, for he was sure that once again she would stop him, as she had stopped him last time. And this would be too much. Her shock and embarrassment at what he was doing to her would be impossible to live down.

He felt a small shudder along the insides of her thighs. Then, to his undying relief, a musical little whimper came from her, and the shrouded sex poised before him stirred in a smooth undulation of female wanting.

Beside himself, he slipped the panties down all at once, buried himself against the russet fur before him, and kissed the core of her at last.

Conscious thought was overwhelmed by passion now. Lou was not entirely aware of the sequence of events as she helped him strip himself, let him take her into the bedroom, and pulled him down on the bed beside her. The whole soft length of her was caressing him now, gentle calves on his thighs, female loins pressed to his own, breasts grazing his chest with a warmth that took his breath away.

And somehow, in all this madness of contact, she retained her dignity, her shy girlish yielding, so that it was always Lou who took, who made the fatal move, while she pliantly and generously let him have his way.

When at last her lovely legs were upraised to invite him, she did not need to guide him inside her. Entering her was like falling through a trap door into a nether world of unbearable pleasure. Nothing in his life had ever been so perfect as this female core that welcomed his frantic thrusts, that offered its kind girlish depths to the arrogant eager penis throbbing with delight in this holy place.

Too late he thought of Vern, and of Vern's agony. And he felt chagrined to have turned this sensitive creature from her generous thoughts for Ursula, her grave provident plans, to this hot frenzy of his own making.

But his shame only made the whisper of her limbs the more maddening, and the sensual grace of her kisses, and the touch of her fingers— and Lou became a heedless animal crouched atop her, pushing and groaning and working with all his might as the soft hands encouraged him, until at last he was torn by the final spasm, and something deep inside him exploded into her, something he had never suspected in himself or given to any woman, something he could never call back.

Utterly spent, he fell atop her and listened to the gasps of his exhaustion as her hands patted his back and shoulders. He lay for a long time in the thrall of her touch, her skin, her smell, and of the fresh girlish smile he could even now feel on her lips.

At last thought began to stir inside him, as it might inside a beast at the dawn of thought itself. Part of him decided that he did not care if he never touched another woman, indeed if he even survived this night. This was what he had been waiting for all his life. He had enough now, and more than enough.

But another part, wiser, was thinking that he could not face the rest of life without the knowledge that he was to have Liz Dameron again. To do so would be like denying a baby the mother's milk it has only now tasted for the first time.

He would do anything, risk anything to have her again. Without that hope his future would be death. It was that simple.

She got up, a statuesque marvel slipping like a ghost through the darkness, and returned a moment later with a fresh drink for him, as though she knew he needed an antidote for the guilt about to fall upon him. He sipped it gratefully.

Then she got back into the bed and cuddled against him for a long while as the liquor warmed his insides. The feel of her young body against his was so natural and wholesome that some of his shame was assuaged. How could this perfect experience of love, this holy fulfillment be wrong?

He did not know how long they stayed that way, her lips placing soft kisses on his chest, her thighs caressing him slowly. He only knew that in what seemed no time at all her touch was making him hard again, and her whisper of reproach was in his ear.

"You have to go. Your wife will be worried."

With shaking hands he put on his clothes. He did his best in the bathroom to wash her marvelous scent off himself. Then she helped him on with his coat, touching at his shoulders as she had done three weeks ago, and took him to the door, back to the place where it had all begun.

She was wearing only a silken robe. He hugged her close, intimately close, pelvis pressed to her, arms curled passionately around her back. He could feel her breasts against his chest. His hands furled her hair, losing themselves in its magic softness as he kissed her. His hips were eager to strain against her even now, but her body sent messages of warning that he had had his fun for tonight, and must be on his way, for he was a man with responsibilities.

"Liz . . ."

He searched for words that would tell her how he felt. They seemed ugly and insignificant in the shadow of what had happened between them. Her smile, warm and languid, lulled him toward silence.

At last an oddly flip notion came to his lips.

"What do I have to do," he asked, "to get you to see me again?"

The next words she spoke made his blood run cold.

"You can give me Vern Innis's job," she said.

XIV

CHRISTMAS WAS in the air.

The semester had ended, and the university was entering into that twilight time when classes are already over, and campus life has dived underground into the frantic stillness of preparation for finals.

There was a hushed tension in the corridors, the packed silent libraries, the dorms stunned by collective worry. Many students already suspected their grades could not be saved by final exams, and that they would not be back next semester. Others saw their hoped-for grade point average slumping well below what was needed to retain their scholarships.

Among all these struggling, terrified young people, Laura alone walked the snowy sidewalks of the campus with her heart soaring.

Though every aspect of her existence was literally up in the air, somehow the ferment inside her lifted her above all care or worry. She no longer felt outstripped by events; instead she sensed unseen faculties growing apace inside her, and arming her for any and all challenges.

She had no serious course worries. She had managed to get A's on her midterms in all subjects. She was well prepared for final exams, her head bursting with material that somehow submitted itself to her will whenever she wished to call it up from memory and organize it for whatever question might be asked of her.

But while her memory labored for her other professors, her intellect devoted itself entirely to Nathaniel Clear. His course had itself been a work of art, and she wanted to give him her best on the final. She had forced him to promise he would give her an A only if she deserved it. But he had laughed.

"That would be like giving Matisse an A for *The Open Window* and then giving him a B for the *Pink Nude*," he said. "But if it will make you feel better, I'll give you a B if you don't show up for the final."

Laura could hardly believe her good fortune as she looked forward to three and a half more years under the tutelage of this amazing teacher. Already he had had a profound influence on her intellectual growth. She was bursting with new ideas about art and artists, ideas that she scribbled hurriedly into a private notebook at home. She could feel them straining toward a coherence all their own, which would one day be *her* contribution as a thinker and writer.

Though she was not an ambitious person, and loath to imagine an influential future for herself, Laura felt she was on the threshold of discoveries, born deep inside her own personality, which might one day bear beautiful fruit. And the old clouded yearnings she had once called her rainy day thoughts seemed on the verge of finding meaningful expression through this bursting new growth.

In every way, Laura was on top of the world. If such a perch was dangerous, she did not care. It was better to scale the heights once in her life than to watch her years pass away in the dreary sameness of the every day. Why not risk everything at every moment? Why not throw all of herself into every impression, every thought, every feeling?

Though to an outside observer Laura might have seemed a sober student, she was living dangerously, to the marrow of her bones. And she could not turn back, because she had already forgotten there was any other way to live.

The Christmas mood of the city was an elixir to her. She found time to go shopping for Uncle Karel and Aunt Martha and Ivy and Wayne, and enjoyed herself even though she knew how little of her heart was invested in these strangers who had already rented her old room to a new tenant, and whom she would see only on Christmas Day.

She journeyed to Fifth Avenue, and was charmed by the sight of children bundled up against the cold and looking into shop windows with wide eyes while their mothers held their hands indulgently. She thought of Santa Claus, the mysterious pagan elf who brought a unique spirit of mischief to the religious holiday of Christmas. And she felt an echo of the playfulness that had brought her to disguise herself as a witch and surprise Nate on Halloween—a prank that had ended in an evening of lovemaking she would never forget.

The only depressing note in her Christmas shopping was that she could find no gift for Nate. She thought idly of making him a garment, such as a sweater, a shirt, or even a pair of slacks for those handsome legs of his. But this seemed too presumptuous somehow.

So she settled on a different plan, one that was daring in a different way. She had recently done a sketch of herself that captured the secret exultation she had been feeling since becoming intimate with Nate. She turned it into a watercolor that was, if anything, even more revealing of how she felt about herself and him. This would be her Christmas present for him.

After all, had he not asked to see something she had drawn? In showing her his painting had he not let her "see him with no clothes on," to use his own words, and asked her if she dared do the same for him? The watercolor would be her way of meeting his challenge, and letting him see what he meant to her, without presuming to put strings on him.

Once this decision was made, Laura felt more Christmasy than ever before in her life. The season was made of magic, and it was all for her.

Finals week began at last. Laura's Modern Painting final would be on Monday morning, and Nathaniel Clear's exam on Wednesday afternoon. Her history final would be on Friday morning, and the dreaded biology next Monday.

She reluctantly put her foot down when Nate asked her to spend Friday night with him.

"After Biology final," she said.

"Come on," he importuned her. "A little rest and recreation is the best thing for a hardworking girl like you. If you don't take a break you'll be too tired to do your best."

"After Biology final," Laura repeated, stroking his rich dark hair as she smiled into his eyes. He seemed disappointed, but she held her ground, though all her feelings were on his side.

She worked like a slave all week long, budgeting her time so that she could quiz herself on biology and history even as she put the finishing touches on her preparation for her art exams. She had drawings of invertebrates and plant cells all over her walls, along with the favorite Matisse reproductions she had bought this semester. The cork board by her study table was covered with historical datelines and biological nomenclature.

Dizzy from overwork, she tried to turn one subject off and the other on at will. When she was wide awake she succeeded; but in her daydreams the nineteenth-century classic portrait got mixed up with the Triple Alliance and the Treaty of Ghent, and the proportions of Ingres' nudes intermingled with the anatomical structures of early mammals.

When Friday came she was so exhausted that she fell asleep in her battered old armchair at three in the afternoon and woke up at eight o'clock with the apartment in darkness. She looked out the window and saw a light snow falling through the airshaft, soundless and delicate behind her hissing radiator.

For a long moment Laura sat numbly in the shadows. There was no point in trying to study anymore tonight. She could feel a lethargy in her nerves that would not allow concentration. As Nate had warned her, she had worked too hard this week. She needed a long rest before hitting the books tomorrow morning.

At length she began to feel restless. On an impulse she put her coat on and went out in search of a breath of fresh air. The streetlights outside glowed with odd humid halos under the powdery snow. The air seemed dewy and not at all cold.

She passed a brightly lit café, saw doughnuts and Danish pastries in the window, and on a famished whim entered the place, drank a cup of hot coffee with cream and sugar, and ate a plain doughnut hungrily. Though it restored a modicum of energy to her tired body, it did not cure the confusion in her senses.

She began to feel bereft and empty as she sat in the overheated café. She recalled Nate's invitation, his smiling insistence, the sensual look in his eyes, and reproached herself for having refused him. How she wished she were with him tonight! She could almost feel the warm haven of his arms. She felt as lonely as a lost child that has strayed far from home.

She left the café and wandered the streets aimlessly, depressed now by the Christmas decorations she saw, for they all signified people's togetherness as they enjoyed the holiday. She noticed young couples out on dates, hand in hand on their way to the movies or to a restaurant. She saw a store closing its doors, the owner turning off the gay Christmas decorations in the window.

Laura felt more alone than ever as she thought of the lonely holiday ahead. Her home with Uncle Karel and Aunt Martha was a thing of the past, and had never really been a home to begin with. Her new life as an independent student seemed dissolved by the emptiness of finals week. The campus had lost its sense of community along with the routine of classes.

All at once Laura regretted her decision to come out for this breath of air. The night alarmed her, for it seemed closed upon itself, with no room for her in it. She felt trapped by the dark city. Even her excitement about school was eclipsed by images of a hundred backbreaking exams and as many course papers standing between her and graduation.

She needed an escape. But there was none.

Then she stopped in her tracks.

She realized that her moody peregrination around the outskirts of the campus had taken her to Nate's street. His apartment building was only half a block from where she now stood. She could see its tall obelisk-like shape and its glowing windows outlined like warm little havens against the night sky.

She hesitated, pondering her situation. She realized how desperately she needed Nate tonight. Her mood was darker than she had thought, and getting worse every minute. She had never felt so alone.

She thought of Halloween. The memory brought a smile to her lips, and she found herself starting down the street toward his doorway. A bold impulse took possession of her, overmatching her natural shyness. Perhaps she would surprise him. Why not, after all? He had almost begged her to be with him tonight. Her unexpected appearance would be as welcome to him as to herself.

She reached the building and stood before the door, wondering whether to go through with her plan. Someone came out. Before the inner door could lock shut, Laura unthinkingly ducked inside past the mailboxes and stopped it.

She looked over her shoulder. The person who had just come out was gone, in a hurry to get somewhere. She had come this far; there was no reason not to go the rest of the way. She let the door close behind her and moved to the elevator.

The impish thrill of Halloween came over her again. She got into the elevator and pushed 17. The little conveyance smelled of women's cologne and tobacco. It shot up through the familiar shaft, silent and quick, its path greased by invisible pulleys that seemed like the inside of a warm body.

The elevator came to a stop. Laura got out slowly. The landing looked familiar, but different, because tonight Nate was not standing in his open doorway, the smile of welcome on his handsome face. The old papered walls, the little Louis XVI table, the faded landscape in its frame opposite the elevator, seemed to disapprove of her presence, like stodgy old neighbors irked by a disturbance of their solitude.

Laura moved forward hesitantly, listening to her steps on the carpet, and hearing for the first time the creak of a floorboard she had never noticed in the past, when she used to rush across the landing into Nate's arms. Feeling somewhat less sure of herself, but driven beyond her scruples by loneliness and longing, she touched the closed door with her fingers, then knocked softly.

There was a long silence. After a hesitation she knocked again, a trifle louder. She looked into the miniature crystal ball of the eyehole, knowing she could not see through it into the apartment, but would be magnified out of proportion to the person who might look out at her.

Now she heard a distant movement inside. She sensed the reaction of a private place invaded by a knock that was not expected. She wondered about the wisdom of her having come here.

But it was too late. The doorknob was turning.

Involuntarily she stepped back a pace. The door opened. Nate stood in its frame, looking irritable and tired in his bathrobe. His expression turned quickly to surprise, then embarrassment, as he looked at her.

"What are you doing here?" he asked. "I thought you had exams."

Laura was noticing how different his voice sounded when she saw him close the door a few inches. She wondered why.

Then she realized he was aware of the mirror on the wall inside the apartment. She glanced at it over his shoulder. From where she stood it reflected the open door of the bedroom. The painting on the bedroom wall was out of sight. But the bed was not.

In it was a girl. The sheet was pulled up over her breasts. Blonde hair fell across her shoulders. She pushed a strand of it out of her eyes, and sketched the ghost of a wave with her upraised hand.

Laura realized that the other girl was also looking into the mirror on the bedroom wall, which together with the one behind Nate allowed her to see straight into Laura's eyes from the bed.

At that instant Laura recognized her. It was Sandra Richter, the pretty senior who was so regular a visitor to Nathaniel Clear's lectures.

Laura turned pale, and looked back into Nate's eyes.

"I'm—" She tried to stammer something by way of excuse. He was looking down at her, his initial alarm already turning to bitter amusement, for he had guessed what she had seen. "I didn't mean . . ."

He shrugged, his lips curled in a grimace of combined resignation and disgust.

"They never do, dear," he said. "They never do."

Laura moved back a pace, watching in a sort of terror as the image of the smiling girl moved out of the mirror, to be replaced by a bland wall and doorframe.

As she retreated, Nathaniel Clear very slowly closed the door. His eyes never left her as the old wood came between them, and she could still see his look of sadness as the narrow slit closed completely.

. . .

A few days later, after the biology final—which, ironically, had turned out to be the only thing separating Laura from insanity throughout the worst weekend of her life—she found a note in her mailbox. The handwriting was feminine, unknown to her.

It read:

Cheer up. You're not alone. It might interest you to know that he always uses the painting. He changes the hair color and the eyes and says, "It looks like you." I'll bet he has a stack of them stashed somewhere. Apparently it always works. Dumber lines have scored, I guess.

Better luck next time.

There was no signature.

Three weeks passed, a proper period of grief. Laura did not go to Uncle Karel's house for Christmas. Instead she sent her presents by mail, with a note explaining that she was visiting a girlfriend's family for the holidays.

Laura stayed alone in her apartment or took walks around Washington Square Park and the neighboring streets as Christmas break wound toward its conclusion. Not long before the end the final grades were posted outside the various department offices.

Laura's grade point was 4.0. She had got A's in all her subjects. The dreaded biology exam, taken at the darkest moment of her life, had been a success.

Laura smiled as she thought of her perfect grades, and the untold story behind them. She could not know that these were the first and only college grades she would ever receive.

Nor would she know, for another week and a half, that she was pregnant.

XV

VERN INNIS DIED on January ninth.

The next day, which would be called Black Wednesday by some Benedict employees and never forgotten within the company, Lou Benedict named Liz Dameron his new Vice President in charge of Product Development.

The Benedict executives were in a state of shock. At first those who knew Lou well, personally as well as professionally, thought he had simply taken leave of his senses. Lou was known above all as a loyal man who never forgot a friend. What he had done to Larry Whitlow by promoting Liz over him—a six-month novice over a seasoned executive! —was simply unthinkable.

Then, as the days wore on and the news sank in, even those whose faith in Lou was the most unshakable began to draw the logical conclusion about his private relationship with Liz.

A week after the appointment, Larry Whitlow sent his resignation in by office mail and walked out of the building without a goodbye to his friend and employer of fifteen years. Larry's silence was the only anthem needed for an era that was now over.

A new age had dawned at Benedict Products.

For Lou Benedict the last two months had been an agony he would never forget.

After the night of his first intimacy with Liz, she never repeated her ultimatum about Vern's job. But her behavior made it more than clear that she had meant every fateful word of it.

To begin, she avoided being alone with Lou, either in his office or her own. She managed to keep other people between them at all times, thus assuring him that she had no intention of giving him an opportunity for further romantic adventures with her.

On the two or three occasions when circumstances, or his own guile, managed to throw them together alone, she let him know by her steely demeanor and the cold warning in her eyes that his slightest move in her direction would bring a punishment he dared not contemplate.

But throughout this period of calculated aloofness Liz also managed to increase her seductions toward Lou. She surprised him with new outfits, skirts and blouses and dresses, so alluring that their businesslike contours were overwhelmed by the sensuality her body brought to them.

She wore new perfumes and colognes, each one more subtly suggestive than the last as it mingled with her own complex scent. She let her beautiful hair flow more freely over her shoulders than in earlier days, so that when she moved along a corridor she looked more like a beauty queen than a corporate employee.

And when she was with Lou—protected, of course, by the presence of other Benedict employees between them—she sent him subtle messages with her eyes, sidelong signals full of combined temptation and warning. "Don't forget what I have for you," she seemed to say. "But there's only one way you can get it."

She no longer came to his office with her reports, as of old, for she did not want to be at close quarters with him outside her own turf. But she telephoned him, at his office and sometimes at home, talking only of business, but in a voice that caressed him with knowing modulations, subliminal hints, musical undertones whose meaning was discernible only to him.

In a hundred ways she was like a female animal at mating time, her every sound and gesture striking at the heart of Lou's need. She was a magnet pulling him away from his work, his family, his friends, wearing down his resistance at long distance, showing off to him each day a bit more of the forbidden fruit he would never taste again if he did not give her her way.

And, what was even more perverse, she made Lou aware that the time running out on himself was also the time running out on poor Vern Innis's days on earth. For it would be Vern's death that would bring Lou his moment of truth. Lou was aghast at his own covetous thoughts about Liz, thoughts that became ever more intense in proportion as Vern, an old friend, grew weaker in the hospital, soon to breathe his last.

But so inhumanly attractive was Liz, so lyrical and sexy and tauntingly girlish in her charms, that the battle raging inside Lou began to move toward an inevitable conclusion. The force of Liz's seduction was too great, and the whisper of his scruples too weak. By letting him possess her once she had dismantled all the weapons that might have helped him resist her now. Terrifying though she was in her silent will and her cruel resolve, he could not banish her image from his heart.

There was nothing left to do but await the inevitable.

And now Vern was dead.

Even as the company was taking in its shock and disapproval over what had happened, it was also being forced to accept the fact that Liz was a factor to be reckoned with as vice president.

She was capable and even brilliant in her new role, despite her youth and the demands of Vern's job. Even Vern's best friends had to admit that she not only had a flair for high-level responsibility, but also brought a wealth of new ideas to an office that had been sadly lacking in them before her promotion.

Vern himself had been a stolid presence in Product Development, a relic of the company's infancy, admired more for his geniality and good humor than for his brilliant ideas. Intellectually he was on Lou's conservative wavelength, and had never thought much in terms of bold expansion of Benedict's product line, but rather concentrated on solidifying markets for the same old electrical parts.

Liz, on the contrary, was able to lay before Lou elaborate drawing-board plans for whole new product lines in small appliances, industrial parts, applications for new metals, precision products to sell to the armed forces for the expanding field of rocket technology—not to mention involvement in the infant computer field, and, her hungriest interest of all, the fledgling industry called television.

The plans Liz brought forward, week in and week out, stunned Lou not only by their boldness but by their absolute practicality. Liz had an amazing command of the company's stock, the measure of its sales against overhead in the current economy, its personnel, and even its history. She could derive future challenges from past mistakes, and lay everything out in dollars and cents so that there was no earthly way to argue with her without appearing to be doing so for petty reasons, or because one was a hopeless fuddy-duddy.

She amazed Lou not only because she was so brilliant and innovative in her thinking, especially for one so young, but also because he could not understand how she found time for all this research and planning.

The more so, he had to admit, because nowadays she was spending so much of her time in bed with him.

In the name of circumspection she had had him rent an apartment in a suburb for their trysts. He met her there several times a week. She would greet him in her nightgown, sometimes still wet from her shower, her fragrance mingling with that of scented soap and shampoo as she looked into his eyes. Sometimes she was dressed only in her bra and panties, to excite him, or even stripped to the buff, her slender body peeking through the doorway like a forbidden delight tempting a wayfarer from the path of righteousness.

He would close the door with a gasp, all control vanishing in that first instant, and bury his face in her breasts, his lips frantic for her taste, his hands trembling to feel the silken smoothness of her flesh.

Her bedroom wiles had changed—Lou was not sure just how. Though on the surface she still displayed that feminine gentleness and delicacy that had been so much a part of her the first time she had given herself to him, it was obvious she was in control now.

There was something predatory about her as she orchestrated the spasms of his pleasure with sure hands, sly murmurs, clever alternations of warning and encouragement that kept him utterly off-balance until, with a last little sigh, she made him come inside her, accepting his orgasm as calmly as though it was a faint breeze fluttering at the surface of her body.

Often she made love to him with such mastery that his climax came before he was ready. Sometimes she would tease him with her hands or lips, just a little too cleverly, just a little too long, so that he wasted his seed without even entering her. He knew—though he did not understand how he knew—that she liked this. She enjoyed making him come before he could make a pretense of satisfying her. This increased her power over him, and turned her apparent acceptance of him into a mocking parody.

The first time he had dared to express his disappointment in words. "I wanted you to have it," he said.

But she had just shaken her head.

"I like it when you come that way," she said. "It shows you really want me."

After a while he was forced to give up on the idea of satisfying her. He realized it was his submission that excited her. She craved the moist look of fascination in his gaze as it traveled up her long thighs, past the sex he adored, the firm perfect breasts, the fiery mane of hair flowing down her creamy shoulders.

His sex was her plaything now. She had made it impotent as a weapon of male domination, and turned it paradoxically into a female organ of sensitivity and yielding, a toy manipulated by her caresses, its spasms ordained by her whim.

Sometimes, when he felt his sex disappear into her, it seemed as though she were taking it for her own, filling her own void and leaving him forever incomplete, so that she was male and female at once, and he merely her eunuch, her slave.

And when he touched her soft skin with trembling fingers as her glowing green eyes scrutinized him in cool triumph, even her naked flesh seemed to be staring at him victoriously, a silken infinity of eyes watching with interest as he sank deeper under her spell.

Only a few short months separated Lou from the old life. But the wall between him and his sanity was miles thick. Liz owned him now. She could do with him what she wished.

He shuddered to imagine what that might be.

Though her work commanded respect, she was no longer liked within the company. The employees working in Product Development were afraid of her, as were her old colleagues in Materials. Even the executive force held her in dread and awe, for her rise had been so sudden and cruel as she stepped over the dead body of Vern Innis and the betrayed Larry Whitlow. No one at Benedict Products felt that his or her job was really safe as long as Liz was there.

For somehow her image had crystallized in everyone's mind as that of a young woman of boundless, ravenous ambition, a creature whose female charms were added to her undeniable executive and managerial ability to make an irresistible arsenal of weapons for getting where and what she wanted.

A woman possessed of matchless gifts, but without a soul.

As time passed, a new and secret wish found expression within the company. Benedict insiders began to hope that Liz would soon take her business elsewhere and leave Benedict Products to lick the wounds she had started in its flesh. For she was indeed a wound in the soul of the company, a wound that might never heal entirely, but would at least scar over if she left in search of a higher-paying, more upwardly mobile position with a bigger company.

"Let her go someplace else and fuck her way to the top," said whispered voices in the company lunchroom. "Why can't she go away and leave us alone?"

And even as these whispers died at her approach, she greeted her coworkers with the same old smile on her face, youthful and bright and friendly. To all appearances she was not at all different from the Liz of old: a hard worker, a conscientious manager, a polite conversationalist and a good listener.

That was what was so frightening. Liz was still her charming self. Yet everyone felt the cunning behind her friendliness, the evil behind her glowing beauty.

Why can't she just go away?

That was the question that haunted everyone. But no one knew its answer.

A new dimension had made itself felt in Liz's recent discussions with Lou about the company. Benedict Products, she explained, lacked the financial base for the sort of product development it must initiate if it was to compete in the postwar economy.

"The company can't stand still," she said, showing Lou fiscal charts and projections that made his eyes glaze. "It has to move forward. If we try to maintain the status quo, we'll become poorer and weaker before we know it, because competition is coming from sources that weren't there three and four years ago."

Lou had to fight to be attentive to her data, for his eyes wanted so badly to focus on the breasts behind her blouse, the thighs stirring under her skirt, the ghost of a smile at the back of her eyes. The sexual spell she cast was overpowering, and it mingled with her arguments in a dizzying way.

But he came back to earth when she revealed the trump behind her reasoning: a merger.

"We need the broader fiscal base of a larger corporation to give us the strength to compete and grow at the same time," she said. "It's the only way."

Here Lou drew the line.

"This is my company," he said. "I built it from nothing. Do you know what *nothing* means, Liz? I started from the ground up. I know every nut and bolt in this place, because I paid for it all with my own money. And nobody's going to take it away from me, or tell me how to run it. Even if I go bankrupt, I'll do it at the helm of my own ship."

She looked carefully at him, seemed to hesitate, and then said no more about the issue. If he sensed that her withdrawal was strategic, he did not admit it to himself. He could not imagine sharing Benedict Products with strangers, perhaps losing the company name, and having to answer to bosses from some conglomerate.

Pleased with himself at having put his foot down with Liz, Lou thought no more about it.

Besides, the company seemed to be doing better and better—that is, if the price of Benedict stock was any indication. The stock had been going steadily up on the regional exchanges, from a modest $7.23 a share to $8.25, and then all the way to $11.66, since Vern's death. Though profit-and-loss figures were only slightly ahead of last year, and though orders for the company's wares were not exactly glutting the sales reps' mailboxes, the price of Benedict stock continued to inch upward.

No one in the company was familiar enough with the subtle new pressures of the postwar economy to interpret this apparently propitious news as a warning sign. It was simply assumed that times were good, and getting better. Why look a gift horse in the mouth?

As for Lou himself, these days he was spending so much time worrying about Liz, fantasizing about her, and losing himself in the secrets of her body and caresses, that he lacked the leisure to ponder the financial intricacies of Benedict Products' market position. His hold on the company had grown more vague, less firm.

Besides, he had another problem to worry about.

Barbara, who had not given him a real smile since the day Liz was hired, was openly hostile since Liz's unbelievable promotion and the embarrassing gossip it had fueled within the company. Though Lou could hardly protest against this reaction, it upset and preoccupied him.

The late hours he kept with Liz were not lost on his wife. Barbara herself had now taken to spending as much time as she could away from home. She was always out with friends, shopping, playing tennis or bridge, visiting, or going to the movies. She left him dinners to warm up when he chose to come home, and curt notes informing him of her whereabouts.

She seemed to take pleasure in confronting him with the stone wall of her absence and her silence. Though it facilitated his relations with Liz, it was eating away at the last foundations of his marriage with alarming rapidity.

The few times he spent with her, they got into quarrels. They fought about money, about the kids, about school, about plans for a vacation Lou wanted to postpone and Barbara didn't. Sometimes the arguments erupted over matters as insignificant as the color of the tie Lou chose to wear to a dinner party, the merits of one cushion cover over another, or the repair shop that had botched the car's muffler. Both of them seemed to know what they were really fighting about, but neither wished to allude to it directly.

The only time the friction between them dissipated was when they slept. But this was because the distance between them at night was greater than ever before. Barbara curled far into her half of the bed while Lou suffered troubling dreams on his own side.

Lou was deeply distressed by what was happening. He had always loved Barbara for her level head, her humor, her steadfastness as a wife and mother, and her forbearance as the mate of a hardworking entrepreneur. She had married him when she was a popular college girl, and had interrupted her education to help him build Benedict Products.

For the last nineteen years he had looked forward each day to the smile she greeted him with upon his return home. But now that smile was replaced by a look of stubborn indifference that never met his eyes, never acknowledged his presence. He could not tell her how much this hurt him, for he knew how richly he deserved it.

The kids, of course, could hardly be unaware of the situation. Paul, the boy, was away at athletic practice all the time now, and the two girls, Cindy and Joyce, seized every pretext to spend afternoons and evenings at the homes of friends.

Sometimes when Barbara was out Lou would find himself eating dinner in embarrassed silence with the three children, asking clumsy questions about their schoolwork as they hurried to finish their meal and be excused from the table.

More often he returned from his trysts with Liz to find that no one was waiting for him. The kids had accepted invitations to eat at their friends' homes, and Barbara's absence was announced by a note left on the kitchen counter. Lou ate by himself, the members of his family having gone their separate ways.

No one wanted to be in the house anymore. Lou was increasingly alone. The family was falling apart under him, its close links being cut away one by one.

And he could not stop the disintegration, for he could not tear himself away from Liz.

One evening he came home rather late and found Barbara alone, waiting for him.

She sat stiffly in one of the living room chairs, looking at him with such authority that he sat down to hear her out.

"I know what you've been doing with Liz Dameron," she said.

He began to protest, but she silenced him with one look.

"Don't make yourself ridiculous by trying to deny the obvious, Lou." she said. "I've had you followed. There are pictures . . . Not that it was really necessary."

She poised herself to go on. He looked at her guiltily. The only thing harder to behold than the reproach in her eyes was the pain. She was not looking at him, but at the disease that had come between them, the cancer that was killing her family.

"I've given this matter a lot of thought over the past couple of months," she said. "For nineteen years you were a very good husband,

Louis. I loved you. And I've decided, I still love you. So I'm going to give you one chance, and one chance only, to make things right between us, for ourselves and for the sake of the children. There are five lives at stake here. If you decide to ruin yours, I intend to save the other four."

Lou's throat was dry. He coughed.

"What is it you want?" he asked.

"I want Liz Dameron out of your company and out of this town," she said. "Right away. I want you back where you belong. It's that simple."

Lou thought for a long moment. Barbara's courage was so touching and human a thing that it almost brought tears to his eyes. He weighed what was at stake, seeing things as though for the first time.

A surge of strength came to him from somewhere. He stood up.

"All right, Barbara."

From her seat his wife gave him a grave, wary look that tore at his heart. Then she got up, turned out the light, and went to bed.

Lou stood alone in the silent living room.

The next move was his.

XVI

LOU HESITATED for over a week before deciding how to present Liz with the news.

Finally he made up his mind to tell her on company time, and within the walls of Benedict, rather than in the apartment, which was a turf she owned so totally that he dared not confront her there. This was a business matter, and must be handled in a businesslike way.

He had her summoned to his office late one afternoon. She arrived dressed in a dark suit with a little silk ruffle at the neck, her briefcase in her hand. She looked at him inquiringly as he cleared his throat. There would be no interruptions; he had ordered his secretary to hold all calls and not to disturb him for anything.

He had dressed more conservatively than usual, for the occasion. He wore a navy worsted suit and a maroon tie, with the tie tack Barbara had given him fifteen years ago. His shoes were freshly shined.

"Liz," he began, trying to sound executive and dispassionate, "I have something important to tell you. I've been doing a lot of thinking lately —about my company, and about my family. And I've come to the inescapable conclusion that things can't go on any longer as they have been going. The best solution, for both you and myself, is that we make a clean break so that I can run Benedict the way I want to, and so that you can go on to the sort of career that is right for you."

She said nothing. The look in her eyes was impenetrable, uncanny in its poise. It was hard to meet it head on without flinching. But Lou forced himself to appear strong and even sympathetic.

"I'll give you the best recommendation I've ever given any employee," he went on. "You've done a great deal for Benedict Products. You've impressed us with your hard work, your brilliant ideas, your grasp of what the company and the marketplace are all about. You'll be a bright prospect for any of a hundred firms here on the coast or elsewhere. Wherever you like."

He steeled himself. "You have a great future," he said. "But it can't be with us, Liz. It just can't. We have differences about the course this company is taking, differences that can't be reconciled. And . . . in other ways . . . it just can't go on. It's bad for Benedict, bad for you, bad for me. I—well, I guess that's all I had to say."

He joined his hands on the desk top and looked at her. She was so beautiful, sitting there in her crisp suit, looking at him through the most heart-melting green eyes in the world. He felt a pang at the thought that in a few moments she would walk out that door never to return. She would clear out her office and leave him to a solitude he had given up imagining, so terrible was the idea of losing her.

Perhaps, he mused, he would one day get over her, as an addict gets over the obsession that ruled his existence for so long. The scars would go deep, but he would face life without her. It was not an impossible challenge.

In any case, there was no choice. This was goodbye.

To his surprise, she opened her briefcase in her lap and pulled out a sheaf of papers.

"Lou," she said, "have you wondered why our stock has been going up recently?"

He frowned, perplexed. "Why do you ask?" he said. "Should I be wondering?"

"I would be," she said, "if my company's stock was suddenly climbing despite the economy, and despite our unimpressive profit-and-loss for the past two years."

Lou gazed at her in bewilderment. "Liz, what are you talking about?"

"I'm talking about the modern world," she said. "The postwar world of business. Lou, in the last five months a large block of Benedict Products stock has been acquired by a corporation called American Enterprise. This stock has been bought through various middlemen, including subsidiaries of American Enterprise, mutual funds, dummy corporations, banks, and private individuals. But all of it belongs to American Enterprise as of the present. The reason your stock has gone up is that there has been greater-than-average activity on it on the California exchanges—and, of course, because the buyers have shifted blocks in order to drive up the price."

Confused, Lou shrugged his shoulders. "Let them buy," he said. "I don't see why that should worry me."

Liz smiled coldly. "The people responsible for this acquisition of Benedict stock," she said, "are not buying without a plan in mind. Just prior to our next stockholders' meeting, Lou, they are going to make a cash tender offer to our stockholders for enough shares to assume a controlling interest in the company."

Lou struggled to take in what she was saying. It made no sense to him.

"Our shareholders won't sell," he protested.

"Yes, they will, Lou," she said. "They'll sell because the price offered by American Enterprise will be too high for them to resist—say, $1.20 per dollar on each share, or perhaps even higher."

Lou mustered a skeptical smile. "And where is this bunch called American Enterprise supposed to get that kind of money to throw away?"

Liz shook her head. "It's not money thrown away. It is money spent to acquire a company. And the temporary loss is tax deductible. It's a sound investment. This sort of thing is being done more and more nowadays. The tax laws favor it, and the new conglomerates have access to venture capital funds to help them cover expenses."

Lou's smile had faded.

"Just what are you saying, Liz?" he asked.

"I'm saying that as of this spring your company will have been taken over by American Enterprise," she said. "Benedict Products will have ceased to exist as an independent entity."

Speechless, Lou wondered if she had taken leave of her senses. Perhaps the story she told was some sort of monstrous fantasy. It certainly sounded like one. Nothing in his experience in business had prepared him for such a tale.

She went on calmly. "The merger will be the best thing for Benedict," she said, "though we'll almost certainly have to change our name, and our executives will have to answer to the people at American. But we'll be an important element in American's product development plans. I've sat in on some of the meetings, so I know what their thinking is. As a matter of fact, it's already been decided that our specialization will be television technology. We're going to be a significant producer of parts for home television sets as well as a research facility for the application of television technology for scientific purposes, particularly in aerospace."

"I don't believe you." Lou's voice shook as he spoke.

Sat in on meetings. The words rang nightmarishly in his brain. Meetings about his company! Rage overwhelmed him as he thought of Liz with the predators in their corporate boardroom, plotting his company's future without his knowledge.

Liz stood up, came forward, and placed a folder of papers on his desk top.

"What are those?" he asked.

"Copies of stock certificates," she said, her soft fragrance suffusing him as she leaned closer to him. "Records of transactions through various brokers and securities agencies." She separated a typed sheet from the rest and showed it to him. "This is the letter that will be mailed to all your shareholders, about a month before the meeting. It makes a cash tender offer for their shares in an amount about twenty-five percent higher than that currently reflected on the exchange. At the same time the tender offer will be officially advertised in all the major trade publications, including *The Wall Street Journal.*"

She stood back, looking down at him, a confused man surrounded by the pieces of paper that detailed his own destruction. How beautiful, how macabre she looked in her cool triumph! A sleek huntress, born for the taste of blood . . .

"How did this happen?" Lou asked, looking at the evidence before him.

"Because of me, mostly," she replied. "I was American's contact within our company. I showed them our books, and helped sell them on the idea of the takeover. I helped them acquire blocks of our stock, and helped them cover over the transactions so your finance department wouldn't find out what was going on."

She shrugged. "They would have got around to us eventually, anyway. But I convinced them that Benedict would be a valuable acquisition right now."

Helplessly Lou gazed up at her.

"Why?" he asked. "Why did you do this, Liz?"

"It was the thing to do," she replied. "It was the only realistic way for us to go in today's economy. This way Benedict, under its new name, will be a company of the future. Had you gone on the way you were going, it would have been a relic of the past."

Lou fought to find words to express the horror he was feeling.

"But I'll lose everything I've worked for," he said. "I've worked a lifetime to become my own man, to own my own business and control my own destiny. Now I'll be someone else's employee. I'll have to take orders from others. They'll be able to keep me or fire me as they choose."

She shook her head. "I've taken steps to protect you," she said. "You'll still be the titular head, no matter what happens. I got you that as part of the deal."

I got you that. Lou's head was swimming as he thought of this green, youthful girl who had paused in her rapacious ambition long enough to "protect" him. The world was turned upside-down.

"Suppose I don't agree to any of this," he said.

"You have no choice, Lou." She folded her arms and looked down at him. "It's over already. If you don't like it, you can let American buy you out personally. Or you can stay, and make yourself a good deal of money as an American executive and stockholder. If you choose to get out, you won't be rich, but you won't be poor, either. You could start over if you liked . . . start another small business, even at your age. In any case, the choice is clear."

"What about you?" he asked.

Her shrug answered him. "I'm staying, of course."

Lou gazed at her in awe. She had enunciated the final irony. She was offering him a chance to stay with his own company—albeit in a diminished and even ceremonial capacity—when he had called her in here to fire her from it!

"I can't believe this," he said. "I just can't believe it."

She let her glance stray from his face to the papers on the desk top, and back to him again. "The books don't lie, Lou," she said. "What's done is done. Benedict Products is through. But your company has a fine future as part of American Enterprise. With or without you."

He looked at her tall, slim body, at the nubile limbs he had caressed so many times, the pretty, catlike eyes, the lush hair and creamy skin.

So this was the face of evil. How could evil couch itself in such simple, girlish human form? Could the devil be that creative, that cunning?

"You're a monster," he said. "You're not human."

Her eyes widened in a look of surprise, and even of hurt.

"What did you say?" she asked.

"I said, you're not human." The words seemed to Lou a perfect syllogism, an incontrovertible statement of the very truth that was destroying his life.

"But I am human, Lou," she said, moving forward a pace. "Don't you see that? I've been thinking of you all this time . . . of your welfare."

She came around the desk with a glance at the closed door, and knelt beside his chair. She touched his arm with one hand, his thigh with the other. Her eyes looked up into his, alive with an intensity that was not far from suggestion.

"I'd miss you if you left," she said. "It wouldn't be the same for me."

Her words were weaving a strange spell even as her eyes held him in suspense. He thought of the many times he had given himself to her, belonged to her as her slave. And he knew she was referring to that now, to her domination and his enslavement, and the perverse pleasure she took in owning his body.

And with this thought he began to feel excitement stirring in his sex, despite the horror in his mind.

"Don't you understand after all this time?" she asked softly. "I am human, Lou. I'm a woman. I need you."

Her words were absurd, but they were like silken cords knotting themselves ever more tightly around his need. He could neither speak nor move. Appalled and on tenterhooks, he listened.

Her hands had moved to his waist. He could feel the warmth of her arms on his thighs, and he knew the hard penis was sending its message of eager alertness through his clothes to the radar she carried in her woman's senses.

The ghost of a smile on her lips told him she knew she had him in her power even now. Yet the look in her eyes was warm, almost protective. There was an odd melancholy in her irises, a womanly gravity and seriousness he had only seen once or twice before. It seemed to paralyze his will, and to make her completely irresistible.

"Come on," she whispered. "Come on, darling. Don't be mean to me."

The bulge under his pants was a mountain now, only inches from her hands. He saw her pause to gauge the silence of the room. He heard the distant chatter of typewriters and the jingle of a telephone in the outer office. He had told his secretaries not to knock at his door under any circumstances.

He could feel Liz reading these thoughts. She glanced over her shoulder at the door. The lock was turned shut.

Slowly she found his zipper and undid it. Her fingers unclothed the penis with the quickness of a thief, and he saw it leap out shameless with excitement, frantic to belong to her.

Now she stood up and began to remove her clothes. She did it without hurry. First the skirt, and the slip; then the jacket and blouse. She looked down at him, her eyes smoky and penetrating, as she reached to unhook her bra.

He knew what she wanted. She wanted to possess him right here within a single wall of his secretary, here in his own office, the office whose meaning would cease to exist within a few months' time, thanks to her. She wanted to savor his destruction, to enjoy him as a princess enjoys her slave, at her cruel whim, her smiles and caresses full of contempt and indolent amusement.

Lou felt as though her gaze had turned him to stone. It remained fixed to him as the panties began to come down. The scent of her naked flesh was perfuming the room. The russet triangle of her sex was offered to him. But not even the impossible beauty of her unclothed body could compete in sheer power with the look flowing from those fatally sexy eyes.

"Come on," she said gently. "It's all right. Don't be shy."

Don't be shy. What madness echoed in her words! She was slipping the trousers down to his ankles, then his underpants. She offered a ripe young breast to his hungry lips, and he suckled it like a baby, famished, pathetic.

She settled herself gently onto his sex, a soft cooing creature armed to the teeth with hooks no man could resist. With his pants pulled clownishly down to his ankles, he began to squirm under her, already feeling her insides slipping over the shaft in welcome.

The last of his self-respect was gone now. And surely it was this monstrous humiliation, the unnameable cruelty behind those soft words and that nurselike smile, that sucked his seed from him in an awful spasm, the male essence gone forever into creamy female loins as the distant typewriters and jingling indifferent phones tolled his end.

When it was over he began to ebb inside her, still tasting the hard tip of the nipple in his mouth, feeling the glory of her body in all his senses, these sensations mingling inscrutably with the doom he knew came only from her. And this was the most fatal and terrible pleasure of all.

At last, when he had caught his breath, he looked at the papers on his desk, at the walls of the office with their old smiling pictures of Larry Whitlow and Vern and the others, and then back to the alabaster nudity of the creature in his lap.

"You win," he said softly. "What more can you take? You have everything."

She smiled against his ear, her nipple moving up and down against his lips. The next words she spoke were a knell sounding over the rest of his life.

"I want you to marry me, Lou."

XVII

New York
January 13, 1952

OLIVE OYL.

The abortionist sat at the small kitchen table in the back room of the apartment, looking out the window at the rooftops of the West Side. Before him was a cup of tepid black coffee to which he had added an ounce of rye to calm his nerves. In his yellowed fingers he held a Lucky Strike, which trembled faintly as its plume of smoke rose in the stale air around him.

It was a gray drizzly day, the kind of January day that chills one to the bones though the temperature is hardly below forty. The cold seemed to come right in the window and laugh at the sniffling radiator.

An ugly day. Not the sort of day that any good could come from. And yet, if Olive Oyl came through in the fifth race at Hialeah, it could be the most important day of this new year for him.

He shifted his weight in the small kitchen chair with a sigh. He was a big man, six feet four inches tall, and somewhat overweight at two hundred forty pounds. He wore horn-rimmed glasses and a soiled pastel shirt, which would be concealed by his white coat before Valerie's girl arrived.

He looked at his watch. Where was she, anyway? She was supposed to be here at eleven-thirty. Without the money she owed him, he could not cover the bet on Olive Oyl.

And he had to win that bet. Otherwise he would not be able to pay his bookmaker what he owed, and have enough left over to buy pills to get him through the next month.

But there was no reason to despair. Valerie had brought him the seventy-five dollars, his share of the first hundred, yesterday morning, and assured him that the girl had the rest. She was a clean girl, according to Valerie. A high school girl from a good family, perhaps, or even a college girl. Nice clothes. Well-spoken. Not a lowlife. She had seemed scared and desperate, but determined. She promised she had the money. Valerie, who knew girls, was sure this one meant business.

He looked at his watch again. Hell, she was only five minutes late. His nerves were playing tricks on him today. He drummed a finger on the chipped tabletop and tried to relax.

The rye was not helping the coffee. He had taken too many pills this morning. There was no choice—his hangover was crushing. But now the jitters were on him bad.

He got up, found his medical bag by the sink, and reached for a Seconal. He ate it without bothering to get a glass of water. He had to get through until after that race. There was no way to do so without this one little dose.

He sat back down at the table, stubbed out his cigarette, and lit another. He drained the spiked coffee at one swallow and closed his eyes.

Life was so unfair. How had he sunk so low?

He had started with a legitimate medical degree, only fourteen years ago. It seemed like an eternity. He had hardly been at the top of his class, but the school was a respectable one, and he had done his residency at a rather good hospital in New Jersey. He had come home to Manhattan to go into private practice because he had grown up here, loved the city, and had high hopes. He expected to make a fine living doing OB-GYN uptown, and maybe even move his practice to the East Side if a few things tumbled his way.

But bad luck had dogged him from the beginning. He had had trouble getting well-heeled patients. Was it because he had not been clever enough to change his name? A Polish last name was not smart for a society gynecologist. Anyway, from the outset all he seemed to get were impoverished housewives, immigrants, and girls who wanted to keep their condition a secret from their parents.

Before long he realized that more of his patients wanted to terminate their pregnancies than to have babies. When things didn't look up, he had no choice but to do a few favors for the less fortunate among them. All they really wanted was a little confidentiality, and he was happy to provide it. The risk seemed minimal.

Then one day one of his patients, a hysterical girl whose boyfriend had knocked her up in the Bronx somewhere, went crazy on the operating table and practically got herself killed. She went home, started to bleed, and blew the whistle on everything. Told her parents about her pregnancy, the abortion—and named him, Dr. Danicevski, of West Seventy-fourth Street.

Before he knew it he was being sued for malpractice. He had a good lawyer, and could have beaten that rap, but when the Board of Medical Examiners got wind of it, they brought him up on a charge of unethical practice and lifted his license, just like that.

He couldn't believe it. For the first few months he thought his life was over. His wife walked out on him and went back to her family in Jersey. He hung around the apartment despondently, and started drinking heavily. It was during those lonely months that he developed his first taste for Seconal.

But just when things seemed darkest, he met Valerie through a mutual friend, a former patient. Valerie knew everybody in Manhattan, the Bronx, Brooklyn. She made him realize that his career was not over —it merely had to move onto a different track. She could send him all the patients he needed.

Before long he had a new name, Dr. Dann—"Doctor Dann the bandage man," he and Valerie liked to joke—and an apartment with an examining room concealed in the back. He treated the same girls he had been treating before—housewives who didn't want another mouth to feed, girls in trouble, girls who knew nothing about birth control and even less about abortion. They were frightened, too frightened to blow the whistle on him. Besides, he took precautions. None of them saw his face or knew his real name. And he moved around quite a bit. In eleven years the police had never got closer than one visit to an apartment he had already abandoned two weeks before.

It was a living. He had fewer patients than when he had been legit, but he charged higher fees. Soon the whores brought him their business, as his reputation grew. He had a loyal clientele, and even did some legitimate OB-GYN for women who trusted him and did not want to take their troubles to their own doctors. He actually delivered babies once in a while. And, through a friend of Valerie's, he helped young women sell babies they brought to term.

He was a respected member of the community, and he felt secure. He no longer missed his wife. Valerie had a friend who fixed him up with all the girls he wanted, and when he discovered that he also had a taste for boys, Valerie had yet another friend to help him with that. He still couldn't service the Upper East Side, whose women went out of the country to Japan or Mexico or Europe for their abortions, but he had his constituency.

The only problem was that the stress inherent in his work had caused him to slip into some bad habits. Booze was one. Gambling another. Seconal and bennies were the third. At first the combination had seemed healthy: booze at night, a man's right, followed by a handful of bennies in the morning to pick him up. Gambling for diversion. But when he lost money at the track he drank more, and then he needed more bennies to pick him up. And the bennies made him jittery, so he needed Seconal to keep him level through the day.

There was no problem about availability. Perry, the drug salesman he had met years ago while still a physician, did some business on the side, and probably supplied half the city for that matter. But Perry had security problems. If the pharmaceutical company he worked for got wind of his under-the-counter sales, he would be out of business. So he was necessarily expensive.

And money was a problem for Doctor Dann. His gambling ate up most of what he had earned, leaving less and less for the pills he needed to do his job right.

This year had started badly. He had lost a bundle on a race two weeks ago, and had to make a considerable loan from his bookmaker. He was low on pills, and Perry had refused to straighten him out until he paid off his outstanding bill from last year. He wasn't sure how much Perry knew about his addiction, but Perry was no fool. He seemed to increase his prices and reduce his availability in proportion to how strung out his clients were.

So there was no choice but to get hold of two thousand dollars right away. That was why everything depended on Olive Oyl. This horse was the hottest tip he had had in a year. He had put a hundred on her nose at 30 to 1. The tip came straight from the stable. If he won he would have enough for Perry, enough to pay off the book, perhaps enough even for a weekend off in Vegas. He desperately needed a rest.

If only the girl would get here!

As he was thinking this the buzzer rang. Quickly he stubbed out his cigarette, got up from the table, and pushed the intercom.

"I'm a friend of Valerie's," came a small voice, distorted by the cheap speaker.

"What's your name?" he asked.

"Laura."

He nodded, pushing the buzzer to open the downstairs door.

Hurriedly he put on his white gown and his mask. Not only would the mask prevent her from being able to identify him, but it would hide the smell of the rye on his breath.

He stood waiting for her. He felt tense. His stomach was raw. He hadn't had anything to eat today, just the coffee and the bennies, the cigarettes and the one Seconal.

After a couple of minutes there was a timid knock at the apartment door. He answered it and stood back as she walked in. She was wearing a cheap wool coat. But Valerie was right: She seemed clean. She had short dark hair, very fair skin, and large black eyes that were looking up at him fearfully.

"Do you have the money?" he asked from behind his mask, disguising his voice in a gravelly rumble. He tried to say as little as possible to his patients. He knew that his great size and the dark horn rims showing over the mask frightened them, and this suited him.

She took bills from her pocket and counted them out, three twenties, two tens, and four fives. He took them in his yellowed fingers, folded them, and put them in his pocket. Then he latched the front door and pointed to the examining room.

"Put your coat on that rack," he said. "Take your clothes off and lie on the table in there."

He went into the kitchen while she undressed. He pulled up his mask, poured one more finger of rye in the bottom of the coffee cup, and drained it at a gulp. He could feel the Seconal beginning to work. At least his hands wouldn't shake now. He washed them in the sink and went back to the examining room.

With her clothes off she looked hardly older than a child. She was very small and scared. Yet he could see from her breasts and the curve of her hips that she was at least eighteen. It was a very lovely little body, come to think of it. She was looking up at him through those big wide eyes.

"Are you going to—give me anything?" she asked.

He shook his head. "Not necessary," he said. "Just lie back and relax."

He never gave his patients anything. Hell, how could he know what allergies they might have? He didn't want some silly girl dropping dead on his examining table because of an anesthetic. Besides, the pain wasn't so bad. They had got themselves into this, after all. They could stand a little scraping and a few cramps to get rid of their burden.

She was lying back, naked, her eyes looking up at the ceiling. He moved to her side, raised the stirrups, picked up her legs one by one and positioned them. He felt her tremble as he draped her with a sheet he had taken from the cabinet.

"Just relax," he said. "This will only take a few minutes." He had already said too much, but he couldn't help feeling sorry for her.

He turned to the sterilizer. He had the curette and speculum well sterilized, as always. This was not only a matter of professional pride, but of prudence as well. These girls didn't know who he was or where to find him, but if he infected one with a dirty curette and she got sick enough, an angry boyfriend or father might follow his trail.

He glanced at the girl as he pulled on his sterile gloves. She was lying with her arms at her sides. She looked pale.

"Are you cold?" he asked.

She shook her head.

"All right," he said. "Don't move until I tell you it's okay."

He took the speculum out of the sterilizer and inserted it between her legs. Using a gauze sponge, he painted her thoroughly with antiseptic. A brief wave of confusion flowed before his eyes, and he shook his head to clear the cobwebs.

Fighting off the unsteadiness in his hands, he dilated the cervix, inserted the curette and began to scrape the uterus in long, careful strokes. He heard a tiny sound from the girl's throat, a stifled cry of pain and fear. He gritted his teeth, fearing that she might burst into wailing hysterics like so many of the others.

But no. She remained perfectly still, and there was not another sound out of her. She was stoic, a real soldier. Thank God for that.

He continued the procedure, being extra careful since he felt so shaky today. One false move and he could puncture the wall of the uterus, causing acute peritonitis. That was what got him into trouble the first time. He did not intend to allow it to happen again.

When he was halfway through he looked at the girl. Her face was distorted by pain, her lips closed tight. Silent tears were streaming down her cheeks. But she did not move.

When he had finished, he swabbed the area thoroughly and packed her with gauze.

"Now get dressed," he said. "I'll be in the other room."

He returned to the kitchen and drummed his fingers on the table, looking at his watch. It would be two hours before he could find out how the race came out.

At length the girl emerged from the back room. She was tottering on unsteady legs, and looked pale. But not pale enough to be bleeding internally. She took her coat off the rack and started to slip one arm into it. She seemed so weak that he took pity on her and helped her put it on.

He still had his mask on. "Go home and rest," he said. "Stay off your feet as much as possible for two days. Remove the gauze after twenty-four hours. Then use menstrual pads as necessary. If you get some cramping, some bleeding, that's normal. It will stop after a while. Now, remember: You haven't been here. You haven't seen me. You haven't seen Valerie. Understand? If you come back here, or send anyone, I won't be here. Understand?"

She nodded in silence, looking up at him. The expression in her eyes got under his skin somehow.

"You're going to be all right," he said, taking pity on her.

She responded with a wan smile and opened the door.

"Goodbye," he said.

When the door had closed behind her, he returned to the kitchen and took off the mask at last. His hands were really shaking now. He took out another Seconal and washed it down with more rye. He would have to lie down and try to keep hold of himself until after the race.

Decidedly, his nerves were shot today. It was more than the race—it was the girl. There was a sort of fragile nobility about her. And the look in her eyes had not been one of fear, as he had first supposed, but rather of grief. As Valerie had said, she was a clean girl. Perhaps a little too clean, he thought.

On the other hand, no one who came here could be completely clean. She would cause him no trouble.

He felt the balance of the drugs in his veins tipping toward somnolence. He was finally beginning to relax. He poured the last of the rye into a chipped kitchen glass and brought it to his lips. He hesitated, then raised the glass to the dirty landscape outside the window.

"Olive Oyl," he smiled.

XVIII

LOU BENEDICT LOOKED into the eyes of Liz Dameron.

Somehow he had never seen them this close before. Or was it the unfamiliar light in the room? Or perhaps the fact that she was undeniably looking at him in a way she had never looked before?

A voice was echoing in his ear, but he did not bother to try to make out the words. The sight of Liz eclipsed them. The auburn flame of her hair framed the beautiful face he knew so well. The sweet girlish complexion, so fresh and creamy with its dusting of soft freckles, each one as pure as the sun itself, had never looked so entrancing.

And the eyes! They were fixed on him, studying him inquisitively. Her lips were smiling, but the look in the eyes was not a smile. It jelled behind the liquid coolness of the emerald irises with an intensity that held him in thrall. A look as deep as the ocean, as remote as the stars. In it there was no human feeling, no recognizable human intention, but instead something larger, something infinitely more dangerous.

He could feel the handful of people in the room, and hear the voice droning on irrelevantly. He knew why he was here: to fall into those green depths at last, though it kill him, body and soul.

She must have felt what he was thinking, for something stirred in her expression. Something displaced itself quietly to make room for him, the better to swallow him.

Someone was speaking to Lou now. The words focused at last in his mind.

"Louis, will you take this woman for your wedded wife, from this day forward, forsaking all others, to have and to hold, for richer, for poorer, in sickness and in health, as long as you both shall live?"

Lou took a deep breath. He had come this far. It was really all over anyway. One might as well finish it.

"I will," he answered.

"Then I now pronounce you man and wife, under the laws of God and the state of Nevada. You may kiss the bride."

Lou mustered a smile. The eyes came closer. The lips were approaching now, soft and sensual as exotic fruit.

He kissed her, heard the desultory cheer of those present, felt a grain of rice drop on his shoulder.

The lips canceled it all. He felt them part, felt the tongue search for his own.

As long as you both shall live.

The last door opened. Beyond it was nothing. Nothing at all.

BOOK TWO

Laura, Ltd.

I

February 7, 1952

"COME ON, DIANA. You're driving me crazy."

A strong arm held Diana Stallworth about her shoulders. Her blonde hair, long and fine, fell across the hand that was pressed to her breast. The seat of the car pushed against her back. She was in the position every girl on a date feared most: effectively pinned, the lips of her date at her ear, his body blocking escape.

He had managed to maneuver one of her trapped hands to the point where she could feel how hard he was under his pants. His excitement was like that of an animal—urgent and breathy. But his whispers were seductive, and he was very handsome. And Diana had had more than enough dates with him already. It was no wonder he thought it was time to get sexually serious.

"Cliff, no," she whispered, afraid that the couple in the backseat would hear them despite the rather loud music of the orchestra on the car radio. "You don't understand. I can't. Really."

The music was Tommy Dorsey, playing "So Rare." The saxophones clucked softly, sensual in their liquid choral tones. The hand on Diana's breast was languorous now.

"Baby," he whispered. "You know you want it as much as I do. I can see it in so many ways. Just let me get inside you where I belong. You'll never regret it. Never . . ."

The lips were caressing her earlobe, and she felt a hot tongue lick at the tender spot, sending alarm flares through all her senses. Her own desire unnerved her, for she knew she could not give in to it.

She had often wondered about what it would be like actually to have a man. To feel the huge hard length of him buried inside her, working and stroking and penetrating deeper and deeper. She had heard girls joke about it for years, at school in Geneva and of course here at Smith. Diana had to play the delicate game of making believe she knew all about the physical sensations and details, while keeping up the pretense that she was true to Hal and did not sleep around.

A pretense that was all too true.

Diana was a virgin.

She had dated some of the most attractive men at Princeton, Dartmouth, Harvard, and Yale—men whose families knew her family, and who knew what the name Stallworth meant in society as well as in business.

These young men knew that seven generations of family breeding ordained that Diana Powers Stallworth was going to become Mrs. Haydon Lancaster as soon as Hal got out of the army and took up the law practice that would lead him—as inevitably as the earth's rotation leads the sun to set in the west—to a brilliant career on Wall Street and perhaps in politics.

These things were facts of life for Diana as well as for her classmates, friends, professors, and dates. Dates who themselves came from important families like the Beekmans, the Webbs, the Alexanders, the Bancrofts, the Auchinclosses. Dates who knew where Diana came from, and what her destiny was, as surely as they knew which fork to pick up first at a Union Club dinner.

They knew, more particularly, that Hal's marriage to Diana was decreed by the fact that Stewart Lancaster had died in the battle of Midway. This was a simple equation of high-society phylogeny.

Had Stewart lived, he would have assumed the primary Lancaster inheritance and obligation. He would almost certainly have married Diana's first cousin Marcia Stallworth. This would have left Hal, a somewhat freer agent, for marriage to one of the Schell girls, Jessica or Cynthia, or one of the Winters sisters, Leigh or Phoebe, or perhaps Holly Seton, whose people were allied by marriage to the legendary Bonds of Manhattan.

But now that Hal remained as the only Lancaster heir—his sister Sybil being considered apart by virtue of her sex as well as her bizarre temperament—he must make his alliance with the Stallworths, whose manufacturing fortune outweighed the Winters' oil money or the Schells' real estate in importance. Since Marcia Stallworth was far too old for Hal, that left Diana.

Thus Hal was earmarked by history and the caprices of fate for Diana. Had she missed him, he might have been wasted on the Schells, and Diana herself stuck with some piece of baggage like Teddy Roche, Quentin Bollinger, or Carter Scott—dull tools she had snubbed irritably at Newport during her girlhood, nondescript young men who would grow up to be golfers, drinkers, and wonderful clubmen, but the worst husbands in the world.

Diana was promised to Hal by tradition. But she had her own reasons for being faithful to him.

Hal was more than just a wonderful alternative to the others. And he was more than just a Lancaster—desirable though that name was in itself.

He was the one and only Prince Hal, blessed by some sort of strange mutation with a gentleness and a sense of humor that none of the Lancaster men had ever had. Thanks to a forbidden spark that had entered the bloodline somewhere, Hal had emerged from it with qualities that set him apart not only from his own people but from all the young men of his generation.

Diana had known this from the first time she met Hal, when they were both still children. He had been tall, and good-looking, with the incisive Lancaster walk and the brilliant Lancaster smile. But there was a sweetness about him, a soft whimsy combined with the glow of male fires underneath, that caused her to conceive a huge crush on him even then.

And that crush grew into something stronger as she realized after Stewart's death that she would one day be paired with Hal by the unalterable politics of breeding.

They were brought together at innumerable family and social occasions, Hal a teenager now and Diana hardly out of bubble gum and candy bars. She looked up to him, for he was so easy within himself, always smiling and curiously relaxed even as he exerted himself at polo, soccer, or tennis with her cousins and his own relations.

After the games they would have dinner with Hal's parents, their pretty adopted daughter Kirsten, and Hal's oddly silent little sister Sybil. Hal charmed everyone. Diana's mother and sisters made no secret of adoring him. His own mother looked across the table at him with a sort of quiet maternal passion that almost made Diana want to look away, as though she were observing something too intimate to see the light of day.

And at those dinners Diana could feel Hal's sidelong smile resting sometimes on herself. She knew even then that she was promised to him, that she would be his wife one day and share his bed. And she knew he knew it, too.

This filled her with the awe of every young girl who is faced with a marriage ordained by factors outside her own free will. But in Diana's case the feeling was more special, for the boy was Hal. Hal, the one and only.

When she learned, in later years, that he was following the Lancaster custom of bestowing his charms on all the best-looking girls in society —his physical gifts being enormous, so it was said, and more than matching the appeal of his handsome face and dreamy eyes—she found to her surprise that she did not disapprove. After all, he was only doing what came naturally to all men, and to the Lancasters in particular.

In fact, Diana was rather proud of him and his new reputation as a lover. She knew that on her wedding night the eyes of everyone in society would be on her, and that all the girls who had known him before her would be thinking, *"Diana's got him now."*

So Diana felt privileged, and lucky.

But her awe did not decrease. She did not feel familiar or easy with Hal. She became more tongue-tied and abashed when she was with him —even though, in his polite way, he drew a bit closer to her, as people always do when they are thrown together with someone by fate and have to make a go of each other.

Diana hoped she would be good enough for him, but she was not sure. And this terrified her, because he was so awfully special, such a prize. When they were together she worried that he was bored with her company—though he never seemed so—and that he could never love her because his independence of spirit had been insulted by having her thrust upon him.

Soon she had returned from Geneva, and was a sophisticated Smith girl. Everyone knew her as a statuesque, icy blonde who turned men on with her body while humbling them with her sharp wit. She could wither a female rival with a glance or a sarcastic word, and could be the life of a party whenever she chose to. She was considered a bit wild, but nevertheless everybody's darling, for she knew every social grace to a T.

But she felt painfully inferior when she was with Hal. She tried to impress him with her worldliness and humor, but also to be womanly and warm with him. Both strategies seemed to fail miserably. On one hand, he made her as tongue-tied as a schoolgirl when they were alone together. On the other, she feared that her clever social manners as observed by him in public must seem to him superficial and shallow.

She even felt funny about exhibiting her considerable athletic skills when they swam, played tennis, or went riding together, for she was afraid she would appear mannish and overly aggressive to Hal.

Yet Hal never once showed a hint of contempt or impatience with her. He was always attentive, polite, and even somewhat tender toward her.

But she suspected that his courtliness had a hint of pity in it. Surely he must realize by now that she was too empty for him. He must be resigning himself to a barren private life with her.

And she did not want that! She wanted desperately to be worthy of him, to be a woman he could love. She prayed that that gentle look in his eyes was one of real affection. Perhaps the glow of his special, unique humor and warmth would one day illuminate the most secret and important parts of her life.

But it was hard to hope. For Hal was a sort of demigod, a creature of extraordinary beauty and masculine charm. And Diana was just another rich, spoiled girl of good family, equipped with a rich girl's tastes and talents, stamped out as stereotypically as any of her contemporaries.

She could serve a dinner for twenty without a false step; discuss Ascot and Dior and Matisse and Flaubert; wear clothes like a model (fashion layouts had already been done on her in *Vogue* and *Harper's Bazaar* by the time she was eighteen); play Mozart on the piano; pilot a yacht; ride to hounds; and organize a Junior League benefit. She could do all these things without particularly enjoying any or needing to commit a deeper part of herself to any—for that was the essence of the rich girl, after all, that lack of an ability or inclination to pour oneself wholeheartedly into any one thing—but do them all gracefully and convincingly.

But she was terrified that it was precisely this facility of hers, this shallow blitheness, that repelled Hal. For her empty skills were shared by dozens of girls just like her. And she could not put her finger on an inner quality, belonging to her alone, that could set her apart.

She felt she must find and cling to that one private thing, that one gift that belonged to her, so she could give it to Hal and thus deserve him.

Thus it was that she kept her virginity, she kept herself pure for Hal.

This sacrifice was unusual, not to say unheard-of, among her peers. In high society virginity was prized in inverse proportion to the empty but crucial ritual of the debutante ball. A girl's family name and probable inheritance counted far more than the mere intactness of her sex. None of Diana's close friends were virgins. One might almost say that virginity was "out." There was something quaint and *fin de siècle* about it that made it irrelevant to today's girls.

But Diana kept her troth plighted to Hal alone—even though she knew he had never dreamed of reciprocating the favor, and even though she feared that the prize she saved for him would have no value to him when she gave it.

And in the meantime, as tonight for instance, the men she dated, hungry for the smooth charms of her body, and encouraged by the flashes of excitement they felt in her kisses, were perplexed and angry when she refused to "go all the way."

After all, none of the other girls in Diana's crowd behaved so incomprehensibly. And since Diana's marriage was a family affair rather than a love match, she was seen as fair game. It was universally deemed in society that one's sex life and one's marriage went together like two adjacent rooms in a hotel, adjoining perhaps, but hardly the same entity.

Hal's reputation for adventuring only made Diana seem the more available. What on earth was she saving herself for? No one understood her.

Thus Diana's position was doubly and triply untenable. But she clung to it, her nerves ever more on edge.

For Diana was human.

"Mmm . . . Come on, Diana. You won't regret it. Here . . ."

The stroking was deeper, slipping subtly up her thigh as the lips whispered provocation into her ear.

"No!" Her whisper was angry. She would have cried out her frustration aloud had it not been for her roommate and her date in the backseat. But the heat in her senses gave authority to her refusal. "I mean it, Cliff. The answer is no."

She squirmed away from him and managed to get a hand into her purse. With desperate quickness she produced a cigarette and lit it with her monogrammed Dunhill lighter.

She breathed a sigh of relief as she exhaled smoke. A cigarette was, as everyone knew, a girl's best weapon against an aroused and persistent male. The common wisdom at Smith was, "just keep lighting them one from another and you're safe."

He released her reluctantly and sat back with a sigh. His eyes were filled with irritable resignation.

"Come on, Doug," he said, apparently sensing by some kind of male radar that the couple in the backseat were no closer to intercourse than he and Diana. "I have to get back to campus."

A groan of assent was heard. Cliff turned the key in the ignition and the large 1947 Packard shuddered into life. They crunched softly off the gravel path onto the roadway.

Little was said on the way back to campus. The two men walked the girls to Parsons House in silence. Outside the foyer the couples paired off and launched into heavy goodnight kisses, more for the benefit of the girls watching from the windows than from sincere affection.

"You can't go on doing this to me," Cliff said quietly to Diana when their lips parted. "This is ridiculous. Christ, Diana."

His handsome face was flushed, his eyes sparkling with anger and frustration despite the dullness liquor had thrown over them. They had all been drinking rather heavily, and Diana felt a pleasant tipsiness soothing her frayed nerves.

"I can't help it," she murmured without much conviction. "You push me too hard. I feel like I can't breathe. I can't stand it."

He said nothing. Beyond his shoulder she could see her roommate, Linda, in the embrace of her date. Linda was held close by the long arms inside a dark Brooks Brothers jacket, her fine black hair splayed across her back.

Diana patted Cliff's muscled neck as she kissed him once more. She felt genuinely sorry. He was a handsome dog, and was probably great in bed. But she would never know, of course. He was not for her.

In a sense this was a pity. A BMOC at Amherst who had his pick of many girls, Cliff came back to Diana every few weeks, as though to test the waters. He did not seem willing to give up on her, though she always froze him when he got too fresh. He was convinced that eventually his charms would get through her defenses, or that her commitment to Hal —whom Cliff had known at Choate—was so shallow that sooner or later she would decide to spice up her premarital life with some red-blooded fun.

Of course, he did not know her secret.

But he seemed to sense a deeper reality: that he, Cliff Hutchinson, was the sort of man Diana was truly meant for. A man not too brilliant, not too original, but ambitious, well-connected, and well-built. Just the sort of shallow, amiable, ordinary man she was designed by background and temperament to spend her life with.

And Diana could feel, painfully, that she had far more in common with poor Cliff than with Hal. She and Cliff were like peas in a pod, identical in breeding and instinct. When she was with him she felt as though fate had made a mistake in betrothing her to Hal, a man she loved but who was not really her type. And she, unfortunate girl, clung to this mistake of the gods, in the hope that she could make Hal a good wife after all.

So that in refusing Cliff, and the others like him, she was refusing a future that belonged rightfully to her, pursuing one that didn't.

It was a lonely undertaking. Meanwhile Diana was a woman, with a woman's needs. She accepted dates with Cliff because she wanted to be touched, to be embraced and coveted—to know that she belonged somewhere. Even though the result was a hot brew of conflicting feelings and aroused senses that pushed her further and further against herself until she stopped him with a spasm of resolve that hurt him and hurt her, too.

. . .

"Well, how was it?"

The girls were going upstairs together. Diana was following Linda's slim, tennis-trained body, and looking again at the sleek dark hair that curled at the collar of her Burberry coat.

"The usual," Diana sighed. "All hands and no brains. Clifford was pretty horny tonight."

"Like fighting off a crazed billy goat, eh?" Linda laughed. It was an attractive, throaty little sound that seemed worldly-wise and somehow sad.

"I guess I shouldn't have bothered," Diana said as they went up the last flight. "It's really a dead end."

Their room was at the top of the house, under the eaves. There was only one other room on the corridor. This was not the first time Diana and Linda had returned together from double dates. Linda was often available with her "need-a-date," Douglas Van Allen, when Diana preferred not to be alone with one of her beaux.

"How about you?" Diana asked.

"Nothing exciting to report," Linda said. "Our Douglas is not much of a he-man."

They had often joked about Douglas, who was so pusillanimous a creature that the slightest tensing of a girl's shoulder in his embrace was enough to make him erupt in apologies. "His balls are in his safety deposit box," Linda would say, "and his prick is in his father's money belt." Her cynical reference was to the Van Allens' great fortune, and to the family matchmakers who wanted to pair her with Douglas.

No one could quite figure out why she bothered to go out with him, for he was inept at conversation and a hopeless lover. Perhaps, it was thought, she liked the security of knowing that her honor was safe. He was not the type to give her a run for her money.

Linda was a beautiful girl, with dark eyes full of intelligence and acerbic humor. She had straight shoulders, fine cheek bones, and perfect white skin. She had competed on the amateur tennis circuit since she was a small girl, and was missing spring semesters at Smith nowadays because of tournament play.

She had been a finishing sophomore when Diana entered college, and now Diana had caught up with her. This year they were finally room-mates, having been gradually drawn together over the past two years by a series of late-night conversations about family, school, and the opposite sex.

Linda was a fine listener, and made few demands on Diana either as a friend or as a roommate. She revealed little about herself, except that she strongly disliked both her parents, hated school, could not find a man she could stand, and played tennis merely to distract herself from her boredom.

She was a well-known player, and had reached the quarter-finals at Forest Hills last year. She played with a graceful ease from which all true enthusiasm was absent. Diana had never seen her practice, but only noticed her walking briskly out of the house, racquet in hand, time and time again.

After their friendship became close, the girls had visited each other's homes. The Prestons, who had made their money in publishing, lived on Long Island, and were very wrapped up in each other. Diana's parents took a liking to Linda, and helped her in her tennis career.

Linda possessed a cool bitterness that protected her from the outside world. Since she did not claim to be happy or to have a great stake in anything, she faced life dispassionately. Diana tapped into this calm cynicism as a defense against her own worries, and joined her roommate in countless wry jokes about the absurdity of the life they were forced to live. Inside she felt a real bond with Linda's sadness, and knew she could always count on her for a sympathetic ear.

At last they reached the door of their room. Diana looked down the corridor to the other door. Yvonne and Priscilla were long since asleep, and their room was silent. They were the dullest and ugliest girls in the house, and had long ago gravitated to each other out of shared abjection and mutual vacuity.

Linda went into the room first, but did not turn on the bedside lamp. Through the curtains one could see a dim glow from the street lamps outside, along with a pale hint of moonlight glimmering off the snow.

Diana breathed a very small sigh, entered the darkness, and closed the door behind her.

The two girls were in each other's arms before the latch clicked shut.

Diana was still holding her wool coat, and let it fall to the floor as the soft hands of Linda Preston closed around her waist.

Diana's breath came short in expectation. The huge waiting that had been building in her all evening was at its peak. The stillness of the room was charged with a delicious thrall.

The hands were moving subtly up her ribs now, as, without haste, the lips of her roommate came to kiss her own.

For a long moment they stayed that way, Diana motionless with hands at her sides while the familiar lips and fingers greeted her anxious flesh. Gradually the feminine shadow before her came closer, until she felt Linda's thighs graze hers. The tips of their breasts touched beneath the fabrics covering them, nipple against nipple, ripe with the secret spark that sent a spasm of excitement down Diana's stomach, darting lower to her knees and up between her legs to her spine.

It always began just this way. First the discomfort and uncertainty of the date, the exasperation of the drawn-out evening—and then Linda. When they did not double-date they would meet in the library adjacent to the solarium, and go upstairs together. Sometimes Diana would come home late and find Linda waiting for her in the room, in bed in her pajamas with a book. Diana would turn to hang up her coat, hear the bedclothes rustle, and wait to feel the cool hands encircle her waist from behind.

At dinner, seated downstairs with the other girls, Diana would catch her breath when a gentle stockinged foot came to brush her leg under the table, a slow, knowing caress from her ankle upward to the place behind the knee that was the most sensitive of all. She would not dare to look beside her to Linda, who was chatting with the others as though nothing was happening. But she would feel reassured despite her embarrassment, for this stolen touch in a public place reminded her that she was wanted.

In the beginning she had been shocked by what she did with Linda. Such acts were unthinkable for a girl of her background. She had wondered in alarm if she was a lesbian, if she was crazy, if she was in love with Linda.

She tried to explain it to herself as a result of the excitement left over from her dates. The storms of wanting created by her young men were conveniently slaked by Linda's careful, tender hands and exploring lips and tongue. This was not such a terrible thing for a girl to turn to when coitus with the opposite sex was ruled out.

But she also realized that what she was doing with Linda was more than this. She needed Linda for something deeper. Diana's loneliness had become more intolerable as she grew older. Her struggles to measure up to what her family wanted of her, to what Hal must eventually expect, to what the future demanded—all this was too heavy a burden to bear.

For she knew in advance she was going to let everyone down. She was no prize as a woman or as a person. She felt shallow and even ugly inside, despite her great physical beauty and her immaculate social graces.

But she was a human being. She needed love. She needed to be taken and accepted for what she was, without having to earn it all through some stellar performance of personal worth that simply wasn't in her.

And so she came to see Linda Preston as her personal blessing, her guardian angel. For Linda, who cared so little about things, who shrugged her pretty shoulders at the unfairness of life, who headed blithely for the tennis courts and exhausting practice at a sport she loathed—Linda wanted her. With Linda she could feel like a woman.

Thus it was always with a sigh of mingled relief, anticipation, and gratitude that Diana stood poised in the embrace of her roommate, held by the hands about her waist, teased by the nipples pressed to her own, thrilled by the tongue slipped into her mouth like a host at some secret communion, already caressing her with soft little strokes that were irresistible.

They were silent lovers. Never a word passed between them during their trysts, nor did either ever refer to them afterward. But they made it a point not to be separated for long at vacations, and not to go home for weekends without knowing when they would be together again.

In their quiet way they wanted to be sure of each other. Nothing was promised, nothing demanded, except the mutual assurance that they would soon be alone again, and lovers.

And now, with that unhurried delicacy that was so characteristic of her, and so alien to the crude urgency of the male, Linda moved her hands to explore Diana's curves, to smooth the hollow of her neck, to cradle her cheeks, to brush back her hair and close her eyes with a soft finger.

And somehow, as her hands slipped downward to pet and soothe Diana's slender body, every fabric she touched came undone like magic, the passage of her fingers loosening, stripping, so that Diana's blouse was already coming off her shoulders, her skirt fallen to her feet, her bra unhooked at last so that her naked breasts could feel the kiss of her friend's lips and the light darting caress of her tongue.

Then she stood trembling slightly as everything else came off, the stockings and slip and panties, until she was completely naked, and Linda stood before her fully clothed.

This was part of the little game they played. And it was, truth to tell, Diana's favorite part. When all her clothes were off, and strewn forgotten into the darkness, she would feel the clothed girl touch carefully at her body, finding pleasure points she knew so well now, places that sent wildfires through the quick of her. Dry palms moved along her breasts and down her stomach, while kisses warmed her all over. A finger stole up the inside of her thigh, making her knees weak.

Linda went on that way until she saw the telltale signs that her roommate was hot with readiness for love and too excited to wait any longer. Then she helped her to the bed and began to take off her own clothes.

Diana watched, her breaths shallow with wanting, as the straight shoulders and shapely breasts came into view, ghostly silhouettes in the shadows, and then the fine slim thighs made firm and strong by sport, the impenetrable smile beneath dark eyes in the moonlight coming in the window.

Then Linda came astride Diana, rearing up athletically, hands poised on the waiting thighs, looking down upon her.

Linda had known from the beginning that Diana enjoyed being the flower, enjoyed looking up from her helpless position at the beautiful body of her lover, and being the trapped victim while Linda, the smiling seducer, toyed with her and savored her submission.

So it was that Linda stayed atop her friend, now arching her back with a purr of pleasure, now crouching to kiss her all over, teasing her with catlike tongue until Diana could stand it no longer and pulled her down to finish it, eager arms holding her close as stifled moans sounded deep in her throat.

When it was over they would lie quietly for a long time, Linda resting her head on her hand as she toyed gently with Diana's tumbled hair, ran a finger between her breasts and down to her navel, all the while smiling familiarly at her, and never saying a word.

Soon they would grow sleepy, for the night was deepening around them. Not without reluctance, they would separate, for they dared not run the risk of sleeping in each other's arms and being discovered in the morning by an inquisitive maid. Diana would lie down in her own bed and feel dreams come over her, comforted by the feel of her friend in all her senses, the memory of her caresses in her most private places.

She smiled in her somnolence, and this smile was no longer a brilliant show for others. It was a private glow of real happiness that was not skin deep, but sprang from the core of her loneliness and her gratitude at being taken for what she was.

For that was enough for Linda. Nothing more was expected, and nothing asked. It might not last forever—terrible nights might lie ahead in the future, filled only by shame and solitude—but for now Diana was wanted.

Her smile would linger for a while before she drifted off. These moments were the best in her life, for only now did she taste the happiness of being a woman.

She slept a dark and mysterious sleep, forgetting all her dreams, and woke up armed somehow to face the new day.

II

THE TAKEOVER OF BENEDICT PRODUCTS by the growing national conglomerate called American Enterprise, coming on the heels of Lou Benedict's marriage to Liz Dameron, was a cataclysm that ushered in a confusing new era.

The company had a new name, for one thing. It was called TelTech, for "television technology," and 90 percent of its product lines in electronic and small appliances were summarily discontinued. The company's facilities were retooled almost overnight, at a cost underwritten by the parent corporation, for production of home television sets. Its Product Development division was given over entirely to research on television technology for the aerospace industry.

Lou Benedict's career employees did not know which way to turn. Old dogs, they were forced to learn new tricks overnight. The pace of work accelerated so suddenly that some of the older employees simply retired, unable to keep up. Others quit to look for work elsewhere, because they were afraid of what might be coming at TelTech.

They were not wrong. There were a lot of firings. New people were imported from the ranks of American Enterprise, strange new faces who were assigned to head new departments. They wore natty Brooks Brothers suits, shoes imported from Italy, and bored faces, as though they were chagrined to be exiled to this remote outpost of the corporate world, far from where the real action was.

The newcomers strolled the corridors of Lou Benedict's office building as though they owned the place. They lunched and socialized with each other, ignoring the old Benedict employees.

Each week, it seemed, there was a new meeting about reorganization, ordered by American Enterprise. New departments were conceived on paper, and within days they would be staffed and in operation, manned by a combination of hungry American Enterprise people—all so young, so coolly energetic!—and confused Benedict employees blinking at their new surroundings and responsibilities.

Over the entire dizzying process, stately, beautiful, and cold as ice, reigned Liz Benedict.

After the takeover Lou had been named Chairman of an entirely powerless and irrelevant Board of Directors of TelTech. His position was a purely titular one, granted because of the stock he still held in the company. Liz herself was given the title of "Vice President in Charge of Personnel," but the higher-ups at American Enterprise considered her the one and only boss at TelTech.

It was Liz's responsibility to cut expenses and increase productivity at TelTech, in the most drastic ways possible and in the shortest amount of time. To this end she fired every Benedict employee whom she deemed expendable, regardless of his or her years of service to the company. Those who remained were forced to accept lower wages. And it was thanks to Liz that Lou Benedict's esteemed profit-sharing plan was now dismantled and replaced by a new and far less generous retirement plan.

Liz set up rigorous, back-breaking training programs for all TelTech employees, forcing those with experience in the new technology to devote long hours, often in the evenings, training those a step below them. Thus the whole company gained in expertise, pulling itself up by the bootstraps and competing fiercely with its rival American Enterprise subsidiaries for dollars and facilities from the parent corporation.

With her crisp business suits, her silky blouses, and her brisk manner, Liz was a hated and feared employer. She was a genius at balancing budgets and showing off quarterly profits to TelTech's stockholders. But the company over which she presided had few if any smiling faces in it, for human beings had no more importance to her than spare parts.

Liz was more than just an overseer of the internal restructuring of her husband's company. She was also the sole responsible link with American Enterprise's top executives and board. She spent a great deal of her time in New York now, at the corporation's Rockefeller Center headquarters, and returned from her trips with devastating new directives for all those who worked under her.

And she had another reason to spend time in New York. Liz was American Enterprise's spearhead liaison with the fledgling television networks and their financial backers. She attended meetings with the network executives and their chief advertisers, and even met some of the fast-rising TV stars such as Milton Berle, Jackie Gleason, and Sid Caesar. Liz was responsible for keeping her finger on the whole burgeoning television industry, with its geometric growth and the billions of dollars it was on the point of generating for advertisers, networks, and producers of television sets.

It was rumored that Liz would not remain at TelTech for long; that her ambition must soon carry her to a higher corporate level. Some employees who claimed to have an inside track to New York even suggested that Liz was considering going to work as a television network executive, that she would produce her own TV shows. There was no limit to the shadowy increase of her power and connections. She had managed to sweet-talk the most influential of her American enterprise bosses while cleverly picking their brains. Now, it was said, she was doing the same to those in the entertainment field.

That was Liz. She maintained a balance of terror with everyone whose life she touched, from her own frightened employees to the colleagues and competitors she seduced with her beauty and exploited with her quick mind. She had found her home in the corporate jungle, and knew how to survive in it and make its cruelty work to her own advantage.

As for Lou Benedict, he spent his days rattling around the corridors of the company that had once been his beloved creation and his second home.

His office, though still the same room where in the old days he had felt such cheerful solidarity with his employees, was empty and silent now. The phone rang only when Liz called from her own office, newly equipped and decorated on the fifth floor, to say she needed him to sign some contracts or other papers.

She would occasionally breeze into the room, dressed in one of the oddly sensual business suits she wore, kiss him perfunctorily on the cheek, get what she wanted from him, and breeze out.

She slept in her own bedroom in the new house they had bought after their return from their honeymoon in the Bahamas. Most evenings Lou would kiss her goodnight while she was still on the phone, papers strewn all over her bed, talking in murmurs to some faceless associate in New York or elsewhere. She would give Lou a little goodnight smile as he went off to bed. He retired much earlier than she, not only because he lacked her youth and energy, but also because the drinks he had had during dinner made him drowsy.

She kept up the pretense of being a real wife, of taking the marriage seriously. She asked his help in choosing drapes or cushion covers or a new chair for the living room. She chaffed him about his clumsiness and his sloppy personal habits—for he seemed more and more to be letting himself go.

They had arguments at dinner occasionally, about people she was inviting over, or about her constant trips to New York, and her failure to call him sometimes when she was at meetings. Lou was drinking more nowadays, and the liquor was beginning to make him contentious.

Many times they kissed and made up, just like a real married couple. But when Lou was in too stubborn a funk for her to cheer him, she said, "Lou, we'll talk about this when you're feeling better," gave him a brisk parting kiss which was more a gesture of discipline than of affection, and left him on his own.

He would spend his evening alone, musing over the torpor of his days, and missing Barbara and the kids. They had moved to San Diego after the divorce, where Barbara's parents lived, and they did not answer his letters, speak to him on the phone, or thank him for the money he sent.

His old life was as forgotten as a previous incarnation. He was Liz's victim now, and her pet. She was solicitous in her treatment of him, and was only truly angry when he deserved it. She saw to his meals, helped him buy new clothes that were more stylish, more "corporate," bought him a new watch for his birthday, cuff links and a tie bar that she even had engraved for him.

And she took him to bed.

It happened less often now. But he spent all his spare time thinking about it, waiting for it, fantasizing about her. When she came to his office he ogled the curve of her thighs, watched her hips move, made out the shadow of her breast under her blouse as she leaned over him while he signed the papers she had brought.

He knew she was perfectly aware of his excitement when she paused close to him this way. The faint smile on her lips told him she knew he would be thinking about her afterward. What she did not perhaps realize was that for Lou the thrill of coveting her from a distance was even more piquant now that she was his wife than it had been when she was his employee. For her distance was more complex now, more incongruous and perverse.

When they made love she treated him like a child, finding his pleasure points with sure fingers and petting him as he came obediently into her. Then he would hear her little sigh of disappointment, and he would know he was a mere plaything to her, the ersatz of the real lay.

She would let him have his pleasure before ten or eleven at night, for she knew the drinks made him sleepy. She would kiss him goodnight afterward and stay up alone to finish her work. Often, in his somnolence, he would listen to her murmuring on the phone in her room, just as a small child hears the movements and conversation of his parents after they have kissed him goodnight and gone back to their adult chores.

Their quarrels brought long periods of painful abstinence when she would not let him near her. But then she liked to take him by surprise. He would shuffle into the bathroom to get ready for bed, and while he was looking at himself in the mirror he would suddenly see her hands open his bathrobe from behind and pull down his underpants, female fingers closing over his genitals while a little purr of triumph sounded in her throat.

One day at the office, within clear view of the open door behind which his secretary sat chatting in her boredom with a passing visitor, Liz pointed out a signature line with her left hand while her right hand stole between his legs and found the testicles under his pants, stroking them for a wild instant before she patted him softly, pulled her hand away, and took her leave with a smile.

Nowadays his intuition told him she was getting it from other men. She was merely amusing herself with him out of perversity, toying with him in her idle moments. He felt jealous over her infidelity, and mused over the idea of reprisals. But he was too much her slave to carry them out. His jealousy had no moral force.

So it was that Lou's solitude grew more profound, and his trysts with his wife less frequent, even as his preoccupation with her grew ever deeper, filling all his waking moments.

She was so young! As age, fatigue, and more alcohol made his own image more sallow and flaccid in the mirror, Liz looked younger than ever, more nubile, more filled with the freshness of a growing girl. In proportion as he disintegrated, this strange creature seemed to draw vitality from her role as the helpmate of his destruction.

There was no sense in lingering over the capriciousness of fate. The gods had chosen Liz to be the one woman who could separate him from his life's work, from life itself—and had sent her to cross his path just when he was most vulnerable to her, just when she could do the most damage.

So he whiled away the days at his desk, dropped in on a few old employees who chatted neutrally with him—for their pity had by now outstripped even their reproach over what he had done to them and to the company—and waited to go home at night. There he drank his martinis at dinner, staggered through his evening while Liz stayed in her bedroom telephoning, and returned to work in the morning with his eyes at half-mast, moving along the corridors in a sort of permanent woozy daze. His secretary shook her head when he came in, and went back to her crossword puzzle, his "good morning" a thick murmur on the office air.

And in his pickled lust he coveted Liz's body when she let him near it. He accepted his lot, for he knew his future belonged to Liz now, not to him. Her very indifference to him, her lack of interest, only increased his insatiable dependence on her.

Sometimes he would look back on his life, a life essentially without sin until so recently, and ask how a fate such as this could have befallen him. How had this thing happened?

But it was not a thing. It was a woman.

Death had come to Lou in flesh and blood, smiling through soft lips, dancing in curved sensual hips, long creamy thighs, perfect breasts, and bottomless green eyes.

In this form death itself was irresistible. There was nothing left but to give up and let it enfold him.

It was only a matter of time.

III

AFTER HER ABORTION LAURA did not speak to a living soul, with the exception of a handful of shopkeepers, for four months.

The first two weeks were a nightmare she would mercifully never remember in all its details. She watched the blood seep out from between her legs, inundating sanitary napkins one after the other. She felt cramp after cramp rake her insides, each one a hideous reminder of the knife that had scored her womb.

She was unable to keep any but the blandest foods down, and subsisted on milk, tea, a few soda crackers, and bowls of cereal. She had constant headaches, but she did not think to take aspirin for them, so pervasive was her inner pain. She never thought of consulting a doctor.

She sat on her bed or in the armchair, got up and crossed to the bathroom as necessary, returned to sit down again—and stared at the walls.

She knew almost from the beginning that she was not going to go back to school. Why and how she came to that inner decision she was not sure. She only knew there would be no more professors, no more exams and papers, no more musty classrooms and dark lecture halls. No more wild hopes.

She ensured her solitude by sending Uncle Karel and Aunt Martha a card telling them that some friends of hers were helping her move to a new apartment for the next semester. She would be sending them her new address, she promised. This message, she knew, would suffice to keep her relatives out of her life. They had washed their hands of her when she left for college, if not long before, and would hardly be curious enough to pursue her.

As winter wore on she stopped caring what day or date it was. She left the calendar at December, so that the gas company's cheap lithograph of a snowy New England scene gathered dust on her wall as the days grew colder and grayer. December was a dead month dumbly surviving itself—like Laura herself, a bundle of dashed hopes and a lingering shell.

Laura existed in a void, cut off from the past as well as the future. And she felt safe here, for this spreading interval was like a twilight of pure arctic emptiness in which she didn't have to feel anything.

She did not notice how much weight she was losing, for she wore the same loose nightgown most of the time. On those occasions when she had to comb her hair before going downstairs to shop, she managed to look in the mirror without really seeing herself. She knew her appearance would not be noticed in the neighborhood stores anyway. In this sense the anonymity of life in the big city came to her rescue.

There was no one to care about her, to worry about her welfare, to come in search of her. She was pleased with this. What happened to her now concerned no one in the world but herself.

She did not think of doing further violence to her body, though a few short weeks ago the notion of suicide had seemed appealing. She was beyond such thoughts now. She had sunk into a miasma of emptiness in which not even self-loathing had meaning.

But she did think about one thing, actively and constantly.

Her baby.

Boy or girl?

She did not know, would never know. But somehow, in all her fantasies, it was a boy.

A tiny, tender boy with dark hair like hers and her father's, and dark, luminous eyes. Eyes that would have reflected her own loving smiles as he cooed from his crib, learned to speak and to laugh, learned to walk on unsteady legs. Eyes that would have looked up at her as she cooked his breakfast, the boy impatient to get the meal over with so he could put on his coat and go out to play. Eyes that would have rested on her as she tucked in his shirt, tied his shoes.

And his smile would have lit up his face when she gave him the toy, the sailor suit, the baseball glove he wanted for Christmas or for his birthday. Perhaps he would have let her hug him goodnight each evening when it came time for sleep, and laughed when she tickled him, and drifted gently off while she told him stories and sang him lullabies.

Laura did not spare herself a single one of these heart-rending thoughts. In fact, she repeated them over and over in her mind, like litanies of punishment and longing.

Perhaps he would have played games with her. "Peek-a-boo, I see you" and "Guess who?" and Pattycake and Hide-and-Seek. She could hear his giggles of amusement, hear his small voice growing stronger as his bright young mind became surer of the words.

You're a big boy now, she would tell him when he had to gather his books and pencils and go off to school. *I'm proud of you.* And when he was old enough to be naughty and need her discipline, he would disarm her with his smile, against which her heart had no defenses.

At first she would have to hold his hand when, as a tiny make-believe goblin, he went out trick-or-treating in the neighborhood. Then, of course, he would be too big for such dependence, and would go with his friends, heedless of her worried glance as he plunged into the dark night dressed in his costume, but answering her look of relief with a smile when he returned safe and sound much later, his bag full of candy and fruit, the echoes of his friends' shouts still sounding outside the door.

My boy . . .

Then he would be taller than she, for Laura was so small. He would outgrow her by the time he was in eighth or ninth grade. And he would put his arms around her in quick, urgent hugs on his way to sports practice or to be with his friends. And though the difference between youth and age, parent and child would separate them as he rushed headlong into his own future and his own identity, Laura's love would make her strong enough to let him go. He would feel this, too, and his acknowledgment would show through when he chaffed her about her protectiveness and her precautions.

"Oh, Mom . . ." Thus he would laugh at her worries. For he himself could not imagine that the world might harm him. His smile would be bright and sure, his eyes shining with the thrill of growing strength and new experience, when he ran in from outside, his hair tousled by the wind, his body hungry for cookies and peanut butter sandwiches and milk.

One day there would be a girl. He would walk with her at school, meet her on weekends, take her to ball games and to the amusement park, stay out talking with her as late as he dared, loath to say good-night, for he was fascinated by her, and unsure in his male instincts whether he was good enough for her.

It would not work out the first time, for he would need to test his heart before the search for the right girl could come closer to the target. But one day there would be a new girl, he would bring her home, and Laura would know without a second's hesitation that this was her at last, the one he would choose. She would see it in the girl's eyes instantly. Good, human eyes, eyes already prepared to live with him, suffer with him, share his joys and adventures and disappointments, warm feminine eyes glimpsed for the very first time.

And when they went off to leave her she would smile, for she would have seen him through to this moment, and part of him would always be hers, just as part of her would always be with him. She would feel sad to lose him, but proud of every cell in his body, proud of every human thought and pain and fear that flashed through him, proud even of his mistakes, his weaknesses. For he was her flesh and blood, he was what she had lived for, he was her heart.

But no. He would never live. It was all a beautiful dream that would never come true. For she had killed it in her own womb, destroyed her love with her own hand.

And it wasn't a dream at all, even though it was now reduced to an agonized fantasy. It had all been real! He had been inside her, the future itself quickening inside her womb, real as her own flesh—and she had destroyed it.

In her long months alone in the tiny apartment Laura covered this imaginary ground a thousand times. She tortured herself slowly, with firmness, with application, using the considerable power of her mind and the most terrible of guilt. She conceived sons and daughters from the deepest part of herself, fleshed them out with personalities, smiles, and laughter, and eventful lives—and then she annihilated them.

Somehow it was the boy she believed in most. She came to know him better and better, more and more intimately. She knew all his gestures, the sweet details of his body, his freckles, the touch of red in his dark hair, the teasing twinkle in his eyes, his height and weight at various ages—and then she killed him, again and again and again, killing her own heart as she did so.

Her imagination was the sharp sword of her penance. For she could see his whole life stretching before her, a kaleidoscope of events in a million colors, their variety tied together by the uniqueness of his personality, a blend of quiet humor and manliness like no other.

And there was more in that image than merely the boy himself, and the man he would have become. She also saw the children he would have sired, and his children's children, a whole beautiful array of human fates all tinged with a bit of herself, for they were all her flesh and blood. She saw their faces one by one, admired them, loved them—and then watched them disappear before her eyes, canceled by the stroke of her own knife.

In slaughtering one individual she had slaughtered the uncountable throng of his descendants, the myriad children who would have been his pride and joy, the generations that would have made her own life worth living. It was a whole race she had annihilated in her womb.

Common sense joined the full power of Laura's intellect in the service of her abasement. After all, she reasoned, were any of these thoughts of hers untrue? Fantastic? Exaggerated? Not at all. Had she allowed this child to live, its future would have been exactly as she had seen it before her mind's eye, in the essence if not the details. And the fruitful race of its descendants would have been just as numerous, as rich in personality and experience, in voice and face and smile, as she had imagined it. A human family of her own blood, reaching out its hand to infinity in the endless future.

And she had destroyed all that. She had murdered everything.

As Laura's physical pain grew less, the void inside her deepened. As her appetite returned, her despair came to silence it. She lost more weight. Physical health was drowned in the chasm of hopelessness.

Laura welcomed the signs of her weakness, the deterioration of her young body. If she had been the blithe destroyer of the best part of herself, why not linger over the disintegration of the rest?

At last, on a sunny day in May, she reached rock bottom.

She was walking down the street to the corner market to buy some milk and fruit juice when she felt the sun on her skin. It had been a cold spring, and this was the first truly warm sun she had felt since last fall, when Indian summer had graced a handful of October days in her previous life.

Laura saw a calendar at the checkout counter of the market.

"Excuse me," she asked, looking at the familiar pockmarked face of the lady who was ringing up her purchases. "Do you know what today's date is?"

The woman looked briefly at her, without warmth, and turned to glance at the calendar. "The sixteenth, I think," she said. "Yes: May sixteenth."

"Thank you."

All the way home Laura looked around her with new eyes. The balmy breeze flowing amid the traffic and pedestrians was full of approaching summer.

So she had missed an entire winter, then, and most of the spring. Her long hibernation had wiped those two seasons out. Such was the profound power of grief.

And now the students who had entered the university with her were finishing their first year, cramming for final exams and preparing to go home for the vacation, perhaps already on the lookout for summer jobs.

In a couple of weeks those students would have a whole semester of grades in their transcript that Laura would never have. In a few years they would finish college, as she never would, and go on to careers she would never pursue.

The world was truly passing her by.

This thought did not alarm her, but brought with it a certain relief. Yes, she mused: Her punishment was growing deeper, more real and permanent. By diverting the flow of her whole life, by abandoning the hopes that had meant everything so short a time ago, she was constructing a monument of absence that did justice to the baby she had killed. She was making her whole life a mirror of emptiness to reflect this holocaust she had wrought. And this was good, this was correct and natural.

Feeling oddly renewed, Laura took her groceries home, made a cup of tea, and looked at herself in the mirror.

Her hair looked too long. It had grown almost to her shoulders.

She sat down before the mirror with a scissors and began to cut her hair. The soft dark curls fell away one by one, and the short hair of the old Laura began to emerge.

Unthinkingly, automatically she worked at the hair, cutting and shaping and combing. When she had finished it looked presentable and even pretty, with the natural waves fluffing out the fine strands. She had a slightly elfin look that was more salient now because her large dark eyes were even bigger in her gaunt face.

On an impulse she went to the closet and found the rolled-up water-color self-portrait that had been her intended Christmas present for Nathaniel Clear. She felt a tremor of dread as she began to open it, but quickly shrugged off her fear. After all, she thought, how could the chagrin of looking at this picture compare with the hell she had endured for the last four months?

The picture was in her hands. Her own face looked up at her, filled with innocence and candor and the bottomless excitement of youth. Now she turned to the mirror. The face she saw there bore no more resemblance to the face in the watercolor than an adult's lined skin to the first baby picture taken of it a lifetime ago.

Her long vigil had done its work, then. She was no longer the person she had been. Her crime and her punishment had forever banished the Laura who smiled out of the painting, the Laura whose brush had painted it. Her youth was finished.

She rolled up the picture and put it away. She cleaned the bathroom floor of her hair, returned to her bed, and sat looking out the window at the airshaft.

In the most paradoxical way she felt alive again. Not in the way an ordinary, healthy person feels alive, or even the way a patient feels who has narrowly escaped the clutches of some malignant illness.

It was not hope—far from it—that had made her cut her hair, that was now urging her to wash her face, to put on decent clothes, to eat something.

It was the final shock of realizing she had nowhere to go but up. The old Laura was dead. She had killed her, along with the foolish hopes that had once tempted her to walk the earth's surface in the absurd confidence that it would not collapse under her. It was all over now. The void inside her was complete. The guilt she had accepted was so final that there were no further battles to be fought against it.

An eye for an eye. For the crime of murder she had murdered her own self.

And now, by a peculiar process of regeneration, a human being was emerging from this destruction.

All that afternoon and evening Laura sat pondering this feeling of being reborn from her own ashes. She could not understand why she could want to live, to endure, to look forward to another day. But somehow she did anyway.

When the darkness of night fell, she felt a strange sense of purpose emerge from the emptiness inside her. She thought of her dead child. It would have been too easy to simply follow him into destruction and nothingness. No: She would build her entire future around his loss. She would know every minute of life as a minute spent without him, a minute spent in the void he had left behind him. She would make of her crime the dead empty core of her future as a woman.

Her life would be her punishment, and her gift to the child she had stolen from herself and from the world. With each new day she would confirm the gulf separating her from the human race, a race to which she no longer deserved to belong. As she had torn her baby from that life, so she would sunder herself from it.

Armed by this knowledge, she dared to call the dead child forward to the screen of her consciousness. She looked long and lovingly at him. She watched the light dance upon his soft eyelashes, tinge his dark hair, linger on his skin.

Then he began to recede from her, and she knew this was for the last time. Her whole past was going with him, and as it left her she sensed that somehow this boy and his loss were permanent parts of her life, realities that her dreams had tried to warn her of long ago, facts that were hidden in the depths of her rainy day thoughts.

The boy's smile was growing more distant now. Yet his loss was still with her. She said goodbye to her own heart as he slipped away.

The dark side of the moon opened its doors to her. She could live now, for the bright sun of human hope was behind her.

Goodbye, she murmured soundlessly. *I love you.*

A silence empty as the tomb enfolded her as she lay back on the bed and fell asleep.

IV

May 31, 1952

LIZ BENEDICT was at the national sales convention of American Enterprise in New York when she met Spencer Cain.

On the first night of the convention she was circulating among the salons at the Waldorf Astoria, shaking hands with executives she had encountered at previous meetings in New York or spoken to on the phone in her daily work at TelTech. She also met people from American Enterprise's far-flung subsidiaries across the country, people who had been just names to her before tonight, but whose functions and importance within the conglomerate she had made it her business to know.

Lou was trailing after her foggily, still drunk from the martinis he had had at dinner. Liquor seemed to go straight to his head these days, reducing him to a staring muteness that annoyed Liz. He had slept through the speeches after dinner. This would have embarrassed her seriously, were it not a somewhat traditional way to listen to convention speeches in American business.

At a little after ten a colleague introduced Liz to a tall, slim, and extremely dark stranger. His name was Spencer Cain. He had black hair with a gun-metal sheen to it, and skin tanned almost olive by the sun of Miami, where his corporation, Rand Industries, was based.

Spencer Cain looked at Liz through tawny eyes that seemed to focus on several things at once: her indifferent husband behind her, her precise rank and function within the American Enterprise hierarchy, the reputation, if any, that might have preceded her—and last but not least, the beautiful body under her clinging dress.

Cain was quite handsome, in a rather sinister way. There was something reptilian, cold and watchful, about his demeanor. And his caressing deep voice added to the impression of danger and ill-disguised sensuality.

For her own part, Liz was well aware of this man's reputation. He was Vice President in Charge of Finance at Rand Industries, a manufacturing subsidiary of American Enterprise. The position was deceptively modest in title and salary, and was only a stopping-off point for Cain, who had held a half-dozen similar positions in other American Enterprise companies in the past few years.

He jumped from one company to another without apparent regard for its products, his movements ordained by the higher-ups in the parent conglomerate. He was known as a brutal manager and ambitious executive whose only aims were bottom-line profit and increased influence for himself within American Enterprise. He was rumored to have powerful friends on the board in New York. At age forty he was clearly being groomed for a senior position in the corporation's headquarters.

His ambition was boundless, and it was said he was willing to do anything within or outside standard business ethics to achieve it. Specifically, rumor had it that more than one of the positions he had held was acquired through the good offices of one or another corporate wife with whom he enjoyed a special relationship. The look in his eyes as he scrutinized Liz instantly confirmed her impression that he had used sex as well as brains to get where he was.

She resolved to treat him carefully, for his position in the corporation was far stronger than hers, of longer standing and higher level.

She let him hold her hand an instant too long as they were introduced. She kept her eyes fixed to his as she presented him to Lou, who muttered disinterested greetings. She could hear quiet music from the bar by the windows. "Lou," she said, "why don't you go over to the bar and have an after-dinner drink? I'll join you in a while."

Lou quietly disappeared. Liz raised an eyebrow as she smiled into Spencer Cain's eyes. He glanced at the receding figure of her husband before looking back at her.

"Your reputation precedes you," she said.

"Not too unfavorably, I hope." His smile was easy and confident.

"On the contrary," she said. "Actually, I've been hearing more and more about Rand from people we both must know. I hear you're doing a great job down there. I can see the sun agrees with you."

"Thank you," he said. "I can see that something agrees with you, too."

He was looking more closely at her. She could feel him sizing her up, his eyes taking in the curves of her body, the straight clean look of her shoulders, the firm breasts under her dress.

"You know," she said, "I believe we have more things in common than either of us realizes. I'll bet we could benefit from comparing a few notes, you and I."

"That sounds like a fine idea," he said. "Why don't we have a drink?"

He was looking over her shoulder to the bar, where Lou was seated alone with a glass of bourbon before him. Cain's eyes told her what he had in mind.

"Lead the way," she smiled.

They went to a secluded lounge outside the hotel, where they would not be interrupted by anyone from the convention. There they spent over an hour discussing their careers at American Enterprise, the corporation's past and future, and the role of their respective companies in it.

Liz discovered that Spencer Cain was knowledgeable about TelTech's specialty, electronics and television technology, having had a high position in a related company in Chicago a couple of years ago.

She also realized that she saw eye to eye with him about the immediate future of the business world as a whole. Despite the expansion of production facilities brought on by the war, recent developments made it clear that the future of American wealth was not in heavy industry. The high wages being won by American unions would soon make it impossible for the United States to compete with foreign producers who enjoyed cheap labor. America's days as the world's foremost industrial giant were at an end.

The future lay in high technology and the spectrum of white-collar jobs and services. America in the 1950s and 1960s must be a world leader in technological innovation if it was to remain a great power. And that innovation must be focused on the right markets at the right moments if the constant danger of recession was to be eluded.

Liz listened carefully to Spencer Cain's conversation, and took pains to compliment him often on his intelligence and expertise. But all the while she was measuring him with the best of her instincts. She began to realize that he lacked the boldness and acuity of her own vision. He was not an intellectual innovator or a serious student of the business world.

Instead he was pure shark: a man on the make in more ways than one, clever enough to find the line of least resistance toward the power and position he sought, and above all so ambitious that he was not afraid to target the top of the mountain for himself, and to direct his steps toward it boldly.

Cain represented business cunning in its purest form. He would go far in the corporate world. He lacked the spark of idealism that sets the great entrepreneurs apart from the mere conglomerators. But this very lack of a higher vision, this ruthless concentration on power alone, made him the more dangerous. He would be a hard adversary to get around.

On the other hand, he would make the most invaluable of friends. And so Liz listened to him attentively, expressing her admiration in a lyrical voice heavy with double meanings. She knew he was interested in her. More than this, her feminine radar told her that he had a weakness somewhere. She could not put her finger on it yet, but she suspected it was tailor-made for her to exploit.

For over an hour they circled each other, wary, avid, testing one another's signals, and preparing for the more intimate test they both knew must come.

Just before midnight they decided simultaneously that it was time to join the battle.

"Look at the time," Spencer Cain said.

Liz merely smiled.

His room was on the twenty-third floor.

The maids had turned down the bed already. The only light in the room was the pale glow of the bedside lamp.

Liz moved into the room ahead of him. As he hung up her coat she turned, her body already sending subtle messages of readiness his way, and looked back at him. His eyes were liquid with desire.

She ran a finger along her flat stomach to the hip under her dress, and gave him the ghost of a mocking smile. All at once she looked extraordinarily young. There was a nubile impudence about her that had not been there before. Her businesslike demeanor had vanished as soon as the door closed.

"Well," she said, her body outlined in the soft light of the lamp. "Here we are."

Her smile lingered long enough for him to see her tongue slide over her lips.

He came forward and grasped her roughly in his arms. His kiss was hungry, penetrating. The fingers clasped about her shoulders were like iron. He was physically strong, there was no doubt about that.

And he was not used to waiting for his pleasures.

She ran her hands down his sides to the slim hips beneath his jacket, and then up along his spine, feeling platelike bands of muscle under her fingertips. It was clear he worked out regularly, probably with weights.

She also took in the signals contained in his kiss. They were ambiguous, but their harshness was revealing. Cain wanted something. Something special. She expected to find out what it was in a few more moments.

"You're strong," she murmured against his cheek, her hands stroking his chest.

"I'll show you how strong."

She pulled back a few inches. They began to undress each other. First his jacket, then her dress, then his shirt and tie, then her slip and his trousers. They were both enjoying the slowness of the process, and the gradual unveiling of their bodies. Her bra came off, revealing breasts so ripe and firm that his breath caught in his throat at the sight of them. Dressed only in her panties, she moved coyly away to pick up her clothes and fold them on a chair.

She turned to see him silhouetted against the light, a tight hard figure of a man whose deep chest was stirring despite himself with the short breaths of desire. His shoulders were very square, his limbs long and lean.

She smiled to see the bulge distending his underpants.

"Hmm," she cooed. "I see London, I see France . . ."

Her brow raised mockingly, she watched the veiled penis throb at the sound of her voice.

"Well?" she asked. "Aren't you going to let me see it?"

Not without a touch of the male's pride in his organ, he slipped off the underpants. A long, hard penis emerged like a sword from its sheath.

Following his lead, she spread her legs slightly and arched her back as she pulled her panties down to her knees. She stood looking at him through upturned eyes, sly and inviting, as she slowly straightened up and let the panties fall to her feet.

Before she could kick them away across the carpet he was upon her, his arms encircling her waist, the long penis pressed hard against her stomach as he pulled her roughly to him.

They stood pressed hard to each other, kissing again as his hands slipped to the soft globes beneath her waist and ground her against his crotch. She heard a groan in his throat. She stroked his thighs coolly, exulting in the excitement her body caused in him.

Somehow she was not surprised when a long, hard finger parted the sweet round loins and probed for the private places between her legs, signaling its hunger for entry where she might not want it to go.

"Mmm," she murmured, her encouragement quickly silencing his scruples.

She heard him sigh. She had half her answer now. But only half—her intuition told her that. It was as though only part of him was engaged in this prelude to sex, while another part remained hidden behind his lips and hands. There was a hint of frustration in his caresses, making them the more urgent.

He picked her up with a quick lunge, gripping her beneath her waist while her legs curled gently around him. He held her that way, showing off his strength, as he kissed her long and hard. Then he bent to place her on the bed.

He kissed her breasts, biting carefully at the hard nipples. Then he kissed his way down her rib cage to her navel.

He pulled her legs apart, breathing his admiration for the long supple thighs, the pearly white skin, the fragrant triangle at her crotch.

He began to explore her, a little more roughly with each passing moment, his tongue and fingers excited by the silken purity of her flesh. Then all at once she felt the first sting of his bite, cautious but eager. The pain shot through her and almost upset her balance, but she silenced it with an inner command to her own senses, and gave him a soft murmur of approval.

"Mmm. More, Spence . . ."

And as she said this, armed by her woman's alertness for the hidden wellsprings of man's desire, the invisible confessions of sighs and lips and fingers, she understood that he wanted her to hurt him, too.

She began to do so, finding the nerves of his need and setting them afire. Soon they were hurting each other in a hundred inventive ways, trembling and working, their bodies clasped nude in the darkness, their moans dying muffled against the soundproofed walls of the room.

She had him where she wanted him, she decided. He liked to hurt women, but was too shy to let them know that he wanted them to hurt him as well, and as much as possible. The male's pride in him did not like to acknowledge this hidden need.

Already foreseeing the future variations they would perform together, she gripped his sex firmly in her long fingers and began to squeeze, a rhythmic little punishment that drew hot gasps of ecstasy from his lips.

She was so sure of her ground that she worked him faster, hearing him moan as his pleasure arose from the pain she was causing. Meanwhile she felt the harsh penetration of his own strokes like a remote tickle at the distant surface of her body, a disturbance muted utterly by her strong will.

At last, beside himself, he came to his climax. She gave a brilliant performance of orgasm herself, sighing her delight at the ecstasy he was giving her. When it was over they lay in each other's arms, breathless and sated.

Spencer Cain was a secretive man, she decided. But not clever enough to hide from her.

So she smiled as she let him go at last, and patted his genitals approvingly to show him her admiration for the size and charms of his organ.

And she tallied her advantage over him.

They made love three more times before she showered and left him. All three times he entered forbidden parts of her and left his orgasm there, for it was clear he could take no pleasure from the natural way to plant his seed in a woman.

She welcomed his perversions, and encouraged them with sure hands that mingled pain and pleasure in a lyrical symphony that she improvised on his flesh.

Between trysts they talked, and drank aged bourbon from the bar the management had concealed inside the room's armoire. She told him of her ideas for expanding the concepts she had developed at TelTech. Her company was only a beginning for her, a tiny springboard for elaborate plans that had international implications. The fledgling television industry, she explained, was not farsighted enough to see technological opportunities staring it in the face. She intended to seize those opportunities and exploit them to the fullest. Perhaps he would like to know more about her ideas, she suggested.

Liz felt that now was the time—when she had him at her sexual mercy—to show him how important she could be to him on a corporate level. She let him see the sweep of her ambition, the acuteness of her view of the marketplace. With his contacts and her originality, the power lying before them was virtually unlimited.

He listened carefully to her murmured ideas. They seemed to excite him as much as her body did. She could feel his libido stir into life each time she surprised him with a concept he had never thought of before, a link-up of facilities and markets more creative than he had imagined possible.

And she held back as much as she offered, making him hungry to hear more.

His penis hardened in her hands as her voice stimulated him. Soon her business talk became love whispers, sensual innuendos, without missing a beat. In a flash she had made him slippery and hot, and he must have her again.

So it was that they talked, and made love, and talked and made love again, as though the two forms of pleasure were indistinguishable. And in her calculated words as well as her painful caresses, she knew the language he longed to hear, she possessed the treasure that sought out his hunger and brought it to its peak.

By the time she got up to leave she was confident she owned him.

She knew both his sexual needs and his intellectual limitations. What she had initially suspected to be an inscrutable sensual enigma behind his lovemaking was, she now realized, a shallow masochism, easily manipulated by her. As for his business cunning, it was all surface with no intellectual depth. He was a dangerous adversary, to be sure, but she was more than a match for him.

They arranged to meet again, two weeks hence, here in New York. The sales conference was a distraction; they needed more time to get to know each other and to discuss the complex plans she had in mind. Plans he wished he had thought of himself.

She left him at three in the morning. She looked sleek and beautiful as ever with her clothes back on. He stood nude in the doorway, showing off his body and his lack of self-consciousness as he blew her a kiss goodbye.

"So long, good-looking," she said with a small wink. "Be seeing you."

"I'm looking forward to it," he nodded.

When she returned to her room she found Lou snoring loudly in his bed, not having bothered to undress. She knew that this passing out fully clothed was his way of reproaching her for having abandoned him. She took no notice of it, but undressed and got into bed with a little smile to herself, lingering only for a moment in thought before falling into a restful sleep.

The next morning four red roses were delivered to her room, with a card signed Rand Industries. It was Spencer Cain's way of bragging over having possessed her four times under her husband's nose.

Liz put one of the roses in her lapel for the morning meetings. Lou did not seem to notice it.

The next afternoon they left for California. As they sat on the plane together, Lou making small talk about subjects to which she paid no attention, she thought back on her trip to New York.

She alone knew how efficient she had been.

She had gone to the sales conference in order to meet Spencer Cain.

And she had succeeded.

V

LAURA BEGAN TO WANDER.

Though she did not realize it, her first step back toward the real world took the form of an apparently aimless peregrination through the noisy neighborhoods of lower New York.

The spring weather encouraged her, and she took in the sights hungrily: the routine of the Village and the Lower East Side, the merchants and grocers and fruitsellers with their Italian and Yiddish and Ukrainian accents, the housewives chatting on brownstone stoops, the hurried delivery truck drivers double-parking in front of stores and businesses on Houston and Delancey streets, and even the numbers runners, the sad-looking prostitutes, the bums passed out in doorways on the Bowery.

The chattering hurly-burly of postwar New York fascinated Laura. She found herself thinking about the great "melting pot" that was her country, a country where she herself had been born, but to which her parents had emigrated from a faraway land, leaving behind them their ancestors, their family and friends.

She thought about the immigrants around her, who had been forced to plunge into the cold competitive water of America, adapting their skills and personalities as best they could to their new environment. Many of them had been left in permanent bitterness by their transplanting, like Laura's father. Their hearts remained fixed forever on what they had lost by being uprooted. Morbid nostalgia for the old country poisoned their experience of the new.

Others lost all contact with their ancestral heritage, and floated in the busy limbo of America, their past now nothing more than a barely perceptible ripple that shone for an instant in their faces or gestures, sang weakly underneath their Bronx and Brooklyn accents, remained as a trace in their cooking, their clothes, an occasional toast they drank in the old country way.

Laura's heart went out to these people for their endurance and for the price they had paid for survival. Even more, she began to see salvation for herself in blending into that impersonal, hardworking throng.

The past, she decided, was something she must lose—just as these people had given up their youthful dreams and illusions. She knew now that she would never be an artist, as her private sketches had once seemed to promise. She would never be a scholar of art, as her fascination with the nude and her intellectual pretensions had made her hope to be. She would never be a professor.

No. Like an immigrant she would abandon those pie-in-the-sky illusions and learn to survive by more realistic endeavor. She would forget herself and dissolve into the outer world of pure survival, of wage-earning, eating and sleeping, and gazing at the sunset over the tenement roofs. She would make a living, like everyone else, and let her inner life die a quiet death, as it deserved.

Laura warmed to her sudden plan. She would live on the surface of life from now on, far from the sinking murmurs of her strange private intuitions. She would be a cog in the wheel of society, just like these subway conductors and delivery truck drivers and warehousemen and stevedores who made the city come to life each morning, just like these shopkeepers and cab drivers and salesgirls who kept the city running all day. She would melt into the ebb and flow of the metropolis, letting herself go easily and naturally, without looking backward.

Thus the essential was decided. But the practical remained.

What was she to do? She had no talents to speak of, except a pointless sketching ability. The intellect she had used in her college work was useless to her now, and faintly sickening to recall. So was her dreamy, introspective personality, and her haunted thoughts.

What could she do?

She was capable of industry. She worked hard and learned quickly. She was thorough and responsible.

This thought cheered her. Why, she could get any sort of job. She could be a shopgirl, a secretary, a file clerk. She could easily be a factory worker. Perhaps starting at the bottom somewhere would gratify her desire to escape her private world.

All these choices seemed good. But suddenly something made her thoughts turn in an unexpected direction.

Her father's face came back to her memory. She saw the look of absorption that used to purse his lips when he was working at his sewing machine. This image reminded her of the sewing talent he had brought with him from the old country, of the Singer machine he had bought with his last pennies, and the living he had eked out in his bitterness.

She thought about him, a man so long dead now, a man whose passions and whose disappointments might have occupied her memory much more through the years, had she not shut him out, burying him deep under her rainy day thoughts. And suddenly it occurred to her that he had passed his talent straight on to her.

Sewing came as naturally to her as breathing. Had she not sewed all her own clothes for as long as she could remember, working with patterns she devised herself? Had she not sewn most of the clothes for Uncle Karel, Aunt Martha, cousin Wayne, and for a sour-faced ungrateful Ivy? Did she not know the dimensions of their bodies as well as she knew her own?

Of course! One doesn't have to start with nothing when one already has something. She possessed a marketable skill right in her fingers, her eyes, her feel for fabric, her understanding of garment and body.

She would become a seamstress.

The decision was simple and logical. More than this, in a curious way it brought her closer to her dead father, and fixed her solidly in the line of faceless ancestors who had been tailors before him, who had perhaps passed down their instincts as well as their experience to him. Instincts that now lived in her own body as surely as the dark hair and light skin she had inherited from Father's side of the family. Yes, Laura thought. Here was the ideal way to lose herself, the perfect way to embark on the future.

She began to make plans. She would put notices in the supermarket, in local stores, on the church bulletin board. She would find clients, women of average means who were hard to fit and couldn't find clothes off the rack to suit them.

She had always had an uncanny knack for knowing what sort of fabric, color, and cut suited a particular person. She could see outfits, contours, even patterns, just by looking in a person's eyes, or by studying the way he or she walked. This innate talent had earned her the admiration of all who knew her back in Queens, as had the mysterious way her own clothes harmonized with her personality.

Yes, she would become a steamstress. She would use what money she could scrape together to buy fabric, and her first jobs would do the rest. She would get her old sewing machine back from Aunt Martha, who never used it anyway.

The uncertainty of starting a new livelihood did not seem to faze Laura in the least. It was as though making the decision had been the hardest part. The actual business would take care of itself. Once illusion was behind her, she could count on harsh reality without second thoughts.

She would start right here, in this empty, cold room with its bare walls, its ugly furniture, its outdated calendar for the year 1951.

Now Laura smiled. It was time to go out and buy a new calendar. She had lived in the past long enough.

Laura took a deep breath.

The die was cast.

VI

LIZ BENEDICT AND SPENCER CAIN met repeatedly throughout the summer and fall. She flew to New York every other weekend. Several times Cain met her halfway in Chicago or Cleveland.

Liz did not need to explain any of her trips to Lou. He was long since resigned to her independent existence. Nor did she need to worry about those who were working under her at TelTech. They all lived in such terror of her executive whims and her influence with American Enterprise that they gave her as wide a berth as possible.

During her many trysts with Spencer Cain she gradually described a master plan of amazing grandiosity. She was careful not to let him take in too much of it all at once. She gave it to him in bits and pieces, hinting ambiguously at its outlines and mechanics, orchestrating his own responses to her while letting him think that these responses were integral to the originality of the plan.

She manipulated his ego just as brilliantly as she used his corporate instincts. It was a bravura performance, for she knew he was mistrustful by nature, and she would need his complete confidence if her plan was to succeed.

Liz knew that the country, and the world, would soon be ready for color television. The enormous and quickly growing market for black-and-white TV sets proved that. But current technology was still incapable of bringing the price of a color receiver anywhere near the budget of an average American family. And the major television networks, though interested in the abstract concept of color reproduction and transmission, were a long way from investing the time and money to make it a reality.

In other words, the time was right for color television, but American industry was not yet capable of supplying a product economical enough for the public to buy.

This was where Liz came in. Through an elaborate and top-secret program initiated and overseen by her within TelTech's research division, a method had been found that could interface a new concept in color television circuitry and projection with the networks' current signaling methods. The process, which Liz's engineers had nicknamed "signal scan," was so simple and efficient that by implementing it the price of both transmission and reception in color could be cut in half. Given today's economy, it was almost certain that home color television could be within the budget of the American family in five or six years.

Liz intended to have the product ready to sell when the market was ready to buy.

Secrecy had been crucial to her plan up to now for several reasons. Not only did Liz want total control over her project; but she had tested the waters sufficiently to realize that no one in the television business would help her anyway.

Her own executive colleagues at TelTech subscribed to the theory that color television was an impractical whim whose realization was a long way off. In their minds television itself, as an alternative to radio, was still only a product in its infancy. There were millions of American families who had not yet made up their minds to buy their first black-and-white TV set. A color receiver, in today's market, would seem an absurd luxury, a curiosity. The demand for it would be so minuscule that the very fact of putting it on the market might backfire and set color television back by thirty years.

This was the prevailing wisdom. But Liz was able to see its shortsightedness and to plan for a market that, though invisible today, would be primed for aggressive exploitation in a few short years.

All this she explained to Spencer Cain. Her logic was inescapable, the more so because his own passing familiarity with television technology allowed him to see the beauty of it. And Liz sweetened the proposal by feigning enough give-and-take in her bedroom conversations to make Cain think that half of her plan was his own idea.

She also explained her timetable for a reorganization of the entire television division of American Enterprise with a view to creating a new television subsidiary that she and Spencer Cain would head. There were patents involved, and complex arrangements for cornering the color television market, which would make both Liz and Cain multimillionaires and corporate celebrities when her plan came to fruition. Their power within American Enterprise would be limitless.

Meanwhile there were things that Liz did not reveal to Cain. The most important was a larger plan she had told no one else about.

Liz foresaw that the technological and financial link-up between her own new company and the major television networks could lead to an even more intimate partnership. By applying pressure in the right ways at the right time, she could gain as much influence over the networks' programming and advertising plans as she would have over the mechanics of those programs' transmission. The ultimate effect of her initiative would be control over the entertainment potential of the medium as well as its technical functions, without running the risk of monopoly prosecution by the government.

But this ultimate objective was her secret. It lay beyond the immediate battle in which she needed Spencer Cain's help.

For the moment Cain was the key to everything. It had not been by accident that Liz had targeted him as her ally. She knew that he possessed an inordinate amount of personal influence with certain key board members at American Enterprise. Cain was their creature, and he had done many rather ugly favors for them in the past, favors for which they were beholden to him.

He was particularly close to a board member with crucial banking connections named Penn McCormick, who had helped Cain more than once within American Enterprise, and who also served on the board of several electronics corporations whose facilities would be crucial to the reorganization Liz had in mind.

Spencer Cain was Liz's conduit to Penn McCormick, and Penn McCormick was the royal road to her future in the television industry.

The only obstacle facing Liz was Spencer Cain's inherent egotism and dishonesty. The very fact that she needed such a man, and needed to be able to trust him in the short run, put her at risk.

She had overcome this obstacle in two ways. First she had made Cain realize that her brains and vision were essential to the entire scheme. She possessed a familiarity with the technical side of the television industry that he could never hope to match. And her precocious understanding of the marketplace as well as the attitudes of the network executives was extraordinary. Cain's influence and aggressiveness were crucial to the plan, but he could not proceed without Liz. She was indispensable.

Secondly, her sexual control over Cain had become total. In the past three months she had gradually let him get to know her body in all its subtle mysteries and dark charms. She had revealed a little more with each tryst, filling out her seduction with clever grace notes of manner and touch, insinuations in her smiles, her laughter, little mocking accents in her voice that drew him ever more securely under her domination.

In bed she played him like a harp, timing her caresses to increase his excitement, measuring out her cruel gratifications of his need to be hurt, keeping him constantly off-balance so as to maximize the desperation of his orgasm.

She was as fine an expert on the rhythms of male desire as she was on the dangers of corporate waters. She knew how to make him wait an instant longer than he had intended for his pleasure, how to make him suffer in piquant ways he had not anticipated, how to make him depend on her wit and resourcefulness in bed just as he did in the corporate arena.

And she timed her visits to New York, her meetings with him, so as to maximize his desire for her, withholding herself when she thought it would make him need her more, just as she withheld enough information about her master plan to keep him always at a disadvantage. So that when they met at last, his wanting was at the same fever pitch as his greed for her ideas.

She saw a hunger in his eyes now that had not been there a few weeks ago. And she exploited it ruthlessly. When they sat talking in their hotel room she would suddenly add a sly accent of invitation to her voice in the midst of a deep technical discussion. This confused him, and made him so hot for her bedroom charms that he moved quickly to her side, his hands eager for her. They had to discontinue their discussion until she had finished giving him his pleasure.

Gradually she came to see that hungry look behind all his expressions, to hear the groan of his need behind all his words, no matter how cool he tried to appear in her company. When she received his phone calls at TelTech, often at odd hours, she knew that his obsession with her had made it impossible for him to get through his day without a renewal of the drug her voice was to him.

Spencer Cain was her creature now. He could not do without her, either in the corporation or in bed. She was his lifeline.

Liz congratulated herself. In the most important move of her business career so far, she had chosen the right pawn. Her instinct had been sure, her seduction faultless.

She alone was the mistress of her fate.

But pride had blinded her to the subtleties of chance. In her growing confidence she had failed to consider all the possibilities.

On November 5 Spencer Cain met with Penn McCormick at American Enterprise's Rockefeller Center headquarters in Manhattan.

McCormick, a soft-looking man in his fifties who had a large family of six children, kept all their pictures on his desk and affected an all-American fatherly attitude toward his employees. He could afford to. Thanks to the great wealth of his wife's family he had acquired sufficient American Enterprise stock to be invulnerable to the various power plays his fellow executives might otherwise have initiated against him. He could not be fired. His place on the board was assured.

McCormick had been Spencer Cain's indefatigable sponsor for six years. The many favors he had done Cain had not been without strings attached. McCormick had ambitions to control the board's major decisions in a variety of key areas, including acquisition of subsidiaries and internal organization. Since the board members were his enemies to a man, the only way he could influence their votes was to be aggressive in privately extending his power over the far-flung array of companies that made up American Enterprise.

This was where Cain came in. By moving from company to company within the conglomerate, Cain could extend McCormick's connections and influence while keeping him abreast of the many intrigues going on in the darker corners that a top executive based in New York could not see. In return, McCormick protected Cain from the bigger sharks who might have liked to share his blood over the years. Thus Spencer Cain was Penn McCormick's eyes and ears as well as his corporate bagman.

And there was another reason for their close relationship.

Today Spencer Cain sat down in the visitors' chair opposite Penn McCormick's teak executive desk and spoke without opening his briefcase.

"Everything is ready," he said.

McCormick looked closely at him. "You've informed Drake and Cathcart?"

These were board chairmen of important electronics firms related by contract to American Enterprise.

Cain nodded. "Their support is assured. They're just waiting for your call."

"And Everett?" McCormick asked, referring to the investment banker whose help in financing the first acquisitions was indispensable.

"He's ready," Cain said. "So are his people."

There was a pause.

Cain spoke. "Will the board go along?" he asked, just to be sure.

"Let me handle the board," McCormick said. He looked sharply at Cain. "Tell me, how is Mrs. Benedict?"

Spencer Cain smiled. "Mrs. Benedict has never been better."

"Then let's drink a toast." McCormick produced a bottle of twelve-year-old scotch and poured two glasses. "To the future."

Spencer Cain raised his glass. "To the future."

When they had finished they stood up and moved to the door.

"We'll move tomorrow," Penn McCormick said. "By Friday it will all be over."

Spencer Cain extended a hand. The older man shook it warmly, and held on to it as he brought his face closer to Cain's.

The look in Penn McCormick's eyes had changed. He spoke in a murmur.

"Am I going to see you tonight?" he asked.

Cain reached a long finger to draw it down his friend's cheek and under his chin.

"But of course," he said, a note of feminine coyness creeping into his voice. "I wouldn't want you to be lonely, Penn."

McCormick nodded. He stood in his doorway and watched as Cain went through the outer office, his eyes lingering on the younger man's lean figure and handsome face.

VII

ON NOVEMBER TENTH Liz was hard at work finishing up TelTech's fall marketing analyses and getting ready for the holiday season.

She was almost too excited to concentrate on her work, for she knew that within a few weeks her life would change radically. She and Spencer Cain had decided it was necessary to move on the new plan before

Thanksgiving. He had assured her that Penn McCormick controlled enough votes on the board to swing the deal.

Before Christmas, Liz and Spencer Cain would be officers of a new corporation. Though they had not settled on a name yet, she knew the company would be a visible and important American Enterprise subsidiary. She herself would be in control of the nuts and bolts of the new operation, but she would have to share title and authority with Spence —a prospect that did not trouble her, for she was confident of her ability to make him do whatever she wanted of him, at least for the foreseeable future.

She was opening her mail as usual, a cup of hot coffee beside her, when she saw a letter addressed to her from the Director of Personnel at American Enterprise in New York.

She opened it. At first its contents were so unbelievable that she had to rub her eyes and peruse it more carefully.

Dear Mrs. Benedict,

American Enterprise wishes to thank you most sincerely for your fine service on its behalf since the acquisition of TelTech, Inc.

Due to an important reorganization now taking place within our corporation, your company will be dissolved as of the present in favor of a new entity. All executive positions at TelTech, including your own, will be eliminated, and a new team assembled to carry out the responsibilities formerly assigned to TelTech.

American Enterprise Corporation wishes to extend to you its best wishes for your future career elsewhere, and to express its gratitude for your fine efforts on its behalf.

The letter was signed by the Director of Personnel, and countersigned by the President of American Enterprise, Charles Powell.

Liz had the phone in her hand before the news had quite sunk in, and dialed Spencer Cain's Miami office.

"Mr. Cain's office," the secretary answered.

"This is Liz Benedict calling from TelTech, California," Liz said. "Mr. Cain, please."

"One moment." There was a pause. Liz drummed a finger on her desk top, angry and confused. She assumed that the termination announced in the letter applied to all TelTech employees, while her new position inside American Enterprise would be handled in a separate communication. She did not like the feeling of being fired, even if it was only temporary.

"Mrs. Benedict," the secretary's voice came back on the line. "Mr. Cain is in conference. Can he call you back?"

"Did you tell him Liz Benedict?" Liz asked. "He'll want to talk to me. I'll hang on."

"One moment." The secretary's voice was cold.

There was a longer pause this time.

"I'm sorry," the secretary said. "Mr. Cain is not available right now. I'll have to leave him your message. What was it in reference to?"

Liz hung up the phone without another word.

She knew what was happening. Spencer Cain would never be at home to her again. Nor would he call, or return her calls.

She was fired. The letter from New York was no mistake. A power play had taken place at the highest levels of American Enterprise. And she was the loser.

That day's *Wall Street Journal*, delivered with the same mail as Liz's termination by American Enterprise, provided her with the explanation she had already half-formulated in her own mind. The article was prominently displayed on page 5.

NEW AMERICAN ENTERPRISE DIVISION TO BE FORMED

Executives of the American Enterprise Corporation today announced the formation of a new division to be devoted to the advancement of television technology, and particularly the development of color television as a consumer product.

The new division, to be named Teltron, Inc., will be based in Boston. Its Chief Operating Officer will be Spencer M. Cain, the present Vice President in Charge of Finance at Rand Industries and former executive officer in several American Enterprise companies.

"We consider this new division to be one of our most important priorities," said Charles Powell, President of American Enterprise. "Spence Cain is one of our most able and energetic people, and just the man for this job. His background in finance and marketing is equaled by his expertise in the field of television technology."

"I'm excited by the challenge," said CEO-designate Cain in a telephone interview. "Color television is the key to the future of the medium in the next decade, and I'm looking forward to working aggressively with my American Enterprise colleagues to see that we are in the forefront of this revolution."

Liz let the newspaper drop to the desk top before her. The photographs of Spencer Cain and Charles Powell smiled up at her from the article.

She understood everything now. Her firing was genuine, and final. American Enterprise's plans for the new division did not include her.

Cain had outfoxed her after all.

Even at this terrible moment, when the base of her power and even her livelihood had been pulled out from under her, Liz had the sangfroid to review the situation analytically, and to appraise how she had been undone.

Cain had taken a business gamble. In losing Liz he knew he had diminished the innovative capacity of his new company. He knew he could never pilot it as expertly alone as he could have with the inspiration and intellect of Liz behind him.

But, by nature a creature of the corporate jungle, Cain had understood that Liz's talent went hand in hand with her ambition. Tying his career to a relationship with her would have been dangerous for him. Sooner or later she might have decided to leave him behind, as he was leaving her behind today.

So he had done the prudent thing. He had opted for pure power and position over creativity. He had used Liz for what she could give him, and then dropped her. If the horizons of his television deal were narrowed by Liz's absence, the position he held within American Enterprise was the more secure.

Cain was an ambitious man. Color television was only a stepping-stone to him. If he could succeed in this plan and concentrate sufficient power for himself within the conglomerate, he might one day end up as president of American Enterprise itself, or at least as a key board member, like his friend Penn McCormick, on whom this little double-cross had obviously depended.

Had Cain continued to depend on Liz, it might have been she who rose to those heights, while he lost out.

Liz smiled to think how prudent Spence had been, how wise. She could not deny that at the back of her mind, all this time, had been the vague but real plan to chop his head off when her control over the television marketplace made her strong enough to do without him. He had understood her only too well.

Her own mistake had been to overestimate her intellectual ascendancy over him, and his need for the technical innovations she could provide the new company.

Worse yet, she had been too confident of her personal power over him.

She looked back on their sexual relationship. She had to admire his guile. He had put on the most subtle act of male dependency she had ever imagined. He had fooled her where it hurt most—in her female instincts.

She recalled their very first night together, when, like an athlete responding with split-second reflexes, she had sensed the secrets of his need and set out to intensify them so as to make him dependent on her. She had known that there was something shrouded and mysterious about his sexuality, something he was keeping back—but she had convinced herself that she unmasked all of it that first night.

Well, she had been wrong. Spence had held back a trump that she did not know about. And, through orgasm after orgasm, he had kept that something hidden. He had been playing a part all the time.

He had outwitted her in bed, as well as at the poker table of corporate competition. It was she who had shown too much of what she had in her hand, and she who had paid the price.

It was a thorough humiliation. No wonder he took his pleasure in having her fired with this cold letter on the same day that the *Journal* announced the dissolution of TelTech. He wanted her to read about her company's fate in the newspaper.

She looked around her office, scanning the pictures on the walls, the view of the city outside the window, the portrait of Lou on her desktop. As she did so she could hear phones ringing and urgent voices talking in the outer office and corridor. The news about TelTech must be spreading among the terrified employees. Her intercom was buzzing frantically. She ignored it.

It was here, in this building, that she had come to Lou as Liz Dameron, an innocent-looking young college graduate, and got a job as lowly materials assistant at Benedict Products. It was here that she had started her upward climb, seizing control of the company without a false step, and handing it over to American Enterprise like a gift on a silver platter.

All her achievements had taken place here. And now they had been taken away from her.

She looked at her filing cabinets, neatly filled with the reports and projections and research that were the stuff of her dedication to TelTech. It was time to clear them out, time to say goodbye to the company she had built on the ruins of Benedict Products.

With an effort of will Liz suppressed the bile boiling inside her. She would be cool today. She would not lose her balance. She would leave the field of battle to the victors for now. But tomorrow was another matter. No one could predict the future. That, and only that, was the final law of business.

She looked down at the picture of Spencer Cain, smiling and handsome.

"I'll be seeing you, Spence," she murmured.

But first things had to come first.

She looked from the picture of Cain to the recently done portrait photo of Lou that she kept on her desk. The photographer had had to do some retouching to conceal the sallow color and sagging lines of Lou's face. Despite his best efforts Lou looked like the pathetic shadow of an executive, a clown masquerading as a man of weight and purpose.

Liz thought about her husband. Over her protestations he had recently changed his will to leave half of all he owned to Barbara and the children. What remained did not amount to much. Hardly enough to keep a woman in clothes and a nice home.

Liz thought about her future. The business world had turned its back on her, and it was up to her to find a way to change its mind. She had a long way to go, and a great deal of fast shuffling to do. It was time to look to top priorities. Time to make sacrifices.

Lou Benedict had no place in that future.

He had served his purpose.

VIII

Sacramento Observer, December 14, 1952

The body of local entrepreneur Louis G. Benedict was discovered early Tuesday in the garage of his Oak Hill home by Sacramento police.

Mr. Benedict, a prominent local businessman and member of numerous civic organizations, was found at the wheel of his car in the closed garage, with the engine still running. The county Medical Examiner determined that carbon monoxide poisoning was the cause of death. A high percentage of alcohol was found in the deceased's bloodstream.

Police were called to the scene by Mr. Benedict's wife Elizabeth, who had found the body upon being awakened by a neighbor, Mr. John C. Glaser, who had become alarmed by the sound of the running engine behind the closed garage door. The two attempted unsuccessfully to revive Mr. Benedict in the interval before police arrived.

Neighbors told police they had heard Mr. Benedict return home Monday night at approximately midnight. Mrs. Benedict, already asleep in the master bedroom at the opposite end of the house, did not hear her husband arrive. The garage door was equipped with an automatic closing device, manufactured by Mr. Benedict's firm. Mrs. Benedict told police she had expected her husband to return late and had gone to bed herself at ten.

Mrs. Benedict was too distraught to speak with the press. Business associates told reporters that Mr. Benedict had been despondent over the recent dissolution of his company, TelTech, Inc., by its parent corporation, American Enterprise Corp. of New York. Mr. Benedict was Board Chairman of the firm (formerly known as Benedict Products). His wife had worked closely with him as Vice President in Charge of Personnel.

Besides Mrs. Benedict, Mr. Benedict leaves a former wife, Mrs. Barbara Benedict of San Diego, and her three children, Paul, 18, Cynthia, 15, and Joyce, 13; a brother, William, of Seattle; and a sister, Mrs. Virginia Fallon, of Denver.

Memorial services will be held at the Jarvis Funeral Home, 1174 Sheridan Avenue, Friday at 10 A.M. Visiting hours are Thursday, 2 to 9 P.M.

IX

HAL WAS SITTING at a small table, looking into his sister's eyes.

Sybil was staring down at the tabletop before her. He let his gaze linger on her pure blue irises, so blue they reminded him of the mountain lakes in the Adirondacks that looked like jewels under the summer sun.

Sybil became aware of his scrutiny. The golden veils of her eyelashes stirred. She was resting her chin on her hand, and though her head did not move, she gave him an up-from-under look of mingled reproach and amusement.

"No peeking," she said. "Come on. I'm trying to concentrate."

"I'm just admiring that pretty face of yours," he said. "You have an unfair advantage. You're taking my mind off the game."

"Brumph," she muttered—an old private joke based on an imitation of their father's authoritative snort.

As Hal watched, she ran her index finger around in a tentative circle over the checkerboard between them, pointed this way and that with a hesitation he knew was feigned, and then, with perfect alacrity, jumped the king on which he had placed so many hopes and dropped the two captured checkers behind her line.

It was difficult to play checkers with her, and even harder to win. She was incredibly adept at catching him off guard, and distracting him with the subtle shifts of her body and apparent moods. Indeed, she seemed literally able to read his mind. After the first couple of moves she understood his game plan, thought several steps ahead of him, and waited for her chance to attack.

Hal could never decide whether it was the combination of her intellect and her ruthlessness that armed her so well against his game, or whether her intimacy with him was the deciding factor. She knew him like a book, of course. When they played "Twenty Questions" she never needed more than two or three to find out what he was thinking of.

At cards she cheated unmercifully—most of all, oddly enough, when she played solitaire. He had taught her chess when she was a girl, and she learned to beat him easily within her first year at the game. But nowadays she made him play checkers instead, out of nostalgia for her early youth.

He looked down at the board. Without that king he would have to be on his toes. He moved one of his men forward, and saw her respond languidly by drawing her king back, an apparently senseless move for which, he was sure, there was a good reason.

"How are the folks?" he murmured, preferring to make conversation rather than to dwell on the silent battle taking place between them.

"Oh, they're fine," she said, not taking her eyes from the board. "Mother says I need to have my hair done. She says I look like something the cat dragged in. By the way, Hal, I'm having a great time in Italy, in case anybody asks. Florence was mahvelous, the Uffizi better than ever. Venice was rainy, but I swam at the Lido anyway. Now it's on to Siena, and after that Orvieto. Never a dull moment."

He ignored her little joke at his mother's expense. Sybil loved to taunt Mother about her concern for appearances. She found Mother's terror of what people would think both cowardly and ludicrous, and enjoyed scaring her with veiled threats of some extravagant action.

Her contempt for Mother hurt Hal, for he remained very close to

Mother. He visited her in New York at least twice a week when he was home, chatting with her in her living room about his busy life and sometimes asking her advice. He knew the side of his mother that was sensitive and even intelligent.

But Mother had never let Sybil get close enough to see that aspect of her. All Sybil knew was a worried, distant woman wrapped up in her own cares, and somewhat shallow in her concerns. Hal did not try to correct Sybil or defend Mother, for he understood that Sybil did not have the same relationship with her that he did. From Sybil's perspective, her resentment toward Mother made perfect sense.

Nevertheless Hal felt a double sting when Sybil made fun of Mother behind her back—first for Mother herself, and second because he felt that Sybil's slurs were an indirect way of reproaching him, out of jealousy or from some other, more obscure motive.

"Have you seen Daddy?" he asked.

"Once in a while," Sybil said. "He breezes in with a quick 'How are you, my dear?' and settles down to talk about the financial news until he's saved by the bell. I might as well not be here. I'll have to kill myself to get his attention."

"Don't talk that way, Syb."

Hal could imagine those deadly scenes. His father had never really known Sybil was alive. His relationship with her was approximately that of a ship's captain with a passenger: a courtly nod in passing, and a flicker of worry in the aging eyes as he tried to remember her name.

Hal looked again at the golden eyelashes, the pale cheeks, the wandering finger moving in its circle over the board like a grim reaper poised to wreak destruction. The anger inside Sybil was all of a piece with her girlish prettiness. She gravitated toward things sinister, dark, and cruel.

Yet behind all that he could see her hurt, and her terrible loneliness. She had no friends. She had made a great point of keeping herself aloof from her contemporaries as she grew up. So it was that today there was no one to miss her, no one to remember her and come to visit, except Mother and Dad. This wrung Hal's heart.

"How's work?" she asked, to change the subject. There was a tone of disinterest in her voice, as well as an inner alertness which made him uncomfortable.

"The same," he said. "I'm going back on Friday, but I hope to be home before the fifteenth."

His destination was Paris. As President Eisenhower's Special Envoy to the NATO leadership, Hal spent three or four weeks at a time in Paris before returning for a week to Washington, where he personally briefed the President on America's uneasy friendship with her war-battered allies. It was during these stateside visits that he stole a couple of days to see his family and Diana in New York.

"How are Mr. Dulles and your other playmates?" Sybil asked.

She enjoyed teasing him about his controversial status among Eisenhower's closest advisors. They considered it unwise for the President to have appointed a registered Stevenson Democrat to such an important post. But Ike had been fond of Hal ever since they first met not long after Hal's return from Korea—not only because of Hal's Medal of Honor, for which Ike had enormous respect, but because, in a subtle way, the two men's views on international policy were similar.

Eisenhower hated the Cold War, and his experience and military instincts told him it would escalate into something bloody sooner or later. Hal, he knew, was an internationalist at heart, a born diplomat whose political life was dedicated to strengthening America by making friends rather than enemies. For this reason Ike clung to Hal, and defended him against the detractors who said he was too young, too rich, too good-looking, and too left-wing for his post. In a political climate filled with strident claims that the State Department was full of Reds and Fifth Columnists, this stance of Ike's took a lot of courage.

As for Sybil, she liked to tease Hal about his working for Eisenhower after having campaigned against him. She was clever enough to understand how a man like Hal could idolize Adlai Stevenson and admire Ike at the same time—but she liked to pretend she couldn't.

"Are the folks in the State Department getting used to having a Commie in their midst?" she prodded.

Hal looked sternly at her. "Ever hear of making the best of a bad situation?" he asked.

She shrugged. "Don't pay any attention to me." She knew how seriously he took his work, so she resisted her temptation to taunt him over the inevitable politicking that was part of any government service. It was common knowledge that Hal's enormous personal charm and popularity with the public were his greatest weapons against the red-baiters who attacked him in the press. Yet she respected him for the heroic steadiness with which he held to his positions in the face of increasing opposition from the noisy right wing of both parties.

Moreover, she enjoyed his high political profile because she knew it was an embarrassment to their father. Reid Lancaster disapproved of politics itself, not to mention liberal Democratic politics. It was only because Hal was the sole son he had left after Stewart's death that he had countenanced his career in Washington. But he hated to talk about it, and was mightily discomfited by the journalists who increasingly asked him to comment on his son's controversial role in the Administration.

Sybil's finger was moving again, poised over the board on which Hal had his men arranged in what he thought was a foolproof attack. He had her two kings outflanked, and he was moving in for the kill behind her best-placed man.

He looked at her hair, which was longer now and fuller. He liked it better this way, even if Mother didn't. Sybil was so unpredictable in her moods and so full of sharp inner edges, like a paper bag full of broken glass, that it was nice to see the outside of her looking a little more sweet and fuzzy.

He had always loved her body, since she was a little girl. There was something soft and kittenish about her that mixed strangely with her tense interior. When she was small he had felt a physical closeness with her, from helping her to dress, cleaning up her spills, and bandaging her little cuts and bruises. Since he spent more time with her than anyone else did, he became as familiar with her body as would a mother, and he cherished its odd charms.

Nowadays when he hugged her, it grieved him to feel how tightly strung she was inside. He often reflected that the dreamy languor of her eyes was like an open window to the Sybil she might have been had she not been born to the Lancasters. She was a fish out of water in her own family.

And just as he respected her for enduring so much loneliness, Sybil admired Hal for his refusal to follow in his father's footsteps as Stewart would have, and for his Quixote-like alienation from the political mainstream. Their chief point of contact and sympathy, now that she was older, was their mutual exile. Though they were not on quite the same wavelength, each was outside the normal alleys of the human race. Hal was no more a real Lancaster than she, for his humor and sensitivity separated him from the clan as surely as her sadness did her.

So Sybil could forgive Hal for clinging to his ideals with an optimism that seemed childish to her, just as he forgave her for stubbornly refusing to open any door that might lead to happiness. She was the darkness, he the light—which was strange, since her blonde body was so luminous in appearance, while he bore the dark piratical Lancaster charms. They made an odd couple, but this fact seemed only to draw them closer.

"How's Diana?" she asked

"Oh, fine," he said. "Every week an opening. She misses you."

Sybil ignored the patent lie.

"Taking good care of her, are you?"

He heard the *double entendre* only too well. She was referring not only to the sex life she imagined between him and Diana, but also to her certainty that he was cheating on Diana with other women.

On one level Sybil thought of Diana as a mere nonentity, a necessary decoration for Hal's life as a socially important male. Far from being jealous of Diana's beauty, Sybil felt sorry for Hal, since the politics of breeding had kept him from finding someone deep enough to do him justice.

Nevertheless Sybil reproached Hal for not being as much a maverick in love as he was in politics. For some reason he had always taken his unofficial betrothal to Diana seriously, and would not disappoint Mother and Dad by abandoning her. He claimed to love her, but Sybil did not believe him. So there was always an acid mixture of contempt and pity in her voice when she spoke of Diana.

"Speaking of openings," Hal added, "we saw *The King and I* with Mother on Friday. I think you'd like it."

"Mm-hmm." Her noncommittal murmur showed her lack of interest. Broadway bored her silly, as did movies and most music. Reading was her only real pastime.

"Also speaking of openings," Hal said, not giving up, "There's a Van Gogh exhibition coming to the Metropolitan next month. We shouldn't miss that."

She brightened. "Wheat fields?" she asked.

"I'll check. I wouldn't be surprised." He knew she adored Van Gogh above all things. When she was small he had taken her to see the Met's Van Goghs, holding her little hand as she stood entranced by the weird canvases, with their landscapes full of claustrophobic skies and clawlike tendrils of vegetation. Van Gogh seemed to be the only mirror in the outer world to the dread pictures she sketched at home.

On this positive note he decided to take a chance. She had moved one of her men forward, and Hal jumped him. Sybil seemed truly trapped now. There was a pause as she surveyed the board.

"Wheat fields," she murmured dreamily. "Cypresses. Houses at Arles . . ."

Then, with a suddenness that jarred him, she jumped both his kings and two of his other men, leaving him with only one piece on the board against her six. He was hopelessly outmanned.

"You did it to me again." He shook his head. "I'm not going to play with you anymore. You've got an unfair advantage."

"What's that, Prince Hal?" She smiled playfully.

"You're a witch of some kind," he said. "Why, back in the Middle Ages . . ."

She raised an eyebrow. He had touched too close to home. He stopped himself.

"Well, anyway," he said, "you're too damned good. And you know me too well."

"Anybody could figure you out," she said. "You're such a hero. You go right in with guns blazing, and leave your flank unprotected. You're not devious enough. You don't know what it is to really be a killer, Hal. You're a lover."

More *double entendres.* It was time to leave.

"I've got to go," he said, gathering his raincoat.

"Duty calls?" she asked.

He nodded. She took the coat and held it out as he slipped his arms into it. When he turned around she picked at a piece of lint on his collar. This was an old ritual. Even as a child she had tied his ties and looked him over critically before he went out, her maternal solicitude belying her tender age. After the war she had massaged his wounded back and torso, becoming expert at reducing the tension in his damaged muscles.

He smiled down at her.

"Seriously," he said. "We'll make that exhibition. You and me. Is it a deal?"

"No third parties?"

"Just you and me."

"My royal Hal. What a prince you are." She curled her lip in puckish irony, patting his chest.

For an instant his smile faded. Her words had reminded him of Kirsten Shaw. Next month would be the two-year anniversary of the car accident that had cost Kirsten her life, on the New Jersey Turnpike en route to a skiing vacation with her fiancé. Next to Sybil, Kirsten had been the woman he felt closest to. Her death seemed to have confirmed the bad luck that was dogging the Lancasters' children. First Stewie, then Kirsten—and, of course, Syb . . .

"Anyway, I'll see you Monday," he said, hiding his emotion.

"I'll be waiting,"

He pulled her close to him and hugged her tight, feeling the strange delicate limbs pliant against his body. If only he could penetrate to the struggles underneath them, as she penetrated so easily to his thoughts! But no. Her doors were shut. He only knew the part of her that mocked him and called him Prince Hal and sometimes gazed at him through eyes filled with a melancholy that stole his heart.

Yet he could not live without her. She was the one who knew the wounds under the smile he wore for the rest of the world, knew how to salve them, and how to make him feel like a prince instead of an all-too-fragile man.

He brought her small hands to his lips, one after the other, and kissed them. She watched him curiously, almost as if it were the old times, and he was tying her shoe or tightening her roller skates.

He studied the hands for a moment. Then he turned them over to look at her bandaged wrists.

"I'd like to see them sometime," he said softly.

"There's nothing to see," she said. "didn't you ever cut yourself?"

"Not the cuts," he said. "The demons."

She looked into his eyes. She seemed very bitter now. How those eyes could go cold as ice!

"I thought you promised to respect a girl's privacy," she chided.

He nodded. "Enough said."

She seemed to soften. "There are no demons, Hal."

He held her by her shoulders. "What, then?"

She sighed. "Just old Mother Earth, Hal," she said. "Just the hungry earth, waiting to swallow us up as soon as we're finished doing this dance."

They stood close together, he stroking her hair while she lay her head on his shoulder. He felt her hands on his hips.

"It's a circus without nets," she murmured, her voice that of a little girl again. "All the acrobats falling to their deaths . . . The tears on the clown's faces, all real . . . The lion tamer torn to shreds by his own beasts . . . It's too risky, Hal."

He nodded, holding her softly.

"I think I've been to that circus," he said.

Touched by his sympathy, she patted his back where she knew the worst wound was.

"My good Prince Hal," she said. "You're the one who knew me when."

"Try to have a good weekend," he said. "For me?"

"I will do that. It's a promise."

"See you Monday?"

She touched a finger to his lips to silence him.

"Monday."

On his way out he greeted the ward nurse and asked to see the doctor. She pointed to the office door, with its frosted glass window on which *J. Faber, M.D.* was painted in block letters.

Hal knocked and was let in by a tall, tired-looking man in his fifties, with graying hair and horn-rimmed glasses.

"How are you, Doctor?"

"Fine, Hal. Good to see you."

They had become good friends over the years. Hal was a regular visitor, and had come to know the doctor well.

"How is she?" Hal asked in the most neutral voice he could muster.

"Did she seem bad today?" the doctor asked, raising an eyebrow.

Hal shook his head. "Pretty much the same. Is that how she seems to you?"

He knew what the answer would be, but he dreaded it anyway.

This was Sybil's third suicide attempt. The first had taken everyone by surprise, when she was fourteen. The second, at sixteen, had been even more serious. Both times there were extended hospital stays.

This time had been less of a surprise, for the family was used to her illness now. But it had been frightening anyway. She had dug into her wrists with a vengeance, taking pleasure in reopening the old wounds, slashing through the scars, highlighting her shame for all the world to see.

The doctor sighed. "Not better, I'm afraid." Hal was the only relative to whom he could tell the whole truth. "She's very adroit at trying to fool me in therapy. From her associations, her dreams, you'd think she was making good progress. But I think I know her now. No, Hal—she's not better."

"Will she ever be?"

The doctor looked thoughtful. "At the moment, her illness means more to her than anything else. Asking her to give it up would be like uprooting a man from his own country. It's all she knows, all she can count on. The world you and I live in is something she gave up on a long time ago. She just doesn't believe it's worth sticking her neck out to live as other people do."

He looked at Hal. "You're important to her, Hal. She looks forward to seeing you. I can feel it. If anyone can keep her connected to life, it's you."

Hal nodded, unconvinced. "Somehow I don't feel like a very strong lifeline."

"Don't give up on her," the doctor said. "Sometimes I think you're her last chance. She's got her eye on you, Hal. She knows how much you care about her. She's waiting for you to let her down. But I know you never will. That gives me hope. It ought to give you hope, too."

Hal nodded, thanked the doctor, and walked out into the rain. When he reached his car he turned around. The asylum looked moody and forbidding, hunched in its thick gardens, the shrubs and trees reaching blindly toward the murky sky, branches like famished arms searching for an ineffable nourishment that was just out of reach. Sometimes he thought he could hear them sigh, when he listened with Sybil's ears.

Well, he mused, at least the exhibition would get her out for a change.

Thank goodness for Van Gogh.

X

January 16, 1953

TIMOTHY RIORDAN was in a hurry.

He had several people to see in Manhattan this morning, and a meeting with a Bronx restaurateur at three-thirty. A business deal he was working on was close to fruition, and he wanted to tie up the loose ends.

It was inconvenient that Catherine had picked this day to fall ill with one of her migraines. He detested running errands for her. But she was his only sister, and the last close relative he had left, so he made a point of taking care of her. She was a nervous, sickly creature, but a good mother to her two children and a loyal wife to Richard.

They had little money, for Richard's salary as a bookkeeper and Catherine's occasional odd jobs as a baby-sitter were barely enough to make ends meet. Tim had given them whatever money he could in the past few years, including most of his veteran's benefits. They were surviving, but hardly in grand style.

Richard had served in the Army during the war, Tim in the Marines. Both had been wounded slightly, and had returned stateside with the unspoken inner wound that all combat veterans bore. But while Tim possessed the brittle cheerfulness of the ex-soldier who prefers even the pressures and inconveniences of civilian life to battle, Richard had not made the adjustment as easily. He had trouble getting along with his bosses, drank too much, and drifted from job to job without advancing in rank or salary.

Tim, for his part, was doing better than he had expected. He had had some dealings in various small businesses before the war, just starting out in his early twenties, and now was well on his way to making a good living as a roving entrepreneur in and around New York. He had helped set up and manage several taverns, a restaurant, and a couple of small retailing businesses.

He was naturally sharp, with a good eye for financial opportunity, and he understood that a man could trust no one in business. It was thanks to his alertness that neither his partners nor his competition had managed to bilk him out of much of his time or money. He had been burned once, but he had approached the individual responsible and made him see reason. The sight of Tim's powerful body and cold eyes sufficed to cow the offender into copious apologies and full financial restitution.

Tim had not managed to put much money away yet, but he had high ambitions. He could see that America had a great future in the postwar era. Despite his healthy cynicism about the business world, he did not share the defeatism of fellow veterans like Richard, whose spirit seemed broken by the scarcity of good jobs and the increasing cost of living. For Tim could compare the world he saw here to the Ireland where his kinsmen still toiled futilely at their trades or at the unforgiving soil without any future at all.

Tim was confident that his own brains and initiative would see him through to financial success. He had a knack for finding ways to fit a new business into the tightest marketplace, and for applying pressure to the people who ran it so that their own weaknesses could not do it in.

But today his own plans must be interrupted by his errand for Catherine. He had to pick up a dress for her at her seamstress's. Catherine had always had an unusual shape, wide in the hips and tiny in the bust and shoulders, and pregnancy had made it stranger yet, and harder to fit. She managed to find a cheap seamstress in the West Village. Tim would pick up the dress this morning and leave it at Catherine's tonight, after his meeting in the Bronx.

The seamstress's address was easy to find, despite the traffic crowding the streets east of Sixth Avenue below Fourteenth Street. He parked his 1946 Packard a block and a half away—parking was becoming more and more of a problem nowadays—and walked back past an assortment of small shops, delicatessens, and fruit markets.

He scanned the mailboxes inside the apartment building's door, found the one he wanted and pressed the buzzer. A small voice answered. He identified himself and was buzzed in.

The apartment was five flights up. Tim took the steps two at a time, forcing himself to ignore the twinge in his thigh that was a reminder of Iwo Jima. He was breathing only the slightest bit heavily when he stopped at the fifth landing. He could hear a baby crying somewhere in the building, and a loud radio.

There was a familiar aroma of cooking, disinfectant, and persistent grime that made him smile. The building smelled of poverty, of tenants down on their luck. He knew that smell; he had grown up with it. He longed to get this visit over with and go on to his busy day.

He looked at the three doors on the landing, and found the one he wanted.

L. Bělohlávek said the small nameplate. *Seamstress.*

He knocked, straightening his tie and composing a friendly smile.

But his breath caught in his throat as the door opened.

Standing in its frame was the most beautiful woman he had ever seen.

Laura looked up at her tall visitor.

"Good morning," she said. "I'm sorry about all those stairs."

"No trouble at all," he said, smiling. "I can use the exercise."

"You're Mrs. Cavanaugh's brother?"

"That's me." He held out a hand. "Tim Riordan. Pleased to meet you, Mrs. Běloh . . ." He struggled briefly with the unpronounceable name.

"Call me Laura. And it's Miss," Laura corrected, closing the door behind him.

"I wasn't sure," he said. "You don't look old enough to be married —though they do marry awfully young in the old country. Why, you look like a schoolgirl, miss."

"Call me Laura." She turned to a small and rather beat-up hanger rack and pulled off a dress with a paper cover over it. "I have your sister's dress ready. I hope it turned out all right. Please tell her to let me know if there's anything wrong. I'll be happy to fix it."

"Oh, I don't think there will be any complaints," he said. "To hear Cathy speak of you, you're Mrs. Chanel herself—or whoever it is that's on top in Paris these days."

"Well, I'm not the ambitious type," Laura laughed. "But I do my best."

He held out the money his sister had given him, and watched her take it. She looked up at the handsome, ruddy face under his curly reddish hair. He had beautiful wavy eyebrows, quick hazel eyes, and a strong jaw. He dwarfed her as he stood before her, and in fact dwarfed the whole cramped apartment, for he was at least six feet two inches tall, and strongly built.

He was the first man who had been in this room since her long self-imposed incarceration. Only women had come here since she first brought the sewing machine from Aunt Martha's last summer and began looking for clients.

Laura's plan had paid off. The notices she had put up on bulletin boards in stores and churches, at the YMCA, the CYO, and various public buildings, had brought her a trickle of initial customers, which expanded into a steady stream.

Most of her clients were local women who could find nothing to fit them off the rack, and needed Laura's expert fingers to make them simple skirts and dresses out of economical fabrics like poplin, percale, and corduroy, which they themselves supplied. Most had struggled for years to alter their own store-bought clothes, for they could not find a seamstress cheap enough to make garments for them.

Her first big sale, almost more than she had bargained for, had come when a local merchant whose wife was a patron of Laura's decided to sponsor a Little League baseball team, and gave her an order for all the players' uniforms. The job was back-breaking and took her two weeks, but she managed it, and the increase in her revenue allowed her to pay off some outstanding bills and put a small classified ad in one of the New York daily papers on a regular basis.

Nowadays Laura had as much work as she could handle. She arose at six in the morning and worked until ten at night, taking time out only for a bite of lunch and a bland dinner. Oddly enough, she felt almost cheerful in her solitude. No one was involved in her life, no one cared how she felt or what she thought. It was easy and comforting to lose herself in the anonymity of the bolts of fabric, the spools of spinning thread, the intricate handwork needed to finish garments.

Now it was with an involuntary twinge of discomfort that she saw this strapping, powerful man invade her tiny lair, bringing the sun in with his burnished skin, and a breath of the fresh outside air on his nice-fitting clothes. There was a little smile in his eyes now, and she could feel the force of a gigantic confidence as he stood before her.

"If you'll pardon a clumsy observation, Miss—Laura," he said, "you look as though you've been working a bit too hard. A small thing like you, you should eat more, and get out a bit. You're pale."

"Oh, I'm fine," she shrugged, noticing the almost imperceptible hint of an Irish turn of phrase in his speech.

"And it's a little cold in here." He looked around the place, his gaze seeming to strip it of its dull familiarity and reveal it in a new light. "Here now, look." He moved toward the window, where there was a cracked pane.

"Nasty crack there," he said. "That could shatter any day. And look: You need caulking around the frame. No wonder it's cold in here."

Before she could protest, he seized the tape measure on her worktable and began measuring the damaged pane.

"I'll take care of it right away," he said when he had finished. "I have my tools right in the car downstairs."

"But . . ." Laura laughed. "Please, don't bother. I'm not cold."

"It's only January," he said. "Wait until winter really gets started. No, Miss Laura, I can't leave a lady in distress. I insist. I'll be done in no time and out of your way."

In twenty minutes he returned with a package of caulking material and a new pane of glass. He set to work on the window and would not accept Laura's offer to pay him.

"Nonsense," he said. "I know the fellow who sells this stuff. He gives it to me for free. I've done him a favor or two in my time."

He worked in silence, with Laura watching him out of the corner of her eye as she sewed a dress. He whistled under his breath, and pursed his lips when the pane came out. She was struck by his patient confidence, and the thick, strong look of his crouched thighs as he bent beside the window. She noticed the freckles on his hands. Everything about him suggested sun and strength.

When he had finished he looked up at her stove.

"Do you smell gas?" he asked.

She shook her head. She had always smelled a little gas when she was near the stove, but thought nothing of it.

He tried the burners, then the oven. As usual, only two of the burners would light.

"Needs cleaning," he said. "I'll bet the landlord drags his feet when you tell him about that."

Laura said nothing. She had never told the landlord about the gas, or the dripping water, or the broken pane, or the outlets that didn't work, or the cracking paint, or the dozen other infirmities of the apartment. When she had been a student she was too obsessed with her class assignments and exams to notice her surroundings. Later, during her solitary convalescence, she had been too wrapped up in her despair. Nowadays it was work that kept her too busy to notice.

"I'll come back tomorrow," he said, "and take care of it for you."

"Oh, please, it's not necessary, Mr.—"

"Riordan," he said. "Tim Riordan. Tim to you, Laura. I insist. Why, one more little clog and that stove could murder you in your sleep. You wouldn't want that, would you?"

She turned pale.

"What's the matter?" he asked. "Did I say the wrong thing?"

"No." She shook her head. She was recalling how close she had come to using that oven as a weapon for suicide. She met his eyes as best she could and forced a smile.

"Well, then," he said brightly. "I'll come by and get it working for you."

"Really, Mr.—Tim—it isn't necessary. I can't impose on you . . ."

"I insist." His frankness was overpowering. He was obviously so determined to help her that she could not oppose him.

"All right, then," she said.

Laura did not realize it that first afternoon, but she had found herself a protector.

Tim Riordan returned with his tool case and easily fixed her stove and oven so that they worked efficiently and safely. He examined the plumbing in her bathroom and the small kitchen sink, and set about repairing it so as to eliminate the drips, the leaks, and the hissing washers.

He found drafts in the room, and fixed the walls with insulating materials. He repaired the door frames, repainted the tiny kitchen cabinets, changed the lock for a better one, and even brought her a carpet that he had procured from somewhere, and which was far more colorful and cheery than the one that had been there originally.

Then, as a surprise, he brought her a beautiful walnut rocking chair to replace the apartment's battered armchair.

"The owners are friends of mine," he said. "They've grown too fat to sit in it. It came from the old country. Probably has quite a history. Anyway, it's the perfect size for a little thing like you, Laura."

He came back every few days, repairing, painting, polishing, all without taking a penny for his help or a no for an answer. As the weeks passed, Laura's apartment began to look like a miniature showplace, cheerful and alive, instead of the drab garret it had always been. Infected by his enthusiasm, she sewed bright new curtains for the airshaft window. As the weather outside grew colder, the apartment seemed warmer and more homey than she had ever imagined possible.

And Tim brought food. He came bearing fresh fruits and vegetables from the produce markets downstairs, and cold cuts from a butcher he insisted was an old friend, who would take no money for them.

In return for all this Laura took time off from her sewing to make him lunch. She sat eating her sandwich or soup and looking at him as he fitted his large body uneasily into one of her old kitchen chairs. They spoke little; both seemed absorbed in private thoughts. But they smiled when they met each other's eyes.

Tim had not told Laura much about himself, but she gathered from hints dropped by his sister that his childhood had not been an easy one. He had been at odds with his father in many ways, and was fiercely protective of both Catherine and his mother, until the mother's death a dozen years ago.

And he had been a war hero. At Laura's probing he admitted he had won a Silver Star and a Bronze Star for his courage under fire, but he would not take credit for heroism.

"It's automatic," he said. "We all did such things. When you see your buddies hurt, you go a little crazy. After it's over you barely even remember it. Then they give you a medal." He frowned. "Medals don't do you much good when you come home and try to find a job," he added. "They turn their backs quick enough then."

He brightened when he spoke of his career and his ambitions. He felt sorry for his relatives who had remained in the old country, he said. America was a land of plenty, for the man shrewd enough to find and exploit opportunities. Tim had nothing but high hopes for his future.

"I'm a born manager," he said. "I understand competition, Laura. The world is getting busier every day. Dog eat dog, dog eaten by dog. You need a quick wit to stay ahead. Trust no one, but use everyone who can help you. Just show me a marketplace, and I'll look in every corner until I find a way to make a dollar out of it."

His current involvements in restaurants and small businesses were only a beginning, he said. He saw a future for himself in the hotel field, which was mushrooming in the postwar economy.

He spoke with affectionate amusement of his sister Catherine, whom Laura knew as a rather sickly and preoccupied woman. He seemed to accept her foibles and those of her undependable husband without criticism, and was devoted to their children.

Laura did not hear him say a harsh word about anyone at all until the subject of Ireland's political troubles came up. His relatives were Catholics who had lived in Northern Ireland for generations, and he had a deep resentment of the English.

"If the limey Brits would stay in their own country and let us solve our own problems, we'd straighten things out in a hurry," he said darkly. "But you can't get a Britisher to keep his nose out of other people's business and his hand out of their pockets. That's God's own truth. Sometimes I wish Hitler had given the bastards what they really deserved."

Abruptly his frown turned to a sheepish smile. "But listen to me," he said mildly. "It's all thousands of miles away and years past, and I'm still shooting my mouth off. Well, old grudges die hard, I suppose. Particularly among Irishmen."

His Irish accent had flared as quickly as his anger, bright as the glint of red in his curly hair, and then died away. He was his familiar self again, soft-spoken and full of solicitude for Laura. He finished his lunch and went back to work on the radiator, and took his leave before two in the afternoon, for he had business on Staten Island.

Laura knew she would see him before many days passed. She worried about accepting so much kindness from him without being able to give anything in return. But she did not have the heart to refuse his help, and by now she found herself looking forward to his visits with something akin to anticipation and perhaps even human need.

Inside herself she was glad for Tim Riordan. At one stroke he had made her realize that she had been alone too long, and offered her the friendship she needed to fill up the emptiness of her life.

She could not know that, for his own part, Tim was entranced by every moment he spent with her.

When he entered the poorly lit tenement and saw her luminous dark eyes come to life in that pretty face with its alabaster skin, he thought he was seeing an angel.

She was the most haunting woman he had ever met. Her tininess, at five feet two and no more than a hundred pounds, seemed to concentrate and amplify her charm. There was a play of darkness and light in her presence that would have seemed almost too mysterious, were it not so perfectly natural.

She was a cautious person, closed upon herself, and perhaps troubled by some secret grief, he knew not what. Yet the more private she seemed, the more intoxicating was the welcome she bestowed upon him.

When he came to the apartment she would look up at him with the sweetest expression of trust and candor. He could feel her eyes resting on him while he worked. And he noticed her slender, graceful hands when she held out a plate or a glass of iced tea to him.

Sometimes she looked almost unbearably fragile. Her vulnerability made him ache to reach out and draw her to himself, to enfold her with protective arms.

On the other hand, as he watched her quick fingers fly over the fabrics, sewing them expertly into handsome garments, she seemed self-assured and even muscular in her talent. It was clear that deep inside herself she possessed a strength and integrity of character that few people had.

And her sensitivity shone through in the amazing creativity of the work she did. The dresses and outfits she had made for his sister seemed to plumb the depths of Catherine's personality, and even to brighten and improve her.

The clothes Laura made for herself were even more impressive. They hugged her lovely little figure while accenting that private aura of hers, with its dark corners and hidden riches, as beautifully as the orchestration of a symphony suits its most distinctive melodies. She shrugged off his compliments when he tried to praise her great talent; but it was there nonetheless.

Yet it was more than talent that attracted him to her. The oddest feeling would come over him when he heard the soft swish of her skirts as she moved around the table to adjust part of a garment. There was an intimacy emanating from her, so feminine that he longed to bury himself in her warmth like a child, to hide from the world's cold cruelty within the refuge of those fresh skirts.

Confusedly he realized that this was a way of being attracted by the hidden sensuality of Laura. Yet he never let himself go to purely carnal thoughts about her. He preferred to linger over her shy dignity, for this was a much more powerful charm than the crude attractions of ordinary women.

Laura was made of a higher feminine substance, and surely of female needs—but needs kept hidden by her strong will and her self-respect. She was all woman, but made to be protected and adored, made for the holy intimacy of the marriage bed, and for babies, and for a home warmed by her unique sweetness.

So it was impossible to want her without wanting to put her on the pedestal she so richly deserved. Yet it was also impossible to idealize her without at the same time falling under the spell of her sex, a sex that was capable of far more than merely inflaming a man's instincts. It was capable of owning his heart.

Or already did own his heart.

Tim floundered in that sweet confusion all the time he was with Laura.

And when he was not with her, he dreamed of her, and counted the hours until he could see her again.

. . .

On a Friday in February he convinced her to go out to dinner with him. It was a business meeting, he claimed; but with a twinkle in his eye he insisted she wear her dancing shoes.

They went to a charming little restaurant on Greenwich Avenue, where Tim chided Laura about her thinness as she did her best to do justice to the delicious but too ample meal. It was the first time she had been in a restaurant since her days with Nate Clear.

She felt uncomfortable at first. She had spent many months coming to terms with the permanent void inside her. Her solitude had been her best weapon, and she had kept the human race at arm's length all this time.

But here was this man, bursting with the hard energy of being male and strong and active, unafraid of the future, brusquely indifferent to the past. And he seemed bent on bringing her back to life. She did not believe he would succeed, but she felt a wistful affection for him, as though he was her last and best lifeline to the planet.

Of course he would never know her secret—though he seemed to sense the grief inside her, and to realize what he was up against in drawing her back to the world. She found this unspoken probing oddly pleasant, like the caress of a strong hand determined to ease her pain without invading her privacy with unbidden questions.

In any case it was best that he not know too much about her. The truth was her own burden, and would only erase that steadfast smile from his face if he were ever to learn it. Laura did not want that.

He convinced her to dance with him when the small trio began playing.

For the first time he held her in his arms. He saw a strange look come over her face, not far from concern, but then relaxing into an acceptance that delighted him.

He was an excellent dancer, graceful and not overbearing in his moves. His big hand was light as a feather on the small of her back, and his smile put her at ease.

Laura felt something precious and cold begin to melt dangerously under the soft touch of male arms and the warmth of the shoulder against her cheek. Pain curled on itself deep inside her, but she held it in check for his sake and let him go on as though nothing had happened.

When they sat down he ordered coffee and looked into her eyes.

"I've been doing some thinking about you, Laura," he said.

She raised an eyebrow. "About me? What is there to think about me?"

"Oh, lots of things," he smiled. "Some more important than others. But the reason I asked you to join me tonight—other than the pleasure of your company—is one of the important ones." He looked seriously into her eyes. "Laura, you can't go on this way."

She looked perplexed. "What way?"

"Working out of a tenement," he said. "Making your customers climb five floors of an old building to get to you. Why, that's a crime, Laura, for a professional with talent like yours."

"Do you mean I should get another apartment?" she asked.

Smiling, he shook his head. "I'm way ahead of you," he said. "Laura, I've had my dealings in the garment business. And I know great potential when I see it. The clothes you make are special. In fact, they're more than special. You make a product that is far superior to what women are buying in today's marketplace. And you do it at a competitive price. Now, what does that tell me? It tells me you've got to expand your operation. It's as simple as that."

She looked at him in some bewilderment.

"Tim," she said at last, "I told you long ago that I'm not the ambitious type."

"But I am," he said. "And I can't stand by and watch a talent like yours go to waste. Now, I'm not suggesting that you try to turn into Chanel overnight. I know how hard you work as it is. I just want you to consider a bit of a change in how you run your business."

"What sort of change?"

He looked at her seriously.

"I've located a storefront for you," he said. "It's on West Fourteenth Street, just a step or two from Seventh Avenue. You'll have access to a wealthier trade there. The place is in good condition, and the rent is cheap. Whatever repairs are necessary, I'll take care of myself."

Ignoring her look of surprise, he warmed to his subject.

"Now, all you'll have to do is move in, and tell your existing customers about your new address. They'll be your base. You'll be a seamstress, but you'll have your own dress shop. You can design and make dresses, skirts, sportswear, just as you please, in standard sizes. Expand just as much as you want. Let your inspiration go a little, instead of just making clothes for unimaginative women. You'll see: in no time at all you'll have a better clientele. I'll handle the business end for you myself. After all, that's my specialty."

Laura considered his suggestion. Though she would never have thought of it in a hundred years, she had to admit it made sense. Her dingy apartment was hardly presentable as a seamstress's shop. And the opportunity to make clothes from her own designs was intriguing.

But where was the money for such a project to come from?

"Tim . . ." she began.

He silenced her with an upraised hand. "If it's money you're worried about," he said, "don't be. I'm an expert at getting businesses off the ground. I'll get you a short-term loan from a banker friend of mine. It will be more than enough. I'll cosign, and make myself personally responsible. I guarantee you'll be in the black inside of three months."

She shook her head and smiled. "I don't know . . ."

"You have nothing to lose," he insisted. "In the unlikely event that we can't get the storefront to fly, I'll reimburse you for whatever you've lost out of my own capital. You see, I'm going to be your first investor. But you won't fail."

Laura laughed. "You certainly make it hard to refuse," she said.

"That's my business, too." Tim looked very pleased with himself, and confident of her capitulation.

She looked into his eyes. Despite herself she was feeling the force of his will and his optimism beginning to course through her own veins.

"Why are you doing this, Tim?" she asked.

Because I love you.

The unspoken words were betrayed only by the softness of his smile.

"Because I'm a pushover for a pretty face," he said aloud.

And he reached a large hand across the table to graze her pale cheek, as sweetly as would an adult with a little girl.

Half-convinced, she asked, "What would we call it?"

He smiled. "It's yours, isn't it? So we'll just call it *Laura.*"

She laughed. "You've thought of everything, haven't you?"

He nodded. "Almost everything, yes. Oh, I keep on my toes, Laura."

He sat back and looked at her, satisfied he had convinced her.

She realized there was no saying no to him. She felt the caress of the eyes resting so gently on her, and admired the man's face made more handsome by his strength and his sureness.

She dared to reach out and grasp his hand, for she needed its support now. A door inside her was slowly closing on the past, and another one opening to a future she could not foresee.

XI

IN 1953 THE AMERICAN FASHION SCENE was dominated by the dynamic growth of the ready-to-wear industry and the development of such new fabrics as puckered nylon, rayon crepe, mohair, stretch synthetics, and Terylene, which in a few years would come to be known as Dacron.

Though the influence of European designers on American taste was said to be diminishing, the power of Christian Dior and his French contemporaries as style-setters remained enormous. Meanwhile Italian fashion had been launched in the United States by a 1951 joint show in which the work of Emilio Pucci was seen for the first time. And in Paris, a former employee of Elsa Schiaparelli had just opened his own salon and was using clear, soft colors to make restrained dresses and A-line coats. His name was Hubert de Givenchy.

Nothing could have been less likely to attract the attention of the fashion world at this busy time than the opening of a modest seamstress's shop near Seventh Avenue in Greenwich Village. But from precisely such beginnings do great successes arise.

Tim had had a painter friend of his create an attractive sign in gold for the shop's window—LAURA, LTD.—CUSTOM FASHIONS. He placed ads in the local papers announcing the opening of the new enterprise, and mailed invitations to all Laura's old customers informing them of her "move up."

On opening day he placed a bouquet of white roses in a vase on Laura's desk. They nervously drank a cup of coffee together, waiting to see what would happen next—and were surprised to see their first customer enter the shop before nine o'clock.

The ice was broken. Soon there was more work than Laura had ever had before. Her old customers were all loyal to her, and new ones were coming every day—attracted, as Tim had predicted, by the upgrading of her premises. She accepted their business gladly, and turned her talents to accomplishing for them what she had accomplished for many women before them: capturing the "something special" about their bodies and their personalities that only her clothes seemed able to bring out.

The shop was tastefully decorated by Laura herself in quiet shades of gray. Discovering an unsuspected talent as a window dresser, she designed a handful of eye-catching dresses and outfits for various occasions, put them on some second-hand mannequins Tim had procured from somewhere, and artfully arranged them in the window. The interior of the shop was designated as a display area, with more outfits hanging on racks, and the back room became Laura's work area. Despite the modesty of the whole arrangement, one had the impression of a genuine dressmaker's salon, with a certain elegance to the trappings.

Once Laura was ensconced in her new surroundings she blithely returned to her old routine of work, beginning early in the morning and not quitting until ten at night or even later. Tim took charge of the business end of the new shop, paying the rent on the storefront, registering the new business with the city and state, and seeing to all the necessary permits and licenses.

He surprised Laura by suggesting that she change her name.

"Not legally, of course," he said. "But just for business purposes. It's called a DBA, which means 'doing business as.' I want people to be able to remember your name easily. I'm afraid Bělohlávek doesn't roll off the tongue all that well."

Laura seemed agreeable. "What do you suggest?" she asked.

"I've been giving the matter some thought," he said with the serious expression she had grown to love. "How would you feel about Laura Blake?"

She raised an eyebrow, staring into space. The idea of adopting a new name was intriguing, but gave her an odd feeling of burning bridges behind her.

"It starts with a B, so you won't have to change your personalized hankies," Tim joked. "And it's easy to say, and to remember. What do you think, Laura?"

After a pause Laura smiled and nodded her agreement. The name was simple, and had an attractive dignity.

"Laura Blake it is, then," he said. "If I had some champagne I'd propose a toast. That may be a famous name some day, Laura."

Laura smiled. She never expected to be famous, but she was pleased that it was Tim who had changed her name, just as he had given her a new life.

Before long Laura was working harder than she ever had before. She was so delighted to see the shop making money that she did not notice her own overwork. It was Tim who, after the first month of operation, informed her that she could no longer handle the sewing and the management of the shop all by herself.

"I'll get you some help," he said simply.

The next day he brought a shy young girl from Spanish Harlem named Rita Suarez to the shop with him. Rita was hardly out of her teens, and came from a large family. From her cautious demeanor Laura could not help suspecting that one or more members of her family might be illegal aliens.

But Rita herself was legitimate enough to have a Social Security card. And thus it was that Laura had her first taste of being an employer. Tim helped her register with the Social Security Administration and the Department of Internal Revenue for tax withholding. Laura wondered how she would pay Rita and keep the shop going on its present shoestring.

But she soon realized Rita was worth every penny of her salary. Behind her expressionless face Rita concealed a natural seamstress's talent honed by generations of practical wisdom handed down from her mother and grandmother. Rita had had a short career in the garment district, until a recent layoff left her unemployed. She had plenty of experience with heavy-duty sewing machines, and could cut and grade patterns with astonishing speed.

Within an hour of her arrival Rita was an indispensable part of the routine of work, and Laura was already freer to devote herself to the creative side of designing garments for her clients before she joined Rita in the patterning and sewing. She was also able to spend more time on fabric-buying trips along Seventh Avenue, leaving Rita in charge while she was gone. Though Rita remained close-mouthed and self-effacing almost to the point of deliberate invisibility, Laura soon developed an intuitive bond with her.

Nowadays Tim would come briskly into the shop after his morning in the city and see the two young women working together. They almost resembled each other, for both were small, both had dark hair, and they concentrated on their work with a stillness that seemed almost religious. Tim felt he had assembled the first two members of a creative team destined for great things.

Events soon began to prove him right. From the kernel of Laura's neighborhood customers grew a larger and larger network, as word spread from sister to sister to cousin to aunt, from mother to daughter to in-laws and friends. Before long Laura's reputation as a custom designer of unique talent was attracting customers from as far away as Westchester, Long Island, New Jersey, and Connecticut.

And now the first big surprise about Laura's salability as a designer became visible to Tim's alert business eye. The women finding their way to the tiny shop were no longer exclusively lower middle class in their financial status or in their taste in clothes. A growing number of them came from affluent suburbs and from the better Manhattan neighborhoods.

These women were hard to fit in one way or another, and were dissatisfied with the clothes they bought even at the finest dress shops in the city. They were more than willing to turn away from Fifth Avenue long enough to give an unknown seamstress a try, particularly in view of the glowing stories they had heard about the miracles Laura could perform. And once they had been the beneficiaries of her talent, they considered her their discovery, and told their friends about her.

Soon Laura, Ltd., was growing almost out of control. Laura tried to keep pace with the work by streamlining her daily routine, but before long it was clear that she and Rita were no match for the new influx of clients.

Thus she was relieved when Tim set up a separate facility for her in a loft a block from the shop and ensconced two new seamstresses there, under Rita's direction, to sew the clothes Laura designed. He also hired an attractive young woman named Meredith Embry to help Laura manage the shop and deal with customers. Meredith, a tall redhead with a ready smile and quick wit, happened to be a perfect size 8, and was soon doubling as Laura's model, salesperson, and all-around "slave," a role in which she was indefatigable and cheerful.

Now the second major surprise about the prospects of Laura, Ltd., made itself felt. More and more of the new clients thronging the shop had come not only for clothes tailored to the peculiarities of their bodies, but because they were intrigued by the distinctive style of Laura's designs. Some of these women were not even particularly hard to fit or dissatisfied with what they could buy elsewhere. They simply wanted a dress or outfit like the Laura creation they had seen on one of their friends.

Laura had never thought of her many designs as possessing a unified style or inspiration. But now she was forced to reevaluate her work. There could be no doubt of it: there was a "Laura look" that characterized all her creations. Like a secret pattern behind a kaleidoscope of colors, it asserted itself in the most disparate of her outfits.

It was an unusual look, quite distinct from anything available in the marketplace. Yet it was more natural and feminine, somehow, than the severe, stereotyped lines of the high-fashion dresses created in Paris and imitated by the major designers here at home. Laura had the singular ability to bring out the shrouded femininity and sex appeal of the ordinary figure in a way that no other designer had thought of.

This special cachet of Laura's designs, even more than her brilliance as a seamstress, caused her business to grow at an ever-increasing pace. Before a few months had passed the loft down the street from the shop accommodated four seamstresses instead of two; then six instead of four. Tim had hired an assistant for Meredith, whose own role at Laura, Ltd., was now that of an executive as well as a "slave."

Tim had been as good as his word, and his prediction had come true. Thanks to his talents as a promoter and manager, and to the eager market for Laura's work, Laura, Ltd., was a genuine business. It employed nine people, had two premises, was listed in the yellow pages of the phone book, advertised in *Women's Wear Daily*, and was a small but real part of the fashion scene.

It was all happening very fast, but Laura remained the still center of this whirlwind of activity. She was unflappable in her efficiency, finding time to design the dozens of outfits that were keeping her seamstresses busy, and dealing with the increasing demands of her customers without showing any signs of overwork or exasperation. Tim was astonished to see her take on so much responsibility without a single complaint.

She was a workhorse as well as a genius, he decided. And thanks to her talent and originality, a seemingly limitless clientele for her work was appearing from everywhere at once. The future of Laura, Ltd., might outstrip even Tim's considerable ambitions for it.

But before this could happen an episode took place that had far-reaching implications not only for the shop but for Laura herself.

XII

ONE MORNING LAURA was interrupted in her sketching by Meredith.

"There's a man here who says he represents the Building Commission," she said. "I don't know what it's about. He says he wants to talk to you."

A small, dark man in rather too flashy clothes was ushered into Laura's cluttered office.

"How do you do, Laura." He held out a hand. "deMarco's my name. Danny deMarco. Glad to meet you."

Laura shook his hand, mustering a smile. She found herself wishing Tim was here. But Tim was out of the city on business this morning.

"What can I do for you?" she asked.

"It's nothing that need concern you greatly," he said, sitting down in the chair opposite her. "It's just the Building Commission. You have a second office going, down at the corner, isn't that right?"

Laura nodded. "That's where our seamstresses work."

"Right." The little man smiled, pulling at his tie. "It's just one of those city technicalities. When a business opens a branch office, the city has to be informed, you see. And you have to pay a special tax for operating two premises where employees are working. See, if the other office was just warehouse space, there would be no problem. But you have employees up there, and in order to satisfy the unions and insurance companies about their working conditions, you have to comply with city regulations on a second premises. And that involves this tax, for which you get a seal. I'll be sending you that."

"How much is this tax?" Laura asked.

"A hundred dollars a month," he replied quickly. "I know that seems like a lot, and believe me, I hate to have to collect it. But that's the way the city is. It's the Building Code, you see. There's nothing I can do about it, even though I have to take the heat from all the businesses . . ."

He held up his palms in resignation, the smile still on his face.

Laura was beginning to feel more nervous.

Something about this little man, with his hurried explanations and his tacky clothes, sounded an alarm inside her mind.

She said, "I'm going to have to check on this with Tim Riordan. He's in charge of money matters, employee arrangements, and so on. He's not here today, but why don't you let me have your number, and I'll have him call you? Or you can make an appointment to see him here. I'm quite sure he'll be in tomorrow morning."

The little man's eyes showed a flash of concern. "Well, the city doesn't like to wait on a thing like this. You could lose your retailer's license," he said. "It's better to get it over with right away. What did you say your man's name was?"

"Tim. Tim Riordan."

"Company attorney?"

"No." Laura shook her head. "We don't have an attorney of our own. But Tim will take care of you."

"Okay, I'll tell you what." The man produced a business card. "I'll be in tomorrow morning. Let's hope your Tim is here. We ought to get this thing straightened out as soon as possible."

Laura took the card and shook his hand. A moment later he was gone, leaving only the smell of his cologne in the office air.

That evening Laura told Tim a little worriedly about the episode. The figure of a hundred dollars per month had frightened her. She doubted that Laura, Ltd., could afford so onerous a tax.

"All right," Tim said. "I'll make sure to be in tomorrow morning when he comes back. Now don't you worry about this, Laura. This is not your department. I'll take care of the fellow."

The next morning Mr. Danny deMarco appeared bright and early at the shop. Tim was waiting for him.

The man went through the story he had told Laura, in the same hurried detail. Tim stopped him before he could finish.

"May I see your city identification?" he asked.

"I gave your boss my card," Mr. deMarco said.

"I mean your identification as a city employee," Tim said.

There was a pause.

"Well, I'm not precisely a city employee," the other man said. "I work for a firm that collects the tax and renders the seal. It's called Building Commission, Inc. It's perfectly legit, if that's what's worrying you, Mr. Riordan. You can check."

Tim got up slowly, moved to the office door, and closed it.

"I have checked," he said. "You don't have any connection with the city, Mr. deMarco. No such tax as what you mentioned to Laura exists, according to the New York City Tax Collector, the Manhattan Register of Permits, and the Building Authority."

He paused, looking through cold eyes at the little man, who seemed visibly discomfited.

"What's your racket, Mr. deMarco?" Tim asked quietly.

"It's not my racket," the man said, his face darkening. "Do you think I'm here representing myself? I'm not that dumb, Mr. Riordan. I work for Frank Rizzo—in case that name means anything to you."

It did. Frank Rizzo was one of the lesser-known but nevertheless important crime bosses in New York. It was widely rumored that his operations included protection for small businesses in the downtown area.

"And?" Tim asked, his tone more respectful now.

"And Mr. Rizzo has an arrangement with people in your business," deMarco said, pulling at his tie with an air of hurt pride. "You're probably new in this business, so you don't know. The city inspectors are dangerous people, Mr. Riordan. You never know when they'll pull the plug on your permit, because they didn't get some payoff they weren't entitled to anyway. Thanks to Frank, you don't have to worry about that. He takes care of the city up front. You pay him this little honorarium, and he protects you."

Tim nodded ruminatively.

"And if I don't pay Mr. Rizzo?" he asked.

Danny deMarco laughed mirthlessly. "Nobody has tried that in a long time," he said. "Frank's business cuts both ways. He has his own reputation to think about. People don't say no to him, Tim. Take my word for it."

Tim looked more impressed now.

"A hundred dollars a month . . ." he said. "That seems like a lot. We're a new business, you know. We can't afford that kind of money. We'd have to go under if we paid it."

A benevolent smile curled the little man's lips.

"Well, why didn't you say so in the first place?" he asked. "Frank is no shylock. Naturally he expects what he has coming to him, but he's flexible. If I can convince him of your good faith, I'm sure I can talk him into an interim arrangement. Say, fifty a month? Payable this week. We'll talk about the future when the future comes. That's fair, isn't it?"

He leaned forward with ill-concealed eagerness. His little hand seemed poised to reach out for the money.

Tim thought for a moment. "I don't have the cash here," he said. "But I'm sure I can get it by tomorrow. Why don't you drop by in the morning, say around ten? I wouldn't want to keep Mr. Rizzo waiting longer than that."

Danny deMarco stood up.

"That's the spirit," he said. "I'll tell Frank's people what you've told me. I don't anticipate any problems. Congratulations on your new business, Tim. I hear this Laura lady is quite a whiz with the women's clothes."

Tim said nothing. He did not like to hear Laura's name on the lips of the strong-arm man before him. He stood up and shook hands. "Tomorrow, then?"

"Bright and early. Be seeing you, Tim."

The next morning Danny deMarco was strolling along Greenwich Avenue, making his rounds, when a deep voice stopped him.

"Got a light, mister?"

He turned to see Tim Riordan standing at the entrance to a dim alley, dressed in a crisp overcoat. For a moment he didn't recognize Tim. Then his face brightened.

"Well, if it isn't Mr. Tim Riordan," he said. "Glad to see you. You looking for me?"

Tim nodded. "I'd like to keep this separate from the office, if you don't mind. It always helps to be discreet." He backed slowly into the alley.

"I couldn't agree with you more," said Danny deMarco, following him. "Discretion is the better part of valor, as they say . . ."

When they had reached a protected corner of the alley Tim reached into his coat pocket.

"How would you like it?" he asked. "Tens? Tens and twenties?"

"Doesn't matter . . ." Danny deMarco began.

Before he could get another word out Tim's fist had leapt from inside his pocket to strike him hard on his shiny little nose. Blood spurted instantly from the injured organ. As he staggered backward a second blow, far more vicious, caught him on the chin.

Danny deMarco hit the brick wall of the alley with all his weight, jolting himself so hard that he fell in a daze at Tim's feet.

Tim knelt to speak softly to him.

"You have no connection with Frank Rizzo," Tim said. "Did you think I was too stupid to check on that? And Frank Rizzo doesn't shake down people in our business. I already knew that yesterday, but I wanted to check you out. You're nothing but a two-bit free-lance, trying a little strong-arm on your own power."

A low, frightening laugh sounded deep in Tim's throat. "A hundred dollars a month . . . You must be doing pretty well for yourself, Mr. deMarco. I wish you all the best in the future. I'll give you a piece of advice, though. You'd better keep an eye on yourself. If Frank Rizzo finds out you're using his name, I wouldn't want to be in your shoes."

"All right, all right." The little man understood the threat. He looked up fearfully at Tim, his face covered with blood. "No harm done. We understand each other. You won't be seeing me anymore."

"That's the spirit." Tim pulled him roughly to his feet and made a show of smoothing the lapels of his overcoat. "Live and let live. Good luck, Mr. deMarco."

Weakly, the little man tried to return Tim's smile. As he did so Tim's fist came from nowhere to strike him full force in the mouth. The sound of splitting lips and broken teeth joined the hard crack of his head against the brick wall of the alley. He fell unconscious at Tim's feet.

Tim produced a handkerchief and wiped at his fist carefully. Two of his knuckles were bleeding. He was not breathing heavily, but he looked pale. He stood for a moment, studying the little man slumped against the wall. He seemed undecided.

Then, with deliberate care, he kicked Danny deMarco in the ribs, twice. His face expressionless, he added a hard blow to each knee, one more to the kidneys, and finally, the hardest of all, a kick to the testicles.

"That's for showing your ugly face to Laura," he said, looking down at the bloody human lump before him.

Without hurry he turned and left the alley.

XIII

ON AN OTHERWISE ordinary Friday in the fall, when business at the shop seemed better than ever, Tim suddenly surprised Laura with an unexpected proposal.

"I hate to upset your ideas about yourself, Laura," he said. "But the simple fact is that being a seamstress isn't the answer for you."

They were sitting in their favorite Village restaurant, the same one where Tim had first proposed that Laura go into business for herself.

Laura was taken aback. "What do you mean, Tim?" she asked. "I thought things were going so well. We have lots of happy clients, and more work than we can handle . . ."

"Too many clients." He shook his head. "That's exactly the problem, Laura. Your talent has outstripped our operation. As we're currently set up, we can't accommodate the market you've created for your work. But that's only half the problem. Have you forgotten your roots, Laura?"

She looked at him, puzzled by his words.

"The whole purpose of your work," he explained, "has been to reach women who can't find fashions they like in the stores, and to give them affordable clothes that will make them look good. Well, you've achieved that remarkably for a select group of women who've found you through word of mouth. But the great population of hard-to-fit women who have limited budgets and can't fit into Dior gowns is still out there. I've been in business long enough to know the handwriting on the wall when I see it, Laura. You've got to reach those women. When you do, you'll be satisfying a market that cries out for your product. And you'll achieve the success you really deserve."

Laura's brow was furrowed. "But how, Tim?" she asked. "What can I do that I'm not already doing? Hire more seamstresses?"

Tim shook his head. "That would only be an expanded version of your current operation. You have to break out of custom fashion, Laura, and break into ready-to-wear."

"But, Tim, all my clothes are tailored to individuals. That's the whole point of what I do."

"Well, you're going to have to change that." Tim's expression was serious and implacable.

"But how?"

He smiled. "You're the genius. That's for you to figure out. When you do I'll be here to sell it for you. But in case you feel tempted to hang back and keep doing what you're doing, Laura, don't forget: There are millions of women who need what you can provide. These women can't find anything off the rack that makes them feel good about themselves. They're crying out for your product. You just need the concept, the bridge, that will allow you to reach them. Once you design that, I'll build it for you."

Laura considered his idea. It was an intriguing conundrum. How was she to discover a "bridge" between tailored clothes for hard-to-fit women, and the ready-to-wear market that was precisely the market that had failed those women?

The problem made her mind blur. But she did not stop thinking about it.

As it turned out, the answer came from the least likely source.

A favorite customer of Laura's from the Upper West Side, Mrs. Kozlowski, was in the shop one day picking up an outfit when she noticed a beautiful dress on one of the mannequins in the display area. It was a slinky, clinging evening dress that seemed designed for one of the willowy models in *Vogue* or *Harper's Bazaar*. Laura had made it on a whim, because she liked the sketch, and had sewn it in mauve silk with black braid trim.

"If only I could wear a thing like that," Mrs. Kozlowski lamented. "But I'd look like a hippo in it. I don't have the legs. Laura, you and Meredith are lucky you have such perfect figures. You can wear such things."

Laura looked up curiously from her desk. She thought for a moment, then got up, came around her desk, and looked from Mrs. Kozlowski to the outfit. An inspiration suddenly seized her.

"Let me try to make this in your size, Mrs. Kozlowski," she said. "I'll make an adjustment or two in the lines, and perhaps change the hem a bit . . . I'll bet I can make it fit you like a glove."

"With that bodice? Dream on, Laura," said Mrs. Kozlowski with obvious skepticism.

Laura studied her customer. Mrs. Kozlowski was an extremely attractive woman to those who knew her well. She had curly chestnut hair, deep blue eyes, a good complexion and a vivacious manner. And she carried herself in a uniquely feminine way.

In short, Mrs. Kozlowski was everything a woman should be. She was graceful, interesting, and, in her way, quite sexy. But she had somewhat short legs and arms, round shoulders, and wide hips. Hers was anything but a mannequin's figure.

Laura had succeeded over the past two years in fitting Mrs. Kozlowski with some clever outfits which showed off her good points without drawing attention to her limitations. But here was a real challenge: to make her look good in a slinky evening dress designed for a much taller and slimmer figure.

And Laura remembered Tim's injunction: The effect she sought must be achieved without custom tailoring the dress to Mrs. Kozlowski's body. Instead, she must adjust the design in such a way that it could be mass-produced both in the original size and in Mrs. Kozlowski's size—and look good on both, straight off the rack.

The problem seemed impossible. But Laura's sharp intellect and innate stubbornness made her think she could solve it.

"I'm going to try this," she told Mrs. Kozlowski. "It will be an experiment. It won't cost you anything. If the outfit works, it will be free—my gift to you. If not, we'll throw it away and think no more about it."

Mrs. Kozlowski shrugged. "Well, Laura, if you think so . . . But don't be too disappointed if I end up as the best-dressed hippo in Upper Manhattan."

For nearly two weeks Laura worked on the problem in her spare time.

She draped fabric in a hundred ways on the model she had in Mrs. Kozlowski's measurements in the workroom of the shop. She tried to reproduce the slim waist and tight bodice of the evening dress in a manner that would flatter Mrs. Kozlowski's odd shape instead of clashing with it.

It was easy to see, Laura soon realized, why high-fashion designers simply ignored such a figure, and concentrated on the svelt mannequins who would make their clothes look elegant and sinuous. It was difficult to achieve the same effect on a smaller, fuller-figured woman.

The result, of course, was that all the Mrs. Kozlowskis of the world had to sigh and shrug their disappointment when they saw magazine ads full of high-fashion designs they could never wear, since the designs were not made for their shapes.

"If only I could wear that!" This was the sad anthem of millions of women who felt cut off from fashion itself, and who were forced to comb the retail racks in search of a tiny selection of less exciting dresses that would look decent on their figures.

What was needed was to bring out the average woman's inherent elegance, her subtlety of bearing, her grace of movement. Laura had achieved this to a great extent in her custom clothes. Now she must achieve it in a ready-to-wear design.

Laura warmed to the challenge before her. She stayed up past midnight working on the design of the evening dress Mrs. Kozlowski had admired. Undaunted by the difficulty of the task she had set herself, she began altering some of the lines of the dress. She changed a seam in the shoulder, a dart in the bodice, and the flow of the fabric in the skirt. She added the thinnest of shoulder straps. She changed the buttons, choosing darker and more visible ones. Then, on an inspiration, she altered the length of the dress by an inch.

All these touches crystallized on Laura's sketch pad. Excited, she took time off from work to go shopping all over town for the accessories she had seen in her imagination. She built the outfit piece by piece at home in her apartment, redesigning the slinky size 8 dress to suit Mrs. Kozlowski's shorter, heavier figure while remaining true to the sleek, sophisticated look of the original dress.

A week later everything was ready. Laura sat in the rocking chair Tim had given her and stared at her creation, tired but happy. She sensed she had done something special.

The next question was whether it would look good on Mrs. Kozlowski.

The following Tuesday was the unveiling. Laura greeted Mrs. Kozlowski at the shop and personally dressed her in the fitting room. She made Mrs. Kozlowski look away from the mirror as she worked. Tim, whose instinct had told him something important was afoot, was waiting in the showroom with Meredith and Mrs. Kozlowski's sister Karen, who had come along for the ride.

The dress fit perfectly, as Laura had known it would. Painstakingly she arranged the accessories, made a small change in Mrs. Kozlowski's hair, and took her out to the showroom.

Tim and Meredith were waiting, along with Karen and a couple of other customers who happened to be in the shop.

"Here goes," Laura said, bringing Mrs. Kozlowski forward.

A collective hush came over the room.

The outfit was a revelation.

Tim whistled under his breath. Meredith nodded admiringly. Mrs. Kozlowski's sister stood with her mouth open, too stunned to speak.

Mrs. Kozlowski had turned to look at herself in the mirror. Her eyes were filled with tears.

"Laura," she said in a hushed voice. "You've made me look beautiful."

There was a long silence. Then Laura heard Tim ask the question that had been on his mind all along.

"You mean to say you can mass-produce this?"

Good old Tim! Business as usual, Laura thought.

"Yes," she said. "The dress will differ slightly from size to size, but each size can be mass-produced."

Tim studied the dress with his educated eyes. It was different from the original from which Laura had started, and yet the same. The overall look was identical—the same fabric, the same sophisticated lines, the same glamour and slinkiness. Yet it was different, because the dress had been cleverly cut to conceal flaws in the fuller figure, while accenting its assets. The whole thing was a triumph of logic, and an amazing display of creativity on Laura's part.

But one question remained in Tim's mind.

"You've done a magnificent job with this particular design," he said. "But could you do as well with another dress? Any dress at all?"

Laura nodded. "Yes, Tim. It's just a question of thinking it through carefully enough. We can start with a dress that only looks good on a size 8 model, and make design changes so that it will look wonderful on the average figure. Then all we have to do is mass-produce those changes in the various sizes. It's hard work, but as you can see, it pays off."

She articulated this revolutionary concept as naturally as if dresses had been manufactured that way for decades.

Mrs. Kozlowski was not listening. She was still staring through misty eyes at her thirty-four-year-old figure, displayed at last in the elegant beauty which seemed to have been imprisoned inside it all these years. Laura had unlocked a door to her body which had been closed all her adult life.

"Laura," she said with a deep breath, "I'd pay you all I have and all I could borrow for this outfit. You've made me feel like a woman. You've made me feel beautiful. I haven't felt this way since before my first child was born."

Tim was shaking his head. "Laura, you're a genius."

Mrs. Kozlowski's sister came forward to hug her, then to hug Laura as well. "When's it my turn?" she asked.

Everyone crowded around, studying the outfit in its details, asking Mrs. Kozlowski to turn around, and congratulating both her and Laura.

It was impossible to explain how Laura had done what she had done. Yet the success of her efforts was gloriously visible to everyone.

Laura could not realize that the praises being sung for her were coming from disparate points of view. The customers studying Mrs. Kozlowski's dress were wondering how soon they could have similar outfits themselves. Meredith was admiring Laura's extraordinary imagination and creativity. Tim was adding up figures and deciding which fashion retailer he would let in on this secret first. Mrs. Kozlowski was dabbing at her tears of joy with a handkerchief and thinking of the miracle that Laura had achieved with her familiar body and a handful of simple materials.

Everyone in the room sensed that they had witnessed something historic. The past was wiped out, not only for Laura and her client but perhaps for millions of frustrated women.

What they saw before their eyes was the future.

XIV

FROM THE DAY of what came to be known in the shop as the "Kozlowski miracle," the routine at Laura, Ltd., was drastically altered. The staff was put on a virtually military footing in order to free Laura for a major new enterprise.

Laura set about developing a whole series of original designs, each one of which would demonstrate the same adaptability to different sizes as Mrs. Kozlowski's evening dress. Laura created formals, sportswear, suits, separates, even bathing suits with the same fundamental concept in mind. Each garment could be mass-produced in all the most popular sizes, provided that certain details of its design were altered from size to size.

Tim, who had been worried from the outset about the cost of this unusual concept in production, spent many hours in secret consultation with a Seventh Avenue fashion contractor named Millie Edelman, whose specialty was the production of complex outfits in small lots. Millie, a hard-boiled veteran of the retail wars with a bluff sense of humor, gave him a mixture of good news and bad.

"I don't say these clothes can't be made, because they can," she said. "They can be graded to different sizes with these little design changes you're talking about, and then the changes themselves can be mass-produced. But you're not going to put J. C. Penney out of business. A Laura Blake dress is going to retail at thirty-five dollars. That's the bottom line. Your average woman is going to have to reach deep to come up with that kind of money. But I'll admit that, to my eye at least, the outfits look like they're worth it. I think you may be onto something here."

As Tim worried about the business end of the experiment, Laura immersed herself in the new experience of creating her own line of clothes. She watched her new designs flow onto her sketch pad and into fabric with a will of their own. Despite her exhaustion she was filled with a hectic energy and excitement that pushed her from discovery to discovery.

There was no doubt about it—the "Laura look" was now a full-fledged reality, a statement about femininity as original as any that had been made in fashion within memory. Laura had found herself as a designer.

But she worried about the salability of her product. Once she learned from Tim that her dresses would cost the average woman a certain financial sacrifice, she wondered if such a woman would consider the expense justified. After all, her designs were more than a little eccentric, compared to the clothes currently available in stores. Women might not know how to use them.

A woman might hesitate to buy a Laura outfit for everyday wear, because it would look a bit too smart, a bit too special. And she might not choose it for an evening out, because it would lack the classic, standard lines of the Dior and Schiaparelli formals. The essence of the Laura look was that it combined elegance with naturalness, dignity with informality.

Tim did not share Laura's worries.

"What you have to realize," he said, "is that you have created a completely new look. Naturally it looks unsalable to you now. That's because there's nothing like it in the marketplace. But the day will come, Laura, when women will pooh-pooh all the *other* looks in fashion, because Laura will be the style-setter. Believe me, there's nothing unsalable about your work. You have Mrs. Kozlowski and all her friends to prove to you that it's wearable, that it's beautiful. Now it's up to us to convince the fashion retailers of the same thing."

For nearly three months Laura worked on her new designs. When Tim and she felt they were ready to go public, he boldly made arrangements for her to hold a show of her own for a select group of New York retailers and fashion writers. Laura found models through various agencies to suit her designs. She also located some nonprofessional girls, very beautiful but with unusual figures, to demonstrate the adaptability of her outfits to less standard sizes.

Out of the hundreds of designs that had come to life on her sketch pad since the beginning of her project, Laura chose those with the most eye-catching lines. At Tim's urging she did not shrink from the originality of her concepts, but brought it out dramatically. If her work must be shown for better or worse to a jaded assemblage of fashion experts, there was no point in attenuating its best qualities. It must speak for itself.

In the weeks before the show the excitement rose at the shop. Engraved invitations were sent to the writers and retail buyers Tim had targeted. The show would be held in a salon at the St. Regis.

March 14 was the great day. Laura herself wore one of her most beautiful designs to the show. Meredith, also wearing a Laura dress, acted as mistress of ceremonies and commentator on the designs. As Tim had predicted, the show was well attended, for none of the retailers wanted to be scooped by a competitor on a potentially lucrative discovery, and none of the important fashion writers wanted to miss what could well be a big story.

But now Laura's worst fear came true.

No one attacked her clothes. No one laughed at them. No one walked out on them.

But no one showed any interest in them, either.

The audience was polite and attentive as the outfits were shown. Meredith described the unique features of the various dresses, and explained the revolutionary sizing procedure that would allow them to be mass-produced in various sizes with small but telling design changes.

When the show was over, the audience left without a word. The next day the fashion press behaved as though the show had never taken place. The only published account of it was an enigmatic little item by a friendly reporter from *Women's Wear Daily* named Sally Giroux.

"Yesterday," the item read, "fashion writers and buyers saw the new line of clothes by Laura Blake, whose shop in Manhattan has been making an impression recently. Miss Blake's designs are interesting, unusual, and worth a look." The item included the address of the shop.

That was all. The fashion world had turned a polite cold shoulder to Laura's work.

Tim was furious at himself and at the fashion establishment. "I'm only sorry I exposed you to this," he said. "It was my fault. I didn't prepare the ground adequately. I ought to know better than anyone else how hostile the fashion big-shots are to new talent. I just didn't think they could be so stupid as to pass up a sure thing." He banged his fist on the office table in his frustration. "I ought to kick myself around the block. I may have set you back years by this premature exposure, Laura. I'll never forgive myself."

But he was surprised to see that Laura was apparently undaunted by what had happened.

"It was good experience," she said. "I think it was worth it, Tim. And don't worry—we'll make it somehow."

Tim looked at her curiously. He could not understand how she could be so impervious to the humiliation of seeing her finest inspiration ignored by the whole New York fashion coterie. Indeed, she was composed and smiling.

What Tim did not realize was that underneath her calm Laura already had a new idea.

XV

AMONG THE MODELS Laura had hired for the show, her personal favorite was a lovely all-American girl named Penny Heyward, whose sparkling personality had made a hit with everyone who worked with her.

Penny had a beautiful figure, but was a bit too short for high-fashion work, and her rather small brown eyes were deemed unsuitable for photo layouts in the major glossy magazines. But in person she was a magnificent mannequin with perfect naturalness of movement and a sharp instinct for making clothes look good.

During preparations for the show Penny, who had a streak of devil-may-care bravado in her, had tried an impromptu experiment with one of Laura's outfits.

"I was meeting a date at the Plaza," she told Laura, "and I couldn't resist borrowing one of your dresses. But you'll forgive me when I tell you what happened! A couple of ladies came up to me and asked me where I got my outfit. Well, since this was the Plaza and they looked well heeled, I took it into my head to play a little game with them. I acted rich, and told them I hadn't bought anything from anybody but Mainbocher in years, but that a friend had told me about this new designer named Laura.

" 'She's got this funny little shop on Fourteenth Street,' I said. 'I had my driver take me down there, just as a lark. But when I went in and looked around I couldn't believe my eyes. That young woman is a genius. Not only does she have an inimitable style, but she managed to fit me in a way no one ever has before. Well, I haven't bought a thing anywhere else since.' "

Penny laughed, adding that she had made the ladies promise to keep her secret, because she didn't want Laura's operation to become too well known among her high society friends.

As it turned out, those very women had since become eager customers, and had brought some of their friends to Laura as well, despite Penny's tongue-in-cheek injunction to secrecy. What Penny had unwittingly accomplished gave Laura an idea, and now she decided to act on it.

She assembled the models from her show whose figures were the closest to those of most average women, and created a new outfit for each one, using the best of her talent to tailor the design to the girl's coloring and posture as well as her personality.

When the outfits were done Laura sent the girls to locations all over Manhattan. But she went a step further than Penny's initial foray at the Plaza. She sent her girls straight to the source of wealthy women's patronage: the fashion retailers and salons on Fifth Avenue, and the most chic dress shops around Manhattan.

Each of the girls was instructed to enter the establishment in question as a simple customer, and to hang around the premises until a stranger noticed her dress and asked where she got it. Mimicking Penny's approach, each girl would tell about her fortuitous discovery of the brilliant young designer, Laura Blake, and how she now bought her clothes only from Laura.

Laura sent out her little army of insurgents and waited for the results. She did not have to wait long. Hundreds of new customers from all over the Upper East Side and the wealthiest suburbs began to appear at the shop, eager to patronize Laura for her unusual designs as well as her now-legendary ability to tailor her "look" to the figure of the ordinary woman.

Laura showed them her line of clothes, and was amazed to see them fall upon the dresses and ensembles like birds of prey, expressing delight and astonishment at how modest her prices were. For these wealthy women were very cost-conscious underneath their glitter.

When Tim heard what Laura had done he quickly jumped on the bandwagon with ideas of his own. A meeting was held with Meredith and the models, and a new dimension was added to the operation. "Laura's mob," as the models were now called, now went beyond the retailing locations for women's clothes. They went directly to fashion shows around the city. And as they sat in the audience, apparently shopping for the works of other designers, their own outfits attracted attention, and they spread the word about Laura, Ltd.

This brought more customers than ever. The models now went farther afield. They began to haunt fur shops, jewelers like Tiffany and Cartier, restaurants like "21" and the Russian Tea Room. They went to galleries, to benefits, to country clubs, to galas. Wherever rich and style-conscious women were to be found, Laura's models attracted attention and sent customers to the Fourteenth Street shop.

By summer the results were amazing. Laura's loft full of seamstresses could no longer handle the demand for her clothes. She contracted the burgeoning ready-to-wear part of her business to Millie Edelman on Seventh Avenue, and reserved her seamstresses for original garments. Tim managed to rent an adjacent storefront to double the size of her showroom, and Laura hired three new saleswomen, experts in female apparel, to assist Meredith in running the shop.

By the time the fall season arrived, the "Laura look" was an underground but very real part of the New York fashion scene. It could be seen in disparate and unlikely places: on a modest housewife out shopping with her children in midtown, and on a fashionable Scarsdale matron shopping on Fifth Avenue; on a schoolteacher in the Bronx, or on an elegant member of the Junior League; on a suburban housewife on her night out, or on a banker's wife at the Metropolitan Opera.

These women were at opposite ends of the financial and social scale. But they had one thing in common. Their figures were those of the everyday woman whose less than perfect shape made it impossible for her to look good in the latest Dior gown. But they all looked marvelous in Laura's clothes—clothes that not only fit them perfectly, but brought out something hitherto unseen about their bodies, something no designer had been able to capture until now.

"The 'Laura look,' " as one thoughtful fashion writer was to describe it much later, "*celebrates the human side of womanhood. The Laura woman wants more than to merely pose before the male like a member of a harem. She wants to be his lover, his companion, his equal, and to merit his sexual admiration even after having had his children. There is a gentleness about this look that is also earthy and sensual; a smiling, musical elegance that commands respect, but also a sexiness too subtle to be put into words.*"

Women fell in love with Laura's clothes. When dressed in them they felt truly feminine—free, attractive, proud to be what they were—and not like poor misshapen versions of an ideal form that had been mismade for 99 percent of the female sex, and came out right for only a handful of leggy models adored by fashion photographers and Paris designers.

Laura's shop was crowded with customers, despite its doubled size. And now, to her satisfaction, she began to receive visits from the very same buyers for major retailers who had been so indifferent to her show. These women, alerted by their bosses to the appearance of something important on the fashion scene, gave Laura's clothes a second look, and were fascinated.

But the minute they understood the sizing problem of Laura's line, and the impossibility of mass-producing the same outfit in all sizes by simply grading the same design up or down, their interest dropped off. They were convinced their large retail employers would not hear of such an idea. It would be too expensive to produce, and too great a marketing risk.

With this negative attitude in mind they decided that, after all, Laura's designs were a little too strange for their taste, a little too far from the fashion mainstream to merit their serious attention. True, they had to admit that many women loved the clothes, and were loyal customers to Laura. But it was a fad, they decided, shared by a few trendy society women, a fad that would die away before long.

Thus Laura's message was ignored by the retailing establishment. But it was carried by a growing number of delighted proselytes to all the corners of the social world. Each day more and more women talked about her and her clothes. Once women's eyes had been opened to the "Laura look," they could not seem to get it out of their minds.

Tim Riordan surveyed this situation with combined admiration and frustration. Laura's work was like a rocket on a launchpad, ready to explode to the far corners of the world, but lacking only the spark to set it off. The national public was ready for her designs, and could afford them. But the middleman—the big retailer—was not there.

Laura would remain a popular but well-kept secret—unless a big break came along soon.

XVI

October 27, 1954

DIANA STALLWORTH stood before the mirror.

She was in her dressing room at home, putting the finishing touches on the evening gown she would be wearing tonight to the ball at the Sherry Netherland.

The ball was being given by the International Committee of the League of Women Voters in honor of the French ambassador. The Mayor would be on hand, as well as several state senators and a great number of people from the U.N. Diana was an active member of the Committee—she had joined it when Hal was named envoy to NATO by President Eisenhower—and would be highly visible tonight. A portrait photographer was to take her picture with the ambassador this afternoon, and the fashion and society press would certainly be on hand at the ball.

In keeping with the Gallic flavor of the evening she had commissioned this formal gown from Jacques Fath. It was a brilliant floor-length strapless design in white silk taffeta. The accessories, including an emerald and diamond tiara, an emerald bracelet and matching earrings, had been designed by Leila Coffey especially for this occasion. The entire ensemble was tailored to bring out Diana's statuesque beauty as dramatically as possible, for she was to represent the solidarity of American society women with the postwar European alliance.

Alongside her was Joy Arendt, her personal make-up girl, who had just finished applying enough color to Diana's naturally golden cheeks to complement the white of her dress.

"How do I look?" Diana asked.

"Sensational," Joy replied, touching at Diana's hair with a small round brush. "I think you're going to be great."

"I hope so."

Diana could not deny that the image in the mirror seemed faultless. Her constant exercise, including riding, swimming, tennis, and golf, seemed to be paying off, along with the elaborate care of her complexion that she entrusted to a skin specialist recommended by friends. She looked youthful, vibrant, and restrainedly sensual.

Nevertheless the woman in the reflection worried her. Granted, she was perfect for a formal gala at the Sherry Netherland, surrounded by dignitaries in black tie and tails. But was she perfect for Hal?

Diana thought she looked too sleek, too studied, too unnatural. Her figure was so ideal for designer clothes that she might have been a professional model had she wished. But she could not get rid of the feeling that she did not look quite like a woman. And, polite as Hal always was in his many compliments on her appearance, she suspected that she left him cold. Despite herself she felt glad that he was in Paris tonight, and would not see her on display among all those strangers.

She sighed as Joy patted at an errant strand of her hair. "I'm really not happy with the way I've been looking lately," she complained.

"What's not to like?" Joy asked in her direct way. "For heaven's sake, Diana. You're America's sweetheart, you've got the most perfect body in the city and the most perfect man to go with it—not to mention a couple of hundred million dollars in the bank to buy bobby pins with. How can you complain?"

Diana frowned. "I can't explain it," she said. "I just don't feel natural anymore. I buy clothes from fabulous people, and they do make me look good, but I just don't feel—well, me enough."

Most of Diana's clothes came from Paris designers like Fath and Trigère, Dior and Balenciaga, and recently the young Givenchy. She always looked perfect, and was considered a trendsetter by everyone who was anyone. But her sleek blonde image was a stereotyped one. She seemed unable to put her finger on anything truly individual about herself when she looked in the mirror.

"Diana, don't be silly," Joy said, concentrating more on her work than on the complaints of her privileged model. "You is you. You're perfect."

"I'm serious," Diana said. "There's something unreal about me—at least in all these fancy outfits and photo layouts. I just don't seem to belong to myself anymore. Maybe I need to come down to earth."

"You know . . . oh, never mind," Joy said suddenly.

"What?" Diana asked.

"Well, this is pretty far out of the mainstream," Joy said, touching up one of Diana's eyebrows. "But I've been hearing about a new designer. Totally underground, you understand. You can't mention her name at any of the major dress shops and get anybody to say they've heard of her. But a lot of women I know have mentioned her name to me. Apparently she does something rather unusual. Different from high-fashion stuff, but pretty special in its way. They say she can fit you perfectly, no matter what your size, and bring out things in you that you didn't even known were there. I have clients who swear by her."

Intrigued, Diana asked, "What's her name?"

"Let me think. Laura . . . Laura . . . I can't think of her last name. But I don't think she uses one. Her place is called Laura, Ltd. It's down in the Village somewhere. You might pay her a visit."

"I'll think about it."

Diana was pensive. The image looking out at her from the mirror, beautiful as it was, had lost all interest for her. And she could not help suspecting that it had lost all interest for Hal as well. Could there be something inside her that a new eye might bring out? Well, she certainly had nothing to lose by finding out.

Laura . . .

XVII

Vogue, January 15, 1955

MEET DIANA STALLWORTH.

If you don't yet know who this supremely poised and beautiful young woman is, then you must have had your head in the sand for the last twenty-four years. For practically from her birth Diana has been a celebrity.

The daughter of Harry M. Stallworth and the former Zelda Gaines, Diana enjoyed a brilliant career at The Regina Colbert School in Geneva and at Smith, and was the undisputed belle of the 1948 season, her debut at the Grosvenor Ball causing a virtual sensation in society.

Now a brilliant, multi-talented college graduate, Diana is also the intended bride of Haydon Lancaster, authentic American Hero (with Congressional Medal of Honor to prove it) and by unanimous consent the most eligible young heartthrob to emerge on the social scene in several generations.

At twenty-four Diana is already a legend in her own time. While her ever-loving Hal continues his work as a special envoy to the NATO countries for President Eisenhower, Diana is working overtime for a variety of charitable causes and writing a series of articles for the *Times* on society in the new age.

Diana has appeared more than once in these pages, wearing gowns by such masters as Dior, Balenciaga, and Schiaparelli. But this month she brings us a surprise. Always an intrepid trendsetter whose iconoclastic nature has made her indifferent to the *qu'en dira-t-on* of high society, Diana has discovered a new designer who has supplanted the great Paris names in her heart.

The prodigy's name is Laura Blake, and until now her work has been a well-kept secret among a handful of forward-looking women that includes some of the best-known names in society.

But not until Diana discovered Miss Blake and lent her own name and exquisite style to her fashions did the brilliant young designer's career begin to sizzle. Already Laura is much in demand, and from here on out her star can only rise.

On page 124 we see Diana in a startling Laura sport ensemble including burgundy wool slacks with matching jacket, cream silk blouse, shoes by Eliade and purse by Ruyer. On page 125 Diana wears a stunning Laura evening gown in peach silk organza with necklace by Zita Villiers. On page 126 Diana sports a midcalf spring coat in beige tweed with fur cuffs and collar, over a skirt-and-blouse ensemble in a light green wool jersey. (Photographs by Cecil Beaton.)

We think our readers will agree that the so-far self-effacing Laura Blake as discovered by Diana Stallworth is someone very special, and destined for a fame to match that of her stellar model.

DIANA LEFT THE MAGAZINE open in her lap and sat looking out the window at Fifth Avenue.

The *Vogue* editorial spread on Laura filled Diana with personal pride, not only because it was she who had been instrumental in bringing Laura to the attention of a wider public, but because the clothes displayed on these pages made her look like a new woman.

Diana had considered her first excursion to the little salon on Fourteenth Street as a lark. Though the dresses in the window were indeed clever and attractive, she had been prepared to believe that Laura, Ltd., was merely a fad fostered by a handful of restless society women.

But when she met Laura all that changed. Not only was Laura an incredible talent—as she proved within half an hour, taking Diana's measurements and sketching half a dozen outfits for her that practically leapt off the page from pure inspiration. Laura was also a marvelous person. She was quite unruffled by Diana's initially snobbish behavior and name-dropping about the Paris designers she normally patronized. Almost immediately she penetrated through the nervousness behind Diana's demeanor and put her at her ease.

By the end of that first visit they were friends. Laura was a person of such sweetness and natural dignity that she was impossible to resist. She was charmingly unaffected and humble about her talent, concerning herself only with the needs of her client. There was not a hint of the fashion *prima donna* about her, as there was in the other designers of Diana's acquaintance.

And when Diana at last tried on the three outfits Laura created for her in the month after that initial visit, she was utterly convinced she had found her ideal designer at last. All three were creations of surpassing beauty that made a compelling statement about Diana's personality. They were more like works of art than mere clothes.

Laura was able somehow to cut away the cold, statuesque image of Diana that other designers cultivated, and to let her inner vulnerability show through. The dresses made her look like a young woman with feelings, with hopes, with strengths and weaknesses, rather than a spoiled, narcissistic rich girl. And all this Laura accomplished in so flattering a way that Diana could hardly look at herself in the outfits without bursting into tears of gratitude. For the first time in her memory Diana could look in the mirror and feel human without at the same time feeling ashamed.

Diana resolved to support Laura with all her powers. She was proud of her role as a style-setter among society women, and she felt she was the ideal person to launch Laura in the most impressive possible way.

She took those first three outfits straight to *Vogue,* and showed them to the fashion editors. To her surprise they seemed unconvinced, and reminded her that only the most established of designers merited an editorial layout in the magazine. Somewhat condescendingly, they offered to accept an advertisement for Laura, Ltd., provided it was paid for.

Diana bristled at this resistance. She reminded the editors of the many stories and layouts the magazine had done on her in the past. Even more compellingly, she reminded them of the stories that would surely appear on her in the future, as her engagement and marriage to Hal Lancaster became a reality. She let them know in no uncertain terms that, if sufficiently displeased with *Vogue,* she could just as easily grant *Bazaar* the exclusive right to document her future with Hal.

The fear of losing "America's sweethearts" to their magazine's archrival convinced the editors. They agreed to do a ground-breaking editorial layout on the clothes of Laura Blake, modeled by the beautiful Diana Stallworth.

And here it was. The layout was stunning. Not only did it show off Laura's genius as a designer. It also revealed the unsuspected, hitherto invisible Diana that Laura had managed to bring out. This was a new Diana, and without question a better one.

Diana had seldom felt so proud of anything she had done. And the benefits went deeper than the glossy surface of the magazine. Diana was thrilled to have been able to help someone as deserving as Laura. But she was sure she had helped herself at the same time.

This afternoon she would send a copy of the magazine to Hal in Paris. The next time he came home she would greet him in clothes Laura was currently designing for her. Now that she had met Laura, and felt so much better about herself, she could face him more bravely. She was in high hopes that her days as a tense and terrified companion to handsome Hal might at last be coming to their end.

Thanks to Laura Blake, Diana was beginning to feel like a woman.

XVIII

January 22, 1955

WINTHROP ALLIS BOND IV was, at age sixty-four, a quietly contented man.

He was Board Chairman of W. W. Bond, the third largest conglomerate based in the United States, and one of the ten largest corporations in the world. As scion of a fortune that had begun accumulating in the railroad economy of the nineteenth century and grown exponentially along with America itself, Winthrop Bond was now one of the richest men in the world.

His work kept him busy. By the time he inherited the company it had already grown from a railroad-and-mining concern into an octopus-like monster with involvements in every far-flung corner of industry, technology, communications, and high finance. Two world wars had completed the process, and W. W. Bond today was a virtual clearing-house for the materials and money that made American business function.

Oddly enough, Winthrop Bond—or Win, as his family and friends called him—was not a businessman at heart. He had never been the mover and shaker behind his company's tumultuous growth. He had inherited his father's position, but not his piratical wheeler-dealer personality. That trait seemed to skip the generations somehow.

The original Winthrop Bond, Win's great-grandfather, had built the business from a shoestring chain of heavily mortgaged firms into a great robber baron dynasty. But grandfather Winthrop II had merely acted as a somewhat feckless steward of the hestitating empire until his son,

Winthrop III, took over as a hungry twenty-year-old fresh out of Yale and increased the size of the corporation by ten times in as many years.

For three decades Winthrop III held sway at the helm, terrorizing his meek family as much as his competition. Then he was carried off by a heart attack—a congenital Bond weakness no doubt hastened by his apoplectic life-style—and the company was left to Winthrop IV.

By then W. W. Bond was a monster almost too big to stop in its growth. Win Bond, born with an essentially conservative personality and a fear of needless risk, managed to keep that growth to reasonable proportions, and along financially secure paths. Thanks to his caution and concern for sound fiscal management, the corporation survived the Great Depression without a false step, and went on to infiltrate the international centers of financial power that led the world into and out of World War II.

During his long career Win had avoided great originality and great foolishness at the same time. As a consequence his company kept a middle-of-the-road profile, and set a standard for earnings and productivity that few competitors could match.

Win could perhaps have done better. He knew that. W. W. Bond might have become, in more aggressive hands, the largest corporation on the planet. But as things stood it was one of the most respected. Win had by no means done poorly.

Win himself retained 26 percent of the company's stock. His personal fortune exceeded three hundred fifty million dollars. He had lived like a king, literally, all his life—that is, surrounded by priceless accoutrements, worried advisors, ringing telephones, and responsibilities both ceremonial and real.

And, like a king, he had been lonely. Close, trusted friends do not come with great power. The man who inherits an exalted position must keep his own counsel. This way of life did not suit Win, who was by nature a tender man rather than a brave one, born to love and be loved, and to shun the cruelties of life.

But Win had possessed sufficient understanding of who and what he was to make a place for himself in his world. He did it by shrinking into one of its blandest and tiniest corners for his private life. His wife Eileen —heiress to the Colston fertilizer and chemical fortune, who had married her family's wealth to W. W. Bond while taking gentle Win to her heart—was his helpmate in this process.

Together they occupied a single floor of the Madison Avenue mansion, where they made themselves a little apartment. Eileen loved to cook, and Win learned to help her with salads and homemade casseroles in the kitchen they had installed upstairs. Visiting their Newport and Bar Harbor homes only on rare vacations for the children's sake, the couple lived quietly in their little digs, sitting by the radio at night, Win reading the financial news or a Western novel while his wife knitted him sweaters and socks.

Their only real "home away from home" was a house Win had built on a cliffside on the deserted Napili coast of the island of Maui. Two or three times a year he would retreat there with his wife for a couple of weeks of tropical languor. The Hawaiian balm of sea, sand, and lush vegetation seemed to bring out the carefree beachcomber in Win, and in that exotic setting, so far from the steel canyons of Manhattan, he felt closer to Eileen than ever.

Win did not consider himself a terribly original or gifted man. He took his few pleasures in a good game of golf, a bit of sailing on his yacht—he was not a strong swimmer, and would never have risked piloting a sailboat on his own—and evenings over backgammon with Eileen.

His only passionate interest was Impressionist painting. The Bonds had been patrons of Renoir and Monet when the painters were still alive, thanks to Win's grandmother Hannah. The family collection included some of their most important works, as well as masterpieces by Degas, Pissarro, and the incomparable Manet.

As a boy Win had fallen in love with those glimmering canvases as he ran along the halls of the Madison Avenue house. The iridescent landscapes filled him with feelings of peace and security, and the Renoir women, so pink and fluffy, reminded him of his mother and grandmother.

When he grew up he took an active interest in acquiring more of them. They were slowly gaining in value in the twenties and thirties, as their importance made itself felt—but to a man with Win Bond's checkbook they were a steal. Win bought Renoirs at $15,000, Monet fields and lilies at $20,000, Degas dancers for $7,500, Manet portraits for hardly more.

Painting was Win's joy and his passion. Today the Bond Collection of Impressionist works was valued at nearly seventy million dollars, and getting richer every day as the works of the French masters took the art world by storm.

Win surrounded himself with the paintings, gratefully closing the drapes on the Manhattan skyline and watching the tiny lamps illuminate the Renoir ladies on the walls of his study. He would sit here for long hours after dinner, feeling the old yearnings of his youth stir to fragile life in the glowing sunlit colors, savoring the security he had once taken for granted in the eternal quiet smiles of the women in their white dresses.

For Win was alone now. Eileen, his only real companion in the world, had died of cancer seven years ago after a long battle with the disease. The ordeal of losing her had left Win a drained man. He had no energy left for anything now except Bond board meetings, reading his novels, and quiet contemplation.

His two children, son Winthrop V (called Tony to avoid the ridiculous confusion of having so many Winthrops in the family) and daughter Gay, had never been terribly close to either parent. They had passed through Win's life like ghosts, making little impression on him despite his worries over a thousand skinned knees, broken ankles, school competitions, piano recitals, tears over boyfriends, fights over late-night dates. Today Tony was a board member and secretary to the Executive Committee, and Gay had married into the Conway merchandising family.

Win had really felt alone with Eileen all along. And when she died, he was left with nothing he valued. He saw the remainder of his life as a gradual lessening of work responsibilities as Tony grew more confident; more absorption in his art collection and its management; and more months each year spent at Napili, where the ceaseless rolling waves reminded him of Eileen and of his cherished, broken dream of spending his old age with her.

He had had a small heart attack three years ago, not serious enough to cramp his life-style. But his doctors had warned him to start taking things easy. They could not know how he welcomed this advice.

Of course, Win was only sixty-four. The family teased him about being the most eligible widower on the American continent, and his fellow clubmen in New York were always muttering jokes about his lucky bachelorhood and the wild times he ought to be having. But his friends had long since given up on introducing him to available women. Everyone could see that he was not getting over Eileen, that he was too old and tired for the exertions of romance, and interested only in solitude and reminiscence.

His grandchildren were a welcome distraction when they came to Napili, which was not often, since the trip was an arduous and time-consuming one. Win remembered their birthdays, and telephoned them long-distance, but did not trouble to make the flights necessary to hold them in his arms, mostly because he did not very much like his own children or their spouses, who were bored with him anyway.

Though contented enough, Win realized he was surviving not only poor Eileen, but himself as well. He was a man who needed to be put out to pasture, but he did not have the heart to leave W. W. Bond to other hands quite yet. His sense of responsibility to his dead father and grandfather would not let him throw off the harness.

But he lived at a safe emotional distance from real life. Inside himself, he was preparing for a quiet end that would not be unwelcome when it came. He existed only for the past which cradled his imagination. There he felt at home, and there he would remain.

Unless something revived him.

The party was a large one.

It was being given at the Republican Club on Sixty-third Street for members of the Association of American Business Leaders, an organization of businessmen whose assets were large and whose charitable contributions were managed as a group.

The whole thing produced some marvelous tax deductions, and was good for everyone. But it necessitated this yearly to-do, in which dozens of corporate leaders with bad manners and loud voices were flung at close quarters with men like Win, whose old money and patrician temperament made the proximity of such hungry sharks an ordeal.

The meeting itself had been deadly. The agenda had been long, involving trusts, endowments, and other means of feathering good relations with the IRS. The membership was restless, for the board chairmen and executives present would much rather be out stealing the public's money than giving it back. The party afterward was dull and smoke-filled, with canapés, champagne, and empty conversation.

Winthrop Bond had shaken as many hands as he could stand before retreating to the eighth-floor library, where he now sat in his favorite armchair staring out the window and fighting the somnolence that was stealing over him in waves. He was drinking a cup of tea—he no longer touched cocktails, for all they accomplished was to give him an upset stomach and insomnia—and he was not at all embarrassed at being ignored by his fellow philanthropists, whose conversation and laughter was a faint murmur from downstairs.

His eyes were half-closing for a delicious forty winks when he suddenly saw two small hands appear from behind the high-backed leather couch facing the fireplace. Pointing straight up, they were a woman's hands, clenched as though to stretch in a yawn after sleep. The creamy skin of slender forearms was a bright glow under the dim reading lamps.

Intrigued, Win opened his eyes wider. He heard a soft sigh, and a little musical hum of awakening. Then he heard the creak of old leather.

Two stockinged feet appeared, dangling off the end of the sofa, and bounced up and down rather gaily. The hands disappeared, and in their place came a mane of lush red hair, rising up from behind the couch like something improbable and childlike.

"Mmm," came a purring yawn as the hands stretched once again. Then, all at once, a young woman stood facing the fireplace, stretching her limbs quite unselfconsciously, and took in a deep breath of air.

Her hair was a bit tousled from her sleep, but all the more beautiful for that. The business skirt and jacket she was wearing looked far too conservative for her catlike body, which was tall and supple. She looked so girlish, so completely charged by youth and happiness, that she actually lit up the musty old room.

She tossed her head to shake the hair from her eyes, and turned toward the windows. She was reaching to insert a bobby pin behind her ear when she saw Winthrop Bond gazing at her from his seat.

"Oh, I'm sorry," she said. "I didn't realize anyone was up here. I just came in to rest a while ago, and the next thing I knew I was dead to the world. I hope I didn't snore or anything . . . ?"

Win returned her smile, and shook his head to reassure her, but said nothing. He was not used to talking to strangers. And indeed, he had not seen a female in this room in his thirty years as a club member.

She was looking down at her suit, which was rumpled from her sleep. "I don't look very presentable, do I?" she said. "I'm quite a sleeper. I can drift off in the middle of Grand Central, if you give me half the chance. I don't suppose you know what time it is?"

Win looked at his watch. "Nine forty-five," he said.

"Oh, my God," she said, touching a finger to her lips. "Is it that late? I was supposed to have called the hotel by nine . . ." She shrugged, smiling at him. "That's another of my faults. I can't keep track of time. It just seems to pass me by."

She knelt down to get her shoes. As she did so the magnificent waves of red hair fell forward, like the mane of an amazon, reminding Win of his favorite Renoir models.

Or was it the prettiest of Degas' dancers she incarnated as she bent to pick up the shoes? She had a dancer's body, with fine shoulders, long limbs, a healthy upthrust back, and pretty rounded breasts under her blouse and jacket.

Her natural grace charmed him because it was so young and fresh. Of course, she was far from penetrating to the withered outposts of his aged libido. He looked at her the way a pensioner admires a schoolgirl playing with a stick and a hoop in the park—sensuality no more than the vaguest shadow behind her bright skin, the piquant tinge of autumn leaves under her feet, or the caressing shadows of tree limbs on her freckled cheeks.

She sat down on a huge leather hassock to put the shoes on.

"Excuse me," she said, "for getting dressed in front of you. I guess I really shouldn't be up here."

Win smiled. "I won't tell a soul," he said, managing a bit of humor.

"I probably should have just gone back to the hotel," she said. "I don't know why, but these meetings knock me out so completely . . ."

Win nodded, charmed by her candor. "That's why I hide out in here," he said. "Of course, I'm no longer young, like you. But no one likes an evening with the Association of American Business Leaders. It's downright unnatural."

Apparently put at ease by his words, she moved toward him, straightening her skirt, and sat down on the arm of the chair opposite his. She was looking at his tea.

"Gee," she said. "That looks good. I never would have thought of it in a million years, but a cup of tea would sure pick me up right now."

"Let me get you one," he said, touching the bell pull beside the reading lamp.

"That's awfully nice of you," she smiled, easing into the depths of the armchair and letting her pretty legs extend straight in front of her as she sighed and stretched once more.

"Earl Grey, like mine?" he asked as a silent waiter came from the doorway.

"Sounds wonderful," she said. He signed to the servant, who faded away as impalpably as he had appeared.

She held out a hand.

"My name's Liz," she said. "Liz Benedict. I'm with Rainbow Concepts, from Phoenix. I was sort of sent as our emissary to the meeting, because Mr. Buhl hurt his back playing golf—whoops! I don't think I was supposed to reveal that—and couldn't come."

She opened her purse and fumbled in it for a moment. Then she blushed.

"I was going to give you my card," she said. "But I seem to have misplaced them. Everywhere I go I meet people I *know* I should give my card to, and I've always forgotten the darned things."

"That's all right," Win smiled. "I know Rainbow Concepts. In fact, if this old memory serves, I think I recall Harris Buhl, too."

"Really?" Her eyes lit up.

He nodded. "I've played golf with him, both here and out west. No wonder he hurt his back. He tries to hit the ball too hard. But he's a nice enough fellow."

Her face was charmingly torn between a smile of recognition and a grimace of embarrassment. "You won't judge our company by me, will you?" she said. "I mean, I'm not much of a representative, but Mr. Buhl is really a wonderful man. He's been awfully kind to me, and he's a terrific boss."

"Yes, Harris is a fine executive," Win agreed. Then his brow furrowed. "I hope you won't think me rude if I tell you a rather embarrassing secret."

"A secret?" she asked.

He nodded. "Now, don't be alarmed," he said. "But the fact is that I own your company."

Her sharp intake of breath told him he had really shocked her.

"Rainbow is a subsidiary of T.C.L.," he said, "which is in turn a division of Continental Industries—which, as you climb up the octopus's tentacles, belongs to W. W. Bond."

Her eyes were open wide. She shrunk back into the chair as though frightened.

"You're not Mr. Bond, are you?" she asked.

He nodded.

There was a silence as the waiter placed her tea on the mahogany table. Then she let out the breath she had been holding, with a soft and perfectly endearing "Holy cow."

He held out a hand. "Winthrop Bond," he said. "The fourth. Don't get me confused with Number Three, who was the real brains of our company, or Number Five, who is my son, and probably destined to take over before long and do a much better job than I have."

She was blushing, and looked genuinely worried.

"You won't hate our company because of me, will you?" she asked. "I really didn't mean to fall asleep that way. I'm not in the habit of running into Bonds and Rockefellers and Gettys at parties. I ought to make myself more presentable."

"Nonsense," Winthrop Bond said, making bold to pour her tea for her. "You're the most presentable person here, if I say so myself."

"You're too nice," she said, pouring a little cream into her cup. "I'm a good account executive—I really am—but I'm just not polished enough, I guess, for the social side of business. I always end up looking like a mess . . ."

How false her words rang, now that she was sitting close to him! There was a sweetness to her bearing that fascinated and touched him. And, behind the candor of her sparkling green eyes, there was a hint of melancholy which only added to her attractiveness.

She was hopelessly, witheringly beautiful, but she seemed not to realize it at all. And her girlish, abashed quality had an elegance all its own.

"Miss—Benedict, did you say?" he began.

"Mrs. I'm a widow. Louis—my husband—died three years ago." She paused. "But call me Liz. Please. Or, if you like," she added on an impulse, "you can call me what my aunts used to—Lisa. I like that better."

She sighed. "At Rainbow it's always Liz this, Liz that . . . I get so sick of it. When I hear the name Liz, I always think of this very efficient woman with a clipboard, who's got everything under control all the time. When I think of me, I think of—well, of a sort of klutz who knows how to have a good time, but who doesn't have much under control."

Win leaned forward. "And what is a good time for you?"

She smiled suddenly. Her look was secretive and a bit embarrassed.

"Well, you'll have to promise you won't tell anyone," she said.

He held up a palm. "Scout's honor."

"My very favorite thing in the world," she said confidentially, "is to go to the circus. I go every time the circus is in town. Alone. Just me. Oh, if I had nieces and nephews, or children of my own, I'd take them, of course. But I don't, so I just go alone. I eat popcorn and cotton candy, and have a wonderful time. Nobody ever notices me, because the circus is so crowded. But that's what I do."

She sat back, looking at him with her curious mixture of diffidence and elfin humor.

He had raised an eyebrow. "That's a very unusual pastime," he said. "I haven't been to the circus in—well, in longer than I'd care to remember. I hate to say it, but I don't think I even took my own children. I let their mother take them. It must be—well, more than fifty years."

He paused ruefully, then looked into her green eyes. "Tell me, though: Why do you like the circus?"

She chewed her lip thoughtfully, as though caught by a genuine riddle. "Well, it's hard to say. There's something about how loud it all is. The noise . . . it could drown out every worry in the world. And the clowns . . . and the girls riding horses, with all the glitter on their costumes. The way everybody bows . . . It's all so silly, in a way, and so pretty . . ."

She paused, struggling to find a way to express herself.

"When I was very little," she said, "my father used to take me to the circus back in St. Louis. He died not long after that, so I've never forgotten. There was this one performer. His name was Mr. Constantine. He was an equilibrist. He wore a top hat and tails, and a monocle, and he carried a cane. When he performed, everything was silent—or at least it seemed so to me. It was very grave and serious—you know?"

She looked past Winthrop Bond, her eyes glistening with memory.

"Well, there was this street lamp in the middle of the ring, that was there for Mr. Constantine. The old kind, with a white frosted glass globe at the top. He would climb this street lamp. When he got to the top he would very slowly work himself up to a one-armed handstand on the top of it. That's when I would notice he was wearing white gloves. He would stay balanced up there, with his legs sort of curled behind him, and the tails of his coat dangling down. His shoes were patent leather, and he wore spats."

She sighed. "Everyone seemed to hold their breath until he got back down, and then there was lots of applause. He would nod very politely, and climb the lamppost again with his cane. This time he would balance himself on the end of his cane, with his top hat in his other hand. He was even more scrunched-up, if you know what I mean, in order to keep his balance. Well, now the audience was even more impressed. Then he did the same thing with a chair, balancing himself with one leg of the chair on top of the lamppost. And the finale of the act was when he balanced himself on *one finger* on top of that white globe."

She looked back into Winthrop Bond's eyes.

"For me that was the be-all and end-all," she said. "I thought that was incredible. Not just the skill, you see, but the elegance, the seriousness, the silence of the crowd—and the terrific relief when he would finish and leap down, safe and sound, and doff his top hat."

There was a pause as she lingered over the memory.

"I begged my poor dad to take me back as often as he could," she said, "so I could see Mr. Constantine again. I guess we only went two or three times before my dad died, but it seemed like those nights at the circus went on forever."

She smiled wistfully. "Years went by before I ever went to another circus. And when I did, there was no more Mr. Constantine. There were just the clowns and the elephants and the ladies on their horses with their skimpy sequined outfits. But I still liked it anyway."

She shrugged. "So now I go alone. I've learned to love all the acts, even the ones I didn't much like as a kid, like the trained dogs and the bears. I just love the smiles and the noise, and all the little kids in the audience. If you look at their faces, you can see that they're really, honestly scared when the drums roll just before the performers do a difficult trick. Their eyes get so big . . ."

She laughed a trifle sheepishly at her own candor, and took a sip of the tea before her.

"Tell me, Mr.—Bond the Fourth?" she smiled.

"Call me Win."

"Well . . . Win. Tell me: What's your favorite thing?"

He thought for a moment. He knew he would have to hide the truth, which was that no single thing had as much meaning for him as what she had described. His own emptiness left him in the lurch.

He thought of the paintings, and the memories of Eileen. He thought of breakfast rolls with fine English jams; of evenings sitting alone in his chair with the *Times*, while the fire burned in his study. No, these were not his "favorite" things. They were just the routines of a man who did not live, but watched life pass him by. They were pastimes intended to soothe his way to the grave.

But then he thought of Napili, and managed to find an acceptable lie.

"I have a place in Hawaii," he said. "Napili—on the island of Maui. The water is very gentle on that beach. You can stand with your tiptoes on the bottom, and feel the waves lift you up and set you back down . . . You don't even have to tread water. The other islands are on the horizon, and the water is very blue. It can take your mind off a lot of things."

"I'll bet," she said. "Sounds nice."

There was another pause. Something in their respective thoughts seemed to have brought them closer together, though there were no words with which to express it.

He noticed the hint of melancholy in her lovely eyes, and decided to speak first.

"Is your mother living?" he asked.

She shook her head. "They both died at the same time," she said. "In a fire, in our house in St. Louis. I was in school, and a note was brought to the teacher. She took me to the principal's office. That's where they told me . . ."

The look on her face almost brought a tear to his eye. It seemed a crime to superimpose such bleak despair over features made only for joy and laughter. But she suppressed it quickly, as though afraid to embarrass him, and gave him a smile that was almost free of pain.

Now he understood the sadness he had noticed in her eyes before. It was a real part of her, though she tried to keep it hidden behind her sunny, quirky personality. She was a sensitive person, and a deep one, but she didn't want to advertise the fact. This only made her all the more irresistible.

For Winthrop Bond was already beginning to think of her that way.

"Tell me," he asked. "How did you come to work for Harris Buhl?"

He thought his change of subject would distract her from her grief.

But the story she told now—albeit with a cheerful cynicism meant to blunt its edge—sent a shiver down his spine, and killed the wistful mood her reminiscences about the circus had created.

She had married her first boss, Louis Benedict, when she was right out of college. She had loved his little company, Benedict Products, and was just learning her trade in the electronics business when the company was summarily taken over by American Enterprise, Inc. and Louis Benedict relegated to a ceremonial directorship.

Winthrop Bond knew American Enterprise and companies like it quite well. They lived and grew by swallowing up target firms through cash tender offers made on a tax-sheltered shoestring, and contributed little to the health of American business. He did not need to be told what had become of little Benedict Products once in the grip of the raiding conglomerate.

Lisa Benedict's husband had died of carbon monoxide poisoning in his own garage after hearing the news that the company he had worked a lifetime to build was being summarily dissolved by American Enterprise. His wife, like nearly all the other employees, was fired during the reorganization. She buried him, sold off their home, took a deep breath, and looked for work. She eventually found it in a modest executive capacity with Rainbow Concepts, working for Harris Buhl.

"So here I am," she concluded brightly, full of youthful determination to hide her hurts and press on into the future.

"You didn't—have any children?" Win made bold to ask.

She shook her head with a little apologetic smile. Behind it he could see bottomless regret.

"Louis was such a busy man," she said. "He loved the company so much. And of course we thought we had all the time in the world. I was so young . . . Then the takeover came, and somehow there was no time for anything but worry. Then, just like that, Louis was gone."

Winthrop Bond was pensive. This girl had been through terrible things. His own tragedies seemed like child's play in comparison to the deaths that had orphaned her twice over—for her husband, from the way she spoke of him, seemed like a second father, a kindly man on whom she had depended for protection and guidance.

Against this background, her warmth of character seemed unbearably brave and touching.

"Tell me," he said, fumbling for a more congenial topic, "there must be other things you like besides the circus. After all, one can't go to the circus every day."

She laughed. "You're right about that. Well, let me see . . . I guess walking. I love to walk. I used to walk to work in Sacramento, and I still do now. I go to parks, and walk along the paths; I like to watch children play." She sighed. "I'd love to walk around New York, but everybody keeps telling me it's so dangerous."

"Not at all," Winthrop Bond said, seized by a sudden idea. "New York is a lovely place to walk. You just have to know how to go about it."

He leaned forward, surprised by his own boldness. "Shall I show you?"

Her eyes widened. "You mean now?" she asked. "Tonight?"

He nodded. "Why not? We've both had enough of this party. My circulation could use a boost after sitting in this chair like an old man. And I'm sure you could benefit from some fresh air. What do you say?"

She seemed to hesitate. She must be thinking she did not know him well, and had responsibilities to her boss and to the meeting.

"I'll have you back at your hotel whenever you like," he said. "I know you need your rest for tomorrow." He frowned, looking at his watch. "Of course, it is rather late. If you're tired, I really don't want to keep you up . . ."

Inside himself he was sorry he had said these last words. But it was too late to take them back.

She seemed to ponder for a last time. Then she smiled.

"I'm not tired at all. I'll be happy to come with you."

"That's the spirit." He was on his feet already, extending a hand to help her up. As her fingers curled around his own he felt ten years younger than he had a half an hour ago.

Despite the late hour they took a leisurely walk down Fifth Avenue. Win's chauffeur, a large, dark man with a face ideally suited to frighten off strangers, followed them at a distance of a dozen yards in the 1947 Rolls-Royce that had been Eileen's favorite car.

Excited by the novelty of her escorted stroll, Lisa Benedict chatted with Win about her work and her hopes for the future. In answer to his questions she told him about her childhood in St. Louis and California, her years growing up with relatives, the schools she had attended. Once again he found her account of things so colored by a stubborn optimism that he had to use his imagination to reconstruct how tragic her orphaned and then widowed existence had actually been.

He had made a phone call from the Republican Club before leaving, and now surprised her by taking her to the executive dining room atop the Bond Building in Rockefeller Center for a late snack of cold lobster salad with champagne and caviar. He pointed out landmarks in the skyline outside the large windows as they were served by two uniformed waiters. Awed by her surroundings, Lisa reproached him for going to so much trouble on her behalf. He merely smiled and admired the glow of her lovely face in the candlelight.

It was midnight when he asked her if she wanted to leave. It seemed far too early to let her go, and yet too late to keep her any longer. She nodded reluctantly, and they left the skyscraper through the huge lobby leading to Sixth Avenue.

On the way to her hotel Win felt tongue-tied. A strange sense of urgency and frustration was thrilling through him. He felt as though he had known this lovely girl all her life. To watch her disappear into the St. Regis, never to be seen again, was too cruel a penance to suffer for the pleasure of having spent this magical evening with her.

"And when will you return to Arizona?" he asked at last, a little afraid to hear the answer.

"The day after tomorrow," she said. "We have our own meeting to go through yet, in the New York office. Not much fun, but I have to be there."

"You'll give my best regards to Harris Buhl when you see him, won't you?" he asked. "It's been a long time . . ."

"Of course I will!" she said. "He'll be thrilled. He's spoken of you so often . . ."

"Good . . ."

He was silent for a moment, screwing up his courage behind a wistful smile.

"I wonder," he began, "if you'd be kind enough to do me one more favor as well."

She looked at him pleasantly.

"When your job brings you back to New York," he said, "I hope you'll get in touch with me, and let me know." He laughed nervously. "I could use a more effective liaison with Rainbow and Harris than I've had in the past. I'd love to see you . . ."

The look on her face made it obvious his subterfuge was not fooling her.

"I'm not a very good liar, am I?" he asked sheepishly. "Let me try the truth, then, Lisa. I had an awfully fine time tonight. You know, I haven't been in that dining room outside of business hours since the building was erected. I'd hate to think I couldn't look forward to it again. That sounds selfish, I know. But if you could see your way clear to pay me a visit next time, you'll be giving an old man a great deal of pleasure."

"You're not an old man." The words were spoken seriously, and accompanied by a firm little smile that touched his heart and filled him with a delightful confusion. "And I'd be happy to see you any time. After all," she said, touching his hand, "a girl can't go walking down Fifth Avenue after dark all alone, can she?"

The glow bestowed by her words lasted him all the way to the St. Regis, and saw him through the distress of watching her disappear into the hotel. On the way back home he was torn by mixed feelings, alternating between the excitement of a schoolboy and the shame of an old man who does not know how to act his age.

Once inside his familiar study, with the warm Renoirs on the walls, he felt his mood dip toward depression. The hope of seeing Lisa Benedict again could not alter the fact that she was leaving right away, and would perhaps not return for a long while. She had her own life out west, a life that must surely include young men, plans for the future. Promises or no promises, he would probably never see her again.

Suddenly Win's exile seemed more painful than at any time since Eileen died. He poured himself a stiff cognac despite the lateness of the hour, and prowled the house in his smoking jacket, unable to sit down. He could not bear the idea of letting Lisa slip through his fingers. But he lacked both the pretext and the courage to hold onto her.

At last he sat crestfallen in his easy chair, rolling the warm brandy in its snifter and staring distractedly around the room. The trappings of his privacy looked so forlorn now, and hardly even familiar. The books, the paintings, the old, old furniture . . .

Suddenly his eyes came to rest on today's *Times*, which the butler had left for him in its usual place on the reading table. He picked it up and began turning the pages, as though in search of something that might rescue him.

He had no idea what he was looking for. But before he knew it, the answer appeared before his eyes like magic.

It was an advertisement in the Entertainment section.

See the Greatest Show on Earth!
Only Six Days Left!

With a sigh of relief Winthrop Bond smiled. His decision had been made for him.

The circus was in town.

XIX

March 5, 1955

LAURA WAS ON HER WAY to Diana Stallworth's Fifth Avenue mansion.

She was sitting in the back of a long white limousine sent by Diana to pick her up at the shop. On the seat beside her were boxes containing a half-dozen spring and summer outfits for which Diana had important plans. Diana had refused to let Laura in on these, but the elegance of the designs they had agreed upon gave a good idea of their purpose. There were two formal gowns, two cocktail dresses in priceless Chinese silk, a striking pants outfit for informal entertaining, and a very sensuous pair of lounging pajamas obviously intended for a romantic evening at home.

Taken together, the outfits seemed ideal for the final stage of a beautiful woman's betrothal to the man she loves, from intimate vows to public celebration. Laura could not help guessing that Diana was about to become formally engaged.

Laura had poured a lot of inspiration and hard work into the designs, not only because she owed Diana so much, but because she had grown to like her.

When Diana had first appeared at the shop six months ago Laura had been prepared to endure her as the latest in the line of wealthy, narcissistic women whose somewhat spoiled whims she must gratify in return for their patronage. If anything, Diana was an even greater challenge than the others, for she was more visible than her peers in society, and often modeled Paris creations in *Vogue* and *Harper's Bazaar*. She must be treated with kid gloves at all costs.

Indeed, at first Diana seemed cold and condescending as she looked around the shop and had Laura take her measurements. A regular customer at the finest Paris salons, she could hardly be impressed by Laura's somewhat crowded, informal premises. She sat quietly as Laura did a few preliminary sketches, and made disinterested conversation with the friend she had brought with her.

Oddly enough, Diana's patrician exterior, and even the gossipy snobbery she shared with her friend, did not make Laura dislike her. Laura sensed something worried and breakable behind that high-society armor of Diana's. Her icy cynicism was clearly a front designed to hide her fears about her own femininity. What she seemed to need more than anything else was reassurance.

Laura was glad to provide it, for she was touched to think that so visible and admired a woman could be the victim of private cares. She found a convenient link from this hidden dimension in Diana to her own personality, and allowed it to express itself in the sketches she made.

To Laura's surprise Diana was ecstatic over the drawings, so much so that her society persona gave way to the spontaneity of an excited schoolgirl when she exclaimed about their qualities. The two women immediately moved from discussion of the garments' general lines to questions of fabric, trim, and accessories. Though Diana was a demanding client, and naturally indifferent to the financial cost of anything Laura might make for her, she was disarmingly flexible about her preferences. She seemed to want Laura to follow her own esthetic instincts in creating the outfits.

One would almost have thought Diana wanted Laura's friendship as much as her best work. This was a welcome change from most of Laura's wealthy customers, and Laura responded by giving her best. The outfits she designed softened Diana's statuesque, almost glacial look, and made her seem human in a way that her collection of haute couture originals had not.

Diana was so thrilled by the clothes that she convinced the editors at *Vogue* to let her do an editorial layout modeling them. The issue was appearing this month, and Laura could hardly be unaware of its importance for her salon's future. Exposure in *Vogue*, combined with the imprimatur of Diana Stallworth, meant instant recognition throughout high society, which was the proving ground of all serious designers.

Since that first commission Diana had come back to Laura several times with requests for outfits of various types. Underneath Diana's manifest enthusiasm for Laura's work there was a mysterious element that was hard to put one's finger on. It seemed to Laura as though Diana was asking for something in all the designs that she either would not or could not name openly.

Laura came to suspect that this something was the look that would appeal to Diana's intended husband, Haydon Lancaster. It was common knowledge that Diana's long relationship with the handsome young Medal of Honor winner and Eisenhower appointee must soon lead to a formal engagement. The combination of Diana's eagerness about the clothes and her worry about how well she would look in them suggested that she had a case of the jitters about her impending betrothal.

Thus Laura was not entirely surprised when Diana asked her to bring the latest batch of designs to her house, so she could try them on amid her own familiar surroundings. She desperately wanted them to be perfect. Laura was happy to oblige her.

Laura had only the vaguest idea of the size and provenance of the Stallworth fortune. She thought it had something to do with chemicals, but she was not sure.

She was entirely unprepared for the magnificence of the house that appeared before her as the driver eased the limousine through the gates at the Fifth Avenue address. An elegantly restrained neoclassic structure in white limestone, the mansion reminded Laura of the great European houses she had seen in architecture textbooks at college. The doorway behind the porte-cochère had a venerable look, with its massive columns and entablatures, as did the pediments and pilasters decorating the six-floor façade.

Even as Laura was asking herself whether places like this could really exist in the New York City she thought she knew, the driver and a liveried servant were helping her out of the car and carrying her boxes with great care toward the house. Laura caught a glimpse of a lawn with sculptured shrubs, and imagined summer lawn parties going on here in stately indifference to the teeming city beyond the granite wall.

"Please follow me, ma'am," said the butler who opened the door. "Miss Diana is expecting you."

Laura was aware that she had come in at a side entrance, and that the grand façade of the mansion designed for the receiving of guests remained out of sight. Yet what she saw before her was already magnificent enough. The butler showed her down a hallway lined with console tables and chairs of various historical periods whose value as antiques must be astronomical. The tables were in carved walnut and mahogany, several with marble tops, and displayed porcelains, both European and Oriental, which Laura was incapable of appreciating. The walls were covered with paintings by artists she had studied at college: Mary Cassatt, Rouault, Chagall, Matisse. All were in ornate frames and lit by individual recessed lamps.

Laura's eyes were fairly popping out of her head as she saw this priceless array of originals pass before her. It was hard to believe that a private family could own such treasures. She could not begin to imagine what prices must have been paid by the Stallworths at Paris or London auctions for these works.

Yet, oddly enough, awed though she was by the paintings, she felt sorry for them as well. They seemed even more imprisoned and domesticated here than they would have been in a museum. Laura suspected that the inhabitants of this house must pass hurriedly along this hallway toward an appointment or errand, paying no attention to these old pictures that had been made virtually invisible by long familiarity. Canvases that an art student would give anything to stare at for hours, they hung forlornly without an audience, reduced to mere decoration.

The butler took Laura upstairs in a tiny elevator and showed her into a brightly lit salon whose savonnerie carpets and Sheraton furniture were matched by an array of eighteenth-century European landscapes in heavy gilt-wood frames, along with some American portraits of Stallworth ancestors. There was also a stunning Aubusson tapestry on the inner wall, and a collection of French porcelains even more impressive than those downstairs.

"Miss Diana will be right along, ma'am," said the butler. "Can I bring you something while you wait?"

"No, thank you. I'll be fine."

Laura turned to look out the tall French windows. The room had a magnificent view of the Park, with the Conservatory pond, the sailboat house, and the bandstand visible in the foreground, and the lake behind. Pedestrians and cyclists were moving along the paths as the Park assumed a postcard prettiness invisible from ground level. Decidedly, there was more than one New York. For here was one that Laura had never known, one whose existence had been as remote to her as a footnote in a history book until today.

Inside the salon sunlight blinked off tiny dust motes near the windows. It was a large room, perhaps thirty feet long, and apparently used for guests who were not close to the family. The furnishings, though impressive, were not very warm.

The only familial touch beside the portraits on the walls was a small grouping of photographs on a pedestal table. Laura drew close to them. They showed various members of the family at different ages.

There was an amusing portrait of Diana and her two sisters. They were much older than she, for in the photo they were already in their teens, while Diana was a mischievous, grinning six-year-old who seemed confined by her lacy party dress.

Laura had heard the sisters' names, Christina and Gilberte, on Diana's lips, but she did not know which was which in the pictures on the table. Each had been one of the most coveted debutantes of her day, and both had made important marriages that allied the Stallworth fortune with others that were sure to complement it.

But Diana, the youngest, had been by far the most beautiful, the most spoiled, and the most admired of the three. Her pure blue eyes, slim figure, and silken blonde hair had captured the imagination of society. She had been singled out by common consent as the most desirable girl in a generation.

Though she was not an academic miracle at her European finishing school or at Smith, more than one of her childish stories, poems, and essays found their way into the pages of *Vogue* and *Harper's Bazaar* over the years. America's highest society could look to Diana as a bright and promising piece of sculptured perfection all its own.

The little table also bore pictures of Diana's sisters with their husbands, and a family portrait from some years ago with their mother and father. Mrs. Stallworth was a dignified-looking woman with wide-set eyes and dark hair. It was her husband, a tall blond man with a barrel chest and square features, who had passed down the light hair to his daughters.

Mr. Stallworth looked like a powerful man, and one who was accustomed to getting what he wanted. Nevertheless, Laura could not help noticing that the pictures lacked one element which must be, in his eyes and in those of society, the most crucial of all—a son.

This was the secret which the glib, familial surface of the photos was trying to hide. Mr. Stallworth—Laura did not know his given name— had no son to pass the family name down to. One could almost feel his effort to conceal his disappointment as he spread the glow of his paternal pride over his three daughters.

How amazing a photograph could be, Laura mused. In these pictures she could see not only the combinations of maternal and paternal traits apportioned differently to each daughter, but also the subtle interplay of personality and relationship that bound them together as a family and perhaps set them at odds against each other.

Obviously the family members had tried to hide their inner selves through studied smiles for the photographer. But it didn't really work. One saw through them to secrets of their flesh and character that were amazingly interesting. More interesting, in a way, than they might be in person, armed as they must be with all the customary mannerisms and social graces of their class.

With this in mind, Laura looked at the most recent photo of Diana on the table. It showed a supremely poised young woman in her twenties, looking as though the world was at her feet. But underneath that classic pose Laura could not help but notice the private worry that had so impressed her in the Diana for whom she had designed her clothes.

It glimmered in the shadows of her perfect complexion and in her jewellike irises, almost as the reflection of a cloud dances among the ripples on the surface of a blue lake.

And now she thought she understood why this was so. Diana was as visible a social commodity as the Royal Family of England, each of whose children must grow up and marry under the watchful eye of a whole nation. The various stages of her youth were as well known to the public as to her own family.

How could any woman be confident of herself under the daily pressure of such scrutiny? How could she assure herself that her femininity was equal to the collective expectations of so many people?

How could anyone, indeed, live among all these priceless trappings of wealth and tradition, without feeling intimidated by them, and by the history behind them? How could Diana fight for her own personality amid such a mire of obligation?

Laura was still gazing at the family photographs, and pondering the strange unbidden thoughts that had come over her at the sight of Diana's home, when a sudden noise from the next room interrupted her. It sounded like a loud sigh, or perhaps a grunt of pain.

Despite her fear of moving from where she had been told to stay, she dared to pace carefully out of the salon and down the hall to the next room. The noise grew more distinct as she went. It sounded like a person gasping from some sort of exertion. Laura could not imagine what was going on, unless someone was moving furniture or repairing something.

Hesitantly she peeked around the corner and saw an astonishing sight. In the midst of another salon, this one with lighter furniture and portraits of Mrs. Stallworth and the girls on the walls, stood a man in a gray sweat suit, his body outlined against the windows.

Laura's mouth hung open in shock.

The man was standing on his hands.

She said nothing, but watched in wonder as he slowly walked from one corner of the room to the other, his legs bent slightly at the knees, his gait easy and even rhythmic as he passed chairs, loveseats, and tables without coming near to upsetting anything.

To Laura's amazement he went on that way for at least two minutes, the only trace of his enormous effort being the occasional abrupt exhalation of breath she had heard from the other room. She had never seen such a physical display before, except perhaps at the circus.

She wondered if he was a bit mad. Perhaps he was an eccentric Stallworth relative whose antics were tolerated by the family.

This impression was accentuated a trifle alarmingly as he noticed her from a dozen feet away and walked directly to her side, grunting as he came.

"Ah-hah," he said, his upside-down face distorted by the flow of blood to his head as he looked up at her. "Company."

Before she could think of a polite greeting he did a quick gymnast's backward flip to his feet and stood before her. His eyes were dark and sparkling, and he looked curiously at her, without a trace of embarrassment, as his heavy breathing sounded between them.

Laura felt oddly defenseless before him, not only because of his vibrant six feet of height and the power of his athletic body, but because she was the stranger in this house, and he its familiar.

But the smile on his face was infectious, and full of welcome.

"Well," he said, still out of breath. "I don't believe we've met before, have we? Are you a friend of Diana's? It's nice to meet you. I'm Hal."

Laura recognized him only at the sound of his last words, for his rumpled costume masked the handsome, elegant male presence that was so visible in magazines and newspapers. So this was *the* Haydon Lancaster, President Eisenhower's admired but controversial envoy to NATO, and far and away the most eligible young bachelor in the nation.

This, then, was the intended husband for whom Diana needed all the beautiful clothes she could find—and thus, indirectly, the reason for Laura's presence here today.

Suddenly Laura's hand disappeared into a large, tanned one that was still moist from its ordeal of supporting an upside-down human body that must weigh 180 pounds or more.

"Oh, forgive me—I'm getting you all wet," he said, staring down at her. "I shouldn't be sweating on you. That won't make a good first impression, will it?"

He laughed. "You see, they're renovating the gym downstairs, and I was pressed for time, so I just decided to use the whole house as my workout room for today. It seemed to me that these old walls could use something more unusual to look at than a cocktail party full of bankers and society people. Besides, it makes a rather attractive gym, don't you think?"

He seemed to be enjoying his own humor, and quite unfazed by the strange circumstances of their meeting. But he was hardly unaware of Laura, for the look in his eyes was quick and appraising, and he had not let go of her hand. Somehow she did not mind the moistness of his palm. Even the perspiration staining his suit and standing out in droplets on his forehead and cheeks seemed natural and somehow endearing.

"Very attractive," she agreed. "You have an unusual way of exercising."

"Oh, that?" He smiled. "It's just a peculiarity of mine. I enjoy seeing the world upside down. Have ever since I was a boy. I used to lie on my back looking up at the ceiling, and imagine it was a clean white floor, to be walked on by creatures we ordinary folks couldn't see. I suppose I had an overactive imagination."

He released her hand. He stood over her, his vitality making her a bit nervous. She felt like a tiny, fearful bird hidden cautiously within itself, compared to his laughing, expansive presence.

As he looked down at her he seemed to sense her discomfort, and to evaluate it. His grin was full of a strange empathy.

"But you haven't told me your name yet," he said. "You're not a spy, are you? Keeping an eye on me for J. Edgar Hoover? Walking upside down could be interpreted as a Communist leaning, come to think of it."

She shook her head, allowing him to tease her.

"Or are you traveling incognito?" he pursued. "Now, that would be romantic. We could use a little romance around here."

"Nothing like that," she laughed. "I'm just here to deliver some dresses to Miss Stallworth."

"You must be Laura," he said, his face lighting up. "I heard you were coming. Diana is crazy about your work. It's a pleasure to meet you in the flesh."

She was impressed by his knowledge of who she was. Clearly he was the type of man who made a point of remembering people and things. Memory must be as much a part of his work as that ready smile.

He looked about thirty, and full of a man's tanned maturity as well as a boyish spontaneity that seemed to suggest that he kept a little bit of his adolescence with him at all times. There was a Peter Pan quality to his charm in person that was not visible in the news photographs Laura had seen of him. It made him seem far more human than the media could communicate, and far more handsome as well. He was like a breath of fresh air in these staid old surroundings.

"And your last name is—wait, don't tell me . . ." He closed his eyes and concentrated, thumb and forefinger pressed to his eyebrows. "Blake. Laura Blake," he announced at last.

"Right again," Laura exclaimed with an involuntary laugh. It astonished her to think that a man as important as he, who had to recall hundreds of crucial names at the highest level of international diplomacy, could know the name of someone as insignificant as herself.

How strange to think that he had been carrying her name around inside his head for weeks, associating it with Diana, and with certain adjacent ideas about dresses and the occasions on which they might be worn, as well as with his musings about what Laura and her shop might look like. This gave Laura an uncanny feeling of being known from afar that was somehow pleasurable.

"Think nothing of it," he said. "Memory has never been a problem with me. I never worry about the things I want to remember. It's the things I wish I could forget that bother me." He smiled. "Don't you ever feel that way?"

There was an instant's silence. Laura was charmed by him, and realized why he made such an impression wherever he went. But she felt a bit uncomfortable, as though in the space of a few words he had shown he could touch more of her than she wanted to have touched, even though he obviously intended no harm.

"Well," she said, dodging his question, "I'm glad the clothes seem to be working out. Diana is a lovely woman, and I'd hate to do less than my best for her."

"Oh, you seem to understand her better than anyone else," he said admiringly. "You bring out the woman in her a lot better than some of those Paris originals she's always bringing home. Of course, that's just one man's opinion . . ."

He looked more closely at Laura. "I'll bet that's one of your designs you're wearing now," he said. "Isn't it?"

Laura nodded, looking down at the simple skirt and jacket she had worn. They looked rather ordinary to her, especially in comparison with the dresses she had brought for Diana.

"I don't know how you do it," he said thoughtfully, stroking his chin as he studied her. "I think you know something about women that fellows like me need to learn. You have a great talent."

"Thank you."

Laura blushed slightly. There was no doubt he was a politician by nature. Decorum and thoughtfulness were joined with a sharp memory to suit whatever purpose he might have in mind. Just as his handsome dark hair, lithe body, and sparkling eyes were made for the press photos that set the hearts of untold numbers of women fluttering—for Haydon Lancaster was considered far and away the sexiest public figure to have appeared on the scene in memory.

He glanced to the room behind her. "Ever been here before?" he asked.

Laura shook her head.

"It's quite a place, isn't it?" he said.

"Yes, it is," she agreed. "Some of those paintings downstairs were in my art books at college. I never really believed private collections like this existed, much less that I would actually see one."

"Here," he pointed to a doorway at the end of the salon. "Let me show you something unusual."

Touching her elbow lightly, he steered her through a set of double doors that led to a beautiful solarium full of exotic plants and delightful rattan furniture.

Laura glanced out the large windows. Central Park looked almost tropical when viewed from such a lush setting.

She turned to smile at Hal Lancaster. As he stood there, perspiration still standing out on his tanned skin and darkening the sweat suit, he seemed all of a piece with this tropical room. He looked exotically alive, and full of strange and powerful energies.

"It's lovely," she said.

"Now take a look at this." He gestured to the corner opposite the double doors. Laura followed his eyes to see a charming little pool filled with tropical fish, its bottom scattered with pennies and other coins no doubt thrown by assorted Stallworth nieces, nephews, and grandchildren over the years. Water was being fed into the pool by a handsome gold fixture in the shape of a fish's open mouth.

Standing beside the pool was a little statue of a ballerina. It was about three and a half feet tall, and the dancer had her arm upraised, almost as though she had just thrown a penny into the pool. She cut a very pretty figure in the playful atmosphere of the room.

But almost instantly the shape of the dancer's face and body alerted Laura to the reason for the smile on Haydon Lancaster's face.

The little girl was none other than Diana Stallworth, captured at age eight or nine as a nymphlike dancer in tutu and ballet shoes by a sculptor who had done her in a style intentionally reminiscent of Degas' ballet dancers. It was easy to recognize Diana's curved lips and bright eyes, her oval chin and slim body, even at so young an age.

"A family conversation piece," Hal said. "Looks like her, doesn't it? I mean, even after all this time."

"It's beautiful," Laura said.

"It was done by a fellow named Foré," he said. "I gather he was quite a sculptor in his time. He died not long after this was done."

Laura recognized the name of Octave Foré instantly. She had seen his sculptures in the Metropolitan Museum. He was a modernist, close to Cubism in most of his work, but for this statue he had reverted affectionately to an impressionist style. He had died about fifteen years ago, Laura recalled. Perhaps he had been ill when he was working on this statue. It almost seemed he was pouring the last of his remembrance of youth and health into it, as though to hold off the decay that was ending his life. The statue was full of haunting preadolescent charm.

"She was cute, wasn't she?" Haydon Lancaster said. "I didn't know her well at the time. Just met her at an occasional party. But what I did know was a tomboy with the sharpest tongue you ever heard. Not a docile little ballerina."

He frowned. "Come to think of it," he said, "her tongue is still pretty sharp. But I'm sure you haven't been exposed to that. It's reserved for her father and me—when we get on her wrong side."

He reached down to caress the little dancer's tutu. And at that instant his sidelong glance came to rest on Laura's small body with a light touch of admiration so delicate, so eloquent that she almost felt she had been kissed.

Obviously Haydon Lancaster was in the prime of his manhood and a great connoisseur of women. Moreover, he was not afraid to let his admiration show.

He said nothing, but watched Laura's eyes follow his hand as he touched the dancer's hips and ran a finger along the small of her back.

Laura almost blushed, so strange was the feeling of intimacy that had spread between them through the intermediary of the statue.

"That's where they got me in Korea." He touched the little back near the base of the spine. "If I didn't do all these damned exercises to keep the muscles strong back there, I'd probably end up walking with a cane for the rest of my life." He smiled at Laura. "This is by way of explanation of my odd behavior."

She said nothing. It pained her to imagine so perfect a male body torn by the cruel weapons of war. Hal seemed so physically confident that one would never think there were deep wounds underneath that innocent sweat suit.

Her smile had faded, for these thoughts filled her with a sympathy for him that was almost painful, and also with a chagrin she could not name.

"Does art interest you, Laura?" he asked, changing the subject. "You're quite an artist yourself, after all. I would imagine you'd have an eye for painting and such."

"Enough to have an idea of what the paintings in this house are worth," she said. "Actually, I majored in art for a while at school. That Chagall downstairs was on the cover of one of my textbooks."

"Are you a practicing artist?" he asked. "Painter? Sculptress?"

She hesitated a fraction of a second before shaking her head. "I—no. Just a fan."

"Well, I am," he said with a proud little smile. "Not an artist, but a sketcher, anyway. Perhaps cartoonist is a better word. I don't know a damned thing about art, but I do get a kick out of drawing. I'm an amateur, and proud of it."

"And so you should be," she said. "I think it's better to have the courage to get your hands dirty than just to watch."

"That's nice of you to say," he said. "But you're not just being a diplomat, are you? Because I have to live with those all day long."

Laura shook her head.

"Well, that's good," he said. "But don't worry, I don't need any encouragement. You know," he added in a confidential tone, "there's a sketch of Diana by me in a frame upstairs in her bedroom. I think she put it up there to make me feel good. And, I suspect, to make sure that no visitors saw it. It's too ugly to put anywhere else. Perhaps you'll see it one day. If you do, please try to keep your laughter down to a giggle."

"I promise," Laura said. "But I'm sure it's wonderful."

"You are a diplomat," he said, his smile full of mischief and a certain tenderness. His look seemed to reach out and take her inside him where his boundless confidence took root. She felt at once denuded by his scrutiny and enfolded by his charm. Indeed, he was much more handsome than his photos suggested.

For a moment the silence between them lingered. His eyes never left Laura. She struggled to find words to break the spell.

"Well," she said at last, "I should be getting back, or Diana will think I disappeared . . ."

"Yes," he agreed, his smile tinged with sadness. "If there's one thing I've learned in this life, it's that people pretty much have to get back. Where they're needed, you know."

How strange his sudden expression of loneliness sounded! It was as though he had all the time in the world to sit and talk and play with her all afternoon, like two children, and was disappointed to see her pulled away from him by adult responsibilities. Yet he was the busy one, the public man, the man of a thousand obligations.

His regret struck a chord inside Laura. Decidedly, he had remained in contact with the child inside himself, as no other adult Laura had ever met was capable of doing. It was not by accident that his whimsical nature had made her think of Peter Pan.

All at once this thought unnerved her, and she felt an irresistible impulse to get away from him, the more so because the smile resting on her was softer than ever.

"It's been a pleasure," he said, holding out a hand.

"Me, too," she said weakly.

He took the hand she had extended and held it as gently as if it were a newborn chick.

Now that a goodbye was between them, the look in his eyes changed. The magnetism in his tawny irises was so urgent that Laura looked away.

A voice from the doorway almost made her jump.

"So this is where you've been hiding. I wondered if you'd gotten lost, Laura. Has Hal been showing you my ballerina days?"

Shining like a mirage in the doorway, dressed in white slacks and a silk blouse that Laura recognized as a Balenciaga, Diana Stallworth regarded her two guests through clear blue eyes.

Hal let go of Laura's hand and moved quickly toward the beautiful girl on the threshold. He kissed her on the cheek and placed an arm about her shoulders.

"You're not going to stain my Balenciaga, are you?" she asked, recoiling a fraction of an inch. Then she returned his kiss and patted his chest possessively. "Oh, well, I guess Balenciaga could use it." She looked at Laura from within his embrace. "How are you, Laura? Glad you could make it so early. I guess this is our big day, isn't it?"

Laura smiled. "I hope everything is all right."

They all moved back to the salon. As she turned away Laura thought she saw the hint of a sidelong glance in Diana's eyes. Diana walked with her usual athletic grace, long thighs and supple hips moving in rhythmic harmony, as Hal kept his hand on her shoulder. Laura could almost feel her happiness as her future husband led the way.

Yet a sixth sense alerted Laura to the same chary unsteadiness she had noticed in Diana before, even at her most brilliant moments. It was, if anything, more noticeable than ever now.

When they were back in the salon Diana extricated herself from Hal. "We girls have work to do, trying on clothes to please you men. Why don't you take your shower, and I'll see you for lunch? Let's make it early. I have to be at an opening at 2:30."

Hal looked at Laura. "See what I mean?" he asked. "Everybody has to be someplace. Nice to have met you, Laura. Take good care of this one." He nodded at Diana.

And with a little wave he disappeared down the corridor, his tread quickly becoming inaudible.

"Well." Diana turned toward Laura with a sudden brisk authority. "Shall we get started?" Her voice was friendly, but somewhat brittle.

One would have thought, for all the world, that something unpleasant had just occurred, and was now thankfully over.

XX

A WEEK LATER Laura was sitting alone in her workroom at the back of the shop.

It was eleven-thirty in the morning, and she felt as though she was in the eye of a hurricane. Business had been growing out of control ever since Diana Stallworth's patronage of Laura, Ltd., became known among the rich and near-rich of New York, Philadelphia, Boston, and even Washington. New clients were waiting in line for appointments, and Laura and her seamstresses were far behind in trying to fill the existing orders of even her most faithful customers.

Never had the smallness of Laura, Ltd., seemed such a constraint. Tim's prediction of many months ago had come true: Laura was not equipped to accommodate the market that her own work had created. Something would have to give soon. Either Laura would be forced to begin turning clients away, or she would have to take the plunge and open a factory of her own to produce her clothes—a daunting financial risk.

At the moment, absurdly, she was alone in the shop. Meredith and Judy, her assistant, were out at a meeting with a fabric designer from Canada whose work had impressed Tim and Laura recently. One of the saleswomen, Sheila, had called in sick, and another, Pam, had had a flat tire on the Williamsburg Bridge and would not arrive before noon. Rita was around the corner with the seamstresses, and Tim, as usual, was off on one of the mysterious but very necessary missions that kept him away from the shop most of the time.

Laura had to hold the fort alone until Pam could get there. An important client from Long Island named Mrs. deForest would arrive at one to try on three dresses Laura had finished this week. There was nothing to do but sit here and wait for her.

Laura was working quickly at a model for a new outfit, her mouth full of pins, her sketch pad open on the chair before her, when she heard a small knock at her workroom door.

She looked up to see Haydon Lancaster smiling in at her, his eyebrow raised.

Oh, no. The unbidden thought struck Laura a hammer blow before she understood what it meant.

"Did I catch you on a slow day?"

For a moment she could think of nothing to say, but simply stared at him without moving.

"Don't tell me," he said. "Everybody's out on an errand, and you're left holding the bag."

Her mouth full of pins, she nodded with a frazzled look to tell him how right he was.

He noticed the sudden pallor that had come over her, and seemed embarrassed.

"Well, I won't burden you with an unwanted visit," he said. "I was in the neighborhood, meeting with a couple of rather unsavory Wall Street fellows this morning, and that photographic memory of mine told me you were around here someplace. So I thought I'd just stop in to say hello."

Laura gave him a pained smile and began removing the pins from her mouth as quickly as she could.

"Whew," she sighed when she had finished. "Hello, Mr.—"

His warning look stopped her.

"Hal," she said.

"That's the ticket," he grinned, entering the workroom unselfconsciously and standing before her worktable. He was dressed in a dark pinstripe suit and the most beautiful cashmere overcoat she had ever seen. He wore clothes with astonishing grace, and had been appearing on more and more Best Dressed lists since emerging as a political figure after his return from the Korean War.

Compared with his elegance, Laura felt frumpy and disheveled in her smock. And despite the infectious smile he beamed down at her, the sinking feeling inside her drained away her strength to greet him properly.

"It's nice of you to stop in," she managed with a smile. "How is Diana?"

"Wild about your clothes, but worried about when to wear them," he said. "She's afraid to waste that green dress on an occasion that isn't worthy of it. So she's holding off . . ."

At these words Laura reflected that a woman in Diana's position cannot wear an outfit more than a couple of times, the way an ordinary woman can. She also recalled her suspicion that the series of parties celebrating Diana's engagement to Hal might be coming up soon.

This thought made her feel all the more troubled to be alone with him now.

There was a pause as he stood looking at her. The fresh, tangy scent of him suffused her, along with a cool breath of the morning air outside.

"Anyway," he said, looking through the workroom's glassed partition to the display area outside, "so this is Laura, Ltd."

"Most of it," she said. "Some of us work in a loft down the street. That's where the sewing gets done. But the clients come here."

He gestured to the mannequins in the windows. "I took the liberty of looking at some of your dresses," he said. "Your advertising doesn't do you justice. You really are one of a kind."

"Thank you," she said. "Sometimes I wish there were more of me. The work gets out of hand."

His dark eyes seemed to soften all at once. Suddenly the clock seemed turned back to that last moment in Diana's solarium when, still holding her hand, he had looked at her with so caressing an expression of warmth and regret that she had feared she might drown in it had not Diana come along to extricate her.

But now there was no Diana. Now they were alone.

"I suppose your day is pretty well filled up," he said. "Clients, and so forth . . ."

"Pretty much," Laura said uncomfortably.

"Look at the time," he said, glancing at his watch. "I didn't realize it was getting on toward noon. I should be running along. I suppose you have someone coming in right away . . . ?"

"Well," she said, "Mrs. deForest isn't due until one. But I have so much to do . . ."

"I imagine you brought a sandwich or something, since you knew you'd be so swamped," he said.

Laura said nothing. The truth was that she had not thought as far as lunch, so obsessed was she with the design she was trying to finish. She often forgot to eat anything during the day unless someone at the shop reminded her. Work kept her too keyed up to think of food.

"You know," Hal Lancaster observed, "if you don't mind a very small criticism, I don't think you eat enough, Laura. You're a little pale, and you look as though you might waste away to nothing if you're not careful. What does your mother say about the way you look?"

"My mother died—a long time ago," Laura said.

His expression changed instantly. His eyes were darkened by a sympathy so intense that Laura felt almost embarrassed by her admission.

"I'm sorry," he said. "Mothers are important. Forgive me if I put my foot in my mouth."

She smiled. "Not at all."

"Anyway," he said, "that's all the more reason for someone to watch out for you. Isn't there anyone to worry about you?"

Laura thought of Tim. He was at her constantly to take better care of herself, to get more rest, to eat more. But his remonstrances could not keep pace with her work load.

On an impulse she decided not to mention him, though. She merely shrugged and looked up at Hal.

"Well, then," he said, "why not let me play the part, for an hour at least? I know a nice delicatessen only a couple of blocks from here. It wouldn't take long."

There was something boyish about him, almost innocent but not quite, that charmed her. She felt her concentration on the design before her begin to flag.

"I really shouldn't leave," she said. "Pam won't be here until noon, and the phone might ring . . ."

"That's only twenty minutes," he said. "You can leave her a note." His logic was quick and unescapable.

"I'm working on something that really has to be finished today," she resisted.

"The work will go faster if you have something to eat. You need energy," he prodded.

"You're awfully nice to offer . . ."

"It's a friendly place," he said. "I know the owners. Mr. and Mrs. Goldman will dote on you. She makes the best potato salad in Manhattan. And, as a matter of fact, I wouldn't be surprised if she could send a lot of business your way. She has an incredible number of friends . . ."

Laura gave him a long, skeptical look.

"Don't say no?" He posed the request as a question, full of gentle cajolery.

Laura gave up. With a smile of amused reproach she let her pencil drop to the tabletop.

"I'll get my coat," she said.

"Ah," he breathed out thankfully, watching her small body as she stood up and removed her smock. "That's nice of you. You won't regret it. I promise you."

He stood back to let her pass. As the empty shop loomed before her eyes, with Haydon Lancaster's tall body at her back, Laura hoped he was right.

. . .

The delicatessen was more crowded than Laura had imagined. It was filled with a noisily talkative clientele whose faces showed satisfaction with the food and ambience, but aggravation over their workdays and absorption in their business problems. Nearly all were local businessmen and secretaries. A few, to judge by their expensive suits and careful grooming, might be Wall Street people or wealthy professionals drawn here by the restaurant's reputation.

Laura watched with a smile as Hal gave their order to a harried, irritable waiter who in turn roared it over the counter to a sandwich chef who registered the order without giving the slightest physical sign of having heard it.

A few moments later a thin, worried-looking man dressed in baggy trousers and a dirty white apron came over to greet Hal and be introduced to Laura. He was Myron Goldman, the owner. He treated Hal with a curious mixture of deference and brusque familiarity that jarred Laura at first.

Then it dawned on her that Mr. Goldman, a busy man at the height of the lunch hour crush, considered it a gesture of great hospitality to take time to meet the young diplomat and his friend. His unsmiling familiarity was in reality a sign of his respect.

He managed to muster a smile for Laura that looked as though it hurt him, and quickly hurried back to his work after authoritatively informing them both that the bagels were just coming out of the oven, and that the cole slaw was extra good today.

When they were alone Hal looked at Laura for a few moments without saying anything, a whimsical half-smile on his face. He touched the water glass before him absently, and then noticed the paper place mat underneath it. It bore the legend, *Goldman's Delicatessen, Finest Kosher Foods*, along with a Hebrew symbol and a little image of a knife and fork.

"Now, don't laugh," Hal said, pulling an automatic pencil from his pocket. "I told you I was an amateur sketcher, and now I'm going to demonstrate. This will show you how implicitly I trust you not to make fun of me."

He began to sketch with quick, nervous strokes, looking from the water-stained place mat to Laura. His eyes narrowed as he studied her face. At one point he hesitated significantly, as though making a decision about which direction to take, and then went on quickly until he had finished.

"There," he said, handing her the place mat without ceremony.

In silence Laura looked at the sketch. It astonished her. Though lacking in polish, it showed real sensitivity and an obvious feeling for proportion, as well as a curious sense of humor. He had caught the oval face above her small body, the shape of her dark hair, and even of her hands. The folds of her sweater were visible, too, ingeniously traced. Even the pendant she wore had not escaped his eye.

"You're really very talented," she said in all sincerity. "You should do more. Have you tried painting?"

He shrugged. "No time. That's the way of the world, Laura. We have to sacrifice one thing in order to do another."

She looked again at the sketch, trying to keep the place mat from trembling in her hands.

"Is there anything wrong?" he asked.

"I'm afraid you capture me too well," she said. "I look scared as a quail."

He seemed distressed. "Is that how you feel? Do I make you feel that way?"

"No," she laughed. "It's not you. It's just me. I'm not the bravest person in the world, I'm afraid." She shook her head, smiling at her own choice of words.

"Oh, I don't know about that," Hal said. "You're the head of a successful, growing business. You employ people, you have a great talent. And look: you're making your mark. After all, people like Diana Stallworth don't buy clothes from just anybody. To me you seem like a bright, gifted, and ambitious young woman who's on her way to great things."

Laura smiled, intrigued to hear herself described through someone else's eyes, but alert to the fact that she was listening to a professional diplomat.

"On the other hand," he added, "some people don't acknowledge their own ambition very easily. I can understand that. They would rather live peacefully in the world than go out and conquer it. I'm not sure that's such a bad thing."

Laura could feel his eyes on her, and for once she did not want to meet them. He seemed to know her far too well. His sympathy only underlined the power of his intuition.

His gaze warmed her pleasantly, but she was feeling the same panicked instinct to escape that she had felt at Diana's. Part of her enjoyed the caress of his openness and charm. Another part wanted to run from him before it was too late.

Why did I come? I must be crazy. The thoughts hurtled this way and that inside her mind, struggling against the lulling gentleness of his manner, yet overwhelmed by it already. Her own image looked up at her from the paper, altered by him to express his interest, his understanding. She wished she were miles from here. She wished she had never met him. But such wishes came too late. Of this she was surer than anything, sure to the point of despair.

She did not tell him that this was not her first exposure to his artistic talent. She had seen his sketch of Diana on the wall in Diana's bedroom, though Diana had not pointed it out. It was vastly different from the one he had just done, in style as well as in subject. Diana had been shown in a cold vertical sweep of lines, and she was not smiling in the sketch. Hal had managed to hint at the tense undercurrent beneath Diana's goddesslike exterior, but without pressing the point.

He was no doubt right about why Diana kept the sketch in her bedroom: to please Hal, and to have him close to her, but also to keep the image from prying eyes.

"Anyway, keep it," Hal said of the drawing in Laura's hands. "I want you to have it."

"Oh, I couldn't," she stammered as the waiter put a plate before her and hurried away to get another place mat for Hal. "Really . . ."

Hal looked hurt. "But you must," he said. "What's the point of making a picture of a person unless you can give it to that person? Besides, keep it to remember me by. You were nice enough to show me a little bit of yourself. Why don't you keep this little bit of me? I'll feel better that way . . ."

His words coiled intoxicatingly around her, full of quiet insights and veiled meanings. She was beginning to realize that there was a lot more to him than a sharp memory and an instinct for diplomacy. He was a terrifically bright man, and a far more sensitive one than his profession would require. This was the real secret to his charm, along with a sweet, rather wistful loneliness that was hard to resist.

"Well, thank you," Laura said. "It's nice of you."

"Not at all," he smiled. "You can throw it away as soon as you get home. But don't tell me."

He spoke as though he were the embarrassed amateur, and she the stern judge. But she could not help feeling that, in the oddest way, he had achieved an advantage over her by drawing this image of her and making her take it. She found her hands shaking again as she folded the sketch and put it in her purse.

She knew she would not throw it away.

"I guess this is a busy time for you," he said.

She nodded. "And you?"

"I have to go to Europe on Monday," he said. "Paris—NATO headquarters. It's a tiresome business, diplomacy. You have to jump through hoops to achieve so little. But the world wouldn't go round without it, I suppose." He looked at her hesitantly. "I won't be back for a while. Maybe a month. How about you?"

"Just work," Laura said. "I think it's going to be a long time before I take my first vacation."

"There's Lancaster's Law again," he smiled. "People pretty much have to be someplace, don't they?"

She nodded. "Yes, I guess they do."

"Well, I'm glad I caught up with you before I had to go," he said.

The sadness was in his eyes again, an odd shadow against which his handsome face stood out like an icon of everything that was young and manly and promising. Laura looked at his dark hair, his hands, the strong shoulders under his jacket. All of it filled her with an involuntary alarm she had never experienced before.

She felt as thought his departure for Europe was saving her by the bell.

But this thought was hardly reassuring. For something told her it would not be long before she saw Hal Lancaster again.

And this thought frightened her more than anything else.

XXI

THE NEXT FOUR WEEKS were a combined ordeal of dread and anticipation for Laura.

She worked harder than ever at the shop, and not by choice. Business was so far out of control that Tim was negotiating with Millie Edelman to double her factory's contract to Laura, Ltd. Everyone from Meredith to Millie to Tim himself was getting more and more tired and irritable, for the only genuine solution to the problems facing their operation was to make a deal with one or more of the major national retailers for the marketing of Laura's clothes. But the retailers were still holding back, even as the "Laura look" became better and better known far beyond New York.

Laura's work load kept her fairly comfortable for the first week. But then a postcard arrived for her from Paris bearing a picture of NATO headquarters. Hal had jokingly drawn a circle around the window of the office in which he worked. His message was brisk and humorous: *Found time for Dior's latest show in the Faubourg St. Honoré. Saw two ladies in the audience wearing Laura dresses. They both looked like the cat that ate the canary. Will keep you posted on further successes.* It was signed *H.*

From that day on, Laura read the New York newspapers from cover to cover, looking for news of Hal. Before long she was an unwilling expert on the daily doings of President Eisenhower's cabinet and the Department of State, but she did not find the news of Hal that she was looking for.

She did notice more than one item on Diana Stallworth in the society pages, however. And no mention of Diana was free of speculation on when she would make her engagement to Hal Lancaster official.

Laura saw Diana once at the shop, when Diana brought in a dress to be altered slightly. The two women had a friendly conversation, and Laura did some tentative sketches for future designs for Diana. But Hal's name did not come up.

By the end of the second week Laura was sleeping badly, and eating less than ever. Her colleagues noticed her pallor, and she made flimsy excuses about their shared overwork and her worries about Laura, Ltd. Meanwhile she was driving herself even harder than usual, but finding it more difficult to concentrate on her designs. Her fingers seemed to be full of memories of their own, and longings that made them clumsy and rebellious.

At night she sat in her rocking chair, staring at nothing, her thoughts filled with images of Hal, his smiles and laughter, his warmth, and the odd amalgam of loneliness and blithe good cheer that set him apart from other men. Laura closed her eyes tightly and fought to banish him from her mind. She knew there could be nothing more insane for her than to linger over the spell he had cast during their two brief encounters.

But it was useless. Far away or not, Hal owned her like an obsession. Her attempts to purge him from her memory only led inevitably back to moments of surprise and chagrin in which she realized that for the last five minutes, or ten, or twenty, she had been lost in languorous daydreams about him.

Laura took a deep breath, squared her shoulders, and returned to her work. But inside she wondered what was to become of her.

At last he returned.

On a Tuesday in April, Laura saw the item she had been waiting for. LANCASTER TO REPORT NATO MEETING TO IKE, read the headline. Hal was to spend several days in Washington before returning home for a visit to New York.

She received a long-distance call from him on his first night in the capital.

"How is work?" he asked. "Are they still keeping you busy?"

"Too busy," she said. "We're swamped every day. How was Europe?"

"Same old thing," he replied. "All the same faces, and none of them particularly glad to see me. I was homesick, Laura. I'm glad to be back."

There was a pause, nervous on both sides.

"I wonder if you'd like to take a little ride with me on Sunday," he said. "Nothing exciting . . . Just around Manhattan. A Sunday drive. What do you think, Laura? Can you spare the time?"

Laura did not have to think. She had done all her thinking already.

"That's very nice of you," she said. "But what about you? Aren't you too busy?"

She heard a low laugh at the other end of the line, as though he found her question absurd.

"Can I pick you up at your apartment?" he asked. "One o'clock?"

"All right. One o'clock." She gave him her address.

"I'll be looking forward to it. Goodbye, Laura."

"Goodbye—Hal."

And so it happened. He arrived in a small European car, and drove her through the deserted Wall Street area toward Battery Park. She was charmed by the skyscrapers looking forlorn and brooding under the gray sky—for it was a wet day, and they were both wearing their raincoats.

"Sorry the weather didn't cooperate," Hal said.

"It doesn't matter," she replied, looking quietly at him as he drove. Somehow the rain suited him. He looked even more vibrant and manly in his light raincoat, immured in the small space of the car with her. The look in his eyes was soft, introspective, as he drove the car along empty streets where only the occasional flash of a yellow cab broke the grayness. Hal himself seemed the only real color in the world today.

To Laura's surprise he stopped the car in the parking lot at the starting-off point of the New York Bay tour boat.

"Do you mind?" he asked, looking at the drizzle outside the windows. "I brought an umbrella, just in case."

"So this was the kind of ride you meant," she said, looking at the few cars from which some brave tourists were emerging with their children to take the boat ride despite the weather.

"Sometimes I feel the need to get offshore," he said. "Off the island. But not in a sailboat out at Southampton, or anything like that. I want to be offshore, but right here in the city. So I can see it without being swallowed up by it. Do you know what I mean?"

Laura looked pensive.

"Penny for your thoughts?" he asked.

"I was just thinking that I haven't seen this place since I was a little girl," she said. "We used to take field trips here, and ride this boat."

He hesitated. "We don't have to," he said, "if you don't want to. We can go anywhere you like . . ."

"No," she smiled. "I want to."

They got out of the car and joined the tourists on the landing. A few minutes later they were on the boat, standing in a secluded spot near the bow, and hearing the old engines rumble as the boat pulled out into the bay.

Governors Island was a grayish hump straight ahead. Laura looked off to the left to see the harbor slips in the East River, and the Brooklyn Bridge, its spans looking ghostly in the drizzle. Somewhere beyond it was Queens, the land of her youth, where she had never felt at home, though so many of her dreams had first come to her there. She began to understand what Hal meant.

The Narrows were in the distance, closed off by Brooklyn and Staten Island, barely visible in the fog. Ahead now was the Statue of Liberty, and to the right Ellis Island, outlined against the green mass of New Jersey.

Hal was standing beside her, looking at Ellis Island.

"Did your people come into the city this way?" he asked.

Laura looked up at him. "That's a good question," she said. "I really don't know. They never told me. I imagine they did." She shrugged. "They died a long time ago. And I guess they weren't interested in discussing such things with a little girl."

Hal looked pensive. "If only they knew what they deprive us of by keeping their memories to themselves," he said. "In one or two generations we forget people and things that were crucial to our families, simply because no one bothers to mention them. Everyone is looking toward the future, so no one realizes the past is slipping away, until it's too late."

He pointed to the island. "My own ancestors came this way," he said. "Oh, they'd like to have us believe they stood proudly on Plymouth Rock. But no. They were poor immigrants like the rest, fleeing here for refuge from their enemies back home. I'll bet half of them were in trouble with the law."

He sighed. "Then they started working. They had been miners back in the old country, so they started where they left off. But somehow the move had changed them, and, like so many immigrants, they got to thinking anything was possible. They saved their money and invested in a coal mine in Pennsylvania. Better to own one here than to work your life away in one back in Newcastle. From there on the pattern was set. Make money, and then watch the money make more money."

There was a silence. The waves were higher now, and spray was coming off the bow. Most of the other passengers were beginning to retreat inside the boat, to look at the sights through the windows.

"I often think back on them," Hal said. "My great-great-grandfather and his brothers, and the rest of the Lancaster cousins. What a clan! They never did anything individually. It was always as a group, with their money and energy pooled together. I admire them for what they accomplished. But you know what, Laura? When I imagine myself in their place, working eighteen hours a day to amass that fortune with the devil at my back, it always seems to me that each of them must have wondered, once in a while, whether he was losing half of himself to build that huge fortune. Whether he was putting blinders on, and closing his eyes to something else that life on this earth might have offered him."

He smiled. "In the funniest way, it's as though they were still miners at heart, toiling deep underground while life went on unseen, at the surface. But apparently the loneliness of it didn't bother them. It would have bothered me."

The rain was still holding off, but the spray from the bay was misting their faces. He reached to turn up Laura's collar, and looked into her eyes.

"Sometimes I don't feel like a Lancaster," he said. "My sister Sybil likes to say I'm some sort of mutation. I've never quite belonged. Stewie —that's my brother—he did. He was a Lancaster to the core. He felt the way Daddy and all our ancestors felt. But I don't feel quite at home inside the skin of a Lancaster. I want something different—but I also feel strange about wanting it. I suppose that's why I decided to go into politics. No one can say that public service is a crime in itself, even if my folks don't approve of it. I'm not sure it's working out, though . . ."

The sound of the waves was muting his voice now, and when he looked at Laura he realized she was no longer listening. She had turned her face to him, a small figure with her hair dampened by the mist, her hands curled at the neck of her raincoat. Her eyes were not upturned to look into his, but were resting on the broad chest close to her face. Somehow Hal felt that this unseeing gaze was focused on the deepest place behind his words, beneath his reason for inviting her on this ride.

Another fine spray of fine mist moistened her cheek. He touched it with a gentle finger, and his hands came to rest on her shoulders, stroking her hesitantly.

Then, on an impulse, he opened his raincoat so as to bring her closer, to protect her from the rain. And he felt her soft palms come to rest against the wool of his sweater underneath, as the hands on her shoulders pulled her closer.

She seemed to give up an inner battle, and be drawn toward him by a force more subtle than the mist, more terrible than the ocean heaving under them. Her hands were pressed to him as much in supplication as in resistance, and her face bent almost tragically to hide itself against that deep chest.

There was something so childlike, almost shamefaced in her surrender, that he drew her an inch closer, as tenderly as a father would gather a child to his arms. She stood motionless, her cheek pressed against his sweater, feeling him breathe, feeling his heart beat as he embraced her.

They said no more. No one noticed them, for the tourists were inside listening to the tour guide's droning Brooklyn accent. The bay passed by them unseen, then the ride back. Only when the boat was approaching the landing from which it had started did he speak softly into her ear.

"Shall I take you someplace where it's warm?"

She did not speak, but the soft body pressed so lightly to him said yes in a thousand small ways that he could not mistake.

He held her hand as they walked down the gangplank and to the car. When they were in traffic he held it again, pressing her fingers with his own as he made quiet conversation to which she did not listen. She had heard enough now.

She did not know what the place was where they came to rest. There was a small, attractive lobby with a homey smell, a voice, a tiny elevator paneled with fragrant walnut.

They came out onto a small corridor with a dark carpet, and made their way to a door with a number on it.

He unlocked the door, and then paused, looking down at her. Her hair was still damp from their ride, and her face had a wounded look almost angelic in its beauty.

"You don't have to, if you don't want to," he said quietly. "I'll understand. Believe me, Laura."

Now the lovely black eyes met his own as a small hand touched his lips to silence him. The look in her eyes was full of a knowledge and a gravity that he had never seen on a human face before. It was like a window to another world.

The door swung open, and Hal Lancaster stood aside with a smile.

"Ladies first," he said.

Laura went through it.

XXII

HAL DID NOT SLEEP a wink that night.

He lay in his bed staring at the ceiling, and seeing sights he had not seen since he was a child. They filled him with wonder, for he had long forgotten their beauty—but also with alarm, for it made him sad to realize how much he had lost in growing up.

As a boy Hal had privately believed that the world had a secret face, full of infinite promise and mystery, which peeked out at him from behind its bland everyday sights. Thanks to a sort of childish sixth sense he saw the things around him as having souls of their own, and the people he knew as being bigger than life, and the days that followed each other, one by one, as mystical adventures leading toward something wonderful.

He would awaken in the mornings, in the days when Stewart's room was right across the hall, and when Sybil, still an infant, was in the nursery, and lie dreamily in his bed, his thoughts cradled by the veiled enchantment of the earth and of his youthful heart.

As he grew older his private vision withered in him, banished by the cares of becoming a young man, and perhaps by the fact that no one else seemed to see the inner color of things that had existed so compellingly for him before. When he looked back on it, which was less and less often, he would recall that something about it was rather sad, and that it required a certain vulnerability or innocence in its beholder. Since he was no longer so innocent, and since he had turned his back on sadness, the beauty he had once lingered over had slipped out of his life.

But today it had returned, like magic. Forgotten all these years, it had come back to him, as though by some incredible chance he had walked down the fated path and stumbled on just the rabbit hole through which he could fall, at precisely the right moment—into the wonderland of his boyhood.

Hal was dazzled. It seemed to him that all his past mistakes, his weaknesses, his wrong decisions and wasted years, were redeemed by the light blinding his eyes now, and the life thrilling through his veins. Indeed, he felt that this was what he had been waiting for all these years, this return to the inner sanctum of himself, where all things were gifted with occult charms, where all people were creatures of legend, where the world was truly a landscape of magic.

And because he had found it again, those long years in exile from it were not wasted after all. It was right there on his ceiling and inside his mind, that secret that made life worth living, that fulfilled the heart beyond all human expectations.

And all because of one misty boat ride, one stolen afternoon, one small woman.

The darkest hours of the night passed like exotic visitors. Sleep was light-years away from Hal, but he did not care.

When dawn was a gray glow outside the window he could stand his solitude no longer. He had to tell someone what he was feeling. He was alive again, for the first time in his memory, and he could not keep it to himself.

But whom could he tell? To what adult person could he entrust his secret?

The answer came almost before he had finished framing the question. Like a child on Christmas morning, he rubbed his eyes, got out of bed and prepared to greet the great day with open arms.

He dressed in slacks and a sweater, went down to his car without bothering to shave, and drove the city streets through the dawn to the Midtown Tunnel. He saw only occasional vehicles, for it was still very early. He took Northern Boulevard all the way to Glen Cove without noticing the sun coming up or the increasing traffic.

He knew the suburban roads by heart, and drove them a little faster than he should have, tapping his fingers on the steering wheel. It was still early when he reached his destination, though he expected people to be up and around.

He parked in the circle before the old building. The pavement was covered by fallen leaves wet from the rain. He entered the foyer, spoke to the woman behind the desk, and was given permission to go along in on his own.

He found the door he wanted and knocked.

"Who is it?" came a voice from within.

"Hal." He wanted to say more, by way of explanation of his appearance at this unlikely hour, but words would not come.

A moment later Sybil answered the door. She saw the look on his face, and something flickered in her eyes instantly. She backed away into the room, almost teasing him to follow her. He closed the door behind him.

She looked excited now, and impishly conspiratorial, as she had been in the old days when they were children and had a secret from their parents.

She sat on the edge of her bed and spoke first, surprising him with her prescience.

"Who is she?" Sybil asked.

XXIII

FROM THE DAY of her boat ride with Hal, Laura was a different person.

She lived only for Hal. She thought of nothing but his face, his smile, the miracle of his touch, during all her waking hours, and his image owned her dreams.

During the days that remained to them before his return to Europe, they saw each other as often as they could arrange it. They made whatever sacrifices were necessary, meeting late at night if they had to, or even at dawn.

When the door first closed on their privacy they could not breathe until they had made love. The hot magic of physical sex was their opening to each other, and to an intimacy of which neither had ever dreamed before. With Hal, Laura felt as though she was in the Garden of Eden, meeting and touching the first man on earth. So overwhelming was her passion that sometimes she found it difficult to look at him, as though the sight of her love would blind her, make him disappear, or consume them both.

Grateful for the darkness, she pulled him down beside her and gave him kisses in which she lost her whole heart to him. When he was inside her he filled her so completely that she could no longer feel the barrier between her flesh and his, but only the mystical fiery difference between male and female, forged in this embrace as if for the very first time, and giving birth to her in that terrible moment as a creature made only to belong to him.

When it was over she would lie touching him, listening to his sweet whispers, or watching him move about the room. And she would ponder the madness that had taken her over. She was no longer capable of ordinary rational thought, of sensible human fear or worry, or even happiness. Love was her only element.

During this time she came to know much about Hal. Oddly enough, she would not have needed to do so, for her love was beyond curiosity. Whoever and whatever he was, she belonged to him utterly.

But what she did learn only made her love him the more.

She soon realized that Hal was a living paradox. Just as his man's body, powerful and sensual, concealed an almost adolescent sweetness of character, so did his entire life consist of a complex surface under which conflicting currents moved.

He had long since repudiated his robber-baron Lancaster heritage, in every way that he could. He had cut himself off from the rigid, distant father whose love and approval he had sought as a boy, and from all the Lancasters, with their humorless devotion to power and acquisition, and their staid sense of who they were and where they belonged in life. Hal was an exile from his people, and he wanted it that way.

His rebellion showed not only in his choice of politics for his livelihood, shunning the Wall Street destiny that his brother Stewart would willingly have inherited from his father. It showed even more in his choice of a liberal, internationalist political stance which was already making him many enemies in the reactionary American political arena dominated by McCarthyism. Hal could not have chosen a better way to frustrate the wishes of his conservative father.

Yet the very stubbornness with which Hal hewed to the line he had chosen was a Lancaster trait, as was his highly developed sense of duty. So, too, was the seductive personal charm with which he disarmed his opponents, and made them think twice about branding him as an enemy to be hated and feared. Hal understood that he would need power in order to get where he was going, and he was clever enough to make strategic friendships that would stand him in good stead down the line. In this, once again, he was a Lancaster.

But the paradox of Hal went deeper. Because he was more sensitive by nature than his ambitious political peers, he possessed a wider and deeper view of the world's problems than they did. Indeed, because his heart was so much younger and unspoiled by cynicism than theirs, his approach to political issues was more mature, more tolerant than their own.

It was this precocious maturity and reasonableness that had so impressed Dwight Eisenhower, and convinced him to keep Hal by his side despite the criticisms of others. Like Hal, Eisenhower knew the horrors of war at first hand, and wanted a secure peace for America in a dangerous world. He was tired of the strident voices around him, which counseled a recklessly aggressive foreign policy, and which warned suspiciously of Communists springing up behind every domestic bush like cancerous weeds.

But the greatest conundrum of all, as Laura soon realized, was that Hal was really not cut out to be a politician in the first place. His gentle, contemplative nature made this painfully clear. Hal was meant for happiness, not for great ambition. He was born to grace the world with his sweet personality, and to learn exciting lessons from its mysterious murmurs. His incomparable sense of humor set him apart from his political peers as profoundly as did his probing intellect.

Had he not been born a Lancaster, Hal might have made a great historian, a political philosopher, or perhaps a journalist. Had he developed his natural artistic talent, he might have become a painter, a poet, a novelist. Certainly he could have been a brilliant political satirist. He showed Laura the caricatures he had sketched of the political figures of the day, and reduced her to helpless laughter with his manic impersonations of Foster Dulles, Joe McCarthy, Sherman Adams, and Dick Nixon.

Hal saw the political arena as a circus full of antic masks that must be viewed with a healthy sense of the absurd if one was not to be daunted by their deadly seriousness. His humor cut through those masks savagely, and yet he tolerantly forgave his peers for the human weaknesses behind their shallow slogans and electioneering. Even the vicious Mc-

Carthy he saw as a tragic figure whom America could best handle by not taking him too seriously.

Thus Hal had made an odd choice for himself in the world, but having made it he intended to see it through successfully. He might be a maverick and a misfit, but he was a survivor. In this he differed from his brilliant sister Sybil, whom he admired for her total alienation from the stereotyped life-style her parents would have mapped out for her, but whom he pitied for the self-destructiveness that was preventing her from fulfilling her great potential as a human being.

But Hal had one crucial thing in common with poor Sybil: the physical wounds that marked his body, and which attested to the fact that, in the final analysis, he was different from other people and always would be. Yet Sybil had inflicted her wounds herself, in her rage against the life she had lived; while Hal had earned his scars in desperate battle for his country.

When Laura contemplated those wounds, and thought about the profound concern for honor that underlay Hal's choice of politics as a career, it seemed to her that all the mysteries about Hal led inevitably back to his Medal of Honor, and to the episode in Korea that had marked his life more than any other. For it was in Korea that Hal became a hero.

An exile in his own family by both choice and temperament, Hal was a fish out of water among his own infantrymen because of social and class differences not of his own making. Thus it was that, at that riverbank in Korea, having made an understandable error in judgment that had endangered his whole company, Hal flung himself with suicidal rage and abandon at the enemy, as though in giving his life for his men he could make final contact with them, and undo not only his tactical mistake but also the riddle of his whole existence.

That moment in Korea was obviously a watershed in Hal's life. Through it he had tried to atone for the death in war of his beloved and admired brother. And he had tried to atone, in a way, for his own exile. But in order to do so he had had to become the leader of men that he was not cut out to be by natural inclination.

And he had had to become that most paradoxical of figures, a hero. For heroes are men who sacrifice themselves for others with a generosity that borders on self-destruction, and an abandon that is not far from suicide.

Laura came to know all these things about Hal, and many more, during her impassioned hours with him. And they all became a part of the strong fabric of her love for him. She loved him for his kindness, his courage, his whimsy, and the sadness of his exile. She loved him for his incompleteness and his mystery as well as his remarkable innocence and honesty.

He knew how to make her laugh as no one else ever had, and he was charmed by the low, husky, and somehow sensual laughter he could bring from her with his humor. But those sounds touched him so near the heart of his male instincts that he could not hear them without gathering her to his arms and silencing her with a kiss.

Laura would gaze at his scars, and touch them with her soft hands, as though trying to salve the inner wounds they hid. But soon her touch was the caress of love, and her whispers of affection were sighs of desire. It was impossible to admire Hal's beautiful youth and vulnerability without falling victim to his terrible sexual powers. And it was impossible to taste the delights of his body without falling in love with his innocent and troubled heart.

So it was with a strange maternal protectiveness that Laura contemplated that hard man's body with its deep white scars and its perfect muscled shape. Sometimes, after they had made love, he would slip on his underpants before getting up to move about the room. She would watch him, and find herself fascinated by the underpants, for they made him look oddly infantile, like a young boy on whom she doted with a mother's delight and loving care.

Yet he was no boy, but a man. She knew that behind that veil of white fabric waited the daunting power of his sex, poised in its lush maze of crisp dark hair to spring forward at the sight of her body, the touch of her hand, the sound of her voice.

Piqued by a naughty impulse, she would say something to tease him, and watch the glittering dark eyes come to rest on her with sudden urgency.

"Come here, handsome."

She spoke the words in the husky little voice he alone had brought to life in her. And, with a nymphlike impudence that never failed to inflame him, she crawled to the edge of the bed, rose to her knees, and put her arms around his waist, kissing his chest, his nipples, his shoulders, as she slipped the soft underpants down his thighs.

But her joke had gone too far, for the terrible erect god between his legs was hungry for her, and could not be denied even for an instant. She pulled him down on top of her, felt the sweet sensual tip of him probing at the threshold of her sex, warm and slow, until with an enormous rush of pleasure it slid to its hilt inside her, forcing breathless sighs of amazement from her lips.

The magic rhythm held them in its thrall once more, joining them ever more deeply, then faster and faster, until he gave his essence to the female depths that clamored for it, the groans of his ecstasy sounding in her ear like anthems of a fate she had waited a lifetime to encounter. She had not thought a man could give himself this way.

When it was over they lay in silence, savoring the storm that had joined them and the calm of its aftermath. They knew their time together was limited, and that the hands of the clock were moving toward the moment when they must part. But they did not care, for the hours of their intimacy existed far from human time, and were, in their way, eternal.

Then they were apart again, separated by a thin veil of time and space, work and reality, which seemed insubstantial as a dream to them both, so concentrated were they on their next meeting.

Laura worked harder than ever, watching her sketch pencil fly over page after page, creating designs of a new sensuality that reflected the tumult in her heart without her realizing it. She sat behind the glass partition separating her workroom from the salon, the surface of her consciousness absorbed by the task at hand, and the vast depths of her emotions hanging in suspense as she waited for the next phone call from Hal.

When it came she held the receiver to her ear and listened to the charmed voice, her eyes half-closed in fascination, her whole body trembling under her smock. She did not bother to wonder whether her rapture might be visible to whoever might notice her through that partition.

So she never felt Tim's eyes on her from across the busy salon, and never realized how deeply he worried for her.

XXIV

AT THE END OF APRIL Hal returned to his mission in Paris. When he left, Laura feared his month-long absence would shatter her newfound happiness and leave her feeling more alone than she had been in her entire life.

Amazingly, his absence had no effect on their intimacy, and even brought them closer. He wrote to her every day, and called her several times a week, so eager to hear her voice that he was oblivious to the enormous phone bills he incurred. She learned about the diplomatic complexities of his work at NATO, and laughed to hear his questions about the smallest details of her much less important activities at Laura, Ltd.

By the time he came home, in early June, Laura felt like a wife whose separation from her husband has merely confirmed the love that is the very stuff of her existence. She knew now that this love had spread to the most secret corners of her personality, and owned her whole heart. Somehow this total surrender made her feel safe from harm. Since her love was all-encompassing, she could not imagine any limit being imposed on it. Blinded by rapture, she could not see a dark cloud on her horizon.

Unexpectedly, it was to be by her own hand that her eyes would be opened.

She and Hal ventured out rarely in the light of day. They had an unspoken understanding about his fame and the familiarity of his face to New Yorkers. So they went only to the most out-of-the-way restaurants, and to movie matinées where the darkness shielded them. They went to museums at odd hours, where Laura showed him her favorite paintings without fear that someone would see them together.

Sometimes, in late afternoon, they would walk along less-traveled paths in Central Park to the carousel. They would sit on a secluded bench, and Laura would dare to hold Hal's hand as they watched the children enjoy the ride. She wondered if he shared the same longings she did at the sight of those tender young bodies going round and round on their colorful horses. Then she put her wonderings aside, for the hand she held told her she already possessed enough of Hal to fill her heart to overflowing.

The only other exception to their rule of never going out in public together was an unusual one, made at Hal's persistent request.

Hal's favorite pastime was swimming. The only thing that made political work bearable to him, he said, was a regular swim to cleanse him of his cares. He convinced Laura to accompany him to a small swimming club in Lower Manhattan that had an attractive pool that was only rarely used by the neighborhood residents.

Laura came to love her swims with Hal almost more than any of their other times together. His childish pleasure in being covered with water was endearing to behold. Like the boat ride that freed him from the clinging shoreline of Manhattan, the pool water gave him the minimal distance from the dry land of earthly worries that he so desperately needed.

His eyes lit up when he saw her come out of the dressing room in her suit. He enjoyed looking at her scantily clad body in public. He convinced her to play with him in the pool, and they treaded water together, effectively disguised by their wet hair, though the handful of other swimmers could not have cared less about the young couple swimming there anyway.

He tickled her under the water, and made her give way to her impulses to touch him as well. The water, slippery and warm, became the special element of their intimacy, for it buoyed them and made their movements languid and sensual. Laura came to share Hal's almost mythic confidence in the power of the water to cleanse away troubles and keep the world at a distance.

She was entranced by his happiness when he was in the pool. Never more than now did she realize how much of Hal was a boy, with a boy's spontaneous delight and innocence, preserved as though by magic inside the body of a man.

So unforgettable was the special smile he wore when swimming that she decided to record it for herself. She asked Tommy Sturdevant, the photographer who handled her fashion work, if he had a camera she could borrow. He lent her a boxy Hasselblad which, he said, would get a good image in an indoor area.

Laura put film in the camera and brought it with her one day. With Hal's amused assent she took picture after picture of him in the water, on the diving board, and on the tiled edge of the pool. His image in the viewfinder intoxicated her. His wet hair looked so dark, and his eyes so happy; his unclothed body was incredibly handsome. Laura could hardly get enough of him. The thrill of capturing him on film made her insatiable for more and more images.

When she reached the last picture on the roll she asked him to pose standing full length before her, with the pool behind. He had just come out of the water, and droplets were streaming down his body, forming a puddle at his feet.

He had never looked so beautiful. But Laura hesitated as she prepared to take the picture. The camera seemed strange in her hands. She felt a sudden fear that taking this picture was a transgression of some sort, like violating something too perfect to be revealed, or capturing a thing that was meant to be fleeting and unrecorded. Perhaps the sight of her love in all its glory should have been tasted and lost in the forgetfulness of their happy day together. Perhaps it was a sin to make it permanent.

But she shrugged off her fear, reasoning that it was no doubt one of her old rainy day thoughts, come from nowhere to trouble a happy time. She loved Hal too much to pay heed to it.

Laura took the picture.

When she had the roll developed she smiled at most of the photos. But her smile faded when she looked at the last one.

It was a full head-to-toe shot, in sharp focus thanks to the camera's excellent lens. Hal was standing with his hands at his sides, looking straight into the camera, his square shoulders and hard pectoral muscles standing out above the firm, manly lines of his thighs and waist. His wounds were visible as ghostly white shades on his tanned skin.

The walls of the pool area were out of focus behind him, and the water itself was an indistinct dark mass rising up in the background like a halo surrounding him from beneath.

Hal was all sunny extroversion, smiling right through the camera with a tenderness meant for Laura herself. His eyes sparkled with a devil-may-care confidence, and he seemed to caress her from the image, as if to say, "No more sad thoughts for you, Laura. You belong to me now." Nevertheless the background behind his smile was rather forbidding, like a dark sky threatening heavy rain.

But the most striking thing about the picture was that Hal was positively streaming with water. It ran down his hair, his cheeks, his chest, and the excellent camera caught all the individual droplets standing out on his skin and dripping off his fingertips to form a smaller shadowy pool at his feet.

There was something disturbing about this watery element that dominated the picture. The freshness of the droplets, like dew shining in the morning sun, came from Hal and his smile. But the darkness of the background and of the pool forming at his feet seemed to evoke bottomless depths of care and sadness. From this perspective the drops clinging to his face and chest no longer looked so sunny. Instead they were like tears of grief flowing over him from some mysterious source.

Grief for what? Laura could not say.

But somehow the forbidding chiaroscuro of the background only made Hal look the more stellar and lovable, for it added depth to his happiness. His smile seemed to say, "What difference does it make if the water is bigger than I am, if the shadows are too dark for my smile to banish them? I'm here with you, and nothing can extinguish our happiness."

And there was more to the photograph. Since it showed Hal with the special look of intimacy that was for Laura alone, it seemed to capture all his smiles, all his kisses, the whole symphony of his affection, since their first day together. What was visible in the picture was not Hal alone, but their love itself.

And if this was true, then the camera, in capturing a fleeting image of Hal and making it eternal, had also captured the participation of time in their love. For that love was bounded by time in a thousand ways, and yet was, somehow, eternal as this image.

After all, had it not been for Laura's visit to Diana's house three months ago, she would never have met Hal, and would have remained only a name to him. But thanks to that visit, thanks to the fact that Diana had become aware of Laura's work and sought her out, thanks to the myriad turnings of fate that had brought Laura from her forgotten childhood in Queens to the shop on Fourteenth Street—thanks to all that, Laura had met Hal, had given him her heart, and could take the picture that documented the beautiful power of their intimacy.

But if time and happenstance had made their relationship possible, they might just as easily end it. Who could tell what tomorrow would bring? How long would the happiness in the photograph go on in the real world? Belonging to Hal as she did today with all her heart and soul, would Laura be lucky enough to belong to him tomorrow? This, Laura realized, was the meaning of the shadows in the picture. They symbolized all the inescapable forces of life that were more powerful than this charmed instant in which she and Hal belonged together so perfectly. And those forces could no more be defeated than the shadows wiped from this picture, or the sad droplets of water wiped from Hal's naked, vulnerable body.

For the first time it occurred to Laura that she was going to lose Hal.

Worse yet, she realized she must have known from the beginning that he could never belong to her. Yet she had come this far with him, and given her heart. She could never get it back.

She showed Hal the whole roll of photos. He laughed, pointing out the amusing qualities in some of them, and recalled the day she had taken them. She held her breath for a brief instant when the last one came up, but he said nothing about it.

"I like this one," she said, pointing to it. "It looks so much like you."

"Does it?" he asked, looking at it again. "To me it's just a somewhat empty-headed fellow standing by a pool, and wishing that the pretty girl behind the camera would stop taking pictures and give him a kiss."

Laura put her arms around him and gave him what he wanted.

There was no more talk about the pictures after that day. But Laura kept the roll, and looked at it often. She took the last picture to a photo lab and had an enlargement made, which she kept among her most private papers. Late at night she would take it out and look at it, frightened by the spell it cast, but too fascinated to leave it alone.

A few weeks later, on a sudden impulse, she had a copy made of the negative and gave it to Hal.

"I want you to keep it," she said, "and have it printed someday. I want you to put it somewhere near you, where the people close to you can see it. That way, when they look at it, they'll see you as I saw you. They won't know about me, but they'll see what you looked like for me."

Then you'll be mine. The thought was too embarrassing to say out loud. And how strange its logic was! As though, by showing him to others through her eyes and her camera, she could possess that precious essence of him that the photo in fact showed slipping through her fingers.

And this, she realized an instant too late, was why she wanted him to have the picture. He was slipping through her fingers even now.

Hal took the negative and put it away carefully. He had sensed the sadness behind her gift.

"I will do as you say," he promised, his gravity touched by a soft glint of humor.

Laura was relieved to see him put the photograph away. In the shadowed water of that swimming pool, the darkest of rainy day thoughts had come to the surface at last, too sad to bear, and yet full of the source of all human happiness, of all human tenderness.

She put the picture out of her mind. She only wanted to see Hal now.

"Kiss me, silly," she said.

And the touch of his lips came to eclipse her worrisome thoughts. She hugged him so close that he made a show of having the breath squeezed out of him. They both laughed.

But the dark water and Hal's smile haunted Laura's dreams that night, and never really left her thereafter.

XXV

June 14, 1955

WINTHROP BOND SAT on the veranda of his Napili house, looking at Lisa Benedict.

She was wearing a strapless tropical silk gown that he had given her on the afternoon of her arrival two weeks ago. Her hair flowed in luxuriant waves over the fragrant plumeria lei about her neck. She had never looked so beautiful.

Win sat smoking a cigarette, dressed in white ducks with his shirt open at the neck, gazing through the plumes of smoke at his youthful companion. Behind her, across the moonlit ocean channel, were the other islands, Molokai and Lanai, crouched on the horizon like quiet conspirators, their shadows dotted by a handful of dim lights.

The servants had removed the dinner things a half hour ago, and he and Lisa had sat here sipping their brandy and enjoying the evening air. Win felt at once more relaxed and more alive than he had been in many years. He was tanned under his shirt from his many swims with Lisa, and his legs had grown stronger from their walks along the beach and cliffs.

The only things troubling his happiness was the lei around Lisa's pretty neck. He had put it there tonight at sunset to commemorate the fact that this was her last night here. Tomorrow morning she was to return to the mainland.

He wondered where he would find the strength to let her go.

—

It was now nearly five months since the evening at the Republican Club when Lisa had crossed his path and touched his heart with her childlike charms. Those five months had changed his life.

He had made good on his resolution to ask her to go to the circus with him. To his delight she had accepted. Dressed somewhat incongruously in a crisp business suit, since she had forgotten to bring any informal clothes with her, and wearing glasses that added a studious look to her lovely face, she had sat close by his side as the performers marched into the coliseum to the fanfares of the orchestra.

He had used his influence to get front-row seats despite the short notice. As the elephants strode past with their hurried, head-bobbing gait, Lisa held Win's arm fearfully, for the animals' huge weight and feral smells were literally on top of them.

After the show started she did not let go, but slipped her palm into his as trustingly as a child. They watched the acts one by one, and he bought her cotton candy and popcorn. She had not exaggerated her love for the circus; she was wide-eyed and intent as she watched the performers. Occasionally she would look at him to share her enthusiasm, and squeeze his hand. Her candor made him feel, in some small but very important way, that he was a man again—at least for her.

The next morning she left for Arizona. Win spent two long weeks trying to forget her, and then gave up. He assessed his situation, calculated the powers he possessed in his unique position in the world, and decided on a bold action.

He telephoned Harris Buhl at Rainbow Concepts to tell him how impressed he had been by the youthful but very efficient Mrs. Benedict at the meeting in New York. In a not-so-subtle manner he let Harris understand that her presence at the upcoming Bond Industries conference in mid-March would not be unappreciated.

The circus was not in town when she came to the meeting, but "21" was. Win took Lisa to dinner, to the theater, and down Fifth Avenue for another long walk, with James at the wheel of the Rolls a few steps from them. He gave her a personally guided tour of W. W. Bond headquarters in Rockefeller Center, and, on her last night, dared to take her dancing at the Café Pierre.

When her visit reached its end he found it impossible to hide his sadness.

"What's the matter?" she asked, sensing his emotion.

"Oh, I don't know," he said evasively. "When a man my age meets a lovely young girl like you, he gets to thinking about all the things he's missed. The opportunities he let slip by. There's so much happiness offered to us in this life—just there for the taking. But so often we turn our backs on it in the pursuit of—of I don't know what. In my case it was some sort of misguided sense of safety."

To his surprise he saw that his words had shocked her.

"Win, you're talking like an old man!" she chided him with a laugh.

"Well?" he gestured to his wrinkled body.

"Win, you're in the prime of life," she said earnestly. "You can do and feel whatever you want. It's all up to you. Don't you see?"

Her optimism touched him. She was too young, of course, to know the cumulative weight of the years, the worries, the capitulations of adulthood. All of that did not exist for her.

"What makes you so sure?" he asked.

"Because I wouldn't be here otherwise," she said smiling into his eyes with a sincerity that disarmed him.

When he had put her on the plane he returned home feeling like Cinderella after the stroke of midnight. He could neither live without her nor summon the courage to bring her back to him again.

Three weeks went by, then six. Win's hand went to the phone a thousand times, only to be held back by his scruples.

You're too old, he told himself. *She's forgotten you.*

Why, a girl of such beauty must have her young man. Lots of them, in fact. She no doubt had dates every weekend, and fought off suitors when she wasn't working. There was no time in her busy, vibrant life for memories of an old man she had met a couple of times in Manhattan, a dull widower whose whim she had gratified by going to the circus with him and having a dinner or two. The whole thing had been infantile, a trifle silly.

But at the end of six weeks, beside himself, he flew to Phoenix to personally attend the stockholders' meeting at Rainbow Concepts. Harris Buhl greeted him like a visiting prince, and now it was Lisa's turn to give him the grand tour, showing him her workplace, her small apartment, and the desert landscape she had learned to love since coming here from Sacramento.

Before he left for New York, Win once more impressed upon Harris Buhl his admiration for Lisa, and hinted that she would make a fine envoy to the parent corporation's stockholders' meeting a month hence. Harris promised she would be there.

It mattered not at all to Harris Buhl, or to anyone else except Win, that the W. W. Bond stockholders' meeting, thanks to a last minute change of venue arranged by Winthrop Bond himself, was to be held in Honolulu.

Everything went off as planned. Lisa's flight arrived at Honolulu

Airport on schedule after its long journey from Los Angeles. Win was waiting at the gate for her, with a lei to put around her neck and a surprise to tell her about.

At the last second he was assailed by doubt. Perhaps his mad scheme would not please her. Perhaps she would be angry at having been manipulated by him.

But his worries were put to rest when he saw her face light up at the sight of him.

"Oh, I've missed you so much," she said as he placed the lei about her neck. "Does it show?"

He smiled, crossing his fingers mentally. "I have a confession to make," he said. "The stockholders' meeting is only the beginning. Harris Buhl is giving you two weeks off. You're coming to Maui with me. You're going to have a vacation." He looked at her a bit sheepishly. "Now tell the truth: Have I made you unhappy?"

For an answer she hugged him to her and kissed his cheek. Then she held him out at arms' length, touching his face with both hands and looking at him through misty eyes. To his surprise she seemed torn between relief and pain, as though fate had cruelly separated them all these months, and at last relented.

"Oh, Win," she said. "How could you ever make me unhappy?"

He squired her around Honolulu during the two-day meeting, showing her Diamondhead, Waikiki, the charming Oriental shops and restaurants of downtown, and driving her through the small lazy plantation towns and fishing villages on the windward side of Oahu, where the island people lived.

When the meeting was over they flew in his private plane to the small airstrip near Lahaina on Maui, and then sailed in his yacht to Napili, the remote location on the edge of the mountains where his house nestled on its cliffside. Lisa exclaimed over the view of the channel and islands from the veranda. The postcard prettiness of Waikiki had not prepared her for the otherworldly splendor of this place.

"It's paradise," she said.

It is now, Win thought, watching the setting sun reflect itself in her green eyes.

They spent a beautiful two weeks together, their days at once lazy and filled with adventure. He took her sailing to Lanai, the island of pineapples, and to Molokai, with its deserted beaches and silent dirt roads. He took her to Wailuku, Maui's county seat, with its charming old homes and vestiges of missionary society, and to the remote town of Hana, hidden in a lush setting of tropical jungle and taro fields, where some of his wealthy acquaintances from the island gathered at the Hana Hotel for drinks.

And he drove her across the isthmus to the volcano, Haleakala, where his friends the Bellamys entertained them for an evening on their cattle ranch. Lisa was surprised and delighted to sit before a fire in the chill night air of the mountain, listening to the singing of the paniolos from the corrals, while the tropical vista of the warm cane and pineapple fields spread beneath them.

He went swimming with her every morning, before the sun got too hot, and took the boat out to show her the stunning tropical fish that spawned around the reef at the edge of the lagoon beneath the house. He had two of his trusted houseboys teach her to ride the surf with a board. She fell off again and again, laughing and waving, and finally, being a natural athlete, managed to ride the board all the way in on the gentler waves. She came to his side, streaming with salt water, out of breath, and stood beside him as he toweled her off with gentle strokes.

The sight of her body in the bright, stinging light of the tropics took his breath away. Her firm rounded breasts were as ripe as the island fruit, her creamy skin as perfect as the white beaches he loved so much, her long gorgeous thighs as irresistible as the balmy breeze caressing him under his bathing trunks.

In the evenings they strolled across the lawn behind the house, with its plumeria trees and thick hedges of croton, hibiscus, and bougainvillea, before sitting down on the veranda to watch the sun set. They heard the mynahs chattering in the palm branches, and watched the waves lap gently at the sand far below. Then his island chef prepared them magnificent dinners of fresh fish, beef from Maui ranches, and exotic salads made with tropical fruit and vegetables grown on his own property.

He told her about his years here with Eileen, and his love for the island people with their friendly ways and subtle dignity. He talked about his children and grandchildren, and got Lisa to tell him more about Louis Benedict, whom she spoke of with a reverence tinged with sadness. Only half aware of his purpose in bringing up the past, Win watched the dying sunlight gild her beautiful eyelashes as she spoke.

As the days passed, conversation became less necessary between them. They seemed to know all they needed to know about each other. Their evenings were spent in quiet communion, rocking together on the porch swing to the sound of the waves, Lisa's hand resting in his. The intimacy that joined them filled Winthrop Bond with a languor that grew a little more seductive with each passing day. He let himself bathe in the spell that Lisa cast, trying to avoid thoughts of what would happen when she left him.

Inevitably, the two weeks dwindled. A growing sense of regret tinged their days together, until, toward the end, they felt their happiness weighted by genuine dread of the future.

And now it was over.

"Thank you," said Lisa, her smile glowing above the white blossoms around her neck, "for letting me see all this."

Win looked at her fresh rosy cheeks in the candlelight of their final evening together.

"Thank *you* for letting *me* see it," he rejoined, reflecting that, though he had owned this place for many years, and spent countless hours gazing at this ocean and these mountains, first with Eileen and then alone, he had never felt the tropics in all his senses until Lisa came here to share them with him.

He touched her hand across the tabletop. His eyes half-closed with longing. He was drained by the days he had spent trying to deny that this moment must come, and felt downright desperate at the thought of letting her go tomorrow.

"Don't be sad," she said, giving him her sweetest smile. "We've had a wonderful time, Win. I'll never forget you and your island as long as I live. Please . . ."

He sighed.

"I'm sad," he said, "because I've exhausted my bag of tricks. I've lured you to New York, and pursued you to Phoenix, and finally shang-haied you all the way out here. There's nothing left now but to let you go. You have your own life to live. I know it has to be that way, but something very selfish in me doesn't like it one bit. Inside I'm hoping I'll at least be able to see you once in a while. Perhaps you'll call me when you're coming to New York. I'll probably find pretexts to stop in Arizona occasionally, on some sort of business. I'll call you, if I have the nerve . . ."

"The nerve?" Lisa looked stricken. "Oh, Win, how can you say that? Is that what you think of me?"

He gazed at her, hypnotized by the green eyes glowing in the candlelight. The evening breeze, scented by palms and tropical blossoms, caressed the hair that flowed over her bare shoulders. She had never looked so lovely.

He tried to concentrate on what was right.

"You have a busy future ahead of you, Lisa," he said. "You'll be a big success at your work. You'll fall in love one day, and you'll get married and have children . . ."

"I am in love." Her voice was dead serious, and full of pleading.

Win felt faint. He tried not to look at her.

"Please, Lisa," he said, making believe he had not heard. "I can't stand in the way of all that. I consider you a valued friend. The most valued, the most wonderful . . ."

"Oh, don't go on, Win," she cried. "Can't you see that I love you?"

He looked at her through wide eyes. His heart beat faster. The explosion that had been building inside him all this time was coming now, unleashed by her words, and there was nothing he could do to stop it.

"Lisa, you can't mean this . . ."

She grasped both his hands. The urgency in her fingers took his breath away.

"Win, I want to belong to you. I want to have your babies."

Tears were streaming down her cheeks. He could see how much this confession was costing her.

He tried to object. "But Lisa, darling, I'm an old man. I'm at the end of my time. You've got so much ahead of you . . ."

She was shaking her head stubbornly. "Not without you."

Taken aback by her firmness, he felt obliged to remonstrate.

"Lisa, you're not thinking straight. Of course, we feel something for each other. We've become close in a short period of time. I can't hide how important you've become to me. But that doesn't mean . . ."

"Oh, think it if you have to," she said desperately. "But don't say it, Win. You're breaking my heart."

And she threw herself into his arms all at once, clutching him with all her strength.

"Don't you understand?" she sobbed, covering his cheeks with kisses as she held him close. "It only happens once, really, and a woman knows for sure. It's you Win, my darling Win. I knew it right away, that very first night in that silly club room in New York. And I tried so hard to please you, to make you like me. I loved you already, but I had to try not to let it show. I didn't want to scare you away because I was too young, and so clumsy. Oh, Win, my heart broke when I left you that first time. And when Mr. Buhl sent me to the sales conference, and you called me, I was so happy, so relieved. I thought you had forgotten me . . ."

A sudden, harsh sob shook her. She wiped ineffectually at her tears.

"Don't you see?" she said. "All this time, I've been trying to hide the way I felt about you, so you wouldn't feel surrounded by me, so you would feel free to choose me if you wanted to. But I can't hide it anymore, Win. I can't say goodbye to you this way . . ."

She wept silently against his chest. He patted her shoulder softly.

How odd it was to feel her cling to him for strength, despite her vibrant youth and his tired old heart.

"Oh, please, Win, please," she said. "Don't say you'll love me, if you can't. But say you'll let me belong to you, or at least try. Please, don't say no. If you do, there's nothing else left."

The hot tears from her eyes moistened his cheek as sweetly as the spray off the ocean. Her hands were on his back, pulling him closer to her, as though this was her last chance to prevent him from slipping away.

Now, all at once, Winthrop Bond understood the feelings that had been growing so crazily inside him during these strange and painful months, and understood why Lisa was so irresistible to him. She wanted him for his manhood. She wanted to give him her children. And it was precisely the instinct to be a man, to be a living part of the world rather than a tired witness to it, that she had kindled in him from the outset.

That was the secret of her strange childish love of the circus, and of the trusting, gentle way she held his hand when they went places. She was not contemptuous of his age, or awed by his money and position. These obstacles did not exist for her. She wanted only to bestow herself upon him as a woman. And she was hungry for his love as only a woman can be. But she had known from the beginning that he would resist her out of consideration for her youth—and this knowledge had been a torment to her.

But all that was behind them now, for the chord she had touched in him with her confession was ringing through him like a symphony, and the last of his defenses against her were crumbling.

She seemed to sense this, for it was with mingled relief and exultation that she took his hand and led him inside to her bedroom. He did not resist.

She closed the door. The moonlight came in at the window, and as he watched she slipped off her dress. She stood before him, pearly and glowing in the moonlight, a miraculous image of nubile womanhood, and as her bra came off he saw for the first time the perfect breasts whose outline had so often charmed and disturbed him beneath her bathing suits.

She came to his side in her panties and touched his lips with hers, softly at first, then full of a timid female hunger that parted his lips so her tongue could slip into his mouth, eager for the taste of him.

His tired senses came to life as he felt her nudity pressed to him, and he could feel her little sigh of joy and excitement when his sex rose against her. Encouraged, she kissed him more deeply, and he dared to touch the silken panties, in the amazing knowledge that she wanted him to slip them down her legs.

What happened to Winthrop Bond in the next few minutes was light-years distant from any sexual experience he had ever had or dreamed of in his long life. The girl offering him her flesh was not doing so because it was expected of her, but because she needed and wanted him, and indeed was desperate for his love.

No one had ever been that way with him before. To everyone he had ever met he was Winthrop Bond IV, a human being born into a position, like a second-rate prince whom people accept as king until the next generation saves them from his mediocrity. For the very reason that he was Winthrop Bond IV, no one had ever paid any attention to him as an individual.

Even Eileen had been brought to do so only after they were already married. And she had merely been doing her best to make contact with the lonely man behind the role she had married by necessity of birth.

But Lisa wanted him, body and heart and soul. She was so hot with her need for him, that her own hunger thrilled through him like fire, hardening his sex and pulsing through his loins. Surprising himself, he entered her with a young man's confidence and gave her the pleasure for which her beautiful flesh was made.

Her moans of encouragement sounded in his ear as she arched her back to pull him deeper inside her. Very soon the tremors of her ecstasy caressed him, and he felt the hot tickle of his own orgasm, stirring at first from very far away and long ago, and then storming forth until it was a burning tide between his legs. She felt it and welcomed it with her soft little cries, and it exploded into her like a part of himself he had kept walled up all these years, a part of him whose existence he had forgotten, until this glorious moment brought it back to life.

"Mmm," she held him jealously close as his gasps resounded over the distant throb of the surf. "Oh, thank you, Win. Oh, sweetheart . . ."

He savored the moment, for he knew it was a miracle he had done nothing to deserve. Life had granted him a second chance, a second manhood far more real than the first, thanks to this sweet and sensual young creature. For the first time in sixty-five years Win felt really wanted.

She lay naked in his embrace, kissing at his chest, her fingers running over his shoulders and down to his hips, their touch electric with lingering ecstasy and fascination.

"Oh, Win," she said. "I love you."

For the last time he looked into those pleading irises, and surrendered.

"Darling Lisa," he said. "I love you, too."

He heard the joyful intake of her breath, and felt her smile in the darkness.

"Say it again," she whispered.

"I love you."

"Oh . . . Oh . . ." She bent to kiss him, and her tears moistened him, pure as holy water. Then she nestled close to him, holding him tight.

"I want to give you babies, Win," she said. "That's what I felt when I first saw you, and that's what I felt just now. I know it's right, Win— I don't know how I know, but I do. You've had children before, but you were made for more. Don't you see? It was fate that I met you. You were meant to be the father of two generations, not just one. And I was meant to be the mother this time."

She kissed his cheek, again and again, with girlish excitement.

"Oh, I know it sounds crazy," she said. "But all my life I've felt I've been waiting for something. I didn't find it with Louis, bless his heart. Maybe that's why I couldn't get pregnant with him. I must have known that my babies were somewhere else, still waiting for me. And when I met you, I could feel it right away. Oh, how much I've wanted you, all these months . . ."

She held him closer, and spoke more urgently now.

"Let me give you babies, Win," she said. "Let me have them, and bring them up. That's all I ask. Please don't say no. Just love me, and I know they'll come. Beautiful boys and girls . . . I can feel them inside me. They're all yours. They had to wait for you. Oh, thank God . . ."

Her face was close to his, her hair shrouding them both, the luxuriant naked expanse of her body like a ghost glowing white in the darkness, sent by fate to change the course of his life.

"Don't say no," she begged. "Just let me belong to you. I'll never let you down, I promise. No one could ever love you as I do."

Win took a deep breath. His manhood was being held out to him on a silver platter. He could not refuse it.

"No," he smiled, curling a hand about her waist to pull her closer. "I won't say no."

She made a small, terribly female sound, somewhere between a sob and a purr of exultation.

"But there's just one thing," he added, grasping her by her strong young shoulders.

"What, Win?" She seemed frightened. "What is it?"

He ran a finger along her cheek and kissed her lips before answering. "You'll have to marry me."

XXVI

Paris
June 16, 1955

HAL LANCASTER WAS SITTING on the sofa in his suite in the Hotel Crillon, listening to the traffic moving outside on the Place de la Concorde.

He was in his shirtsleeves. His feet were on the coffee table before him, which bore a plateful of half-eaten sandwiches and a couple of empty bottles of French beer. His eyes were closed.

The radio was on. An announcer's mellifluous French was reading the news. Hal was not listening, because he found it an ordeal to think and speak in French after a long day at the conference table.

But Tom Rossman, Hal's hand-picked assistant and close friend, was listening intently to the broadcast. Today's meeting with the French had been ultra-sensitive and marked by dozens of ambiguous signals on both sides. Tom wanted to hear how the French radio network would report it, for he knew that the French government controlled the radio news broadcasters, and expressed its own party line through them.

The President's NATO staff, including Hal, Tom, and the representatives of General Gruenther, Supreme Allied Commander in Europe, had been jumping through hoops for months to get the French government to agree to the formation of the European Defense Community, or EDC. Such a step, which would lay the groundwork for a united European defense against potential Soviet aggression, was Eisenhower's personal dream for the postwar West.

Today's meeting had taxed the Americans' diplomatic skills to the utmost, and they had left in a state of collective exhaustion. Hal was to return to Washington tomorrow, and he knew he would only be able to report small progress to Eisenhower. He hated the onus of returning home time after time with frustrating news, the more so because the hard-liners at State and in the National Security Council had never approved of Hal's appointment to his post in the first place, and were continually trying to prejudice Eisenhower against him.

But their efforts failed, for Ike trusted Hal's instincts about the French and EDC more than those of anyone else. However unpopular he might be among right-wing Republicans in Washington, Hal was sure of a friend inside the Oval Office itself.

For this reason Hal was always glad to get home. And, on a far more personal level, he lived for his trips to Washington, because they brought him within a short flight of New York, and Laura.

In fact, preoccupied though he was with his long day's work, his thoughts at the moment were far away from NATO. He knew that he had a chance of seeing Laura in just three days if he made it to Washington tomorrow, and he was devoured by his need for her.

He looked at Tom, who was sitting on the edge of an armchair, dangling his glasses against his knee and cocking his head in the characteristic way he had when he was concentrating hard on a problem.

Tom was Hal's closest friend in government. They had been classmates at Harvard Law, and had entered politics at about the same time. But they came from radically different backgrounds. Hal, the product of an old Anglo-Saxon family and the beneficiary of a traditional education at Choate and Yale, was worlds apart from Tom, who had come from a poor family in the Bronx and seriously considered not bothering with college at all until his last-minute scholarship to Columbia changed his mind.

Tom was marked as deeply by the ethnic roots of his immigrant family as Hal was by the Lancasters. But the two men had in common a willful exile from their parents' politics. Just as Hal had renounced the Lancasters' right-wing Republicanism, Tom had turned his back on his parents' New Deal nostalgia, convinced as he was that the postwar world posed new problems that required new leaders.

The two young men, both Democrats, had found their way to a common ground in Dwight Eisenhower's progressive White House, and hit it off from the moment they first met. Hal saw in Tom a perfect foil for his own personality. Tom had a sharp, cynical wit, a cunning sense of political poker-playing, and a nervously analytical mind that saw into the dark corners of issues that Hal's own instincts might not notice.

Meanwhile Tom had felt from the beginning, though he never said so aloud, that in Hal Lancaster he had met a potentially great leader of men. Hal had a precocious breadth of political wisdom that came from the combination of his deep-rooted idealism and his innate flexibility as an individual. Added to this were his courage and a willingness to sacrifice himself for others, which one comes across once in a lifetime among public servants.

Tom had decided that wherever Hal was going in public life, he would help him get there. By the end of the first year of their friendship, they had a wordless understanding to the effect that their careers would remain linked from now on.

They played handball together, and Tom was able to use his quickness to beat Hal about half the time despite Hal's superior physical ability. And they played poker, at which Tom had the apparent advantage because of his suspicious nature and canny sense of attack and defense, but found himself undone often by Hal's surprising ability to bluff his way to victory when he held a poor hand.

Tom had married his college sweetheart, a pretty young woman named Nora who was affectionately tolerant of Tom's high-strung personality, and loved him for his humor and his youthful spirit. Hal spent many evenings and Sunday afternoons at their modest Washington home, and had become the adopted uncle of their six-year-old daughter Joan, a strong-willed firecracker of a girl who loved good movies, and could recite most of the dialogue from *Gone With the Wind* upon request.

Both men were eager to fly home tomorrow, for they desperately needed a break from the snail's pace of the NATO negotiations, and missed those closest to them.

This thought was on Hal's mind as he watched Tom sigh, turn off the radio, and begin straightening his tie.

"Tom," Hal said from his reclining position on the sofa, "if you have a minute, there's something I'd like to talk to you about."

Tom looked at him curiously. "What's on your mind?"

"Something hypothetical," Hal said. "Not about NATO. It's about me."

Tom put down the sport jacket he had picked up and moved to the edge of the bed. The look in Hal's eyes told him the subject was serious.

"Suppose, just for the sake of argument," Hal said, "that in a couple of years I were to run for some important office. Senator, Representative, Lieutenant Governor—anything. By that time, of course, I would be married to Diana. Do you think that would help me win the election?"

Tom laughed. "Does it help the Pope to be Catholic?" he asked. "What do you think?"

Hal did not laugh. He seemed pensive.

"So you think it means that much," he said.

Tom's smile had faded. "If you're asking me seriously," he said, "yes, I do. Not only is Diana free publicity, in the best sense of the word, she's high-profile, positive publicity. You can't buy that for a million dollars, Hal. You and Diana are America's sweethearts. Diana doubles your newsworthiness. And what's more, she's newsworthy on her own. She's in fashion magazines, and on all the society pages . . . People are crazy about her. Christ, she'd make the greatest first lady in history. A man could get into the White House on her smile."

Hal nodded.

"And if I didn't marry her?" he asked.

Tom was about to laugh, but then he saw that Hal was in dead earnest. Frowning, he took off his glasses and dangled them nervously between his legs.

"You're not kidding me, are you?" he asked.

Hal said nothing. The look on his face answered the question eloquently.

Tom thought for a long moment, staring out the window behind which the dusk cloaked the French capital.

"Well," he said at last, "there's more to this than just subtracting Diana from your image. You also add something negative to your image. You become the man who dumped Diana Stallworth after a love affair that was the talk of the nation. The man who turned his back on his past, his family, his obligations. That will hurt you, Hal. It will hurt a lot."

Hal was looking at his friend through clear, watchful eyes.

"How much is a lot?" he said.

Tom sighed. "As of today you're the country's favorite young bachelor, a white knight. If you marry Diana, you become half of America's favorite couple. But without her, you're alone. You're on your own. And you've got to add into the calculations the fact that you already have the reputation of a political maverick. Putting it all together, I'd have to say that it would set your career back by five years, maybe more. I also think you'd probably be diminishing your political potential by one office, maybe two. You'd never be President, Hal, and maybe never Vice President."

There was a pause. Tom cocked his head in concentration.

"There's one more thing," he said, "though I hate to mention it. Money. You'd be less bankable, Hal. Not only from a party point of view. Don't forget your family."

Both men knew that the Stallworth fortune had been informally wedded to that of the Lancasters for a dozen years in anticipation of

Hal's marriage. If Hal backed out now, his gesture would not only be the ruination of a fiscal alliance involving many millions of dollars, it would be a personal slap in the face which his father would never forgive. Reid Lancaster was a rigid, vengeful man. He had never wanted his son to be in politics in the first place. He could go a long way toward financially limiting Hal's ability to run for public office.

"Now, over time, you might manage to repair some of the damage," Tom said halfheartedly. "Nothing is forever in politics. We all know that. The public has a short memory. But it would depend on circumstances—both political and, well, personal."

He cleared his throat. "Let me ask you something, Hal: Do you have someone else in mind?"

"I can't answer that," Hal said.

"Hypothetically, then," Tom prodded.

Hal gritted his teeth. "Hypothetically, okay. Let's say I had someone else in mind."

"She would have to be another Diana," Tom said. "Someone from the same background. Someone with the same connections. Someone your family could welcome with open arms. That way the public might be persuaded to perceive you as having switched from one princess to another. That's a less serious crime." Nervously, he looked at Hal. "Would the girl we're talking about be that kind of girl?" he asked.

Hal gave his friend a wan smile. "I can't answer that," he said.

Tom looked very worried now.

"Hal, my advice to you would be to take your time and consider this very carefully. The public is waiting for you to marry Diana. They'll wait a bit longer. Don't rush into anything."

Hal said nothing.

"Look, Hal," Tom said. "I want you to understand something. Your career is not a matter of mere curiosity to me. Wherever you're going, I want to help you get there. I know something about this crazy country of ours, and I know it's going to need you in the years to come. Ike is keeping us out of war, but it's taking every bit of his know-how and stature to do it. And Ike is not going to last forever. We're going to need wise leaders in this nuclear age. You've got the head for the job, and the heart. Don't take yourself out of the race before it begins, Hal. Don't do something today that will make you unelectable when we need you most."

He stood up, put his glasses back on, and looked down at his friend. "Think of your country, Hal, as well as yourself," he said. "That's all I ask."

Hal nodded, measuring Tom's words. Then he stood up, smiled, and stretched his tired arms.

"Tell you what," he said. "I'm going to take a shower. Order me a martini when you get downstairs. I'll see you in a couple of minutes."

"Okay." Tom headed for the door. He still looked worried.

"And thanks," Hal said.

When Tom was gone Hal sat down again and gazed out the window. An ambiguous smile played about his lips, though his eyes were pained.

He had known in advance what Tom would advise him. But he had to hear it from Tom anyway.

He had already made his decision. Tomorrow he would fly home. He would speak to Diana. Then he would ask Laura to marry him.

Hal was smiling at his own past naiveté. In all these years of decision-making, love had never entered into his calculations. But now, gloriously, incurably, he was in love. His heart had belonged to Laura since the first time he laid eyes on her.

And that fact made everything else moot. Laura must come first.

Love was a new experience for Hal. In the beginning the feeling had been so painful, so consuming, that he thought it might drive him out of his mind. For the first time in his life he understood those lovesick young men who pined for a girl, gave up everything they had for her, even killed themselves for love.

Laura was his heart. Without her he would be nothing.

Girls had always been something given to Hal on a platter. They threw themselves at him without restraint, and were transparent in their hunger and their motives. Clumsy and shallow in their attempts to be feminine, they made Hal feel alone even in the most frantic of their embraces. Since they were always there for the taking, it was impossible to feel any great need for them. Why desire that which one can have at one's whim?

But Laura was different. Laura kept within herself, because she had a self of her own. Unlike other women, who were interchangeable with each other in personality as well as intellect, Laura was one of a kind.

Yet even as her depth and dignity set her apart from the female sex Hal had thought he knew so well, she gave more of herself to him than any woman had ever been able to give. When she touched him, smiled at him, made love to him, she gave her whole heart.

And because of that, she owned his.

As Tom had explained, without Diana, Hal would be perhaps 25 percent of himself politically. But without Laura he would be half a man forever. Hal could not face the rest of his days on earth without her. It was that simple.

He would pay any price, make any sacrifice to win her. She was life itself.

Relieved to have made his decision, Hal looked at the phone. It must be nearly noon in New York. Laura was almost certainly at the shop, busy with her customers. All he had to do was call her, hear her voice, and he would have the courage to face the rest of it.

He began to reach for the phone. It rang before he could touch it.

He picked up the receiver.

"Lancaster here," he said.

"Glad I caught you, Hal." It was Colonel Sprague, General Gruenther's chief aide. "We need you to stay over. The French have a counterproposal on EDC. They're going to put it on the table tomorrow. The General has just spoken to Dulles in Washington. Ike wants us to drop everything and see if we can get a concession out of the French in the next week or ten days. Sorry to mess up your plans, but I'm afraid you'll have to cancel your trip home."

Hal gritted his teeth. "No problem. I'll meet you at headquarters in the morning."

He hung up the phone. For a long moment he thought of calling Laura anyway. Then he decided everything must wait until he got home.

He could live without her answer for ten more days.

XXVII

ON JUNE SEVENTEENTH Laura received a call from Diana Stallworth's secretary inviting her to tea with Diana the following Monday.

The invitation was not surprising. Diana was one of her best customers, and certainly her most famous, and it had been nearly a month since she had completed her last commission for her.

Nevertheless Laura felt a pang of apprehension. She did not look forward to being at close quarters with Diana just now.

Laura arrived on time, her sketchbook in hand. She was shown to the second-floor solarium to which she had first been introduced by Hal four months ago. She sat on one of the lovely rattan chairs, and watched the fish swim in the little pool beside which the tiny ballerina stood in her bronze tutu, her sculptured eyes looking childlike and innocent.

At length Diana appeared, wearing a yellow silk blouse and dark gabardine trousers that Laura had designed for her. As Laura stood up to shake her hand she saw that Diana was carrying a small zippered portfolio, which she placed on the table beside the tea things.

"You take lemon, don't you?" Diana asked, displaying the acute memory that was part of her hostess's arsenal of skills. She poured carefully. Laura saw that her hand shook slightly.

"How have you been, Laura?" she asked, holding out the cup.

"Oh, the same," Laura answered perhaps a bit too blandly. "And you?"

"Perfect." Diana's smile was brittle, her voice tense. An alarm went off at the back of Laura's mind, but she resolved to ignore it.

"I brought my sketch pad," she said, pointing to the pad. "What sort of things did you have in mind?"

Diana shook her head. "This meeting is not about clothes, Laura."

Laura said nothing. She watched as Diana reached for the leather portfolio and opened it. Inside were two large manila envelopes. Diana opened the first of these and handed it to Laura.

"Take a look at these," she said.

Laura gave Diana a searching look before taking out the contents of the envelope.

They were photographs, perhaps two dozen or more. They were all of herself with Hal.

Laura turned pale. Someone had apparently followed her and Hal to all their favorite places, and managed to get pictures of them on many of their days together. There was a picture of them smiling as they waited for a cab; and another that showed them seated in the shadows of an intimate restaurant, deep in conversation, their eyes fixed on each other.

One of the photos showed them walking together in Central Park, in their favorite secluded lane near the carousel. Another showed them on their way into a movie theater. Inevitably, the dogged photographer had managed to catch them holding hands on a nightlit street. Worst of all, there was a picture of them kissing, as Hal held her about her shoulders when he was sure they were unobserved.

Surprisingly, the swimming pool was not included. Somehow the photographer had missed that.

But everything else was there. The pictures showed the furtive, sweet glory of their closeness, as they talked, laughed, exchanged looks full of lovers' tenderness and, inevitably, touched each other.

Quietly Laura gathered the pictures together and placed them on the table. She looked up at Diana.

Diana was staring at her through tear-stained eyes.

"I thought you were my friend," she said, a sob shaking her voice.

The sinking feeling inside Laura deepened. The pain on Diana's face was real, and Laura was the cause of it.

Diana wiped at her eyes with a handkerchief and took a deep breath.

"I'm sorry I said that," she said. "What we have to talk about has nothing to do with friendship."

These words hurt Laura almost as much as those that had preceded them.

"Laura," Diana said, measuring her words with difficulty, "I like you a lot. I have great respect for your work, and for you as a person. And, to be honest, I can easily see why Hal finds you attractive. You *are* attractive. In your own special way you're a very beautiful woman."

She paused, as though wondering where to begin something very painful and difficult. She looked at the little ballerina beside the pool.

"I've known since I was nine years old," she said, "that I was going to marry Hal Lancaster. That's been a fact of life, for me and for Hal, all these years. For better or worse, we belong to each other. Now, I'm sure it's hard for you to imagine us living this way, knowing a thing like this from such a young age, adjusting to it, growing into it. Most people wouldn't understand it. But Hal and I come from a society in which such a thing is a way of life. It is literally part of us—and we're part of it."

She paused. Her brow furrowed in concentration.

"Laura, I've loved Hal since I was no bigger than that statue. And, believe it or not, he loves me. Perhaps in a different way than what he feels for you; perhaps not. I don't know. But, believe me, the bond between us goes very deep. Hal has stuck by me through many difficult times of which you know nothing. He is going to marry me, for a thousand reasons you cannot begin to know. I've loved him and suffered for him all this time because those reasons are mine as well as his."

She sighed in sudden frustration. "I don't know how to explain this to you," she said. "I'm not sure I should even try. I'm not sure it's any of your business."

Laura said nothing, but her heart went out to Diana, whose face bore a mask of pain she recognized only too well. Laura recalled her own sleepless nights thinking about Hal, wondering where he was, whether he was happy, whom he was with. She recalled her floods of private terror and resentment against anything that might separate her from him. All of that was clearly visible in Diana's tortured eyes at this instant. For how many months and years must Diana have suffered that agony?

Diana took a deep breath.

"Laura," she said, "Hal is at the beginning of a great political career. One only has to look at the newspapers, or talk to anyone in Washington, to know that. Eisenhower is going to be the last Republican president for a while. The next political era will be dominated by the Democrats. Along with Jack Kennedy, Hal is the most promising Democrat in the party. Many people—and I'm one of them—consider it a foregone conclusion that Hal will run for the Presidency in the next ten years. I'd like think that when he runs, he'll win."

Again she paused to concentrate on what she was trying to say. There was a hint of condescension in this, as though Laura was too inexperienced or ignorant to understand what was at stake. Yet something deeper and more sincere shone through despite the pose.

"Do you know what this means, Laura?" Diana asked. "It means that everything Hal does today is being done by a future presidential candidate—perhaps a future President of the United States. Every move Hal makes affects his chances to fulfill his destiny and his responsibility to his country. Imagine how tragic it would be if something he did today, however minor, however forgiveable, were to compromise that destiny . . ."

She sighed. "As I'm sure you know," she said, "Hal chose politics as a career over his family's objections. That's how important this career is to him. And the Lancasters respect Hal enough to have decided to put all their resources behind his political future. This is, however, a sword that cuts both ways. Hal will need every bit of support he can get from his family if he is to achieve the great things ahead of him."

She shook her head as though frustrated with herself.

"But that's not the real point," she said. "Money is not the issue. If it were, Hal would have turned his back on his family long ago. No, Laura. Hal is a man whose roots go deep into the past, far deeper than the outward aspects of his personality might suggest. Like me, he takes his life's blood from that past, and from a future to which he belongs, like it or not. If you—or anyone, for that matter—were to ask him to depart from that, to abandon it, he would be leaving a part of himself behind. And he would never, never be a whole man again. He would not be the Hal you have known. Believe me."

Diana looked into Laura's eyes.

"I know Hal must feel something for you," she said. "But nothing he feels can negate what he is. Laura, this may hurt, but I'm going to say it anyway, because it's important for both of us. I'll bet Hal has not asked you to marry him."

She watched her words take effect. A long silence held the two women in suspense as, with the greatest effort of her life, Laura fought to keep her emotions from showing in her face.

"I thought not," Diana concluded with more sympathy than triumph. "He never will. If you knew him as I do, you'd understand why that must be."

She took a deep breath.

"It might occur to you, Laura, to put what I've said to the test. In your place I know I would be tempted to. But if you do, I think there's something you should know."

She opened the leather portfolio, removed the second envelope from it, and handed it to Laura.

Laura took the envelope and emptied its contents into her lap. It was another pile of photographs. Almost before she saw what they were, tears made her vision start to blur.

The photos were of Hal with other young women—four or five different girls at least. Some of the pictures were more recent than others. Laura recognized Hal's cashmere overcoat in one picture. In another, he had a deep tan she had never seen, and his hair was longer than usual.

The girls in the pictures had two things in common. They were all pretty—oh! how painfully pretty!—and they all had the same expression on their faces, whatever their physical differences. It was the composite expression of joy, of discovery, of trust, and of infinite excited hope that was on Laura's own face in the pictures of her with Hal.

That radiant glow of female exultation struck at Laura's heart as she flipped through the photos, seeing the girls on Hal's arm, holding his hand, walking on the beach or a city street with him, savoring his beauty with their happy eyes.

With a sigh Laura put the pile of pictures on the table alongside the ones of herself, and looked at Diana.

"There's a photographer for a major New York daily—I won't say which one—" Diana said, "who's been watching Hal like a hawk for years. Ever since this man first . . . approached me, I've had a rather dingy but mutually satisfactory relationship with him. I buy the negatives from him, he agrees not to make them public, and I—well, I get an idea of what Hal is up to. I know that sounds cheap, and pathetic . . ."

Despite the agony in her heart Laura felt a profound sympathy for Diana. After all, it must have hurt Diana as much to look at those pictures as it was hurting Laura now. And Diana had had much more time to linger over them, and to calculate their significance for her own life with Hal.

Silent tears had started down Diana's cheeks as she looked at the piles of photos. "I have to do it," she said. "I have to protect him. No one else is watchful or clever or committed enough to bother. Hal is a passionate man. You know him, Laura. You know his war record. Hal has tremendous courage—he would gladly sacrifice himself for others at the drop of a hat—but he has a poorly developed idea of how to protect himself."

She gazed at the multiple images of Hal on the tabletop.

"That's what he is," she said, "and nothing it going to change him. That is the man I am prepared to accept for my husband, and to take care of as I was destined to do."

There was a silence. At length Diana found strength somewhere for a wan smile.

"You see, Laura," she said, "that's what we women are put on this earth for. To protect our men, without their knowing they're being protected. They are not as wise or as brave as they want so much to be, and that's why they need us, and our love."

She took a deep breath. "I don't know whether Hal will be a faithful husband," she said. "I hope he will be. But if not, I will live with that eventuality. I know what he feels for me, and God knows I'm giving up my life for what I feel for him. I know you understand what that means. I've invited you here today to ask you to make a sacrifice for him, just as I am."

But he doesn't love you!

The thought had leapt into Laura's mind before she could stop it. The whole logical edifice Diana was building so eloquently, even so heart-rendingly, was a mere house of cards when confronted with that devastating fact. Hal did not love her. How could a marriage between them make any sense? It was insanity, even a sin, and it could only lead to tragedy for them both.

But the protest in Laura's heart was silenced by another fact, unknown to Diana, that had a destructive logic all its own.

Hal had never said he loved Laura. And Laura herself had never told him she loved him. Part of her had feared the words as something that would bind him, that would kill the spontaneity of their love, and turn it into an obligation. She had wanted to free him for whatever future he chose. As for the rest of her, she had simply loved him beyond words, and not felt the need to say how she felt.

And as for Hal himself . . . who knew why he had kept his silence, and what that silence had meant? Laura could not see into his heart. Until this terrible moment she had not felt she had to. Only now did she realize what a curse her blindness had been all along.

She looked at the images of Hal on the table, and then at the image of him she had carried inside her all this time. She saw a last receding vision of a world in which things were as they were meant to be, a world in which people were happy, in which love brought them together instead of sundering them—and she watched it disappear before her eyes.

In its place she saw Hal marching grimly through his days on the planet, exiled from himself, and yet wedded to his mission by an impersonal force that would never allow him to deviate from it.

Perhaps he had chosen a destiny that, in the last analysis, no woman could share. No wonder, then, that Laura felt a strange kinship with poor Diana at this moment.

She looked down at the little bronze ballerina, a figure frozen at a time in life when a little girl can have no inkling of the agonies her heart will have to face when she becomes a woman.

Then she looked up at Diana, who was gazing past her as though at a faceless rival more implacable than any mere flesh-and-blood woman.

Laura smiled, her eyes full of pity and surrender.

"What do you want me to do, Diana?"

XXVIII

June 21, 1955

Dear Hal,

This is a painful letter for me to write, so I'll make it brief for both our sakes.

I cannot avoid telling you that I am involved in a relationship of some standing, which I think ought to be pursued. Under the circumstances I don't think we should see each other anymore.

The friendship we've had over these past months has been a wonderful thing for me. You've made me feel stronger, happier, and better about myself than I have felt in a long time.

I want to wish you all success in your public and private life. I have learned to admire and respect you greatly, and I think you deserve the best of everything.

Please, Hal, don't try to call or write me about this letter. Help me to leave things as they were, so that they can be remembered that way.

Live your life, Hal—and be happy! The Hal I knew will always be part of me. I couldn't prevent that if I wanted to—and I don't ask more. Please don't either, for it will only make you unhappy, and that is the last thing I want.

Laura

XXIX

LAURA DID NOT KNOW how much time passed.

She went through the motions at work, devoured by her hectic daily routine. She felt as though her insides were packed with ice, or with a substance infinitely colder and harder than ice, a substance that killed everything it touched.

She wondered whether others could see her grief. Was it possible that she could turn this dead flesh to the world without anyone noticing? For she felt literally murdered inside, the life of her heart annihilated by what she had done.

She had stopped thinking of what had happened in terms of right or wrong, fairness or unfairness, logic or illogic. She only knew that everything that mattered to her was over, and that the days ahead were of no consequence whatever. This acknowledgment brought her a sort of peace. She had no important decisions to make, no crossroads to face, for she had already left life far behind her.

Ironically, as she watched from her remote perspective, she became aware that the fortunes of Laura, Ltd., were finally taking a dramatic upward turn. Thanks to the publicity garnered for her clothes by the favor of Diana Stallworth and the concomitant patronage of high society, two of the major national retailers had finally overcome their resistance and signed contracts to market her designs across the country.

The clothes would be sold under the Laura, Ltd., label, with tailoring modifications for the different sizes according to Laura's specifications, and displayed in salonlike surroundings designed to communicate both the prestige of the line and its affordability. Major national advertising campaigns were planned by both retailers, including layouts in *Vogue*, *Harper's Bazaar*, and all the other important glossy magazines.

All this had been orchestrated contractually by Tim. The amounts of money involved staggered the imagination. Only now did Laura realize what it meant to have her designs sold at hundreds of retail outlets from coast to coast. Overnight she would become one of the most important designers in the nation, and one of the wealthiest businesswomen any-where.

Laura accepted this hoped-for reality with an inner combination of amusement and indifference. She put on a happy mask for her coworkers, immersed herself in new designs for the coming seasons, and watched her life run its course as though it were a mechanical contrivance. The success for which she had worked so hard was entirely eclipsed by her grief. She existed only to watch time pass around her, and to hope that the void inside her would deepen enough to make existence more bearable tomorrow than it had been today.

At last, one rainy afternoon, a voice came to wake her from the doldrums into which she had gratefully sunk.

"Long day, pretty girl?"

It was Tim. He had stepped quietly into her office, dressed in a handsome blazer and gray flannel slacks, a crisp red tie completing the impression of sparkling male confidence as he smiled down at her.

"Let's have dinner tonight," he said. "There's something I've got to talk to you about."

For a moment she lacked the strength to respond to him. The pain inside her pulled her away from him.

Perhaps mistaking the weakness in her eyes for mere exhaustion, he moved around the desk and stood rubbing her shoulders. This was a familiar gesture that had often comforted her in the past when the pace of work got her down.

She looked at their dual image in the wall mirror. With his powerful arms and shoulders he was bent over her like an adult helping a child with a skate key. She had always been impressed by that almost comical difference in size between them. Indeed, her trust in Tim had always been a bit childlike, for his great muscled strength went hand in hand with his unflappable calm, his mastery over the outside world, and his steadfast devotion to her.

"It's not business," he said. "It's something personal. I think you can help me out."

She felt warmed by his hands, and tranquilized by his smile in the mirror. How foolish she had been to take him for granted all this time! She was so lucky to have a friend like him. Perhaps it was time to count her blessings.

"All right," she said, touching his hand with her own. "It's a date."

They had dinner at Michelini's, their favorite Italian place in the Village. It had been the scene of more than one celebration and more than one "disaster dinner" as the fortunes of Laura, Ltd., fluctuated over the past three years.

On the table was a single white rose. This was Tim's accustomed gesture of affection when he had a special reason for being with Laura.

Laura could not eat more than a few bites, but tonight Tim did not upbraid her about her thinness and lack of appetite. She felt strangely relaxed. She was outside herself, dispersed among the muted sounds of glasses and silverware, of waiters' shoes brushing the carpet, of snatches of conversation. She drank gratefully of the wine in her glass, for it sent a warm glow into her frozen insides.

When their coffee had been brought she looked at Tim. His eyes were resting on her quietly.

"Well?" she smiled. "What's the problem?"

She thought of his sister, and of the family back in Ireland. What sort of problem could be on his mind? Strangely, he didn't seem worried. Instead he looked somehow excited, as if he was holding back a secret like the cat that had eaten the canary.

"I'm not sure how to begin," he said, touching his tiny espresso cup with a hand so large that she might have feared it would shatter the frail china, had she not been certain those fingers could never harm a thing.

"Laura," he said, "you're the person I trust most in this world. In fact, you're the *only* person I really trust. That's why I'm going to ask your advice on a very private matter."

She nodded. "All right."

"There's a girl," he said. "I've known her for quite a while. We're friends. But I've only recently realized that I'm crazy in love with her."

He stopped himself. "Well, that's not precisely true. I knew it before. I tried for a long time to tell myself that it was just that I liked her and admired her. But I knew it was more. Now I can't hide it any longer. But the things is, you see, we've been friends for so long that I'm afraid to say anything. Maybe I'm just an old shoe to her. Maybe she made up her mind a long time ago that we're just friends."

He looked at Laura. "What would you do in my place? Make a clean breast of it, or lay low? I can't go on this way. It's killing me to keep this secret to myself."

Laura smiled to hear his words. How lucky he was to have someone to love! Even if the someone was close and familiar, and didn't know it. At least he could look at the beloved face whenever he wanted, and hear her voice . . .

But, she reasoned, one must grasp all the happiness one can in this world. And if defeat were the fated ending, one might as well confront it without delay. The chance might be taken away if one did not act quickly.

"Tell her," she said firmly. "Don't wait. And don't be scared, Tim. She's probably crazy about you. Hasn't she given you any sign?"

He shook his head. "If she has, I'm too thick-headed to have noticed it. That's the whole problem. I'm not clever enough to handle this sort of business. I'm too crude a bloke, Laura. For that reason alone, she'd probably never have me."

"Tell her anyway, Tim," Laura insisted. "You're being much too hard on yourself. Besides, why take chances with something so important? The worst thing you can do is to keep your feelings secret from the very person they concern the most."

"You mean," he said, "ask her to marry me?"

"If that's what you want." She nodded. "For heaven's sake, Tim, she's probably been pining for you all this time. As a matter of fact, she's probably already given up on you. You should set her straight now, before she starts looking elsewhere—if she hasn't already."

Laura said these things with a conviction that amazed her. Yet she felt oddly detached from them, and from Tim. How could the dead presume to advise the living?

Tim looked sadder now, as though he had sensed her private hopelessness.

"Just you wait and see," Laura pursued. "You'll make her the happiest girl in the world."

"What if she says no?" he asked skeptically.

"She won't," Laura smiled. "Not if I know women. You're a wonderful man, Tim, and a very handsome and desirable one. Women notice you wherever you go. You know that. You're kind and strong and good . . ."

He laughed. "If I was fishing for compliments, I came to the right place," he said. "But what if she says no anyway?"

"Then you'll be no worse off than you are now," Laura said. "At least you'll know where you stand. Besides, this world is too uncertain for us to wait around for things to happen. Grab your happiness, Tim. Fight for it. Even if you lose, you'll have gone down swinging. That's all that matters."

Laura listened to the solid wisdom of her words, aware that they spoke the most important truth that she herself had failed to heed. It felt good to say it out loud, for so much of her pain went with it.

But what happened next wiped the smile from her face.

From nowhere Tim produced a tiny velvet box, wrapped with a gold ribbon, and placed it on the table before her.

"Open it," he said.

She looked up at him. The cool green of his eyes had deepened, and seemed to pull her into itself like a bottomless lake.

A silence fell between them, poised and pregnant. The box sat on the white tablecloth, a tiny thing that somehow seemed to grow larger before her eyes, as though it contained a whole world that was calling out to her to enter and explore it.

Curiosity killed the cat. From the depths of Laura's memory came the ancient injunction with which her mother used to warn her when her childish inquisitiveness tempted her to mischief in the old house in Chicago. Her mother had been dead for many years, but the warning still sounded in Laura's mind with uncanny authority.

Laura dared not confront the truth that was staring her in the face. She wanted to close her eyes, and to take back the words she had said so heedlessly.

But it was more than curiosity that was trying to make her open this box. The force gathered inside it was big enough to swallow her whole, to engulf her past and direct her future steps where it wished, regardless of her terrors, of her lost hopes—regardless of everything.

If she touched it, if she opened it.

She felt faint. She watched helplessly as her hand, moving with a will of its own, slowly gathered the tiny box, touched at the ribbon. The box opened. Inside it was a small but beautifully tasteful engagement ring whose diamond gleamed in the half-light like a talisman.

That luster seemed to leap from the stone into the green eyes of Tim Riordan, which had not left hers for a second.

"I . . ." Laura tried to speak, but words would not come.

"It's your size," he said. "After all this time I know those hands of yours pretty well, Laura. It will fit. I promise you that."

Now she saw a large hand cover her own, the fingers encircling the hand and box and ring so easily that she felt dwarfed by a fate infinitely greater than herself.

"I love you, Laura," Tim said.

She closed her eyes without thinking. The echo of the words sounded in her ear like an anthem. Despite herself she felt a seductive acquiescence in all her senses.

"I've loved you since the first day I saw you," he said. "When I climbed the stairs to that dark apartment, and saw this tiny angel of a woman with her lips full of pins, her fingers flying over that fabric, I lost my heart. All at once I understood what had been missing in all the women I had ever known, the reason I couldn't love them, trust them, respect them—it was all in you. You were what I had been waiting for

—but a thousand times more so, a thousand times more beautiful than my dreams."

He sighed. "I took too long, I know. I let you get used to me. I let you think friendship was all I wanted. I shouldn't have—but you were so fine, Laura, so delicate, so pure . . . Just being in a room with you made me feel like a bull in a china shop."

His hand cradled her own. "But, oh, how I wanted to tell you I loved you, adored you, how I would give anything to spend the rest of my life with you. Keeping my silence was the worst torture I've ever endured. I'm telling you now because I'll burst if I try to hold it in one moment longer. I love you, Laura. I want you to be my wife. With you, I'll be the happiest man in the world. Without you, nothing. Say yes, Laura. Say you'll be my wife."

Her eyes had opened as he spoke. They were full of tears now, and her hand trembled around the tiny box.

He saw her distress and patted her hand gently. He looked ashamed of himself. "I'm sorry, Laura. Don't let me force you. My God: It was you who gave me the courage to ask. What a fool I am. Just answer what your heart tells you. Don't be afraid to say no, if that's what you feel. I'll take it like a man."

Laura looked into his eyes, and saw the entreaty in their depths. He was putting his future in her hands. She had the power to make him happy, or to condemn him to the pain that was twisting inside her even now.

He had meant so much to her! It was his pride in her, his steadfast support that had prodded her to all her achievements these past years, and given her precious balance when she thought the maelstrom of her life would suck her under. Tim was the very ground she walked on.

And now she faced the truth. Indeed, she had always known he loved her. Why had she never acknowledged this to herself, when it was such a basic fact of her life? *He loves me, Tim loves me . . .*

Five minutes ago she had felt more alone than she had ever felt in her whole life. But now the sound of his voice and the touch of his hand were penetrating to her cold dead center and warming it, pulling her back to life despite the stubbornness of her own need to hide from the world.

His hand still covered hers. His eyes were fixed to her, their expression full of reassurance, and yet somehow intoxicating, somehow dangerous.

A temptation was growing inside her. It was as though a genie in a bottle had been freed by the sound of those three small words, and was upon her now with a charm capable of paralyzing her will, of turning her into someone new who could only do the very thing she had thought impossible until this moment.

She felt a voice rising within her, sprung from that unseen change, filling her to overflowing and coming quickly to the surface, abetted by the strength of his will and the weakness of her own.

The box was open. He was slipping the ring onto her finger. Surrender coursed through her thrillingly, for she was not alone now, and need never be alone again, if only she let him have his way.

"Well?" he asked, expectant as a boy. Again she saw that curious light of mischief behind the pain in his eyes, as though he knew her defenses were no match for the power of his love.

Laura held her breath. The ring on her finger joined the voice in her ear to pull away her last balance.

"Yes, Tim," she said, taking the final step that pulled the ground from under her feet, and holding onto his hand as to the only lifeline that could save her from herself. "I'll marry you."

XXX

December 15, 1955

Dearly beloved, we are gathered here in the sight of God, and in the presence of these witnesses, to join together this man and this woman in holy matrimony, which is an honorable estate, instituted by God . . .

WINTHROP BOND STOOD beside Lisa, in full view of the assembled Bond relatives and friends from the business world as well as the best of New York society. Nearly everyone present was younger than Win, as was the beautiful bride whose smile beamed through her veil at him.

The relatives bore stiff and disapproving looks, some of them focused on the magnificent bridal gown Lisa was wearing, others on Winthrop's balding head with its white hair.

The minister, dressed in his vestments, was himself an aging figure with bifocals and hair the color of Win's. He looked down his nose at the bride and groom, his breviary in his hands.

Not a single person in Christ Church, the largest and most prestigious Methodist church in New York City, approved of this marriage. Each and every one, despite his or her sensitivity to Lisa's charm as revealed at the engagement party, thought Win was not only sealing his personal doom, but committing an unforgivable sin against the immortal Bond fortune: wedding it to nothing.

Four generations of cunning, ambitious, desperately hardworking Bonds had not built this legacy in order to see it wasted in this way. The relatives had outdone each other in eloquence as they struggled to convince Win that his marriage was a crime not only against themselves, but against history and the American way.

All for naught. Win had control of the entire fortune, and the decision was his to make.

So there was little joy in the church today.

But Winthrop Bond did not care. He had enough joy in his heart for a multitude.

Lisa stood beside him, glowing with her excitement over what was happening. She had never looked so youthful, so candid in her emotion. He had eyes only for the radiant smile behind that veil, and for the kiss, the voice, the love that that smile signified.

Win cared nothing for the disapproval of others. The watchful faces in this church belonged to his past, a past that was over now. His future was an open book, and he was content to read it in the eyes of the lovely creature at his side.

In recent weeks his sister and the cousins had done their best to talk him out of the marriage. They had even presented him with an absurd detective's report about Lisa's past, a past they claimed to be dubious in the extreme. But Win could not be moved. He had already heard Lisa's side of the story, and had had leisure to understand its ring of truth.

More than this, he knew *her*, knew Lisa in a way that none of his dour relations could know her. She was a kindhearted, vulnerable girl who had suffered greatly in her life, and who loved him and wanted his babies. And the truth in her jeweled green eyes was infinitely more eloquent than any dubious calumny concocted by a paid detective.

It was Win, in fact, who was grateful to Lisa for overlooking appearances and accepting him. She could easily have contented herself with a vision of him as the dull scion of a family of robber barons, a burnt-out shell of a man with nothing to recommend him. But she had looked deeper, and found a man she could admire and accept, a man ready to be reborn with the help of her love.

For better, for worse, for richer, for poorer . . .

The words sang like a poem. The lovely eyes, with their touch of haunting melancholy behind the bright girlish sparkle of their surface, were looking at him now, full of love and joy and infinite promise.

The past was past. Nothing mattered now but Lisa.

As long as you both shall live . . .

. . .

Therefore marriage is not to be entered into unadvisedly or lightly, but reverently, deliberately, and in accordance with the purposes for which it was instituted by God.

Diana Stallworth looked from the face of Hal Lancaster to the grave but approving visage of the Episcopal bishop of New York. Behind her, she knew, were the assembled Lancaster and Stallworth relatives, hundreds of them, here from all over the world, as well as more than a few celebrities, high officials from Washington, and representatives of the best families in the nation.

Diana was wearing a gown of ivory silk with a beaded lace bodice designed for her by Christian Dior. A photo portrait by Irving Penn of her in her wedding dress would appear in this month's *Vogue*, along with an account of her wedding and a special layout on her trousseau.

Outside Saint Bartholomew's Church at this moment were journalists from fifty countries eager to get pictures of her and Hal as they left the church. Television cameras would record their progress by limousine to the Stallworth mansion on Fifth Avenue for the reception, and their departure for their honeymoon in the Greek Islands, a honeymoon during which Hal would find time for meetings with several important European leaders.

This wedding was the biggest event in American social and political life since the Roosevelt years. Hal and Diana cut the figure of an heir to the throne and his chosen queen. Their marriage was seen not only as the long-awaited union of two beautiful people and two historic families, but also as Hal's auspicious political debut. It was taken for granted that he would run for some sort of high political office in 1956. With Diana by his side, it was difficult to imagine him losing an election.

The collective approval of so many millions of observers, as well as their puckish excitement over what must happen tonight between Hal and Diana on board their ship, was reflected in the gentle twinkle of the bishop's eyes.

No one was against this marriage. Everyone applauded it. The whole world thought Diana a beautiful and lucky young woman, wedded at last to this Prince Charming in flesh and blood, this fairy tale come true, Hal Lancaster.

Diana was petrified.

As she listened to the bishop's words, praying she would be able to repeat the vow without stumbling, she looked through her veil at Hal. His eyes were resting on her affectionately, and in them she saw a private look of reassurance tinged by humor. "Don't worry," he seemed to say. "This is all just a big circus. When it's over we'll laugh about it together." Diana wanted to weep with gratitude for his support.

His boyish look, so subtle and charming as it mocked the solemnity of the occasion, filled Diana with joyful longings. Could it be that, like any other happy bride and groom, they would end up in each other's arms tonight, then tomorrow and the next day and the day after that, laughing about this menagerie of relatives and guests as they reminisced about their wedding? A reminiscence soon interrupted by love, by kisses and hugs and the lovely security of being together . . .

But for Diana tonight would be the very first time. She had kept herself pure for Hal, through all these difficult years. And tonight she would know if the treasure she had saved was worthy of him.

This thought made her happy fantasy vanish, and almost wiped the smile of loving expectation from her face as she looked at Hal. She was no longer so sure of anything.

After all, she reflected, did she really want to see that look of cool unruffled mastery on her groom's face at this ultimate moment? Wouldn't she have preferred a more serious face, even a worried or nervous one, from her lover on the day he asked her to accept him for life?

Diana did not want this ceremony to be shallow and unimportant. She wanted it to be the solemn rite that closed a door on her lifetime of self-doubts, and joined her to Hal in a union powerful and intimate enough to make her truly his wife, his lifelong and eternal mate.

But was that happening now?

She could not help wondering whether in that little smile Hal was keeping his distance, and not giving himself to her entirely. Perhaps he was not only making fun of the public aspect of this wedding, designed to please the families' atavistic instincts and the curiosity of the admiring public that would one day be his political constituency. Perhaps he truly felt that it was merely a charade they had to go through, a performance which meant nothing.

Diana's hands began to perspire at this notion. The old feeling of clumsy unworthiness was upon her now, cruel, mocking, making her feel ashamed and ridiculous at the most important moment of her life.

Diana Stallworth, posing as Haydon Lancaster's wife! Poor little rich Diana, trying to cut a feminine figure in her Dior gown as she prepared for a role whose demands were light-years beyond her capacities.

Now she thought of the sly cynicism behind so many of those expectant smiles in the huge audience. Everyone knew Hal would be unfaithful. All the Lancaster men were unfaithful. This marriage ceremony was hardly a vow of fidelity. It was merely the preamble to a luxurious honeymoon, a thousand cocktail parties and political receptions, an endless array of prying journalists, a house in New York and another in Washington. And children—for children were necessary, children were expected . . .

It was nothing.

Nothing will come of nothing.

Diana could not recall what book she had read that line in. It was in some course at Smith, a line written by a great master about whom she could not have cared less. Now it came back to her like a dark warning, more terrible than any caution this aged bishop could intone. Yes, nothing could come from nothing. And from this marriage, conceived in sham, nothing good could emerge.

Diana struggled to put this thought out of her mind. Panic had made her body tense. Her hands felt like ice.

The bishop was speaking to them both now, his tone grave.

"I require and charge you both, here in the presence of God, that if either of you know any reason why you may not be united in marriage lawfully, and in accordance with God's word, you do now confess it."

Hal was looking at the bishop, and beyond him. There was a shadow of pain in his eyes, a look so private that in watching him Diana felt she was eavesdropping criminally on a dialogue between a man and his own soul.

She knew he had had many women. Of these, a great number must have loved him. How could they not? He was the most lovable man in the world, a man whose charms were so delightful that other men seemed like crude beasts of burden in comparison with him.

Diana had had her encounters with some of those unfortunate women, and detached them from Hal when she thought it was necessary to prevent things from going any further. The last had been little Laura

Blake, a creature of such sweetness and vulnerability that Diana had almost hated to have to burst her bubble about Hal. But what choice had she had? It was only a matter of months before her wedding. Hal's dalliances with pretty girls must stop, in the interest of his own reputation as well as the credibility of his marriage.

Diana had long since accepted Hal's promiscuity as a trait passed down through the Lancaster bloodline. Even though she knew it should not make her jealous, she hated thinking about those other women who had given as much and more to Hal than she, who had known him and needed him in so many ways.

And now, as she studied that haunted look in his eyes under the bishop's warning words, a terrible thought suddenly occurred to her. What if one of those many young women had meant more to Hal than any of the others? What if, sometime, somewhere, he had given his heart?

If this were true, then he had lost the chance to marry the one girl who really meant something to him. Through today's ceremony, indeed, he was renouncing his chance to be with her forever. And thus, behind his decorous smiles for Diana, he must be hiding a burden of grief that he must forever endure alone, which Diana could never comfort, for she herself was the cause of it.

This notion twisted in Diana's heart like a poisoned knife. She clenched her teeth and fought to put it out of her mind. Hal's eyes were turning back to her now, and she put the full measure of her love and her loyalty into the smile she gave him now.

The bishop joined their hands and spoke to Hal.

"Haydon, will you have this woman to be your wife, to live together in the covenant of marriage? Will you love her, comfort her, honor and keep her, in sickness and in health; and, forsaking all others, be faithful to her as long as you both shall live?"

"I will."

Diana's frozen hand was in Hal's now, and his warmth was so beautiful that it almost seemeed capable of melting the chill inside her soul.

"Diana, will you have this man to be your husband, to live together in the covenant of marriage? Will you love him, comfort him, honor and keep him, in sickness and in health; and, forsaking all others, be faithful to him as long as you both shall live?"

"I will." She prayed the tremor in her voice was audible to herself alone.

Nothing will come of nothing.

• • •

Will you accept children lovingly from God, and bring them up accord-
ing to the law of Christ and his Church?

Tim Riordan looked at the Catholic priest.

"I will," he said.

His voice sounded hollow in his ear, for he was overcome by the solemnity of the occasion, and the huge weight of the Catholic Church gracing his marriage.

Laura to be his wife!

Tim could not believe his good fortune. For three years Laura had owned his heart, occupying a place deeper inside his mind and imagination than any woman since his mother when he was a tiny child. The sheer force of his love had been such that he could not tell her of it. It had nearly killed him to see her become used to him and go about her business in his company, while with each passing day his obsession with her grew to more unbearable proportions.

But now it was over. Now the miracle had happened, and she had accepted him. This sweet, gentle little creature with her soft hands, her grave dark eyes, her enormous talent, and her secret feminine warmth —now she would be his wife.

It was too good to be true.

He looked at her as she murmured her response to the priest's question. Her expression was both tender and serious, tinged as always by the shadow of ancient hurt and by her courage to overcome that hurt. What sensitivity hid inside that tiny body! And what terrific strength . . .

Though there had always been something sad behind Laura's beautiful eyes, in the last few months Tim's intuition had told him she had suffered a more recent wound. He had wondered if it was a man.

He had not dreamed of broaching the subject to her directly. Not only would it have been an invasion of her privacy, but now that she had accepted him he knew she would never tell him another man had ever competed with him for her heart.

The important thing was that he had her now. And he would never let her suffer a moment's unhappiness again.

Occasionally he found himself thinking about the man who had been close to her—assuming there had been one. At these moments Tim felt strange emotions in himself. The faceless image of the man who had hurt her, who had perhaps ill-used her, dropped her, filled him with a rage so black that he could have strangled the culprit with his own hands.

On the other hand, the idea that there might have been a relationship that she herself ended in favor of Tim himself, or even a relationship that had simply ended in failure, was less terrible. Tim so admired Laura that he could even forgive a rival who had been lucky enough to be graced by her love. Indeed, he felt a kinship with the man who had fallen under her spell and, like himself, spent long nights haunted by the image of her.

Tim looked at her now. The happiness in her eyes as she looked at the priest was almost too beautiful to behold. Yet it was not without its perennial shadow of mystery. He worshiped her for every facet of her personality, from the charms he knew so well to the depths he was too crude to be able to fathom.

Tim did not know whether he deserved her. But he knew he would love her with all his heart, for as long as they both should live. He willingly plighted his troth to her in the sight of God.

And some day—he hoped soon—the children of their union would begin to come. When he saw the fruit of his love emerge from Laura's womb, his cup would have run over entirely, and life for him would be a dream come true.

The priest, having heard their vows, was speaking now.

"You have declared your consent before the Church. May the Lord in his goodness strengthen your consent and fill you both with his blessings."

The dark eyes were smiling at him from behind the veil. The small hand was offered to receive his ring. Tim touched her gently, afraid as always that his brute strength might break her if he did not rein it in with his love.

Whatever his own shortcomings, he knew one thing for sure. Laura had suffered her last loss, her last hurt. From now on she would have Tim to take care of her, day and night. And if anyone ever tried to harm her, or dared to cause her a moment's pain, Tim would destroy him without mercy. His whole being flung itself into this resolve, with a certainty and a commitment bordering on rage.

"What God has joined, let no man divide," the priest concluded.

Anyone, Tim thought.

Amen.

BOOK THREE

Prince Hal

I

1958

CBS News, January 11

A tragic story from Washington heads the news tonight. Senator Garrett Lindstrom of Michigan, a respected member of the Democratic leadership through two and a half terms, and author of several important bills in the field of appropriations and taxation, has died in what authorities are calling a suicide.

Senator Lindstrom's body was found this morning by his wife in the basement of their Georgetown home. The senator had apparently hanged himself from a basement rafter. His death came six days after a scandal that forced him to announce his resignation from the Senate. The *Detroit Examiner* last week published a story accusing Lindstrom of having leaked classified information relating to current Senate Appropriations Committee hearings. The leak, according to the story, was made to a young Washington woman with whom Lindstrom was having an illicit affair.

Four days after the story was printed, Lindstrom, faced with disciplinary action by the Senate, admitted having inadvertently leaked the sensitive information. The same evening he made a televised speech to the people of Michigan in which he resigned his Senate seat.

THE OFFICE WAS in darkness. The television screen was a blue glow against a wall lined with old bookcases and photos in small black frames. Oversized leather furniture loomed heavily in the shadows. The place smelled of books, cigar smoke, and tradition. Beyond the windows with their venetian blinds, the Washington Monument could be glimpsed, along with the glow of the Mall against the night sky.

Behind the large desk sat a man in middle age, puffing quietly at a cigar as he gazed at the image of Douglas Edwards on the screen. Across the room from him, on the deep leather couch, sat a young woman, watching the news report intently.

On the screen there now appeared the tired, haggard face of a handsome man in his forties. It was Garrett Lindstrom, saying his farewell to the people of his state.

"All my life," he said, "I have only had one ambition: to be a member of the United States Senate. For fourteen years my dream came true. I was privileged to serve with some of the most distinguished legislators in my nation's history. Now, because of a tragic error in judgment for which I alone am to blame, I have not only destroyed that dream, but dishonored the institution that I served with my whole heart for so many years. I can only apologize to my fellow senators, to the people of Michigan, and to all the citizens of the United States of America for what I have done, and ask you to believe that my error in no way reflects upon the entire Senate, or Congress, but on myself alone."

The image disappeared, replaced once more by the face of Douglas Edwards.

"Senator Garrett Lindstrom," Edwards said, "dead at forty-six by his own hand. The young woman to whom the late senator leaked the sensitive information remains a mystery. Her name is reportedly Miss Dawn Thayer. Sources have told CBS News that Miss Thayer until a few weeks ago was employed as a secretary in the Department of the Interior. According to spokesmen for the Justice Department, Miss Thayer related the information she learned from Senator Lindstrom to a reporter of her acquaintance, who in turn passed it to the editors of the *Detroit Examiner*, which broke the story last week. We have not been able to reach Miss Thayer for comment. Her whereabouts are unknown."

A blurred image of Senator Lindstrom with a young woman filled the screen. The girl had long, wavy blonde hair, and wore sunglasses. She might have been any of a thousand attractive young secretaries, lobbyists, government employees, and party girls who lived in Washington.

The man behind the desk motioned to the girl on the couch, who arose, turned off the television set, and closed the oak panel that hid the screen in the bookcase. She returned to the couch and sat looking at the man.

Her eyes were filled with tears. She trembled slightly.

"No one was supposed to get hurt," she said. "You told me that no one would get hurt. You promised me."

The man looked at her appraisingly. He seemed unmoved by her display of nerves. He puffed at his cigar before speaking.

"I kept your real name out of it, didn't I?" he asked quietly.

"Real name!" Her voice shook. "Don't you think they'll be able to find me if they want to badly enough? They leaked the story, didn't they? You didn't stop them from doing that, did you? And Lindstrom . . ."

He shook his head with a smile.

"Leslie," he said, "you must try to understand that there is much more here than meets the eye. In fact, your role in this entire business depends on the fact that you must not know what is behind it all, and what the repercussions are. Now, don't underestimate me. I told you I would protect you, and I will do so. You were a wonderful Dawn Thayer, and you did the job I assigned you to do. Do you think I would forget a thing like that?"

"You said no one would get hurt," she repeated, stubborn even in her panic.

"Now, listen to me," he said. "You may not realize this, Leslie, but you have served your country. You were not involved here in a mere vendetta between one man and another, or between two groups of men. You were involved in a struggle between good and evil, between our way of life and those who would destroy that way of life. You have performed a valuable service to your country under difficult conditions. And your country will take care of you. Do you believe that?"

There was no answer.

"Technically, of course, you've committed a crime," he added, his tone more menacing now. "A crime for which you could be punished severely by the courts. But it is precisely in perilous times like these that our duty to our country compels us to go beyond the law. You see, my dear, whether you realize it or not, you're a hero. And as such, you will be protected."

She looked up at him, hearing the mixture of cajolery and danger in his words. She was as afraid of him as she was of the authorities.

This was the way he wanted it.

The long blonde wig used for the photo that had just appeared in the news report was gone now, replaced by natural chestnut curls that fell only to her shoulders. Without the sunglasses she had attractive hazel eyes and a pretty complexion. She looked more like a small-town girl than a Washington beauty—though even now he observed the perfect figure under her conservative dress. Her sexuality was very natural and unpretentious. She had a nice face and an honest, down-to-earth manner.

He looked at the shadowed office behind the girl. The walls were cluttered with pictures of himself with all the important leaders of the last twenty years, from Roosevelt and Cordell Hull to Acheson and Truman and Stevenson, Eisenhower, Rayburn, Taft, Lyndon Johnson. In the photos he himself could be seen growing over the years from a robust young senator with a large head and curly hair to a barrel-chested, balding man in middle age whose gray eyes had grown sharper and colder as the political wars hardened him.

He was a man conscious of the sacrifices he had made, the battles he had won, the political blood he had shed in order to achieve the highest power a senator can achieve. Today he was chairman of the Senate Appropriations Committee and ranking member of the Foreign Relations Committee. Those titles, though hugely important, could not communicate the extent of his power. By any accounting he was the one man in the Senate who could, through methods known only to himself and his intimate associates, swing enough votes to pass any bill he really wanted to pass. No senator dared refuse his friendship, on either side of the aisle. No man dared risk his enmity, whatever his politics.

His name was Amory Bose.

Gar Lindstrom had made the mistake of getting on the wrong side of him.

Lindstrom had been more than a liberal opponent of Bose's right-wing power base on the Appropriations Committee. He was a dedicated enemy who was quickly making friends hostile to Bose, on the committee and throughout the Senate. And Lindstrom was a canny enough organizer to put the power of these friends together—given enough time. Worse yet, he was a moral fanatic of Lutheran background, and for several years had been conducting a private investigation into the tactics by which Bose gained and used political influence in the Senate.

Indeed, Gar Lindstrom had been much more than a nay vote to Bose. He had been the worst single threat to Bose's power in twenty years.

That was why Bose had hand-picked Leslie to take Lindstrom out of the ball game.

She had come along at the perfect moment. She was still relatively clean, almost unknown, innocent-looking, and, in her way, very sexy. Bose had investigated her background thoroughly before making the decision to use her. And his instincts had paid off.

She had played her part to perfection. Thanks to the natural sweetness underneath her faintly tarnished exterior, she had gained Lindstrom's confidence right away. He became dependent enough on her sympathy to let a few secrets on Defense appropriations slip when he was in her arms. That was all Bose needed.

Ellison Gardner, the editor of the *Detroit Examiner*, had owed Bose a major favor for fifteen years, and was willing to print what he was told, when he was told. The story came out under a banner headline, with the damning photo of "Dawn Thayer" on Lindstrom's arm, and the rest was history.

Naturally the girl was frightened now that Lindstrom had done the unexpected and killed himself. But Bose knew how to soothe her and keep her quiet. As for Bose himself, he was privately delighted that Lindstrom would not survive to write his memoirs. Men like him were better off dead.

Bose looked at the girl. She was pensive, wondering what sort of horror she had got herself into, and when the news media would track her down.

"I've found you a new job," he said. "You'll disappear into the big world of working girls. In a few days Lindstrom will be forgotten. No one will come after you. I'll see to that."

"I don't want to be here in Washington," she said nervously. "I've got to get away from here."

He thought for a moment, then nodded. "All right. I can get you something in New York. I think that's the best place for you. Simply stay where you are for the next few days. Don't call anyone or see anyone. I'll have Earl get in touch with you."

The girl shuddered inwardly at the name of Bose's special assistant, the fat, bespectacled man named Earl, with his cruel eyes and threatening demeanor. It had been Earl who first found her, it was thanks to Earl that she had gotten into this mess.

She had come to Washington straight from Illinois, where she had been a wayward teenager oppressed by her straitlaced Swedish parents. Her low grades in school belied her high IQ, for life in the boondocks stifled her willful nature. She was a girl in search of excitement and adventure. And she was good-looking.

Like many of her contemporaries, she ended up in Washington, where she found a secretarial job after a Civil Service exam, and drifted more or less willingly into the Washington party scene, meeting a variety of lower-level politicians, and allowing them to romance her. Though not a naturally promiscuous girl—her background had left its mark—she was not loath to spend the night with a man if he treated her well enough.

She had been in town less than a year when the man named Earl introduced himself to her at a party and asked her to have dinner with him. She was afraid of him at first, but agreed when he said he had an important proposition to put to her that would advance her career in a hurry.

Their dinner had taken place in Amory Bose's office in the Old Senate Office Building. She knew enough about Washington by then to know who Bose was and how important he was.

Bose had both impressed and intimidated her. He made her stop all her social and romantic contacts. He told her he had something much more important than that in line for her. The power of his personality was daunting. He could be fatherly when it suited him, or cruelly coercive. She noticed that the picture of his college-aged daughter on the desk top bore a certain resemblance to herself.

When he asked her to go to bed with him, she did not refuse. Something authoritative in his demeanor made her both fascinated and afraid to displease him. She was a bit unnerved by his sexual preferences—he wanted only oral sex, and he said strange, ugly things during his excitement—but she was sufficiently swayed by his fame and position to overcome her scruples.

After a while he told her about Lindstrom. He shrouded the affair in secrecy from the start, telling her it was important for national security reasons that she not know the background of it all or where it was leading. She was to make friends with Lindstrom, get him into bed, and await further orders. There was ten thousand dollars in it for her if she did the job right, and job security for the rest of her Washington life. But secrecy was crucial.

Bose had a friend introduce her to Lindstrom at a party. Oddly enough, they hit it off quite naturally. Lindstrom was an attractive man, and he shared with her a straitlaced Midwest background. She liked hearing him talk, and liked the way he treated her. He was a nice man, and an honest one.

Going to bed with him was a pleasure. He was gentle and really quite romantic. Afterward he sent her flowers, notes, little presents. He was so kind, so considerate, that after a few dates she could hardly imagine her affair with him as being wrong. He was a sweet, overworked, lonely man who only wanted a little female warmth and companionship.

On Bose's orders she got Lindstrom to talk about the Committee. There was an important Defense Appropriations bill under discussion, with heavy pressure from the Joint Chiefs and the National Security Council to recommend passage. It was on this bill that Lindstrom was at loggerheads with Bose. Emboldened by the fact that he knew Eisenhower did not really want the bill passed, Lindstrom was mustering support to kill it in committee and save the nation four and a half billion dollars. Bose wanted it passed, for the sake of some powerful friends at Defense, and because it would make a good plum for his Senate campaign later this year.

Lindstrom made the mistake of confiding to Leslie some of the classified plans for the new missiles the DOD wanted the appropriation for. They were souped-up ICBMs, which Eisenhower had already declared unnecessary in comparison with the current B-52 fleet.

Leslie reported what she had heard to Bose. After that, Bose sent her to Lindstrom with a small microphone planted in her purse. She made sure to leave the purse near the bed in the hotel rooms where she had her trysts, so that the bug could pick up her murmured bedroom conversations with Lindstrom.

This went on for no longer than a week. Then all at once a story with banner headlines appeared in the *Detroit Examiner* about Lindstrom leaking classified information to a "girlfriend" of dubious reputation. The one picture that Bose's people had managed to get of Leslie with Lindstrom accompanied the story. The next thing she knew, Lindstrom's face and her own were all over the media.

Then Lindstrom was dead.

Leslie was shaken and frightened. Events had far outstripped her wildest imaginings about Lindstrom and her mission. All she had to protect her now was Bose himself. And he frightened her as much as what he had made her do. She was not in a mood to dally with him any longer.

"All right," she said now. "I just want this to be over. I'd like to leave for New York right away, if you don't mind. I'll get a room at the Y or something."

"All that will be taken care of. You just stay where you are for a few more days, and don't talk to anyone. Earl will find you a place in New York. Your job will be waiting for you when you get there."

She stood up to leave. There was still reproach in her eyes, and fear.

"Goodbye, then," she said.

Bose shook his head in the shadows of the office. He looked almost amused at her consternation.

"That's not a very friendly farewell," he said. "Can't you be a little more affectionate, Leslie?"

She sighed. She knew what he wanted.

"I really can't, Mr. Bose. Not after—not after what's happened." She looked nervously at him. "Gar Lindstrom had a family. A wife, children . . . I hope you can understand. I just can't. I've got to get away from here."

His face had darkened.

"It's you who don't understand, my dear."

The words chilled her to the marrow of her bones. She understood the threat. She was smart enough to realize that a man powerful and audacious enough to engineer the destruction of a United States senator would not hesitate to crush a pawn as insignificant as she.

Charily she approached him. He had pushed the large armchair away from the desk. He was sitting with his legs spread, a rather coy posture, his cigar still burning in his hand. He looked ugly and somehow devilish in the shadows, with the smoke curling around his large head. His sensuality frightened her.

She came to his side. He ran a hand up her thighs to her buttocks and fondled her gently. Despite herself she trembled at his touch. This did not seem to bother him. Just the opposite, in fact. She heard a small grunt of excitement. The stubby fingers slipped over the silk of the panties, then under the elastic band. He pulled them down to her knees, then watched her step out of them. He held them in one hand while she knelt to undo his zipper.

She remained fully clothed as she took him in her mouth. He sat in the chair, his eyes seeing nothing, the panties held to his lips as her head moved over his sex. She tried to control her trembling. She did not know which was worse, her disgust or the chill of terror inside her.

She could tell he was enjoying her fear. There was a little sigh of satisfaction as his hips rolled against her face. She felt like a slave, on her knees before him in her dress, the awful sex moving in her mouth, the power and perversity of the man poised to spew itself into her.

"Doesn't that taste good?" he asked. "I know you girls love the taste . . ."

She could feel him looking at the picture of his daughter on the desk top. Hot tears started out in her eyes. She had never felt so degraded. It seemed as though she had the devil himself in her mouth. Surely no punishment could be too severe for such a sin.

"Is this what you did to Lindstrom?" he asked. "I'll bet you gave him a good time, didn't you? Tell me, Leslie: Where do you like it? Where do you like a man to come? Did Lindstrom give it to you where you like it most? Did you tell him where to stick it? Come on, now, tell Amory the truth. Don't be bashful."

He droned on, his voice shaken by pleasure. The images called up by his words were more and more cruel, more and more perverse. He detailed the parts of a woman's body in a sick litany, evoking their attractions in order to insult them one by one.

"You'd cry if I didn't let you have it, wouldn't you?" he asked. "Wouldn't you cry great big crocodile tears? Just like poor Mrs. Lindstrom is crying tonight? Crying because you killed her husband?"

She wanted to vomit. But she controlled herself. She stayed with him as he bucked and strained and gasped his enjoyment. When his orgasm came she managed to finish it without retching. She just wanted to get out of there as soon as possible, and alive.

She got to her feet and moved away from him. She saw him toying with the panties, a sated look in his eyes. She was not about to ask for them back.

He watched her put on her coat and pick up her purse. "I'll be in touch," he said as she opened the door. She nodded without answering.

The phone rang as the door was closing on her frightened eyes. Amory Bose answered it.

"Yes?"

"This is Warren Hough, Senator. Sorry to bother you this late."

He recognized the familiar voice of his chief of staff and longtime campaign manager.

"What is it?" Bose asked.

"Something important. I thought you should know right away. I found out from a friend that Haydon Lancaster is going to announce for your seat tomorrow. He's going up against you in the primary."

Bose's face darkened. This was the last news he wanted to hear. Just as the Lindstrom business was tidied up, here came a new problem out of left field.

"You're sure about this?" he asked.

"Positive." The voice on the phone was uncomfortable, apologetic.

Bose thought for a moment. The panties were still in his hand, forgotten now.

Frowning, he spoke into the phone. "All right," he said. "No statement until you hear from me. If the press corners you, just tell them the Senator welcomes all comers, it's a democratic society, may the best man win. And so on."

"All right, sir. See you tomorrow morning."

Bose hung up the phone.

He thought of Lancaster, the photogenic young war hero with his pretty wife and his glamorous reputation, his left-wing politics and his inevitable ambition. He should have known this was coming.

Good and evil, he thought.

You're finished, Lancaster, he mused as he fondled the panties. *You don't know it yet, but you're finished.*

• • •

Leslie moved as quickly as she could to the ladies' room. Thankfully, there was no one in it. She went into one of the stalls and threw up into the toilet. She retched long and hard. She had never felt so filthy in her life.

Filthy and scared. Amory Bose was like a poison that seeped into one's very bones, a taint that could not be eradicated. She trembled to think of the future, of Earl, of Bose's tentacles, of what else he might ask her to do. For she was an intelligent girl. She knew that men like Bose did not simply let go when they had their hooks into people.

When she had lost the worst of her nausea she left the stall, went to the sink, washed her face, and fixed her hair.

In two days she would be out of this town. But how far away would she have to go to escape Bose?

It was not a matter of distance, she knew. No distance could make her safe from him.

It was a matter of power.

With this thought in mind she looked down at her bra and touched it carefully.

Inside it was a tiny microphone.

Leslie had taken the precaution before coming here. Bose himself had given her the idea when he armed her with a bug for her trysts with Lindstrom. Her conversation of tonight, as well as Bose's filthy sex talk, had been recorded on a machine in a parked car a block from the Capitol.

The good Lord had not given Leslie a brain for nothing. Someday, somehow, that tape might make all the difference in the world.

With a last sickened look at her face in the mirror, she left the bathroom.

II

January 13, 1958

"MRS. LANCASTER, may I say that you're looking very beautiful, as usual?"

"Why, thank you. You're awfully kind."

Diana looked a trifle nervously at the dozen or so journalists assembled in the downstairs salon. Two of them were TV reporters sharing a feed, and the hot lights they had set up were blinding her. She hoped her make-up would last; she was still baffled by the subtleties of television make-up, and had spent half an hour retouching her eyes in anticipation of this interview.

Today was an important day. This was the first time the press had been invited to the house Hal and Diana had moved into on Fifth Avenue. In accordance with the occasion Diana had invited the most influential of those writers who covered the gray area in which society and politics dovetailed.

They had been given the grand tour of the house by Ellen, Diana's secretary, and Susan Pfeiffer, Diana's personal public relations assistant. Since the unveiling of the place was considered a major event, the reporters had taken their time, making careful notes on the priceless furnishings and paintings that had been contributed by various Lancaster and Stallworth relatives, from the Meissen vases in the living room to the almost legendary Turner landscape which dominated the upstairs sitting room.

It was a fabulous house, with six bedrooms, two salons, a dining room large enough to accommodate any political group Hal took it into his head to invite, a library for his many books, a beautiful solarium in back, and a completely finished fifth floor with billiard room, study, and a reading room for Diana.

All in all, it was just small enough to pass for the posh Manhattan digs of a young childless couple instead of the headquarters of an extended family. Diana's father had had to use all his contacts and a considerable amount of muscle to get it away from its previous owners, an elderly stock trader and his wife who needed the income from this sale to finance their retirement in Palm Springs. It was the only place in this part of Fifth Avenue that Harry Stallworth deemed suitable for a young man of Hal's background and future.

When the journalists had completed their tour they sat down to interview Diana. They were impressed by the show, of course—though hardly awed. These were two dozen of the best-known and most jaded reporters in the country. They had all covered Diana many times, both before and after her marriage.

They knew they had been invited today because both Diana and Hal sorely needed their bylines and their goodwill. Public exposure, with the right tone, was a must for the Lancasters now more than ever, since with Hal's hat in the ring against the redoubtable Amory Bose for the Democratic Senate nomination, a tough campaign loomed ahead.

With this in mind Diana's people had prepared the ground carefully for the occasion. The journalists had all been sent engraved invitations, and a month ago each one of them had received a lavish and carefully chosen Christmas gift from the Lancasters—a bottle of aged Armagnac for Naomi Russell of the *Times*, who was known to be a great tippler of brandy; a champagne cooler of solid silver for Vera Strick of the *San Francisco Chronicle*, who had done a feature on Diana last summer; a pair of jade earrings with matching necklace for Madeleine Baron of the *Washington Post*; a set of crystal glasses for Erica Crittendon of CBS, who loved to entertain; and so on.

These reporters had to be treated with kid gloves, for each possessed a large audience and could do Diana a lot of harm with a few well-chosen innuendos. But Diana had conscientiously courted them all, and so could reasonably expect a good result from this long morning's work.

That did not mean it was going to be easy.

The questions began with Patricia Hand of UPI.

"Tell me, Mrs. Lancaster," she said, "now that your husband has challenged Amory Bose for the Democratic Senate nomination from New York, have you found that the pace of your married life has changed? Are you seeing less of your husband?"

Diana smiled. So far so good.

"A bit more, actually," she said. "At the outset there were a lot of meetings which kept Hal busy. But he's very good at budgeting his time. And now that he's no longer working overseas for the President, I'm lucky enough to have him home much of the time."

Naomi Russell of the *Times* took up the question.

"Isn't there a built-in conflict," she asked, "between your husband's busy career and your home life? Do you ever feel like a political widow?"

"Not at all," Diana smiled softly. "Hal and I both understand that he has chosen a career in public service that will make demands on his time and energy. We've managed to find ways to make our time together as effective and valuable for us as it can possibly be. For instance, I'm up early to have a long breakfast with him, and we have dinner together quite late, when the day's work is finally over. We often find time to sit in front of the fire at odd hours, and talk over what's been happening lately."

"Your husband's career has been controversial up to this point," observed Jessica Vogel of NBC, to whom Diana had sent a signed print at Christmas by a New York artist she was known to admire. "His political views are sure to be a hot topic in the Senate campaign. Tell me, does he ask your advice on the more sensitive issues? In your case as in others, can we say that behind every great man there is a great woman?"

Diana laughed modestly.

"Not a great woman, no. But I must say that Hal tells me about the political problems that are on his mind. I think any man would confide his major concerns to his wife. When he asks my advice, I give it—that is, if I have anything constructive to say. But I don't expect him to follow my advice in every case. He has a mind of his own, as you well know."

Diana was being very gentle. There was something almost languid about her responses and her demeanor that contrasted remarkably with the rather mercurial girl she had been not so many years ago. All the reporters knew that this image was carefully calculated, and few believed there was anything genuine behind it. But that hardly mattered to them.

It now fell to Madeleine Baron to open the topic that was the press's bread and butter where Hal and Diana were concerned.

"Mrs. Lancaster," she said, "not only are you a beautiful woman whose looks are admired everywhere. You're also married to the man who is considered, among all American politicians, to be the most attractive, indeed the most sexy. How do you handle the attention this double role brings to you?"

Diana smiled. "Well," she said, "I must admit it's not easy being married to a man who has so many female admirers. I make it my business to see that he doesn't get a swelled head."

The joke fell flat among the unsmiling, indifferent reporters. But Diana's pleasant smile and attempt at wit would come across well on television, and would be reported prominently in their articles. She was not here to make friends, but to make a media impression. And they were not here to like her, but to get valuable copy out of her.

"But seriously," Diana added, "I consider myself a very lucky woman. I've known Hal since he was a sensitive and terrifically handsome young boy. I've watched him grow into a dedicated, hardworking man who is not only very attractive, but also a fine, loving husband. I feel my job is to be as good and supportive a wife to him as I can."

There was an almost audible smirk of incredulity in the room.

"Since you mention it," asked Alexa Burke of the *Chicago Tribune*, "of course everyone is aware of the public side of Haydon Lancaster's charm. But what about the private side? I'm not asking whether he snores, or leaves hair in the washbowl—but what is he like to be close to?"

They all knew what she was asking, and their pens were appropriately poised. There were three key topics in any interview with Diana: her wealth, what Hal was like in bed, and how soon Hal would run for president. No matter how monotonous the questions and answers were for Diana and the reporters, the public never tired of them, and they had to be asked.

"Hal is a very thoughtful man," Diana said sincerely. "Very tender and gentle, in all ways. That's how he was when I first met him, and that's how he is today. He doesn't put a woman on a pedestal; nor does he patronize her. He treats me as his equal. Yet he treats me as the person he loves. I don't really know how to say it any other way. We're very close. We need each other, and we don't do well when we're apart. I miss him terribly, and he misses me."

Her jugular was exposed now, thanks to her blunder in mentioning her separations from Hal. Too late she realized that one of the vultures present was sure to strike.

It turned out to be Vera Strick of the *Chronicle*.

"Naturally, you know you're among friends here, Mrs. Lancaster," Vera began. "Most of us have known you for years, and always enjoy seeing you and talking to you. But I think the public is curious about the rumors that you and your husband have, in fact, been seeing less and less of each other. It is common knowledge that you spent an extended stay at Newport last summer while he remained in New York except for one weekend; that you spent two weeks without him in Nassau last spring; and that during his four-month stay in Helsinki for the arms talks, you joined him only twice. People are wondering how you keep a marriage going without seeing each other."

The knife was plunged firmly into the wound. Vera Strick sat back with a satisfied look on her hard features.

Diana mustered her brightest smile.

"Those separations were painful," she said, "for both of us. At the time, given the pressures on Hal, we saw no other alternative. But as things turned out, being apart was too much of a strain for us. We only ended up paying the biggest phone bill in history. We've decided that with the Senate campaign ahead of us, we're going to stick together, come what may. Besides, we have more fun together anyway. We're each other's best booster and comic relief."

The answer had been rehearsed at length, at Susan Pfeiffer's suggestion. Her sharp eye for the press had warned her that the separation issue was sure to be a danger today.

The reporters raised eyebrows in acknowledgment of Diana's polish and preparation. Vera Strick jotted down the response without expression.

Diana breathed an inner sigh of relief.

But she was not over the worst yet.

Erica Crittendon of CBS asked the next question.

"I don't wish to intrude on what is of course a private matter," she said. "But naturally everyone is waiting for you and your husband to start a family." She gestured to the spacious salon in which they were sitting. "This is an awfully big house for a childless couple."

She let the word *childless* sink in for an instant. "Of course, it's none of our business—but are you intentionally waiting to have a family, or are you . . . trying to start one now?"

Diana hid herself a trifle more desperately behind the soft glow of her blue eyes.

"To answer your question honestly," she said, "Hal and I decided when we got married to give ourselves some time to be alone together, rather than to rush things. As I say, we are very close, and we want to build a life around that closeness. But now we feel that we're ready to start a family quite soon. I wouldn't say that we're precisely 'trying,' nor that we're 'waiting.' We're simply letting things come naturally."

She had rehearsed this speech for nearly two weeks. It had been decided that the titillating phrase "come naturally" would enhance the image of Diana as the only woman in America who knew her handsome husband's charms in bed, while assuring that the couple's childlessness was intentional. The idea was that the lack of children came not from an absence of intimacy, but rather from the natural interval of sexual enjoyment to which this vibrant young couple had a right.

Children would come in their own time; meanwhile Hal and Diana were America's sweethearts, in bed as well as on the society pages. Such was the campaign.

Of course, everybody in this room knew it was not true. Diana was having trouble conceiving, despite the ministrations of the best gynecologists in New York, and her lengthy separations from Hal were hardly facilitating the making of a baby. Moreover, Hal's dozens of flings and one-night stands with other women, which were an open secret with the press and the political fraternity, could hardly be helping the situation.

The unsmiling women in this gathering had more than an inkling of the truth behind this marriage made in heaven. But they could not dream of printing that truth.

Nor could they imagine what it was doing to Diana.

The pressure on her to give Hal an heir went infinitely deeper than the mere romantic fantasies of a whimsical public, and deeper even than the concerns of their respective families. It sprung from the empty center of her marriage itself, a marriage already so barren in its essence that only children could save it.

Inside himself Hal must have concluded long ago that his life with Diana was merely an obligation to be endured for form's sake. He could not hide this fact, not even behind the bedroom charm that was an extension of his princely regard for his wife's needs and feelings. She knew now that he did not love her and would never have married her had their respective social positions in life not forced them together. Two years of marriage had amply convinced her of this sad reality.

The doctors having decreed that he and Diana must have sex on a set of dictated nights each month, calibrated precisely to the intervals surrounding ovulation, Hal dutifully came to her with his beautiful body, aroused her with his caresses, and took her with strokes so slow, so terribly deep and exciting, that her orgasms were little gasping explosions that echoed in the silence of the dark house.

He could not know that her cries and murmurs carried far more pain than pleasure, and more anguish than delight.

Diana knew how aware he was of her lonely dilemma. His obliging, deferential manner made it obvious. But he could not know that the most intimate of his caresses only made her feel more alone than ever. There was nothing he could do to help, of course, beyond the mere bestowal of his seed. The rest was up to her.

When she knew it was time to make love she grew unbearably tense, worrying that her terror would make her dry between her legs, so that he would think she was frigid, and hate her for it.

Ironically, she was anything but indifferent to him. Indeed, she could never watch Hal walk through a room without being moved by his smile, his humor, his handsome body. But being close to him was an exquisite ordeal. There was a withdrawal at the heart of his tenderness, an absence that filled her with cold fear and with a terrible loathing of herself.

Worse yet, she knew she was sharing this lovely male flesh with strangers. She could feel the mocking ghosts of those other women all around him when he came to her, women he was screwing, women who must surely be spreading whispers about his prowess all over New York and Washington and Paris and Bonn and London.

She could feel the traces of their hands and mouths all over him, feel the traces of their hungry sex on that proud, tremendous penis that entered her, and almost hear the echo of their sighs of pleasure in her own moans of orgasm.

So it was that when he was deep inside her, the heat she felt was also a coldness, harsh and burning as dry ice, the more painful because Hal was not really there, because she was alone.

Worst of all, she could not bring herself to blame Hal for a philandering that not only descended to him from generations of Lancaster men, but which he probably needed for human warmth, human contact, since Diana was so far from being able to fulfill him as a wife.

So she gave herself to him in terror and in loneliness, haunted by the faceless shadows of the other women whom he had gratified with his seed, wondering whether she could conceive a child out of what he had left for her, and suspecting in advance that it was all a waste of time, a waste of his effort.

Nothing could come of nothing. Since their intimacy was empty, so must her womb remain empty.

Each month Diana waited for her hopes to be dashed. And when the day came, right on schedule, the discharge between her legs making her feel more unclean and unworthy than ever, she would tell Hal the unwelcome news, and he would pat her on the shoulder and try to encourage her.

"It will come," he would say. "Don't put pressure on yourself."

How lonely those words made her feel! And how desolate was the brief interval of days before he came to her once more, manfully prepared to try again to impregnate his barren wife.

All of these watching journalists knew of her shame and her humiliation. But none knew about her pain, or cared.

Nor could they know, she hoped, about the other secret she was trying to keep from them, and from the world, nowadays. A secret she was finding it harder to hide with each passing month.

Diana was drinking more now.

Each day she drank because she was frightened by life, in one or another of its perils. Today she had drunk because she was frightened by reporters.

The gentle, languid manner they were noticing in her this morning was in fact the glow of two strong vodka martinis.

Diana was expert at holding the drinks she took as tranquilizers before interviews. She never slurred a word, never looked haggard or unkempt, never said an offensive thing or lost track of the questions at hand. But she was quietly, gently plastered—and those closest to her were beginning to realize it.

No one said a word, of course, because Diana had reached that twilight moment in the life of every drinker when the liquor accentuated her best qualities while not yet disturbing the outer surface of her personality—at which it was, however, patiently eating away. Thus

Diana was a bit more charming, more happy, more tactful, even more intellectual when she was drinking—which was, nowadays, most of the time.

Most mornings she needed a pick-me-up to cut through the faint haze of her hangover from the night before. Then she drank a cocktail or two with lunch—vodka left only telltale signs on her breath—in order to blunt the edge of the morning's challenges and to smooth the way for the afternoon.

Then it was a race between the clock and her nerves as she waited for the cocktail hour. Sometimes a dip into the tiny flask in her purse was necessary to see her through. Then cocktails before dinner, wine with the meal, and a stiff vodka consumed furtively afterward, completed her drinking day.

For the last year or so Diana had felt calmer than in a long time. Alcohol seemed precisely the tonic she needed. It provided the little breathing space between herself and reality, the minimal cushion that could ensure both good behavior and a measure of well-being. Looking back, she wished she had had it during her courtship and the first year of her marriage.

But the balance was delicate. The armor of her courage was beginning to crack at inopportune times. The little flask was refilled each evening now, instead of once a week. And this morning, when she had stolen the two stiff vodkas in preparation for the reporters, was only one in a series of mornings requiring that extra dose to hold off one threat or another.

And now that the morning was coming to its end, and lunch was still almost an hour away, Diana needed a drink. Badly.

She was in luck, for the journalists had finished their questions, and were packing away their notepads as the camera crew turned off the lights and asked Diana for a couple of final close-ups.

"Thank you very much for coming, ladies," Susan Pfeiffer was saying. "We have some *hors d'oeuvre* for you, and some *petits fours*, and coffee, tea, champagne—and of course your press kits are ready for you, should you wish to take them along. We hope to see you again soon. Don't say anything nasty about us, now!" She finished with a laugh.

It went unnoticed. The journalists gathered in three small groups—they were rivals, as it happened, and had grown to loathe each other through many years of press junkets, parties, and shared assignments at close quarters—and began moodily eating the canapés offered by the waiters and sipping their champagne.

Diana, standing with Susan in the front of the room while the cameramen packed their things, could instantly see she was a fifth wheel. The reporters ate of her offerings as though they were at a convention. As they consumed their free lunch they fell into catty conversation about various society figures, occasionally darting hostile glances at those of their number who were in rival cliques.

"You okay?" Susan murmured, touching at Diana's elbow as she looked out over the room.

"Fine," Diana assured her with a brave smile.

"You did great," Susan said. "You came through with flying colors. Just remember, they need you so much more than you need them . . ."

If only that were true, Diana mused sadly as she gazed at the white-gloved, bitchy throng before her. Yes, they had to publish the party line she gave them, because their livelihood depended on her and on people like her.

But she knew how they really felt about her. At the first opportunity they would gladly give her the first push into hell—provided they were sure they could get away with it. Even as they got a story out of her while she was afloat, they would attack the instant they smelled blood in the water. That was what journalists were, after all: sharks who celebrated their prey in word and image while waiting to devour it.

In any case, Susan had the roles reversed. Diana needed them even more than they needed her. And Hal needed them, too. The image of the Lancasters as America's Sweethearts was a crucial adjunct to Hal's own image as the most stellar and attractive of up-and-coming political leaders. And Hal would need every bit of public relations clout he could muster to defeat the powerful Amory Bose. Hal's advisors knew Bose would play rough. He would not give up his Senate seat lying down. Hal needed to have the press on his side. And so did his wife.

So Diana had to stand here, like an overdressed ugly duckling, ignored by her own guests, and hold herself ready to enter into the small talk they would not condescend to make with her. After twenty or thirty minutes of circulating uncomfortably on the outskirts of their three little closed groups, she would see them out with a graciousness that belied the hurt they were causing her now. Then she would be alone to lick her wounds and try to salvage her tattered pride.

If only she had children! The thought came unbidden, almost surprising in its novelty—for she almost never thought about the actual flesh-and-blood children who might emerge from her lonely struggle to get pregnant for Hal. Suddenly, right at this moment, she wished she had her own offspring to take care of, to dress and play with and read bedtime stories to. Children whose voices would fill this house after these awful women had gone, children whose warm little bodies and whose need for love would fill the rest of this day for Diana as their happy mother.

But even as she lingered over this fantasy, Diana had to admit to herself that she wanted Hal far more than she wanted his children.

If she could spend five minutes of earthly time at the center of his heart, she would die happy. To belong to him just once, and to have him accept her, would be worth a thousand children.

But that was not to be. Diana had no escape. There was no place for her but this hot seat that showed no signs of cooling, and which could only become more painful yet in the event she became a senator's wife, giving lavish parties in the heart of Washington, that cruelest of all societies.

But there was no point in looking forward to that horror yet. Better to confine herself to seeing this bevy of pencil-bearing sharks out of her house, and then to face the more immediate perils of the day ahead.

In twenty minutes she would be alone.

Then she could have a drink.

. . .

As it turned out she was not so lucky.

The journalists were slow in leaving, and she had to rush through a change of clothes and make-up in order to arrive at the Plaza by twelve-thirty in time for lunch with several members of the Junior League. She could not keep them waiting, for they were part of a statewide organization called Women for Lancaster, which would be a valuable asset to the campaign against Amory Bose. It was a feather in Hal's cap to get any part of the Junior League involved in Democratic politics. Diana had to do her utmost to cement this unlikely friendship.

By the time her chauffeur got her to the Plaza she was almost shaking from thirst. She entered the Oak Room, with its familiar Tudor beams and unpleasant echo, and saw the *maître d'hôtel* smile at her in greeting.

She was moving toward him when she heard her name spoken.

"Diana! What a small world . . ."

The voice was familiar. When Diana turned in its direction she saw a table for four, and a face hardly changed by the passage of nearly six years.

Linda Preston stood up and came to her side with the same athletic stride she had known so well when they were roommates at Smith.

"Remember me?" she asked. "Long time, no see."

"Linda!" Diana brightened, and kissed her old friend on the cheek. "My God, you look wonderful. How are you?"

"Same old me," Linda said. "You look fabulous, of course. Come on, I want you to meet my husband."

Linda led her to her table, where a handsome man in his thirties was looking up at her expectantly. With him was an older couple, very prosperous-looking, but with the air of professional people rather than society folk.

"Diana Lancaster," Linda said, "meet Scott Stephenson. Scott, this is *the* Diana."

"I'd know you anywhere," the man said, rising to shake Diana's hand. "Any roommate of Linda's is a roommate of mine." He was an attractive and athletic-looking fellow, a bit too tanned for this time of year. Diana wondered if he was one of the San Francisco Stephensons. Her instincts alerted her to the high-society breeding behind his down-to-earth manner.

"Scott's a lawyer here in town," Linda said. "He's probably sued at least one of your family's companies, or been sued by you. He's with Wellman, McLean, Sebring, and Stephenson." There was more than a hint of pride in Linda's voice over her husband's high position in the firm.

"I'm pleased to meet you," Diana said. "I suppose Linda has told you all sorts of tall tales about our wild days at Smith."

"Nothing a good lawyer couldn't get you out of," he laughed. "It's wonderful to meet you at last. Of course I see your picture in the papers all the time; but we always talk about you as 'our' Diana. It's great to join up the past and present."

Linda introduced Diana to the older couple—Mr. and Mrs. Sebring, of the firm—and asked if she could join them for a drink. With a glance toward the Junior League's table, which was still empty, Diana accepted. The waiter brought her a vodka gibson, from which she took an intentionally small sip as she looked at her old friend.

"You really do look marvelous," she told Linda. "Do you have children?"

"Two." Linda nodded enthusiastically, touching her husband's hand. "A boy and a girl, four and two. I'd show you pictures, but I'm not that bourgeois yet."

Seated between the two couples, Diana felt at sixes and sevens. Linda, after all these years! The wife of a Manhattan attorney, and a mother. The shock of the passage of time, telescoped in an instant by a once-familiar face calling out Diana's name in a restaurant light-years away from their old room at Smith, had killed what was left of Diana's equilibrium.

"Are you still playing tennis?" she asked, having noticed that Linda, looking young and pretty as ever, had something of a tan herself.

"Not seriously," Linda said. "I was doing some amateur until my first pregnancy. But babies make it so hard to come back. Now I just play to stay in shape. With huz here." She squeezed Scott's arm.

"She beats me every time, too," he smiled. "She has no sense of fair play."

"You have to know how to handle her," Diana said, twirling her gibson glass. "When we were roommates I had the sense never to play with her. We got along fine that way."

Diana hazarded a second sip of her drink. It would be her last. She was desperate for a decent swallow, but she knew she could not go beyond two small sips in such company. She dared not give total strangers the idea that Diana Lancaster liked to drink. That would be the end of Hal.

In two more minutes she would excuse herself and pop into the ladies' room for a deep drink from her flask before returning to face the Junior League. That private jolt would have to see her through the lunch hour.

"Tell me," she asked Linda with real interest, "how did you two meet?"

"I was playing a tournament in Winston-Salem," Linda said, "and this one"—she gestured to her husband—"had the temerity to seek me out on the way to the locker room and ask me for a date."

She laughed. "I was flattered—particularly since I had got killed six-two, six-love that day—so I said yes. We had dinner, went for a boat ride—and you know the rest."

"How are your parents?" Diana asked.

"The same," Linda shrugged. "Mother is in Hilton Head, with her set of beaux, and Dad is still in East Hampton. Nothing changes. They both enjoy the grandchildren, I'll say that for them. And they can almost stand each other when we get together for Thanksgiving."

The divorce of Linda's parents came as a surprise to Diana, for they had seemed so close to each other when she knew them. To Linda it must be such a fact of life that she forgot it was news to her old friend.

"Do you have pictures of the children?" Diana asked impulsively. "I'd like to see, really."

Linda fished in her purse and produced two small snapshots, one showing a very pretty blonde baby girl, and the other a boy with fine dark hair, perhaps three and a half when the picture was taken.

"Katie, and Scott Junior," Linda said with a mother's quiet pride.

"They're beautiful," Diana smiled. "I'm so happy for you."

She caught a sidelong look in Linda's eye. If Diana's tone had betrayed her desperate longing for children, her old roommate would be quick to notice it. They knew each other's signals very well, despite the passage of the years. Realizing this, Diana felt even more trapped than before.

But Linda merely smiled as she put the pictures away. "They're a handful," she said, glancing at her husband.

Scott Stephenson was looking at Diana with a mixture of politeness and cool curiosity. Obviously he had heard a lot about his wife's two years in close proximity to the famous Diana Stallworth, and was intrigued to meet her in the flesh. He seemed impressed, but was too restrained to show it openly. He was a lawyer to the soles of his feet, Diana could see.

Linda kept glancing at him, almost possessively, whenever the rhythm of the conversation seemed to justify it. She seemed very happily married. She almost glowed.

Diana felt a sharp pang of jealousy. Here was Linda, doting on her husband, a proud mother of two pretty children, and as lovely to look at as she had been in the old days. Still athletic and youthful, she stood on a solid bridge between her past and her future, living a life uncluttered by lies and subterfuge, and enjoying the precious fruits of simply being a person like any other.

To think that she and Diana had started from the same place, so few years ago! The comparison of their fates in the adult world made Diana feel sick at heart, sick of belonging nowhere and of mucking up everything she tried to do.

"Well," she said, hoping she did not look as pale as she felt, "I'm going to have to run. I have to meet some ladies of the Junior League who are campaigning for my husband."

"You haven't told me anything about him!" Linda complained. "I want to hear your stories, too."

"I'll tell you what," Diana said, finding a piece of paper in her purse. "I want you to call me soon. I'd like you both to come to dinner. And why don't you bring the children out to our place at Southampton this spring? We'll have a picnic. Wait 'til you see how great Hal is with children. He's still a kid at heart himself. Really, Linda, it's been so long! I can't believe we got so out of touch. Here, I'll give you my phone number . . ."

She had found her pen, and was writing her name, *Diana Lancaster*, when a sudden tremor shook her hand.

A faint touch, feathery light and warm, had brushed her leg beneath the table, starting at the ankle and slowly working its way up her calf and behind her knee in a caress intimate as a kiss between lovers.

Forcing herself to control the shaking of her pen, Diana wrote down the phone number and looked up. Linda was sitting quietly beside her, leaning forward, her pretty face eclipsing that of her husband who was sitting on her other side.

The electric touch of stockinged foot against calf went on an instant longer as the familiar dark eyes held Diana, full of veiled meaning and a certain sympathy. How futile it was to try to hide from Linda!

Then Diana was on her feet, saying goodbye and bending to kiss her old friend's cheek.

Linda had taken the phone number, and held it up as she smiled her goodbye.

"Don't be a stranger," she said.

III

DIANA LAY AMID the tumbled covers of the bed, watching her friend move about the silent hotel room.

Linda was naked. Looking for a cigarette, she padded about the place, her tanned skin still tight and firm despite two childbirths. Her athletic life-style showed in her perfect legs, square shoulders, and long, slender arms. Her hair was expertly coiffed in a page boy that made her look even more fresh and girlish.

In bed, just now, she had made love to Diana with exactly the same grace and calm she had possessed years ago, soothing her with kisses and caresses so subtle that they brought her a kind of wanting almost indistinguishable from tranquility.

Yes, she was the same Linda. She still knew all the private places, the special positions, the clever play of lips and fingers most sure to excite and pleasure her friend.

It was Diana who was different. Not only because her breath smelled of liquor from the flask that stood on the bedside table. She had been so pent-up on arriving here that at first Linda had thought they should just call the whole thing off.

Diana had not been with a woman in all these years. After her engagement to Hal she had realized it could mean his whole career if she let herself go even once and somehow got caught. The journalistic community was more than ever on the alert for one false move.

In all this time the private side of her had had no outlet—the side that could let its hair down, admit to its need, and stop worrying about being good enough for the world. The side that could relax and bask in the glow of simply being wanted.

So she had been almost like a woman possessed when, at the door, as in the old days, Linda had stripped her with careful hands, parting her lips with soft kisses and darting a sweet tongue into her mouth. And she had watched trembling from the bed as Linda took off her own clothes, bent over her like a gentle mother, and covered her with herself.

How delicious it was to feast her eyes on those firm breasts with their warm nipples and mauve aureoles, before feeling them come to rub against her own! To contemplate the fragrant dark triangle between Linda's silken thighs, and then to feel it brush her own sex with the old tickly roughness that inflamed her so.

It had all been slow and tender and even romantic, this welcome tryst after so long a separation. Even in the spasms of her ecstasy Diana had felt a new peace flowering within her. Her sighs were as full of gratitude as of pleasure.

When it was over Linda held her in her arms protectively, as though aware how deep was the pain she had just soothed.

"It's been a long time for you, hasn't it?" she murmured.

Diana could only nod.

"You feel lonely," Linda said. "I mean, I can feel it in your body, Diana. You feel tense, and sad. You're keeping yourself so far inside . . . It isn't good for you."

Diana shook her head, biting her lip. Tears welled in her eyes.

"I can't," she said, clutching Linda's hand without looking at her. "It's for him, you see. For Hal. I have to think of him. We shouldn't even be here, Linda. If anyone saw us . . . I'm so conspicuous. Everyone knows what I look like. I have to be good, for Hal." She sighed despairingly. "Otherwise, I'm finished."

Linda kissed her cheek and slid a long thigh across her legs.

"So there's been no one?" she asked.

"Not since you."

"Hurts, doesn't it?" Linda traced a small circle around one of her friend's nipples.

Diana nodded, closing her eyes.

"You want to watch the booze," Linda said, glancing at the flask on the table. "That's no solution. Believe me, I know."

Diana opened her eyes to look at Linda. "You, too?"

"I had a little fling with martinis a few years ago," Linda said. "Right after Scottie was born. Gin was my poison. I thought I was just playing around with it, but all of a sudden the stuff had its hooks in me. I managed to kick it, but it hurt for a year afterward. Take my word, honey—it's bad medicine. It will make you step in every hole you try to avoid."

Diana looked at Linda through the combined haze of her sexual afterglow and the alcohol in her veins. She nodded, but ignored the warning. How could she throw away the precious philter that was her life's only blood?

And how could she explain to Linda, the happy possessor of a private and anonymous life, what it felt like to have to go before the press, the Lancaster relatives, the political kingmakers and the assembled pillars of society, day after day, and play the adored wife of a man who privately looked upon her as an object of pity? How could she explain the humiliation, the loneliness, the worthlessness?

It was impossible. Evoking her shame in words would only make it worse. She must keep silent.

But now she was not alone. Linda was here beside her. And one taste of her charms had convinced her she could not live without her any longer.

"Listen," she said, curling up with her head against Linda's breast. "You can't leave me now. I couldn't go back—without knowing I'd see you again. Please, Linda . . ."

"Ssshhh," Linda smiled, stroking her friend's hair. "I won't let you down."

"But it's so dangerous," Diana said, turning to face her. "My schedule is so busy. Everyone knows where I am. It's so hard to get away. It's so dangerous . . ."

"Hush, now," the sweet voice said. "Linda will find a way. You just relax. I can come into town anytime I feel like it. I'll just say I'm shopping. Call me when you're available, and I'll come in. We'll have lunch, then a little cloak-and-dagger, and then we'll be together. I know what to do."

Diana snuggled closer to her.

"I'm such a mess," she said. "Can you still want me?"

Linda silenced her with a kiss.

Words were not necessary now. They had always had a passionate physical attachment, but also a deeper bond born of a loneliness that came from their separate pasts to mark them as spiritual sisters. Six years apart had not lessened their intimacy. Today had shown that.

How odd the passage of time was, Diana mused. It took away so much, and was so relentless in its cruelty—but then, like a coy Santa with a bag full of surprises, it brought out gifts whose loss one had accepted long ago and almost forgotten, offering them with a flourish just when they were needed most.

Diana thanked her lucky stars. Finding Linda again this way was like a new drug added to the alcohol, a human drug that could alleviate her unbearable pain and give her the precious illusion that things were not so bad, that life was worth living after all.

Long ago, when Diana was a little girl on her father's knee, the world had seemed like a vast playground spreading out before her to sunlit horizons, a good solid earth to walk and play on, a place to have fun and be loved in. Since then it had turned to quicksand, sucking her deeper and deeper into its mire no matter how hard she fought to escape it.

Now that Linda was here—Linda, so calm and balanced, so easy in her body and her sexuality—it almost seemed that the clock could be turned back, or at least slowed in its pitiless grinding away of life. Linda was proof in flesh and blood that it could feel good, and be good, to be alive.

For a while, at least . . .

Yes, Diana decided. She was in the market for last resorts, and Linda was made to order. She would get as much comfort out of her as she could, and give as much of herself as Linda cared to take. Linda was an unexpected lifeline thrown to her from nowhere, and she was in no position to spurn it.

She would hang on somehow, until . . .

Until what?

As the future receded, withholding its helping hand, Diana reached for her flask again.

IV

HER NAME WAS TESS.

It had been her father's name for her when she was a little girl. No man had called her that since his death, and she intended that none ever would. As a child she had guarded it inside her as a way of keeping him alive. Now she kept it as the private touchstone of her character, a secret she must never reveal to the outside world.

Not only was Tess her only real identity, but it was a refuge as well. For behind her masks there was no ordinary human personality, confused by fears, loves, insecurities, and resentments raging out of control. She had long since killed those weaknesses in herself—how, she did not know. Perhaps it had happened when her parents died, leaving her alone in the world; or even before that. Perhaps, indeed, the process had begun before her birth, in the mysteries of her heredity.

In any case her inner being was a restful place, untrammeled by worry. She enjoyed its emptiness, because it gave her control and peace of mind. And it armed her with irresistible weapons for whatever challenges she might face.

Long ago it had alerted her to the flaws in her mother's relationship to her father, and allowed her to triumph over her mother through wiles she had not known she possessed until the moment she began to use them. Later it had allowed her to manipulate all the important males in her life—relatives, teachers, priests—and to wrest from the females all the power she liked. Fate had given her a beautiful body and a sharp, cunning brain. The combination was more than a match for the poor defenses of ordinary human beings.

It was a comforting ice that filled her heart. If it cut her off from the warmth of other people, it also protected her from the wounds they might cause. And she enjoyed living from conquest to conquest, walking over whoever stood in her way. Since power replaced all human considerations in her mind, she never felt lonely. Need and love were for others; stillness and peace were Tess's domain.

It was thanks to this inner void that she had found Lou Benedict and used him, despite her youth, to position herself for an important future in the corporate world. And it was thanks to the mental clarity behind her mask that she had found her way to American Enterprise and used its inner workings to lead her to the threshold of great achievements.

Her only setback had come at that crucial moment. But this defeat was due only to her inexperience, and was only temporary. She had landed on her feet, her instincts leading her unerringly to Winthrop Bond, the only man in the nation capable of restoring to her all that she had lost, and opening the door to infinitely more.

Today it was as Mrs. Winthrop Bond that she sat on the sofa of the Sutton Place penthouse her husband had bought for her. Outside the windows the afternoon haze shrouded the Queensboro Bridge, the East River with its busy traffic of barges and small boats, and the narrow expanse of Roosevelt Island.

But she was not looking out the windows. Her eyes were on the man seated on the couch opposite her. He was a dark, virile-looking figure, with something coiled and dangerous about him despite the conservative pinstriped suit he wore. His open briefcase was on the coffee table before him. A manila file folder was in his hand. He awaited her permission to begin what he had to say.

As Tess looked at him she thought about the ground she had covered since her marriage, and the road still ahead.

She had given Winthrop Bond a perfect marriage over the last two years. Under the guise of the sweet, rather childish Lisa she had delighted him with a thousand little kindnesses and displays of affection. In bed she had given him every pleasure his tired libido could imagine with her beautiful body and her subtle caresses.

Most of all, she had restored to him his youth, and given him a contentment he had never expected to enjoy in this world.

Lisa was an eager lover, and she made Win eager as well. They would have made love every night had the doctors not given them a rigorous schedule designed to maximize the chances of Win fertilizing Lisa with his aged seed. Win had been carefully examined, and not found infertile, although present-day science could not know these things for sure.

At first there had been some questions about his cardiac health. He had had a heart attack six years ago, and his concerned young wife wondered whether he could withstand so much strenuous sexual activity. But his cardiologist assured them both that it was the best thing for him.

So far Lisa had not succeeded in getting pregnant. She covered herself with shame over this, and had herself examined by the best gynecologists that Win's female relatives could recommend. She wanted Win's babies so badly that she seemed on the verge of worrying herself into physical illness. The doctors told her to be patient. Win held her in his arms and told her to be happy and love him. The rest would come in its own time.

Despite this one problem Lisa was the ideal wife. Since marrying her Win was a new man. His family and friends had never seen him so full of life and humor and happiness. He and Lisa had chosen the new penthouse and decorated it together, abandoning most of the furnishings from his old Madison Avenue place, and opting for a brighter, more open look. The walls were covered with modern paintings by artists like Kline, Motherwell, Dubuffet. They had also completely redone the Napili house, where they spent as much time as they could.

Win had changed his will immediately after his marriage, leaving the vast bulk of his fortune to Lisa. Since that moment no one in the family dared show the young wife anything but a smiling face. Yet this was not so difficult, for Lisa's sweetness and youthful charm were hard to resist. Thanks to her, Win was closer to the family than ever before, entertained the relatives more often, and saw more of his children and grandchildren. And gentle, happy Lisa was the mistress of ceremonies of this renaissance.

But Lisa was too full of talent and energy to devote herself exclusively to the duties of a housewife. She had a career now as well.

Not long after their wedding she had spoken to Win about American Enterprise, and about the new television division that had been built on the ruins of TelTech, her late husband's company. She was consumed with guilt over what had happened to Louis Benedict's dream. Moreover, a vibrant and creative young woman, she was still interested in the technical aspects of the new field of television that had once absorbed her, and was sorry she had lost her chance to contribute to it.

Win Bond, touched by her regrets and loath to see her talent go to waste, had decided to try something bold. Using his considerable influence, he arranged a complicated corporate deal with American Enterprise, involving the mergers of several subsidiaries of both companies and the transfer of considerable assets. As a result of the deal, the new television division of American Enterprise became a W. W. Bond company, and was renamed Bond Television Research, Inc. at Lisa's request.

Lisa became Chief Operating Officer of the new company, and a member of the board. Corporate headquarters were, of course, in New York, convenient to the television networks with whose executives Lisa had increasing contacts. Somehow she found time for this great responsibility and her wifely commitments to Win as well.

She was filled with excitement and new ideas. She showed him the brilliant plans she had devised to lower the cost of color television and make it affordable for the average American family within the next three or four years. She got him interested in the booming television industry, and introduced him to the fascinating and talented TV people she met in her work.

Lisa was thrilled by her new career. She was doing justice to the memory of her late husband, so that his life's work would not be wasted. And she was giving her own natural creativity an invigorating outlet.

Soon she became something of a celebrity because of her dual role as the youthful wife of America's richest man, and an innovative business-woman in her own right. Her extraordinary beauty attracted the media. Articles began appearing on her in the major business magazines, and in the fashion glossies as well. She was seen on Win's arm at the charitable events they had organized together, including the dedication of a hospital wing, the opening of a research facility at Columbia, and a donation of two dozen of Win's Impressionist paintings to the Metropolitan Museum.

Mr. and Mrs. Winthrop Bond became famous as one of America's most admired corporate couples. If they seemed mismatched in age, they more than made up for it in their affection and enthusiasm for each other.

Tess watched this whole process from behind her mask, and was pleased. She considered Lisa her finest creation. Lisa's youthful ardor, her sweet, quirky personality, and her touching dependence on Win, were an irresistible combination. More than this, her fixation on Win as a father figure, and her exaggerated hunger for his babies had brought out instincts in him that another woman would have overlooked, but which had made the marriage inevitable once he fell under Lisa's spell.

Today Lisa was making Win happier than he had ever dreamed of being. In return Win loved her, had given her the power she needed, and had willed his fortune to her. It was a fair exchange, and it suited Tess's purposes perfectly.

Babies, however, were not part of Tess's plan. Therefore she had taken steps to make sure Win did not impregnate her. She secretly used a diaphragm when making love to him, and applied the most sophisticated spermicidal cream available in Europe, both before and after coitus. She privately patronized an expensive Manhattan gynecologist who was an expert in contraception. In the event that her precautions failed, this physician could be counted on to give her a safe and discreet abortion.

It was a good life. And it was leading toward an even better future.

But Tess had not forgotten her past. She had unfinished business to settle.

That was why the man sitting on the couch with his briefcase was so important to her.

His name was Ron Lucas. At great cost to herself in time and money, she had located him a year ago in an out-of-the-way corporate position in New York, and convinced him to go to work for her as a special executive assistant.

Ron was not a classically handsome man. Yet there was an obvious strength behind his dark features that inspired confidence, and a smouldering, feral quality about him that was as frightening as it was attractive.

He came from a lower middle-class background—his father and grandfather had been New York City police officers—and was a decorated war veteran. Already a wayward son before Pearl Harbor, he lost all sense of family continuity during the war and emerged from it with an outlaw's instincts.

The quiet brutality of the business world had completed the process of alienation. Ron had learned to live without values or scruples. He was ruthlessly efficient as a businessman, but did not rise as quickly as he might have, because his manner was so threatening. He had not bothered to learn the art of flattery.

When he met Tess, an invisible bridge made itself felt between his own inner void and her ambition. Perhaps he saw a reflection of his exile from humanity in her, or of his silent rage.

In any case, he hired on and quickly showed himself to be loyal to her as no ordinary corporate employee could ever be. He acted as her advisor, executive assistant, bodyguard, detective, and enforcer, all rolled into one. She knew he would kill for her if she asked him to. But things had not got that far yet.

She would have willingly gone to bed with him, as a courtesy, had he asked. But he had not. He preferred a platonic footing of mutual respect and loyalty in their relationship, and she was happy to oblige him.

Ron understood that Mrs. Winthrop Bond was going places. And he intended to help her get there.

Today the file he had brought with him concerned Spencer Cain.

Tess had not forgotten Cain. When the television deal with American Enterprise was consummated under Winthrop Bond's aegis, she saw to it that Cain was summarily fired. She also used the octopuslike influence of W. W. Bond throughout corporate America to make sure that Cain did not find a high-level position elsewhere.

She used Ron to track Cain's downward progress through the business world, and to act as her agent in seeing that Cain lost each new position he found. A determined man, Cain managed to wangle his way into executive positions in smaller companies, positions that might be springboards to advancement and power. But Tess pursued him relentlessly, and got him fired for trumped-up reasons behind which her revenge was thinly veiled.

Tess looked from Ron to the file before him.

"Where is he now?" she asked.

"He's running an automobile dealership in San Diego," Ron said. "He managed to finance it by taking out a personal loan from a local businessman. He had no collateral, so I had it checked out. The man is a homosexual. He and Cain have been photographed together going into motels. I suspect Cain is blackmailing the fellow."

Tess nodded. "Is there more?"

"Yes, there is," Ron said, his faint smile acknowledging her intuition. "The auto dealership is a front. Cain is smuggling cocaine and heroin from Mexico, and selling them to dealers in southern California. That's his real business."

She looked pensive. Of course, she mused. It made perfect sense. Cain was a shark, and a fighter. Having been hounded out of the legitimate business world, he would quite naturally move outside the law in search of success. In his place, with an implacable corporate enemy pursuing her, she would have done the same thing.

She had to admire his resourcefulness.

She looked at Ron. "Is he making any real money at this?"

Ron shrugged. "I don't have that information yet. But to judge by the people he's dealing with, there is probably big money involved if he stays afloat long enough."

There was a pause, full of reflection on both sides. At length Ron pointed to the file. "What shall I do about this?"

A mental balance seemed to teeter behind Tess's beautiful eyes. She drummed a finger against her thigh.

"You have documentary proof of the drug dealing?" she asked.

He nodded. She need not have asked. Ron never brought her information for which there was no proof in black and white.

Tess made up her mind. "Well, Ron," she said. "It seems a crime is being committed. I think it is your duty under the law to share the evidence you have with the authorities."

He looked at her. "FBI?" he asked.

"It's their jurisdiction," she replied with a smile.

V

FATE WAS A STRANGE MISTRESS.

In her wildest dreams, Laura would never have imagined that anything other than financial collapse could come between her and the career of fashion designer.

Yet, amazingly, it was in the midst of her greatest professional success that things started to change for her.

Laura, Ltd., was a rapidly expanding business empire in the winter of 1958. Since the first exposure of Laura's designs to a national audience through mass-market retailing, the "Laura look" had become a virtual obsession among women who wanted to look their best and could not find attractive clothes to fit them anywhere else.

There were Laura, Ltd., salons in Chicago, Boston, Atlanta, San Francisco, and Hollywood now, staffed and managed by fashion professionals Tim had personally chosen. Meanwhile more national retailers had jumped on the bandwagon, both in the United States and Canada, to market Laura's clothes in their hundreds of outlets. Laura's designs sold out almost before stores could arrange them on the racks. Reorders were so frantic that the manufacturers had to restructure their factory hours to accommodate the avalanche of demand.

The "Laura look" was visible everywhere. Laura hardly needed to advertise it herself, for it could be seen not only on millions of women going about their daily business, but in hundreds of advertisements for products of all kinds, as well as on television shows and in the movies. It seemed that every creative director who wanted his female models or actresses to look good draped them in Laura clothes for the purpose.

Eager imitators of Laura's style were popping up all along Seventh Avenue, of course, and selling their wares across the country. But this fact did not trouble Tim or the major retailers who had contracts with Laura. Not only was it impossible for the imitators to duplicate the complex sizing procedure that was integral to the Laura line. The designs Laura created were so original and easily recognizable that customers at all levels were not satisfied with the imitations, and came unerringly to Laura herself.

Laura was fast becoming the greatest single star in ready-to-wear women's fashion. At the same time, through her custom work for influential clients from high society and the entertainment industry—not to mention members of royalty from several foreign countries—she was hailed as the most elegant and forward-looking designer to emerge in America in recent memory. Her designs continued to appear in *Vogue* and *Harper's Bazaar* along with editorial kudos calling her "America's answer to Chanel."

European fashion editors were quick to find their way to the new sensation. Soon the "Laura look" could be seen in the pages of *Elle*, *Moda*, and British *Vogue*, among other magazines. There were offers from major retailers in France, Italy, England, Spain, and the Scandinavian countries to market Laura's ready-to-wear designs. And Tim had received urgent calls from potential investors who wanted Laura to open her own salons in Paris, Rome, and London.

Laura was a celebrity. Articles about her were appearing throughout the business and fashion press, and requests for interviews were a daily occurrence. She accepted as many as Tim thought appropriate, and spent the rest of her time in sketching new designs or in consultation with fabric designers in New York and elsewhere as she prepared for each season's new line.

As always, Laura went about her business with a calm application that amazed Tim. She was as impervious to the pressures of success as she had been to the strains of early privation. She remained close to Rita, to Meredith and Judy and Millie and her other friends, and budgeted her time so as to allow herself quiet evenings with Tim.

They had moved into a large co-op on Central Park West. It was a gorgeous place, with a magnificient view of the Park, a uniformed doorman (Laura had never thought she would live to see that), a rooftop swimming pool for the summer, and friendly neighbors, most of whom were wealthy professionals or theater people.

The only significant change that Laura had made in her work was that she now did most of her sketching at home, and visited the salon in its new Sixty-third Street location only when she needed to show her work to Rita and the others, or to help finish a new model.

She loved sitting at her design table, facing the window on Central Park. Whenever she felt tired she could turn off her lamp, rest her eyes, and gaze across the greenery to the lake, the Conservatory pond, and the Upper East Side.

When she did so she could not help letting her eyes linger on the windows of the house across the Park which she knew belonged to Hal Lancaster and Diana. She had looked at the place from a safe distance two years ago when they first moved into it, and now could easily recognize its brownstone front from her own window. On dark afternoons and in the evening she could see a pale green lamp in the topmost window, perhaps a desk lamp in a study or bedroom. For a dreamy instant she would imagine what life was like for Hal and Diana in that pleasant-looking home. Then she would catch herself, and go back to work.

It was at home, in this new work setting, that Laura's life changed in a way she could never have expected.

One cloudy afternoon she was alone in the co-op, working hard on a new design, when a visitor arrived.

It was Penny Heyward, the bright and attractive model who had played so important a role in making Laura's clothes visible to the public when Laura, Ltd., was still an underground fashion secret. Penny was still one of Laura's favorite models, and was featured in all her fashion shows, wearing Laura ensembles suited to her uncomplicated, all-American looks.

But today Penny seemed distraught. She was dressed in jeans, a sweatshirt, and tennis shoes. Her hair was tousled by the harsh wind outside, and held in a loose ponytail by a rubber band.

"Laura, I've got to talk to you," she said.

Laura invited her in and gave her a cup of tea. Penny's face was a mask of worry. Gone was the sunny look of girlish innocence that was her trademark as a model.

Somehow Laura guessed what was on Penny's mind before she could say it.

"Laura, I'm pregnant."

Pale with anxiety, Penny explained her situation.

"I thought my period was just late," she said. "It's happened before. But I went to see the doctor about a flu I had, and he took blood tests, and the next thing I knew the nurse was calling with the news."

"Is it good news?" Laura asked, sitting with her legs curled under her on the couch.

Penny grimaced. "I don't know, Laura. The guy—well, he's great, in his way. But I'm not really sure I love him. And I'm even *less* sure he loves me. It just—came at the worst possible time."

She looked pleadingly at Laura. "I suppose I shouldn't be dragging you into this, but you're the only person I really trust. My family would never understand. I don't see how I can—well, I just don't know what to do."

Laura was instantly aware of what was in the other girl's mind. Pregnancy and childbirth spelled the end of a modeling career, particularly for a girl with a face and figure like Penny's. Therefore Penny was facing a professional crisis as grave as her personal one. Laura had to suppress the twinge of pain that shot through her senses as she realized Penny was considering abortion.

She hid her feelings, and resolved to listen sympathetically to whatever Penny had to say. Clearly Penny needed a friend, and Laura was not about to let her down.

The afternoon was an absorbing excursion into a private life Laura had known nothing about before. Penny told the story of her parents' troubled marriage and divorce, and of her own childhood, which had been rendered more difficult as she grew into a strikingly beautiful teenager. She had grown up too fast, going into modeling at seventeen. And today, at twenty-three, she did not feel equipped to bring a baby into the world. She was too haunted by her own past, and too uncertain about the future.

Laura confined herself to showing as much support and affection as she could for Penny, and drew her out on her confused feelings while gently convincing her not to rush into any plan regarding her condition. As afternoon's light began to wane Penny said she was feeling better, and promised to keep Laura abreast of whatever she decided in the coming weeks.

Laura found herself so startled by the unaccustomed depth that worry had etched in Penny's lovely features, that on an impulse she asked permission to take her picture before she left. Shrugging, the preoccupied girl agreed. Laura found Tommy Sturdevant's old Hasselblad on her bookshelf, loaded it with fresh film, and took a handful of pictures of Penny in close-up, her tired face limned by the pale light coming in the windows from the gray sky.

Then, after being hugged by a grateful Penny, Laura bade her good-bye and watched her leave the apartment.

It was nearly two weeks later that Laura finally thought to have the roll of film developed.

The photographs of Penny were a revelation.

The person in the pictures was someone Laura had never seen before. She was far from the sleek, elegant Penny of the fashion layouts Tommy and Laura had so often worked on. Nor was she the Penny who used to breeze through the office when it was time to pick up clothes for a shoot—a girl confident in her ability, charming in her humor, but not particularly remarkable as an individual.

No—this was someone new. Laura stared at the pictures in the silence of the apartment, trying to put her finger on what was so bewitching about them.

Of course, there was a sadness, a worry in the pictures that she had never seen in Penny before. And the exhaustion of having confided so much of her life to Laura as she stood on the threshold of an uncertain future was painfully visible in Penny's features.

But beyond this, it seemed as though a mask had been taken off for the very first time, revealing through the camera a Penny who was somehow more real than the Penny whom Laura and her colleagues knew so well. This creature of light and shadow was not only deeper than the flesh-and-blood Penny, but also more beautiful, incomparably more beautiful, despite her lack of make-up, her drawn features, and her lumpy sweatshirt.

The Penny Heyward of everyday life was like many other girls—while the face captured in the photographs was like no one else in the world. It could neither be compared nor equated with anything outside it.

It was unique. And because of this it was, for the very first time, truly human.

Laura could not take her eyes off the pictures. Though the emotion they stirred in her was confused, she felt that she was seeing something very important in them, something surprising and new and amazingly specific. Looking at them was like tasting an apple for the very first time, or smelling a flower, or feeling rain fall on one's skin, or seeing a sunrise, without ever having had the experience before.

Laura sat immobile before the pictures for two breathless hours. They filled her with awe, and with a curious insatiability, a hunger to get closer to the secret they were holding out to her. All at once she began to feel that the documents before her were opening a door she should have come across years before, and could not dream of turning away from, now that she had found it.

She found herself regretting all the stylized fashion photos she and Tommy had taken of Penny—even though they had been necessary and important in their time. In comparison to the photos before her now, they seemed like absurd images of a feminine ideal as superficial as it was stereotyped.

She even began to regret her whole career as a fashion designer, whose vocation was to cover women with costumes designed to flatter their narcissism and make them attractive to outsiders, rather than to reveal the raw, haunting beauty underneath their surface.

Indeed, she cursed all the weeks and months and years of her life in which she had not known about this amazing ability of the camera, in which she had spent her time doing anything else but searching out and uncovering revelations like the Penny in the pictures.

Common sense told her these thoughts were crazy. How could a handful of black-and-white photographs change her whole life, and make all her past endeavors seem irrelevant and senseless?

But it was not that simple, Laura realized. An obscure inner voice told her that everything she had done in the past—her sketching, her studies in art, her work as a designer—had been precisely a preparation for the unexpected moment when luck and fate could reveal to her the magic that a camera was capable of working in her hands.

The notion that chance had been necessary to open this door for her was both fulfilling and frightening. After all, what would have happened if Penny had not come over to ask her advice about her unexpected pregnancy? What if Laura had not felt the sudden need take Penny's picture? What if life had simply gone on as before?

I've got to take more pictures.

This thought brought with it a nervous exultation not far from dread. For Laura sensed that the pictures she had taken were more than mere documents about another person. In some strange way they had brought her face to face with her own self, a self she had turned her back on long ago and not dared to confront since.

The haunting patina of melancholy in Penny's face bore the shadow of the rainy day thoughts that had stood between Laura and the sunlit exterior of the everyday world since she was a little girl. Indeed, one good look at the pictures revealed the inescapable fact that no one but Laura could have taken them. If this was true, then Laura would be turning her back on her own heart if she did not take more pictures.

But if Laura had found herself through the camera, she had lost herself as well. For Laura was a fashion designer, not a photographer. Her busy life had no room in it for the camera.

Unless, that is, she changed her life.

I've got to take more pictures.

Laura sat alone on her couch, the photographs spread around her, the Hasselblad held tenderly in her hands. She looked at the small black box with its glass viewfinder, its calm inhuman lens ready to take in the world. It seemed to her that this lifeless eye, once joined to her own, and opened by her hand, could never be shut again. Nor could the door she had opened into the future be closed.

It was not only Penny Heyward who had come to life in the pictures. It was Laura Blake, the only Laura, the Laura who had been waiting all these years to taste the reality of life.

Sitting alone in her silent home, awed by the revolution the innocent little box had created inside her, Laura felt fate take her in its arms.

VI

FROM THE DAY of her great photographic discovery Laura led a Jekyll-and-Hyde existence, like a woman possessed by a private addiction hidden from the outside world.

She forced herself to put as much energy as she could into her fashion work, though the sketches she drew seemed abstract, inhuman, and almost interchangeable with each other. She labored meticulously over the new garments she was finishing for her loyal clients, though she could not help feeling that the art she had so painstakingly mastered was really only a way of hiding the essential instead of revealing it.

And all the while she secretly looked forward to her next outing with the camera.

When she could steal an interval away from work she would ride the subways, stroll around Times Square, walk the paths of Central Park and Washington Square Park, haunt bus and train stations and busy streets, watching the incredible variety of New Yorkers pass before her eyes.

In no time, it seemed, she would see someone whose face bore a strange aura that told her she could take a picture of him or her. She could never figure out how she knew, for the feeling came over her weakly, uncertainly, as though by a throw of the dice.

But the second sight that overtook her at these moments gave her the courage to approach these total strangers and ask permission to take their pictures.

"You look wonderful today," she would say with a smile. "I'm a photographer. Would you mind if I took your picture?"

Most of them looked at her suspiciously. But she managed to disarm them with her candor, and something sympathetic in her personality gained their confidence. Before long she would entice them to a park bench, a table at a café, a seat on a subway platform. She would get to know them quickly, listening to their stories about their lives, their observations about life in the city—and photographing them all the while.

Sometimes she went home with them. The sight of their apartments or furnished rooms took her breath away, for it revealed a lot about who they were, much as the natural habitat of an animal reveals how it has adapted to the world. Some of them showed her pictures of their relatives. At this Laura's cup ran over, for the human richness of their families as reflected in their own faces was a gift almost too precious to receive.

But even those who remained strangers, seen and photographed only for an instant before disappearing into the crowd, spoke to her camera with an eloquence that thrilled and amazed her. Individuals who at first had been mere commuters, pedestrians, drifters, prostitutes, hustlers— the anonymous flotsam of New York's cruel, impersonal streets—took off their visible masks and revealed inner faces beautiful as the greatest of Rembrandts to her camera.

In some cases Laura's first instinct had been wrong. The person she chose had nothing to give her. The mask he or she wore was too stubborn for the camera to penetrate.

But these exceptions only seemed to prove the rule. With the camera in her hands Laura walked the earth as though possessed of a witching rod that could sense human secrets and pull her magically in their direction.

Each time she developed her pictures Laura had the same feeling of shuddering thankfulness she had felt with Penny Heyward, as though something precious had given itself to her by a lucky chance, something that had almost slipped away, and would never have been seen had she not come upon it and captured it.

Oddly enough, despite the diversity of the faces, which were so unlike each other, there was something melancholy behind all of them, and something triumphant as well, a sort of halo that confirmed them in their uniqueness and set them apart from the rest of humanity. What the shadow meant Laura did not know. Neither did she understand the glow that pierced it. Were these things part of the mystery that belonged to her subjects? Or did they come from the depths of her own heart as she opened it to them through her camera?

Laura could not get to the bottom of this paradox. But it only made her eager to take more pictures. The insatiable compulsion that had taken possession of her the first day with Penny's photos grew greater as did her excitement about what she was doing.

The faces in her pictures were like the inhabitants of a new world, a world glimpsed once upon a time in her rainy day thoughts, and now spreading out before her as fast as she could photograph it. She pined all day long for the hour she could steal with her camera before Tim got home from work. She ached all week for Saturday morning, when she could go out for three or four hours and take pictures of people.

In a few short months Laura's life was transformed from an orderly concentration on one career to a hectic, disturbing oscillation between a past that was rapidly losing its appeal and a future that was taking possession of her.

She told herself she must keep the change from Tim as long as possible—she was not sure why. Then she pondered that short, frightening word: *change*. The transformation, the metamorphosis . . . Was nothing the same anymore, then?

As though to test this hypothesis, Laura tried an experiment. Like Dr. Jekyll first trying the fatal serum on himself, Laura set up the camera on a tripod in her living room and turned the camera's glass eye on herself.

When she developed the pictures, not without hesitation, her suspicions were confirmed.

She, also, was one of the faces on which the shadow played, on which the strange glow beckoned. She, also, was one of the different ones.

Now Laura knew there was no turning back. It was too late.

VII

IT WAS SIX O'CLOCK on a snowy Thursday night in February.

Laura was sitting on the couch in her living room. Beside her was Tommy Sturdevant, the fashion photographer who did all the magazine layouts for Laura, Ltd. Tommy was pointing to three large sets of proof sheets on the coffee table. They showed a dozen of Laura's most important new outfits—the centerpieces of the national summer line.

Laura had personally selected the four mannequins who modeled the designs. They were all old favorites, and complemented one another brilliantly. Each embodied a different look, to which Laura carefully adjusted not only the outfit she wore but also her position in the layouts vis-à-vis the other girls.

There was Daria, with her fragile and mysterious European look; Roxane, the classic long-necked high-fashion mannequin; Gretchen, whose dark skin and pale blue eyes made her perhaps the most exotic and ambiguous of them all; and Wendy, whose all-American *Seventeen* looks contrasted piquantly with the others.

Wendy was a second choice for this layout. Laura would have used Penny Heyward were the latter not on leave of absence from the agency, having decided to have her baby after all. But Wendy had a charm all her own that made her an effective vehicle for the "Laura look."

Tommy was serious and respectful as he discussed the pictures with Laura. Since his early days with her he had learned that she took a detailed and perfectionistic interest in the photographic presentation of her designs to the public. She was present at every shoot, and always had important suggestions to make about backgrounds, make-up, and of course the girls' postures and expressions.

Laura had hired Tommy several years ago after he had been recommended by one of Tim's retailer friends. He had a reputation as one of the most sensitive and talented young photographers around. Laura was pleased she had snared him on his way to a great future, but while he was still sufficiently unknown to be within her price range.

From the beginning they had worked well together. Tommy's relaxed attitude toward life in general shielded him against the terrible time pressures and sudden shocks of the fashion photography business. He kept calm when outfits and layouts had to be changed at the last minute, a situation that forced everyone to wait around the studio as precious time and money slipped through their collective fingers. And he was able to soothe the models' frayed nerves when their hair or make-up had to be redone after many exhausting minutes in front of the camera.

More importantly, Tommy had an intuitive understanding of Laura's approach to clothes as well as fashion layouts. She always tailored each outfit for color, cut, and fabric to one specific model, and she expected Tommy to tailor the photograph to that particular combination so as to make a graphic and psychological whole. She would not approve a photograph until it brought out something about the model as well as the clothes. Tommy took this as a refreshing challenge—for so much of fashion photography was a drab chore to a creative photographer—and threw himself into it wholeheartedly.

Their partnership had borne fruit as Laura grew from a struggling underground designer to one of the biggest names in the business. The "Laura look" now extended beyond the clothes themselves to the unique, unusual layouts Tommy and Laura created to advertise them. Many critics were saying that the Laura photographs in *Vogue, Harper's Bazaar,* and elsewhere were instant classics of fashion photography, worthy of inclusion in museum shows.

Tommy was delighted by this attention, since he knew it was good for his career. Indeed, he was already getting commissions from important designers in America and abroad, which kept him busier than ever before.

But he was modest enough to admit to himself that it was Laura's contribution to his work that was giving it the extra depth the critics so appreciated. While his own approach to fashion work was sleek and somewhat glib, Laura brought a shadowed complexity to their collaborations that Tommy could never have achieved alone. Her perfectionism highlighted Tommy's own talent while giving it greater weight.

Over the years Laura had become more interested in the technical subtleties of photography. She spent much of her spare time in Tommy's studio, helping him develop and print pictures. Spongelike, she absorbed all the tricks he had learned from an advanced degree in photography as well as ten years on the job. This pleased Tommy, in a paternal way, and he had insisted that she accept the Hasselblad as a gift from him. Half-jokingly he told her that she had missed her calling, and should have been a photographer.

Laura had not told Tommy about her recent experiments with the Hasselblad. She did not want to mix business with her private obsession, the more so since her photography seemed to sap her enthusiasm for fashion altogether. And perhaps she did not want to share something so terribly personal with another photographer. So she continued her close working relationship with him, as well as their easy and somewhat superficial friendship.

Though not a classically handsome man, Tommy had a refreshing charm that made him appealing to the opposite sex. Laura suspected that he had had flings with more than one of her models. He was a bachelor, and apparently too irresponsible for marriage. His one-time fiancée, a charming girl named Marcie whom Laura had once met, had finally broken off her engagement to him, for she was unwilling to gamble a lifelong commitment on Tommy's undependable personality.

Like many artists, Tommy was perfectly focused on his professional skill, but scatterbrained and disorganized outside of work. He spent his evenings carousing with friends, romancing girls, and losing money at card games. Laura could easily imagine that no self-respecting female would take him seriously for long.

But at work Tommy and Laura made perfect foils for each other, since his fancy-free way of skating on the surface of life harmonized well with her intent, searching nature. Their closeness was of the type that so often develops in a working environment. An outside observer of Laura and Tommy in the studio might have concluded that they were intimate friends who knew all there was to know about each other. The truth was that their relationship stopped at the door of his studio.

Tonight they were both in high spirits, for the proofs were some of the best they had ever produced together. The editors at *Vogue* were eagerly awaiting them. And the clothes themselves represented Laura at her innovative best. This gave her a sense of relief, for in recent months she had felt so cut off from her fashion work that she wondered whether her designs were worth anything anymore.

She had offered Tommy a glass of wine, and he was sipping it in silence as he sat beside Laura on the couch before the coffee table.

They heard a key in the door and looked up to see Tim come through it, looking particularly handsome in his overcoat and gloves. His ruddy cheeks were still rosy from the chill outside air, and his eyes shone with that sparkle of hardworking energy that always warmed Laura when he came home at day's end.

Laura loved that look, and the huge male power he brought with him when he met her at night. Since work kept them physically separate nowadays, except for a few hurried lunches, she looked forward to his return at six o'clock.

Their greeting was a ritual. "How's my girl tonight?" he would say, watching her rush to his side so he could take her in his arms. He would hold her close, hugging and kissing her in silence, and would not let go until he had had his fill of her. Then he listened closely and patiently to her news about her latest sketches and ideas, only confiding what his own day had brought after she had finished. He seemed to want to remind her that she was the creative center of Laura, Ltd., and that his far-flung endeavors as her representative were strictly secondary to her own work.

Laura adored those quiet moments of greeting. She was proud of her husband, and she loved to look at his athletic body as he held her out in his arms. His sparkling eyes and ready smile were like a caress meant only for her.

Two years of marriage had made her feel protected as she had never been before. She had always known how loyal Tim was to her. He would do anything in the world to keep her from harm. And now he added the sweet attentions of a husband to his steadfast qualities as a friend and business associate.

So she smiled as she looked up at him tonight. Her work with Tommy had been a great success, and she was glad to see her husband.

"Welcome, stranger," she said. "Come on in and have a drink with us."

To her surprise Tim did not seem pleased by her greeting. There was an icy look in his eyes that she had never seen before.

For an instant she could think of nothing else to say. She saw his eyes dart from her to Tommy, and back again.

It was Tommy who spoke next.

"What's the matter?" he asked Tim from his reclining position on the couch, his glass of wine in his hand. "Haven't you ever seen your wife with another man before?"

Laura laughed. She was reaching to give Tommy a playful poke in the ribs when Tim's voice suddenly rent the air between them.

"All right, Tommy," he said, "Get out."

Tommy looked up in surprise. He had never heard Tim use such a tone before, and assumed he was joking.

"Don't take it so hard," he said, reaching to pat Laura's hand. "It was just an irresistible attraction. It came over us so suddenly . . ."

He was grinning at Laura, still not taking Tim's remark seriously.

Then something astonishing happened.

Tim abruptly crossed the room with long, frightening strides, grasped Tommy by the lapels of his leather jacket, jerked him bodily to his feet as though he were a child, and pushed him to the door.

"You heard what I said," Tim breathed through clenched teeth. "Get out. I mean now."

There was an instant of silence. Tommy, nonplussed, was looking back at Laura as though for an explanation. Tim's face was red, his eyes glittering with a terrifying anger.

Tommy began to say something, but his words were lost as Tim found the doorknob, opened the door, and flung Tommy into the corridor. Laura watched in horror, unable to believe her eyes.

She saw Tommy turn around to give Tim a look of surprised hurt and anger. Tommy said words of reproach that did not register in her confusion. She did not know whether Tim heard them or not, for he was slamming the door unceremoniously in Tommy's face.

Laura sat paralyzed on the couch, looking at Tim's powerful back as he took off his coat and hung it in the closet. She had never seen him behave this way. He was like another person. She struggled to take in what had just occurred.

Without a word Tim went into the kitchen. She heard the cupboard open, then the refrigerator as he got himself a glass and made himself a drink. The sound of liquor pouring made a bizarre echo in the stunned silence of the apartment.

There was a long pause. Laura could feel the tremor of unresolved panic in her nerves. Somehow she felt terribly guilty. And she could feel that Tim was experiencing something similar in the kitchen. But she was riveted to the spot, and could not move.

At last, after an interval that seemed endless, he appeared in the kitchen doorway, holding his drink, and stood looking out the window at the Park and the cityscape of the distant Upper East Side.

For a long moment he was motionless. Then he turned and came toward her.

He sat slowly in the chair on the other side of the coffee table and looked down at the proof sheets as he sipped at his drink. Laura waited, unsure of her ground. He seemed to collect his thoughts before speaking.

"Laura," he said at last, "I'm sorry. I guess I've been working too hard."

She stared at him in silence. The pain inside her was intense. She did not know what to say.

At length he looked up at her with an odd, somewhat sheepish smile.

"I didn't realize I was the jealous type," he said.

Jealous. In all these charged moments it had never quite dawned on Laura that jealousy could have been the cause of what happened.

She looked at him through wide eyes. "Tim . . ." she said gently.

"No, don't excuse me," he cut her off, his lips tight with self-reproach. "It was my fault. I don't know how it could have happened . . ."

"Tim, are you crazy?" Laura almost laughed despite her distress. "You have nothing to be jealous of. Nothing in the world. Has this been bothering you before? Why didn't you tell me?"

He shook his head in frustration. He seemed angry at himself.

"I know it sounds crazy," he said. "But the idea of another man . . . looking at you . . ." He breathed a deep sigh. "I can't handle it. That's all. I just can't."

There was a silence. Laura still could not believe her ears. The idea of Tim being jealous about her was so foreign. He might as well suspect her of being a bank robber, a foreign spy, a saboteur.

Besides, in her marriage with him she had never dreamed of Tim coveting her in quite that way. He lacked the possessiveness of a jealous husband. He was always so gentle with her, so respectful of her independence as a person.

"This is news to me," she said simply.

He did not meet her eyes. His hand was clenched about his drink. His voice seemed to come from very far away.

"I know it's crazy," he said. "I've never doubted you for a minute, Laura. All I've ever wanted in this world is to take care of you. I just can't stand the idea of someone—trying to come between us. Trying to get his hands on you . . ."

"But Tommy Sturdevant!" she exclaimed, not sure she was really getting his point. "Why, Tim, you know what I think of Tommy. He's a sweet and helpful colleague, but he's nothing at all to me. Nothing! How could you possibly . . . ?"

There was another silence. Then Tim looked up guiltily, the glimmer of a smile returning to his eyes.

"Can you forgive me?" he asked. "At least it proves I love you."

A half-smile of confusion played over Laura's lips. She did not know how to respond.

"I'll apologize to Tommy tomorrow," he said. "I'll tell him I thought he was someone else. I'll tell him I was seeing double. I'll think of something. But for God's sake, Laura, don't look at me that way."

Laura held out her arms to him. She had never needed him so badly.

He came to her side, took her in his embrace and kissed her. The warmth of his arms made her feel safe.

"Don't make me afraid," she whispered against his cheek. "You're all I've got."

"I love you, Laura."

For what seemed a long time they held each other, the forgotten proof sheets on the coffee table before them, as though shielding each other from a storm that had come upon them both from outside, a tempest they needed the bonds of their affection to hold off.

Laura touched her husband, her small hands seeming to test him to make sure he was still there. She felt his soft kisses on her cheeks, her brow, her eyes. The fear inside her began to give way to gratitude that he was still Tim, and was still hers.

At last he parted her lips with a kiss that sent a shiver of need through her senses. Something told them both that they must make love. He took her gently to the bedroom, turned off the lights, and helped her off with her clothes. He enfolded her tiny body in his arms with the familiar delicacy she had come to know so well.

They made love slowly, passionately, each touch seeming a rediscovery of flesh known once in all its intimacy, but lost since and now thankfully recovered. If there was something quietly desperate about their caresses, the old tenderness between them covered it over. Soon they were joined in a shudder of wanting urgent as it had never been before. When it was over they lay panting in each other's arms.

"I love you, my darling," Tim whispered. "Don't ever doubt that. If I lose you, I'm finished."

Later they had a quiet dinner together, lazily prepared in their pajamas. They drank white wine, which calmed the strange flutter of lingering distress and satisfied desire in Laura's senses.

Afterward they cleared away the proofs on the coffee table and curled up together on the couch, listening to soft music with the lights off and looking out the windows at the Park and the East Side. For a long time they said nothing, buoyed by the happiness of being together.

Then they both slowly realized that what had happened tonight could not be put to rest yet.

It was Tim who spoke first.

"You know," he said, "when I was little I had to be the head of the house, pretty much. My father was a salesman. He was on the road for weeks at a time. My mother wasn't very strong, and Catherine was four years younger. There was never enough money, so I had to work odd jobs to make ends meet. Sometimes I even had to borrow. It wasn't easy, but we made out."

He sighed. "Then, every so often, he would come home. My father, I mean. It was bad, because my mother knew he was cheating on her when he was on the road, and we all knew he was spending our money on liquor and women instead of sending it home. But he'd breeze in as though nothing had happened, with booze on his breath and nothing in his pockets but his shanty Irish charm. He'd apologize to my mother, and turn her head with that smile of his—and she'd take him back."

He held Laura's hand. "I used to sit there and watch this happen, watch them go upstairs together, and my blood would boil. A week later he'd be gone again, selling on the road, gambling and drinking and whoring away whatever he made. And it was up to me to make ends meet. I wanted to kill him . . ."

The memory made his body tense. Laura had never heard the story before. She knew only that his father had died in the old country long before she met Tim.

Tim held her close. "I don't know whether this will make any sense or not, Laura," he said. "But I just can't stand the idea of you being around anyone . . . irresponsible. I need to feel that you're safe . . . protected. I shouldn't have worried about Tommy. I know he's nothing to you. It was just one of those split-second things. I really have been working too hard."

Laura nodded. She reproached herself for not having given more thought to the awesome weight of Tim's work. All this time he had freed her for her creative work by taking the enormous responsibility of the financial side of Laura, Ltd., on his own shoulders. Too often the business had been on the brink of bankruptcy, and it had taken all Tim's guile and all his contacts to keep it afloat. He had never asked for or been supported by anyone, any advisor, in that work. It had been his lonely burden. How it must have drained him!

"Tim," she said, "I'm sorry. I know how terribly hard you work. But what I don't understand is how you could doubt *me*, of all people. Don't you know me well enough to know that when I married you, it was for good? You're the only man for me. Why, Tommy Sturdevant is nothing but one of the faces in the office."

"But you see a lot of him," Tim corrected.

"It's true that I see a lot of him," Laura admitted. "But that's because of photography. Tommy is not a man to me, Tim. He's an employee, a colleague—and sometimes a teacher. His private life couldn't concern me less."

"You spend enough time in his darkroom."

Laura caught the note of argumentative triumph in her husband's voice. At the same time she understood that her private outings with the camera in recent months had not escaped Tim's attention, and had their own obscure place in his reproach about Tommy. But Tim could not realize how absurd his suspicions were.

Nevertheless, he had put her on the defensive again.

"Tim, you're crazy," she said. "You're making mountains out of . . ."

Too late she saw that her choice of words was unfortunate. Tim was staring at her hard. His look was dark and full of suspicion, as though he had turned in upon himself and was measuring her from a distance, like an enemy in a hostile outside world. There was something cold and rigid about that look, something almost hateful. Worst of all, it shut her out completely.

Laura began to sense the depth of her predicament.

"Tim, don't look at me that way. Please."

To her immense relief, his face softened. He took her hand.

"It's not you I doubt," he said. "That's what I've been trying to say. I trust you completely, Laura. But other people . . . that's another matter. I've learned not to trust people until they earn it."

"But Tommy Sturdevant?" she asked in dismay, squeezing his hand. "Can't you see how wrong you are, Tim?"

He looked away, as though to change the subject. She could feel that they were speaking at cross-purposes somehow. But she could not figure out how to make contact with him, how to banish his silly suspicions.

At last he took a deep breath and turned back to her.

"Laura," he said. "This isn't easy for me to say, but I'll say it anyway. I wish you were pregnant. It's been two years . . . Maybe, in some way, that would make a difference."

His words struck an odd chord. Somehow she had known that this was on his mind. They had been trying to have a child almost since their wedding. They both wanted a baby, so they had watched the calendar, and Laura had seen a gynecologist for advice. To date, there had been no result.

The doctor, a genial Upper West Side practitioner named Dr. Ensor, had reassured Laura. "We can't rush Mother Nature," he said. "These things take time. Being too eager can make it worse. Just relax, Laura."

For the first few months Laura had taken him at his word. But in the dark of night she lingered over the memory of what she had done to herself in the aftermath of her affair with Nathaniel Clear, so long ago. It had never occurred to her, in her grief over losing the child, that she might have permanently hurt her own body. But now the thought struck her a painful blow, and filled her with an anxiety that grew with the passing months.

At last she forced herself to tell Dr. Ensor of her worry.

"Did you think I didn't know about that?" the gynecologist had smiled. "I have eyes to see, Laura, and a little bit of experience with women's bodies."

He looked at her as she sat before him in her smock on his examining table, tiny as a little girl.

"I should have set your mind at rest a long time ago," he said. "But I sensed you didn't want to talk about the past. Laura, I found no evidence that the abortion you had has in any way influenced your capacity for normal conception. The man who worked on you may have been outside the law, but he did know his stuff. I'm quite sure that your excessive worry about this has been the cause of your trouble in conceiving. The woman's body is a mystery, believe me. Emotions can play just as big a role as physical problems in preventing pregnancy. So concentrate on relaxing. Morbid worry is your worst enemy."

He had looked at her carefully.

"Does your husband know about your abortion?" he asked.

"I—no," Laura answered, embarrassed to admit the truth.

"He wouldn't understand?" The doctor's smile was probing.

"No. No—I don't think he would."

"All right, then. You just sit tight and concentrate on your calendar. And have your husband see his own doctor and check into his fertility. Just to be on the safe side."

Tim had done as the doctor suggested, not without a few grumbling remarks about his manhood. Sure enough, he was pronounced perfectly fertile. Since then he and Laura had gone on trying, without discussing their efforts or their worries. After all, they had not been married for very long. Everything takes time, as the doctor was so fond of saying.

Now, hearing Tim mention their failure after today's disturbing events, Laura was assailed by guilt.

"Tim," she said, "there's nothing in the world I want more than to have your baby. Maybe I want it *too* much. Dr. Ensor seems to think so."

"Or maybe you know that *I* want it too much," Tim said, generously taking the blame on himself. "I don't think I've been very easy to live with, Laura."

"How can you say that?" she remonstrated. "You're the most wonderful husband in the world, Tim. Every day with you is a joy."

Until tonight . . .

He looked at her. In some way they both realized that their conversation had brought them full circle.

"Then do me one favor," he said.

"What's that?" Laura asked.

"Love me," he said, sadness mixed with the entreaty in his handsome eyes. "Love me as I love you, and forgive me for being a crude pig-headed bloke. And forget the fool I made of myself tonight. All I need in this scurvy world is your love, Laura. Will you believe that?"

"Then you have nothing to worry about," she said, snuggling closer to him. "That's the one thing that belongs to you. Forever."

"Ah," he sighed, hugging her. "That's my Laura."

A half hour later they were in bed together, and she was close to him, listening to the soft murmur of his regular breathing as he slept.

She watched him, filled with wonder and relief. What was there to fear in the world, as long as she had him?

But she did not go to sleep. She kept her eyes on him through the darkest hours, wondering what dreams might be hiding behind that handsome sleeping face.

Dawn was turning the windows a pale sickly gray when Laura finally drifted into troubled slumber.

VIII

IT WAS LATE the next afternoon when Tim knocked at the door of Tommy Sturdevant's studio.

The place was a cavernous loft in lower Manhattan, filled with props, lights, and rolled-up backdrops for modeling layouts. There were small tables with empty beer bottles, coffee cups, and ashtrays full of cigarette butts. The walls were covered with posters made from Tommy's work and that of other photographers. A large blow-up from one of Laura's shows was prominently displayed.

Tommy was in the darkroom, and gave Tim a somewhat guarded hello as he came out.

"What's up?" he asked, mustering brittle joviality despite his obvious coolness. "Got anything for me?"

"Just an apology," Tim said, not taking off his leather coat.

Tommy was wiping developing fluid from his hands with a dirty rag. He looked at Tim carefully.

"No apology necessary," he said. "Everybody gets snappish sometimes, Tim. It's the nature of the job. We've all had too much work lately. I shouldn't have been there without calling you."

"No." Tim shook his head firmly. "You were doing your job. You had a right to be there. It was none of my business. I was out of line. It was completely my fault. But you're right about one thing, Tommy. I've been working too hard. I'm letting things go to my head. I know there's nothing between you and Laura. She respects your work, and she's grateful to you for all the help you've given her—as I am."

"Christ," Tommy shrugged with a grin, "she's the one who ought to be giving me pointers. She's the best natural photographer I've ever seen. All I've taught her is a few mechanics. She's got the eye."

Tim nodded without smiling. Tommy's praise of Laura's abilities did not seem to please him. He had not moved from where he stood. He seemed a menacing presence somehow in his long leather coat that clung to powerful shoulders and thick arms.

"Well," he said, not taking his eyes off Tommy, "I thought I should set things straight. I was out of line, and I know it. I hope you can see your way clear to forget the whole thing."

"Forgotten already," Tommy smiled. "Want a beer?"

"No, thanks. I have to go."

But Tim had still not moved. There was something stubborn about his immobility, as though he had not finished what he came to say, and wanted to make a point of which he himself was not entirely aware.

"Well," he said. "As I say, I know there's nothing between you and Laura."

"Me and Laura?" Tommy laughed. "Man, you've got the wrong guy. Laura only has eyes for you, Tim. Anybody can see that. She knows what I am. She wouldn't waste a look on me."

"Just keep it that way."

All at once the menace behind Tim's apologetic demeanor showed through. Now Tommy understood why Tim had not turned to leave. He had had this one more thing to say.

Tommy could think of no rejoinder.

"I believe you," Tim concluded. "But if I ever found out you were fooling around with my wife, I'd kill you with my bare hands."

He stood for moment, looking not at Tommy but past him out the loft windows, as though his gaze were fixed on a private demon that had driven him here to make this threat under the pretext of an apology which obviously meant nothing.

Genuinely alarmed, Tommy stood with the dirty rag in his hands, staring at the hard face of his visitor.

After five more seconds that seemed like an hour, Tim turned on his heel and stalked out of the studio without saying goodbye.

IX

February 4, 1958

"MR. LANCASTER, I'd like to know what makes you tick."

Carol Alexander was the most highly regarded young political reporter in the nation. She had begun her career at the *St. Louis Post-Dispatch* fresh from her *summa cum laude* degree in journalism from Columbia, and had quickly earned the respect of her jaded superiors at the paper by turning a routine story about political corruption in the construction business into an in-depth exposé that was picked up by the national press, and won her a Pulitzer Prize.

After turning the series of articles into a book that garnered her every available journalistic prize and a National Book Award, she moved on to *The New York Times*, where she was greeted with suspicion by the senior reporters and editors, to whom her youth and striking good looks branded her as an empty-headed prima donna hired for her "star quality."

Once again she silenced the doubters, this time with an amazingly detailed study of political patronage in the Civil Service that became front-page news and won her a second Pulitzer. Even the most savvy of her associates could not figure out how she had got her hands on such sensitive information. But everyone had to admit it made a great story. And the fifteen indictments brought by the State's Attorney in the wake of her revelations only helped to establish her as a major force in the city's press hierarchy.

Carol Alexander was well on her way to a distinguished career as political reporter and analyst, a career that almost certainly would have landed her a column on the editorial page, when she once again did the unexpected. Turning her back on the prestigious *Times*, she accepted a job as a political correspondent for one of the fledgling television networks.

Nearly everyone in journalism thought she had taken leave of her senses. After all, how could a job with an unheralded network news service compare with the prestige of *The New York Times?*

But Carol Alexander loved the new medium. She enjoyed doing live interviews on the air, for they were so much more spontaneous and immediate than the laborious print interviews she had done as a newspaper reporter. She took pleasure in forcing her interviewees to show their faces directly to the camera, so that the public could evaluate their demeanor as they tried to elude the merciless probe of her questioning.

As a TV reporter she continued using her disarming beauty as a weapon to keep her subjects off balance. And she showed herself off to the public as well. Her regular reports on the evening news became a high point of the broadcast, not only because of their incisive and often controversial content, but also because her rich dark hair, creamy complexion and beautiful, striking eyes made her by far the most attractive correspondent on any network.

At age twenty-eight, Carol Alexander had found her niche as an important new face in journalism. Few political leaders dared refuse her requests for interviews, though none looked forward to her biting, pitiless questions or to the vast store of knowledge she put behind them. Besides, if there was a subtle form of blackmail in her approach to her subjects, it came in such an attractive package that few could resist the stimulation of being in her company for an hour.

Today Carol Alexander was sitting in Haydon Lancaster's State Department office, dressed in a gray suit with crisp skirt and tailored jacket, a pastel blouse, and a neat black silk foulard that made her look very feminine despite her brisk manner.

Her cameraman was behind her, pointing his lens at Haydon Lancaster, who sat behind a large desk piled with folders and loose papers. The walls were covered with bookcases containing every available government report on Indochina, Formosa, and mainland China. For the last year and a half Hal had been Dwight Eisenhower's eyes and ears where the Far East was concerned, and had acted as an important informal liaison to the area's leaders.

Under normal working conditions Hal would have been in shirt-sleeves, his tie loosened, the phone cradled under his chin as he rooted through the papers on his desk in search of the latest piece of urgently needed information for Ike or the NSC. But today the phone was off the hook, and his eyes were riveted to those of Carol Alexander.

If he noticed her lovely complexion, the body she kept trim through rigorous exercise, or the soft lips that glistened beneath her clear eyes, he gave no sign of it. He knew how formidable an adversary she was, and he took her seriously.

She had just finished putting him through her patented meat grinder, questioning him on his stand on every major issue of the day, from farm prices to the stock market to Taiwan and the Suez, with special emphasis on his controversial views on the Cold War and the arms race.

Of course, she had a right to ask these questions. As a candidate for the United States Senate, Hal was expected to have strong positions on the major issues and to be able to defend them. Nevertheless he had had to do the fastest shuffling of his life to keep up with her. He had never faced a reporter so well-informed and so quick to move in for the kill when his guard was down.

She questioned whether his six-year experience as Eisenhower's envoy to NATO, to the Geneva Conference, and to Indochina qualified him for a position in the nation's most important legislative body. She insisted he explain why his State Department experience gave him anything to offer the people of New York as their representative. She wondered aloud whether his fast-growing popularity on the national scene did not stem more from his sex appeal and family history than from his actual positions on the issues.

And just when he thought the inquisition was over, she had attacked from a new angle by asking him a personal question on camera.

"Mr. Lancaster, I'd like to know what makes you tick."

Hal smiled. "How do you mean that?" he asked amiably.

"When I listen to you talk about Communism," she said, "I hear a left-wing internationalist liberalism couched in the trappings of Cold War anti-Communist militance. I can't help wondering which side of the fence you're really on. And I suspect that the people of the state of New York, and indeed the nation, are wondering the same thing. Are you for real, Mr. Lancaster? Or are you a puppet of your party and your family's wealth, using warmed-over political positions to get yourself a free ride into the Senate?"

Hal smiled, trying to hide the blood drawn by her slashing words. Never had he heard his own views dissected so cruelly, and with such brilliant erudition. Carol was not precisely right about him, of course. But she had articulated the most aggressively anti-Lancaster position in the most eloquent terms possible.

"I see what you mean," he laughed good-naturedly. "A sort of wet-behind-the-ears Adlai Stevenson, wearing a John Foster Dulles mask so no one will see him for what he really is."

"You said it—I didn't," she smiled, shrugging her assent to the unflattering characterization.

Now Hal grew serious.

"A lot of people have trouble understanding my attitude toward Communism, Carol," he said. "But to me it's simply common sense. Our country is living proof that free enterprise is freedom itself. Through free enterprise each man works for himself rather than for the state. Our job in today's international arena is to convince developing countries that democracy is the only realistic safeguard against repression. I believe we are a shining example of that fact, and that because of this no sensible nation in either hemisphere is likely to refuse our friendship."

His expression darkened.

"Now, to me its obvious that none of the Communist dictatorships can offer that kind of example, or that kind of friendship. This is our great strength. But if we base our foreign policy on the mistaken belief that the developing countries of this world will 'fall to the Communists' like a bunch of puppets with no will of their own, we're not only overestimating the appeal of Communism, we're selling both ourselves and the developing nations short. This is an attitude that is sure to get us into war, and soon. A fellow named McCarthy has already shown us what damage it can do right here at home. I'm proud of what President Eisenhower has done to fight against it in foreign policy. And I intend to pursue that fight wherever I can. I hope, incidentally, that that will be in the U.S. Senate, starting next year."

The half-smile on Carol Alexander's face was not visible to the camera. It acknowledged Hal's cleverness in turning her provocative comments into the platform on which he could restate his views in their most advantageous light. He had a way of combining his almost boyish handsomeness with a measured, mature tone that was amazingly seductive, particuarly in a broadcast format.

She hesitated before asking her next question. There was no point in berating him anymore about his positions. He had outwitted her with his intelligence and with the charm he sent directly through the camera to the audience. She would look childishly aggressive if she pushed him any further.

So she opted for the human approach.

"We come back to our starting point," she smiled. "What does make you tick, Mr. Lancaster?"

Hal laughed. "When you find out," he said, "I hope you'll let me know. That's a question I've never been able to answer."

"Let me put it this way," she said. "You come from a great American family. You have all the wealth you could ever want. You have a beautiful young wife and an unlimited future. Today you're in the midst of a promising political career that many observers believe will make you an eventual candidate for the White House. One would think you have everything your heart could desire. Yet when I listen to you talk, you sound like a man who is not satisfied at all with what he has—a man, in fact, who is not even sure what he wants out of life."

Hal's smile gave way to a very serious look. "For the record?" he asked with a glance at the cameraman.

"For the record," Carol nodded.

He thought for a moment before answering.

"You know, Carol," he said. "I've found in public service the ideal outlet for the part of me that wants to be—well, a soldier. The Korean War left its mark on me in an odd way. I almost died in it, and on the battlefield I realized for the first time what it would be to give myself, all I was and all I had, for my country. Somehow, at that moment, I forgot my own self-doubts, and my worries about what I wanted out of life and who I thought I was. Everything was very clear. All that mattered was the men I was fighting with, and the cause we were fighting for."

He paused, a wistful expression in his eyes. "Ever since that time," he said, "I've felt that the soldier's role suits me. In other words, I may never know the important answers about myself, or about the meaning of life. But I would like to help in some small way to make this country safe enough, secure enough, so that my friends, my family, and hopefully my children, will have the leisure and the peace of mind to find out what makes *them* tick, to make all the great discoveries about themselves and about the world around them which will go to make our future as a people."

The infectious smile returned to his lips. "I hate to belabor the metaphor," he said, "but another nice thing about politics is that I get to be on the front lines. Politics is where things get done, and where the action is—win or lose. It's an exciting life. The all-or-nothing aspect of it, particularly in running for office, attracts me, and reminds me of soldiering. On the other hand, if you're right in saying that something about me seems unsatisfied, perhaps that's because I've grown up with all the benefits my country can shower on one undeserving individual. I can't help feeling a little guilty about that. I'm sure that something in me wants to give back all I can, in order to even things up somehow."

He shrugged. "I don't claim to know myself as well as some men do. But if you put all that together, Carol, it is probably as good a description as any of what makes me tick."

Time had run out. Carol Alexander's smile was at once cynical and admiring.

"Thank you for spending this time with us, Mr. Lancaster," she said. "And good luck in the primary."

"Thank you, Carol. I suspect I'll need it."

The interview was over.

Carol stood up and held out a hand.

"Well," she said briskly, "thanks again, Hal. You're always the best interview in town."

Smiling, Hal shook her hand, feeling the odd alertness of her strong fingers. Inside he was relieved. For such a young woman Carol was as tough as anybody in the business. He was glad the interview was over. But he wouldn't feel really secure until he saw it on television, and knew how good or bad her editing had made him look to the viewers.

"You were terrific, as always," he congratulated her. "But I'll admit I'm glad to get you out of here. I always feel better when you sheath that saber of yours."

She gave him a quick look whose meaning he could not fathom.

"All in a good cause," she said.

"Come on, I'll walk you down." He ushered her past the camera crew, who would take their truck back to the studio, and moved into the corridor with her.

They headed past the seventh-floor offices of the State Department Building toward the elevators to the parking garage. Hal watched Carol walk beside him with her strong, athletic strides. In person she was even more attractive than her on-camera image, for her somewhat stiff television voice was replaced by a more lilting, friendly tone.

"I hope you won't mind," she said, "if we have some comment from interested observers as part of the report."

"Uh-oh," he smiled. "Does that mean what I think it means?"

"Afraid so," she said.

What she meant was that she would be giving Amory Bose an opportunity to vent his spleen against Hal on the broadcast. Hal could not blame her for it, since Bose made tremendous copy with his vituperative attacks on Hal, whom he had been labeling a card-carrying Communist to anyone who would listen since the day Hal announced for the Democratic primary.

In a way Hal was not displeased with this vendetta, for not only did the thunder of Bose's hatred increase Hal's own public profile, but Hal was confident of his own views and of the image he was projecting through interviews such as the one he had just done with Carol. Bose's strident red-baiting tactics were so clumsy that Hal felt he could turn them to his own advantage in the long run.

"Well, may the best man win," Hal said simply. "I just hope that when you interview him you give him as much vinegar as you did me."

"I think I can promise that," she smiled.

She had learned to respect Hal since he came to Washington. His good looks and family connections had disposed her against him in the beginning, but in interviews she had found that nothing could shake his sincerity. In a curious, indefinable way, Hal was truly his own man. He was neither the puppet of the liberals nor a creature of the Democratic machine. He went his own way, without a lot of friends in the Washington hierarchy, and took his message—fleshed out, it was true, by enormous personal charm—directly to the people.

She admired him for this, though she suspected he was not protecting himself sufficiently. His unorthodox approach to politics might prove his undoing one day.

"Is your car in the south lot?" he asked as they entered the elevator.

She nodded. "Double-parked."

"Well, we might as well go through the basement, then," he said. "It's quicker."

She said nothing as they slid downward through the shaft.

The basement corridor was lined with obscure State Department offices. It was deserted this afternoon, not only because it was Friday but because it was past five. Carol's story would go directly to the editors at the network, who would prepare it for tomorrow's evening news. She would probably have to work very late tonight. Hal felt sorry for her, in a way, for she had to spend so many hours in tiresome drudgery far removed from the interviewing she loved.

They paused before a door whose frosted glass window bore the number *063*, but no sign.

She stood in silence as Hal took a key from his pocket and slid it into the lock. The door opened inward.

With a quick look up and down the hall she followed him into the small office.

The shades were drawn. There was nothing in the room but a set of old filing cabinets, a large table, and a deep leather couch.

She put her purse and briefcase down as he closed and locked the door. He did not turn on the lights.

When he turned back to her she smiled and held out her arms.

He pulled her to him gently, and felt her hands close around his back and slip quickly beneath his waist.

Her kiss was hungry, almost animal in its urgency, the light catlike tongue darting back and forth across his own. She tasted wonderful. The fragrance of her hair suffused him, along with the fine natural scent of her skin.

Her breasts, small and firm, were pressed hard against his chest. He heard a sort of harsh purring in her throat as she pulled him to her, rubbing her sex against the already-hard penis under his pants.

Her torso was very slim. He could feel her rib cage, and her small waist in his hands. Her legs were strong, hardened by her exercises and the fast walking her job required. They were closing around his waist now, for he had lifted her up. Her gray woolen skirt was hiked up so that her sex hovered around his own, covered only by the silk of her panties.

As she kissed him more deeply his hands moved over the diaphanous fabric. Something about girls' panties had always had a mystical allure for him, as though the white petal were a virtual part of their bodies, a little maidenly veil over the loins, a pearly door to the fresh sanctum of their sex.

With Carol the feeling was particularly piquant, for her skin was so white and smooth, her legs so long, the ripe little globes so firm and sweet. And now her excitement was making it clear she wanted her sex to be naked for him right away. She was whimpering, trying to hide her sighs so that no one would hear from outside. Her hands were all over him, her kisses almost frantic.

He braced her on the table long enough to slip the panties down her legs, and then lifted her again, his hands under her buttocks.

"Oh, God," she whispered. "Please, Hal, get it in. I can't stand it. Please . . ."

He set her down on the table for a few seconds, an almost absurd vision of naked female limbs poised on the old brown tabletop under the prim gray skirt—just long enough to loosen his belt and zipper.

The slacks fell down around him, and before he could lift her up again she had pulled down his underpants. Warm female fingers hurried over his sex. He heard her exclamations at the size of him, little oohs and aahs of admiration.

Then, thanks to a lithe movement of her hips and the pulling of her legs, he was inside her, buried to the hilt in the warm honey of female flesh, the tip of him probing at a core that drew gasps of delight from her lips.

"Oh, yes, Hal," she breathed against his cheek. "Oh, my God . . ."

He lifted her up again, hands clasped beneath her waist, and felt the eager legs clutch harder at him as the long penis slid back and forth inside her.

Each little push seemed to make her more helpless, and her words sang in his ear like prayers.

"Deeper, honey. Oh, deeper. Oh, God, you beautiful thing. Unh . . . Unh . . ."

She was beside herself. He mused that she must have wanted him badly, back there in the office. Something of this pent-up female hunger had been subtly present in the harsh rapier thrusts of her intellect as she had interviewed him. And now she was making love with the full urgency of her strong, ambitious personality, craving pleasure just as she craved success.

It was a fascinating riddle to see the hot female animal come out from under that icy control of hers, hungry for cock, covetous of his sperm, desperate for his thrusts. Fascinating, but not quite human, not quite feminine. For it was not himself she wanted, but only the pleasure she could take from him.

He kissed the hollow of her neck and felt the soft mane of her hair fall over their faces. Her hands were fluttering all over his back, his waist, his thighs, her sighs sounding in his ear.

"Oh, Jesus," she moaned. "Jesus, Hal, don't stop . . . Oh! . . ."

Her orgasms were coming fast now, first one, then another and another, her body squirming fast and hard as he held her in his hands.

"Just a little more," she whimpered. "Oh, Hal, just a little . . ."

She need not have feared he was going to finish. His strokes were steady, unhurried, touching at the quick of her in slow thrusts that allowed her to grace the moving penis with her own sighs, to covet it with her ecstasy and let her inner needs explode around it.

Hal's women all knew this special delight of feeling that his "up" would never end, that it would just go on calmly and carefully screwing them until they had had their fill and were limp with pleasure. It was not out of male narcissism that he overwhelmed them this way, but rather from a sort of loyalty, a friendly cooperation. The terrible prowess of his organ joined with the unique charm of his personality—so tender and thoughtful behind all that statesmanlike cleverness—in a recipe that literally drove women wild.

Carol Alexander was no exception. Her hair awry, her hands grasping, her whole body atremble, she was coming to her final climax now, taking of the deepest and most total orgasm a man could ever give her.

"Baby doll . . . Give it to me . . . Come on, Hal . . ."

Her words infected him with their own excitement. But even as his semen began to quicken in his loins he remained mysteriously apart from the shuddering creature in his arms. He felt exiled within his own self, his heart of hearts as alien to this hot rhythmic pulsing inside him as was Carol's true personality to the blind female animal working insanely at his sex.

In ten minutes, he knew, she would be her cool evaluative self, scanning the world with alert eyes for advantages, opportunities, her quick mind fed by truth just as the hot place between her legs was fed by the seed she had got from Hal.

This made Hal feel sad, and more than a little lonely.

What did it all mean? Why did he do this to women? What was this hunger that drove him to their arms, when he could no longer rise to the surface of himself as they did, lose himself in pleasure as he made it possible for them to do?

It was worse for him now than in the early days, the days of his adolescence, when sensual Kirsten Shaw and her countless successors had tickled his youthful imagination along with his libido, and made his orgasms feel like little fantasies come true, fantasies not quite real but enjoyable for all that.

Nowadays the separation was more profound, more complete. For he had been touched once in that secret place of his own exile, touched where he lived, where his smile ended and his heart began. And now the hollow left behind was bottomless.

He dared not think of Laura when he gave his body to these other creatures. Had he done so, thinking to please himself with fantasies of her while he enjoyed the flesh of the others, the pain would have killed him. He was prudent enough to know that.

So he retreated into his own emptiness, and let the women taste of his body, soft remote creatures lissome and empty as Kirsten, poor dead Kirsten, his first teacher, his first playmate.

And the cold center of him remained a mystery, as much to Hal himself as to the women who longed for his attentions.

How honest he had been today when he told Carol he simply had no idea what made him tick! But how much pain those blithe words had hidden . . .

All these thoughts rose within him at the same instant as his orgasm. They came, as though bidden by some cruel spirit, to remind him that he was not really here, that his heart was not in this hot working of flesh against flesh—but also that he was not really anywhere else either. There was no safe home within himself to compare with the coldness of this exile.

As for Carol, her mind was gone now, and her words tumbled out like the ravings of a witch driven mad by her own spell.

"Give it to me, Hal. Oh, please, baby. Let me have it now . . . Oh! . . . Oh . . ."

His powerful hands pulled her harder onto the shaft as the sperm shot out, a hot salve darting to the deepest core of her need. She gripped him frantically, tensing in spasm after spasm against him—and then collapsed, sighing and moaning, her loins undulating with the last of her delight as the long penis rested calmly within her.

He lowered her gently to the couch, feeling the perspiration dry on his stomach as her mingled perfumes surrounded him. Her hands were in his hair, her thighs still curled about his waist. For a long time she purred and held him and kissed him until he finally ebbed and left her.

"Honey," she whispered. "Thank you. Thank you so much."

He smiled against her cheek.

"Jesus," she said. "If you could bottle that, Hal, you could throw away the Lancaster fortune and make one ten times as big."

"Can't bottle it." There was something sad, and final, under the humor of his words.

She sat up, her skirt still pulled up to her waist, and reached to fondle his penis gently, to touch in wonder at the balls whose seed had just settled inside her.

"You're a nice boy," she said in an odd, wistful voice.

She bent to kiss the sex, and patted his hip possessively, before standing up to find her panties. She pulled them up her legs, tucked in her blouse, straightened the skirt, and turned to the large metal storage cabinet. Opening it, she looked into a small mirror inside the door. She took a brush from her purse and began fixing her hair.

Hal watched as she easily pinned the hair back and took out a compact to dab at her make-up. Already she was herself again, polished and beautiful, cool knowing Carol, the brilliant young journalist whose own future was her only real concern. The hidden animal desperate for sex was gone again, satisfied for today.

He watched her, admiring her strong personality as much as the perfect legs and small, pretty breasts that made her so attractive. Like Alice through the looking glass, she was disappearing before his eyes, vanishing into herself.

He fixed his own clothes now, putting on the underpants she had pulled down moments before, tucking in his shirt, straightening his tie in the mirror behind her. Her aroma clung to him charmingly, and he felt a twinge of melancholy at the thought that he would have to wash it off soon.

As they prepared to part, her eyes met his.

"A great American—and a great lay. Too bad that's a slogan you can't use, Hal," she said.

Her words hurt him, but he did not let her see it. He simply smiled, and ran a finger down her cheek.

"I'll be back on Tuesday," she said. "In Weaver's office, for a press conference. I'd like to see you. Can you make it?"

She was all business. How coldly she saw to the needs of that hungry thing between her legs! She might as well have been ordering groceries over the phone.

He thought for a second. He looked doubtful.

"Call me Monday," he said. "We'll see."

She came forward to kiss him on the lips. "So long, Senator," she said. "Keep it bent."

She opened the door a crack, looked up and down the corridor, flashed him a last half-tender look, and was gone.

After a decent interval Hal himself left and went back up to his office. He had some work to finish before he could go home.

It was always fun to see Carol. Maybe he would find time for her Tuesday after all.

He had had intercourse with her the very first day they met, nearly four years ago, when she was still with the *Times*. She had been less sure of herself then, but already possessed of her sharp intelligence and her instinct for the political weak spot.

And her eagerness for sex with him.

That first day they had had a quick lunch together and taken a walk before finding their way to an empty office not much different from this one. And, like so many women, she had made love that day exactly as she did today. Her style never changed.

But she never bored him. He liked the way her brains dissolved into the cries of her flesh when she made love. Such a clever mind, only abandoned at a certain price to her—and only for a couple of minutes. He admired her quick recovery almost as much as her surrender.

And he knew that, inside, she was as lonely as he was. For that, above all, he genuinely liked her—even though the contact of their flesh could never bridge the gap of their mutual solitude.

She was a great reporter—and a great lay. Hal smiled at the thought.

But what about underneath? Who was Carol behind her ambition and her sexual appetite? He would never know.

Perhaps he did not deserve to know, Hal mused. Perhaps the pleasure he enjoyed in her arms, and in the arms of others like her, was a punishment garbed in the sweetest disguise, the better to find his heart and scar it.

Oh, well, he thought. Better to hold in one's arms the very thing one cannot have than to be completely alone.

Hal squared his shoulders under his jacket, peeked out the door, and reentered the world.

X

"This is Carol Alexander reporting from Washington. One of the biggest stories in the nation's capital this year concerns neither Indochina nor the Middle East nor the arms race, but a dynamic young State Department official who has set his sights on the Senate seat now occupied by perhaps the most powerful man in Congress.

"The young man's name is Haydon Lancaster, and as a controversial Eisenhower appointee he has captured the imagination of millions of Americans in the past few years with his good looks, his legendary family name, and his hardworking political style. He faces a difficult and perhaps dangerous race against incumbent Amory Bose for the crucial seat. The decision will not be an easy one for the Democratic voters of New York State, who must choose between an elegant and attractive challenger and a distinguished senior senator whose influence in Congress is itself almost legendary."

THE CAPITOL DOME loomed rosy and majestic in the dusk behind Carol Alexander. She was dressed in her familiar wool suit, her navy blue silk tie appearing dark gray in the colorless television image. But even the crude technology of black-and-white television could not hide the sparkle of her eyes, her beautiful complexion, or the intelligent femininity she projected.

As Carol added some biographical remarks about Haydon Lancaster, the scene shifted to his State Department office for the edited version of his interview with her. One did not have to be a professional journalist to see that the beautiful young correspondent was asking tough questions. She played the devil's advocate, challenging Lancaster on each of his major positions in turn, and forcing him to explain why a man of his inexperience and privileged background was a credible opponent for the respected and feared Amory Bose, whose stature as a legislative power broker matched that of any man in recent memory.

On the other hand, one did not have to be a fan of Lancaster to appreciate the deftness and extraordinary self-possession with which he answered the most difficult questions. Not only did he display a virtually encyclopedic knowledge of the major foreign and domestic issues of the day. In addition he comported himself with so imposing a combination of dignity, coolness, and charm, that it was difficult not to find oneself on his side almost immediately.

The medium of television was ideally suited to Lancaster's dark good looks and infectious humor. He did not have to reach out and grab at the audience with the strident bluster of the average politician. He achieved an infinitely deeper effect by simply letting his natural charm flirt with the camera. One could almost feel the eyes of his millions of female admirers glued to their TV screens as he spoke in calm and unruffled tones to his attractive interviewer.

Perhaps sensing that the combination of Lancaster's sex appeal and his obvious competence was virtually irresistible, Carol Alexander placed a brief interview with his opponent near the end of the telecast in order to balance what had been a virtuoso performance by Lancaster.

"The senior senator from New York, Amory Bose," she said by way of introduction, "is far from dismissing Haydon Lancaster as an inexperienced and thus unworthy opponent. Not that Chairman Bose does not reproach Lancaster for his youth and his overprivileged past. But beyond this, Bose considers his opponent a true menace to the American way of life in the decade before us."

The face of Amory Bose filled the screen. The backdrop was a wall full of law books in his Senate office. His thinning hair and ruddy complexion gave him a distinguished look, as did the handsomely cut Brooks Brothers suit he wore. His eyebrows, untouched by gray, stood out incisively above his piercing eyes.

Television treated Amory Bose neither kindly nor unkindly. He looked middle-aged, well dressed, and poised. The personal force that set him apart from his colleagues on the Hill was too subtle for the TV cameras to capture. Yet something of his confidence in his great power communicated itself to the viewers.

Bose was expert at incarnating a fatherly benevolence in interviews when he wished. But tonight his eyes glittered with undisguised anger and even revulsion as he spoke of Lancaster.

"Carol," he said, "I'm grateful to you for giving me this opportunity to speak my mind about Mr. Lancaster. Many of us, viewing this man with his considerable charm and eloquence, may be fooled into believing that he is nothing more than an intelligent and ambitious young fellow who wishes to serve the public interest in the United States Senate. I am here to tell you that this is not the case. If you study Haydon Lancaster's speeches, his record in the State Department, the interviews he has given, and his avowed intentions as a maker of policy, you cannot fail to conclude, as I and many other concerned observers have, that Haydon Lancaster is a clear and present danger to our democratic political system, and indeed to our very way of life."

The Senator paused to let his words take effect.

"Haydon Lancaster," he went on, "is nothing less than an unwitting agent of the international Communist conspiracy. He is a man sworn to appease the Communists wherever they may undertake adventures against freedom, a man sworn to uphold the principles of the Communist Party in matters of economy, labor, foreign policy, and, of course, education. Haydon Lancaster is nothing more or less than the ideology of Communism itself, sugar-coated by a pleasing appearance, an amiable personality, and one of the oldest and most respected family names in America."

"Don't you find it incongruous, Senator," Carol Alexander asked, "that a man such as you describe could have emerged from what is considered a right-wing family background?"

"That is exactly my point, Carol," Amory Bose replied. "We who have dedicated our lives to the struggle against Communism have long ago learned to remember one crucial fact. When Communism sets out to infiltrate a free society, to weaken and destroy that society, it does not come bearing the ugly face of an enemy. It comes disguised in the mask of attractive promises, of clever arguments in favor of reason, of accommodation, of understanding and peaceful coexistence. Those of us who have been in the trenches fighting Communism all our lives know how to recognize this smiling face when we see it, and to see through its false promises and cajoleries when we hear them."

"These are strong charges, Senator Bose," the reporter said. "Can you back them up with documentary evidence?"

"I have already made available," Amory Bose said, "through my own office, and through the *Congressional Record*, incontrovertible proof that Mr. Lancaster's policy positions are without exception those of the left wing in this country, and proof that Mr. Lancaster's avowed intention as a United States Senator is to dedicate his vote to the interests of the Communist bloc as a worldwide power and to the principles of the Communist Party."

Predictably, Bose was hedging. He could not openly claim that Haydon Lancaster was a Communist, for there was no evidence to that effect. He could only suggest in the strongest of innuendos that Lancaster's politics were the same as those of the left wing. Since this also was open to debate, Bose had to use the best of his eloquence to cover his opponent with scorn and suspicion while silencing the voices of those who might wish to defend him.

Carol Alexander respectfully allowed the angry senator to vent his spleen for a full three minutes. His message was clear: Haydon Lancaster was a subversive menace to the Senate and to America.

"If this man, or men like him, reach the centers of power in the executive, legislative, or judicial branches of our government," Bose concluded, "we can kiss our constitutional freedoms goodbye. Haydon Lancaster stands for a weakening and dissipation of those freedoms, and a wholesale destruction of our democracy as we have fought and died for it."

So powerful was Bose's display of righteous fury at his opponent that his three minutes had virtually superceded Hal Lancaster's lengthy interview. Sensing this imbalance, Carol Alexander chose to end the report with the intimate remarks she had elicited from Hal about his war experiences in Korea and their effect on his choice of a political career.

"I've grown up with all the benefits my country can shower on one undeserving individual," Hal was seen to say, his face boyish and endearing as he spoke his modest words. "I can't help feeling a little guilty about that. I'm sure that something in me wants to give back all I can, in order to even things up somehow."

The camera froze the handsome image of Hal's face as Carol Alexander spoke.

"Communist dupe or great American?" she said. "Traitor or potential President? Haydon Lancaster is different things to different people. He already has a place in military annals as a winner of the Congressional Medal of Honor. Now he wants a major place in American legislative life. If he defeats Amory Bose in the Democratic primary this spring, he will have made history, for no incumbent senator of Bose's importance has ever lost a primary. Perhaps this is one reason why Amory Bose has made it a personal mission to stop Lancaster, and indeed to hound him from our political midst.

"Where does the truth lie?" she asked. "That is a question for the people of New York to decide this year. And if Haydon Lancaster prevails in New York, the ultimate question of his political future may one day be decided by the entire electorate in a race for the presidency of our country. This is Carol Alexander. Thank you and good night."

. . .

Elizabeth Bond sat before the television set in her penthouse study, gazing at the frozen image of Haydon Lancaster.

She was pensive. She had turned on the news out of mere curiosity tonight, for she knew the network executives were trying out a new sponsor whose influence she might need in the future. But when the Lancaster interview had begun, something made her stop what she was doing and devote her whole attention to him.

Before tonight he had been just a name to her. But the magnetism he projected on the television screen impressed her as a student of the medium. And his poise in responding to the reporter's penetrating questions was extraordinary. He managed to cut a very controversial figure in the paranoid American political arena, and yet to turn all the suspicions about him to his own advantage.

"Potential President . . ."

Carol Alexander's words echoed in Tess's mind. Could one look at Lancaster's handsome young face and imagine it in the Oval Office?

Tess considered herself as sharp a judge of the probable future as anyone. The weighing of contingencies, the calculation of distant threats and advantages, was as much a key to her personal life as to her professional career. Yet she had never focused her intellect directly on politics before.

But tonight she was thinking about Haydon Lancaster. A Medal of

Honor winner. A man of great personal wealth and even greater charm. A political thinker of obvious seriousness. A focus of controversy.

The husband of an heiress, a spoiled young woman who had been the darling of high society since long before her debutante days.

But the couple was childless.

Tess gazed at the sensitive eyes, the strong chin, the lush dark hair. Could this be the face of the future?

Why not? After all, anything was possible. Tess had proved that over and over again. Her mission on earth, indeed, was to prove it.

Haydon Lancaster, she mused. President of the United States.

A voice interrupted her reverie. It was Win. He was in his pajamas and bathrobe, ready for bed.

"Lisa, are you coming?" he asked, putting a frail hand on her young shoulder.

She looked from the aged fingers to the handsome face on the screen.

"Be right there." She spoke in Lisa's voice. She had to bring herself back to Winthrop Bond by force, for in her mind she was already far beyond him.

The idea coming to life inside her seemed too bold to be taken seriously. Not even a woman of her guile and resourcefulness could contemplate a conquest like that of Haydon Lancaster. He was hopelessly out of reach.

On the other hand, she mused as she got up to join her husband in the bedroom, the world was an unpredictable place. Anything was possible.

She entered the bedroom, curled up beside her husband, and put her arms around his neck.

"Darling," she said. "Don't you think we've both been working too hard lately? I'm dying to go back to Napili for a week or two. This winter has been too much for me. I want to get some sun with you, and a good long swim."

He kissed her cheek and smiled.

"Lisa, that's the best idea I've heard all day."

XI

The Wall Street Journal, February 21, 1958

Winthrop Allis Bond IV, board chairman and majority stockholder of W. W. Bond, Inc. has died in a swimming accident apparently caused by heart failure.

Bond, the reclusive scion of one of America's most influential business families, was vacationing at his retreat in Hawaii when the mishap occurred. His body was found floating in the surf outside the coral reef near his private beach by members of his household staff. His wife Elizabeth attempted artificial respiration before driving Bond to Maui Memorial Hospital, where he was pronounced dead on arrival at 10:22 A.M. Pacific Standard Time.

The examining physicians found evidence that Bond suffered a heart attack while swimming and lost consciousness. He had suffered a mild coronary thrombosis in 1952, with minimal damage to the heart. According to family members, Bond was not a strong swimmer, but knew the ocean waters near his house well. No autopsy was performed.

Stock prices declined sharply yesterday morning at news of the billionaire's unexpected death, but rebounded later in the day. Spokesmen for W. W. Bond assured stockholders that an orderly transition of authority within the conglomerate will take place over the coming weeks, with no changes in corporation policy or personnel anticipated. Bond's son by a previous marriage, Winthrop V, a board member and high-ranking executive officer of the company for the past decade, will succeed his father as board chairman in accordance with the company's bylaws.

In addition to his wife and son, Winthrop Bond leaves a daughter by a previous marriage, Gay; a sister, Jessica; and four grandchildren.

Funeral services will be held Monday at the United Methodist Church, Wailuku, Hawaii.

XII

IT WAS A NIGHT FOR CELEBRATION.

Laura's spring show had just taken place at the Waldorf, and was a huge success. This had come as a relief to Laura, for the designs she had produced for the season were as unusual as any she had ever conceived. They represented Laura at her most eccentric and forward-looking, and bore clear traces of the ferment going through her as a person and an artist at this particular moment of her life. She could not help wondering if she had gone too far this time.

But the major buyers and journalists at the show had seemed impressed, some of them even ecstatic. Orders were pouring in, and there was talk of the show reaching a height of international stylistic influence beyond anything Laura had achieved before. It looked as though Laura, by going a bit farther out on a limb than even she had hitherto dared, had pulled off one of her greatest coups as a designer.

Tonight Laura and Tim planned to celebrate the good news with an intimate dinner at home. There was champagne waiting in the refrigerator, and Laura had already prepared the table with candles and her best linen before going to work. She and Tim had joked about their "date," but the affectionate looks they had exchanged left no doubt it was an important occasion for both.

Their relationship was badly in need of renewal. In recent months the bonds between them had grown tenuous, and their marriage more troubled by forces neither could quite understand.

On the surface it seemed that Laura's secret obsession with photography was the cause of everything, for it was affecting her profession and her home life at once.

She had installed a darkroom in her walk-in closet, and now processed all her own pictures at home. This was a financial necessity, given the expense of commercial photo labs, but it was also a symbolic gesture. Laura hoped that by bringing her avocation under her own roof she could get Tim to accept it as a familiar and therefore innocent fact of life.

But Tim behaved precisely as though the darkroom were not even there, and in fact as though Laura's photography simply did not exist. Whenever she mentioned to him that she was going out to take some pictures, or that she had to do some developing in the darkroom, he gave her an absent, irritated look, as though she had suddenly announced an incomprehensible plan of action that interfered with their domestic routine.

As a result of this, Laura became afraid to mention her photographic outings in advance. She knew Tim would disapprove, and that the mention of photography would poison the atmosphere between them.

In the early days of her photography Tim had told her she was crazy to wander around New York's less savory neighborhoods by herself in search of subjects. She had tried to explain to him that the camera was ideal protection for her, and that no one had menaced her in the slightest degree. She had never convinced him.

But now the argument no longer came up, for Tim had replaced his remonstrances with cold silence. When Laura went out with her camera she would leave him friendly notes—*Went out for an hour. See you before nine. Love, Laura.* Tim would ignore them. When she came home, encumbered by her camera bag, she would find him moodily reading or watching television. Her note would be on the kitchen counter where she had left it.

Often she was filled with inner excitement over the pictures she had taken, and eager to get into the darkroom to develop them. But she could not share her exhilaration with Tim, for she knew it would annoy him.

On the rare occasions when he broke his silence about her photography, it was to reproach her in the most unkind of terms. One day a pressing photography session with a new subject caused her to be late with some sketches she had promised Meredith for early morning. Tim had seized on this little mistake to upbraid her. "Are you a photographer or a fashion designer?" The almost contemptuous curl of his lip had made her feel guilty and confused.

Yet she could not deny it—she *was* both a photographer and a fashion designer. Her photography was far more than a hobby. It was as deep a part of her as fashion design had ever been. And though it was not yet a profession, it had just as much meaning as one, and just as profound a claim to her time and energy.

This fact was as full of joy as it was of insecurity. For the camera had become the outlet for something which had been pent-up inside Laura all her life. The pictures she took of strangers were open doors to her own heart. When they crystallized before her eyes in her processing tray she felt a mixture of awe and relief, as though the essence of herself was being restored to her after having almost slipped away. She felt a new contact with the human race, deeper and more exciting each day.

But she could not share any of this with her husband. Indeed, the gulf between her and Tim seemed to be widening. There were times when he himself did not return from the office until very late, times when he missed dinner with her, times when he came home with liquor on his breath, his mood brittle and dangerous.

She dared not question him about these absences, for she understood he was giving as good as he got. If she could presume to be two hours late in coming home, then so could he.

Once she was convinced she smelled woman's perfume on him when he came home late and got into bed with her. She forced back her words of anger and distress, for she correctly assumed he was intentionally angling for an argument.

Later she tried to find a propitious moment for a serious discussion with him about the problem that was darkening their marriage. But he stopped her with a brusque excuse about not having time to talk. The look in his eyes made it clear he wanted no accommodation to the present situation. He wanted a return to the old life, when Laura, Ltd., had been her only work, and her all-encompassing bond with him.

As time went by, in the absence of heartfelt conversations, they had sudden moments of irresistible need for each other, in which their old warmth joined them once more in wordless physical closeness. They made love in the early morning, or in the evening before dinner, and sat quietly in bed together, listening to the city breathing outside the windows, and feeling a seductive echo of their old intimacy.

But, as they both suspected, it was just an echo, and no longer a firm foundation for love and confidence. This made it the more bittersweet, for they knew it came from a halcyon time that was no more, and resounded in the cold silence that had now fallen between them. And they sensed, even in the hottest of their embraces, that the gulf deepening at the heart of their relationship was not banished, but would reappear as soon as the routine of their days resumed.

Laura did not know how to fight against this gradual sundering that was pulling her away from her husband. She knew Tim would never be satisfied until she gave up photography altogether. He saw her solitary outings with the camera as forbidden, almost perverse adventures. They filled him with something bordering on jealous rage. He turned up his nose in disgust when he glanced at the pictures she had taken of people who were considered the dregs of society.

But Laura could no more give up photography than she could give up her very self. In the short space of one year the camera had become as crucial to her as any other part of her life. So she had no choice but to keep trying to fit it in with a husband and a livelihood that remained in bitter conflict with it.

Tonight's celebratory dinner at home, Laura hoped, would be one of those precious moments when her old closeness with Tim would eclipse their recent estrangement.

Her hope was not merely emotional, but physical, too. She had not been intimate with Tim in nearly two weeks, the pressures of the spring show and of their private conflict having come between them. She wanted him desperately. Her body ached for the warm touch of his hands, the slow excitement of his embrace. She hoped that tonight would bring them together again.

But in the afternoon something happened to upset her plans.

The office was relatively quiet in the aftermath of last night's show, so Laura had stolen an hour to take her camera to the Bronx, where she knew she would find one of her favorite new subjects, a teenaged prostitute named Maria.

Maria, whose mother was of Hispanic birth and her father an unknown quantity, was a prodigious photographic subject. Underneath the garish make-up and clothes she wore to ply her trade, she had the fresh beauty of an angel. And beneath her hard-boiled whore's exterior she was as sweet and shy as a Sunday school student.

Maria was a walking paradox, a flesh-and-blood incarnation of the battleground between Good and Evil, for her natural personality was as saintly as her profession was squalid and demeaning. Over the last four weeks Laura had assembled a heartbreaking series of pictures that captured the two sides of Maria, and today she intended to add to it some shots taken on the street, where Maria actually plied her trade.

But, to everyone's surprise, the police had picked today to round up the girls in Maria's area, and Laura had been standing with her camera bag no more than six feet from Maria when she was arrested.

On an impulse Laura had gone along to the precinct house, following the police van in a cab, and had put up bail for Maria in return for the privilege of photographing her in this less profitable sector of her working life. The red tape of processing at the police station had taken a long time, and Laura had ducked out long enough to call the office and leave a message for Tim that she would be home late.

She had managed to get several dozen pictures of Maria's face, eloquent in its patience, during her time in the detention room and at the bail hearing. She had also got intriguing images of the other whores, the bored police officers, and the judge. She had been so fascinated by the air of languid cooperation, almost of family feeling, between law enforcement officials and offenders, that she lost track of the time.

It was not until nearly nine-thirty that, exhausted by her adventure with Maria, Laura finally arrived home, lugging her heavy camera bag, famished and out of breath. She took the elevator upstairs and entered the apartment.

She smelled cigarette smoke in the living room. Tim was home, then. "Tim?" she called.

She hung up her coat, left her camera bag in the foyer, and moved toward the kitchen.

She passed through the dining room. The table was set for dinner. Two candles were lit, and had burned halfway down. There was champagne in the pewter bucket.

Laura could feel violence in the air. But her reaction time was not quick enough to prepare her for what was to come.

As she entered the kitchen Tim loomed up from nowhere in front of her. He was in shirtsleeves, his powerful chest showing behind the open neck of his shirt. His face was red.

His eyes told her he had been drinking.

"Tim, I'm so sorry," she began. "I couldn't help it. I hope I haven't spoiled everything. I had so looked forward to tonight . . ."

Her words trailed off, for he was advancing toward her so menacingly that she backed away into the hallway that led to the bedroom. He looked huge, frightening. His silence unnerved her.

"Didn't you get my message?" she asked. "I called the office as soon as I realized I was going to be late . . ."

"Message?" he said through clenched teeth. The word came out slurred by alcohol, but sparked by smoldering anger, so that it sounded like an accusation.

"I left it at the office," Laura said, her voice shaking. "Maria, my friend, got arrested, and I had to post bail for her . . ."

Tim was shaking his head in disbelief. "Message? What message? There was no message."

Laura was still backing away. She had entered the bedroom without realizing it. The bed stopped her at last. "As I said, I called Meredith . . ."

"*What message?*"

"Tim, if you'd just listen . . ."

"A special dinner," he murmured darkly. "Just the two of us, Remember? A special occasion. But you weren't there. It was just the one of us. And there was *no message*. Don't try to tell me there was a message. I'm not that stupid."

He seemed crouched before her, coiled to spring at her like an animal. The sight of him made her turn pale.

"Tim, you've got to listen," she said. "I tried to . . . I left it . . ."

Before she could say any more his hand came from nowhere and slapped her so hard that she was flung backward onto the bed like a rag doll. Her cheek went numb. She saw stars. For a moment she was too dazed to move.

She looked up at him. He was glaring down at her, his eyes lit by a fury so terrible that she wanted to cry out.

"Message . . ." He intoned the word with a vicious sarcasm. The hatred in his voice made her blood run cold.

He took a sudden step toward her and held out his hand to strike her again. She cringed into the bedclothes like a child. His eyes were like red coals, the irises on fire with rage. She knew he had been drinking. But liquor alone could not unleash such an awful look.

"You can tell me any lies you want about where you were," he said. "Go ahead, use that brain of yours. Be smart. Make up any story you want. But don't tell me there was a message, you little liar. There was no message. *Do you hear me?*"

He was leaning over her, his large hand clenching and unclenching like a weapon. He held it over her, and watched her cringe away from him, clutching desperately at the pillows.

She could not find words to say to him. The hot pain in her cheek and eye joined with the infinite menace of his posture to reduce her to silence. Her attempts to reason with him were forgotten now, eclipsed by sheer physical fear.

"Come on," he said, grasping her suddenly by the shoulders. "Say it, liar. There was no message. No message. Say it. Say it. *Say it!*" As he repeated the words he shook her with terrible force. He was as huge as a lion, she as helpless as a doe in his hands. Her head was flung backward against the pillows again and again, making her limp and dizzy.

She did not speak. She was too frightened to say a word. She could only stare in amazement at his eyes, which were fixed on her with an intensity from which all human feeling had been banished. It was the look of a beast, full of hatred for its enemy and hunger to destroy it.

At last he flung her down and stood over her, the breath rasping in his throat, his body silhouetted like a monster by the light from the doorway behind him. Laura lay on her back, gazing up at him through eyes wide with terror.

Than all at once his posture changed. He sighed. The spell that had come over him seemed to pass. The animal heat of his crouching, predatory posture disappeared, and once again it was her husband standing over her, looking exhausted and frightened himself.

Seeing this, Laura's eyes filled with tears, and a sob sounded in her throat. She still shrunk from him among the tumbled bedclothes, but her heart went out to him.

At last he sat down on the edge of the bed, hiding his face in a large hand.

"Oh, my God," he sighed in a deep, hoarse voice. "Oh, my sweet Laura."

Without looking at her he touched gently at her hand. She came to his arms.

"My God," he murmured close to her ear. "Forgive me."

She kissed his cheek, and felt hot tears there. She joined her own to them as she nodded, pulling him closer to her. Still she could not bring herself to speak. She clung to him with all her strength. And in the arms holding her there was a desperate surging energy almost as terrible as the anger that had possessed his hands a moment ago.

"Forgive me," he repeated, his tone so inconsolable that her heart broke to hear it on the lips of so proud and strong a man.

She hid against his chest, clinging to his warmth as to the only rampart between herself and an outside world cold as the hardest of ice, a world that could freeze the life out of anything it touched.

But she knew that her embrace was not enough to bring him as close as he once was, and should be. And the power in his arms would never again be as reassuring as it had been before. For the very strength of those male muscles still stung her cheek, and the terror that had made her recoil from her husband still throbbed in all her senses.

The enemy was inside now. A line had been crossed tonight, a step taken that could never be retraced. Laura could not turn back the clock. She could only cling to what she had left.

But even that was not enough. After a while Tim began to let her go. She could feel him receding from her, as his pride and his fear made him shrink from what he had done.

He did not want her forgiveness. He wanted something more, something that could erase not only his rage but also the reason for it. And that reason was his wife herself, whose separate existence had somehow become a thing he could not tolerate.

They sat together in that frail embrace, feeling it weaken on both sides, until at last he got up and left the room, without looking back at her. This time there would be no instant reconciliation. Things had gone too far.

Laura lay in silence. She heard the hall closet door open and close. There was a rustle of fabric as he pulled on his coat. She felt her voice rise in her throat to call out to him. Too late: the apartment door was already closing behind him.

Laura was alone.

XIII

THE NEXT MORNING, his mind painly wrenched by the memory of what had happened last night no less than by a crushing hangover, Tim arrived at the office early. He was following an old pattern of taking out his frustrations and dark moods by doubling the amount of his work.

In the silence of the deserted office he sat at his desk and shuffled slowly through the papers and memos in his IN box. Most were notes of congratulation on the success of the spring show from retailers, fashion editors, and business contacts.

Near the bottom of the box he found a folded note. The handwriting was Meredith's.

Five thirty, it read. *Laura has an emergency—She's at the police station in the Bronx bailing out "Maria," whoever that is. She'll be home by nine or so. "Tell him I love him, can't wait to see him." Love and kisses—M.*

Meredith had written the message with her usual humor, using quotes for the parts she thought he should hear verbatim.

Tim's headache abruptly got worse. He closed his eyes. The only sound in the office was the coffee perking in the next room.

So she had left him a message, just as she said. It must have got lost in the shuffle of yesterday afternoon's business, for he had not found it when he cleared his desk before leaving at six.

Tim's stomach felt queasy. His head was spinning. The words on the piece of paper were blurred by the memory of his own hand flying toward Laura's face. The image hung before his mind's eye like a nightmare.

Tell him I love him, can't wait to see him.

So she had wanted him last night, just as he had suspected. She had looked forward to the evening with the same emotions as he.

But in his case the long hours of waiting had turned his wanting into a black rage that could not be denied, a rage he had fought against for many weeks, but which had finally pushed him over the edge into the unforgivable.

Early this morning, in the wee hours, he had returned to the apartment. He saw that Laura had cleared away the dinner things on the table, folded up the linen, put away the unused champagne, and straightened up the apartment before going to bed.

He imagined her coming out of the bedroom alone after he left her. He imagined the look in her eyes as she put away the hopeful trappings of their aborted dinner. In his mind's eye he could see her sadness, her loneliness, her lingering pain and fear over the way he had treated her. And he could see her slipping into bed alone, to sleep without her husband by her side.

Uneasily he peeked into the bedroom. She was fast asleep, her tiny body like that of a child under the covers. The sight of her had so wrenched his heart that he could not think of sleep himself. He stood looking at her for a long while, not daring to get into bed with her, yet unable to take his eyes off her.

At last he had gone to the living room, lay down on the couch until five-thirty without sleeping, feeling the false balm of the alcohol resolve itself through cottony numbness into a splitting headache, and got up to shower and come to work.

Now he looked at the memo again, still haunted by the visions of her cringing away from him like a terrified child, images of her asleep alone in his bed. Her sleep had shut him out, as had her fear earlier. And, before that, her need for him.

I love him. I can't wait to see him.

Even the notion of her wanting, her desire for him, had undergone a change during the troubled months that had led to last night. He used to think of her female needs with a kind of humble gratitude. He was touched by the naturalness with which she accepted him, opening her small body so willingly to his caresses and his passion.

But no more. Now that soft little body, with its creamy skin, its secret warm places, its wellsprings of female hunger, no longer belonged to him. It was hidden behind the veil of her separate, unknowable existence, an existence he could not hope to share or really understand.

He found himself unable to think of her womanhood without being tormented by images of forbidden thoughts she withheld from him, forbidden pleasures she might taste far from him or might wish to taste. Though he had long since overcome his absurd jealousy about insignificant Tommy Sturdevant, he still found his daydreams haunted by faces not so unlike Tommy's, handsome faces to which Laura raised her lips eagerly, delightedly, and men's bodies caressed by her soft hands in moments of shared surrender, shared excitement . . .

He tried to shrug off these painful fantasies. But when he did so he was confronted by the thought of her past. He knew she had known men before him. He had sensed this when he first met her. Something in those melancholy eyes of hers made it clear she had felt something for a man at some time, and been hurt.

In the beginning Tim's sympathy for her had been part and parcel of his admiration. But now the past she had lived through before she met him was at the core of his nightmare fantasies. A past in which she might have known pleasures he could not give her now, pleasures over which perhaps her memory lingered, allowing her secret thoughts to stray down guilty paths to dark ecstasies she had enjoyed in the arms of another . . .

Tim shook his head violently, struggling to fight off his own thoughts. Why, he wondered, had his love for Laura changed in a few short months from the sweetest adoration into this terrible pain, this witches' brew of longing and suspicion that last night had finally pushed him over the edge? Why? What had happened to his love, and to Laura's?

Instead of an answer, his mind showed him the image of her shrinking from him across his bed, her whole being absorbed in those terrified dark eyes that looked up at him.

Heaven help me, Tim thought with a prayerful shudder, seeing his wife slip so far away from him that only the will of God could bring her back.

XIV

THAT FRIDAY LAURA had an appointment with her doctor.

She had to flip a mental coin before deciding to keep the appointment. Her cheek and eye were still black and blue from the blow of Tim's open hand, and she did not want to face a question from the alert doctor about what had happened.

But she had had the appointment for three weeks already, and Dr. Fried was so busy she knew she might not be able to get another one soon, so she decided to keep it after all. She had been troubled by episodes of fatigue and weakness in recent weeks, and she wanted to rule out the possibility of anemia or some other physical trouble. In reality she suspected the morbid stress she was under was the root of the problem, and she wanted to hear Dr. Fried's opinion of this.

After the nurse had taken her blood pressure she waited a long time, dressed only in the smock she had been given, sitting on the examining table and looking at herself in the mirror. She looked pale and much too thin. The black-and-blue mark on her face was obvious despite the make-up with which she had tried to hide it.

When the doctor came in he immediately asked, "What happened to you?"

Laura was not a good liar, but she did her best. "I got smacked in the face by my own camera in the studio yesterday," she said. "It was one of those crazy things . . . I lost my balance and it fell on top of me."

"Mm-hmm . . . ," he murmured noncommittally, touching at the sore spot with a finger and thumb. "Doesn't look too bad . . . Should clear up in two or three more days. You're lucky it didn't get your eye itself."

He raised an eyebrow. "Your husband isn't still beating you, is he?"

She laughed and shook her head. Dr. Fried was an incorrigible joker who loved to belabor her with funny stories during his examinations. But she knew how watchful he was behind his mask of humor. She hoped the easy smile she had put on was hiding her chagrin from him.

He gave her a thorough physical, and then had her put on her clothes. A moment later she joined him in his office.

"So," he said. "You're feeling tired. Out of sorts. Not quite yourself. Have you been working too hard?"

She nodded. "I'm afraid that's nothing new," she said.

"Husband treating you all right?" he asked, looking at her critically from behind his desk.

"Fine," she managed.

There was a pause. Laura was preparing to broach the subject of the stress she was under, but could not seem to find the right words.

"Any nausea?" the doctor asked.

She shook her head.

"Dizziness? Blurred vision? Insomnia?"

"No . . ."

"When was your last period?" he asked.

She half-closed her eyes, mentally counting the days. "About three weeks ago," she said. "I'm due, I think."

"Overdue is more like it, I suspect," he said. "Laura, I won't be sure about this until I send you over to Dr. Ensor for a test. But I've got good instincts, and I'm usually not wrong. I think the reason you feel drained is that there's a little person inside you who needs a lot of your energy."

Laura looked at him in shock. "You mean I'm pregnant?"

"That's what my crystal ball says," he replied. "I'll make you an appointment with Ensor for this afternoon. We'll know what's cooking the day after tomorrow. Can you wait that long?"

Laura could see herself in the mirror on the wall. She was pale as a ghost, the black-and-blue marks on her face looking more salient than ever. But her eyes were sparkling with a new light.

"I—yes, I can wait," she said.

"Good. Now try to relax. And no bumping into any more cameras," he said. "This is not the time for accidents."

Laura nodded. "I promise."

"All right. You run along now, and start thinking about how to break the good news to that husband of yours."

As she left the office, those final words resounded inside her like a challenge, vying crazily with the painful feelings that had haunted her all week.

Yes, she must tell Tim.

Everything was changed now.

XV

The New York Times, April 5, 1958

LANCASTER SHOCKS STATE IN PRIMARY VICTORY

BOSE ANNOUNCES AS INDEPENDENT

In a victory which has defied the predictions of pollsters and Democratic kingmakers, Haydon Lancaster yesterday defeated U.S. Senator Amory Bose by a solid margin in the statewide Democratic primary election.

Lancaster's victory was doubly shocking because no incumbent Democratic senator has lost a primary in several generations. No incumbent of the stature of Amory Bose—Chairman of the Senate Appropriations Committee and ranking Democrat on the Foreign Relations Committee —has ever lost a primary.

Experts are still assessing the reasons for Lancaster's victory. The efficiency of his campaign organization at mending fences with party leaders suspicious of Lancaster's youth and political views has been cited, as well as Lancaster's personal sincerity and willingness to deal fairly with party regulars.

But the concensus among election observers seems to be that the Democratic voters themselves made the difference. Lancaster's high public profile, combined with the acrimonious campaign waged against him by Amory Bose—a campaign in which Bose sought to convince voters that a battle between Good and Evil was at stake rather than a mere contest between two men—seems to have redounded to the challenger's advantage.

The turnout yesterday broke all records for Democratic primaries. Observers at the polls reported that an unprecedented number of female Democrats turned out to vote. Given Lancaster's popularity among women, this fact is seen as a key to the unexpected victory.

But the primary seems to have been only a prelude to the real fight for the Senate.

Even as he conceded defeat in the early hours of this morning, Amory Bose announced that he would run for the Senate as an independent. He urged his many supporters to stand by him, and vowed that under no circumstances would he drop out of the general election and release his voters to support Lancaster as the Democratic candidate.

"My views about Haydon Lancaster as a man and as a public servant are well known," said Bose. "I would do a disservice to my own supporters, and to the people of this state, if I did not do everything in my power to deny this man access to a seat in the United States Senate. My knowledge that I alone stand between him and a position of such responsibility gives me strength and confidence for the battle ahead."

Few of those present at Bose's concession speech doubted his word. Amory Bose has made his vendetta against Haydon Lancaster into a virtual crusade. That crusade seems likely to continue until the November election for the U.S. Senate.

HAL LANCASTER was between the frying pan and the fire.

In the week following the primary, his victory over Amory Bose began to look less like a triumph and more like the prelude to a battle in which, astonishingly, Hal was the underdog. With Bose still in the race an an independent, commanding the votes of so many Democrats loyal to him, Hal could not count on the wholehearted support of the party organization in his campaign against the Republican nominee, Lawrence Ingersoll. The election would be a three-way race, and a close one.

Ingersoll, a wealthy industrialist with a lot of his own money, had been considered a token opponent without a chance for victory, until Bose's unexpected announcement. Now, however, he was seen as a credible dark horse in a race against a divided Democratic party, and the Republicans were throwing everything they had behind him.

Ingersoll had in common with Amory Bose his conservative politics. Therefore Hal could count on being branded as a left-wing radical by both men. The votes he lost due to his age, his inexperience in New York State politics, and his controversial image, would almost certainly go to Amory Bose. Viewed from this angle, Bose could be seen as the favorite in the very election from which his primary defeat would seem to have barred him.

Hal's best chance in the election was to convince the voters that his responsible State Department position in Dwight Eisenhower's White House proved that his loyalty and political convictions were above reproach. This platform was a mixed bag, however, since Senator McCarthy and his minions had been branding precisely the State Department as a hotbed of Communists and fellow travelers for years.

But Hal had other weapons: his precocious maturity of outlook, his command of the important issues, his eloquence, and, most important of all, the youth and undeniable charm that had carried him to improbable victory in the primary against the most powerful and entrenched opponent imaginable.

Bose and his people knew this only too well, and were responding to the threat with every weapon in their arsenal. Within hours after his concession speech Bose was on the campaign trail all over again, assailing Hal in the most strident terms as a Communist sympathizer and enemy of freedom. Advertisements paid for by Bose's reelection committee were appearing daily in major newspapers and magazines, warning the public that "documented proof" of Hal's Communist views and affiliations existed, and repeating words such as "traitor," "treason," and "conspiracy" with monotonous insistence.

Bose's strategy appeared to be working. The polls taken in the wake of his announcement as an independent showed him holding a strong position alongside Hal among the voters, with Ingersoll in third place. Bose's fear tactics seemed to be striking a chord in the public mind.

Thus the campaign ahead seemed like an uphill battle instead of the easy victory that Hal's advisors had expected. It looked as though Hal would have to start all over again, this time in a three-man race, to win the confidence of the people of New York and parry the vicious barbs of Amory Bose.

It was at this difficult moment in his already controversial career that Hal encountered a new face which was to become important for him.

Her name was Elizabeth Bond.

Hal had been surprised when Tom told him that the widow of the famous Winthrop Bond was interested in him. The Bond family had been an enemy of the Democratic party for many years. In fact, the Bonds were so close in political stripe to the Republican Lancasters that there had once been talk of a possible match between Hal and the daughter of Winthrop Bond, a girl named Gay. But the girl had been deemed a bit too old for Hal, and the idea had been dropped when Hal was still a boy.

In any case Hal could not believe his ears when he was told that Winthrop Bond's widow had already contributed a hundred thousand dollars to his campaign without ever having met or contacted him before. He half-suspected that, with her enormous corporate interests, Mrs. Bond would be expecting to influence his Senate vote on tax incentives for multinational corporations. And when Tom informed him that the lady was a leader in television technology and had close connections with the major networks, he naturally assumed she would want his vote on monopoly legislation concerning the television industry.

But when he met Mrs. Bond at a fund-raising banquet not long after the primary Hal momentarily forgot all these thoughts. The most astonishing thing about her was her youth and beauty. She could not be more than twenty-eight or twenty-nine years old. Were it not for the conservative business suit she wore, she would have looked more like a college coed than a grown woman.

"I'm delighted to meet you," Hal said, shaking her hand. "I was an admirer of your late husband."

"He was an admirer of yours," she said, "in spite of his family's political inclinations. As a matter of fact, it's partially because of his enthusiasm that I'm here. I try in as many ways as possible to carry out my husband's wishes."

As they spoke the spell of her beauty deepened. Hal was impressed by how Irish she looked. The pearly complexion touched by freckles, the brilliant auburn hair flowing to her shoulders, the white hands and fresh cheeks, and above all the sparkling green eyes—all this made Elizabeth Bond look like a sprightly schoolgirl sprung from verdant country hills, rather than the widow of an old New York millionaire.

Hal had learned that she had no family of her own, and was more or less marooned among the Bonds since her husband's death. She had been close to Winthrop Bond, but not to his family.

And she was still grieving for him. The more she talked about him, the more Hal realized that she had been far more attached to him than rumor and speculation would have suggested. She seemed devastated at not having been able to give him a child before he died. She apparently took this as a personal failure for which she had to atone by seeing to it that his vast fortune was administered as he would have wished.

Her veneration for him—which struck Hal as a bit odd, for he knew Win Bond by reputation as an ineffectual figurehead without either great charm or executive force—was joined to a deep personal sadness, and to a resigned and even somewhat contemptuous view of herself.

"Instead of Win's children," she said rather bitterly, "I have his money. It's a poor excuse for what I wanted. But I have nothing else to give, so I spread it around as helpfully as I can. I give to children's hospitals, orphanages . . . I visit them sometimes, and since the staffs are grateful to me for my money, they let me hang around. I try not to be a nuisance, but it's hard to tear myself away. I take the kids to amusement parks or on picnics, and sometimes to the circus. I'm a pretty good companion, because I keep my self-pity to myself."

She smiled. "I'm afraid I'm one of those women who disguise their need for chidren as a love of mankind. Sublimate—isn't that the word

Freud used for it? Well, I'm no psychologist. But I do know I have a hole inside me, and too much money, and too much time on my hands —so I spend it in trying to do some good for someone."

She looked at Hal. "That includes trying to help people like you— people who want to do something for the human race. Like keeping us from being massacred by our own weapons and our prejudices."

"Well, if you don't mind hopping onto what might be a sinking ship, welcome aboard, Mrs. Bond," Hal said.

"Call me Bess," she told him. "All my friends do."

"Bess, then," he smiled.

Their first meeting ended with some casual conversation that led inevitably to the question of the Presidency. Concerned that Elizabeth Bond might share the common perception of him as an ambitious young war hero who only wanted the Senate as a stepping-stone to the White House, Hal assured her that he saw Jack Kennedy as the party's best hope in 1960, and fully intended to campaign hard for him.

She seemed to take him at his word.

"What about after Kennedy?" she asked. "No one can predict the future. How would you feel if you ended up in the White House yourself?"

Hal thought for a moment.

"Scared," he said at last, an infectious grin lighting up his face.

She nodded, an odd light flickering in her emerald irises. It almost seemed to him that he had passed some sort of test, for the smile she gave him now was even warmer than before.

At first Hal took Elizabeth Bond's friendship with a grain of salt. He knew enough about political contributors to know they did not spend their money without expecting a return on their investment. But as time went on, and he saw Mrs. Bond more often, he began to realize that she wanted nothing at all from him by way of favors to herself or to W. W. Bond, Inc. She simply wanted him to get elected to the Senate, and to vote his conscience, especially on nuclear disarmament and the Cold War.

Hal could hardly believe his good fortune. He had stumbled upon that most rare of political creatures: the wealthy contributor whose only interest was ideological and purely philanthropic. Elizabeth Bond was spending her husband's money to try to do good for the world—nothing more.

She surprised Hal in more than this. He realized that she had an amazing analytical grasp of all his positions on the key issues, both domestic and foreign, as well as a profound and sophisticated understanding of the balance of power in Congress. She knew not only why she wanted him elected, but also what the political effects of his election would be.

And on a more immediate level she had brilliant ideas about how to get him through his tight three-way race to the finish line on election day. She was a shrewd judge of political realities, and had valuable advice to give Hal about special interest groups, Democratic kingmakers in Albany as well as New York, and the whims of the voters who were his grass roots support.

Before long he found himself listening respectfully to her ideas on his speeches, and to her very cunning suggestions on his campaign advertising, particularly on the developing art of television advertising. The sharpness of her intellect was joined to her boundless confidence in him, a confidence that was not shaken by his modest standing in the polls.

"Don't be afraid to be yourself," she told him. "You're young, dynamic, attractive. These are your strengths, Hal. Have faith in them. Communicate them to the public. Use the media to help you in this. And mark my words: Bose and Ingersoll will cancel each other out. Their own venom is making them look more ridiculous all the time. And most important, they're both old men—old and worn-out and cynical. No sensible voter will look at the three of you and choose one of them. You'll see."

Within a few weeks of their meeting Elizabeth Bond had become an unofficial member of Hal's team of advisors. He spoke to her on the phone several times a week, and invited her to lunch with Tom and the others. Her beautiful, composed presence made a pleasant contrast to the rather sweaty professionalism of the others.

She was also a consistent spectator at his fund-raisers and major speeches. Hal found himself picking out her face in the audience when he spoke, and giving a bit extra for her sake.

He enjoyed knowing she was out there, taking in his every word, expecting him to give his best but never doubting him. Since his family had never really approved of his political career, he had always felt more or less alone in his upward struggle. But now he had a booster, someone who believed in him. It was a pleasant feeling.

And there were more practical expressions of her loyalty. Hal did not know the precise extent of her contributions to the campaign—he left that to Tom—but he knew they were very considerable. He also began to notice that he was getting amazingly good press from the network news organizations. Not only were the constant accusations about his loyalty played down by the network reporters, but his eloquent responses to them were given crucial air time, along with flattering views of his youthful face in contrast to the jowly, aging visages of Bose and Ingersoll.

If Bess had anything directly to do with this, she was a valuable friend indeed. If not, she was perhaps a good luck charm. In either case she was someone to be treated well and listened to carefully. Hal's astute political mind told him that.

She invited Hal and Diana to dinner at her Sutton Place penthouse.

"Be nice to her," Hal warned Diana, not without a hint of duplicity. "We need every cent she can spare us."

He breathed an inner sign of relief when the two women got along well together. Bess accomplished the amazing feat of treating Diana—a woman at least as old as herself—like a daughter. Diana, ever conscious of preserving her youth, jumped on the opportunity, and seemed far more relaxed and happy in Bess's company than she had ever been with Hal's political friends.

"I like her a lot," Bess said later of Diana. "There's a lot more to her than meets the eye."

Hal did not mention the strange fact that Diana had said precisely those words to him about Bess.

"There's a lot more to her than meets the eye."

After that pleasant dinner Hal's relationship with Bess Bond was assured. Though it was not precisely a friendship—she was restrained almost to a fault in her treatment of him, and never asked a question about his personal life—he soon felt a trust in her, and a confidence in her steadfast loyalty, that few friendships offer.

He found himself looking forward to seeing her after his hard weeks of campaigning around the state. There was a stillness and calm about her that acted like a drug to soothe his nerves when he was with her. And he enjoyed her personality. She had a somehow composite essence, strangely divided between her fresh girlish body and the ageless sadness in her eyes. It was as though there was more than one woman inside her. Hal's artist's eye could not fail to be fascinated by this complexity.

As they grew more used to each other's company, there were lighter moments in their conversation. She teased him with the rumors she heard about him at her beauty parlor. She claimed they were an accurate measure of his popularity.

"What are they saying this week?" he asked.

"They say you're sexier than Kennedy," she said, "but that you don't have his killer instinct. That you're almost certainly a better lover than he is, but that you might not be as good at walking over the people who stand in your way. The attitude is wait-and-see—with emphasis on the 'see.' If looks alone mean anything, you've got the women's vote locked up."

"That's nice to know," Hal smiled. "Maybe I ought to schedule a few major speeches at beauty parlors around the state."

Bess invited Hal to visit an orphanage she helped to support in upstate New York. He came on a brisk October day, and impressed everyone with the simple but entertaining talk he gave to the children. He was touching in his ability to gain their confidence and get them talking about their innocent ideas of how a country works. They warmed up to him almost as though he were a sort of Pied Piper who himself possessed the secret to a child's wishes and dreams. Some of them even spontaneously held his hand.

"You were wonderful," Bess told him afterward. "You really have a gift with them."

"To be completely honest with you," Hal said, "—and I suppose you ought to know this, being a contributor—I don't think I've ever been entirely comfortable as a grown-up. I felt more at home as a boy. Perhaps part of me feels I've lost something I shouldn't have, along the way." He laughed. "That must be why I play a childish game like politics."

She gave him a wistful look.

"What this country needs," she said, "is precisely a man like you. A man who still has some of the child left in him. Some joy, some spontaneity, some hope for this world of ours." She smiled. "It comes out on film, you know. I noticed it the very first time I saw you on television, in my living room at home. Perhaps the real reason I wanted to meet you was to find out whether it's there in person as well."

"And?" he asked.

"And I'm not disappointed," she said.

Hal looked at her curiously. He realized that the bond he felt with her had a lot to do with her frustrated maternal instincts. Her childless state was a crucial element in her personality.

The same, he reflected, was true of him. Whenever he thought of his own lost childhood, and the disappointments of growing up, he found himself thinking of the children he wanted so desperately to have, children who seemed to elude him somehow.

But this train of thought was too painful to follow, for between his memories of boyhood and his secret dreams of children there lingered a sweet face that he had to force from his memory at least a hundred times a day. That part of his soul was owned by Laura. If he allowed himself to think about it, his despair would sap him of the strength to go on making a pretense of living.

Oddly enough, Elizabeth Bond played the unforeseen and convenient role of standing between Hal and the worst of his inner distress. Bess was so open about acknowledging her own unhappiness, that by listening to her and hearing her words echo inside himself, Hal could indirectly face the fact that his own life had led away from his dreams, toward something that he could not help thinking of as a poor substitute.

Yes, he decided, Bess was more to him now than a mere contributor. She seemed to understand him so well that she freed him from the burden of understanding himself, a burden he had never shouldered willingly and had never been able to count among his accomplishments.

As they left the orphanage Bess saw him looking at the children who were waving goodbye from the playground. If she divined his mixed emotions from the wistful look in his eyes, she did not say so.

Instead she changed the subject.

"Tell me," she asked. "How does Diana feel about being a Senator's wife?"

Hal laughed. "She's a lot more prepared for the job than I am," he said. "She'll have everyone in Washington in the palm of her hand before I get my office furnished. No, you don't have to worry about Diana."

Elizabeth Bond looked at him through clear, smiling eyes.

Yes, I do, Hal, she mused. *Oh, yes, I do.*

XVI

ON MAY FIRST the unexpected happened.

Hal was on the campaign trail, preparing for a speech in the upstate city of Rochester, when Tom Rossman rushed into his hotel room and turned on the television set.

On the screen was Amory Bose, giving a news conference. The look on Bose's face was stern and self-important, as though in keeping with an occasion of high seriousness. He was brandishing a sheaf of documents in his hand and speaking to reporters in a voice quavering with anger.

"You missed the beginning," Tom said. "He claims he's got evidence you were a spy for the Russians during your NATO days."

Hal leaned forward to listen to the broadcast.

A reporter was asking where Bose had got his information.

"I cannot reveal that to you at this time," Bose said, "because it involves classified information. But I can personally vouch for the accuracy of this material. What I have here is no more nor less than documented proof that Haydon Lancaster, during his days as a White House appointee, a representative of our nation to the NATO alliance at one of the most sensitive moments in our history, was responsible for the passing of top-secret, classified information about U.S. military installations to agents of the Soviet Union."

Hal watched in silence as Bose answered more questions. Though Bose refused to reveal the details behind his allegation, he was obviously enjoying being the center of attention. He teased the reporters with hints about the high-level secrets he had discovered, and their significance for national security. But he was withholding his trump card, no doubt in order to milk more press attention from it.

Hal felt a chill come over him as he listened to Bose speak. He was not sure what Bose had, but he was politician enough to understand the importance of this attack, and its crucial timing. He and Bose were dead even in the polls as of last weekend. In the past four weeks Hal had managed to close the gap, thanks to his own brilliant performances as a speaker, and to the good press he was getting from the networks and many newspapers and wire services.

Now was the perfect moment for Bose to strike a blow that would shock the voters into believing his oft-repeated claims that Hal's liberal politics had treasonous roots.

But what was the evidence? What could Bose have unearthed that would embolden him to hold a nationally televised news conference?

Before the broadcast ended, Hal's aides were already on the phone to Washington, to New York, to all the news media, trying to find out something, anything, about the material Bose was waving before the cameras. But no one seemed to know what was behind it, or how serious it really was.

Hal and Tom had to wait for the evening news an hour and a half later before some light was thrown on the accusations by an NBC reporter.

"According to Amory Bose's unnamed sources," the correspondent said, "Haydon Lancaster had a relationship with a Belgian NATO secretary named Jacqueline Brichot during his days as President Eisenhower's envoy to the NATO leadership in Paris. In the course of this relationship, Lancaster wittingly or unwittingly passed sensitive classified information about United States military installations in Europe to the young lady. The information ended up in the hands of Soviet intelligence agents."

A rather unclear picture of an attractive young woman appeared on the screen.

"This is Jacqueline Brichot as she appeared six years ago, just before Haydon Lancaster's arrival in Paris," the reporter said. "Miss Brichot later died in what Senator Bose has called 'mysterious circumstances.' It has not yet been possible for NBC News to verify or authenticate the charges against Lancaster. The documents in question have been withheld by Senator Bose because of their sensitive nature."

Hal looked long and hard at the picture of the girl on the screen. He seemed thoughtful.

When the broadcast was over Tom Rossman sent the other aides out of the room and turned to Hal.

"Listen," he said, a cautious look on his face. "I was there with you, remember? I'm the one who knew you when. Just between you and me, is there anything in this?"

Hal did not answer. He seemed lost within himself.

"Hey," Tom said. "If you can't tell me, who can you tell?"

Hal looked into his old friend's eyes. The truth of Tom's words was too obvious to deny. He was Hal's campaign manager and closest friend. He had to be told whatever there was to tell.

"There is nothing in this." Hal's voice was firm, but his eyes looked troubled.

"All right," Tom said. "Then what do you want to do about it?"

Hal was silent. That, indeed, was the question.

The next twenty-four hours were among the worst Hal had ever experienced.

While his staff frantically scrambled to find out what was behind the Bose allegations, Hal had to deal with an avalanche of press attention unlike anything he had ever imagined in his worst nightmares.

The phones at his campaign headquarters, his State Department office, and at home were ringing off the hook. His aides, secretaries, and current and former government colleagues were besieged by reporters eager for any and all comment on the charges against him.

Clearly the press smelled blood. For too long the name of Haydon Lancaster had been synonymous with glamor, privilege, and the brightest limelight of fame. Now it seemed that the youthful idol's feet of clay had been revealed at last, and the fickle news establishment, sensing a public backlash against Hal, was moving in for the kill.

After some hesitation Hal decided not to cancel his speaking schedule. He gave a speech before the Rochester Chamber of Commerce on Tuesday night, and another one before the Upstate New York Democratic Party on Wednesday morning. Mobs of reporters from all over the country turned out for both the speeches. Hal parried their questions as best he could with a straightforward denial, saying that he wondered why Senator Bose did not make the substance of his charges public, so that Hal could defend himself against them. In reality this was what Hal feared the most. But there was nothing he could do but bluff.

Hal knew this strategy could only work for a few more hours at most. Bose had captured national air time with his accusations, and would certainly get more throughout the weekend. There could be no more serious allegation than espionage. Unless Hal got to the root of the charges and refuted them convincingly, the election would be a lost cause.

As luck would have it, one of the most alert professional pollsters conducted a telephone poll of New York Democrats Wednesday night. The results were published in the Thursday morning newspapers. Hal's standing with the voters had already dropped ten percentage points— points that landed squarely in Amory Bose's column, making Bose the favorite to win the election easily.

Thursday was a nightmare. As Hal struggled to hold off the press, his aides called in every favor they were owed in an effort to get their hands on the substance of the charges made by Bose. But the information was under wraps. Even Bose's closest subordinates seemed vague about precisely what was involved.

Significantly, the information Bose had alluded to in his press conference had not yet been passed along to the Justice Department. This could be good or bad news. It might mean that the evidence was not as convincing as Bose had claimed. Or it could mean that Bose simply wanted to keep both Hal and the press hanging for a few more days before he dropped his bombshell.

At the end of the day Hal flew to New York City to be closer to the source of the problem. He joined Tom and the others at campaign headquarters to discuss strategy, and they all watched the evening news together, their eyes darting nervously back and forth over the three television screens in the conference room.

The news was worse than they had expected. Bose had given a second and more detailed news conference, timed so as to be covered live by the networks at the top of the evening news. He appeared in company with a small man of nondescript appearance who, he revealed, was the brother of the dead girl, Jacqueline Brichot.

"Mr. Vincent Brichot," Bose said, "is a Belgian citizen. He has personal knowledge of the circumstances that led up to his late sister's relationship with Soviet intelligence agents, and to her liaison with Haydon Lancaster in Paris. Mr. Brichot is here to authenticate the documents I have produced, and to personally testify to Haydon Lancaster's complicity in this shameful episode."

The man named Brichot, who spoke with a rather undifferentiated European accent, said only a few words to the press. Bose would not allow him to answer substantive questions about the affair. Nor would Bose himself be any more specific than he had been last night.

Bose was asked why he did not make public the information on which his charges were based. "I will turn all the documents over to the proper authorities at the proper time and in the proper way," he said. "It will certainly be referred to the Department of Justice, to the Department of State, and to the President, not to mention the FBI and the Central Intelligence Agency. I fully expect prosecution to follow."

The news conference was an exercise in grandstanding, intended to bedazzle the press and public with a "surprise witness," while withholding all relevant information that might shed light on the issue at stake. But it was a perfectly timed and modulated press event, for it gave visual credibility to Bose's charges against Hal.

To make matters worse, Bose showed off to the reporters photographs of Hal on the streets of Paris in the company of Jacqueline Brichot, an attractive young woman with dark curly hair and a slim figure.

At the end of the news conference Amory Bose turned to the camera.

"Ladies and gentlemen," he said, "Mr. Haydon Lancaster has finally shown us his true colors. Those of us who have spent our political lives trying to save the American public from this man, from his subversive ideas and his un-American intentions, are now confirmed in our mission. I'm only glad we have unearthed the whole truth before it was too late. I call upon Mr. Haydon Lancaster to meet me in a public forum, if he dares, and to answer the charges against him. If he refuses, then I call upon him to immediately withdraw from the New York State Senate race, and allow Mr. Ingersoll and myself to campaign against each other as loyal Americans."

An ironic smile curled the Senator's lips. "Let me say that I personally recommend the latter course of action," he said. "For if the American people become aware of the treasonous activity documented in these files, I would not bet a nickel on Mr. Haydon Lancaster's future in this country."

The news conference was over. The satisfaction on Amory Bose's face was evident as he dismissed the reporters without answering any further questions. He had brilliantly manipulated the press, making Hal seem to be tried and convicted of espionage without having produced an ounce of proof.

Hal's aides were split down the middle on what course of action to adopt. Half of them thought the prudent strategy was to blandly deny the charges and challenge Bose to prove them. The other half felt that such a course was suicidal, given the public attention Bose had already captured and its effect on the polls. Only through some sort of confrontation could Hal save himself.

Hal listened to the debate among his advisors for an excruciating two and a half hours. Each of the aides was loud and confident in his advice, and even seemed taken aback when another pointed out how wrong it was. Their voices increased in empty conviction as the logic behind their suggestions grew weaker. For the first time Hal understood the true solitude of a political leader. The discussion was degenerating into a virtual shouting match. And yet it was Hal's fate that was at stake, and not that of those debating about it. This lent the meeting an air of unreality that made it all the more painful.

At ten o'clock Hal broke up the conference and sent his staff home, saying there would be another meeting in the morning. They all needed time to think over the situation, and to digest what had been said tonight.

When he was alone Hal took a stiff drink of brandy from the office bar. It did not help. He paced the silent room, mulling over his situation. He understood that his entire political career was on the line, and that Bose's public grandstanding was not all bluff. Action must be taken, and right away, to regain at least a portion of the initiative Bose had seized, and to reassure the public that Hal's candidacy was not yet dead.

But how?

Frustrated, Hal put down his drink, left the office, and took a cab to his health club on Fifty-fifth Street, where he went down to the pool and swam twenty hard laps, struggling to clear his mind of the combined cacophony of reporters' questions and aides' eager suggestions.

By the time he emerged from the water he was physically exhausted, but less panicked by the situation before him. He felt prepared to face it down calmly, whatever it was.

He returned to the office, not yet feeling ready to go home. He thought of Diana, who was with her relatives at Southampton, and cursed himself for not having called her long ago to tell her where he was and what his plans were.

He picked up the receiver and touched the dial. But his hand, with a will of its own, dialed a different number, a number he had not realized he knew by heart.

There were several rings before a soft female voice answered.

"Hello?"

"Bess? This is Hal. Hal Lancaster."

"Hello, Hal. It's great to hear your voice." She had brightened at her recognition of him.

"Well," Hal began uneasily. "I . . . Have you seen the papers?"

There was a pause.

"Yes, I have," she said.

"I hate to bother you this late," Hal said, watching his fingers twist a rubber band on the desk top. "Do you suppose we could get together for a drink somewhere?"

He was amazed by the flutter of nervousness in his voice. He felt as jittery as a schoolboy asking a girl out for the first time.

"Why don't you come over here?" she said. "It will be best all around. I'll tell you how to come in the back way, so you won't be seen. It's probably better for you not to be meeting women in bars at a time like this."

Her humor had a calming effect on him. Her voice sounded completely composed, and, most important, utterly loyal.

"Thank you," he said.

"It's I who should thank you," she corrected. "I'm glad it was me you chose to come to."

He memorized her directions and drove to her Sutton Place building, where she buzzed him in through a small back entrance. He took a tiny, unfamiliar elevator up to her penthouse floor. She was waiting for him on the landing, with the door to the apartment open behind her.

She looked radiant. She was dressed in pale silk lounging pajamas of a subtle green that set off the glow of her eyes. Her hair was let down, and flowed over her shoulders in a crimson mane. She smelled magnificent, her natural scent mingling with a sensual perfume he had never smelled before.

She let him in the doorway and took him in her arms to hug him. For a moment his eyes closed at the feel of her long, slender body, whose softness he was touching for the very first time. As he opened his eyes he saw the penthouse spread out behind her, looking like a warm green refuge against the night, with its long couches, soft lights, and the mysterious paintings on the walls.

They hugged for a long moment, their embrace soothing Hal's tortured nerves. She leaned her head on his shoulder, for all the world as though it were she who was tired, she who needed his strength and support, instead of the reverse.

Then she smiled. "Not followed?" she asked.

"Lost them in a wild car chase," he said, a twinkle in his eye.

"Good work," she smiled.

She helped him off with his coat and led him into the living room. She turned off all the lights except the one closest to them, and brought him a scotch and water.

"So," she said, sitting beside him with her legs curled under her. "Tell me all about it."

He told her the problem, insofar as he himself could understand it at such short notice. She listened in silence, nodding slowly as he spoke.

When he had finished she smiled.

"I'm very glad you came," she said.

"I'm not sure why I did," Hal sighed. "I really shouldn't be bothering you with this."

"On the contrary," she said. "I'm delighted, for selfish reasons. I want to share the bad times with you, as well as the good. I joined your team for better or worse, Hal. I'm glad you thought of me now, when there is a problem, instead of shutting me out."

He returned her smile as best he could. He wanted to say something, but could not find the words. He was astonished at how deeply he needed her. He had never needed Tom Rossman in this way, or anyone else. He had always relied first and last on his own political instincts. But tonight he had come running for help and support to a woman he barely knew.

"You look worried," she said, studying his face. "Tell me, Hal—is there something here to be worried about?"

He hesitated for a long moment, and then breathed a deep sigh.

"I knew the girl," he said. "We had an affair. It was during my first year at NATO. I met her every so often at a little hotel on the Left Bank. It was nothing serious. But . . ."

Bess nodded. She seemed neither shocked nor disapproving. "And the rest?" she asked. "The business about the documents?"

Hal ran a hand through his hair. "I've racked my brains about that, over and over," he said. "The girl was a NATO secretary. Her section was far removed from mine. I don't know what sort of material she had access to, or what she might have stolen. If she was working for the Russians, it's possible there's something to this whole story. But I can't see how she could have gotten anything through me. She was never in my hotel suite at the Crillon, or at my office. I might have had my briefcase with me a few times when we met, but I was pretty careful about security. I don't think she could have gotten anything that way." He sighed. "But I'm not absolutely sure."

Bess seemed thoughtful. "So the probability is that Bose's people have something on this girl, who is dead and can't defend herself—and they're using your relationship with her as a way to tie it to you."

Hal nodded. "As near as I can figure it." The anxiety in his voice embarrassed him.

Sensing his confusion, she slipped her fingers into his palm and gave his hand a firm squeeze before letting it go.

Again her face was very serious.

"Am I correct in assuming," she asked, "that you had no contact of any kind with Soviet personnel in Paris? Nothing that could be taken in the wrong way?"

He shook his head. "Nothing. We stayed on our side, and they stayed on theirs. I met their ambassador at the embassy once or twice. That's all."

"The photographs of you with the girl," she asked. "Are they genuine?"

"I don't think so," Hal said. "I'd have to see them close up, but they looked odd. I suspect they're fakes."

"But you did have an affair," she said pensively. "So even if everything else can be disproved, there is always the chance that Bose will throw that charge at you as a last-ditch attack."

Hal nodded. "I hadn't thought of it that way," he said. "But I suppose you're right."

The notion of seeing his political career ruined by a sexual peccadillo came to him almost as a surprise. Somehow he had never taken such a possibility into his thinking. Now he recalled his many affairs, and his halfhearted attempts to protect himself and his women from prying eyes. He had been living in a fool's paradise, he mused. Perhaps he deserved what was happening to him now.

He looked at Bess. Her beautiful face was at rest as she considered the issue at stake. Long golden eyelashes shrouded her irises like palms over a tropical sunset. The girlish, innocent lines of her face hovered over the deeper, more womanly expression of her concern in a flicker of light and shadow, girl and woman eclipsing one another like dancing reflections on a silent pool. She had never looked more lovely.

"Hal," she said at last, "what kind of poker player are you?"

He looked quizzically at her. "How do you mean?" he asked.

"Are you willing to bet all you have in order to call your opponent's bluff," she asked, "if there's a chance for you to take home all the chips in one hand?"

Hal thought for a long moment. He realized what she was asking. Bose was playing rough. He had more than a mere Senate election in mind. He was after what amounted to political murder. Hal would have to play rough himself, and expose his flank in the process, if he was to get out of this mess.

But what choice was there? His whole political career was at stake, and there was no time to lose. If ever there was a time for desperate measures, this was it.

Suddenly an image of Korea flashed across Hal's mind. Yes, he thought—he had been on the battlefield once before, with the enemy's hatred aimed at his heart. He had survived then. Why not now?

"Yes," he said to Bess. "I'm that kind of player."

"In that case," she said, "we have a lot to talk about. And not much time to talk about it in."

She got up, went to the window, and closed the drapes. The nocturnal skyline disappeared behind her. She came back and sat down beside him, her face grave, but still calm.

"I have a small confession to make," she said. "Since I first heard about your trouble I took the liberty of doing some thinking about it for myself, and of checking out a few things. If you can forgive me for that, I'd like to tell you my own thoughts."

"You don't have to get involved in this," he warned her.

"I already am involved," she said, taking his hand once more. "We'll solve this together, Hal."

Hal looked down at the slender fingers curled around his own, and up into the green eyes with their imponderable depths.

"Politics is a dangerous poker game," he said. "Are you sure this is what you want?"

Her smile removed his last doubts.

"This is what I want, Hal," she said.

XVII

ON THE MORNING AFTER his meeting with Elizabeth Bond, Hal held a news conference of his own.

He agreed to Amory Bose's terms. He would meet Bose in a public forum and answer the charges against him. The details would be worked out in the next twenty-four hours, and the public meeting would take place as soon as possible.

Hal was cool and even humorous as he greeted the press.

"Well, I always wanted to be the center of attention," he joked, "but in the last three days I think I've seen enough of you ladies and gentlemen to last me the next decade."

Then he became serious. There was an impressive maturity in his manner as he assured the audience that a matter as grave as this could not be disposed of without total candor on his part. The people of the State of New York, and the people of America, he said, had a right to know where the truth lay.

When the brief news conference was over the reporters rushed to their telephones. Hal was calling Amory Bose's bluff.

If it was a bluff, that is.

Within six hours the venue for the confrontation had been chosen. Hal and Amory Bose would meet on the *Washington Today* program on Sunday morning. *Washington Today*, hosted by a distinguished political columnist named Farrell Keyes, was, along with *Meet the Press*, the most popular and critically acclaimed interview program on television, and was obligatory viewing for everyone in Washington as well as people around the country who had an interest in politics.

The broadcast would be live. Amory Bose would have the opportunity to present his evidence to representatives of the press in a public forum, and Hal would answer it.

The forty-eight hours before the broadcast were the most tense that Hal's advisors had ever spent. As of Saturday morning Hal's standing in the polls had plummeted below that of Lawrence Ingersoll. Amory Bose was now the favorite to retain his seat in the Senate by a landslide.

Hal had quietly dispatched Tom Rossman on an undisclosed mission to Europe in the early hours of Friday morning. To his other aides he would say nothing about his precise intentions regarding *Washington Today*. He wanted them to be in ignorance, so that none of them could leak anything to the press that might compromise the plan of action he had devised.

Hal flew to Albany to give his scheduled speech Saturday afternoon before members of the state legislature. He confined his remarks to economic and educational issues facing New York State, and assured those who asked questions about Amory Bose's charges that all would be made clear on Sunday morning.

By the time of the *Washington Today* telecast Hal's aides were in a virtual panic. Hal ordered them to remain at campaign headquarters to watch the broadcast on television. He went alone to the studio, where Tom, having returned from Europe in the nick of time, was waiting for him.

An air of anticipation reigned in the small studio, for television observers were predicting that today's broadcast would have the highest rating in the history of Sunday morning television. Hal greeted Farrell Keyes, an old friend, and sat chatting with Tom while the make-up girl applied touches of highlighting to his face. Despite the tension just below the surface of his charm, Hal seemed calm and confident.

The show began with a brief statement by Farrell Keyes, describing the controversy and stating the ground rules of the present encounter. Amory Bose would be heard first, followed by Hal, with a period of discussion and mutual rebuttal to follow.

Now the camera turned to Amory Bose. Looking every inch the

sternly patriotic Senate patriarch, filled with righteous wrath against his disloyal opponent, Bose detailed his charges. His statesmanlike demeanor commanded respect and awe as he accused Hal of high treason and conduct unbecoming an appointee of the President of the United States.

Then he introduced Vincent Brichot, the brother of the dead girl who was at the center of the accusations against Hal. Brichot, speaking in a quiet voice, explained that his sister had become enamored of a Soviet soldier during the war, and, succumbing to his blandishments, agreed to help Russian intelligence agents in the tense early days of the postwar period.

According to Brichot his sister had intentionally used her wit and charm to find a job with the Belgian NATO mission in Paris. When she was unable to lay her hands on documents of sufficient importance in her own office, she had befriended Haydon Lancaster, become his lover, and used her power over him to gain access to classified information about planned deployment of American missiles at bases in Europe.

Vincent Brichot had become aware of his sister's illegal activities and tried to stop her. But she had warned him that his life would be in danger if he got involved.

Not long thereafter, Jacqueline herself died "suddenly and mysteriously," in her brother's words. After her death Haydon Lancaster left Paris to take up his new post at the Geneva Conference.

Vincent Brichot, who admitted he was not a brave man, had considered that his sister's death closed the door on her folly and the whole sordid episode. He had thought no more about it until he learned that Haydon Lancaster was a candidate for the United States Senate. His conscience would not let him stand by while such a man penetrated so influential a body. So he had come forward and told what he knew to Amory Bose, a senator of impeccable reputation and authority.

During Brichot's speech, pictures of Hal with Jacqueline Brichot were held up to the camera, along with photos of Hal's office at NATO headquarters and the Hotel Crillon where Hal had stayed during his NATO service. The only thing missing from Brichot's presentation, beside the classified documents themselves, was the identity of the Russian agent or agents with whom the late Jacqueline Brichot was involved. About this nothing was said.

When Brichot had finished speaking, Amory Bose turned to the camera. His face was darker now, and angrier. He pointed a finger at Hal.

"I ask this man, Haydon Lancaster," he said, "to refute these charges if he can. I ask him to offer the American people some proof that he is a loyal servant of this democracy. I ask him to give us some reason to believe he did not act as a conscious agent for the Soviet Union, and as an enemy of freedom, while he was working for the very organization dedicated to protecting Europe from the Communist conspiracy that has enslaved millions of innocent people. I ask Haydon Lancaster to prove that he is an American—and to prove it NOW!"

The silence in the studio was deafening. The cameras turned to Hal. Surprisingly, he looked calm and composed.

"I'm happy to have the opportunity," he said, "to clear the air about an issue which has not only hurt my reputation and standing with the American public in the past unfortunate week, but has distracted the people of New York from the real issues at stake in our campaign for the Senate. I believe I cannot only refute Senator Bose's charges as to their substance, but also shed some light on the meaning of accusations like these in a free society."

Hal looked into the camera. "I have brought my own guest to this program," he said, "and with the permission of the moderator I would now like to introduce her to you. Ladies and gentlemen, Mrs. Marie-Claire Brichot, the mother of Jacqueline Brichot."

A small Belgian woman in her sixties was escorted onto the sound stage and sat in the chair next to Hal.

Hal turned the questions over to Farrell Keyes, who regarded the surprise guest with interest.

"Mrs. Brichot," her asked, "are you the mother of the young woman named Jacqueline Brichot?"

"I am." The woman spoke with a slight French accent.

"And do you know Mr. Lancaster, seated here?"

"I do not."

"Did your daughter work at NATO in Paris during the 1951–1955 period?"

"Yes, sir. She worked as a secretary at the Belgian mission, because she was bilingual, speaking French and English fluently."

As the woman spoke, her resemblance to the girl in the photos became evident. Her eyes, and the shape of her face, made it clear she was Jacqueline Brichot's mother.

"Are you aware," the moderator asked, "of any evidence that your daughter had contact with Russian agents, or that she stole or otherwise received documents from anyone at NATO concerning American troop or weapon deployments in Europe?"

"I am not."

"To your knowledge, did your daughter have a love affair with a Russian military officer during the war?"

"She did not."

The audience was watching closely. The woman spoke with undeniable sincerity. But so far she had proved nothing, refuted nothing. Nevertheless it was obvious she was here for a reason.

"Did your daughter die under mysterious circumstances, Mrs. Brichot?" the moderator asked.

The lady shook her head. "Jacqueline died of leukemia," she said. "She had suffered from the illness for many years. She was first diagnosed during her school days, but her illness was not of the severe type, and she spent many years in remission. Then, at age twenty-four, her red blood count began to diminish, and she had to receive transfusions every week. She died a year later."

"Therefore," said Farrell Keyes, "there is nothing mysterious about your daughter's last illness."

"Not at all. I have with me the medical records of her entire illness, from age eleven until her death at twenty-five. She was under the care of the same physicians throughout."

Keyes looked intrigued. "Let me ask you another question, Mrs. Brichot. How many children do you have?"

"Two."

"I take it, then, that you have one surviving child, your son."

The lady shook her head. "My children are both dead."

There was a shocked silence. Amory Bose looked briefly at the man sitting next to him, and back to Mrs. Brichot.

"But Mrs. Brichot," Farrell Keyes said, "it is your son, Vincent, who brought the information to Senator Bose which is the subject of our meeting today. What are you trying to say?"

The woman smiled sadly. "My daughter Jacqueline had an older brother, Vincent. He was killed by the Nazis in 1942. Therefore, as I say, I have no surviving children."

Farrell Keyes seemed confused. "But Mrs. Brichot, if you have no son, then who is the individual sitting next to Senator Bose, the individual who has brought forth the information we are concerned with here today?"

With contempt in her eyes, Mrs. Brichot looked at the small man seated next to Amory Bose.

"I have no idea," she said.

From that moment on events followed each other in a rush. Hal produced evidence to show that the photographs of himself with Jacqueline Brichot were fakes. He also produced records to show that the documents purported by Amory Bose to be military secrets were in reality declassified documents available to the public. And, last but not least, he stunned the national audience by revealing the true identity of the so-called Vincent Brichot who was sitting next to Bose. His name was Leon Matone. He was a pathological impostor known to police departments in several states as well as the FBI. Hal produced copies of Matone's criminal record and photographs documenting his career as an impostor.

As this damning information sank in, the cameras remained pitilessly focused on the flushed face of Amory Bose. He no longer looked so statesmanlike or dignified. His carefully tonsured hair was awry, and a thick line of perspiration was dripping off his upper lip. As he fought to find words to defend himself and his star witness, the now-silent "Vincent Brichot," he looked embarrassed and ridiculous. Gone was the righteous patriot defending his beloved Senate against Communism. In his place was a blustering demagogue caught with his pants down.

"I hope," Hal said by way of conclusion, "that Mrs. Brichot's visit has helped us set the record straight about the charges made in this campaign. I would like to add a brief word about the real reason we are here today. We happen to be in the midst of a very painful and uncertain period in our history. We find ourselves in a cold and apparently hostile world, in which a faceless, soulless enemy seems poised to attack us with sinister weapons, not only from without, but from within."

The camera moved closer to Hal's face.

"Now," said Hal, "because of this fear, this uncertainty—which will pass, I am quite sure, for you and I know that Americans are not by nature a fearful people—we have recently found ourselves listening to political voices that counsel us to distrust each other, to think of our neighbor as our enemy, to suspect that our neighbor's thoughts might harm us, and that our neighbor's loyalty to our country is not the same as ours. These voices have alarmed us, and upset us—but they certainly haven't convinced us."

At these words there was a sudden pulse of recognition in the studio. Those present could feel that something important was being said.

"We're getting a painful but valuable lesson in our time," Hal continued. "We're seeing what it's like, in a small way, to live in those repressive societies where no man trusts his neighbor, where every man's loyalty to his country is suspect, where freedom itself is looked upon as an undesirable shelter for untrustworthy men and traitorous thoughts. Yes, we're finding out—and we don't like it. We don't like the taste of fear. We're a proud people, not a fearful one. We're a country of love and brotherhood—not of suspicion and distrust. Americans work together for one goal—they don't work against each other. We are a people united by freedom—not a house divided by hate."

The hush in the studio was electric.

"And any man, or group of men, or nation," Hal said, "who thinks Americans can long be fooled into working against each other rather than for each other—that man or nation is making a terrible mistake. For we are indeed a stubborn people. We can criticize our government and each other all we like—and, being Americans, we surely will. But let anyone else try to turn us against each other, and he'll have us all to reckon with. There is no weapon on this earth more deadly than the will of a free people to stay free. For, ladies and gentlemen, freedom has no enemies. But any enemy of freedom has found himself the most terrible foe in the world."

There was a pause as these words sank in. Their message seemed to throw a new light on the entire controversy that had led to this telecast.

A few moments later the show had ended. Already there was no doubt as to the outcome of the Senate race in New York. Amory Bose had killed his own candidacy in one self-inflicted blow, and assured the election of Haydon Lancaster to the seat Bose had occupied so powerfully for sixteen years.

In thirty minutes of network air time on a Sunday morning, the course of Senate history had been changed, and with it the face of American politics.

XVIII

IT WAS A NIGHT for celebration.

The combined Stallworth and Lancaster relatives had arranged a gigantic party on short notice. Several hundred guests, including representatives of the business and social communities as well as the political fraternity of public servants and journalists, were invited to Harry Stallworth's Fifth Avenue mansion. A dozen representatives of Dwight Eisenhower's White House were in attendance—there was a congratulatory gift for Hal and Diana from Ike himself—along with as many members of Congress, who wanted to express their eager anticipation at the prospect of working with Hal after the election.

The festive atmosphere was tinged with awe, not only because of Hal's narrow escape from a terrible threat, but also because the very idea of the destruction of a political figure as powerful as Amory Bose sent chills down the spine of anyone who knew Washington. If fate could strike down an eminence like Bose, then anything was truly possible in this crazy world.

Of course, as everyone agreed, Bose had brought the disaster upon himself. In his zeal to ruin Hal he had lost his sense of balance and caution. He had not double-checked his own information or the man who had provided it. Moreover, he had forgotten that the memory of Joseph McCarthy's censure by the Senate was still fresh in the public mind. The television image of a mud-slinging senator brandishing "documented proof" that turned out to be plain fraud was already a sore spot in the American consciousness. By going the way of McCarthy, Bose had sealed his own political doom.

But everyone was too happy for Hal to waste more than a few whispers on Amory Bose. The party was a great, uproarious success, with unlikely friendships springing up throughout the Stallworth house between hoary, hard-drinking political reporters and society ladies, stalwart Republican clubmen and the young Democrats who were Hal's friends in Washington, wealthy captains of big business and the very senators whose committees on the Hill were hell-bent to regulate their corporations into fiscal respectability.

The spell cast by Hal Lancaster's youth, his charm, and his new success seemed to bring everyone together and to make old enmities irrelevant. It almost seemed as though a new world was dawning. No one could forget Hal's eloquent statement of his political convictions on the *Washington Today* broadcast. In a few brief words Hal had opened a door that led beyond the gray world of the Cold War to a bright future in which happier people would laugh about the suspicions that had once divided them.

Even tonight, as he stood watching the festivities, Tom Rossman was thinking about the felicitous phrase Hal had coined, *"Freedom has no enemies."* He saw it as a slogan not only for the balance of the Senate campaign, but for a whole career that would one day lead to the White House. Tom was a keen observer of the Washington scene, and something of a historian as well. He simply could not see how a leader who combined Hal's precocious wisdom and peacemaker's skills with all that charm, all that sex appeal, could fail to become President one day.

But there was plenty of time to think about that in the future. For tonight the theme was celebration and relief.

The party went on until very late, with music, dancing, and more than a few pranks by pixillated guests that lent the staid Stallworth premises an antic quality that had never been seen there before. Hal gave a brief speech, and kept everyone in stitches with "in" jokes about the separate and equally insular societies of Washington and New York. A cake in the shape of the Capitol dome was cut, and many magnums of Dom Pérignon champagne were poured.

By midnight Hal was exhausted, and had to make apologies and go home to bed. He had had precious little sleep in the last four days. Moreover, tonight was the first time he had seen Diana since the crisis began, for she had been with her cousins in Southampton all along, out of harm's way where Hal wanted her.

It was time for husband and wife to enjoy their private celebration of victory.

Hal held Diana's hand and made tired small talk as the Stallworth chauffeur took them home. When they had arrived he took a long hot shower, toweled himself off, and emerged naked in the bedroom, where the inviting-looking double bed awaited him.

Diana was standing in the doorway.

"Am I too late to be with you?" she asked.

He smiled at her. Despite his fatigue, he knew he owed her a few moments of intimacy after their long separation.

"It's never too late," he said.

She crossed the room and kissed him. He realized she was a tiny bit unsteady on her feet. Too much champagne at the party, he guessed. Of late he had suspected that Diana was drinking more than she should. The family made her nervous, and the press and public even more. She sometimes used a drink to help her maintain the mask of artificial charm that her official role demanded of her, when cold sobriety would perhaps have been a better armor.

Hal lacked the leisure to worry about this. But he did notice that Diana's statuesque exterior seemed to show infinitesimal chinks, almost like cracks in a perfect paint job. She was as beautiful as ever, but somehow brittle.

He watched as she went into the bathroom. He lay on the bed in the half-light, waiting for her to come out. He heard the soft clink of a perfume vial or other container from behind the door. She seemed to take a long time, so long that he almost fell asleep naked in the sheets, his hands clasped behind his head.

At last she emerged, wearing a sensual-looking silk camisole he had never seen before, very low-cut and clinging, her beautiful legs emerging tanned and shapely from the matching panties.

She came to the bed and lay down beside him. She said nothing, but he could feel the message coming from her flesh. They had not made love in nearly a month. The demands of his campaign, combined with the subtly widening gulf between himself and Diana—a gulf they had never acknowledged directly—had made lovemaking more and more difficult to initiate.

Hal knew that now was the time for a renewal of physical intimacy with his troubled wife. He had been neglecting her for too long, allowing her to spend long periods away from him, and not paying the proper attention to her when she was near.

His little infidelities with women inside and on the fringes of politics were insignificant in themselves, but he knew that Diana suspected them, and that this painful knowledge was keeping her apart from him.

Then, too, there was the problem of children. Everyone believed Hal and Diana were trying mightily to conceive a child. The truth was that the stress of recent months had forced them to put this dream on a back burner. By mutual consent they had slipped into foregoing sex when they felt too tired or preoccupied to approach each other. And this new habit had unfortunately increased their physical estrangement to the embarrassing point of making conception virtually impossible.

So tonight, after a terrible crisis in the campaign that had ended in triumph, Hal knew it was time to make love to his wife. In spite of his fatigue and hers, in spite of her mood, which he could feel was a shaky one, in spite of all he had on his mind tonight and all he had to do tomorrow—it was time.

He turned out the light. He touched her shoulder tentatively. With the chary softness of a child she curled her fingers about his own. He turned to lie on his side, and ran his hand down her stomach to her hips, and back upward to her breast. He felt her respond to him instantly. Her breath was coming short. He saw the outline of the beautiful, firm breasts in the shadows as his thumb grazed a pink nipple.

Slowly he caressed her, trying to soothe the familiar tension in her nerves even as he sought to excite her. It had never been very easy, and tonight it seemed harder. His touch brought sharp tremors under her skin, but they seemed almost painful in their intensity. She seemed terrified that the signs of her desire would not come quickly enough, or would not convince him when they did come.

How different she was from other women, who threw themselves at him like panting animals! Yet he could take no pleasure from her restraint, for it was so full of chagrin and worry. She drew back from coveting his body openly, and even seemed ashamed of her own nudity.

But often enough he was able to overcome all that and get through to the sensuality under her tense exterior. So, tonight, he would do his best.

He turned her to him. Her hand touched his shoulder, almost in supplication. She seemed coiled tight as a string. He drew her face to his and kissed her.

All at once he smelled liquor on her breath. Vodka, he thought. A great deal of vodka. Somehow he knew she had had more since she came home with him.

Now he recalled the little sound he had heard from the bathroom when she was performing her ablutions. He deduced that she must be keeping a store of vodka somewhere among her toiletries.

Hal drew back from Diana, weighing the fact that his wife had had to sneak a furtive drink in the bathroom to give herself the courage to come in to make love to him.

He looked at her blurred form, still within the grasp of his hands, but cut off from him by the darkness. He felt a twinge in his senses, more of pity than of distaste.

Then he patted her cheek, very gently.

"It's late," he murmured. "It's been a tough weekend. Let's get some sleep."

She was lying on her side, looking at him. He could feel the mute pleading, the fear and reproach in her eyes.

There was a long, painful pause. Then, silently, Diana turned away.

A great coldness had fallen between them. Hal lay gazing at the ceiling and listening to the muted sounds of the city beyond the windows. He let his thoughts wander over the past week, over the melodramatic twists of his political fate, over Amory Bose and Lawrence Ingersoll and the many other faces he had had to deal with and worry about through this exhausting time.

His thoughts drifted further afield, back to his childhood, to Stewart, to little Sybil, to summers at Newport, school days at Choate, the pungent tang of earth and grass on athletic fields, the smell of horses, the lulling embrace of boyhood fantasies, limitless youthful hopes, and the slow sinuous path away from them toward the preoccupations of manhood.

How devious time was! As his childhood waned, Hal had felt smarter, stronger, and for a while looked back on his innocence as a naive thing better outgrown. Then, too late, he had seen the adult world for what it was—a collection of lonely, shallow creatures, each so little different from the others, and all concerned only for themselves.

Except one. Had Laura not crossed his path, and he not been a little too slow to tell her she owned his whole heart, a little too shy to get on his knees to her and tell her he would throw it all away for her—had he only been quick enough, or indeed never met her at all, then everything would have been bearable. For he would not have known any better, and the world he knew would have seemed the only one there was.

But it was too late for that. Too late for everything.

Hal did not know how much time went by before he realized he was not getting to sleep. He glanced at Diana. Her breathing was regular now, even a bit heavy. The vodka, no doubt.

He glanced at the clock by his bedside. Only one o'clock. So early! In New York City this night was young. Innumerable adventures would take place in its darkened streets before dawn. People's lives would be changed by those events, irrevocably . . .

Hal opened his eyes wide now. He knew he was not going to get to sleep. It was too late. He had let his thoughts stray down the wrong paths once again.

A sudden impulse told him he could not stay here, contemplating his own nerves and listening to Diana sleep.

He slipped soundlessly from the bed, got some clothes from the closet, and dressed in the bathroom. As he did so he noticed Diana's toiletries and opened one of the largest cologne bottles. Sure enough: he had found her flask.

He looked at himself in the mirror. The face was haunted. A strange light glowed in the tawny irises. He smoothed his hair with a few quick brush strokes, shrugged at the stubble on his chin, turned off the light, and went out.

He left the house, got into his car, and drove through the empty streets of the city. He knew where he was going. He wondered how he had held off this moment for so long.

He reached his destination within five minutes. He parked in an illegal space, walked through the shadows to a door, entered a foyer, and rang a buzzer. To his surprise the voice answered right away.

"It's me," he said. "Sorry to bother you. Can I come up?"

Without another word the door was buzzed open. He went up the back way, as he had been taught so recently.

When he reached the landing he looked at himself in the mirror. He did not look his best. He could almost see the demons gnawing at his soul. He wondered if his appearance could frighten someone away.

He knocked quietly at the door, three little taps barely audible even to him.

It swung open almost at once.

Bess was dressed in a light silk nightgown that shimmered in the pale light of the landing. Behind her the apartment was in darkness. Her hair was down over her shoulders. He saw the swell of her breasts, fresh and ripe under the nightgown, and the creamy skin touched by freckles like drops of sunshine.

The look in her eyes was kind. She had read his thoughts, perhaps long ago, and her smile gave him the answer he wanted.

Without a word he went in and swept her into his arms, closing the door behind him.

Their first kiss took his breath away. He almost wanted to weep, so urgent was the longing inside him, and so lovely the feel of her slim body, like familiar flesh touched again at last after a long and unfair separation.

When their lips parted he held her close, his body on fire under his clothes, his cheek pressed to her own.

"Finally," she murmured.

"You're sure . . . ?" he heard himself whisper.

She silenced him with a kiss.

It was she who led the way to the bedroom, as though aware that he had exhausted his capacity for decision during this terrible week. It was she who unclothed him, helped him to the bed, and gave him her kisses, her sighs, and the secrets of her flesh as a mother gives a child the nourishment without which it cannot grow and live.

They said no more that night.

XIX

THE NEXT AFTERNOON TESS had a meeting with Ron Lucas at two o'clock.

Ron arrived punctually at the penthouse with his briefcase. He sat on the couch and looked calmly at Tess. She knew him well enough to see the slight smile under his cold exterior. He was pleased with the way things had worked out.

"I'm proud of you, Ron," she said. "You did a fine job."

He nodded. He did not know how to acknowledge a compliment, as she had learned long ago. But she knew her praise was what he valued most in the world. She could see the effect her words had on him.

"The documents you gave Matone were the key," she said. "Without them he could never have convinced Bose he was the girl's brother."

Ron nodded. "It was touch and go there for a while. We expected Bose to try to check the fellow out in Belgium. I had a man there just in case. But, luckily for us, Bose fell for the whole thing, hook, line, and sinker."

"He hated Hal too much," Tess said. "His hatred made him careless."

If there was one thing she had learned in the competitive world, it was that one could not defeat people by hating them. Hatred brought them too close for one to control. Only by viewing them from afar, like insects surveyed from a great height, could one foresee their plans and destroy them without putting oneself at risk.

Amory Bose was a man whose own passion had ruined him. Tess felt a mixture of contempt and pity for him. If this was what the Senate considered a power broker, she thought, she would rule that body inside a year. Such clumsiness as Bose's offended her fine sense of strategy.

She looked at Ron with satisfaction. It had been Ron's idea at the outset not to choose just anyone for this job, but to use someone who had a police record, who was a known impostor. Leon Matone had been the perfect choice. His considerable talents had hoodwinked Bose into putting his own neck on the chopping block without realizing it. The idea was not only to save Hal, but to humiliate Bose and make him look as ridiculous as possible.

That had been achieved. As of today Bose was not only a disgrace to the Senate and to his party, but the laughingstock of American politics as well. His grotesque showing on the *Washington Today* program was the lead story in every paper in the country. BOSE'S FOLLY, read one headline. REDBAITER BOSE EATS CROW ON NATIONWIDE TV, read another. HUMBUG! read a third, over a wire service photo of Bose's jowly, glaring face.

Victory had been won, thanks to some careful planning by Tess herself, and thanks to the irresistible charm and dignity of Hal Lancaster, which had recaptured the heart of a fickle public poised to reject him.

And Ron could not know that last night an additional prize had been attained, one that changed the face of all Tess's plans and opened the door to a future she had not dared to envisage so soon.

What a lover Hal was! Even now her body tingled at the memory of her intimacy with him.

She had heard of his prowess, of course, and expected him to be physically gifted. But there was much more to Hal than mere cock.

He made love with a sweetness, a vulnerability, that touched her heart. In the nakedness of his body she felt the unseen depths of hurt behind his celebrated smile, resources of which he himself was apparently unaware, but which sang with a strange eloquence in his every caress.

And it was this delicate inner quality of his that made the experience incredibly, shockingly sensual. With his slow strokes he had forced her to orgasm after orgasm, in which, gradually, she realized more of herself was involved than in any tryst she had ever enjoyed before.

His faith in Elizabeth Bond, in her devotion, her fierce maternal pride in him, and her depth of character, was such that Elizabeth actually came to life inside Tess under his kiss, like a frightening alter ego possessed of a reality Tess had never intended her to have. And, for better or worse, Elizabeth gave Hal her heart as well as her body—a sacrifice Tess would never have made for any man.

At the final moment, when the terrible thrusting power of him upraised her, and her ecstasy burst through the last barriers, Tess had felt a sort of chemical change inside her, as though the unknowable mystery of Hal was flowing right through her. Was it something missing, at that ultimate instant, or something extra that exploded from his body to hers? Something he withheld, or something he gave?

Whatever it was, it brought forth a thing unsuspected inside Tess herself, a womanly, possessive need she had never felt within her before. This shocked her, and left her unnerved as she lay in his arms afterward. All at once she realized that she did not want these arms ever to let her go; that the thought of walking the earth without Hal to guide her steps was an agony she could not bear.

When she let him out of her apartment this morning, she knew that her relationship with him was no longer a mere game. It was dead serious, more serious than she had ever intended it to be.

And so it was time to take action.

She looked at Ron.

"On that other matter, Ron," she said. "Do you have everything necessary to make a move right away?"

He opened his briefcase and took out a folder. He had anticipated her wishes, and brought the material along. How well he knew her!

She took the folder and looked inside. It was full of pictures of Diana Lancaster.

She was not alone in the photographs. There was a woman with her. A very attractive young woman, the wife of a New York lawyer, according to Ron. A onetime amateur tennis player, nationally known until her retirement a few years ago.

The pictures showed the two friends having lunch uptown, getting out of a cab together, looking in a shop window, going into a small hotel.

And in bed.

The photographer had had to use a telephoto lens from the building opposite. It had all involved a lot of planning and expense. The pictures were grainy, but their content was unmistakable. The two women were lovers.

Tess closed the folder and handed it across the table to Ron.

"Use it," she said.

XX

"GIVE IT HERE, Raymond."

"Throw it!"

"Come on, sucker, it's mine!"

"Alex, make him throw me the ball!"

The blacktop surface of the playground was littered with broken glass, pebbles, and trash. A space had been halfheartedly cleared in front of the basketball backboard. The hoop bore a single hanging strand of the chain net that had once been there.

An old volleyball, stolen from somewhere, and marked up with paint from a graffitist's palette, popped up from the throng of pushing, shouting boys, spun through the gray air of afternoon and fell silently through the empty hoop, bouncing into the garbage-strewn area beyond the blacktop.

There were seven boys playing. All were black. All were skinny and full of energy. As they flung back and forth under the basket, jostling one another, one could see from the shape of their limbs that they were undernourished. Yet they were growing fast, bones lengthening, voices soon to drop, childish gestures of face and hands soon to be replaced by the mannered languor of self-conscious inner-city teenagers. Growth and decay were running a race inside their bodies, with the dubious future of ghetto manhood at the finish line.

Laura was taking pictures fast, moving around the periphery of the game, snapping her Leica with expert control of focus and aperture, advancing the film quickly, and even changing rolls with the same facility that one of these boys might display in removing the wrapper from a candy bar.

But her camera was ignoring all the boys except one. It had eyes only for him.

His name was Alex. At fifteen he was the second oldest of the group, and without question its leader. He stood in the center of the game like a symbol of authority, occasionally disciplining the others in low tones, directing where the ball was passed with his look or his nod. It was obvious his heart was not in the childish game, for he was old enough now to be preoccupied by more serious concerns. But he fulfilled his role as leader with a calm appreciation of his own importance.

In her box at home Laura had nearly five hundred pictures of Alex. She had first encountered him four months ago, in Morningside Park near 113th Street, and convinced him to be a subject for her camera. Since then they had become friends. She came to photograph him as often as she could. When she was on his turf, he considered himself her protector.

His older sister—a whore since girlhood—was now seventeen. He had three younger siblings, two sisters and a brother. His mother, a woman of thirty-nine, had had a stroke two years ago, and lay helplessly across her bed while her children ran wild about the house.

Alex was the man of the family, for the father had disappeared years ago. Alex made a pretense of going to school at P.S. 18 on Morris Avenue, and maintained a C-minus average without ever opening a book or deigning to respond to a teacher's question. He spent his afternoons roaming with his friends or alone, hustling, stealing, and fencing stolen goods.

He bet the numbers each morning. He smoked Pall Malls and Lucky Strikes, which he stole by the carton, drank whatever liquor he could hustle, smoked marijuana every day, had tried heroin and cocaine, and was a minor drug dealer.

He used the money he made to maintain his family. He went grocery shopping with his sister every evening, and presided over the dinner table like a stern father, instructing the youngest children on table manners, and feeding his disabled mother with a spoon while she groaned incomprehensible complaints.

In his hard-boiled urban way Alex was a saint. His devotion to his family—a family he had not sired, and could not save despite his best efforts—was touching to behold. He cared for his mother with tender understanding, and disciplined his brother and sisters with a patience beyond his years. The fact that the girls would almost certainly become whores, and the boy a doomed street punk, did not tarnish the luster of this display of love.

Alex was also a genius. Of that Laura had no doubt. Five minutes' conversation with him on any topic made it obvious he had an enormous intellect and a brilliant imagination.

And Alex was a criminal. He had committed burglary, armed rob-bery, assault, extortion. He had pimped. He had committed arson count-less times. The only reason he had not spent his youth in reform schools was that he was too clever to be arrested.

In other circumstances Alex would have grown up to be a surgeon, a philosopher, a statesman. His innate courage and sense of justice might have made him a great moral leader, as soon as he outgrew the transgressions of youth. His creativity might have equipped him for a fine career as a playwright, novelist, or poet.

Instead of these things Alex would probably die in prison. Failing that, he would fall victim to gang violence or to a drug overdose. Yet his genius was written all over his face, and was magnified through the lens of the Leica. Laura had seen this the very first time she laid eyes on him, and had sought him out ever since.

What made it particularly urgent that she photograph him with the best of her inspiration was time itself. Alex was growing before her eyes. Today he was two inches taller than when she first took pictures of him. Soon he would no longer be a boy. The light of infinite possi-bility in his eyes might flicker out at anytime, as the mystical metamor-phosis of adolescence gave way to the grim manhood of poverty.

So it was that Laura had lugged her heavy camera bag all the way up to the Bronx this afternoon, after spending a hard morning finishing her latest batch of design sketches at home. She had wanted some good pictures of Alex with his little gang.

Despite her overwork Laura felt good today. Not only was her pho-tographic inspiration humming at a higher intensity than ever before, but she had the baby inside her and a new relationship with Tim to keep her warm.

Since her pregnancy had been confirmed her marriage had taken a strong turn for the better. Tim was loving, concerned, and terribly sorry for what had happened the night he struck her. They both realized that a tragi-comedy of errors, involving her lost message to him and her absurd adventure in jail with Maria, had created a disaster that never would have happened had they not both been under such terrible stress.

Laura loved Tim. Even the night he had struck her she had not thought of abandoning him. He had clearly been in the clutches of emotions too powerful for him to cope with, emotions that came from the painful depths of his past, emotions for which he was not responsi-ble.

And she admitted to herself that she had been putting unfair pressure on him lately, by her absorption in a new vocation into which she seemed to be rushing headlong, at the expense of the career he had given all his energies to help develop. Tim could only feel she was leaving him in the lurch just as their long efforts together had finally brought success. And, understandably, given the hard life he had had as a boy, he had translated his dismay into jealousy, a jealousy he himself could see was absurd, but which, in certain circumstances, got the best of him.

The depth of his guilt over what had happened was obvious. And now that Laura was carrying his child, her commitment to him and to their life together was proved, over and above any career choice she might make.

Even now Tim was softening about her photography, accepting her outings with the camera and her hours in the darkroom, and doing his best to understand that she must pursue the creative course that had the most meaning to her. He seemed ready to help her arrange a transition that would allow her to fulfill her responsibilities to Laura, Ltd., while pursuing photography with her remaining energies. Together they would work it out somehow.

His only objection to photography nowadays was a half-jocular one.

"You're overworking yourself to death," he said. "A little slip of a thing like you, dragging that camera bag all over New York. You'll wear yourself out. You should be taking it easy."

She let him complain, for his words bore the echo of the protective concern he had expressed for her when they had first met during her seamstress days, as well as a hint of admiration for her intrepid courage with the camera.

"The doctor told me to be active," she defended herself. "Medical science no longer believes women should be immobile when they're pregnant. You heard him yourself."

"Active means active," Tim retorted. "It doesn't mean doing two jobs with one body, and roaming neighborhoods where you might have to run for your life at any moment."

But a half-smile vied with the disapproval in his eyes. She knew he respected her devotion to photography. Though he still did not look at her pictures or discuss them with her, he accepted her avocation as a part of their life together that need not drive a wedge between them.

Laura and Tim were happy now. The baby had opened a new door for them both. They were determined to go through it hand in hand.

The basketball game broke up as Laura finished her roll, and the boys began pestering her to take a group picture of them. Laughing, she agreed, and told them to assemble before the chain-link fence rimming the playground.

She picked up her camera bag, carried it to the fence, reloaded the Leica, and stood before the group.

"All right," she said. "Everybody close together, now . . ."

The younger boys were jumping up and down, and Alex had to quiet them with a warning. It took a while to rearrange the group so that everyone was in the frame, with Alex at the center.

Laura was standing before them, her camera poised. Suddenly she hesitated.

"Wait a minute," she said, holding up a hand as she sank to one knee. In her jeans and leather coat she looked smaller than the boys, so delicate that one might have taken her for their mascot.

She looked down at the blacktop as though to steady herself. Then she focused the camera again.

"Come on, Laura!" somebody shouted. "We ain't got all day!"

"Sorry," she said weakly. "I . . ."

Suddenly her face fell. The words died in her throat. She looked pale. Alex pushed at the boys in front of him, to clear a path to her.

He was too late. She had fallen to the blacktop with the camera beneath her. By the time he reached her she was unconscious.

An hour later it was all over.

Laura lay drained and hopeless in the maternity ward at Montefiore Medical Center in the Bronx. She watched mutely as a nurse passed through the semi-private room, on her way to other patients who were here for joyful reasons.

The baby was gone.

Just like that.

The residents on duty in the emergency room had had to handle the treatment of her miscarriage, monitoring her vital signs and making sure she did not lose too much blood. Luckily for her, they said, she had been unconscious at the time.

Yet perhaps it was not so lucky, Laura thought. If she had gone through the agony with her eyes open, it would have had some reality. As things stood, it was as though she had simply drifted off to sleep and awakened to a world in which her baby was dead.

Dr. Ensor had made the rushed journey from his office downtown to take charge of her treatment. He had decided she should stay the night before going home in the morning. There was no sense in moving her now.

She had been awake when he arrived. From the look in her eyes he could see she was in the grip of terrible emotions.

"Laura, don't start blaming yourself for what happened," he had warned. "Are you worried that you overworked yourself into this? I really don't think that was it at all. These things happen. It's nobody's fault . . ."

She grasped his hand and spoke in a low voice.

"You know what I'm worried about," she said.

He patted her hand. "Well, you can lay that to rest as well," he said. "I've examined you thoroughly. The abortion you had was competently done, and left no damage that I can see. You'll have plenty of babies, Laura—all you want. We may have to be a bit more cautious next time, but believe me, there's no reason for pessimism. What happened is a mystery. Medical science is a long way from knowing all the answers about the female reproductive system. The main thing is not to blame yourself. That will only make things worse all around. This is just a setback, Laura. Can you believe that?"

She nodded, more for his sake than for her own. She just wanted him to leave her alone with her grief. She felt every bit as destroyed as if her baby had come to term and been stillborn. It seemed as though death itself had taken up residence inside her scarred womanhood, death that had clawed at her with its iron fingers six and a half years ago, and now returned to take this new life from her, and with it all her hopes.

Sensing her mood, the doctor gave her a strong sedative before he left. She tried to stay awake for Tim, who would be arriving soon. But the drug combined with her shame and depression buried her in unconsciousness.

With a dark sense of relief she watched the world recede from her as oblivion took her to its arms.

It was six-thirty when Tim arrived at the hospital.

He had been out of the city, visiting a retailer in New Haven, when the urgent news reached him by telephone. The rush hour had delayed him by at least two hours on the way in. Cursing, he had inched his way through stop-and-go traffic while his wife lay helpless in a strange hospital only a few miles away.

When he arrived Dr. Ensor had long since departed. The residents on duty explained to Tim what had happened. He was dazed by what he heard, incapable of taking in the news altogether, and above all concerned for Laura.

He was shown to her room, given a measure of privacy by the folding partition, and left by the nurse with the warning that he could only stay until the end of visiting hours.

"She won't know you're here, anyway," the nurse said. "She'll be out like a light until morning. I'd suggest you go home and get some sleep yourself, and be here when she wakes up."

"I'll just stay a little while, then," Tim said.

When he was alone with Laura he looked at her tiny form under the sheets, and at her pale, sleeping face. He could imagine the grief and shame that must have tormented her when she realized what had happened. He would do everything he could to make her understand that this was not her fault, that the future was an open book, that he loved her.

He tried not to dwell on the painful thoughts crowding his mind. He recalled how happy Laura had been these past weeks, how he had sat on the living room couch with her head on his lap, touching softly at her stomach and looking forward to the miracle of childbirth.

So long ago, when he had first fallen in love with Laura, she had seemed made to bear beautiful children. Something about the freshness of her skirts, her soft white skin, the warm female presence under her crisp clothes and busy fingers, had seemed the essence of motherhood. That was the Laura he had fallen in love with—the Laura he had seemed to lose during the recent painful period of their marriage, and to recover joyously when the news of her pregnancy came.

He tried not to blame her for overexerting herself with her camera. It galled him to think she had been way up in the Bronx, on dangerous streets, taking pictures of young punks, when this happened to her. He had tried so often to remonstrate with her about her photography, but she could not be reasoned with. The camera was like an obsession eating at her soul.

Yet the doctor had not thought she was delicate, had not warned her to take it easy. Perhaps no one was to blame for what had happened. Perhaps this was just the latest piece of bad luck that was dogging their marriage, coming between them, pushing them always a step further from happiness.

It had seemed that the baby would patch things up. Her pregnancy was like a miracle, coming to allay his suspicions about why she had taken so long to conceive, to silence his worries about her commitment to him and about the other interests that ceaselessly drew her away from him.

But now they would have to start all over again.

With this thought in mind Tim noticed the chart hanging on the hook at the end of Laura's bed.

Furtively he got up, taking a brief look out the door to make sure the nurse was not coming back, and then picked the chart carefully off its hook.

There were several pages, filled with incomprehensible notes in the doctors' sloppy handwriting. Tim flipped through them absently, in vague search of some clue as to why this misfortune had happened.

All at once a notation caught his eye.

A previous pregnancy was terminated in January 1952 by induced abortion (curettage).

Although the procedure was not performed in a hospital setting, patient had no major hemorrhage, infection, or other serious sequelae.

The relationship between the previous abortion and the loss of the present pregnancy is not clear.

Tim stopped short. He read the note again. His eyes were wide open. The earth seemed to wheel dizzyingly under him. His hands were frozen about the clipboard.

Abortion . . .

He looked from the uncanny word to his sleeping wife, and back again.

Abortion.

Tim felt a chill, dark and cold as the grave, inside him. It started in his stomach, crawled down his legs and up his spine, and struck finally at his heart. The frozen anguish inside him took his breath away.

Abortion!

He looked at the date on the chart again. Six years ago. A year before she had ever known him. One year before the peregrinations of his life had led him up that flight of stairs to the tiny flat where she did her sewing.

Before he had ever had a chance to protect her, to keep her from the world's harm, to shield her from her own weaknesses—before that, some man had lain with her, planted his seed in her loins. A baby had grown inside her, and she had destroyed it.

Abortion!

Now Tim's pain became a black, mindless, blinding rage. Everything blurred before his eyes, from the silent sleeping woman, so distant and unknowable in her unconsciousness, to the white sheets, the drab room, the silent corridor outside. The whole senseless, murderous world receded before the explosion inside him.

Tim's baby was dead. The woman's loins that were its home had expelled it like a thing unworthy to live. And it was as though part of

Tim himself had been killed, and the blood of his ancestors, annihilated for no reason, up in smoke, murdered by an unseen hand which had marked the flesh of his love and made it unclean.

The pain coiling on itself in his heart seemed to cry out the destruction of his hopes, his marriage, his future, everything he had ever trusted in his life or held dear. In every cell of his body he felt the triumph of death over life, the victory of betrayal over love.

Now everything was clear to him. Now he knew the secret behind it all, the guilty secret that had gnawed at his happiness through years of doubt and struggle.

With a cold stealth that amazed him, Tim replaced the chart. He looked back down at Laura, his eyes shining with a sudden power of judgment that showed her in a light he had never seen before. He saw truths she had hidden from him with all her guile, sins she had thought to conceal from him even in the marriage bed. But she had not been clever enough. Now he knew. And the knowledge burning its way through his soul would come back to haunt her one day.

He got up slowly, picked up his coat, and walked out of the room, leaving Laura behind him.

XXI

DIANA WAS IN THE GREEN ROOM of a midtown television studio, moments away from an interview to be taped for broadcast on the evening news.

She was wearing a classic Norell suit, spare and clean in its lines, with a string of pearls and earrings to match. She was at her most elegantly informal, as befitted a busy public woman pausing in the middle of her day to chat with the press.

The interview would be fluff, of course. Diana would be asked about her campaigning with Hal for the Senate seat, her plans for life in Washington, her pride in her husband after his brilliant showing on the *Washington Today* program.

She had been inundated with requests for such interviews now that Hal's standing in the polls had shot to a commanding level. It was taken for granted that she would soon be the most beautiful Senate wife in Washington, and a glamorous representative of New York before the entire political world. As such, she was as hot an interview subject as Hal himself.

Diana struggled to clear her mind for the interview ahead. She was fighting the combined effects of two hundred milligrams of Equanil and two strong glasses of vodka within the last hour. She felt like a skater whose blades turned the ice to slush underneath her. The very device that allowed her to undertake the ordeal before her was sapping her of the strength and nerve to go through with it.

Since the night after the *Washington Today* show Diana's life had slipped its tether. When Hal turned her off so brutally, after having been on the verge of making love to her, she knew something terrible had happened. The last ounce of her self-respect had vanished at that moment. She suspected he knew she was drunk, and even wondered if he knew about her bottle in the bathroom.

Whatever the case, she knew all too well that he wanted no part of her. His refusal of her body had been full of pity and contempt. And when she woke up the next morning, she was alone.

Ever since then her public responsibility to Hal had been tripled, and her ability to handle it reduced to a fraction of what it had been before. It seemed as though she and Hal had come completely apart just as the national public was excitedly greeting them with open arms as the future darlings of the Senate.

The depth of the lie was too much for Diana. She had been lying all her life; but somehow since her marriage she had expected Hal to be the net under this high-wire act of deception.

Now Hal was no longer there. She had only the vodka and the tranquilizers, with their perfidious gifts and the terrible tribute they extorted from her. They were the ground on which she walked—but that ground was quicksand. They gave her a voice to answer the terrible, smiling interviewers. But that voice was full of tiny stumbles, infinitesimal slurs, horribly audible to Diana herself, and perhaps—perhaps—audible to others now.

The drugs were her medicine and her poison, her blessing, and her curse. She would have given anything to throw them off, to try to live again. But she had never really lived in the first place. Deception had been the very fabric of her life. So there was nothing to go back to.

And Hal was no longer with her. She was alone.

Five minutes remained before the interview. She looked around the green room, with its magazine-laden tables, its battered couches, the bland travel posters on the walls, the sad coffee urn and the plate of pastries. Television green rooms, she had learned long ago, were depressing places. The producers seemed to take pleasure in not bothering to put up a front of elegance or glamor. That illusion was for the television screen itself. Everything behind the camera in a TV studio was dirty, cluttered, dark, and somehow disgusting.

Diana was reaching for one of the magazines when a knock came at the door. A messenger stuck his pimply face in.

"Mrs. Lancaster?" he said.

"Yes?"

"Package for you, ma'am."

He entered and handed her a large manila envelope. It bore no postmark, no return address, but only her name in block letters.

The messenger left without asking her to sign for it.

Puzzled, Diana opened the envelope, assuming it had something to do with the broadcast.

As the contents slid out into her lap, her breath caught in her throat.

The naked breasts of Linda Preston shone white and creamy in a blown-up eight-by-ten photograph. They were pressed against Diana's own breasts as the two women embraced amid the tumbled sheets of a hotel room bed. Linda was crouched over Diana, her hips and thighs limned in light and shadow, her lips touching Diana's own in an intimate kiss.

With a gasp Diana pushed the picture back into the envelope. She looked around her, thanking her lucky stars that no one else was in the green room.

Then, furtively, she took another look. There were half a dozen photographs in the envelope, all as explicit as the first. The prints were grainy, but eloquent and almost poetic in their depiction of guilty sex between women. She and Linda were shown in all the languid positions of their love, legs and arms intertwined, lips and tongues and fingers moist with passion, faces distorted by excitement as they delighted in each other's nudity.

Diana thrust the pictures back into the envelope. She got to her feet, felt a wave of dizziness, and sat down again. She wondered how many minutes or seconds remained to her before the producer came in to take her to the studio.

She took several deep breaths to try to clear her mind. Then she peeked into the envelope in search of a letter or note. There was none.

What did it mean? What did they want? Who could have done this to her?

At last she thought to examine the envelope itself. She found what she was looking for on the inside of the flap.

There were four words, printed in black marker.

WAIT FOR MY CALL.

Diana closed her eyes as tight as she could for a long moment, as though to blot out the nightmare she had just seen. A single tear found its way through her lashes and down her cheek.

Then she stood up, walked out of the green room, and out of the studio, without telling anyone she was leaving.

XXII

Women's Wear Daily, July 1, 1958

LAURA BLAKE A WINNER AGAIN

For the second year in a row Laura Blake has won the coveted American Fashion Critics' Coty Award for the best original work by an American designer.

Ms. Blake, whose salon, Laura, Ltd., has become an international sensation over the past several seasons, received the award at a ceremony held at the Waldorf-Astoria last evening. In attendance were many of her peers in the high-fashion world, as well as representatives of the fashion journalism and retailing fields.

In her brief acceptance speech Ms. Blake gave special thanks to her husband, Tim Riordan, for his tireless work in expanding Laura, Ltd., from a tiny Greenwich Village dress shop to perhaps the most talked-about and prestigious fashion establishment on this side of the Atlantic.

"If I have won this very special award for a second time," the diminutive designer said, "it's only because Tim has kept me on my toes and driven me to efforts of which I would not have been capable without him. Tim already has my love, and I want him and the world to know he has my undying admiration and gratitude as well."

TIM RIORDAN HAD NOT TOUCHED his wife in two months.

During that time he had watched her change from the grief-stricken victim of a miscarriage into a worried convalescent, not sure of her ground either in her own emotions or in her marriage—and finally into a wife so frightened of her husband's private thoughts that she threw herself into her work as a desperate refuge from her own dread.

Tim had brought about this transition. He had done it by withholding part of himself at each stage of his wife's return to normal living. He had said all the correct things, but without real warmth. He had comforted his wife, pampered her and encouraged her, but without love.

And he had withheld his body from her.

As the weeks passed he watched her fight her way back from her grief and guilt over the lost baby. He watched her pale body grow stronger again, watched her go back to work. Gradually, as her strength returned, she began to expect the renewal of a normal relationship with her husband.

When they were together her eyes strayed to the hard contours of his body. Her voice bore the subtle undertones of feminine interest when she talked to him. Her attempts to express affection showed that she was ready to take him into her bed again, and needed him.

Tim watched all this, and used the weapon of his distance to put Laura off. Each time he could feel the longing in her mood, he managed through a look, a yawn, an ambiguous word, to freeze her.

Meanwhile he threw himself into his own work as never before, staying out until eight o'clock or even later. He went to bed early and rose at dawn. Thus he only had to spend an hour or two with Laura at night. During that time he kept her at arm's length through the calculated modulations of coldness and withdrawal in his demeanor. Then he bade her goodnight with a brief kiss and slept with his back to her.

As time passed he saw her growing puzzlement, her sadness, her frustration. He realized she was suffering a double torment, first because she was struggling to overcome a painful physical and emotional episode, and second because, having lost the baby she wanted so much, she desperately needed the support her husband was quietly denying her.

She could not fail to conclude that his refusal to offer her his body was only the surface of a more profound rejection. Nor could she suffer this treatment without interpreting it as a reproach for her having lost the baby. On the other hand, she could not of course know how deep the source of her husband's bitterness went. About this she could only wonder, a little more painfully each day.

Tim watched this wound fester in her as the weeks passed, one by one. He contemplated her anguish, and did nothing to assuage it.

He was able to carry out this slow and subtle form of psychological torture, despite his love for Laura, because he was as removed from himself as he was from her. It was as though another person was doing this to her. Tim watched himself like a bystander as he put her off, made her feel guilty and unworthy and tainted and unforgiven.

This odd detachment was a talent he had never discovered in himself before. Yet in a sense it came naturally to him. Ever since boyhood Tim had been the sort of man who keeps things inside. He had always buried his hurts and resentments beneath the surface of his hard-headed, active personality, where they could not confuse him. True, this habit had sometimes led to sudden explosions of rage when the emotions he had denied burst forth to have their say at last. But on the whole it had kept his life on an even keel and allowed him to achieve great things in the business world.

Now he simply took his natural inclination a step further. He held his emotions so far inside that even he could not feel them. He watched their effect on Laura without sympathy, without pity, for he had pushed the core of himself so far out of sight that he truly did not know what he felt anymore, or what he intended.

Tonight he was to find out.

The ceremony at the Waldorf had meant something to Laura, he could see that. Her words had genuinely touched him. She had taken this occasion, in front of all these people, to speak directly to him, to try to tell him she loved him, to try to tell him things could be all right again.

They took a cab home, and he wore a polite smile as they went up to the apartment, his manner just cool enough to let her know that her speech about loving him had not changed things.

But her tone of voice on the way home had indicated she was not giving up on him yet. She was going out on a limb to try to contact him. She held his hand in the cab and in the elevator. There was a chary tenderness in her voice, and the hint of the old seductive lilt that had so charmed him in the old days, when they would make love to celebrate some victory or other at the office.

He had had two drinks at the awards ceremony. Though not normally a heavy drinker, he had enjoyed the warm swirl of the liquor in his senses, and the increased detachment it brought. So he made himself another one now, a strong one, and sat down on the living room couch, still dressed in his blue pinstripe suit, his tie not even loosened.

There was a pause while Laura went to the bedroom. The drink tasted so good, and Tim's detachment felt so intoxicating, that he emptied the glass at one gulp, got up, and poured himself another. He sat down again in silence.

At length she came out. She had taken off the pretty black dress she had worn tonight and was in her nightgown. Her hair, so curly and natural, looked somehow girlish. He noticed the perfect shape of her calves as she sat down next to him on the couch. Her hands were so white, so delicate . . .

She was saying something, he was not sure what. The wall of detachment around him and inside him blurred the words. But he could tell it was small talk about the award, about work, small talk filled with amorous overtones, but also tinged by worry, for she could feel his distance, and was screwing up her courage to reach out to him across it.

He heard his name on her lips. She curled up next to him, her head on his lap. As she watched, he brought the drink to his lips and took a modest swallow. He felt her touch his thigh, her fingers moving timidly over the fabric of his slacks.

He let his hand come to rest on her shoulder. The fingers went halfway down her back, she was that tiny and his hand that large. How thin she was! She had not gained enough weight since the miscarriage. Too much worry, too much work . . .

His hand had slid downward to her hip. She rose to her knees beside him. He watched her face come closer. She kissed his cheek, once, then again. The lips were parting his own now. He let her kiss him. He could feel her hunger, her loneliness. The sweet little tongue darted into his mouth, caressing him, teasing him, offering him her flesh. He could feel her offered to him, the slim little body with its warm secret places, the woman's senses hot with longing.

Suddenly he heard a cry. He looked down at her as though from a great height. He saw that his fingers had clenched in her hair, gripping it hard and using it as a handle to pull her head down toward the couch.

"Tim . . . Tim, you're hurting me!" There was a terrible urgency in her voice, but also an unreality that he found curiously restful. Holding her down with one hand, he picked up his drink with the other and finished it.

She was kicking and flailing, but her frail body was no match for the power of his grip.

"Look at you," he said.

"Tim, stop . . . Let me go!" Tears of pain and fear were running down her cheek.

"Look at you," he repeated, impressed by the lucidity of his own words. "Is this the way you were with him?"

"With who, Tim? What are you talking about?" The words were gasps of pain in her throat. "There's no one, Tim. There's never been anyone . . ."

Calmly he pulled her head this way and that, hearing her cry out as he tore at her scalp.

"Were you like this?" he asked. "All hot and bothered? Did you put your hands on him and kiss him, like this? Is that what it was like?"

"Tim, please . . ." She was weeping desperately. "There is no one . . ."

"You're not a very good liar, you know," he said, his teeth gritted as he twisted her head back and forth. "Tell the truth, now. Was it fun when he fucked you? Did you enjoy it? Did you call him Darling, and kiss him all over before he put it in you?"

"No one . . . Please, Tim, don't . . . There is no one . . ."

"Did you enjoy yourself?" he asked. "Did you come? Tell me, how many times did you come, Laura? Surely you can remember that."

Anger had joined the terror in her under his insults. She flailed desperately, and struck out at him with her fist. But he pushed her head into the cushions hard, and bent to whisper harshly in her ear.

"Think, now," he said. "How many times did you come that night, Laura? How many times did you come the night he made you pregnant? Hmm? How many?"

He felt her start under his words. The message had got through.

"That's right," he said, his face close to hers, his hand pushing her head down. "That's right, my dear. I found out."

He released her all at once. Her face was red from being forced into the cushions. She was looking at him in shock.

"How did you . . . ?" she asked numbly.

"Find out?" he asked, gazing at her through glittering eyes. "How did I find out about your little accident? How did I find out about the baby you killed? How did I find out that you ruined your body? How did I find out why our baby died? Well, that's an interesting question, isn't it, love? How did Tim find out? How did he find out when I used all my wits to keep it from him so long? How in the world did he find me out anyway?''

An odd calm had taken possession of him, deeper even than rage. So calm was he that he felt nothing when he saw his hand strike her, when he saw her try to get away, and saw his long arms catch her and pin her head in his lap.

"Tell me something," he said. "Does *he* know you killed his baby? Of course, he can't know you killed ours, too, can he? Or does he? Do you still see him? Do you still fuck him? Do you get together and laugh about the babies you've killed?''

He did not know whether she was saying anything in response. The world was behind a screen that hid certain sights and sounds while letting others through. He saw the tears in her eyes, saw her look of terror and agony, but could not hear the words on her lips. She was like a silent movie being played a very long time ago.

"Ah, don't try to wiggle out of it," he said. "You've made your bed. Now you'll have to lie in it. You had your fun, and you killed to cover it up. And now you've killed my baby as well. You've spoiled your womb with your fun, Laura. But I found out, didn't I? What do you have to say for yourself, now? Tell me that.''

She had stopped struggling. She was not looking at him. Her eyes were staring at nothing. But the sight of her body beside him, the flimsy nightgown exposing the breasts and thighs, pushed another invisible button inside him. He grabbed her, got to his feet, carrying her like a doll, and bore her to the bedroom, where he threw her on the bed. She cringed away from him into the sheets, as she had done before.

This annoyed him. So he leaned down over her, grasped her hard by her shoulders, and pulled her close to him. He worked together a gob of saliva inside his mouth, and spat in her face.

Then he let her go. A look of horror and disbelief was in her eyes. He saw the liquid evidence of his scorn dripping down her cheek. His lips curled in a twisted smile. He watched her for a moment, his arm upraised, his every sinew poised to attack her. Then he seemed to think better of this plan. He turned all at once and left the room, closing the door behind him.

For a long time Laura lay in silence. She could hear the distant sounds of Tim moving about the apartment, the vague violence of him pushing a chair aside, tearing off his coat, slamming a door. Then there was the sound of the refrigerator being opened, of ice clinking in his glass, of the bottle being put back on the kitchen counter after he poured more liquor.

She got up, went to the bathroom, and washed her face. She changed the nightgown, for it was stained with Tim's spittle, and put on another one. Then she returned to the bedroom, got into bed, and sat staring into the darkness.

It's over.

For a long while she could focus only on those two words. The details of what had occurred tonight no longer mattered. What did was the consequences.

She realized now that in some sick way Tim had planned this all in advance. He had found out about her abortion somehow, sometime. He had been putting on an elaborate act all this time, going through the motions of everyday living, and waiting for her desire for him to reach the point where she would dare to make the first move so he could attack her.

How long had he known? How long had he been planning this revenge?

She could not know. But the look on his face moments ago had made clear that his hatred had been simmering for a long time, cooked by his own patient hand to the boiling point.

She wondered what she ought to do. She wanted to get up, to pack a bag, to leave him. But she knew he would not allow that. He was ensconced between her and the apartment door, waiting like a jailer. He would not let her out. She dared not think of what would happen if she showed her face to him again tonight. She cursed herself for not having put a telephone in this bedroom when they moved into the apartment. It would mean everything to have a lifeline to the outside world tonight. She needed help.

She sat in the silence of the dark bedroom, hearing the muffled sounds of Tim's brusque movements, the awful intervals of his coiled silence, the terrible clink of the ice in his glass as he poured more anger down his throat.

Laura was afraid.

But deeper than her fear of what might happen tonight was her despair over her entire marriage, and over the future that now stretched before her.

For the man in the living room was no longer her husband. The love she had taken for granted, even in her worst moments with him, was gone now. He hated her. He lived only to revile her, to punish her.

The extent of his subterfuge amazed her. It awed her to think that he had waited for this moment through so many weeks even as he was pretending to be her husband. What kind of man could have prepared his revenge so coldly, so patiently? What kind of man could have stood by day after day, savoring her worried looks, fending off her timid approaches one by one, waiting for her longing to reach the bursting point before he struck out with his knowledge and his hatred?

Tears rolled slowly down Laura's cheeks as she faced the truth. Her husband was lost to her. Perhaps, in fact, he had never been hers as she thought he had. Perhaps she had never really known him, never really been admitted to his heart. Certainly she had never dreamed that behind his moods and his jealousy lurked this cold, hateful executioner.

She realized she herself bore a lot of the responsibility for what had happened. Perhaps she should have told him about the abortion long ago, before they were married. But she had been too ashamed. She had sensed that Tim's upbringing, his religious convictions, had not equipped him to accept such knowledge. And she had wanted to close a door on her past in marrying him.

That had been her undoing.

It was a combination of circumstances, a coalescence of tragic events and equally tragic misunderstandings. But nothing could change the way it had ended. With the spray of Tim's spittle on her face, the cruel dart of his hatred in her heart, their marriage was over. So it was more than mere terror that she felt now. It was grief for the life she had tried to build with him, a life that lay in ruins around her.

Laura sat alone in the silence, listening to the sounds of her husband behind the closed door, and wondering how to escape him, how to begin the separation that would break her heart.

It was three in the morning when she heard his hand on the knob. She had not slept, nor had she moved.

She saw the door open. He came in and closed it behind him without turning on the light. She knew he was terribly drunk. She did not know whether he could see that her eyes were open.

They remained that way for a terrible poised moment, husband and wife separated by darkness, each sizing the other up like an enemy, neither knowing what was coming next.

Then Tim lurched forward and sat down on the bed beside her. The smell of whiskey overwhelmed her. His hands touched her arms.

"You said you wanted it," he murmured thickly.

"Don't touch me," she warned in a quavering voice.

"No, no . . ." He shook his head angrily, as though she were trying to weasel out of the truth by a specious argument. "You said you wanted it, didn't you? Don't lie to me, now. You said it, didn't you?" He was still holding her tight by her arms.

"I didn't say anything. Leave me alone, Tim." She was trembling uncontrollably.

There was an instant's silence. Then, to her horror, she saw him raise his hand to strike her.

She was too late to defend herself. He hit her a tremendous slap across her face with his open hand, so hard that she went numb under the blow.

"You wanted it, didn't you? I didn't get you wrong, did I?" He grunted these words as he fought to catch both her hands in his own. Despite her struggles he managed to grasp both her wrists in one large hand, freeing the other to strike her again.

"Say it," he said, slapping her hard with the back of his hand. "I had it right. You wanted a little, didn't you? I saw through you, didn't I? You wanted some, didn't you? Didn't you? Didn't you?"

With each stabbing question he struck her again, now with his open palm, now with the back of his hand. The blows jerked her head back and forth, making her see stars. She fought against him, kicking and squirming and pulling with her hands, but he was twice her size. The blows rained harder on her face, again and again. She tasted her own blood. Dizziness overcame her.

And all the while his terrible questions continued.

"You like your fun, don't you? You killed our baby, didn't you? You spoiled yourself for my child, didn't you? And you killed his baby, too, didn't you? Who is he, Laura? What's his name? Who's the fellow you ruined us for? Who's the man who fucked you? Was it fun? How many times did you come? Come on, you can tell me. Say it. Say it. Say it!"

He hit her many more times, heavy maniacal blows rhythmic as the tolling of church bells. She slipped toward the edge of unconsciousness. She could feel her blood all over her nightgown, hot and sticky and pungent. She stopped fighting him. She wondered dazedly whether he was planning to kill her.

He felt her give up her struggles. Abruptly he let her go and stood up. She watched in confusion as he fumbled with his belt. His image was not clear, for she was seeing double.

She began to come to herself as she realized he was taking off his clothes. His balance was so skewed by drink that he had to struggle with his pants, his shoes. He muttered obscenities as the effort absorbed him.

Laura was brought awake by panic. She saw her husband rear before her like a beast in the darkness. She knew she lacked the strength to defend herself against him. If he took her now, by force, she would be finished.

She looked around her frantically. There was no means of defense against him. She began to squirm across the bed, hoping to run from him, but he caught her with a large hand and flung her back against the headboard.

"Bitch," he said, tearing off his pants at last. "Stay where you are. Now it's my turn."

He stood over her, his sex erect as a weapon between his legs. The size of him terrified her.

He bent over her, felt her body tremble at his approach, and laughed.

"Don't be scared," he said. "It's just me. Good old reliable Tim. I'm just going to give you a little fun, like you wanted. Remember, Laura? Just what you wanted."

His face came closer. She tried to push him away, but he slapped her again, with such force that she almost passed out. She felt his hands on her breasts, his knee shoved between her thighs.

"Come on," he said, patiently hitting her again. "Relax and enjoy it. Don't you want to be fucked? What's a little fucking between husband and wife?"

He jerked her knees apart with his hands. As he did so she hit out at him.

"Tim, don't! Get away from me! Don't do this!"

He felt the sting of her slap on his cheek. It seemed to set off a fatal spark inside him. He hit her hard with both hands, ten times, fifteen, spewing blood all over the room as her head flung back and forth. When she was quiet he pushed her knees up roughly with his hands and spread her thighs. He held her down with a large hand on her chest as he prepared to enter her.

Through her daze Laura felt the tip of him poised between her legs. He was pushing her down with such force that she was buried in the sheets. Desperate, she felt behind her with her free hand. She touched the lamp. It was too big for her to get a grip on. In another instant he would be inside her.

Suddenly she found the bedside alarm clock. As she struggled to get a grip on it she heard Tim's low laugh. His knees were pushed under her hips now, the hard man's sex nudging at her, preparing to push its way into her.

With all her strength Laura brought the metal clock over her head and struck him in the face with it. He cried out suddenly and fell away from her.

She pulled back against the headboard and listened to the darkness. He was moaning. She could see him holding his face. Something told her she had hit him in the eye.

Her only thought was for escape. If he recovered his senses, he would attack her again. There was no telling how badly he might hurt her now.

She leapt to her feet and stood six feet from him, ready to fly through the door the moment she saw a chance.

But she began to realize that the pain of the blow to his face was being eclipsed by the effect of so many drinks on him. He was doubled over on the floor, holding his eye, moaning incoherently, a rhythmic animal growl unlike any sound she had ever heard before.

The sounds grew more indistinct, muffled groans, confused gurglings, and lapsed toward silence. Laura stood stock still, waiting.

At last Tim curled into a fetal position on the floor, his hands still clutched to his face. He began to snore stertorously.

She dared not come closer to see whether she had hurt him badly. This was her chance to get away. It might be her last.

While her husband slept, Laura moved furtively toward the closet, in search of clothes to wear for her flight from him.

XXIII

TIM WOKE UP ALONE.

It was dawn. The pale light outside the windows joined the crushing aftereffect of the drinks still in his system to leave him dazed and motionless for a long time. At first he did not realize where he was.

Before he could quite come to himself, an excruciating pain in his left eye made him groan aloud. He touched at the eye. It was swollen shut. Dried blood was a thick crust on his cheek.

For a long moment he dared not move. Then, slowly and painfully, he turned his head to look for Laura.

She was nowhere to be seen. The bed was empty.

Through his good eye he could see that the bedsheets were covered with dried blood. There were spatters on the wall as well. He thought of his eye and wondered what had happened. A vague image of terrible violence swept behind his memory.

Laura was gone.

He listened to the silence of the apartment. She was not in the living room. Nor in the kitchen, making the morning coffee. He could feel her absence. She was not here at all.

He looked for the alarm clock. It was nowhere to be seen. It must be five or six o'clock in the morning. How long had he slept? Where was Laura?

The questions were like accusations. His pain was so intense that he curled up on himself like an infant, shutting out the world.

But he could not shut out the image that hung before his mind's eye. Something terrible had happened to him and Laura. An impersonal, murderous violence whose roar he could still hear somewhere inside him.

What had happened?

He struggled to remember. She had been sitting by his side, smiling. They had had a good time at the awards ceremony. Her arms were around him, she was kissing him. She was so pretty, her soft lips offered to him, the small hands caressing him with their feathery touch . . .

But after that it was a blank. The sweet little body of his wife, ready for love . . . And then a horrid, black violence attacking them both in the dark of night, flinging and thrashing them this way and that like a demon.

And now she was gone. He was here by himself, a blinded, bloody man confused and anxious and alone.

It took him twenty minutes to pull himself together and get up. But once he was on his feet a sense of purpose animated him.

He staggered to the kitchen to put a pot of coffee on. There was no sign of Laura. Everything was in perfect order. Nothing in the living room or kitchen was out of place.

He came back to the bathroom to look at himself in the mirror. He saw that his eye was swollen shut, black-and-blue, and covered with blood. There was more blood caked on his chest, his arms, even his thighs. He swallowed a handful of aspirins and got into the shower.

The hot coursing water made him feel a bit less confused, though his legs were trembling underneath him. His stomach was sick, and he felt weak and woozy.

When he had dried himself off, he surveyed the bedroom. The clock was on the floor near the windows. The dial, itself stained by blood, was stopped at 3:12. Tim put it back on the bedside table. Then, mechanically, he stripped the bed, remade it, and threw the bloody sheets and pillowcases down the incinerator shaft.

Not without hesitation he opened Laura's closet. Some of her clothes were gone. He checked the bathroom, and saw that some of her cosmetics and toilet articles were gone as well.

With a sigh he opened the hall closet. One of her suitcases was gone. He found himself musing that it must have been heavy for her to carry. She was such a small woman. . . .

He could hear the coffee perking now. He prowled the house in his bathrobe, checking all the rooms, unaware of the unconscious purpose driving him.

Nothing was different. Except for the undeniable signs of violence in the bedroom, the house was as before. Every tabletop, every chair in place. The kitchen counters, the closets, all the same as always.

And now he realized what he had been looking for.

A note. There was none. She had not left him a message.

She had just walked out.

He considered this fact as he poured his first cup of coffee. He sat down by the kitchen window, feeling the aspirin in his bloodstream fighting the monstrous dose of poison he had administered to himself last night.

He sat staring out the window, not hearing the little groan that was sounding in his throat. He looked blankly over the Park, with its trees and lanes and hillocks, somnolent and still under the gray morning sky, with the East Side beyond, the buildings lit by pale lights in windows, lights soon to go out as the city awoke to the day.

The coffee coursed through his insides like fire, making him nauseous as it bathed the walls of his stomach, already burned by liquor. Pain throbbed worse than ever in his head, his eye. His limbs were weak, his mind confused, his memory a nightmare.

But worst of all was his solitude as he sat staring out the window. Laura had left him no note. Just walked out on him.

But they were happily married!

This thought came to Tim like a savior, pulling a hasty screen over the most complete loneliness he had ever felt.

They were happily married. They were Laura and Tim. Everyone knew of their happiness. Friends said they had an ideal marriage. They were so close, so affectionate. An ideal couple.

His business sense and her creativity went perfectly together. He was outgoing, she more introspective. He was practical-minded, she more cerebral. He was the doer, she the creative genius. He was large, she was small. He was light, she was dark. She had often told him that he lit up her shadowed inner world and kept her happy when, left to her own devices, she would have been sad.

"You're my smile," she would say.

And she would draw him to her small arms and kiss him, hugging him close with a happy little sigh. When those soft arms were about him he felt as though he was in heaven. She was wrong about the smile, of course—though he had never told her that. It was she who was his light, his smile.

He had known since the first moment he ever saw her that Laura was his one chance for a kind of happiness he had not thought himself cut out for. A higher kind of happiness, an infinitely more perfect joy and peace than the dreary world of his past had ever allowed him to envision.

And now, of course, she belonged to him. If he ever lost her, there would be no hope of ever achieving anything comparable with another woman. Laura was the one and only. She was more than his wife. She was his whole life.

Why, they were a perfect couple! A marriage made in Heaven—everyone said that.

And that was why, come to think of it, he had suffered so much for her.

He had understood from the first moment he met her that she had known great unhappiness in her life. Her inner pain was visible in her dark, thoughtful eyes. From the outset Tim had set out to protect her with all his strength, for he knew how cruel and perfidious the world was.

And it was from that protectiveness that his jealousy had sprung. How his suspicions had tormented him! Worse than the most malignant of diseases, they had eaten away at his insides.

And, of course, this was because his jealousy had had its grain of truth. His suspicions of poor Tommy Sturdevant might have been exaggerated, but they were not wrong in principle. No man with a heart, with normal male instincts, could resist Laura. Her beauty, her depth and sweetness, were incomparable attractions, possessed by no other woman.

No, he had not been wrong about Tommy, notwithstanding all Tommy's self-serving denials. A man can see through another man easily enough. And, despite Laura's innocence, was it not obvious that she needed protection from herself, from her own vulnerability? Other men, more sensitive, more attractive, might succeed where Tommy had failed. Determined, subtle seducers . . .

Did not the very fact of Laura's abortion prove that?

In a strange way it made sense that Tim's worry about her photography had dovetailed with his suspicions about other men. There was something wayward about her wanderings through dangerous neighborhoods in search of subjects taken from the dregs of society. Something wanton, like a tempting of fate.

And, sure enough, it was photography that had caused her miscarriage. She had been dragging her heavy camera bag around the South Bronx, miles from where she belonged, taking pictures of a bunch of teenaged hoodlums, when the misfortune happened.

Had not Tim been right all along about her senseless obsession with the camera? It was a crazy tangent that cut her off from her real profession as well as her marriage. And in the end it almost killed her.

The suffering Tim had endured on Laura's account in the past year had almost driven him out of his mind. But the news of her pregnancy had seemed to undo all the damage and give them a new start on life together. The baby inside her was a living bond between them, a flesh-and-blood rampart against all the doubts and uncertainties haunting their marriage. A child would have been the foundation for a whole new life, the first of a new generation that would spring from their blood and their love. Nothing in the cruel world could have destroyed that.

But now it was gone, nipped malignantly in the bud, destroyed in the very womb where it should have been protected.

Destroyed by Laura alone?

No. The chart in the hospital proved that she had been possessed by a man before, and had spoiled herself because of him.

Even before Tim married Laura he realized she had been hurt by a man. It was written all over her. The sadness behind her dignity, the lingering pain in the heart of her charm—it was obvious.

But he had not realized the extent of the damage, the depth of the taint.

He had dedicated his life to protecting her. On the very day of his marriage he had vowed that if ever a man tried to harm her, he would squeeze the life out of him with his bare hands.

But it was already too late! Too late for them, that very first day in the Catholic Church! The man who had hurt her had done much more than Tim could have imagined. That man had not only scarred her heart, but had left his scar in her womb, in the purest and most precious part of her.

And all this time, when Tim was tying himself in knots with his worry over Laura, giving her his own seed over and over again in hopes of giving her a child, losing sleep over her night after night—all this time that killing seed, that murderous scar, had been waiting to destroy his child. And all it had taken was a bit of ill-advised exertion with a camera to annihilate the hope of his marriage to Laura.

Because the other man had got there first.

The chart in the hospital had been more than a document. It was a malediction. It proved that Laura had never belonged to Tim with a pure heart. It proved she had sullied herself with another man. It proved she had already murdered one child. It proved that her Catholic vows of marriage were a blasphemy. It proved that the delay and difficulty in her conceiving Tim's child were no accident, but had their roots in her womb, and perhaps in her heart. Finally it proved that the foul taint of the man who got there first had killed Tim's child as well.

When Tim's eyes were opened to these unbearable truths, he had nearly gone crazy. The agony he had endured during those first weeks after the miscarriage was a thing he would not have wished on his worst enemy.

But even in the depth of that torture he had forgiven Laura. He had understood that she was, in the old phrase, more sinned against than sinning. And he loved her enough to stay by her side, in spite of all her mistakes.

But last night something had snapped, something had exploded. The pent-up grief and despair he had endured all this time lit the fuse to a storm of violence that had attacked them both, Tim and Laura, in the heart of their love and their marriage.

But they had survived it!

That was the miracle. That was the essential. Wherever Laura was this morning, she was all right. And Tim, though deeply drained and hurt by what had happened, was still alive, and strong, and himself.

The world was still the world. Outside these windows the Park was filled with trees and shrubs growing toward the sun, and children getting up to a new day, and mothers walking those children with love in their hearts. Life was still life. What had happened last night was not the end of the world.

The damage could be repaired. Tim and Laura must fight this thing together. He was prepared to do anything to get her back. After all, his bridges were burned behind him. There was no life without Laura.

And his own heart was pure. Had he not, in fact, already forgiven her for sullying her body, for destroying two children, for lying before the Holy Trinity of the Catholic Church in her marriage vows? Was he not prepared to take her back, if only she would join hands with him, forget the past, and build a new future?

She must come back. All she need do was plight her troth to him once more, accept his forgiveness and grant him hers.

Tim warmed to this logic, drinking his coffee, gazing out the window as the sky brightened for the new day.

All she had to do was come back, admit her own faults, and be his wife. The rest would take care of itself. Their love was still real. One night's battle with a demon did not end a marriage consecrated by God. . . .

They had a long way to go, an uphill struggle. But they would make it. There would be more children. They would be more careful next time. The finest specialists would oversee her pregnancy. She would take more precautions. She would spend nine months in bed if necessary.

But Laura would bear him a child—because she owed him that. Her marriage vows demanded it. A law higher than any worldly sanction decreed that, notwithstanding her lies, notwithstanding what she had done to herself, she owed a child to her husband and to God.

They were married. Her life was with him. His destiny was also hers. She had betrayed that destiny once. She must not do it again.

With this thought Tim got up and prepared to return to the world, to find his wife and get her back.

Yes, things made sense again. He understood his marriage now. Mistakes had been made on both sides. But mistakes could be forgiven. If violence had occurred, violence could be forgiven, and thus undone. If a child had been destroyed, another child could be conceived.

Once she came back.

Once she assumed her responsibilities, accepted the sacred covenant that bound her to her husband, and renounced her sins in favor of her life with him.

Tim had put his shirt on. He began to tie his tie with shaking fingers. Despite the pain in his eye and the worst hangover of his life, he felt confident. The awful solitude yawning inside his heart would not last long.

Laura would come back.

And when she did, he would go beyond all the things he had already forgiven her for. He would even forgive her for running out like a thief in the night, without even leaving him a note. She should not have done that. No, she should not.

But he would take her back, The world was still the world, and she was still his wife. They would solve things together, admit their mistakes and forge a new life together, as their vows demanded.

As soon as she came back.

XXIV

TIM ARRIVED at the office at eleven.

He was dressed in one of his handsomest silk suits, freshly shaved, his hair neatly brushed, his shoes carefully shined.

The only outward sign of what he had been through since yesterday was the patch over his eye, which gave him a curiously rakish and attractive look. The doctor had determined that there was no serious damage to the eye, but the trauma to the area would require several weeks to heal.

Tim had returned to the apartment after seeing the doctor, and had found that there was still no sign of Laura. The coffee things were where he had left them. The note he had written for her was still on the kitchen counter.

Miss you bad, it read. *Be back soon. Please don't go away.*

Before leaving for the office he looked again at the note, and decided to change it for another. The wording seemed too weak, too apologetic. He rewrote it carefully.

Be back tonight, the new note read. *Miss you. Don't go away.*

This note was better, he decided. It had a note of authority as well as of affection.

When he arrived at the office he was surprised to see that Toni, the secretary, was not at her desk in the reception room. Instead there was a strange woman in a business suit sitting at the desk. At the sight of him she got briskly to her feet and approached him.

"Mr. Riordan?" she said, holding out her hand to shake his. "How do you do?"

Tim looked at her sharply, without accepting her handshake.

"Who are you?" he asked. "Where's Toni?"

"Mr. Riordan, my name is Nancy Underwood. I'm an attorney representing your wife Laura. I'm here to pass along a few items of important information to you. Why don't we step into your office where we can have some privacy?"

After a hesitation Tim followed her down the hall to his office. When she opened the door he saw to his surprise that the place had been cleared of all his things, from the papers on his desk top to the photos on the wall.

Tim was beginning to get angry.

"What's going on here?" he asked.

"Please, sit down." The young attorney had a look of firmness and authority. She seemed confident, and very professional. Something told Tim this was not the time to get tough with her.

He sat down in the visitors' chair. She sat on the edge of the desk.

"Mr. Riordan," she said, "I'm here to inform you that a court order obtained this morning enjoins you from setting foot on these premises pending action by the Family Court of New York regarding the assault on your wife that took place last night. As you can see, your office materials have been removed. By the decision of the Court, in consultation with Laura and her counsel, your office has been moved to the Sixty-third Street premises of Laura, Ltd. You are free to continue your professional activity on behalf of the company at that location. However, you are enjoined from approaching or communicating with your wife at any time prior to the hearing that has been set for July fourteenth. Do you understand what I've said so far?"

Tim had turned red. Anger boiled inside him as he looked at this crisp, aggressive young woman who was trying to tell him where he could work, where he could and could not go. But he sensed he must be careful. The situation was a delicate one.

"Yes," he said. "I understand."

"Fine," she said coolly. "Now, I give you this paper"—she handed him a legal-sized folder—"to inform you officially that with the Court's authority your wife has filed for a legal separation from you. You are advised, of course, to obtain representation for yourself in this proceeding. You will have an opportunity to remove your personal effects from the apartment at 315 Central Park West this afternoon, in the company of a court officer. After that you will not be permitted access to that location, as provided in the temporary restraining order I have just handed you. Do you understand?"

Tim said nothing, but simply glared at her. In the few minutes since he had met this young attorney he had conceived a bottomless hatred for her. Her firmness, her waving of papers and court orders in his face, and the hint of distaste in her attitude toward him, made him want to strangle her.

"If you attempt to see your wife," she continued, "you are liable to criminal charges. Since an assault took place last night that endangered your wife's physical and emotional health, the Court has decided that no personal contact shall be permitted until the separation proceedings are completed. Do you understand me?"

"What about my health?" Tim pointed to the patch over his eye with a twisted smile.

The attorney acknowledged his remark with a cool glance full of contempt.

"Do we understand each other?" she asked, never taking her eyes off him.

He looked at her appraisingly.

"Let me ask you something," he said. "If an assault took place, why have no charges been filed against me? Why haven't I been arrested?"

"At your wife's request, no charges have been filed," she replied. "Her interest is in a clean separation rather than retribution."

She stood up. "That concludes what I had to say to you, Mr. Riordan," she said. "Your counsel will find all the necessary papers in the folder I've given you. It's been nice meeting you. With your permission, I will escort you off these premises."

Controlling his anger with effort, Tim allowed himself to be walked through the outer office and through the doors of Laura, Ltd., to the street outside.

When he arrived at the Sixty-third Street building he found his office set up as neatly as possible on the first floor. As he set about rearranging his papers and files, he reflected on what had happened.

Laura had not had the courage to face him. She had not seen him, even once. She had simply run out in the middle of the night, before either of them had the chance to explain what had happened, to begin patching things up—and she had hired legal interlopers to stand as a barrier between herself and her own husband.

She had banished him from his place of work—a place he had built virtually with his own hands—and from his home. She had left a cold, reproachful representative of the legal establishment behind to insult him with ultimatums while Laura herself hid away somewhere.

Tim burned with the humiliation of being treated like a criminal by a total stranger in his own office. It was unbelievable. And Laura had not only allowed it—she had arranged it.

He could still feel the embarrassment of having entered his place of work when it was full of employees who already knew that this lawyer was waiting like a guard at the reception desk to intercept him. There must not have been a person in the place who had not heard the news, who was not waiting for him to appear, who did not know his business before he did.

All because of Laura.

He thought of the humiliation of going back home later today to find another legal representative there, who would watch over his shoulder as he cleared the underwear out of his drawers, packed his shirts and socks and toothbrush to go to a hotel. The invasion of his privacy was unspeakable.

And Laura had done it.

She had had a private episode with him last night—a violent and upsetting one, perhaps, but above all a private one—and instead of facing him and working it out maturely in the privacy of their marriage, she had slinked out under cover of darkness while he slept, and surrounded herself with a rampart of legal whores to defend her, while his own reputation and dignity suffered from this childish show of force.

She had not even had the guts to face him. She had not left him a note. She had simply run away like a coward.

So be it, then, he shrugged, He would clear out his things, obey her rules, and bide his time.

And some day he would get his revenge.

With that thought Tim turned to the phone on his new office desk, and began the search for a lawyer.

XXV

July 14, 1958

LIEUTENANT DAN AGUIRRE sat in Courtroom 3 at the Lafayette Street Courthouse, watching Tim Riordan.

Aguirre did not look like a policeman. In his gray pinstriped suit and tie he might have been an attorney, a banker, or perhaps a bright young physician. His demeanor was calm and professional. His tanned complexion and droopy mustache added mystery to his face without quite betraying that he was a man of action.

He was leaner than his peers on the police force, and stronger than most, though the powerful muscles of his tall body were concealed by the conservative suit he wore. The reflexes and instincts which equipped him for split-second life-and-death decisions on the streets of New York were hidden behind his handsome face, just as the horrors he had witnessed in his fourteen years on the force were masked by the cool eyes with which he took in the scene before him.

The courtroom was quiet, almost somnolent. Judge Margaret Tagliaferro was on the bench, listening to a statement from Riordan's lawyer, Kevin Matz. The judge was a small woman in her fifties, with salt-and-pepper hair, bifocals that she was fond of dangling from her thumb as she concentrated, and a lively manner.

At the moment she was listening carefully as Matz, a polite young attorney who had once clerked for Judge Tagliaferro herself after his graduation from Yale Law, completed his presentation.

"Your Honor, my client wishes to express his sincere regret for an incident which he admits and considers to be entirely his own fault. He stands ready to make any reparations necessary and possible toward Mrs. Riordan, whom he believes and stipulates to be entirely blameless in this matter. He wishes further to express his gratitude to Mrs. Riordan for generously abstaining from filing charges against him for his behavior on the night in question. He further thanks her for allowing him to continue in his position as Vice President and Chief Executive Officer at Laura, Ltd., until such time as he can secure alternative employment."

The attorney paused to glance at his client. "Mr. Riordan, however, respectfully declines his wife's generous offer of continued employment, and tenders his resignation effective immediately, out of consideration for his wife's concern for her personal security and privacy in the wake of the unfortunate event that led to these proceedings. Instead he offers his services as a consultant to Mrs. Riordan in her business, at no charge, such services to be provided upon request through an intermediary chosen by the Court. Mr. Riordan feels this is the least he can do by way of reparation. In addition, he accepts all terms and stipulations requested by Mrs. Riordan and decreed by this Court relative to their separation. He renounces all claim to community property, and will cooperate fully with this Court in divorce proceedings to begin at the Court's discretion."

Detective Aguirre was still looking at Tim Riordan, who was seated at the table beside Matz. Riordan was an intriguing presence. He was a large man, but the stillness of his posture seemed to shrink him somehow. He was looking at the judge with a respectful, even mild expression. His hands were folded on the tabletop. He wore a dark suit, and his manner was conservative to match it. He seemed withdrawn so far inside himself that his surface was as innocent as that of a schoolboy. The only thing remarkable about him was the patch he wore over one eye. It made him look vulnerable, wounded, and added to his chastened appearance.

Kevin Matz had made it obvious to the Court that Mr. Riordan sincerely regretted the misfortune he had caused. His only desire was to repair the damage in any way he could. He accepted his wife's decision to separate from him, and would not contest the divorce to which she had a legal and moral right. He still loved her, and only wished to expiate the crime of which he alone was guilty.

But Detective Aguirre was studying Timothy Riordan carefully. For this there were two reasons.

In the first place, Dan Aguirre had been on the police force for fourteen years, and had a degree in criminology from Columbia to go along with his considerable street experience as a cop. He had seen thousands of faces in those years. He understood a lot about women, and even more about men.

That was why he knew that there was more to Tim Riordan than was revealed by the quiet eyes looking up at the judge.

In the second place, Dan Aguirre had been present at the 20th Precinct, by happenstance, the night that Laura Riordan had dragged herself, half-dead and beaten to a pulp, into the station house at four in the morning to ask for help. It had been Aguirre, a seasoned veteran of the court system, who had recommended Nancy Underwood to Laura Riordan.

He glanced at Mrs. Riordan's face now. It still bore bruises, evidence of split lips, and black-and-blue shadows, two weeks after the incident. But her condition now gave no clue as to what she had looked like then.

Dan Aguirre could read human bruises as a paleographer reads hieroglyphs at an archeological dig. He had understood what kind of man Tim Riordan was that first night, without ever seeing him. The man had left his signature—distinctive as a handprint—on his wife's face.

So Dan Aguirre sat watching with interest as Riordan's attorney finished his presentation to the judge.

"In conclusion, Your Honor, Mr. Riordan wishes to express his regret to this Court and to Mrs. Riordan for the very necessity of these proceedings. He offers to pay court costs as an expression of his sincere regret. He thanks Mrs. Riordan, her counsel, and the Court for having given him the opportunity to fully apologize for his conduct."

Kevin Matz sat down beside his client. The judge dangled her bifocals for a moment, her sharp mind alert to the forces at work in the courtroom.

"The Court is impressed by Mr. Riordan's sincerity," she said, measuring her words. "Since no charges have been brought by Mrs. Riordan against her husband for assault, the Court feels it is appropriate to assign the following guidelines for a legal separation. Mr. Riordan is not to contact his wife or approach her except through his own attorney and hers. Should Mr. Riordan attempt to contact her in any other manner, such contact will be deemed a contempt of this Court, and appropriate measures will be taken by the legal authorities to restrain any such contact and to protect Mrs. Riordan's safety and privacy pursuant to this order. Mr. Riordan may contact Mrs. Riordan for business purposes only through an intermediary approved by this Court. Divorce proceedings will be entertained by this Court in accordance with the laws of the State of New York."

The judge looked at both counsels.

"Court is adjourned," she said.

Laura stood up and shook Nancy Underwood's hand.

"Thanks for everything," she said, managing a smile which still hurt her lips, though the night of her injuries seemed a lifetime ago.

"That's what I'm here for," Nancy said. "I'm only glad things went so smoothly."

Together they moved toward the heavy oak doors at the rear of the room.

Tim and his attorney were going in the same direction. The four of them reached the doors at the same moment. Since the hearing had been so amicable, they shook hands all around, the attorneys, attorney and client, and finally Tim and Laura.

There was a brief instant while Tim held Laura's hand, as the lawyers were busy congratulating each other. Tim was still smiling. His handshake was gentle, but he did not let go right away. He leaned downward to whisper in Laura's ear.

"You owe me a child," he said quietly. "No court can change that."

Laura turned pale. Her hand went cold in his grasp. As their faces separated she saw the look in his eyes. It was a look of infinite hatred, but so cleverly hooded by his outwardly amicable expression that no one but she herself could see it.

Then he was pulling back, joining his attorney, and walking out the door.

Nancy Underwood noticed Laura's pallor and took her aside.

"What did he say to you?" she asked.

Laura hesitated, watching Tim's large form move down the hall in the company of his attorney.

"Nothing," she said after a pause. "I just . . . It was just being that close to him. Never mind, Nancy. Really, I'm fine."

"Are you sure?" The experienced attorney was giving Laura a searching look.

"Yes," Laura lied. "I'm sure."

XXVI

The New York Times, November 8, 1958

LANCASTER WINS IN LANDSLIDE OVER BOSE, INGERSOLL

Haydon Lancaster yesterday made modern New York State electoral history in unseating Senate incumbent Amory Bose, who ran against him as an independent, and defeating Republican Lawrence Ingersoll for the U.S. Senate.

It was the first time in New York history that the incumbent, having lost the Democratic nomination in the primaries, ran as an independent and was defeated by a member of his own party.

Lancaster received 65 percent of the vote, to 21 percent for Ingersoll and 14 percent for Bose.

The election followed a hard-fought campaign in which Lancaster's loyalty and patriotism were questioned by both his opponents. Most observers agree that the turning point came in May, when Lancaster defended himself brilliantly on nationwide television against a Bose accusation of treasonous activity during Lancaster's tenure as a NATO envoy. When the Bose claim was revealed as a fraud based on false documents and the word of a known impostor, the results of the election became a foregone conclusion, and Bose's illustrious sixteen-year career in the Senate was doomed.

Lancaster made a gracious victory speech before a cheering mob of supporters at the Waldorf-Astoria early this morning. He thanked his many campaign workers for their tireless efforts on his behalf, and apologized to the crowd for the absence of his wife. Mrs. Lancaster is at the side of her seriously ill mother, Mrs. Harry M. Stallworth III, in Palm Springs.

A reception will be held tonight for Lancaster at the home of his parents in Manhattan. It is expected that his major supporters will attend, as well as representatives of all three branches of government eager to congratulate him on his victory.

TESS FOLDED *The New York Times* and put it down on the table. She was standing in the upstairs study of the Lancaster mansion, having stolen a few moments here away from the mob of guests thronging the house.

The newspaper account of the election could not communicate the fervor of Hal's supporters or the excitement of the crowd here tonight. Everyone seemed to sense history in the making. It seemed as though half of Washington society had made the journey to Manhattan to congratulate Hal on his victory and to try to get on his good side for the future. Senators, congressmen, lobbyists, journalists, federal judges, and even members of the Cabinet and their wives were here.

A personal message of congratulation from the President had had special meaning to Hal. *This is one time I'm pleased and proud to see a Democrat get into high office,* it read. *I'll be looking forward to working with you for the rest of my term.*

Hal was downstairs circulating among the assembled well-wishers, aided by his parents and by Tom Rossman. Not that he needed any help. He remembered every name in the disparate crowd, and knew just how to make each guest feel welcome and important with a brief word and a flash of his famous smile.

The lie about Diana seemed to be holding up so far. Her mother was far from seriously ill; but it was true that Diana was holed up in the Palm Springs house, out of sight and out of mind. Thanks to Hal's good relations with the press, and some quiet intervention by Tess herself with the television networks, Diana's disappearance from the scene in recent weeks had been covered up nicely.

It was an open secret in government and society circles that Diana had got herself into some sort of trouble. Few people were surprised by this, for her unstable personality and problems with alcohol had been noticed far too often in the past couple of years. On the other hand, the rumor that her indiscretion had been of a sexual nature, and a taboo one at that, did come as a surprise, for Diana's heterosexual inclinations and fidelity to Hal had been taken for granted by everyone.

There was a private family understanding to the effect that sometime after the inauguration, perhaps next spring, Diana would fly to Reno and divorce Hal. The grounds would be irreconcilable differences, or whatever else would sound most innocent.

Divorce was not a good thing for Hal at this stage of his career. But the double standard applying to women in the public mind would come to his rescue. Though it was widely known that his passionate nature had led him into many more or less insignificant affairs, no one blamed him for this. On the other hand, the rumor that Diana had been unfaithful to her Prince Charming was less forgivable. And the sexually forbidden stripe of her indiscretion put the frosting on the cake. She would disappear from Hal's life without leaving a politically ugly scar.

Of course, down the line, if Hal ever decided to run for President, his divorce might prove a hindrance. But Tess suspected that the public perception of Hal's blamelessness in the matter of Diana would smooth things over. In fact, she intended to use her influence with the news media to make sure that this was the case.

After all, Hal was a man of destiny. Neither Amory Bose, nor divorce from Diana, nor a future opponent could hold him back from the eventual victories that belonged to him.

It was a happy night for Hal, and even more so for Tess.

She decided to take a brief stroll around the upper wing of the mansion before going back downstairs to join Hal. She was a bit lost in this part of the house, having only recently become a Lancaster familiar. Thus it was that, without really knowing where she was going, she ended up in the large study that had come to be called the "playroom" in memory of the days when Hal and Sybil had played checkers and gin rummy there as children.

The room was empty. Tess closed the door behind her. On the wall over the fireplace was the famous swimming photograph of Hal, which had been blown up by Sybil into an enormous life-sized image, perhaps seven feet high, in a customized frame. The picture, which Hal's parents loved as much as Sybil did, had been installed here as a sort of heirloom, because nowadays Sybil considered this "her" room, whenever she was home from the hospital.

Tess stood looking at the photograph. It was haunting, for it captured the vibrant youth in Hal's face and body so eloquently. It was a peculiarly ambiguous image, for it made Hal look almost like a boy, and yet brought out something ageless and sensitive in him, that special quality that Tess herself had learned to adore so ardently, especially since she had become his lover.

Perhaps, she mused, she might have it copied for herself. She would love to have this picture in her own penthouse. Having it near her would be like living under the mysterious light of Hal's smile.

She was standing by the bookcase, thinking these thoughts, when she saw a plume of smoke emerge from the deep couch before the fireplace and curl upward toward the recessed lights illuminating the picture.

Tess moved forward slowly, until she could see over the high back of the couch.

Curled upon herself like a little girl, gazing up at the picture while a cigarette burned unnoticed in her hand, Sybil Lancaster lay on the couch. There was something almost fetal about her posture. Though she was dressed in a sleek evening dress that showed off her bright complexion and blonde hair, she looked like a starved waif buried in the huge expanse of overstuffed leather.

"Sybil!" Tess greeted her with a smile. "What a surprise. I wondered where you might be. I haven't seen you all evening. Did you steal away to get some privacy? I can't say I blame you."

Sybil did not even acknowledge these amicable words. Her eyes remained glued to the picture, their expression vacant.

Tess felt distinctly uncomfortable. She had never really been alone with Sybil before. They had only met twice, at Lancaster family dinners where Sybil paid no attention to Tess, and vanished almost as soon as she had made her obligatory appearance.

Tess knew, of course, from Hal, that Sybil was in and out of institutions, and was a very sick girl. Her intuition had told her, as well, that Sybil had a strong possessive attachment to Hal. Sybil had never warmed up to Diana, and apparently liked Tess even less.

Tess had treated her with every courtesy, and even tried to affect a big-sister air with her so as to forge whatever friendship she could—but to no avail. Sybil's behavior toward her, in their few moments together, had been cool, distant, and oddly knowing. Tess had recognized in her a nasty rival for Hal's affections, and had soon decided to give her a wide berth.

So now she was standing here, trying to think of a decorous way to retrace her steps and get out of the room, when she thought she smelled something unpleasant.

She looked down at Sybil. All at once she caught sight of the cigarette burning in the girl's hand. The ember had already reached the bare flesh of her fingers, and was slowly burning them as Sybil lay oblivious, staring at the picture of her brother.

"Sybil!" Tess cried in alarm, grabbing for the nearest ashtray and shaking the butt from Sybil's fingers into it. "For God's sake . . ."

Sybil at first did not even look up at her. Her hand was as limp as a rag. Her eyes seemed glazed.

Then, at last, she looked from her burned fingers to her unlikely rescuer with a little smile that seemed to bespeak triumph as well as indifference.

"Don't move," Tess said. "I'll get you some lotion and a bandage."

Preferring not to alert the house to the accident, Tess hurried along the hall to the bathroom and returned with some ointment, a washcloth, and bandages. Shaking her head in wonderment at Sybil's madness, she knelt to cleanse the wound.

"This may hurt," she said. "Are you sure you're all right, Sybil? Really, you ought to be more careful . . ."

She wanted to be friendly and protective, for she hoped her solicitude would facilitate better relations with Sybil. At the same time she did not know what to say. How does one address an insane girl who has just let a cigarette burn her fingers out of sheer psychotic distraction? Absorbed in her own delirium, Sybil could not even feel the most painful of sensations.

Sybil had still not said a word. Tess was torn between pity and embarrassment as she cleansed the fingers carefully, sucking in her breath as she saw the burnt skin blister, and began putting ointment on them.

Sybil lay inert as something dead, her glassy eyes still locked to the smiling face of Hal in the photograph. Hal seemed to grin down benevolently on both of them from his place on the wall.

As Tess applied sterile gauze to a piece of bandaging tape, she heard Sybil speak at last.

"Poor Diana." Sybil's voice was husky and very small.

Tess pondered this odd remark as she bandaged the wound. Sybil had never given any sign of harboring sincere feelings about Diana.

Nevertheless, one had to make some sort of response.

"A sad young woman," Tess said. "She's had a lot of bad luck. I hope things get better for her. She's suffered enough . . ."

"There were others before you."

The words had cut Tess off. They were enunciated with deliberate clarity, though Sybil was still not looking at her.

Tess looked cautiously into Sybil's eyes.

"Me?" she asked. "What do you mean?"

Sybil gave her a glance full of knowledge and disinterest, as though she certainly knew everything, but could not be bothered to press the point.

Tess said nothing more.

"A lot of others," Sybil continued in her small, penetrating voice.

"I know," said Tess carefully, finishing the first bandage and beginning the second. Sybil's words worried her. It occurred to her that Sybil, having known Hal intimately for so many years, must know secrets Tess herself could not know.

"But he never cared for any of them," Sybil said.

Tess was silent, feeling this double-edged remark sink in. She sensed that Sybil possessed weapons that might have deadly force when used against a woman in Tess's delicate position as Hal's lover.

But she was not prepared for what came next.

"Except one," Sybil concluded. Her gaze at last left the picture on the wall and fixed itself upon Tess.

How frightening they were, those blue eyes of Sybil's! So limpid, so deep, and yet so horribly empty. There was something cold as arctic ice about them, and also ugly, something suggestive of an ancient festering sore, an irreparable pain turned into infinite hatred of herself and the world.

That hatred now came forth in a voice filled with triumph.

"Only the one," she said, digging the knife deeper into Tess's heart even as it was Tess herself who worked on the wound in Sybil's hand. The words were spoken tonelessly, without inflection of any sort, absolutely malignant in their intention.

Tess turned pale. Her fingers trembled as they worked on the bandage. She could feel Sybil's eyes on her as the words echoed in her mind. The message contained in them seemed to have penetrated to her heart before she could evaluate it intellectually. And this had obviously been Sybil's intention.

Tess was a strong woman. She had destroyed determined adversaries, enemies possessed of more power than herself at the time she bested them. Her personality was built on her certainty that she would fight any battle to get what she wanted, and that she feared no human being.

But Sybil was not human. The disease consuming her had dissolved her humanity into a macabre brew of sick deliria, and replaced it with something evil, something one could not perhaps fight with human weapons.

With this thought Tess forced herself to meet Sybil's eyes. She tried to put on her own iciest stare. But she still held the girl's hands in her own, and she knew Sybil could feel her alarm. The combined spell of Sybil's insanity and hostility was unnerving.

Tess felt herself weakening. If the subject had been anything except Hal . . . But it was too late. The wound Sybil had opened was getting wider, deeper, slashing through the armor of Tess's pride and all the scars over her feelings, directly to the woman's heart she had never possessed until Hal gave it to her.

And from that open wound came two words, words she would have given anything to suppress, words sure to give satisfaction to the soulless creature who had attacked her so surgically, words she could nevertheless not hold back.

"Which one?" she asked.

She was still holding the burnt hand in her own. She stared at Sybil. Sybil's eyes were leaden, opaque, yet lit by a serpentlike contentment, like a predatory snake patiently digesting the defenseless mouse it has just devoured.

Tess looked up at the picture of Hal on the wall, and back to Sybil.

"Which one?" she hissed, the words an explosion on her lips.

Sybil said nothing, but fixed her with the same sated stare.

"Which one?" Tess could not see how wide her eyes were. Nor did she realize she was squeezing Sybil's burnt fingers with all her strength, pressing the fresh burns together, trying to get through the layers of insanity to human vulnerability, human pain.

But Sybil merely raised an eyebrow in ironic acknowledgment of this futile torture. Her eyes seemed to laugh mirthlessly.

Then she spoke in a lyrical, mocking tone.

"Ask the fellow in the pool," she said, glancing up at the picture of Hal.

Tess followed the direction of her gaze and looked at Hal's smiling image. The last thing in the world she could ever do, of course, was to ask Hal about the truth of Sybil's words. The potential for destruction in his answer was unlimited.

Tess released Sybil's hand, giving up the charade of aggravating the wound she had just bandaged. The real wound was in Tess's own heart. And Sybil had planted a seed in that wound, striking at the perfect moment with the brutal instinct of a matador, just when Tess was congratulating herself on her victory over Diana and the bright future that lay ahead of her with Hal.

It was a wound whose possibility Tess had not suspected two minutes ago. But now that it was open, now that Sybil's coy silence and the doubt it sowed were spreading through it, deepening it to lethal proportions—now Tess knew it would never heal. She would have to live with it, lose sleep over it, struggle in vain to close it, from now on, and perhaps forever more.

Sybil had done that.

And Sybil's faint little smile, as she lay back on the cushions to look at her brother's picture, was proof that she knew precisely what she had done, knew her shaft had gone home, knew she had found the Achilles' heel of this woman she had met so recently.

Tess stood up. She herself looked up at Hal's handsome, boyish face in the picture, joining Sybil in contemplation of it. As she did so she felt a deathlike dread, and a curious unfamiliar warmth, spreading through her senses.

She turned and left the room silently, to look for Hal. She had never needed him so desperately as she did now.

XXVII

December 21, 1958

IT WAS A LONELY LIFE.

Laura had been on her own for five months. She had not seen Tim since the day of their separation hearing in Judge Tagliaferro's court-room. True to his word, he had cleared out his desk at Laura, Ltd., that very day and shown his face no more. Divorce proceedings were moving slowly, and would probably not be final for another eight or nine months. But Laura felt completely sundered from Tim. Their marriage seemed an ancient thing, the more painful for its remoteness.

Nowadays Laura knew all the strange emotions that are reserved for people whose marriages have failed, emotions that a single person who has never been married cannot really imagine, no matter how lonely he or she may be.

A sense of worthlessness, of abandonment and emptiness now greeted Laura as she awoke each morning, and stayed with her all day long. Her abjection seemed as natural to her as breathing out and breathing in.

Having had a man, loved him, and lost him, she was like half a person, a virtual ghost haunting the premises of her former life. However troubled that life might have been, it had offered a warmth and a feeling of being wanted that were now gone forever.

She had changed her routine so as to do her sketching at the office now. When she could find time she went out with her camera, visiting her favorite subjects or wandering the city in search of new ones. Often she did not return home until her fatigue was so overpowering as to drive her into sleep without time for morbid reflection on her solitude.

The apartment was a torture chamber. She hated the silence, and the pathetic feeling that these spacious rooms were here for her alone. Without the quick active step of a man to echo off these walls, the sound of his deep voice, the warmth of his body beside her in bed at night—without all that the place was like a tomb, and she herself like a mummy whose decayed existence only served to commemorate her past happiness.

But her outings of late had become doubly painful, for it was the Christmas season—the worst time of year for lonely people. Fifth Avenue was alive with festive decorations and eager shoppers. Santas were ringing their bells on street corners, and children pulled their mothers to brightly lit store windows to gaze at the colorful displays of toys and gifts.

Faced with this distressing holiday that celebrated the closeness of families and the bursting happiness of children, Laura found herself gravitating with her camera to the darker corners of the city where lonely people endured their solitary existence in abstraction from the season around them. But her pictures of poor and homeless people were too painful for her to look at, for they reflected the emptiness in her own heart all too poignantly.

So she returned to Central Park, which had become in an odd way the geographical and spiritual center of her peregrinations, as it was for so many New Yorkers. Here she took pictures not only of children with their mothers, but also of glassy-eyed vagrants on benches; not only of young couples in love, but also of elderly widows walking their dogs in moody silence; not only of energetic teenagers rollicking along the paths in groups, but also of the solitary strollers who passed them without seeming to notice their levity. Strollers on their way to nowhere, like Laura herself.

Central Park had everything, and everyone. It contained the inexhaustible variety of human faces spawned by the metropolis. To a photographer's eye it was a paradise of opportunity. But nowadays it was a difficult spectacle for Laura to look at, for so many of those faces were lonely.

Nevertheless she came back, for, impersonal though the Park might be, it was the only home she knew, and these anonymous passersby were the closest thing she had to members of her own spiritual family. Even if loneliness was her only bond to them, it was a powerful bond, and not one she was ready to sever any time soon.

So it was that today, as darkness was falling over the city and the chill in the air announced an impending snowfall, Laura was wandering the lanes of the Park, between the pond and the Wollman Rink, where skaters with bright scarves flowing behind them in the breeze lent a picturesque grace note to the stark landscape.

Laura knew it was time to go home and fix herself something to eat, but she could not make up her mind to stop her wandering. She had her camera in her hand, but had only used it a few times this afternoon, taking pictures of people far away from herself. She felt cut off from them, and the chill in the air seemed to match the cold void inside her.

She turned a corner, walked up a flight of steps, and suddenly heard the piping of the calliope from the carousel. She moved in the direction of the music, saw a handful of children on the merry-go-round, and sat down on a distant bench to watch them.

It was late, and darkness was falling quickly. The mothers who sat on the benches nearest to the ride were looking at their watches and beginning to fidget. The children's faces bore that composite look of stubbornness, resignation, and delight that meant they knew their play must end soon, but intended to enjoy it until the last possible second.

Laura raised her camera to her eye and focused it on the whirling children. She wanted to take at least one picture of the scene before her, but something stopped her, and she put the camera away.

With a sigh she realized it was the happiness of the children that had sapped her courage. They reminded her of the two babies she had lost. She could not bear to open her camera's eye to a happy six-year-old tonight, when her chance to have a child of her own had passed her by twice over.

How many sleepless nights she had spent thinking about those two unborn children, and what they would have meant to her life! Not only would their existence have filled her heart to overflowing, but the very fact of their birth would have changed the course of her life in ways she could hardly imagine today.

If Nathaniel Clear's child had been born, Laura might never have become a seamstress, might never have met Tim, never have become a fashion designer. She might have chosen some completely different walk of life as a way of supporting herself and her baby.

Might never have met Hal . . .

And if Tim's child had been born, her marriage to him would have lasted longer, perhaps much longer. But it would have ended. Of that she had no doubt. And she shuddered to think of the terrors that innocent child might have witnessed between her and Tim.

These thoughts filled Laura with despair, for she knew that, however much her heart might long for those lost babies today, it was nevertheless best that they had not come into the world, for she had failed to prepare an adequate and safe nest for them. The men who had sired them had been badly chosen by her, and thus she was not a fit mother to offer them the happiness and security that would have been their birthright.

What cruel tricks life plays, Laura mused. Sometimes the gifts it holds out with a tempting hand are things that would destroy us if we ever possessed them. Thus, sadly, we are better off not having received them, for in our weaknesses and our imperfect judgment we would not have been capable of doing justice to them.

Laura felt at home with this thought, for it had been an old acquaintance all her life. She was through trying to outwit the world. She accepted its rules. But her only serious complaint against these capricious and fickle gods was that they had to bring innocent unborn children into their games. A woman can stand any misfortune to herself, any humiliation. But when fate takes away the children from her womb, the game becomes too cruel to be endured.

With this thought, Laura watched the mothers get up from their benches, as though by an invisible signal, to tell their children it was time to go. The merry-go-round was slowing down now. In a moment everyone would be gone, and Laura would be alone under the falling night.

Despite this depressing thought Laura could not seem to drag herself to her feet. She felt more tired, more empty than ever before.

Suddenly a gentle touch on her shoulder startled her out of her reverie.

"Fancy meeting you here."

Laura looked up. When she saw who it was her breath caught in her throat.

Hal was standing beside her in a dark overcoat she had never seen before, smiling into her eyes as a snowflake or two came out of the dark sky to melt on his shoulder.

A tear came to Laura's eye despite herself at the sight of him, and she had to fight it back with all her strength.

"It's been a long time, Laura," he said, bending closer to her.

Hal. My Hal.

Laura could not find words to say to him. Never in her life had she felt so rescued by a single person, and at the same time so torn.

She opened her mouth to speak, and then hesitated. All at once she realized that words were important now. She could not tell him what was in her heart.

He spoke for her.

"I was taking a little stroll, to collect my thoughts," he said. "It's an old habit of mine. It helps me to sort things out at the end of a long day. I was feeling kind of lonely. Then I saw you sitting here, and, to tell you the truth, you look like I feel. I hope I didn't embarrass you by coming over."

Laura managed a smile. "Not at all, Hal. Would you like to sit down?"

He sat beside her, his gloved hands on his knees. The melting snowflakes were in his hair now. She thought she saw a strand or two of premature gray.

Time had changed him, in a way the newspaper and television images could not capture. He seemed smoother, calmer, but no less himself. He had never looked so handsome.

He gazed at the carousel, almost empty now, and paused to listen to the calliope.

"Seems like old times," he said quietly.

It was true. She had sat here with Hal many times during their time together, watching the children play and guiltily dreaming of one day bringing his child here herself. Now, as she sat here beside him, she realized why her lonely steps had brought her to this place tonight.

"You look wonderful, Hal," she said.

He shrugged. "But different," he said. "Don't you think?"

There was a resignation in his tone that belied the smile on his lips.

"Different," she said, "but still wonderful."

She studied the subtle, eloquent changes that time had etched in his handsome features. As she did so she realized that the intervening years had given her new eyes to see him with—the eyes that made pictures with her camera.

"Are you still working as hard as ever?" he asked. "I've read about your success. I was proud of you."

Laura shrugged. "I'm still at it," she said, "but not in the way I once was." She showed him the camera in her hands. "I'm a photographer now, too. I don't know how much longer I can go on being a designer. It's hard to serve two masters."

She wanted to explain the change in her life, but its enormity drained away her strength to talk about it. Life was an ocean that had borne her light-years away from the dreams she had once cherished. And yet, incredibly, it had set her down in this familiar place by the side of the man who still owned her heart. It was too much to explain, too much even to think about with him looking at her that way.

"I understand," Hal said. And she could see that he really did.

"You know," he said, "your swimming pool picture of me has been in our house all this time. My sister had it blown up to life size and put it on her favorite wall."

"Ah." She nodded, touched by the bittersweet implication of his words. So he had known her as a photographer, after all.

"I kind of thought you would go a long way," he said. "From the first day I drew that sketch of you in Goldman's Deli, I could feel that there were too many Lauras in there for one profession to take in. I'm happy for you, Laura."

She looked at him softly.

"And you?" she asked. "I heard about the election. Congratulations."

He shrugged. He said nothing.

"I see you on the news all the time," she added. "I'm a fan. I voted for you."

He brightened, as though surprised and delighted. "That was nice of you," he said. "Somehow it never occurred to me that you might be watching . . ."

"You were a wonderful campaigner," she said. "And I know you'll be a great senator. I'm proud of you, too, Hal."

He looked at her with an expression so complex, so full of darkness and light, that she had to look away.

"How is Diana?" she asked.

He hesitated for a long moment before answering. She felt him look away from her.

"Fine," he said at last, his tone deliberate.

There was a pause.

"Your husband?" he asked.

The truth tensed painfully inside Laura's breast. How much it would mean to her tonight to unburden herself to Hal! But the faraway tone of his voice, and his pained demeanor, reminded her that a world separated them. She could not make it disappear with a few truthful words. What good would it do?

"Fine," she said. The word came out with a brief tremor of her lips, accompanied by a look she knew he saw, a look that gave away more than she would have wished.

"Children?" he asked, raising an eyebrow amicably.

She shook her head.

"Me neither," he said.

There was a long pause, after which, driven by some mutual inner desperation, they both spoke at once. They laughed at the accident, and lapsed into silence again, as though each was relieved not to have been heard.

"You look so good," he said at length. "I never thought you could look so good."

The caress in his words made her feel faint.

"Me, too," she said weakly, admiring the light that danced around his smile amid the dewy snowflakes.

"Happy?" he asked, genuinely hopeful that she would say yes.

Laura pondered the question. After all this time, and all that had happened, it was the most unanswerable question in the world.

She gave him a little shrug, confused and abashed. She said nothing.

He did not seem to notice her discomfiture. He was looking at her through eyes full of fascination, as though simply having her here was a joyful surprise that must silence all thoughts of unhappiness.

"I still walk around the house on my hands," he said, his old humor come to greet her as it did so long ago. "But I knock over more vases now. Maybe I'm getting old."

He looked away from her, into the gathering darkness.

"And I still swim," he said.

Oh, Hal . . .

Laura looked down into her lap, where the camera was cradled in her hands. The tears were coming to her eyes again, but she managed to hide them.

For a long moment neither of them said anything. She wondered if he regretted the cruelty of this chance meeting as much as she did—and if he was as grateful for it as she was.

"I come here all the time," he said. "Usually when it's getting dark, like now."

Laura's eyes opened wider as she realized how often the skein of their lives must have brought them within a few days, a few hours, of a meeting like this. For she had often paused to sit before this carousel during her walks through the Park.

Hal sighed. "I think of you, and of us . . ."

Don't say anything more. Please . . .

". . . and I dream that one day you'll be here," he added. "I'm afraid I'm still a boy at heart, Laura. Growing up was never my strong suit."

She watched one of the stubborn tears fall from her cheek to the hand holding the camera. Her strength was gone. She wanted to hate him for his words, but her heart was melting.

"Anyway," he said, "today my dream came true."

She looked up at him. The acquiescence in her eyes turned back the clock like magic. He had seen it that first day, on the boat in New York Bay, when she had leaned against him helpless as a child, and put her fate in his hands.

So he dared to speak now.

"Laura," he said, "shall I take you someplace where it's warm?"

She gazed at him with infinite sadness, infinite relief.

The darkness around them was luminous, tinted by the blue of fallen snow, as they stood up together and turned to leave the Park.

. . .

They went to a quiet place not so very different from the setting for their trysts years ago. But tonight their meeting was not of the world they had once known, or of any world to which their separate steps had taken them.

Their lovemaking was beyond pain or pleasure, for each touch was not only a celebration of the chance meeting that had brought them together after all this time, but also a goodbye, for they both knew that fate had allowed them to meet once more only for this farewell.

Laura gave all of herself, and knew that in this moment she had all of Hal that she would ever have, all that he had saved for her, all she could ever expect in this life. And as she held him to her breast, she felt that there was nothing more to be lost and that in this goodbye Hal belonged to her at last.

When it was over they lay for a long time in each other's arms, silent, as though an invisible law forbade all words between them. She felt his fingers graze her cheek and curl around her hands, over and over again, full of wonder and resignation.

After a while it became too painful to endure, for they both knew their parting was at hand, and these soft caresses were opening wounds that would soon be too deep to bear.

They sat up and began to dress. They did not look at each other. When Laura was finished she noticed her camera on the floor by the door. It seemed to beckon to her with a strange energy. She looked at Hal, who was dressed only in his slacks, still bare-chested.

"May I take your picture?" she asked.

Without a word he nodded, and stood waiting for her. She picked up the camera, came close to him, and took a picture of his face, framed by the hair their lovemaking had tousled, and by his bare shoulders.

She lowered the camera and looked into his eyes. Suddenly she felt gripped by a mortal dread.

"Maybe we shouldn't have," she said.

Hal shook his head. "No," he said. "It will be easier now. It was best."

"Do you think so?" she asked, her eyes full of pleading. For once she felt weak enough to lean on him, even though tonight she knew he was to slip through her fingers for good.

"I know so," he said, enfolding her in his arms. "If you promise to remember. If you won't forget . . ."

"Never."

Blinded by tears, she hugged him with all her might. He felt more solid, more beautiful in her arms than ever before, now that she knew she was letting him go. And the strange idea came to her that only the everyday things of this world are ours for the taking, only unimportant things are tame enough to belong to us. The things that are forever must escape our grasp—for it is we who belong to them, and not the reverse.

She stood back and watched him dress. The familiar flesh, with its handsome straight contours, and the wounds she had touched so tenderly, disappeared for the last time under his shirt. She watched him as though in a crystal ball as he stood before the mirror, ran a hand through his hair and knotted his tie.

He picked up his overcoat and came toward her. His eyes were tight with pain, but they rested on her with a last caress.

"Shall I go first?" he asked. "Perhaps it would be easier . . ."

She looked up at him beseechingly. She could not decide this.

"We'll go together, then," he said. "You and me."

He opened the door and held it for her. The cruelest world imaginable waited in that opening. But it was Hal, her Hal, holding out his hand to help her through it. And for this reason she knew it was a world she could still live in somehow.

I love you.

The words could not come out. For his sake, and hers, she held them in. But she gave them to him with her eyes, and saw them in his.

And that would have to be enough.

"Laura?" All at once he smiled, and his face was full of the boyish whimsy she had fallen in love with so long ago, the first day she met him. He was holding out his hand for all the world as though they were leaving for an exciting adventure, one that would never end.

She mustered a smile from somewhere in her breaking heart. She took his outstretched hand and squeezed it tight.

The door reared before her with Hal still silhouetted in its golden light.

Laura went through it.

XXVIII

IT WAS THE SIXTH OF JANUARY.

Laura was on the subway, heading downtown to the Village. She had left work twenty minutes ago, saying goodbye to Gail McLemore, the new manager who had taken Tim's place at Laura, Ltd. She was on her way to her new home, a spacious loft on West Street, far from the beaten track but with a skylight and huge windows that made it an ideal location for a photographer's studio.

It was Friday. Laura was going home to a new routine. She now divided her days equally between work at the office and photography at home or in the field. She was taking her first photography courses at the Parsons School of Design on Tuesday and Thursday evenings. On weekends she wandered far afield in search of pictures, often taking the train to Connecticut or New Jersey.

Laura's new life had come upon her suddenly, enforced by her own impulse to leave the past behind her. She had moved out of her Central Park West co-op and into the loft just after Christmas, and since then had been very gradually putting some order into the clutter of her possessions while struggling to keep her two careers going.

She was hovering on the edge of the biggest change of all, abandoning fashion design altogether to devote herself completely to photography. She had an unspoken understanding to this effect with her managers at Laura, Ltd., who were aware that a transition might soon take place that would allow the company to continue operating under its now-famous name, but without Laura at the helm.

Just before Christmas Laura had received a phone call from the associate editor of *Photography* magazine, who told her that her series of photographs of Alex, her young friend from the South Bronx, had been accepted for publication in the magazine in the spring. The editor was eager to see more of her work, and was amazed when she admitted she had never formally studied photography.

Laura had submitted the "Alex" series as a sort of throw-of-the-dice test of her talent. She had never expected them to be accepted by an organ as influential as *Photography*. But when they were she had felt something more than mere happiness. She realized that the slow metamorphosis that had been overtaking her life for the past several years was now complete. She could not hold on to her past any longer. It was time to move forward into the future. She intended to complete a degree at Parsons and become a professional photographer.

There was no other way for her.

Laura was in an excited mood as she climbed the stairs of the subway station to the street. The weekend stretched before her, with several photographic projects in the works in Manhattan and on Staten Island. And she had a large backlog of exposed film to develop and print at home. She could hardly wait to get there, make a hurried dinner, and get to work.

She walked quickly through the dusk, carrying her sketching portfolio and a new, smaller camera bag that doubled as a purse. It was a cold, slushy night, the sort of night that makes New Yorkers curse as they fight their way through the rush hour. But Laura was oblivious to everything except the task ahead of her.

She turned into the alley that led to her building. She was one of eight tenants in the ancient place—a piano factory twenty years ago, and now a cavernous shell in which the loft dwellers coped with the dust and poor insulation in order to enjoy the space and light of their apartments, and the magnificent view of the Hudson River. Laura liked the no-frills atmosphere of it all, for it made her feel free to throw herself into her new life without fear of getting her hands dirty.

There was an old, battered sedan stopped in the middle of the alley, and she had to edge around it to get to her door. The uneven pavement was full of puddles from the melting snow, so she had to step gingerly in order to avoid getting her feet soaked. Her keys were already in her hand.

She was so preoccupied by where she was going that what happened took her completely by surprise. Later she would curse herself for having been so off guard.

The front door of the car opened as she tried to inch past it, and she was seized by a powerful hand and dragged into the wide front seat before she could scream.

The door closed. A hand was over her mouth. She flung this way and that, trying ineffectually to call out. The portfolio and camera bag had fallen into the wet alley.

How she knew it was Tim she was not sure. He was wearing a sweater; she could feel the wool against her cheek. There was something strange and feral about the smell of him that was not the Tim she remembered. But she knew it was him anyway.

Her struggles were futile, because there was no one in the alley to hear her, the more so since the car's doors were shut. But she fought him all the more frantically, for she was consumed by a sudden anger at his intrusion into her life. She kicked at the dashboard, tried to bite his hand, flailed at him with all her strength.

But he was too strong. He grasped both her hands in one of his, and with the other stuffed a gag into her mouth. Then he tied a handkerchief around her head. His dexterity impressed her, but did not come as a surprise. He had always been good with his hands.

Despite her jerking movements he managed to bind her wrists together in front of her. Then he tied them to the door handle on the passenger's side. He reached down to tie her feet together, and attached them in turn to some sort of bar under the seat which she could not see.

She gazed helplessly out the window, her face below the edge where no one could see her. She saw only the roof of her building, and the wet snow falling from the dark sky. She heard Tim get out of the car to retrieve the fallen portfolio and camera bag. He threw them into the back seat, put the car in gear, and drove slowly through the alley.

Laura looked at his face for the first time. His jaw was set. He was driving carefully. His face looked familiar, but the expression in the handsome features was foreign to her. Despite the cold determination in his eyes, she sensed that he was in the grip of something beyond his will.

They drove through city streets illuminated by misty street lamps until they reached what Laura guessed was the FDR Drive. From the landmarks she could see through the window she understood that they were on their way north, toward Harlem and the Bronx.

As the car picked up speed Tim spoke.

"Don't be afraid," he said, his voice low and deliberate. "You're in no danger."

The gag in Laura's mouth made it impossible for her to answer him.

For a moment he paused, as though thinking through a prepared speech. Then he nodded to himself and began to speak.

"I've given this thing a lot of thought," he said, glancing from the road ahead to the rearview mirror. "And, Laura, I honestly don't think you can say you've done that. You acted in haste, and out of—emotion. You acted out of panic. In a sense, I don't blame you for that. You were confused and frightened. But you closed the door on things before you had all the facts. If there's one thing I've learned in business, it's that one has to be in possession of all the facts before one can make a judgment."

Again he nodded to himself, as though pleased with his reasoning. He did not look down at her, but kept his eyes on the road.

"You need to have . . . You have to have something to compare a thing to," he went on. "That's why I'm giving you this chance. You see, when you made your hasty decision, you were under the sway of a set of circumstances that were in effect at that moment, but might not be in effect—in effect tomorrow, or next week."

Underneath his somewhat stilted delivery Laura could hear something nervous and disjointed which made her even more afraid of him. There was an insane tension in him which his measured words were trying uncertainly to control.

"As I say, that's why I'm giving you this chance," he said. "This chance to go back to things as they were in the beginning. Once you've seen that, and refreshed your memory, you'll be able to compare it to —to what happened, and to compare the two things. You'll see where you went wrong—where we both went wrong—and you'll understand."

He glanced down at her for the first time. His eyes seemed glazed. He wasn't really seeing her. He was seeing a fantasy, a desperate dream concocted to turn back the clock and make his nightmares go away.

"Because that's all I ask, you see," he said. "That you understand. That you make the effort to understand. You see, that is where you let me down, Laura. You didn't even try to understand. You just ran out on me, ran out on our marriage, and surrounded yourself with an army to keep me away from you. You owed me more than that, Laura. You owed our marriage more of a chance than that."

He paused, as though satisfied with his own logic.

"Now, I know that mistakes were made on both sides," he said. "I was, and am, willing to understand, to forgive, to patch things up. I've made my mistakes; all I ask is a chance to correct them. But you wouldn't give me that chance. That was not fair of you, Laura."

He went on that way, in an increasingly rambling tone, as they sped north. Laura was glad she was gagged. It would have been senseless to try to argue him out of his logic, for he had long since convinced himself that he alone was right. And anything she might have said would probably have increased the anger inside him—an anger of which he was pitifully unaware—to the boiling point.

The uptown landmarks were gone now, and the night seemed darker. Sleet was dropping against the windshield in little sprays. The world was sinking into a sinister dewy blackness.

Keep calm, Laura told herself. *Just don't panic.*

She cursed the laxness of her precautions that had allowed him to abduct her at the threshold of her own home. But he had fooled her by laying low all this time. She had believed he had accepted their separation and started a new life of his own.

But what was happening now did not come as a complete surprise. Tim's stubbornness was perhaps the most important element of his character. He had not given up on her in all these months. She should have been forewarned by his last menacing words in Judge Tagliaferro's courtroom, and by the look of hatred in his eyes.

Perhaps, she mused, no precautions would have been enough. Tim was too resourceful a man to be put off forever. Sooner or later he would have got her alone in any case. What was saddest about this whole mess was the condition he was in. Laura's heart went out to him, for she realized that the violence he had subjected her to before their separation was only the beginning of a disintegration whose ravages were all too apparent in his face tonight. The old Tim was gone. The man behind the wheel of this car had lost his grip on reality.

But this thought did not comfort Laura. She knew that, wherever he was taking her, she would be in danger. He hated her with a passion that he himself did not understand. He did not know his own violence. The words he was mouthing now were like sparks sputtering from a damaged electrical wire containing millions of volts of lethal current.

"I never claimed to be perfect," he said. "But we had a marriage. A marriage is a sacred thing, Laura. You accepted the sacrament of the Catholic Church. Yet you ran out on me and left me alone. And my child . . . You ran out on my child, Laura. You conceived it, but you weren't a fit mother for it. But, you see, I've forgiven you for that. We'll try again. There is a higher law . . . You owe me a child. We owe each other a child. We'll start over, at the beginning. It will be different this time, you'll see. But just don't try to run out on me again, Laura. Because that was a big mistake. A big mistake . . ."

All at once despair eclipsed the rest of Laura's thoughts. She knew he blamed her for everything, and that his blame was the real heart of his feeling for her. There was no love in his words. Somehow, even at this late date, that hurt more than anything.

Why had she ever married him?

She looked back to their courtship and tried to see what had gone wrong with her at that moment. Tim had fooled her with his steady, thorough personality, a personality whose caution about the hostile outside world had been part and parcel of his fierce protectiveness of her.

She had thought he considered her an exception to his suspicions of the world. He had seemed so steadfast and kind in his devotion to her. But now she realized that his bitter distrust of the human race had never really spared her. The passage of time, and her own painful growth as a person, had given her eyes to see this, though it was far too late to do anything about it. She had not heeded the warning signs when she had the chance, because she needed him so desperately, and needed to be loved.

Now she understood, to her terrible chagrin, that something more fundamental, and more tragic, lay behind her disastrous decision to become Tim Riordan's wife. It was Hal. Had she not been mired in the unbearable grief of her loss of Hal, she would not have been weakened enough in her judgment to accept Tim. For she did not love him in the way a wife must love her husband. She had spent long years trying to deny that fact, but now she could escape it no longer.

And Tim, from the beginning, from the very night when he pushed his ring across the table to her in its seductive little box—Tim must have sensed the truth even then. He must have known he was getting her on the rebound. And he must have hated her for this. But he did not know himself well enough to see through his love to his own resentment.

The seeds of their destruction were in that box, in his offering it and in her accepting it. It should have fallen to Laura to prevent everything by refusing him. But she had not. In accepting his ring she had sealed the doom of the very marriage she was making possible.

And so, in a way, Tim was right about everything. She had entered into the grave covenant of marriage too lightly, without knowing her own heart. And when time and Tim's rage forced her to reap what she herself had sowed, she had tried to get rid of him too easily. Indeed, the minions of the law and of the courts were small protection against Tim now. She could not turn her back upon her past mistakes so blithely. She must be punished.

As the car hurtled into the night with her fashion portfolio and her camera bag dumped in the backseat, and her failed marriage clutching at her in the form of her stubborn, hateful husband, Laura felt as though all the threads of her life were twining together in a noose tied around her neck. How could she fight against such a fate?

So she closed her eyes, defeated, and waited for the car to reach its destination. What must be would be.

They pulled off the highway and began to lurch down dark, bumpy streets. Through the window Laura saw the roofs of old brownstones and row houses, then of factory buildings.

Soon there were no traffic lights. Then the buildings were unlit. Finally they came to a stop in a street that was entirely dark, without street lamps or traffic.

Tim turned off the car. He looked down at Laura.

"I want your word that you'll come quietly," he said. "As I've told you, you're in no danger. I won't hurt you. There's no one here to see us. I'm going to take off your gag, because no one will hear you even if you scream. When we get inside we can talk. All right?"

Laura nodded.

He unbound her hands and feet, and took off the gag. She sat up and looked out the window. The street was completely deserted, with old factories on either side. There were a handful of cars against the curbs, nearly all their tires flat.

Tim got the camera bag and portfolio from the backseat, stepped out of the car, and came around to the passenger side. He opened the door and helped Laura out. Her hands were numb, and she felt unsteady on her feet.

"All right, let's go," Tim said. He touched her elbow to point her toward a dark, massive building with ancient frosted glass windows, many of which were broken. Laura wondered what awaited her inside it. At the moment she was too resigned to feel fear. The pain and despair emanating from Tim had turned her soul to ice.

She heard him fumble in his pocket for keys as they approached a heavy metal door. He held her arm tightly as he turned the key in the lock.

As the door swung open a voice from inside the building surprised them both.

"You're under arrest, Tim. Let go of her and put both your hands behind your head."

Before Laura could recognize the voice Tim had curled his arm about her neck and pulled her back a pace.

"I'll break her neck," he said.

Laura felt the breath squeezed out of her by the terrible power of his muscles. She believed he might kill her. The darkness all around her, and the angry arm about her neck, might be the last things on earth she would experience.

But all at once there was a flurry of movement in the shadows. She heard the door banged back against its hinges, and another sound, which might have been a fist against human flesh. She felt herself released, and heard the weight of two bodies falling to the littered concrete walk before the door.

Detective Dan Aguirre burst from the interior of the doorway to strike Tim a hard blow across the face. In the instant Laura was released, the officer tackled Tim with an expert motion and pinned him to the ground.

Tim let out a roar and flung his body to left and right. Thanks to his enormous strength he was able to throw the detective off him. He scrambled to his feet, a bearlike silhouette in the shadows.

Aguirre was on his feet as well. "You have the right to remain silent," he said. "If you waive that right, anything you say can and will be used against you in a court of law. You have the right to an attorney . . ."

The two men circled each other slowly as he spoke. Laura saw Tim smile. It was a desperate, maniacal smile. Poised for battle, he did not try to run, but stood with his hands outstretched before the detective, who was nearly as tall as he, but much more slender.

"You have no authority over me," Tim said. "You're just one of her whores . . ."

Before he could finish the detective lunged forward and struck him a terrible blow to the stomach. As Tim doubled over he was hit again, this time squarely on the jaw. He staggered. The detective, quick as a cat, was behind him, pushing him hard to the ground. Laura watched in horror as he dug his knee into Tim's back and began putting handcuffs on him.

"No!" she heard herself cry out as blood from Tim's mouth flowed onto the wet pavement. "Don't hurt him. Please don't hurt him . . ."

Tears were flowing down her cheeks. She felt as though she were being torn apart inside. Her heart went out to Tim, who was looking up at her from his bound position, a twisted smile of triumph on his bloody lips. In his sick way he must believe he had proved his point, proved that she had allied the world to herself against him.

"If you cannot afford an attorney, one will be appointed for you . . ."
Detective Aguirre spoke through his own gasping breaths as he jerked
Tim to his feet and pushed him toward one of the nondescript cars lining
the street. Laura stood watching the scene in horror. She saw Tim forced
into the back of the car, his head pushed down by the officer.

A moment later Dan Aguirre was walking back up the sidewalk to
her. Though he was still out of breath, he had the same smooth pan-
therlike appearance she had noticed the first time she saw him, six
months ago. The dark skin of his face shone over the turtleneck sweater
he had on under his leather jacket. His mustache drooped about his lips,
making him look like some sort of nocturnal matador. In her previous
brief contacts with him she had been impressed above all by his calm
stillness, and had no inkling of the terrible predatory athleticism he had
just displayed. His physical presence frightened her.

"Are you all right?" he asked, picking up the camera bag and portfolio. "Do you need a doctor?"

She shook her head. He saw her tears and took her arm gently.

"It's all right now," he said. "It's all over. You have nothing to be
afraid of."

"I'm not afraid," she said in a colorless voice.

He looked at her and nodded. "I know," he said.

She glanced at the car, and back into the detective's eyes.

"How did you . . . ?" she asked. "After all this time . . ."

"I saw the way he looked at you in the courtroom that day," the
officer said. "I've been keeping my eye on him in my spare time. He
led me to you, Mrs. Riordan. He's been watching you for three
months." He nodded to the dark building. "I knew about this place. I
saw him pick you up tonight. I got here two minutes ahead of you."

Laura looked from his handsome features to the slumped form of her
husband in the backseat of the car. Her world reeled before her. All at
once she felt faint.

Dan Aguirre was still one step ahead of her. He caught her with a
strong arm before she could fall to the dirty pavement, and carried her
to the car.

A moment later, with Laura in the front seat and Tim manacled in
the back, they were on their way back to Manhattan.

XXIX

NBC News, January 20, 1959

"And will you to the best of your ability carry out the duties and respon-sibilities of your office as set forth in the rules of the United States Senate?"

"I will."

With those words Haydon Lancaster today became the junior Senator from the state of New York. In an off-year election that provided few surprises in congressional and gubernatorial races, Lancaster's improbable victory over Senate Appropriations Committee Chairman Amory Bose was the event of the season.

In unseating the most powerful Democrat in the Senate, Lancaster captured the public imagination as no other young political leader, with the possible exception of John Kennedy, has done in a generation.

Thus Lancaster's Senate inauguration today may signify more than the mere accession of one man to high public office. Lancaster may have written the first page of a history that many observers believe will not end until he himself is in the White House.

ON THE SCREEN was an image of Hal Lancaster completing the oath of office and acknowledging the cheers of the crowd assembled in the Senate Chamber.

Amory Bose sat in his private law office in Albany, watching the broadcast. His face was red. Despite the most expensive and dirty cam-paign he had run in his life, he had not succeeded in defeating Lancaster. Worse yet, in running as an independent he had garnered only 14 percent of the vote, to Lawrence Ingersoll's 21 percent.

To have polled even less than a Republican! And this on the heels of having lost his own party's nomination in the primary. No humiliation could be worse for a man of Bose's stature.

Bose stared at the television screen as his cigar burned unnoticed in his hand. Lancaster was smiling and waving to the crowd. To Bose it looked as though Lancaster was laughing at the destruction of an entire world—Amory Bose's Senate. Lancaster had not just won an election. He had slaughtered an era.

But his victory would be a Pyrrhic one, though he could not know it now. In making an enemy of Amory Bose he had lit the fuse of a bomb that would one day, when he least expected it, explode in the face of his own dreams.

Bose would see to that. He had not spent thirty hard years in politics without learning a thing or two about human nature and human weakness.

He would bide his time. He would assemble his ammunition carefully, lovingly. He would wait until the right moment, the moment when defeat would be as devastating to Lancaster as it had been to Bose in this election.

Then he would strike.

Enjoy it while it lasts, Lancaster, he thought. *Sow your wild oats. Enjoy yourself. Your day to reap the harvest is coming. And when it does, I'll be the one to break your heart.*

. . .

Hal = not Hall

Tess sat in the Senate Chamber watching Hal accept the oath of office. The entire room, from senators' desks to spectators' gallery, was full of love and congratulation for him. He was the prince who had slain the dragon, banishing the despot whose stranglehold on this body had been a scandal for more than a decade. With his arrival, and Amory Bose's departure, a more exciting and less fearful era seemed about to begin.

For Tess it was a special moment. Not only had she been instrumental in bringing this handsome young man to the first great triumph of his career. She had achieved a victory of her own whose enormity no one in this room could appreciate.

Yet, surprisingly, it was a victory that was perfectly visible at this moment to anyone who had eyes to see with.

For Tess was here, and Diana Lancaster was not.

Tess had pulled off the impossible. She had separated Hal from his wife, she had broken up America's sweethearts, without hurting Hal politically. Here he was, acccepting the oath of office, without Diana. The fine surgery by Tess that had made such a moment possible would never be known. It was for her alone to savor.

And Hal himself would never know the real truth. All he would ever feel was his relief at being free of Diana and of his unhappy marriage, free to breathe the clear air of a new future.

And, in time, Hal would decide that he needed a new wife. A wife he could trust, a wife whose steadfast love and support he could count on. For his mate he would choose a young, beautiful widow. Widows make good press for divorced politicians. A widow is cleansed by her own sorrow. More yet, a youthful widow can offer her fertility to a virile young leader without the taint of sexual scandal. She does not fit the role of a paramour who estranges a man from his wife.

Yes, when the time was right Hal would turn to Bess with his loneliness, his need, his hopes. And Bess would be there to gather him to her arms. But he would not turn to Bess out of mere expediency, for he would know that her attachment to him came from the depths of her sad young heart.

This was a possibility that Tess had not taken into her calculations when she first set her cap for Hal. The false personality she had created for herself as the soulful, melancholy Mrs. Winthrop Bond had come to life under Hal's smile, and become, somehow, a real woman who actually did love Hal with all of herself.

This was an odd turn of events that Tess viewed with a certain detached admiration. She had assumed many guises in her time, but none until now had possessed so much reality, and so much life and initiative of its own.

Indeed, Bess Bond, with her maternal protectiveness and fierce devotion to Hal, might win his heart in a way that the real Tess, a cold and empty huntress, never could have. And this fact contained food for thought, and perhaps for eventual worry.

But there was more. Tess did not doubt her ability to carry off her plans for Hal. She had never recoiled from a challenge in her life, and even the challenge of making Hal her husband, of scheming her way into the White House as First Lady, did not daunt her. She was born for success, because she was afraid of nothing and would stop at nothing.

No, Tess was not afraid of action, or of risk.

The only thing that gave her pause was the strange ferment going on inside her own heart over Hal.

Its terrible power had been shown to her on the night when Sybil, with the cruel instinct of an executioner, had planted the idea in her mind that ever since had continued to fester, turning slowly in the wound it had created.

He never cared for any of them.

Except one . . .

Had Tess's love for Hal been there already, like a potential energy of some strange sort which made her performance as Bess the more credible? Or had it been brought into being at one stroke by Sybil's quiet, triumphant words?

She did not know.

But in the echo of those words she had looked back to her first intimacy with Hal, and to all her trysts with him since, and she had come up against that strange something in his lovemaking, that peculiar absence or distance at the heart of his caresses, which seemed to prove that Sybil was right.

Which one?

Part of Tess wanted more than anything else in the world to know that answer. But another part wanted even more not to know. For Tess realized that such information could destroy her.

A woman can detach a man from anything. But removing another woman's image from his heart is another matter. That illness is inoperable. The successful surgery would kill him.

So, as certain as Tess was that she could conquer enough of Hal to make him her husband, just as certain was she that she would never possess all of him. Worse yet she knew that with each passing day she loved Hal with a bit more of herself. The remotest corners of cold emptiness that had remained intact inside her only a few months ago, before Sybil's fateful pronouncement, were now filled with the prohibited warmth of Hal, and with the agony of doubt that grew more painful with each of his caresses.

Which one?

Tess was a newcomer to love, a novice at suffering. Thus her surprise at the feelings inside her was equaled by her panic over the feelings that might be hiding inside Hal. More and more of her lived only for him. But the doubt inside her was a cancer that could not support life. And today, as she savored her triumph in the Senate Chamber, she knew all too well that her private torment went deeper than any victory.

Which one?

The words were a knell over her past and her future alike. She knew there was no silencing them now. Wherever she was going in her life, she must go there with Hal. And so the words would follow her.

Which one?

. . .

Sybil was sitting on the edge of the bed in the room she had rented in an expensive uptown hotel. The television set was turned on. The face of her handsome brother was on the screen. He was addressing a news conference in a press room of the Capitol, answering questions about his stunning victory over Amory Bose and his triumphant inauguration to the Senate.

One of the reporters had just asked the predictable question. What did the prospect of a career in the Senate mean to Hal?

Hal's face grew serious.

"Today is an important beginning for me," he said. "But it's also a beginning for all of us. The future is spread out before us, beckoning to us to be at our best as we prepare for it. But the future is an alien land. It doesn't follow today's rules. It will be populated by new people, people who no longer share our preoccupations of today, our old habits, our fears. These people will be our children and grandchildren."

He paused thoughtfully.

"The paradox we face," he said, "is that we can't know in advance what that future world will be like. The things that seem the darkest and most terrifying to us today may well be things our grandchildren will laugh about as ancient history. On the other hand, the decisions we make today will certainly affect the world those grandchildren live in, for good or ill. Therefore we must not allow the fears that haunt us today to force us into precipitate actions that will harm that future, which is not ours to live in."

There was another pause. Dozens of flashbulbs were popping in the press room, but the assembled reporters were respectfully silent, listening hard to what Hal was saying.

"Most of these worries of ours deserve to be just footnotes to history," he went on. "I think it's our responsibility to make sure that words like Suez, Quemoy, Matsu, Formosa, Congo, Dominican Republic, Laos, and Vietnam, go down in the history books as trouble spots that did not lead the world into war. We will need the precious combination of our strength, our patience, and above all our modesty to see that that happens. Fear is a dangerous counselor. If we listen to our wisdom instead of our fears, we may succeed in preserving a future in which our children will be able to think thoughts and dream dreams far beyond what we're capable of now. All I ask is the chance to be one of the men who gave of their best for the sake of those children."

Spontaneous applause erupted among the jaded reporters listening to Hal. They were accustomed to stereotyped sentiments and timeworn formulas from politicians. The freshness and thoughtfulness of Hal's words had touched them.

Sybil smiled wanly at the screen.

"Good old Prince Hal," she murmured aloud. "You still want the good guys to win, don't you?"

Even over the crude television transmission of the event she could feel the awe of the audience in the press room. They knew they were listening to something more than an ambitious politician. They were hearing the voice of a statesman.

Sybil studied the image on the screen. She had known Hal since he was a young boy, fighting to find an identity for himself amid the chaos and shallowness of the Lancaster blood. And now, even though something of that boy might have been lost along the way—after all, how can any person live on the earth without giving up those parts of himself for which the earth is not a fit habitat?—he had found in politics an outlet for his love, his idealism, and his crazy appetite for self-sacrifice.

No doubt his political destiny would be a great one. Maybe he would end up in the White House after all. How could the American people say no to that handsome face, and to the voice of compassion and maturity that was Hal's alone?

But that was in the future. And, as Hal put it so eloquently, the future is not for us.

Sybil looked at the screen. She knew that Diana was not at Hal's side today. And somewhere near him, she suspected, was Elizabeth Bond. In more ways than one a torch was being passed on this day.

With this thought Sybil got up to turn off the television. She approached it and bent close to her brother's image. The reporters were asking him further questions about the issues of the moment. She did not want to hear anymore.

Then, on an impulse, she changed her mind and left the set on.

The sound followed her as she walked into the bathroom. She turned on the bath water and began taking off her clothes. She folded her skirt and blouse carefully on the bed, then her slip. Finally she took off her bra and panties.

She took a long look at herself in the bathroom mirror as the tub filled up. As she watched, the flesh in the glass seemed to melt like warm wax, distorting the face like the grotesque images in a fun house mirror.

Now she looked into the eyes. How well she knew them! They had a dewy, drowned look to them, their clear blue surface like a reflection of sky on the surface of a muddy pool full of fetid growths and sinister creatures.

Well, she would look at them no more.

She gave the monster a little smile and opened her vanity case. Inside it she found a fresh pack of razor blades. She opened it, placed it on the edge of the tub, and got in.

The water was up to her collar bones as she sat back. It was too hot, but she did not feel it. With another faint smile she noted that the faucet dripped. Good, she mused. A little accompaniment. The irregular plopping of the world's decay, to join her own.

The bathroom door was open, so she could see the screen of the TV, a pale lidless eye flaunting Hal's image at her across the space of two rooms. The hollow voices of the reporters could be heard shouting over each other, full of their hunger for Hal's success, hoping to bite off a bit of it for themselves, at least long enough to hold their viewers until the next commercial.

And Hal was smiling, for all the world as though he did not mind being eaten alive by this predatory horde. So profound was his hope for mankind that he either did not see the horror all around him, or thought that it did not matter.

Prince Hal! A boy adrift in a man's ocean . . .

Sybil carefully removed one of the razor blades from the package. Holding it between two fingers, she leaned back in the hot water.

She found the largest vein in her right arm and drew the blade carefully along it, from the wrist upward.

Her first try was unsuccessful. The blood starting out along her forearm was clearly from a superficial cut.

She tried again, searching patiently for the vein, dissecting the flesh until she actually saw the vessel. It was slippery and hard to get a purchase on, but after a moment she succeeded.

When she opened it a huge rush of blood spilled out into the water. In fascination she watched the rhythmic plunging spasms of the stream as the heart pumped its liquid out.

"The things that seem darkest and most terrifying to us today may well be things our grandchildren will laugh about as ancient history . . ."

The words sloped brusquely downward before her mind's eye, as though dragged down a steep hill.

She knew that not much strength remained to her. She transferred the razor blade to her right hand and slashed hard at her left arm. This time she was not neat or careful, but merely plunged the razor in, digging and pushing until, to her relief, she saw the blood erupt again, unmistakably coming from the big vein.

Already she was feeling lightheaded.

She let the blade fall into the water, and carefully placed both her arms under the surface so that the flow of blood could not be impeded by clotting.

On the distant TV screen Hal was still smiling and answering questions. Sybil closed her eyes. She wanted to leave Hal in his absurd luminous box in the other world, and take her leave of him in peace.

But it was no good. He was not really in the other room. He was here in the water with her, giving her his old smile of reproach and encouragement, still trying to coax her from her unhappiness, even as the crimson current swirling about her began to suck her down.

His smile made her think twice. Was she making a mistake? Perhaps he needed her. Perhaps she should have stayed on the planet's surface after all, forsaking her cherished niche beneath it, in order to watch over him.

But the witch woke up. She hurried down to the cave. And when the prince turned around to look at her, the dragon bit him and pulled him down into the water and he died.

Where had those words come from? Though their source remained a mystery, their truth sounded familiar. All at once Sybil thought of her beloved swimming picture of Hal, which so eloquently captured his smile and the water flowing down his body like a fatal rain from unseen clouds. From the first moment she saw it, the picture had proved to her that Hal's destiny was not really of this world, no matter how hard he tried to pretend otherwise.

Were princes put on earth only to die for something better than the earth? Was that the paradox floating in this bloody water with her?

Of course, she mused. Hal had been a step ahead of her all the time, despite his apparent naiveté and her voracious cynicism. He chose to be a hero because he knew that heroes sacrifice themselves for something outside them. No wonder he could be so brave, and so tolerant of the shallow absurdities of politics. He knew he was not made to battle the stubborn earth for his own happiness, but to be a smile and a voice in which other people could find their hope.

Sybil thought of Stewart, of Mother and Dad, of poor Diana, of subtle, dangerous Bess whom Hal would probably marry soon—men were such fools!—and of the forgotten girl whom he had truly loved and given the best of himself to. What a comedy of errors!

All dragons come out the winners, she decided. The smile Hal wore for the public was part of the sham that was human hope itself. In order to believe in the future, we must turn our eyes away from the wet reptilian arms pulling us all under, ever downward toward the bottom of the darkest lake. And that was the hero's role, that circus sham, that high-wire act that turns all eyes toward heaven, and away from hell.

Say goodbye, Prince Hal . . .

All at once Sybil felt a new pain, a gathering spasm worse than anything she had suffered before. Her flesh was preparing to die, to give up the ghost. Her operation was a success. It was time for the patient to die.

A pity to be alone now, she thought idly. If Hal were here to hold her hand through this, it would be so much easier.

But it would have hurt him too much to see her go. He would have fought against her. And she had never really learned how to say no to him.

So it was better this way.

Say goodbye . . .

The red pool rose around her, waiting, hungry.

Sybil smiled as the water closed over her face.

. . .

Laura sat watching the final image of Hal on the television in her loft as the news conference ended. He was waving to his admirers, his eyes full of smiles for the masses who believed in him, but also touched by melancholy, as though part of him saw beneath this political ceremony to something deeper and more human than the world of statesmen can encompass.

Yet she knew that an important part of Hal was engaged in his political mission. In these years of fear and suspicion Hal's voice was the only one capable of the modesty, the humor, the love of mankind that could restrain his country from actions that might destroy the very future he spoke of so beautifully.

Laura did not notice the tears in her eyes as she turned off the television and stood gazing out the loft's windows at nothing. She felt only tenderness for Hal now. The pain of losing him had become so much a part of her heart that she no longer felt it as a loss.

She knew now that she had loved Hal with all of herself. She could accept the fact that he was gone, for she knew that her heart belonged to him, and would be with him wherever he went. It had taken their last meeting to plight that final troth, to give that last remnant. They had waited painful years for that final rendezvous, a tryst arranged by fate to allow them their goodbye and the memory of their love.

Laura had outgrown the illusion that love brings people together. Now she understood the painful irony of fate: that love sunders and separates, forcing those joined by it to watch each other recede along divergent paths chosen by capricious gods. But if love is deep enough, a kind of redemption comes from even such a loss. There is a joy in giving one's heart that needs no requital, when one has known a Hal, and belonged to him.

Laura had failed to learn this lesson in time to prevent her marriage to Tim, and the unhappiness of her marriage had been her punishment.

She had paid the price for committing the most tragic sin a woman can commit: marrying without love.

But now it was all over. Her love life was behind her, a closed book. Though she felt alone today, looking out these strange tall windows at a New York City she had never seen until a few weeks ago, there was a harmony inside her, a cleansing hollow around which she could still build a life. Her future remained for her to do with what she might.

She was standing there, feeling the wintry soul of the city flow into the room around her with the harsh light from the windows, when the telephone rang.

She moved without hurry to pick it up.

"Hello?"

"Mrs. Riordan? I'm glad I caught you in. This is Nurse Jacoby from Dr. Fried's office. You had a physical with the doctor on Monday, didn't you?"

"Yes, I did," Laura said. "There's nothing wrong, is there?"

"Not at all. But I do have some surprising news based on your results. I hope it will be good news . . ."

Laura felt a sudden presentiment that made her knees go weak. The phone trembled in her hand.

"Yes?" she asked. "What is it?"

"Well, you're pregnant, Mrs. Riordan," the voice said. "According to our calculations, it's been approximately four weeks. By this time in September you'll be having a baby."

BOOK FOUR

Pandora's Box

I

1964

Washington Post, April 12

LANCASTER AND ROCKEFELLER ON COLLISION COURSE

As the primary season approaches its halfway point, both parties are showing signs of confidence in their search for unbeatable candidates for President.

The assassination of John F. Kennedy has given the Republicans an opportunity to seize victory from the jaws of what had promised to be a Democratic dynasty. With Kennedy dead and Lyndon Johnson generally perceived as a caretaker president, the Republicans are eager to field a powerful candidate whose views will be acceptable to the majority of Americans.

That candidate would appear to be either Nelson Rockefeller, Governor of New York and influential Republican stalwart for many years, or Barry Goldwater, the ultra-conservative Arizona senator whose popularity among Republicans has increased greatly over the past few seasons.

The only handicap faced by Rockefeller, who easily won the crucial New Hampshire primary in March, appears to be his 1962 divorce from his first wife and his remarriage in 1963 to the former "Happy" Murphy. Rockefeller is plunging ahead despite this hurdle, convinced that his centrist views and vast governmental experience will carry him past Goldwater this summer and the Democratic nominee in November.

The big news on the Democratic side has come from an unexpected direction. Haydon Lancaster, Senator from New York since 1959 and a popular national figure since his early days in appointive office in the Eisenhower administration, has won five of the seven primaries to date, with handy victories over opponents Johnson, Hubert Humphrey, and Robert Kennedy.

Lancaster, a respected senator and author of several important bills in domestic and foreign policy, is something of a political curiosity. Though a dedicated liberal Democrat on domestic issues (he was making an eloquent plea for Kennedy's Civil Rights bill on the Senate floor the afternoon Kennedy was shot in Dallas), he has been unafraid to separate himself from the party's hard-line anti-Communist foreign policy, and has been an outspoken critic of the intervention in Vietnam.

Lancaster does not shrink from public expressions of his admiration for Dwight Eisenhower's restraint in foreign policy, and this has got him into not a little hot water with both parties. Centrist Democrats suspect him of being a Republican in Democratic clothing, while hard-liners of both parties see him as being soft on Communism. Several conservative critics have predicted that it would be impossible for Lancaster to work as President with either Congress or the Pentagon because of his controversial views on major issues such as Vietnam.

Lancaster's energetic supporters see him as a tailor-made replacement for the slain Kennedy. Like Kennedy, Lancaster is young, handsome, charming, and a brilliant speaker. Like Kennedy, he is a war hero, though Lancaster's Medal of Honor for almost inhuman bravery in Korea far overshadows Kennedy's PT 109 exploit in World War II. Like Kennedy, Lancaster comes from a wealthy and influential family—though the Lancasters, old-money Republicans, can hardly be compared to the self-made Irish Kennedy clan of politicians.

Interestingly, Lancaster's chief political weakness is identical to that of Rockefeller: he is divorced, and has a second wife, the former Mrs. Winthrop Bond IV. Given the public appeal of his earlier marriage to Diana Stallworth, it would seem that Lancaster's divorce would hurt him seriously with the voters. But the primaries so far tell a different story. Mrs. Bess Lancaster has been an attractive and eloquent campaigner for her husband. Observers are speculating that Kennedy's election as the first Catholic President may have loosened public attitudes. The American people seem to have no quarrel with the notion of choosing between a divorced Rockefeller and a divorced Lancaster in November.

The battle promises to be hard-fought and exciting. It pits either Rockefeller or Goldwater, who both have powerful organizations, against youthful, statesmanlike "Hal" Lancaster, a war hero whose controversial political positions and marital history seem only to add to his glamor. The Republicans feel that their chance to wrest the White House from the Democrats has come earlier than expected. But Lancaster, who seems the favorite to take the remaining primaries by storm, and carries a luster equal if not superior to that of JFK, could well enter the lists as the most daunting enemy the Republicans have faced in many a year.

Unless something happens, and soon, to tarnish Lancaster's shining armor.

II

THE MUSEUM OF MODERN ART
PROUDLY ANNOUNCES
AN EXHIBITION OF PHOTOGRAPHS BY
LAURA BLAKE
"PANDORA'S BOX"
APRIL 15–JULY 1, 1964

"PEEK-A-BOO. I see you."

She was standing in the doorway, outlined by the light from the hall that made a halo about her slender body. The image was golden and warm, the dark silhouette of the face adding to its charm.

The boy giggled and squirmed under his covers. Somehow he could feel her smile brightening as she took a pace toward him. Her humor seemed to reach out and tickle him from across the room, even as her warmth caressed him despite the distance between them.

The poster was on the wall outside the door, a new addition to their home. He knew it meant something important to his mother, for she had taken him excitedly to the museum to show him the three large rooms filled with her photographs. The pictures themselves were like old friends to him, for he had lived with them almost since he could remember. But in the museum they were blown up to enormous sizes, and looked almost scary as they hung in the silent galleries.

She was still coming slowly forward. It was like this every night. First there was the delicious waiting as he heard the muted sounds of her movements in the living room, or the closing of a cupboard in the kitchen. Then the wonderful anticipation as her steps came closer in the hall. And finally this headlong stream of warmth, an intoxicating bath of love, as she came into the room to take him in her arms.

"Ready for pleasant dreams?" she asked.

He nodded.

She came to his side. As she did so her shadow mingled with the glowing image thrown onto the ceiling by the night-light beside his bed.

She had painted it herself a long time ago, before his memory began. It showed the smiling face of a curious little elf, whom they had decided after numerous consultations to call Felix. The face was cheery and mischievous when looked at directly on its glass globe, but somewhat sinister when projected in hues of purple, red, and green all over the ceiling.

Since he was still young enough to be afraid of monsters, he had been uncertain about Felix in the beginning.

"You mustn't be scared of Felix," she had told him. "For one thing, he'll scare off any monsters who might want to come into your room. Monsters are terrified of elves. And for another thing, you'll hurt his feelings if he thinks you don't like him."

So he had come to love the grinning little face that was transformed by the projected light into a huge luminous mask of glee. And when his mother came into the room at night, familiar Felix would adjust his ceilinged form to her own shadow, just as she joined a bit of her essence to his in passing close to him.

Now she sat on the bed by his side. He heard the soft swish of her skirt, and felt her weight on the mattress, pulling the bed down toward her in a little slope. Every night he would feel that gentle incline drawing him closer to her while she said goodnight. It seemed a bit uncomfortable at first; but then he forgot it as the wonder of being so close to her eclipsed all else.

When she would get up to leave, the bed would spring up again, so that he was level—but alone. And for a moment he would miss the incline that was part of her approach, that way of pulling the world down so that he tumbled joyously toward her. Then sleep would come, and he would forget the whole lovely process until the next night. And even his forgetting was part of the routine that made his days so sweetly similar to one another.

"Well, now," she said, taking one of his hands in her own while with the other she caressed his hair. "Has your day been a good one?"

He nodded. "I liked my picture."

"So did I."

He had painted a portrait of her in his preschool art class. It was hanging on the refrigerator now, having supplanted his previous painting, for which she had found a new place among her photographs on the walls of the loft.

It had been a very typical day. She had been up long before him, doing her darkroom work so as to be free to chat with him over breakfast. She had bundled him up warmly, for the chill in the outside air was still wintry, and walked him to school before noon. She had then spent her day at the Museum of Modern Art, preparing for her show with the museum's exhibitions staff, and had been at school to pick the boy up at two-thirty.

She tried hard to organize her busy life so that she could be with him as much as possible. She found it physically painful to be separated from him by work. She always did her darkroom and printing work after he was asleep or before he woke up. She took him everywhere with her. Most of her photographic subjects, however unconventional their own lives, were friends of his now, and looked forward to seeing him, giving him little gifts and hugs and kisses.

They were no more able to resist his charm than she was. There was a sweet mildness about him, combined with traces of gentle humor and an almost saintly understanding, that stole everyone's heart. His soft skin and handsome features, his fine black hair and grave little eyes, were full of a childlike introspection that was irresistible.

His name was Michael. How she had settled on it during her solitary months of pregnancy, when her world was topsy-turvy as she prepared for a new career as well as a baby, she never quite knew. It had simply come, with its odd poetry and its masculine depth: Michael. It was not a name she associated with anything or anyone—but she knew somehow that it would be perfect for her baby. Just as she knew, somehow, that the baby would be a boy.

"And what will you dream about tonight?" she asked, holding his hand.

He looked thoughtful. "About Alfalfa," he said.

Alfalfa was his imaginary friend and alter ego, a mischievous imp who broke every rule of good behavior and was constantly in trouble, for he was entirely made up of the infantile egoism and naughtiness that Michael, a naturally quiet and diplomatic child, hid in himself. Michael's few transgressions around the house were often blamed on Alfalfa, who did not know any better.

"When you dream about Alfalfa," Laura said, "please tell him we forgive him for breaking that glass in the kitchen. We haven't seen him for two whole days now. I think he feels bad about breaking the glass, but he's too stubborn to admit it, so he's hiding. Don't you?"

"Yes." His soft-spoken manner charmed her, as always. He was a boy of few words. His eyes most often told the story of what he was thinking and feeling.

"Well," she said. "I see a delicious-looking pair of lips. Who's going to get a goodnight kiss from them?"

He raised a humorous eyebrow to tease her.

"What?" she asked, feigning a stricken look. "You mean I have to go to bed without a goodnight kiss? I won't be able to sleep a wink."

He touched his lips with a smile.

Laura bent to kiss him. When she felt his lips on her own she closed her eyes and, as every night, something deep inside her stirred almost painfully. It was so beautiful to feel the utter intimacy of his love and trust. Yet it hurt to realize that because their existence was bounded by time, she could have this Michael, the Michael of this precious moment, only for tonight.

Tomorrow a new little boy, a day older, a day braver and smarter and more independent, would greet her. So that in having him tonight she was also losing him, and in giving him her love she was also arming him to slip away into his own future. This knowledge filled her with a strange ache of longing and delight that almost made her sigh out loud when she embraced him.

She had to force her feelings down beneath her calm surface, to smile and rumple his hair and take her leave, for all the world as though their soft little moment at day's end were eternal, as though this life they had together would never change.

"I love you," she said. "Have a good sleep, now. And pleasant dreams."

"Goodnight, Mommy. I love you." He hugged her and, with a gesture that was peculiar to him, let his fingers run along her arm to the palm of her hand as she released him.

She saw him watching her as she paused at the doorway to blow him another kiss. She left the door ajar. She could see the dim projection from the nightlight across the ceiling as she turned away.

. . .

Mommy.

As she went into the loft's living room the word echoed inside her, still pronounced by his lips. It was the most wonderful word in the world, and it sang through the sweet agony that owned her heart when she had to leave his side.

At this moment each night she reluctantly tore herself away from her absorption in her love for him, and turned back to thoughts of her professional life.

The entire loft was full of photographs, pinned to cork supports on all the walls. Some were experimental shots that Laura wanted to live with for several weeks at a time in order to decide how important they were to her. Others had long since become part of her personal canon, and were included in the show at the Museum of Modern Art. And many were of Michael.

For Michael was part of the show as well.

It had taken Laura three and a half years to complete the photography program at Parsons after leaving Laura, Ltd. By the time she was halfway through the difficult curriculum she had sold photographs to most of the major photography magazines, won two international prizes for her work, and been recognized by the faculty and her awed fellow students as the greatest prodigy in the history of the school.

The riot of attention her work attracted left Laura more than a little unnerved, for photography had always had a private and even forbidden aspect to her. She had never expected anyone else to welcome her work or approve of it.

Yet she knew her pictures were important. She never doubted it. If she felt far less than important as a person, she knew the faces she put on celluloid told a crucial story, and possessed truths that could come into the world only through themselves.

This knowledge did not make Laura feel brilliant, or even particularly confident. Instead it filled her with a mixture of relief and lingering anxiety, as though she had almost lost her chance to capture those images, and been just lucky enough to snap them before they disappeared. She never felt herself equal to the truths they told—but she felt a sense of responsibility to them, for they showed themselves to no other photographer. And, as a consequence, her work was instantly recognizable wherever it was shown.

Since the camera's magic enforced a profound modesty on her, Laura never dreamed of letting her growing celebrity go to her head. Instead she approached her craft as a humble artisan. She devoted herself to her demanding technical courses at Parsons, and resolved to make her living as a photographer. She put most of her residual income from Laura, Ltd., into a trust fund for Michael, and lived modestly with him on the money she made from selling pictures.

She did free-lance work of all kinds, from portraits to weddings to industrial photography, commercial photography, and even fashion work. The latter sometimes brought her into contact with old friends who were still nonplussed by her having abandoned her brilliant career as a designer.

And in what time remained to her she took thousands of pictures of her favorite subjects, people who haunted the margins of society, and who, in their loneliness, their endurance, and even their self-deceptions, spoke somehow to her heart and came to share a portion of her soul. The painfully intimate close-ups she took of these key faces formed her artistic oeuvre, whose fame had already spread so far that the Museum of Modern Art had done her the high honor of offering her a one-woman show this spring.

It was nearly three years ago that the separate paths represented by her love for her little boy and her devotion to the camera had crossed.

Of course she had taken hundreds of baby pictures of Michael. But these were merely snapshots to document his growth. Somehow Michael and her camera's artistic eye remained on different wavelengths. When she took pictures of him she was a proud mother, and not an artist.

Then one day she felt an odd tingle in her fingers when she trained the lens on him. The camera seemed to want to take a serious photograph of him, but to warn her at the same time against doing so. She tried to resist the temptation, and gave up. She brought the camera close to his little face, spoke to him in gentle murmurs to open him up to the lens, and, with a little furtive thrill, took her first "real" pictures of him.

What a chill she felt as she developed those first images! Thanks to his closeness with the woman behind the lens, Michael allowed the camera to see directly into his youthful soul. For the first time Laura saw things about him that she had never really seen with her loving maternal eye alone—a seriousness, a melancholy, and a mysterious individuality that left her in awe.

Despite the touching innocence of the boy's youth, there was something in the pictures more grave than even adulthood could bear witness to. Something Laura would have been tempted to call fate, if that word did not frighten her too much when applied to Michael.

Michael had been one and a half years old that day. In the years since then Laura had taken thousands of pictures of him. She set aside special times for their work together, and called the camera "Poppy" to humanize it for him, and to make him respect it as a separate power of vision, and not merely an extension of herself.

By the time the Museum of Modern Art made its offer of an exhibition, there was no doubt in her mind that Michael must play a key role in the show.

After careful thought Laura divided her photographs into three groups, each one to occupy one of the three rooms set aside for the exhibition. The first group embodied the most important of the pictures with which Laura had begun her career. It included the pictures of Penny Heyward and her pregnancy, Laura's first real photographic essay. It also included the now-famous "Alex" series, which was part of the permanent collection of the George Eastman House in Rochester, and would come to the Museum of Modern Art on loan for the exhibit.

The theme of this room would be the past. Penny's modeling career was just a memory. She had two children, and was a housewife in Connecticut. Alex, tragically but not unpredictably, was dead now, a victim of gang warfare in the South Bronx.

The second room represented the present, and encompassed a selection of Laura's current subjects, including anonymous poor people and a handful of famous public figures who had either asked her to photograph them or been assigned to her by one or another magazine for which she did free-lance work. This room showed the play of light and shadow, space and time, mask and reality in the faces of human beings caught between what they wanted to be and what the world was making out of them.

The third room would be all for Michael—identified only as "Boy" in the pictures—and embodied the future itself, as it shone in the camera's attention to the spontaneous beauty of youth. Laura could not help feeling that this room was the most important. For photography, in her mind, was like motherhood. With her camera Laura captured fleeting images for eternity, and in so doing confirmed their fugitive reality— just as her love for Michael confirmed the fact that she could not keep him forever as he was now, but must let him go with each of her kisses, send him into his separate existence with all her love.

Yet, loss was at the heart of photography, and so was death—because pictures of people survived not only after the people were altered by time, but even after they had vanished altogether from the earth. Photography documented an inevitable loss, for even as the human creature offered his image to the camera, he was borne away into a fate where the camera could never follow. For the camera's eye could not see into passing time, future time, but was only expert—yet, oh, how expert!— at the instant, the fleeting, the momentary.

"If the photographic image weren't fugitive," Laura had once told an interviewer for an Italian photography journal, "it wouldn't contain any truth. I don't know how I know this, but I do." Yet if photography was about loss, it was also, quintessentially, about love—at least for Laura. She tried to let her subjects into her heart, and to give of herself to them just as she gave all her heart to Michael in the knowledge that he must nevertheless slip through her fingers into his own future.

And if it seemed somehow a sacrilege, a transgression, to duplicate this intimate relationship through the camera by seizing the transitory beauty of her boy, she must do it anyway. For she used the camera as an act of love. This was her art, and also her life.

So, despite her inclination to keep Michael only for herself, she had decided to show his pictures to strangers.

Her show was entitled *Pandora's Box*. The words had come to her from nowhere one day as a title for one of her best pictures of Michael, and had stuck in her mind with such stubbornness that she finally decided they must stand for her whole exhibition and perhaps for all her photography.

She could not help worrying that in going public at the Museum of Modern Art with the most private core of her vision she was somehow showing too much. Part of her was afraid that her work would be ridiculed. A deeper part felt that she perhaps had no right to show something as intimate as what emerged from herself and her subjects in her pictures.

Nevertheless it was with an electric sense of anticipation that Laura watched the last days pass before the show opened. She could hardly wait to see the museum open its huge doors to curious spectators wandering through the rooms where the pictures taken from her own heart, enormously blown up, would stare down at them in all their nakedness.

And above all she wanted to be there when those strangers entered the third room, the precious inner sanctum, where Michael was shown.

III

April 15, 1964

THE HOTEL ROOM was in shadow.

Only the pale blue eye of the television set illuminated the place. On the screen were images of Hal smiling and waving to cheering crowds. A network commentator's voice could be heard describing the primary campaign.

"Haydon Lancaster continued his odyssey through the Midwest today," the commentator said, "taking his message of internationalism and peace based on economic and military strength to an obviously admiring public. The man who has been called 'Prince Hal' by close friends and family looked like a prince indeed on the campaign trail. His attractiveness and humor, combined with the eloquence of his speeches, seem a combination that his Democratic opponents will have a hard time beating. He has already won five primaries, and the Lancaster juggernaut shows no signs of slowing down.''

Tess lay naked under her silk nightgown. She nodded to herself as the report came to an end. The commentator had done his job well.

Tess's subtle endeavors on behalf of Hal with the networks—a handshake arrangement with no traces left behind—had ensured that the news departments would treat him kindly. So far the strategy had worked. The negative points of Hal's divorce and remarriage, combined with his controversial views on foreign policy, had been played down. The video portion of the nightly broadcasts showed generous views of his handsome face, his charm, the warmth of his contact with large crowds—and stressed his success.

The people at the networks owed Tess a lot of favors. And she had called them in for this campaign. She could confidently look forward to good press for Hal from all three networks throughout the primaries and—knock wood—the general election. It was in the bag.

Hal, of course, would never know how much she had done for him behind the scenes. There was no reason for him to know. Hal's job was to be the best candidate, the best future leader of the American people. Tess's job was to get him into the White House.

The time was clearly right. Lyndon Johnson, a caretaker in the Oval Office, was ready to pass the reins to someone else. Neither Robert Kennedy nor Hubert Humphrey was a match for Hal—the primaries had already shown that. Meanwhile Rockefeller and Goldwater would cancel each other out in the Republican race. The winner would emerge from the San Francisco convention at the head of a hopelessly divided party.

Hal was the man of the hour, the man of destiny. All he had to do from today on was avoid needless campaign blunders, and the White House was his.

The broadcast was over. Tess turned off the television and lay back in the darkness. She was exhausted from her campaigning of the last week —speeches every day, sometimes two and three major appearances, not to mention dozens of press interviews in airports, on planes, and in TV studios. She had not had a decent night's sleep in weeks. Were it not for the anticipation thrilling through her senses at this moment, she would have drifted off into welcome slumber.

The bedside clock showed ten-twenty. It could not be long now . . .

The phone rang. Tess picked it up hurriedly.

"Hello?"

"It's me. Where are you?" The voice was male, deep and caressing.

"Six-twenty-two." She looked at the key on the table beside her.

There was a pause. The voice on the other end of the line was silent. She wondered if he had heard the hunger in her voice.

"See you in a minute."

She hung up, got out of bed to unlock the door, took off her nightgown, and lay back naked in the darkness. Her body was tense with wanting.

The seconds passed like hours. She heard steps in the corridor, sat up as they approached, and then breathed a pained sigh as they died away.

Hurry. She was tingling all over. She could not stand this much longer.

At last more steps approached the door. There was a pause. Then she heard a tiny knock, just the tapping of a fingertip against the door.

She said nothing. The door opened slowly, just enough to reveal the tall figure coming through it, his overcoat on his arm, a small suitcase in his hand.

Neither of them said a word. Darkness settled again as the door closed. She lay back, gazing up at the ceiling, a smile on her lips. She could feel him moving toward the head of the bed.

He stood there, invisible, looking down at her. Then he removed his jacket and threw it on the chair by the vanity. She could see the white form of his shirt like a pale ghost in the shadows.

Her breath caught in her throat as she heard the soft rustle of his clothes coming off. The emptiness inside her coiled to a painful throb of intensity. Not only was her sex on fire—her whole womanhood was enslaved to this moment.

At last she could see that he was naked. He stepped forward, touched the edge of the bed, and bent over her.

She felt his tongue slip into her mouth at the same instant that a warm hand cupped her breast. The kiss deepened slowly, sensually, as his fingers ran down her stomach and paused at her thighs. He caressed the creamy curves, enjoying the feel of her nudity in his own senses, and then spread her legs with a gentle hand. He heard her gasp as he touched the center of her.

She pulled him closer. He knew she could not stand for him to wait. So hot was her desire that, the first time, she liked it all in one rush. So he knelt over her, his hands stroking her cheeks and shoulders and breasts with a strange knowing softness, and slowly came closer until the tip of him probed at the center of her.

A half inch, then an inch—and her moans told him to hurry, to come deeper. He poised himself cautiously, always gentle—for that was the key to his sexiness, that slow delicate touch—and the long man's sex slid smoothly inside her to the hilt.

"Oh!" she cried, a little girl helpless against his wiles. Her body tensed madly against the careful shaft, and he felt the tremor of hot female sinews giving him their first orgasm, and singing to him of their hunger for more.

Her legs were around his waist now, pulling him deeper and deeper as her hands caressed his thighs. The lovely rod did not move, but remained buried in the quick of her, awaiting her sign to begin its slow strokes.

"Oh, my baby," she moaned. "Oh, I've missed you so."

She felt his kiss against her cheek. Their bodies were locked in an embrace so urgent, so tight, that she thought she might faint from the sheer intimacy of it.

"Darling," she whimpered. "Please, more . . ."

He began to move inside her. The mystical staff moved in and out, in and out, its rhythm slow and steady, but somehow more sensual, more knowing with each thrust. And she trembled and shook and begged and murmured, her fingers all over him, her lips kissing his cheeks and mouth and eyes, orgasm after orgasm buffeting her as a tremor beneath the earth shakes tallest buildings at the surface.

Soon his own need began to thrust her to the last terrible heights. Her little cries surrounded him, helpless and panicked and delighted. The moment expanded dizzyingly, the slow hot penis working inside her as she gave her creamy flesh like a spellbound female slave, all thought giving way to wild pleasure inside her mind, all care for herself dissolved in the impossible ecstasy he was giving her.

At last it came, the lovely white stream that leapt inside her like a fountain of youth, gracing her most secret place with its hot mystery. An eerie moan sang in her throat as she gave herself.

When it was over she lay limp and genuinely faint, still clinging to the hard sex with all her sinews, kissing his lips and holding him close as her thighs caressed the straight contours of his waist.

And now, only now that the first time was over, and the sharpest ache of her need for him was slaked, did she say his name.

"Hal . . ." The murmur came out of her depths. "I love you so . . ."

For an answer he cradled her warmly in his arms and kissed her again. The whole sweet length of him seemed dedicated to her comfort, her pleasure.

But she needed something more.

"Say it." She smiled against his cheek, her finger touching his lips.

There was a pause.

"I love you, too, Bess," he said.

"Ah . . ." A little shudder went through her. The sound of those precious words brought its own response, a last tiny spasm of female satisfaction.

With her eyes closed in grateful bliss, Tess lay in her husband's arms.

If only it were that simple.

They met on the run these days, the opportunities for their trysts enforced by the pace of the campaign. They would take separate planes to the nearest point available by direct flight from their respective locations. They would have a quick dinner, if there was time; some conversation about the campaign, full of guarded optimism and careful planning for the coming week. A bit of banter about Washington gossip, Lancaster gossip, just to take their minds off their shared obsession—and, of course, lovemaking.

On the surface it seemed the vibrant if tiring life of a politician running for very high office, and the wife he loved and depended on. When Bess and Hal were apart, they called each other at least once a day. The ups and downs of the campaign brought them closer together. When they could steal a moment of privacy, their pent-up need for each other joined the affection of their four-year marriage to make them eager lovers.

If only it were that simple!

After a few more moments in Hal's arms, Tess watched him put his clothes on. Reluctantly she slipped from the bed and joined him. They went downstairs for a drink and a late dinner. Then they returned to the room and made beautiful love together, savoring in slow motion the pleasures that had overtaken them so suddenly when he first arrived.

When it was over, Hal fell asleep in her arms, and she lay cradling him like a mother, listening to the sounds of him breathing, and imagining the unseen dream thoughts that might be occupying his mind. How tired he was from this draining campaign! But he was a strong man, and a balanced one. He was able to withstand the pressure, keep his sense of humor, and be a good husband to her.

After a while she slipped away from him and padded on bare feet to the bathroom. She opened her vanity case, found a bottle of Nembutal, and shook a 100-milligram capsule into her hand. She paused, looked down at the pill, and then shook out another one. She swallowed them both with a glass of water from the bathroom tap and returned to her husband's side. He had not noticed her departure. Exhausted sleep made him oblivious to everything around him.

Tess knew she would not sleep well tonight. Sleep came less and less easily to her nowadays. She feared that soon the Nembutal would go the way of the Seconal and Miltown and the others before it, the drug's powers incapable of combating the emotions that kept her awake into the dark hours.

She looked at Hal with a pained smile. He was such a wonderful husband. He treated Bess with the sincerest of affection and regard. More yet, his eyes lit up when she came into view. He entrusted something precious of himself to her, in his laughter, his hugs, his little endearments, the sly practical jokes he occasionally played on her— and above all in his trust in her judgment and her absolute loyalty to him.

Yes, Hal gave her something of himself.

But he did not give all.

Tess knew that there was something about her that he genuinely loved. Something that made him feel safe and loved and protected and even happy.

But was it all of her?

Was it, indeed, her at all?

The dilemma that had her in its horns had been in force the day she married Hal. And in the years since, it had grown ever more painful without becoming any clearer or easier to understand.

She only knew that her ever-increasing need for Hal was indistinguishable from a kind of private torture that his charm and sweetness made worse instead of better.

When she had first set her sights on Hal, she had never dreamed she might fall in love with him. In fact, she was so sure she could never love any man that she would have staked her brilliant mind and her highest ambitions on that proposition.

But Hal had got under her skin. Was it simply the fact that he was, in himself, so very lovable? He was indeed, as his nickname suggested, a prince. No woman could fail to feel the seductions of his nobility as a person, seductions which became irresistible when allied with the beauty of his perfect man's body.

Or was it the terrible malediction which mad Sybil had announced on the day of Hal's election to the Senate that had somehow catalyzed Tess's cold heart into life, and placed the image of Hal at its center like a fatal disease? The curse that Sybil left behind her as she went to her grave . . .

Except one.

Only one.

Tonight, when Hal gave his seed to his loyal wife of four years—a wife whose body, thanks to her youth but also to her childlessness, still had the perfect nubile contours of a maiden—the sensuality of his touch was the same as it had always been. It was a kind and husbandly giving of himself, full of his desire to bring pleasure to his wife.

But there was still that mysterious absence, as though part of him were not there, or as though in the deepest part of Tess he was missing the mark, giving himself to something outside her, and missing what she tried with all her heart to give him.

It was clear that he did his best to hide that little absence, that little mystery, and to reduce it to a minimal undertone of his love that his wife would not notice. But she noticed it all the more. And it proved to her over and over again that Sybil's dart had struck home, that there had been someone else. Tess, a master at interpreting the subtleties of men's need, could not fail to sense the truth. Sybil had not been bluffing. Sybil, from beyond the grave, was still turning the knife in the wound.

For five years Tess had spent her life in three quests. The first, of course, was to prepare Hal for the White House. She was on the verge of seeing this plan through to success.

The second was to give him a child. Here she had failed miserably. They had been trying since the day they got married. She had consulted the finest gynecologists in Europe and America. She had dared to experiment with fertility drugs prescribed by experts. She had agonized day after day, night after night, about the contraceptive measures she had used during her previous marriages, and whether they had upset her reproductive system somehow.

Nothing worked. And with each passing month she saw that the disappointment Hal hid from her so bravely was taking its toll on his happiness. Though he tried to shrug off the problem, Tess realized full well that he wanted children far more than he wanted political distinction. His childlessness with Diana had been a crucial factor undermining his marriage to her. And when he had married Bess he had been confident that children were in the offing. But no, the curse was upon him again. For Bess did not seem to be able to get pregnant.

Tess's third quest was to make Hal love her.

The idea would have seemed absurd to an outside observer. After all, she had made her conquest, wrested him from his former wife, and indeed had so much of him that one might wonder why she would want more.

But the irony of her quest did not make it any the less serious. Deadly serious, in fact.

For Tess was in love with Hal. Not as loyal, melancholy Bess, or as girlish Lisa Bond, or as feline, sensual Liz Benedict, or as any of the other alter egos she had found it convenient to use in her life—but as Tess herself. And she wanted more than anything else to be loved by Hal for herself, and not for the mask she had created in order to hook him.

But this was impossible. Hal had married a subtle impostor. It was loyal Bess, the motherly young widow, to whom he had given his confidence and finally his hand in marriage. He knew nothing of the real woman behind this mask. And as for Tess, whose predatory life had required that disguise be her constant armor against the world, she knew even less about her true self than did her husband. For she had been too busy making conquests all her life to bother building a real personality of her own, with strengths and weaknesses like those of any normal human being.

So she faced the tragic dilemma of being forced to hide behind her mask even as she cursed it for standing between herself and her husband. She dreamed schoolgirl dreams of being caressed and wanted by her Prince Charming for who she really was, when all the while she knew that she herself would no more wish to confront her real face than Dorian Gray would want to look at the sins he had kept in his attic through so many evil years.

Such was her disarray that Tess was not sure of anything anymore. She wondered whether her mask was cracking under the strain her love was placing on it. She mused over strange thoughts. Would she herself have been capable of winning Hal as Bess had? What would happen if Hal ever realized who the real woman behind Bess was? Would he turn away in horror?

These were terrible questions, and they filled Tess with fear and trembling. They opened the door to agonizing doubts whose existence she had never dreamed of before. And, most painful of all, they directed her sharp mind and fertile imagination to the one theme that was surest to punish her—the faceless woman who, according to Sybil's curse, had owned Hal's heart.

She had not been able to prevent herself from having Hal investigated. The operatives she had hired, the best in the nation, unearthed and assembled evidence of dozens of affairs Hal had had with all sorts of women: journalists, political assistants, Washington wives, actresses, a young fashion designer, a Broadway musical comedy star, even a female circuit court justice.

There were photographs to document most of these relationships. But they meant little. For by the nature of Hal's promiscuity and of his discretion it was impossible to know which of these partners he had truly cared for, which one had made the difference in his heart.

So Tess was back where she had started from, the day that the ember of love waiting to spring to life in her heart had been sparked by the cruel words of Sybil Lancaster.

She was a woman in love, a woman who is not sure she is loved. And for this disease there was no cure. It became more acute, more painful, each time her husband touched her, each time he smiled to greet her after a long absence. Possessing part of him was a torment infinitely more horrible than merely possessing none of him.

Tess was jealous, not only of the mystery woman she could not find and could not name, but of herself as well. For in winning Hal for Bess she had lost him for herself. He belonged to a stranger, and behind her mask Tess was the loneliest woman in the world.

And so, as each month went by without a child, and as the White House drew coyly nearer, while her husband's solicitude grew imperceptibly tainted by the strain of childlessness and the fatigue of great ambition, Tess's ordeal became more painful.

Come, you spirits
That tend on mortal thoughts, unsex me here . . .

The lines from *Macbeth*, learned she knew not when, came back to her memory with an uncanny brilliance, striking at the core of her feelings. If only she were not in love! If only things had the same meanings today that they had had before Hal. But no. The game was different now. What Diana must have suffered in her years with Hal, Tess was suffering a million times more. Because to Diana, Hal had been merely a polite stranger—while to Tess he was so near, and yet so far . . .

Tess lay now in the darkness beside her husband, listening to the rhythm of his breathing. In his sleep he had the face of a boy. How innocent he was, and yet how capable of causing pain! Perhaps the two things went hand in hand somehow. This was an enigma she was too exhausted to linger over.

The two Nembutals were spreading cottony confusion through her senses, but sleep still seemed a long way off.

Methought I heard a voice cry "Sleep no more!"
Macbeth doth murder sleep . . .

Tomorrow she would say goodbye to her husband, send him off to his political war, and fight fiercely for him in his absence. Then, a few days hence, she would be in his arms again, and taste the precious part of him that kept her going, that was her life's blood. A remedy that was, alas, also a poison, for it combined with her love to make a drug that caused a kind of pain only a woman could endure.

She touched Hal's hair with a gentle finger. She felt his body stir. A sigh escaped his lips, and he reached out in his sleep and took her in his arms.

For whom did he sigh? Whose arms did he dream of tonight?

Tess closed her eyes.

Sleep no more . . .

The words were still dancing inside her mind like mocking demons as she plummeted into troubled slumber.

IV

April 17, 1964

DIANA WAS STROLLING alone in Central Park.

She was at loose ends. She was still trying to recover from a lunch with the unmarried Stallworth ladies—cousins Renée Stallworth and Becky deForest, along with spinster aunts Rachel and Lulu, and of course Mother—a lunch that had taken so much out of her that she had actually slept for an hour afterward in her suite at the Pierre.

Tonight she had to be at the Fifth Avenue house for dinner with some family friends who had known her since childhood. They were bringing a single friend from Europe, a Scotsman named Guy McElvain who was the proprietor of a huge castle near Aberdeen. A longtime bachelor, he would be a perfect social match for Diana and, most importantly, through him she could get out of the country.

Lunch had been painful, difficult. None of the Stallworth women had ever forgiven Diana for what happened with Hal. Two hours with them, struggling against their strained levity and their obvious distaste for her, were really too much to bear.

Diana was a skeleton in the Stallworth closet. The relatives seemed to want to shield her from the outside world, but at the same time to forget about her existence. Family councils designed to get her out of the way were a regular occurrence in the Stallworth clan. The social gatherings to which she was invited were stiff affairs in which only the bravest and kindest of her relatives bothered to pass a pleasant word with her.

They were all politely waiting for her to disappear. And no one wanted that more than Diana herself.

This morning she had taken a couple of Benzedrine tablets with her coffee, as part of the elaborate preparation for the long day ahead. But somehow the morning's medley of moods had left her too desperate to face lunch without extra fortification. She had added a Miltown to her midmorning vodka, hoping to regain some sort of balance. Her intention was to get through lunch on one gibson at the table and a quiet sip from her flask in the ladies' room.

But the Miltown had weakened her in some unpredictable way. She was in such disarray by eleven that she bolted two more drinks in the next forty-five minutes and tottered into lunch like a mechanical toy with a screw loose.

Her hour of exhausted sleep after the noontime ordeal had been anything but restorative. It was three-thirty now. She faced the evening to come, as so often, like a grim adventure that she had little hope of negotiating without further damage to her pride, her nerves, and of course her reputation.

Such was life these days. Each morning she awakened to an uphill battle for survival which became, before she knew it, a downhill slide through hazy daylight toward sinister evening. The first slipping of the quicksand under her feet came when she looked at herself in the mirror, and saw the mask that alcohol was patiently modeling out of what had once been her beautiful face.

In order to forget that face she made her daily capitulations to the tranquilizers, the stimulants, and the drinks. She held the world at arm's length through morning; then the gibsons at lunch sent her reeling foggily into afternoon, a shadowy ordeal in which her hours alone were almost as catastrophic as her obligatory contacts with the family members closest to her.

Then came night, upon which the curtain was raised by strong cocktails and furtive swigs from her flask. She rarely tasted or remembered her dinner. The evening passed in a dream, and the next morning she had the dubious leisure to wonder whether or not she had offended anyone, said anything to embarrass herself, slurred her words more than usual, perhaps knocked over a vase, stumbled, or even fallen down.

And all the while she knew that everyone was watching her, everyone was wondering how fast she was sinking, and how she dared show her face in public.

Like death warmed over. The familiar phrase had become Diana's private anthem for herself. At age thirty-three she could feel the distant tentacles of death in the pills that threw an ugly gauze over her brain, and in the alcohol that stank in her mouth and pickled her body. The world was a dark ocean waiting to suck her under. For a little while longer she could try to float her way through it on a small oily bubble of alcohol—but not for long.

No one would miss her. The family would be only too happy to see her haggard face disappear along with the hopes that had once been so foolishly invested in her. Her shame was doubly unforgivable because she had been handed everything including the great Hal Lancaster, the one and only Prince Hal, and been too weak to hang onto it.

Soon, one way or the other, she would slink out of this world, trying to leave as little memory of her shame behind her as possible. To next year's debutantes, or to their daughters after them, she would be just a name with a faint tinge of scandal attached to it, like a faded corsage from a ball where something unpleasant occurred many years ago.

Nevertheless her shame would outlive her, and continue to haunt the Stallworth girls for generations to come. For she had once been the wife of Haydon Lancaster—and she had lost him . . .

It was in flight from thoughts such as this that Diana had stumbled from the Pierre across Fifth Avenue into the Park this afternoon, wearing dark glasses and a scarf to make herself as anonymous as possible. Today was so evil a day that if she did not get a breath of fresh air and a glimpse of the human race outside her shrinking private world, she would not be able to face the evening, and would have to beg off her faint chance with the Scotsman.

She wandered down the paths, watching joggers pass her by on light feet, their shoes making little crunching noises on the gravel. She saw mothers walking their babies in prams, old ladies on benches feeding pigeons, boys playing catch with grass-stained footballs, young couples in love walking hand in hand under the smiling sun.

Despite the sickly backdrop of confusion against which this human medley played itself out, it had a springlike freshness to it that kept Diana walking. She prayed that another half hour of this would get her in shape to finish the day somehow.

Then, all at once, she realized she was lost.

She saw a large lawn, a hillock, a marble monument of some sort, and in the distance, behind the trees with their new leaves, the brick ramparts of the West Side. There was no one around. Diana had no idea where she was.

This frightened her. She had played in the Park as a girl with her nanny, and knew every foot of it from Grand Army Plaza to Ninety-sixth Street. It was as impossible for her to be lost in Central Park as to forget which fork to use first at a society luncheon.

Yet nothing looked familiar. The large oaks, the path, even the blue sky tinted yellow by her sunglasses—everything was strange. It was as though a spell had been cast over the Park, turning it into a bucolic no man's land.

Diana began to think about retracing her steps, and negotiating her way cautiously back through this alien landscape and her own confusion to familiar terrain. She would need a stiff drink when she got home. Better to abandon her foolish plan of a little invigorating fresh air than to risk untoward adventures like this.

She was turning on her heel to go back the way she had come when all at once she saw the woman and the boy.

They were playing together on a gently sloping lawn. There was a picnic blanket, a basket, and a large floppy bag beside which a camera sat on the grass.

The mother—for something in their quiet intimacy made it obvious she was the mother—was on her hands and knees, creeping slowly toward the boy, who was making a game of pretending not to see her as he hid his face behind his arm. He was dressed in cotton pants with an elastic waistband, and a light spring jacket.

He might have been five or six—Diana was not good about children's ages—and quite good-looking, with his fine dark hair and alabaster complexion. As he glanced up at his mother, giggling at her approach, Diana caught a glimpse of his dark eyes, beautiful as those of a girl.

The mother was wearing blue jeans and a sweater. She was very small and had medium-length dark hair. As she crept toward the boy, whose body wriggled with anticipation, something youthful and spring-like seemed to emanate from them both, harmonizing with the fragrant stillness of the Park.

"Peek-a-boo," the mother cooed. "I see you . . ."

The voice rang out so clearly that Diana realized she was much closer to them than she had thought. So close, in fact, that if she were to make the slightest move they would hear her, and turn to look. She did not want to break the spell of their private play; nor did she want them to notice her before she could find a way to slip out of their sight.

The mother made amusing murmurs of menacing approach in a husky little voice as she crept closer. At last she reached the boy, who made an effort to squirm away before she caught him with slender white hands and pulled him to her. His laughter danced on the air of the Park like bubbles on the surface of a stream.

The mother had pulled him down on top of her, and he was giggling into the hollow of her neck as she embraced him. Her eyes looked up almost lovingly into the sky above her, and a little sigh of maternal happiness stirred in her throat. She held the boy close, making believe she was holding him prisoner. A soft smile lingered on her lips.

Though she was still in profile, and altered by the strangeness of the park as well as Diana's own muddled perceptions, she looked somehow familiar. Diana stood still, hoping to get a better look.

"Got you!" the mother was saying.

"No, I got you!" the boy corrected.

"Oh, ho. You think you're pretty smart, don't you?" the mother smiled, turning over abruptly so that the child was pinned underneath her, his hands on her shoulders. "I guess you think you can twist me around your little finger, don't you?"

"Mm-hmm," the boy nodded, touching her cheek. He was very masculine in his way, despite his smallness and the tender beauty of his features. The obvious intensity of the mother's love made him confident of his place in her heart, and therefore of a certain male power he possessed over her.

Diana was admiring their closeness when the timbre of the female voice at last sank in, and she realized why the young woman looked so familiar.

Because the mother was so tiny herself, the boy appeared bigger as she held him in her arms. Now Diana could measure her small, perfectly formed limbs, subtly changed by childbirth and by eight or nine years of living since she had last seen her. She could also see behind the longer hair to the short haircut she had always worn in the old days.

But the name would not come. For an instant Diana cursed the liquor that impeded her memory, much as an arthritic curses the permanent affliction that makes it painful for her to unscrew a bottle cap.

Motherhood had made the woman even more beautiful than she had ever been before. There was a glow of love in her face, so fresh that

Diana almost wanted to turn her eyes away in shame before such perfect happiness.

Diana felt a catch in her throat as the past came to take her in its embrace. In another time, another world, she herself could have borne that glow of mother love, and held a lovely boy like that in her arms. The beauty of that swanlike mother's neck, the laughing eyes tinged with maternal passion, the voice filled with humor and joy, could have been hers.

But not in this world. In this world she could only stand here like a wrinkled crone and gaze upon such impossible bliss as upon a scene from a fairy tale, brought magically to life in this mystical outpost of the Park.

Still the once-familiar name would not come to her mind. All she could do was watch and listen.

The mother was still holding the boy underneath her.

"I look up," she said, craning her neck to see beyond the tree limbs, "and I see deep blue sky and one shy cloud."

"It's the first one out," the boy said dreamily, grazing her neck with the backs of his fingers.

"Ah," she nodded. "Do you think it's embarrassed to be the first, with no others to keep it company?"

"It's bashful," he agreed. "It's blushing."

"You're right," she said, still looking up. "It's a little pink, isn't it?"

"And what do you see when you look down?" he asked.

"Hmmm," she said, looking at him with a mysterious grin. "When I look down, I see a handsome fellow . . ."

A whisper of breeze in the trees drowned out the rest of the words. Diana was gazing at her in wonder. With her elfin, nymphlike form, she seemed an eternal girl, and yet blessed with the infinite depth of motherhood. A tear had welled in Diana's eye at the sound of her endearing words.

But now she saw her face more clearly, and a name came from nowhere to join it.

Laura.

Diana stood transfixed. The name rang inside her like the tolling of a bell, sending echoes through her memory.

Laura . . .

The last time she had seen her was the day she had summoned her to the Fifth Avenue house to separate her from Hal. So long ago! An eternity . . .

On that day Diana had thought she was protecting what was rightfully hers. And in later times, after having married Hal, she had always looked back on Laura as the loser—the more so because, during their brief painful interview about Hal, it had been so terribly obvious that Laura really cared for him.

But now the kaleidoscope of the years had turned, and all the pieces were in different places. Diana's life with Hal was just a memory, and her life as a woman almost over. But here was Laura, her old natural sweetness having flowered into something so beautiful, and almost unbearable to look at—because fate had given her a son.

Diana stood listening to their murmurs, the soft lyrical whisper of a mother conversing with her boy in words tinged by the music of love. She struggled to get her bearings. Something about this scene didn't make sense. It was as enigmatic as the unreal stillness of this lost corner of the park she had thought she knew so well.

Memory and her social sense came to her rescue. Hadn't Laura married that fellow who helped her run her business? Diana couldn't recall his name. A strapping Irishman with a brisk and rather sexy manner. He was very protective of Laura.

Yes. It was coming back now. Diana had seen the announcement of their marriage in the papers, and pointed it out to Hal. She had remarked on the fact that their marriages had taken place the same day. Yes—it was an Irish name, Regan, Rowan, Reardon, Reilly.

Could this be the Irishman's boy?

Something more complicated came to join these thoughts in Diana's mind. She recalled reading stories about Laura's leaving fashion design at the height of her enormous fame. She had been surprised by it at the time, and later wondered what became of Laura.

Well, here she was.

The child had turned his mother over and was lying on top of her now. It was his turn to play the aggressor. His hands were on her shoulders, his little face raised toward the sky.

"I look up . . ." he said.

That was when he saw Diana.

The little dark eyes took her in expressionlessly, measuring her with a child's candid curiosity. Diana was unnerved. She knew she had only a few seconds to make her exit before the boy pointed her out to his mother. She could not let Laura see her spying on her. Worse yet, she could not face a conversation with Laura, and the look in Laura's eyes as she realized what the years had done to Diana.

Still she could not tear herself away from the little boy's gaze. His eyes seemed to steal some of the sun's brilliance as they took her in, accepting her in pure innocence as part of the great wide world around him. The irises were dark, gentle. Something about them hypnotized her.

To Diana's relief he said nothing to his mother. He simply looked away from the stranger and back down to Laura.

"And what do see when you look down?" Laura was asking.

"Peek-a-boo," he said. "I see you!"

Diana could still not tear herself away. She studied the boy's hair, so dark and fine, like Laura's. And his brow, his chin, the shape of his face, which seemed to conceal a secret that would not let her take her eyes off him. Meanwhile the sound of his voice struck a chord within her, so distant and muted that it was like a lullaby heard once and long forgotten, but unmistakable when it recurs, for it penetrates directly to the heart.

And now Diana understood that something was wrong here, very wrong. The haunting beauty of the scene bespoke the mystery behind it, a riddle that was already solving itself inside Diana's soul.

She recalled from somewhere that the marriage to the Irishman, Rowan, Regan, or whatever, had not worked out. There was something ugly about it. A divorce . . .

And there were no children. The marriage had ended in trouble, something involving the courts. There were no children . . .

Diana's breath caught in her throat. Dizziness overtook her as she backed away furtively along the path, hoping they would not notice her in her retreat.

But the boy was looking at her again. She saw a tiny light in his eyes, acknowledging her presence and her withdrawal, even as he lay atop his mother, his body pressed to her breast like a newborn babe, in the most intimate position as she murmured her affection for him.

Diana turned away as the words springing from her heart came to her lips with a will of their own.

My God, he's Hal's.

She reached out to grasp at the branch of a nearby hedge for support. The lawn and sky wheeled before her like a maelstrom.

She has Hal's child.

Diana closed her eyes, trying to banish the image that had plunged straight through all the years, all the alcohol, all the illusions that had clouded her life since she last saw Laura. There was no doubt about it. None at all.

What she had seen was more than the simple, undeniable resemblance that made Hal shine in all his princely beauty behind that boy's face, and made Hal move in his limbs and sing in his voice.

No, it was more than that. It was something in the precise modulation of the intimacy between mother and son, the specific tone of their affection for each other. It was as though certain human beings could only love in one musical mode, could only laugh in one key. And this key that was theirs alone, this mysterious coefficient added to the scene she had just witnessed, was Hal. Not the Hal that Diana herself had known and tried so futilely to satisfy—but another, happier Hal, the Hal who lived inside Laura's heart and in the flesh of her boy.

Yes, that was it. What Diana had just seen in this hidden grassy glade was the cosmic conjugation of Laura and Hal, and their love, which was incarnated in this sweet little boy who looked so much like his father.

Diana's heart, broken long since by a thousand failures, seemed to shatter only now inside her breast. For only now could she really see Hal, the real Hal—as he had been for another woman. Only now could she feel the full weight of what she had lost, and look in the face the wheel of destiny that had destroyed her life.

She has his boy. Hal gave her a child.

Like a blind woman Diana floundered through the alien Park, not knowing where she was going. She was too beside herself to think of the drinks ahead, or of the phone call she would make to Mother to tell her she was too ill for tonight's dinner. Such mundane considerations were banished by the revolution taking place inside her mind.

He gave HER his child.

Suddenly everything was clear. In a crazy way Diana understood why she had never been able to give Hal children. She even understood why Hal had never been able to have children with his second wife, Elizabeth Bond, a beautiful and healthy young woman who by all accounts should have succeeded in giving him a child where barren Diana had failed.

It all made perfect sense. This was the way the fates had arranged it. Hal belonged to Laura. There was nothing of him left for the determined, ruthless women who had managed to make him their husband. It was the loser, Laura, who had picked up all the marbles and gone on with her life.

Laura was the shadow behind the mirror of Diana's disintegration all these years. Laura had been the other side of the cosmic coin, the face of Diana's lost happiness, all along.

An infinite rage at herself and at the world gripped Diana as she plunged along the pathways leading out of the Park. She thought of her long agony as Hal's fiancée, her futile worries about herself, her humiliating attempts to be a wife to Hal, the destruction of their marriage, and now her slow decay, unnoticed by the busy world that had its eyes fixed on Hal and his career.

Now she knew why.

She understood at a single stroke why she was alone this way, why she had always been alone, exiled in a life drawn ceaselessly downward toward hell. It was a cruel game the patient fates were playing with her, a game whose pawns revolved around this lovely young mother playing in the Park with the beautiful boy whose eyes contained the light that had long since been stolen from Diana's life. The light of Hal's love . . .

She saw the Pierre come into view across Fifth Avenue. In another couple of minutes she would be home. She wanted the biggest drink of her life. But something told her she was not going to have that drink. Not yet, anyway. There were questions to be answered. The scene she had just witnessed seemed to have come from another world, somewhere on a mystic orbit separated from the ordinary affairs of men. She had to find out where its reality lay, and what it might mean in practical terms.

But the deeper meaning was already clear, fatally clear. It was graven in Diana's ruined life. And as she rushed through the lobby of the Pierre past astonished bellmen who had never seen even Diana in such a state, she saw her crime, her stupidity, her punishment.

And her revenge.

V

April 23, 1964

TESS WAS ALONE in her hotel room in Cleveland.

She was lying on the bed with her shoes off, exhausted from three campaign appearances around the city today. She would already have been in a tub of hot soapy water were it not for the fact that the evening news was on television. She wanted to see the day's reports about Hal before her bath.

A knock at the room door forced her to get to her feet. It was a messenger with a package for her.

"Do I have to sign for it?" she asked.

"No, ma'am."

"All right," she smiled. "Thank you."

She closed the door and drifted exhaustedly to the edge of the bed, holding the package in her hands as she watched Walter Cronkite's face fill the TV screen. She fiddled with the sealing tape holding the flat package closed as the broadcast began.

"A bombshell of sorts hit the Haydon Lancaster primary campaign today in Ohio," Cronkite said, "when a leak to the press from an unnamed source suggested that, for unknown reasons, Lancaster is about to withdraw from the campaign for the Democratic presidential nomination. Peter Winston has details."

Tess paused, the package in her hands, and stared at the screen. There was an image of Hal smiling in the glare of dozens of photographer's flashbulbs.

"Haydon Lancaster seemed surprised by the rumor," the reporter said, "and joked with the press about it."

Tess watched Hal's familiar smile as her hand felt inside the package.

"If I'm going to withdraw," Hal was saying to the eager mob of journalists, "I'd better save the fried chicken from this week and take it home to my wife."

Puzzled, Tess looked down at the contents of the package. There was a single piece of paper with a message typed on it in block letters, along with a handful of eight-by-ten photographs.

The reporters were still asking Hal questions as Tess read the message before her.

YOU HAVE ONE WEEK TO CONVINCE YOUR HUSBAND TO WITHDRAW FROM THE CAMPAIGN, MRS. LANCASTER . . .

At first the words made no sense. Tess looked back at the television set.

"Despite the strange rumor, which seemed to have reached all the major media at once," the reporter said, "Lancaster had a busy day in Ohio, speaking to a group of farmers in the early morning and to an AFL-CIO rally before noon. To enthusiastic audiences Lancaster continued to state the theme of his campaign, that in the tumultuous times we live in our leaders must show patience and good judgment, rather than extreme reactions left over from the Cold War . . ."

The words blurred in Tess's ears as she turned back to the typed message in her hands.

Tess had turned pale. Her hands were frozen in her lap. She looked up to see Hal waving to a cheering crowd of union members. Then she thrust the typed message aside to look at the pictures accompanying it.

They showed a little boy, perhaps four or five years old. Two of them were rather grainy snapshots of poor quality. But the rest were magnificent portraits in close-up, haunting in their concentration on the boy's expression and personality.

Tess stared at the pictures. The boy was very beautiful. He had delicate features and astonishing dark eyes that looked into the camera with a touching innocence. There was a sweet humor somewhere in those eyes, combined with a precocious, manly tenderness and melancholy that were almost unbearable to look at.

He was Hal's. Tess understood that from the first second.

One could look at these photographs a dozen ways, and learn a hundred things about the boy from them—but all these things, in perfect unanimity, confirmed that he was Hal's. Not only was it proved by the brute resemblance in the hairline, the chin, the brows, the dark eyes, the shape of the nose. The *way* he looked out from the image annihilated all doubt. That unique combination of candor and complexity could only have come from one source.

Tess was looking at Hal's son.

She glanced back at the TV screen. *CBS News* had gone on to another story. She switched to another network. For a brief instant she saw Hal, on his way from his limousine into a building, pausing to speak to a group of reporters.

"Is there any truth to the rumor you're going to withdraw, Senator?"

Hal grinned. "You'd better ask my wife about that," he said. "She's been at me for months about being out of the house so much. If she's decided to ground me, I won't have much choice. I never did learn how to say no to her."

Hal parried the most strident of the questions with a sure hand, telling the reporters that a campaign wouldn't be a campaign without dramatic leaks, but that in this case there was no substance to the story. He was in the fight to the finish, he said.

Struggling to control herself, Tess looked back down at the pictures, and wondered about the fact that the timing of their arrival matched the strange leak that had the press baying at Hal's heels. This was no coincidence.

She was in deep trouble, and she knew it. A lifetime of coping with disasters and winning bloody battles had given her the instinct to know when her jugular was exposed, with the enemy closing in for the kill. Now was such a time. But the victim was not herself alone. It was Hal.

You have one week . . .

Tess took a deep breath. She knew there were emotions inside her that must have their say sooner or later. She understood that a great suffering was to be hers. But all that mattered now was to use every last ounce of her intelligence and resourcefulness to find a weapon against the threat at hand.

She got up, turned the volume of the TV set all the way down, and picked up the phone. She called Hal's hotel in Columbus. The phone was answered by an aide who told her that neither Hal nor Tom Rossman had returned from the late afternoon interviews yet. They were expected soon, and he would have Hal call her.

Without putting the phone down Tess asked the operator for a long distance number. She kept her fingers crossed as the faraway phone rang.

At last it was picked up, and a familiar voice answered.

"Ron," she said, "thank God you're there. This is me. Listen, we have bad trouble."

There was a pause.

"Does it have to do with the news?" Ron asked.

"I think so. I'm not sure of anything yet. Ron, there's something I have to show you right away. I'm in Cleveland, at the Midtown Plaza Hotel. Where can we get together quickly?"

"I can get a flight out of LaGuardia tonight," Ron said. "I'll call the airlines and get back to you. How bad is the problem?"

Tess opened her mouth to speak, and stopped herself. She looked at the telephone in her hand. Anything was possible, she decided. Whoever was behind this elaborate blackmail scheme was certainly capable of bugging a hotel phone.

"I can't talk about it over the phone," she said. "Just hurry. I'll wait for your call."

She hung up the phone and stood up. The tremor in her nerves kept her on her feet, moving back and forth in the room like a caged animal. She saw the pictures lying on the bed, but did not have the courage to look closely at them again. Her mind was a blank, devoid of all thought, all strategy.

The sudden ringing of the phone came like a savior. Thinking it was Ron, she rushed to pick it up.

"Bess?" It was Hal's voice. "I just got your message. Have you seen the news?"

"Hal." The beloved voice brought tears to Tess's eyes. For a long moment she fought to get control of herself. She could not let Hal know how worried she was.

"Hal, what's going on?" she asked. "I've been watching the news . . ."

"Your guess is as good as mine," he said. "But I don't think it's anything to worry about. Somebody is trying to throw up a smoke screen to make me look bad. I've talked to Tom about it. He thinks the opposition isn't satisfied with the way the primaries are going, and wants to stir the soup to see if they can take away some of our momentum. It makes sense, I think."

"You haven't—heard anything more?" Tess asked.

"What do you mean?"

Tess bit her lip nervously. She dared not reveal how much she herself already knew. "I mean, you don't know any more than you've heard from the press?"

"Not a thing," he said, his relaxed tone reassuring her. "By the way, have they been on you about this yet?"

"No, not yet," she said. "I haven't seen any reporters since early afternoon."

"Well, they probably will," Hal said. "Tom says just keep smiling. Put them off with a joke if you can think of one, or tell them flat out that the story is a fake. We'll just have to ride out the storm, Bess. This is the price you have to pay for being the front-runner. But don't worry. This thing will die down in a couple of days. If there was anything serious behind it, I'd have heard by now."

"Yes, Hal," she said weakly. "Of course."

She did her best to match his relaxed banter as they finished out their conversation. When they hung up she closed her eyes and took a deep breath.

He doesn't know.

She had found out what she needed to know. Hal was completely unaware of the real threat behind the rumors about his campaign. Tess alone was in possession of it.

She realized she must keep it that way.

She moved to the bed and looked from the pictures of the little boy to the ultimatum on the typed sheet.

You have one week to convince your husband to withdraw . . .

"One week," she murmured, her tired eyes staring at the pictures. Would one week be enough?

She closed her eyes tightly and made fists with both her hands.

Keep calm, she told herself. *Don't panic.*

But as she sat alone, waiting for Ron to call her back, Tess had never felt less calm in her life.

VI

April 24, 1964

THE NEXT MORNING at ten Ron Lucas was sitting with Tess in her hotel room. Foggy conditions throughout the Midwest had forced cancellation of his flight last night, and he had not been able to make the trip until just after dawn.

Tess had not slept a wink all night. She held in her hand a telegram, delivered to her room at 7 A.M.

SIX DAYS, it read.

She had canceled her morning speech to the Cleveland Chamber of Commerce so she could be here to speak with Ron. She watched his face as he studied the pictures and the typed warning. When he had finished she handed him the telegram.

"This came a couple of hours ago," she said.

Ron looked at it and nodded. He held up the photographs.

"What is your opinion of this?" he asked. "Do you think it's for real?"

Tess nodded. "I think that is Hal's child," she said. "I could be wrong, but I don't think we can take the chance."

"Do you know who this boy is?" Ron asked.

She shook her head. "I haven't a clue."

He touched the telegram and the typed page. "Who do you think sent these?"

"I have no idea," she said.

Ron looked pensive.

"The one-week time limit," he said. "I don't like that much."

Tess nodded. She did not need words to tell him how afraid she was.

"And the news leaks," he said. "They're linked to this, I suppose?"

Tess shrugged. "They must be. There's a limit to coincidence."

"Have you talked to your husband?" he asked. "How much does he know?"

"He knows nothing," she said. "I'm the only one who knows."

There was a pause. Tess wondered how visible her terror was in her eyes.

"What do we do?" she asked.

Ron looked at the materials spread across the bed. "The first thing we have to do," he said, "is to find out where this came from. That may not be as difficult as it seems. I can get into the other campaigns if I have to. But the time limit makes it tough."

Tess nodded. "You'll do it," she said.

"The other problem is more serious," he said, picking up one of the photographs. "We have no information to go on. No identification. Just these pictures. I can't exactly put a five-year-boy through the FBI's mug files. There won't be any records of his face anywhere. He's too young to have left any traces in the world, except a birth certificate. Too bad they weren't helpful enough to include that with their package."

Tess clasped her frozen fingers together. "What will you do?" she asked.

"Find the mother," he said. "If the people behind this have bought her, that's one thing. If they haven't, and she doesn't know about this, that's another. Either way, we'll have to deal with it."

Tess could only nod. As usual, Ron went to the heart of the problem. He neither underestimated the danger nor shrank from attacking it with all his powers.

"I'll make some calls before I leave here," he said. "Then I'll direct things from New York. Be sure to keep me informed of your whereabouts. I'll call every couple of hours. Are you going to go on with your campaigning?"

"Unless you need me," she said.

"Good," he said. "I'll be in touch."

He picked up the pictures. "I'll need to copy these."

Tess nodded. She was glad to see him take the pictures away. She could not bear to look at them any further.

He got up to leave. A man of few words, he had no need to say anything else for now.

He paused at the door and turned to Tess.

"There's just one thing," he said. "Does your husband know about this boy?" He held up one of the pictures.

Tess tried to shake her head. But Ron was slipping away from her, behind a black veil that fell from the ceiling to cover everything in a shower of darkness. She tried to speak, but the words that came were an echo from somewhere beneath the earth, which was already rising to engulf her.

Ron saw the look in her eyes an instant too late. Before he could catch her she fell to the floor in a dead faint.

. . .

An hour later Ron was on his way back to New York, and Tess was standing before the mirror in her hotel room, applying make-up to her haggard face as she prepared to make her afternoon address to the League of Women Voters.

She felt a small measure of relief now that she knew Ron was working to help her. But she was only too well aware of the difficulty of the task ahead. Together they had less than six days in which to find a determined enemy and to disarm that enemy. It was not going to be easy.

And if their efforts failed . . .

Tess had now had sixteen hours in which to imagine that eventuality. The very thought was too horrifying to linger over.

If she could manage to bury this secret forever, then everything could be saved: the campaign, the election, and her marriage to Hal. Once in the White House, she would have the power she had dreamed of all these years, and she would use it to make Hal a happy man as well as a great president.

Everything could be saved—if she kept the world from finding out the truth.

And—an odd notion that struck her with tremendous force—she must prevent Hal from finding out, as well.

She was all but certain that he did not know about the existence of his son. Had he known about the boy, he would have visited him over these past years, sent him presents, telephoned him. His pride and love as a father would have forced him to do so. And Tess, whose surveillance of Hal had been close, would have found out about it.

So Hal did not know. But in six days, unless she prevented it, he would find out.

This she could not allow. There was no telling what that knowledge might do to him, and to their marriage.

It was not Hal's shame over having sired an illegitimate child that Tess feared. It was his love for such a child.

And, perhaps, for its mother.

Now the terrible words of Sybil's malediction came back to haunt Tess with a power beyond any they had possessed before.

Except one.

A cruel, almost mystical intuition told her that the little boy in the photographs was a child of love. Hal could not have conceived him with just any woman. This child had not sprung from a thoughtless man's sowing of wild oats.

No. That boy had come from the mystery woman whose hold over Hal's heart had been the bane of Tess's existence through all these painful years. And if Hal found out about the boy—in a storm of scandal that would surely destroy his political career at one stroke—he would find out about the mother, too.

That would be the end of everything. For, having nothing further to lose, no reputation to protect, no career to safeguard, Hal would fly to the arms of the woman he loved, the woman who had borne his son, and would not waste a backward look on the life he had lived so bravely and unwillingly all these years.

This was the nightmare that had kept Tess from sleeping a wink since she first saw those pictures. This was the disaster she must prevent at all costs. She was not fighting merely to save one man's campaign for high office. She was fighting for her very life as Hal's wife.

Tess applied a last touch of color to her pale cheeks. In the mirror, to her amazement, she saw a lovely and composed woman, about to make a lighthearted speech to the League of Women Voters, and to answer the rumors about her husband's campaign with blithe denials.

All her life she had been a master at hiding the truth. Today, and in the days to come, her lifelong gift for subterfuge would be tested as never before.

And in this astonishing turn of her fate there was a peculiar irony, which Tess's hardheaded personality would not allow her to measure, but which she felt as the twisting of a private knife in her heart. The sin she was trying to cover up might as well be, in a strange way, her own. Why, otherwise, would she be so desperate to keep it from Hal as well as from others?

But there was no time for thoughts such as this. Her backbone, strong as steel, was coming to her rescue. She would fight this battle and win, if victory was humanly possible. With Ron's help she would save Hal from the anonymous threat to his campaign. She would see him through the rest of the primaries. He would win the nomination. In November he would be elected President.

Once in the White House Hal would change the course of history, and halt the sick veering toward chaos and confusion that had begun in the wake of Kennedy's death and was gaining in momentum every day. He would steer America away from its fearful obsession with international confrontation. He would halt the arms race with the Soviet Union, as Kennedy had tried and failed to do. He would end the manic adventure in Vietnam before it grew into a tragedy as bad as Korea or worse.

He would see Kennedy's poverty and civil rights programs through to their logical conclusion. And he would invent new programs, bold initiatives that would solidify America's position as a great world power while safeguarding the moral leadership the country was in danger of losing.

He would do all these things, and more. And Tess would be at his side as he did them. She would give him children, lots of children, the children she knew he wanted more than anything else. Her strength would support him, her love fulfill him. Their life together would be a long and happy one.

If she survived this coming week. If she kept her secret.

He would never know about the little boy in those terrible photographs. Because Tess would never let him find out.

And when it was all over, and the danger was behind them both, she would seek out the woman who had brought this shame on Hal, and she would destroy her.

VII

THE NEXT TWO DAYS were busy ones behind the scenes in Washington.

On Tuesday evening, Miss Juliet Summers, a Washington secretary and longtime lover of the campaign manager of one of the key Democratic presidential candidates, accepted a date from a handsome and wealthy-looking stranger who squired her through a romantic evening of dinner and dancing before taking her to a remote location in his Lincoln Continental and holding a knife to her throat.

The stranger politely asked her whether her lover had confided anything to her about his campaign's involvement in the current spate of rumors about Haydon Lancaster. When she protested her complete ignorance of the affair, her clothes were cut patiently away with the same long knife, and she was held naked by her hair and asked the same question again. Gasping through her tears of pain and terror, she repeated her story. This time she was believed.

Also on Tuesday evening, Mr. Alan Graff, a male assistant campaign manager for another major candidate, was stopped on F Street by an unknown man, helped into a car and shown photographs of himself in compromising unclothed positions with a variety of men, young and old, one of whom was the candidate's senior aide.

Mr. Graff, threatened with exposure of his homosexual adventures to his wife and three children, had heart failure in the presence of his interlocutor, and had to be rushed to Georgetown Hospital. But not before he had convinced the stranger, in what he feared were his last breaths on earth, that he knew nothing of the matter in question, though his candidate's campaign was certainly being helped by Lancaster's current problems.

On Wednesday the Associate Chairman of the Democratic National Committee, a known intimate of a third crucial campaign manager, was privately contacted and presented with documentary evidence of his illegal laundering of several million dollars in campaign contributions through a variety of paper corporations and a bank in Puerto Rico. This individual, when informed that the misuse of such sums, a federal offense, would be traced directly to him and made public in two hours if he did not cooperate, managed to convince his visitors that he knew nothing of the Lancaster scandal.

Also on Wednesday, the Arlington, Virginia, apartment of the female journalist who had originally received the damning leak about Haydon Lancaster's imminent withdrawal from the primary campaign was burglarized. Numerous documents relating to her personal life, including affairs she had had with more than a handful of Washington celebrities, were stolen, and a meeting held with her the next morning.

It was explained to the attractive young reporter that the sexual favors she had exchanged in return for several important stories, and the relationships she maintained with certain public figures about whom she had written admiring profiles, would soon guarantee her banishment from the journalistic community without hope of her every plying her chosen profession again, unless she revealed to the two strangers before her the source of the leak about Haydon Lancaster.

Unfortunately, she was only able to explain that the leak was anonymous, and showed the visitors the typed message from her answering service by which it had first come to her.

The investigation did not end there. Nearly everyone connected with all the major campaigns had benefited monetarily, at one time or another, from the flow of cash across the elusive borderline between government funds, campaign contributions, and plain graft that made Washington such an exciting place to live. Ninety percent of those concerned had illicit lovers. Of these, perhaps forty percent were homosexuals. All these individuals were followed, contacted, and threatened with exposure or worse unless they told what they knew of the Lancaster matter.

The word spread quickly. Washington entered a period of quiet panic as its collective sins came within inches of seeing the light of day. No one realized that the information behind this campaign of intimidation had been patiently gathered by Ron Lucas and his operatives over a period of several years, at the behest of Bess Lancaster, in anticipation of this very day and this contingency.

But it was slow going. Whoever was behind the Lancaster leak was very clever, and had covered his tracks well. The people most likely to know the source of the leak were in fact ignorant of it. Washington knew no more about the sudden cloud over Haydon Lancaster's campaign than did the press or the American people.

Ron Lucas kept his operatives working around the clock. He realized that time was short, and that he must keep his investigation discreet. Whoever was behind the threat Tess had received was using only the innermost circle of his people, or perhaps even a solitary outside contact.

Meanwhile everything Ron already knew about the past of Haydon Lancaster, from his days as a youth at Choate through his early government career to the present, was sifted and resifted in an effort to find out the identity of the unknown little boy who might or might not be his illegitimate son.

Every known mistress of Haydon Lancaster who might logically have been impregnated by him within the last six years was followed, her mail intercepted, her home burglarized.

Yet the answer still eluded Ron and his team.

After forty-eight hours he was prepared for more drastic measures. Information had been compiled on all the major candidates that, in the right hands, would be sufficient to force their withdrawal from the presidential race. Unless the source of the threat to Hal was found soon, a campaign of mass blackmail against the most illustrious names in American electoral politics would begin. The collective terror caused by so extreme a move would be such that whoever dared to cast the first stone at Hal Lancaster would himself be destroyed in a matter of hours.

The effect of this blood bath on the political process, and perhaps the history of the country, would be devastating. It might well annihilate the political careers of some of the finest executive talents available to the nation. But unless another way was found in a matter of hours, the most violent solution would be the only one left.

Then all at once the answer came.

VIII

April 26, 1964

FOUR DAYS, MRS. LANCASTER

TESS HELD THE TELEGRAM in her hand. Her fingers trembled despite her best efforts to control them. She had not slept more than two hours per night in the past three days. Each morning, like clockwork, the greeting from her blackmailer had arrived bright and early.

She was in Nebraska now, making campaign appearances in as many places as her schedule and stamina would allow. Hal was crisscrossing the country between here, West Virginia, Maryland, and Ohio. Primaries were to take place in all four states on Tuesday, as well as crucial caucuses in five other states. The blackmailer had chosen his moment wisely. A disastrous showing for Hal in those nine states could turn the entire campaign around in one day, and virtually ensure the nomination for one of his opponents.

Tess had not seen Hal since the terror began. Their respective schedules were too tight to allow them to meet. Her contacts with him had been limited to hurried telephone conversations and anguished moments before the television screen, where she saw him besieged by jackal-like reporters asking whether it was true that his withdrawal from the race was imminent.

Despite Tess's private pleas to the networks, the orgy of broadcast coverage of Hal's beleaguered campaign had increased in intensity. Not even Tess's great power could restrain the press when it scented blood. It seemed that Hal, the golden boy, the handsome war hero with a privileged past and two marriages to beautiful women, had been found to have feet of clay after all. Every newspaper, magazine, television and radio station in the country wanted to be in on the human sacrifice when and if the unknown scandal became public and forced the candidate to resign from the race and perhaps from his entire career.

Ron was sitting opposite Tess in his own hotel room, his briefcase in his lap. Tess knew her future was in his hands, so she steeled herself to hear what he had come to tell her.

"I'm ready," she said. "How bad is it?"

Ron opened the briefcase. "There's something I want you to hear," he said.

He produced a small tape recorder, placed it on the table beside Tess, and turned it on. A conversation could be heard, distorted by echoes and room noises, but audible nonetheless. There were two voices, both male.

"*Did everything go all right today?*" asked one voice.

"*Yes, sir.*"

"*How's Diana?*"

"*Fine. I saw her at noon.*"

"*Holding up, I take it?*"

"*My man is keeping an eye on her. She's drinking enough to keep her calm, but not enough to make her do anything rash.*"

Tess had pricked up her ears. She thought she recognized the voice asking the questions, though the tape's distortions were making it sound strange. The name was on the tip of her tongue.

"*Well,*" said the familiar voice, "*she needs support. She's confused and desperate. She must be feeling a lot of guilt. Suicide is a possibility. Stay on top of her and keep me informed.*"

"*Yes, sir.*"

"*Now, remember: if the kid doesn't quit, and we have to go public with this whole thing, the press will think of Diana first. They'll be all over her. I want our people to be in control if that happens.*"

"*I hope it won't be necessary, sir. I don't think he'll hold out until Tuesday. Not the way the polls are going.*"

"*You may be right. Let's hope so. This business should never become public knowledge. It could hurt the party too much. We really have no way to go but the way we've chosen. It's up to Lancaster now."*

There was a loud sound, apparently near the microphone, which covered the next few words.

". . . the wife?" Tess heard the tail end of the sentence.

"She's pulling a lot of strings. She's even got a lot of people scared. But so far she's off the scent."

The deeper voice, more familiar than ever now, spoke. *"She won't give up easy. She's a fighter. But we have her in a corner. Her people haven't thought of me yet. They're sticking close to the major campaigns. That's their mistake."* There was a sound, perhaps a low laugh. *"I know her. She always goes straight to the top. That's why she's going to strike out this time."*

Ron turned off the machine.

"There's more," he said. "But that's the gist."

Tess looked thoughtful. "I know that voice," she said. "Who is it?"

A slight smile curled Ron's lips.

"Amory Bose."

Tess smiled bitterly. She cursed herself for not thinking of Amory Bose throughout these last terrible days. But she understood why he had slipped her mind. As an insignificant New York legislator, he could not possibly gain a political benefit from Hal's withdrawal from the Presidential race. Besides, she had bested Bose so many years ago that she had virtually forgotten his existence.

But he had not forgotten her. And the passage of the years, bringing as it did the dwindling of his political fortunes, had only sharpened his thirst for revenge. There was poetic justice in hearing his voice on that tape. But Tess had no leisure to linger over it, for Hal's career was at stake, and time was running out.

"How did you find him?" she asked Ron.

"When we didn't get anywhere in Washington during the first two days, I began to think we were on the wrong track," Ron said. "So, instead of looking for people who stood to benefit politically by your husband's defeat, I started thinking about people who might have a personal ax to grind. We extended our surveillance, and got this tape last night."

"Who was the other voice?" Tess asked.

"Bose's right-hand man. A fellow named Earl Weisman. He's a good man, and a tough one. He's stuck with Bose through the lean years. Not a man to take lightly."

"And Diana?" Tess asked. "I presume they mean our Diana?"

Ron nodded. "It seems fairly clear that it was Diana who came across the existence of the little boy and passed the information along to Bose, through her own motives. Diana is a bad alcoholic, as you know. Her life has been going downhill faster and faster since the divorce. I think we're dealing with a woman scorned, a woman who stumbled on a way to get back at her husband."

Tess leaned forward, her mind working fast.

"If that's true," she said, "you can find out from Diana who the mother of the child is."

Ron shook his head.

"I don't need to do that. I already know."

Tess's breath caught in her throat. She spoke in a tremulous, almost faint voice.

"Really?"

Ron smiled. "I thought that was going to be the hardest, but it turned out to be very simple."

He opened the briefcase, put away the tape recorder, and took out a file folder full of papers and photographs. He spread several of the pictures across the tabletop. They showed a young woman, very attractive in an unusual way, with dark hair and light skin.

In two of the photos she was outdoors, on city streets, walking with the little boy whose face Tess already knew.

"Who is she?" Tess asked. "Do I know her? She looks familiar somehow."

"That's understandable," Ron said. "Until a few years ago she was quite famous as a fashion designer. Her name is Laura Blake."

Of course. Tess looked at the pictures more closely. She had seen that face in profiles published by several of the major fashion magazines in past years. The "Laura look" had been an international sensation, and still existed today in popular women's off-the-rack fashions sold at dress shops and department stores. Tess herself had come close to trying out some of the Laura, Ltd., designs before her marriage to Hal, but had decided to stick with Givenchy, her favorite designer.

"I see," she said, studying the pretty face with its haunting eyes.

"She left fashion design at around the time the little boy was born," Ron said. "She went to photography school at Parsons, and made quite a name for herself all over again. She's had her photographs published in some important magazines. And, as a matter of fact, she has a one-woman show going on at the Museum of Modern Art right now. It opened last week."

Tess cleared her throat. "How did you find her?" she asked.

"When we started the investigation, I thought we were looking for a needle in a haystack, since all we had to go on was the little boy's pictures. But fortunately for us, we had been collecting pictures of your husband's . . . women friends, all these years. It occurred to me to compare them with the boy. If there was a resemblance, all we had to do was check out the woman in question to see if she had a child."

Tess nodded, her eyes still riveted to the face of Laura Blake.

"Well, at first we didn't find her, and I thought it was a dead end," Ron went on. "But then it occurred to me that we might not be going back far enough. We had been concentrating on women your husband had known in the last six years or so. This Laura woman had an affair with him that ended before his marriage to Diana. That's nine years ago. But when I got a look at a picture of her, there was no doubt in my mind."

He took a large photograph of the little boy out of his briefcase and put it on the table alongside the other pictures. Then he pointed to one of the images of Laura with his pencil.

"Look at the eyes," he said. "Notice the shape of the brows. And the chin—see what I mean? Also the complexion, and the nose. Just put her together with your husband, and think of the little boy."

If he saw the effect of his words on Tess, he gave no sign of it. Her hands were clenched into fists under the table. Her whole body was as cold as ice.

There was no doubt as to the truth of Ron's assumption. The boy's resemblance to Laura was as striking as his likeness to Hal. As Tess looked from one picture to the other, the boy's lovely face began to look like those campaign buttons that flash two separate images as they are looked at from different angles. The features of Laura, then Hal, then Laura again, danced over the little face like projections from a magic lantern, crystallizing again and again in the haunting features.

"I was fooled at first," Ron was saying, "because she knew your husband so long ago. The boy is only four and a half years old. But there must have been a later meeting, one we didn't know about. There's no proof of it, of course—except the boy himself."

Tess felt a twinge of pain in her heart at the sight of the woman who was most likely the rival she had hated and feared all these years. With some difficulty she thrust her feelings aside and concentrated on the business at hand.

"How did she meet Hal?" she asked.

"We're pretty sure it was through Diana," Ron said. "Diana was one of her big-name clients back in the fifties. That's the obvious connection. I imagine Diana herself made the introduction."

Tess absorbed this blow as well, her face showing no expression.

"What do you know about the boy?" she asked.

"His name is Michael. He's in preschool in lower Manhattan. He and the mother live very quietly, in a loft in the Village. She works as a professional photographer, and lives on her income from that. She has her attorney and accountant handle most of the residual income from the Laura, Ltd., business. It's a schizoid sort of existence, living as a struggling photographer while the fashion money keeps piling up in the bank. But I guess that's the way she wants it."

He reached into the briefcase and brought out a large glossy booklet.

"This is her exhibition catalog from the museum," he said. "You might want to look through it at your leisure. By the way, the boy figures in the exhibition. There's a whole room devoted to him."

Tess flipped briefly through the booklet. Her eye was caught by poetic, oddly disturbing close-ups of people from all walks of life. Though there was a magnetic pull to their faces and to the way the camera looked at them, she turned the pages quickly until she found pictures of the boy.

They were amazingly eloquent. The boy's expressions were unforgettable. The fact that he was never named, but merely called "Boy" in all the captions, added somehow to his mystery. Tess felt involuntary tears quicken in her eyes as she saw so much of Hal glowing in the little boy's pensive features.

Tess closed the book. Inside the front cover was a self-portrait of Laura Blake done especially for the show. She was indeed a beautiful woman, just into her thirties perhaps, and in the prime of her womanhood. There was a gentle openness about her face that harmonized touchingly with her obvious depth.

"What do you know about her background?" she asked Ron.

"It's sketchy so far," Ron said, pulling a yellow legal pad from his briefcase, "and not very interesting. She was born on April 22nd, 1933, in Chicago. Her mother and father were Czech immigrants . . ."

"April 22nd?" Tess interrupted. "That's odd . . . I was born the same day." She thought for a moment, then motioned for him to continue.

"Her father was a tailor," Ron said. "Both her parents were killed in a highway accident, when the family was moving to Milwaukee. Laura was brought up by relatives in Queens, went to NYU for a semester, and then dropped out to become a seamstress. She met her future husband, a fellow named Riordan, and he helped her start the Laura, Ltd., business. As far as I can understand it, the marriage went sour at about the time that she began to lose interest in fashion design and got into photography. The divorce was ugly; her husband actually served time in prison for kidnapping her after the separation. There were no children."

Except one . . . Tess smiled bitterly. Indeed, it was not a very interesting story. Not until Hal came into it, that is.

"Do you feel confident that Hal knows nothing about the boy?" she asked Ron.

Ron shrugged. "It's an educated guess," he said. "This Laura is a very private woman. She probably would not have wanted to tell him. On the other hand, he might have found out for himself. But I can't find any evidence of him writing to her, calling her, sending her money, and so on. So I'd say he doesn't know."

"That means he hasn't been . . . seeing her, in all these years," Tess added, a trifle too hastily.

"Possibly," Ron nodded.

Tess took a deep breath.

"What do we do?" she asked. "Approach her?"

Ron shook his head. "I wouldn't advise that. I have evidence that she's being watched. If we approach her, we'll tip our hand to Bose. I suggest we keep an eye on her from a distance. She's not hurting anybody. She probably knows nothing about what is going on. Our problem is with Bose. The question is how to get him to back off. Only if we fail at that should we consider doing something about the boy, or the mother, or both. But if we can't handle Bose, it might be too late anyway."

Tess looked at the telegram on the table. "We have four days," she said.

"That's the problem," Ron said. "Bose is out of high office now, exiled in state government. When he was a power in the Senate he had a reputation for some pretty dirty dealing. But he covered his tracks well. He insulated himself from the strong-arm stuff that was done in his name."

Tess looked into Ron's eyes. "Have you got anything we can act on?"

Ron shook his head. "Nothing solid yet. We didn't realize he was in the ball game until last night. But he must have slipped up somewhere along the line. We'll find out where, and we'll hit him with it."

Tess's eyes narrowed. "Within four days," she said.

Ron shrugged.

Tess's eyes narrowed. "I don't like the way this shapes up," she said. "I know Amory Bose. Thanks to Hal and me, he lost everything, politically. He'll sacrifice whatever he has in order to get revenge. He won't scare easily." She shook her head. "Not in four days."

Ron looked at her. "There is one possibility," he said. "Do you remember the Garrett Lindstrom episode? He was a senator from Michigan who leaked some defense secrets to a girlfriend. The story got out to the press, and Lindstrom ended up committing suicide."

Tess nodded. "Vaguely, yes," she said. "That's a long time ago."

"Well, the word I have is that the girl worked for Bose," Ron said. "There was never any proof of it—just a very quiet rumor. She dropped out of sight immediately after the episode. I had a man working on it when your husband was running against Bose, just in case. We found out where the girl went. She got a job as an executive secretary in New York. She's still there. As I say, she was the one who did Lindstrom in. But there was never anything to connect her to Bose. And there's no way I can think of to find out."

"Except to ask her." Tess was tight-lipped, her eyes bright with concentration.

Ron nodded.

"It never hurts to ask," he said.

IX

April 27, 1964

LESLIE CURRAN HAD just returned home from work.

Her apartment on Riverside Drive was an opulent one for an executive secretary. The rent was paid by her employer, the senior vice president of a major Manhattan investment banking firm, who lived with his wife and children on Long Island and visited Leslie three or four times a week.

Leslie was now twenty-nine years of age. Since leaving Washington six years ago she had held several well-paying jobs in New York. Each had involved a relationship with her boss, an attractive uptown apartment, and the various perquisites and restrictions that go with being a kept woman.

Leslie had done well for herself. But she was not a happy woman.

She had not been brought up for this sort of life. After nine wayward years she longed for a husband and family of her own. But her brief year in Washington had left its mark on her. Since coming to New York she had lacked the combination of willpower, self-respect, and hope that would have been necessary to change the drift of her existence.

She hated to look at herself in the mirror, though the years had done little to fade her beauty. She avoided thinking about herself, and concentrated on going through the motions of work at the office, trysts with her boss, and weekends shopping or at the movies.

Leslie was living a life of quiet desperation in the nicest possible surroundings. As a result she had found herself returning in recent years to something she had thought she left behind her a long time ago: religious worship. She went to church regularly, read the Bible at night, and wore a medal about her neck which bore the image of the Virgin.

Such was the pattern of her life. But that pattern had changed in the last year. She had met a new associate at the firm, a young man from Michigan named Jerry Brantman. Jerry was not terribly good-looking or ambitious, but he was nice to Leslie, and respected her. When he dated her there was a touching nervousness about him, as though he were afraid he was not good enough for her.

Jerry was a "nice boy." She wondered why she always thought of him that way, though he was two years older than she. Perhaps it was because he reminded her of her high school days in Illinois. He came from a similar background, and had about him the unmistakable cachet of the Midwest. He was candid, serious, sincere.

Leslie was at a crossroads. She felt that Jerry loved her. But she knew he was aware of her relationship with Mr. Knudsen, as everyone else at work was. If she took the chance of ending her relationship with the boss, and let her feelings for Jerry show just enough to give him courage, he might ask her to be his wife. She would gladly give up the life she had led all these years for the opportunity to make a good young man happy, to bear his children and make him a home.

But the face in the mirror seemed to stand between her and such a decision. It bore a taint she could never erase, a taint that was incompatible with a normal, happy life. Whenever she was forced to look at it she turned away in alarm, and put off all thoughts of making a decision about herself. She went about her usual business, keeping dates with her boss whenever he crooked his finger, finding time to go out with Jerry, staying up late in order to get to sleep, reading her Bible and going to church on Sundays.

The fork in the road was too daunting. Leslie hung back from choosing a path. Yet she knew she could not wait forever. Jerry was thirty-one now, and eager to marry and start a family. He would not wait forever. And Leslie was getting older every day.

Today Leslie was in a hurry. She had to shop for a new dress and have her hair done before meeting Mr. Knudsen for dinner at an out-of-the-way restaurant. The evening would be a typical one, with the two of them returning here by nine for an hour in bed, and Mr. Knudsen arriving home on Long Island by eleven after his "hard night at the office."

Leslie was preparing to take off her clothes and jump into a hot shower when a knock came at her door. She looked through the eyehole and saw a face that took her aback.

After a moment's thought she opened the door. In its frame stood Mrs. Haydon Lancaster, the famous and beautiful wife of the presidential candidate.

"I—well, this is a surprise," Leslie said. "Mrs.—I mean . . ."

"Bess Lancaster." Tess held out a hand. "I'm sorry to barge in on you this way, Miss Curran, but it really couldn't wait. I wonder if I could have a moment of your time?"

Leslie saw the seriousness of purpose in Tess's eyes. Despite the alarm signal sounding at the back of her mind, she stepped back to let her visitor in.

"You have a lovely home," Tess said, sitting down on the couch Leslie pointed out.

"Thank you," Leslie said guardedly. "To what do I owe the honor . . . ?"

"I know you're a busy young woman," Tess said, "so I'll come right to the point. I need your help, Miss Curran. And, I think, I can help you as well. In fact, I'm sure I can."

Leslie thought for a moment before she spoke.

"That's very nice, Mrs. Lancaster," she said with a pleasant smile. "But the fact is that I don't need any help."

Tess was looking into Leslie's eyes. A lifetime of judging other people's strengths and weaknesses came to her aid as she tried to evaluate Leslie Curran. She looked like the kept woman she was, according to Ron's information. Yet there was an innocence about her, and a brittle surface under which Tess sensed great fear.

"Do you keep up with the news, Miss Curran?" she asked.

The girl nodded noncommittally.

"Then you have heard about the problems facing my husband in the primaries," Tess said, doing her best to sound cool and authoritative.

"Someone is trying to intimidate Haydon Lancaster into dropping out of the presidential race. Someone who, as it happens, was once close to you."

She paused to let her words sink in. The girl turned a shade paler than she had been a moment ago, but continued looking at Tess with a hospitable smile.

"Haydon Lancaster will not drop out of the race," Tess said firmly. "The fact is, Miss Curran, that Haydon Lancaster is going to be the next President of the United States. The people of this country are waiting to cast their votes for him. They know that he, and he alone, can lead this country out of its current confusion and into the rest of this century without compromising its honor or its strength."

Her lips curled in a smile that bespoke warning as well as friendliness. "Now," she said, "some ugly battles may stand between my husband and the White House, but I assure you that when the dust settles he will be our President. The reason I am here, Leslie—may I call you Leslie?—is because one of the people who could be hurt in this process is yourself. As you know, you were involved in an episode in Washington a number of years ago that resulted in the death of a fine and respected United States senator. His name was Garrett Lindstrom. Yours, if my memory serves, was Dawn Thayer."

This time the young woman could not hide the emotion that quickened in her face.

"In the wake of that episode," Tess went on, "you enjoyed a certain degree of protection from the man who employed you in Washington. That protection brought you to New York, and started you on your subsequent career. I am here to tell you, Miss Curran, that that protection is about to end. It will end within days, perhaps within hours of this moment. You see, a lot more is at stake today than six years ago. Some powerful men are being pushed to last resorts. The protection of a girl like yourself—her reputation, her livelihood, even her personal safety—can no longer be a primary concern at such a time."

The girl stirred on the couch, but said nothing. Tess knew she had her attention.

"As you know," she said. "Amory Bose is not the man he once was. His powers are a shadow of what they once were. Yet he is correspondingly desperate. He is willing to sacrifice anything and anyone necessary in order to hurt my husband. I am not going to allow him to succeed."

Leslie cleared her throat. "What is it you're asking of me, Mrs. Lancaster?"

Tess leaned forward in her chair. "I want you to help me prove that Amory Bose was behind the Garrett Lindstrom affair," she said. "If you do so, and right away, the crisis going on in Washington this week will end immediately. Haydon Lancaster will become our next President. I will personally see to it that you are protected in the future. I can guarantee you a job, a life, even a new identity if necessary. And, of course, all the money you need or can use. As you know, Miss Curran, I am a woman of considerable means in my own right. Do what I ask, and I will guarantee your future myself.''

Tess wondered whether she had tipped her hand too early, and struck the right balance between warning and cajolery in her presentation. She could not know. Her own nerves were out of control.

Leslie was looking at her carefully. She realized that if Lancaster's wife had come here to ask her for compromising information on Amory Bose, she must not yet possess such information on her own. She was in the position of a beggar, and was trying to hide that fact behind her commanding demeanor. In a word, she was bluffing.

But this thought did not make Leslie feel safe. For in her mind's eye was the image of Amory Bose, with his smoldering cigar, his threatening manner, and his perverse enjoyment of other people's fear. Alongside this image was that of Earl, Amory Bose's ruthless, terrifying right-hand man. She had not seen either of those faces in six years. She did not want ever to see them again.

"I can't help you, Mrs. Lancaster," she said.

The polite smile on Tess's face disappeared.

"I don't like to repeat myself, Miss Curran," she said. "More is at stake here than you can realize. Please don't sit there looking at me as though I am a woman without weapons to make good her promises. I assure you that I have them, and I will use them. I have, for instance, considerable influence with the television networks and their news departments. The Garrett Lindstrom story is old news, but it could be reopened by a single revelation—particularly in this election year. Don't run the risk of embarrassment, Miss Curran. Don't run the risk of prosecution. Help me, and I'll help you.''

Leslie was thinking hard. She knew the woman sitting before her possessed considerable power. But it must have failed her, for otherwise she would not be here, begging a nobody for information about a six-year-old scandal.

She was bluffing. Leslie had to bet on that. She lacked the courage to brave the wrath of Amory Bose.

"I can't help you," she said again.

Now Tess's armor cracked despite herself. Tears welled in her eyes, and she fought them back with an effort. She could feel the vulnerability of the girl before her, but her own terror for Hal was sapping her sangfroid and making her lose her balance. Her attempt to give orders had failed. The time had come to beg.

"Leslie," she said. "Think of your country. What we do today matters not only for ourselves, but for our descendants. Can you see that? Hal is the only man in Washington who has the courage to get us out of that sick war in Indochina, who can halt the arms race, who cares enough to help our poor people and minorities . . . Think, Leslie. A good man can make such a difference in the White House, a difference that can affect millions of people. Help me. Help me, and I'll make it worth your while. You won't be taking so serious a chance . . ."

"I cannot help you." Leslie's teeth were gritted. She was terrified by the other woman's emotion, but more terrified by the thought of what might happen if she did what she was being asked to do.

Tess was at her wits' end. She scanned the attractive apartment as though in search of some magical element that might come to her rescue. As she did so she noticed a small painting of the Crucifixion that hung on the wall near the sofa. She looked back to Leslie, and saw the religious medal hanging about her neck.

"You believe in Jesus," she said.

There was no response. The girl's eyes were open wide, as though in awe of her visitor's desperation.

"Listen to me," Tess said, her voice cracking with emotion. "Six years ago you helped to destroy one good man. Save another one today. Wipe out your sin. Wipe the slate clean, Leslie. You'll never regret it."

There was a long pause. Leslie Curran sat motionless on the couch, gazing at Tess with something like true sympathy.

Then she spoke.

"I can't help you, Mrs. Lancaster," she said. "Now please leave. Just leave me alone."

X

TEN MINUTES LATER TESS was sitting in the back of her limousine, on the way across town to her penthouse. She needed some time alone to think, before going to LaGuardia for her flight back to Nebraska.

She had bungled the approach to the Curran girl, and she knew it. The girl must have had more protection than Tess had calculated, or perhaps more to fear than she realized. In any case, she had been unmovable.

Worse yet, Tess had not been clever enough to get an idea as to whether the girl in fact possessed or could procure information that might connect Bose with the Lindstrom scandal. Ron's lead had turned into a dead end.

She had failed miserably. There was nothing left but to confess her failure to Ron, and hope that he had other ideas.

As she opened her purse to put her handkerchief away, she noticed the crumpled telegram she had received this morning.

THREE DAYS, MRS. LANCASTER

She could not bear to look at it. She averted her eyes, and looked out the window of the limousine.

As she did so she caught a glimpse of a poster on the side of a crosstown bus passing by.

At the Museum of Modern Art
"Pandora's Box"
An Exhibition of Photographs by
Laura Blake
Until July 1

Tess looked at her watch. She was due at the airport in an hour and a half for her flight. She thought for a moment, and then spoke to her driver.

"James," she said, "take me to the Museum of Modern Art."

The trip to Nebraska would have to wait.

Tess disguised herself as best she could with a scarf and sunglasses before entering the museum. She paid for her ticket to the exhibition and found her way through the galleries to the wing where it was taking place.

The uncanny feeling that had been building in her as she approached this place grew stronger yet as she looked at the Laura Blake photographs on the walls. Nearly all of them were tight close-ups of people who had been caught with oddly revealing expressions on their faces. Blown up to eight or ten feet in height, the photographs were overpowering. They were almost too human, too vulnerable, and would have been sickening to behold had Laura not also brought out a strange nobility in her subjects.

The first room was full of pictures of people from all walks of life. Many of them seemed to be poor. The second room included pictures of celebrities. They seemed to document the frail egos of their famous subjects, who were eager to have Laura make them look good, but were also afraid of what her camera might reveal about them. She penetrated their masks pitilessly but resisted the temptation to make them look ridiculous. Instead she brought forth their humanity in a generous and forgiving spirit.

Not without trepidation Tess entered the third room. Hardly had she taken a step into it when she began to feel her composure come apart.

The walls were covered with enormous, gloriously eloquent pictures of the little boy, Michael. They captured him from age two to the present, showing about a dozen avatars of his growing personality, each of which was a masterpiece. His face seemed both to conceal and to reveal a thousand moods, a thousand possibilities.

This room was different from the others, not only because of the camera's powerful concentration on one subject, but because of the intensity of love emanating from all the pictures. Though not a connoisseur of photography, Tess realized instantly that she was in the presence of a genius at work. Laura Blake's pictures were full of a feminine giving, a capacity to love, to understand, that took one's breath away.

Though the first two rooms had communicated this rare ability in dramatic ways, the third room, Michael's room, carried it to its ultimate extreme. The photographs were alive with a mother's love for her son. Not that they were sentimental or cloying—the contrary, in fact. They were haunting, even frightening in their revelation. Laura had used the power of her feeling for the boy to lay bare his separate existence, rather than to idealize or prettify him. As a woman Tess could understand the sacrifice this had entailed.

But to Tess the pictures were much more even than this. For the boy was Hal, her Hal, the part of Hal that she would have given anything to possess, even to touch just once.

If only he were mine. The words coursed through Tess without her noticing their ambiguity. She only knew that the sight of the boy filled her with an infinite hunger and an equally infinite sadness.

And to think that this child, displayed here so openly and magnificently for all the world to see, was the same little boy in the ugly, secret envelope Tess had received only a few days ago, the envelope that contained the seeds of her destruction, and Hal's, too. The same boy! It was just a question of the sign, the coefficient one added to that grave little face.

The whole world could see Hal in these pictures, if only something were to direct its attention to his hidden presence. With this thought Tess began to feel dizzy. She moved on unsteady feet toward the middle of the room, where there was a bench she could sit down on. For a moment she thought she was not going to make it. The nightmare collection of pictures, staring down at her with their candid innocent eyes, were too much to bear.

A quiet voice shook her from her confusion as she felt a hand on her arm.

"Are you all right? Can I help you?"

Tess turned to see a small woman smiling at her. She was dressed in an attractive spring outfit, with a bright skirt and patterned top. Her hair was shoulder-length, her eyes friendly. Since she carried no coat or wrap, one would assume she worked at the museum, or was perhaps a student.

But in the next instant the truth struck Tess a hammer blow.

It was Laura herself.

Mercifully, the bench was right behind Tess. Laura helped her to sit down.

"Would you like a glass of water or something?" she asked.

Tess shook her head. "I'm sorry," she said, touching a hand to her breast. "I must have had a little fainting spell. I didn't eat anything today. It's nice of you to keep me from falling down in front of everybody."

"Not at all," Laura said. "I'm always hanging around here, trying to see how people like the pictures. I can't seem to tear myself away. But quite honestly, I wouldn't have known what to think if someone fainted in front of them."

Tess forced a smile.

"Well, don't worry about it," she said. "If I had fainted, it wouldn't be out of disapproval. They're beautiful pictures. So beautiful . . ."

She looked into the eyes of the woman who had now sat down beside her.

"You're Laura, aren't you?" she asked.

Laura nodded. "That's right," she smiled. "I hope it doesn't embarrass you to have the photographer standing around while you look at the pictures. Don't worry. If you feel like laughing at them, I have a thick skin."

"Oh no . . ." Tess could hardly bear the thought. "I can't believe that anyone could ever laugh at such pictures. The opposite would seem more likely. They break your heart. I almost wish I had never seen them . . ."

The awful irony behind her words was perceptible only to herself.

"I'm—I'm thrilled to meet you," she managed to add. "I haven't known your work before this exhibition, but believe me, I'm a fan now." She looked into her lap, and held up a hand in frustration. "I should have brought my copy of the catalog. I'd love to have your autograph."

"I'll get one for you before you leave," Laura said. "It will be my pleasure."

Tess felt weaker than ever. Sitting down did not seem to have restored her equilibrium. The proximity of the other woman seemed to drain away the last of her strength.

All at once she sensed that her disguise was not fooling Laura. The look in those lovely dark eyes left no doubt of it.

"Do you know who I am?" Tess asked.

Laura gave her a soft, understanding look. "Not if you don't want me to," she said. "I can understand your not wanting to be recognized. I know how busy and important you are. I appreciate your taking the time to come here."

Tess could think of no answer to this. She cast about for something to say. The first thing that came to mind popped out of her mouth unbidden.

"Your boy . . ." She gestured to the pictures. "The catalog said he's your son. I . . . he's very beautiful. You must love him very much."

Laura nodded. Obviously words could not convey the depth of feeling that shone in the photographs.

"Your husband . . .," Tess blurted out. "He must be very proud, too. I mean, to see the little boy this way . . ." She realized what she was asking, but could not stop herself.

Laura's smile had a shadow now, but was no less sincere.

"We're divorced," she said. "He lives in California."

"Oh, I'm sorry," Tess said. "Did I say the wrong thing?"

"Not at all," Laura smiled. "I asked them not to mention my marriage in the catalog. My ex-husband doesn't . . . Well, it was a clean break. You see what I mean . . ."

"Of course!" Tess promised, doing her best to hide the tremor in her voice. "Really, I'm sorry I asked. It's none of my business."

Laura said nothing. She seemed neither embarrassed nor reproachful. Her eyes bore the same look of simple welcome and friendliness as before.

"The catalog," Tess pursued confusedly, "mentioned that you were *the* Laura, from Laura, Ltd. I can't tell you how much I admire your having moved from one career to another with so much success. It must have been quite a challenge for you."

Laura shrugged. "Oh, it doesn't feel like that when you're doing it," she said. "It's more like a growing experience, or a—well, a change of life. The one thing simply takes over from the other, as you do it more and more."

"I feel guilty, because I can't say I've worn your clothes," Tess said. "So many of my friends did . . . I still can't understand how I missed you."

"Well, if you'll pardon a little hard truth," Laura said, "you've always looked so magnificent in Givenchy that I doubt I could have done you justice."

Tess blushed. Her mind was racing as she tried to imagine what might have happened had she met Laura years ago, been her client, worn her clothes. Could it have made any difference? What impact might it have had?

But it was too dizzying to try to factor such a possibility into the already tangled equation that was her indirect relationship to this gentle young woman.

"My husband," she said. "His first wife, Diana—she looked so marvelous in your designs. I . . ." Her words trailed off. It seemed that every subject she tried to broach with Laura was in some sense taboo.

But Laura merely smiled. "I think it was a case of the woman making the clothes instead of the clothes making the woman," she said. "Diana is such a great beauty . . ." Her expression had not changed a bit. If the reference to Diana was hurting her, she did not show it.

"By the way," she added, "congratulations on your husband's success. I don't know anyone who isn't planning to vote for him. I'm positive he's going to get the nomination. And he'll be a wonderful candidate in November."

Tess managed a wan smile. "I appreciate the sentiment, particularly now," she said. "We're under a bit of a cloud, as you probably know."

"Oh, it's nothing that won't pass, I'm sure," Laura said.

"Thank you," Tess replied, darting her hostess a sidelong glance that Laura appeared not to notice.

Tess could not believe her ears. How could they be sitting here talking so politely, so amicably, about the man they both loved, the man who was the father of the boy in these pictures, the man whose fate hung in the balance at this very moment because of that boy and because of this attractive young woman smiling into her eyes?

How could such things happen under heaven? What madness possessed the gods above, that they could arrange such cruel games for human beings to be forced to play?

Laura was looking at Tess a trifle more closely.

"If you'll pardon a photographer's observation," she said, "the pictures in the press don't do you justice. Even in that disguise you're a very beautiful woman."

"Oh, I—thank you," Tess stammered. "Really, you're too nice. I don't feel very beautiful these days."

"Well, don't encourage me," Laura laughed, "or the next thing you know I'll be asking you to let me take your picture."

Tess was thoroughly confused. The kindness in the other woman's eyes seemed deeper even than the pain she was feeling now. There was something almost godlike about it.

But at the same time there was a penetration, an intuition in those dark eyes, that made one fear that one could keep no secret from them for long. Tess began to wish she could get out of here as quickly as possible.

"You know," Laura said, "I met your husband once, long ago. When I was delivering some clothes to Diana. He was famous even then, and I was a nobody, but he was awfully pleasant to me." Suddenly she put her hand to her lips as though to catch herself. "Oh, I'm sorry. That was so long ago. Before his marriage. I hope I didn't put my foot in my mouth."

"Not at all," Tess said, relieved that the other woman was on the wrong track. "That was way before my time, as you say. Believe me, I have no hard feelings at all for Diana. The fact is, she and Hal had had their parting of the ways almost before I came along. I knew her very little, but she was rather like a daughter to me. You see, I had been widowed twice, even back then."

She laughed. "I must seem like some sort of ancient crone to you. Sometimes my own past amazes me. It just goes back and back and back . . ."

There was a silence. A strange sisterly intimacy seemed to join Tess to Laura, making her want to unburden herself of all sorts of things. But she saw the danger of this, and kept her silence.

It was Laura who broke the spell.

"I'm going to have to run in a moment," she said, looking at her watch. "There's a photography critic coming to interview me and the exhibition director. We have to be extra nice to him. Are you sure you're feeling all right?"

"I'm fine," Tess insisted. "Really."

"Oh! Wait just a moment," Laura said, standing up. "I'll be right back."

She disappeared for a long moment. Tess sat gazing helplessly at the images of the boy shining down their youthful enigma from the cold white walls. Her world was careening out of control. Laura was such an admirable young woman. She obviously adored that boy with all her soul. It was as hard to dream of cruel vengeance against her as to plan one's own destruction.

But that very sweetness of Laura, those wide deep eyes so full of wisdom, of humanity and readiness for love—it must have been this that attracted Hal . . .

Tess closed her eyes. It was all too terrible to think about. She had to get out of here before the mysteries of this place drove her insane.

At length Laura reappeared, carrying a copy of the exhibition booklet.

"For you," she said, handing it to Tess. "I autographed it for you. Really, I'm so grateful you came."

"It was a pleasure," Tess said, shaking the other woman's small hand. "I can't tell you how much I admire your work. Keep it up. I hope to be seeing a lot more of it in the future."

"I'll do my best," Laura said. "And good luck to you with the campaign. I just know it's going to turn out wonderfully." She leaned closer to murmur, "I won't tell anyone you were here if you'd prefer I didn't."

Tess looked thoughtful. "You know," she said, "that might be a good idea. I'm supposed to be giving a speech in Lincoln, Nebraska, right now, but I had to fly back here on some urgent business, and I wanted to see your exhibition while I had the chance."

"It will be our secret, then," Laura said.

Tess nodded, noticing the odd sound of these words.

Laura walked her back through the exhibition galleries to the museum lobby. As they prepared to say goodbye, Tess asked the question that had been on her mind since she first walked in.

"Tell me something," she said. "When did you first realize you wanted to be a photographer? I mean, what started it all? You were such a brilliant designer . . . It couldn't have been easy to tear yourself away from something you cared so much about."

Laura smiled ruminatively.

"You know," she said. "I've asked myself that question many times. There was a day when one of our models, a girl named Penny, came over to my place to tell me some news that had her worried. I took pictures of her that day, and they cast a sort of spell over me. I've often told people that that was where it all started . . ."

"But it wasn't?" Tess asked.

Laura shook her head. "Not exactly," she said. "There was another time, years before that—though I didn't see the importance of it until much later. I was with—I was with my husband at a swimming place, and I took a picture of him beside the pool." She laughed. "I don't know whether it was the camera, or just falling in love. Anyway, I kept the picture. Maybe that's where it all started. I don't quite know."

She shrugged. "I don't imagine that really answers your question, does it?"

Tess smiled. "Some things don't have easy answers," she said. "Thank you so much, Laura. I hope we meet again."

"Thank you for coming. And send—" Laura stopped herself. "No, never mind. I was going to say send your husband my best wishes for the campaign. But he wouldn't remember me after all these years. Besides," she grinned conspiratorially, "you weren't here, were you?"

"Mum's the word," Tess nodded. "Goodbye, Laura."

"Goodbye."

Tess went out through the revolving door. When she was outside she looked back to see Laura walking away across the lobby.

The whole world was spinning as madly as that revolving door. Tess could hardly breathe.

Why did I come here? she asked herself miserably. *What is the matter with me?*

How much wiser it would have been to have hated this woman from a safe distance, rather than to have set foot within the orbit of her unique, disarming charms. It would have been so much easier to contemplate the things she might have to do, and then to do them, or have Ron do them, had she not come here and had this encounter.

Tess began to move on unsteady legs toward her waiting car. But she stopped in her tracks as, all at once, Sybil's riddle came out of the past to take her breath away, shining with a crystalline purity of truth that only increased its malignance.

Ask the fellow in the pool.

If the look of love shining in the pretty face of Laura Blake and glowing out of her boy's photographs had not convinced Tess of her worst fears, then that last unwitting admission about the swimming pool, tempted out of her by a question Tess had not thought of asking until the last second, had closed the door on all doubt.

It's her, Tess admitted to herself. *She's the one. The only one.*

Tess got into her car and told the driver to take her to the airport. Her suitcases were still in the trunk; she would not get home after all.

She sat in the backseat with the exhibition booklet in her lap. She did not need to look at it again. She had got what she came here for—and much more.

Now it was time to go back to the world, and fight her last battle.

If she lost it, and lost Hal with it, she knew that not even the saintly beauty of Laura and her little boy could survive the holocaust that must follow upon that loss. For by then the world would have ended.

And the end of the world leaves no one alive.

XI

Albany, New York
April 28, 1964

AMORY BOSE KEPT TESS WAITING for over an hour.

She arrived at his State House office punctually at four. His private secretary's eyebrows rose at the appearance of so famous a visitor, and she immediately informed her employer by intercom of the arrival.

Then nothing happened. Tess sat on the sofa in the outer office, gritting her teeth as she watched visitor after visitor go in to see the Senator. Despite her own gathering rage and humiliation she felt pity for the poor secretary, whose embarrassment was growing more intense with each passing minute.

At five o'clock the secretary went home, and Tess was left alone, listening to the murmur of voices from behind the inner office door. She opened her purse to find her compact. As she did so she noticed today's telegram, folded neatly among her keys and other personal items.

TWO DAYS

Tess took a deep breath. She was going to get through this somehow. Despite the gaunt, haggard face in her compact mirror, despite the thousand hectic little tremors in her nerves and the fact that she had barely eaten or slept in five days, she was going to survive this week.

At last the door opened. A male visitor was shown out and Amory Bose stood smiling down at her.

"Dear lady," he said. "It is indeed a pleasure to see you. Do come in."

He was in his shirtsleeves, with a pair of gray suspenders stretched over his portly figure. She had not remembered him as being quite so rotund. He looked older, more florid, and oddly satisfied. The expression "in the pink" came to her mind.

He ushered her into his office, pointed to the visitors' chair without a word, and sat down at his desk. A cigar was burning in the ashtray.

"These surroundings hardly do justice to your beauty, my dear," he said. "To what do I owe the honor of a visit from so distinguished a personage?"

Tess thought for a moment. She saw through Amory Bose's courtliness. He had brought her here to humiliate her. Therefore there was no point in wasting time trying to cajole him with polite formulas. This was power politics, so she might as well get right to the point.

She opened her purse, took out a small tape recorder, and turned it on. As Bose watched her, the smoke from his cigar curling upward toward the office's high ceiling, the conversation Ron had recorded between Bose and his assistant about Diana and the blackmail campaign against Hal was played back.

Bose did not take his eyes off Tess. He smiled and puffed at his cigar as his conversation with Earl sounded in the air between them.

"*She won't give up easy,*" came his own voice, referring to Tess herself. "*She's a fighter. But we have her in a corner.*" As he heard these words Amory Bose gestured to Tess with his cigar, a little smile of acknowledgment on his face.

When the tape had ended Tess put the recorder back in her purse and looked Bose in the eye.

"Well, Amory," she said. "Let's not waste time. What's your price?"

He raised an eyebrow. "Price, madam? Pray, what do you mean?"

With an effort Tess suppressed the pounding in her nerves and kept her eyes locked to his.

"We both know where we stand," she said. "You know me, Amory, and I know you. Now, just tell me what you want."

"What I want?" he rocked back in his chair, a sudden laugh escaping his lips. "What I want? I wonder, madam, how you could possibly understand what it is I want?"

Tess said nothing. Amory Bose was glaring at her with an expression somewhere between outrage and triumph.

"Let me tell you something, Mrs. Lancaster," he said. "Thirty-five years ago, when I was still a boy in my teens, I worked twelve hours a day picking apples in my father's orchard so he could make enough money to keep the parcel of land his people had been working for four generations. I don't know if you remember your history, Mrs. Lancaster. If you did, you'd know that most of the those apples ended up being sold on the streets of New York City by men who had lost their jobs, and couldn't make a nickel for their next meal any other way."

He paused to puff at his cigar.

"Well," he said, "despite my hard work and that of my father and brothers, he did not manage to keep his land, dear lady. The First National Bank of Olean, New York, took it away from him. And that same bank took our house as well. That little bank had had a mortgage on our house and our land for many years, and it foreclosed."

He smiled. "Now, do you know who owned that bank, madam? It was owned by a holding company in New York City, a company whose majority stockholders were a family named Lancaster."

He paused to smile at Tess as his words sank in.

"So you see, Mrs. Lancaster," he went on, "the same people who owned the coal mines and manufacturing companies and banking firms that ran our nation—the people whose speculations brought on the Depression—those people owned our little bank, and that bank owned me and my father and mother and my brothers and sisters."

He laughed. "Now, that's quite a joke, isn't it, Bess?" he said. "The sweat off my back and my father's back was for someone else all along, wasn't it? For someone who sat in an easy chair in the Union Club in Manhattan, and never gave much of a damn about who was working twelve hours a day to help pile up all that money in his Chase Manhattan accounts. And since he didn't know or care who was sweating to make him so rich, he didn't notice when those little people were ruined to help his banks balance their books. Did he?"

Tess listened in silence. She had not realized the depth of Amory Bose's personal grudge against Hal's family.

"When I went into county politics," he went on, "and started trying to squeeze a price support or two out of the government for our farmers, I found out just how patriotic those Wall Street fellows really were. That's why I became a Democrat, Mrs. Lancaster. I knew that the rich would never give up a cent of their money for poor folks, unless you *made* them do it. And there was only one way to twist their arms: politics."

Tess cleared her throat. "My husband is a Democrat, too, Amory."

Amory Bose leaned back to laugh.

"A Democrat!" he said. "Madam, you really ought to brush up on your history. Your husband is not a Democrat. He is a spoiled, rich society brat who has had his political career handed to him on a silver platter by his family—a Republican family, I might add. He understands nothing about how this country works. He only knows how to count the money that comes from the sweat of people he never sees. And that, my lady, is why he does not understand the threat that the Communists pose to our way of life. You see, Soviet Russia is a land where the common man slaves away his soul without ever owning his own property or his own destiny—just as the America of the Lancasters and of other robber barons like them, is a land where the common man works for someone else. So, madam, your husband may be many things —but he is not a Democrat."

Tess was taken aback. For the first time she realized that there was a grain of sincerity behind Bose's right-wing demagoguery. Not only did he hate Hal for personal reasons, he truly saw Hal as a danger to the nation. Bose was a genuine fanatic.

"And now," he concluded, resting the cigar in the ashtray and folding his hands on the desk top, "now you come here to tempt me with money. I can understand that, coming from you. Your husband was born with it. And you, you married into it—twice. You think I and every other working American will bow down to you for money. How sadly you misunderstand me, madam. How sadly you underestimate me."

Tess fought for clear vision. She knew now that she was not dealing with a mere political enemy. Bose had waited a lifetime for this revenge, and he would not be easily turned away from it.

"Amory," she said carefully. "I'm not asking you to like Hal. We can get along without having to love each other. That's politics, after all. I'm only asking you not to stand in his way."

"Stand in his way!" Bose thundered, his voice echoing off the old office walls. "Why, Bess, what could possibly stand in his way? He's got a name, a family, a Medal of Honor, a beautiful and wealthy young wife—who, incidentally, carries considerable clout with the media, as we well know—and he's got all the sex appeal, all the charisma he could possibly need. Now, what could possibly stand in his way? The White House is being held out to him for the taking, isn't it, like a toy to an ambitious child? Just as the Senate seat I had worked for all my life was held out to him six years ago? Isn't that right? Now, what could stand in his way, my dear—except one little mistake he made on his way to the top? One little bit of wild oats he sowed, that sprouted up in a little corner of our land where no one could notice it? Until now?"

Tess saw the bottomless hatred in his eyes. She met them with difficulty.

"Let him who is without sin cast the first stone," she said quietly. "If you start a war in the press, Amory, you won't emerge unbloodied. Can you take the chance of your own past becoming public?"

He looked at her, an almost benign smile on his face, like the cat that swallowed the canary.

"I've been in politics a long time, Bess," he said. "I'm an old poker player, from way back. What's more, I know you, my lady. I know how you operated six years ago, and I know how you operate now. If you had cards to play, you wouldn't be sitting here. You'd have played them already."

Tess's heart sank. Indeed, Amory Bose held all the cards. She had come here today to try to tempt him with money, and to bluff him with threats. But he had seen right through her. He had waited many years for this moment, and now it was his.

He could see her deflate before him. She looked pale, weak, and, for the first time in her life, defenseless.

"All right," she said, a tear running down her cheek. "Suppose I convince him to withdraw. I don't know how I'll do it, but suppose I convince him. Will you withhold the information you have? Will you leave him his political future?"

An enigmatic smile curled Amory Bose's lips. He sat back in his chair, savoring her desperation.

"Will you do that?" Tess asked. "Will you spare him?"

She was aghast at what she was asking, and what she had already offered. But Hal's entire future was at stake, as well as her last hope for her life with him.

"Will you leave him his future?" she repeated pathetically. "If you do that, I'll get him out of your way for this year."

She could see he was enjoying her humiliation. He picked up the cigar and puffed at it, never taking his eyes off her.

She looked up at him through tear-stained eyes. "How can I convince you?" she asked. "I'll do anything . . ."

Suddenly there was a lewd gleam in his eyes, a look of sadistic anticipation. He raised an eyebrow inquiringly.

All at once she understood what he wanted.

It was a high price. But she would pay it for Hal.

She stood up and moved around the desk to his side. As she did so she glanced at the frosted glass window in the ancient oak door. She knew the outer office was empty. Everyone had gone home.

"Anything I have," she said, "is yours. Just say the word. Tell me what you want."

She saw his eyes dart down to her breast, and back to her face. She understood the signal. Fighting against the trembling in her fingers, she touched at the tie of her blouse. It came undone. He was watching her with interest, the cigar in his mouth.

She undid her skirt, and it fell to her feet. The blouse followed, and she was dressed only in her bra and panties. Amory Bose looked her over slowly, an expression of sensual appraisal glittering in his eyes.

Feeling a deathly cold surround her, Tess slipped off her underclothes and stood naked before him.

"Anything . . . ," he repeated musingly, the cigar smoke curling around his face.

Shuddering in her nudity, she nodded. "Anything."

For a moment he admired her breasts, the clean slim thrust of her shoulders, the creamy flesh of her loins, her thighs. Then he grasped her wrists. She felt a downward pull. She sank obediently to her knees before him. Keeping the cigar in his mouth, he touched coyly at the zipper of his trousers, then patted his own stomach.

Tess felt a wave of nausea inside her. Sex had never meant anything to her in a lifetime, except with Hal. In her day she would have pleasured a hundred Amory Boses without a second thought if she believed it could help her get where she was going. But at this moment the idea of what was waiting behind that zipper made her sick with loathing.

Yet she was prepared to suffer any humiliation, any abasement, for Hal.

Bose was staring down at her, a cruel smile on his face. His hips rolled slightly in an obscene gesture of invitation.

"Anything?" he asked slowly.

Unnoticed by the nation outside this office whose fate depended on what she did now, unseen by her husband who was campaigning thousands of miles away, Tess took the biggest step of her life.

She reached to undo the zipper.

XII

Laguna Beach, California
April 28, 1964

"WAKE UP, SLEEPYHEAD."

A pair of warm lips kissed Tim Riordan slowly. As his eyes opened he could see lush blonde hair, long and wavy, above large blue eyes, a complexion tanned gold by the sun, and the fine sculptured features of a beautiful young woman.

Julie was still in her shortie pajamas. He breathed in her fresh, breezy fragrance, and held her close for a moment to savor the feel of her body.

"Good morning to you, ma'am," he murmured, smiling.

She snuggled close to him. He sensed her nudity under the skimpy pajamas—the long legs, the firm breasts pressing against his chest. There was a touching candor and devotion about the way she offered him her body. It was all of a piece with the natural sensuality that was so much a part of her. Even now, separated from her only by this flimsy veil of fabric, he felt himself stir under his pajamas.

"I love you," she whispered, kissing his earlobe.

"And I love you."

It was so easy to say the words to her. They seemed to spring from him of their own accord. Like a ray of sunlight that brought an immediate reflection, she drew a flood of affection from him without his having to reach into himself to bring it out for her.

She pulled him closer. Her hands were around the small of his back.

"Say it," she murmured.

"Say what?" he asked, running a large palm over her haunches and watching her eyes glow with feline pleasure as he stroked her.

"You know. Say it."

"Mrs. Riordan," he said. "Is that what my lady wants to hear?"

"Mmm," she purred, her long thigh covering his own, her lips kissing softly at the hollow of his neck.

Tim smiled. The happiness he felt this morning was something he had waited for all his life.

He had met Julie eight months ago. At that time he was riding the crest of his successful new life in Laguna Beach. He had used his credentials and residual savings from his earlier career in New York to build a new and lucrative livelihood as a construction and management consultant for hotels and restaurants up and down the coast.

His reputation for business savvy, thoroughness, and shrewd judgment of people soon made him sought after as perhaps the hottest start-up man in the field. His services were in demand by investors throughout southern California, and he had made himself a small fortune almost overnight.

Tim had invested his money wisely. He owned commercial real estate that was doubling in value almost yearly. He had built a handsome house on the ocean overlooking the San Pedro Channel to Catalina, with a 25-foot sailboat moored in the marina next door. He owned a Mercedes 180 and a Ferrari Tipo 555. His closets were full of suits designed by Lisle Hayne of Los Angeles, and a wide variety of casual outfits that were tailored to hug his muscled and now deeply tanned body.

Within a year of his move from New York he was one of the most eligible bachelors on the Coast. But, a perfectionist, Tim was not easy to please. He played the field for several years, biding his time and savoring the finest fruits of female charm that southern California had to offer.

The luster of newfound freedom, success, and beautiful women for the asking was just beginning to pall when he met Julie.

She was working as a secretary at the Playa del Mar Hotel, in which he had a small interest. He had crossed her path one night on his way to a meeting, and been struck by the willowy softness of her body and the subtly sensual look in her eyes. He had introduced himself, asked her point blank whether she was available, and invited her to dinner.

They had been intimate that first night, on his boat. Julie was magnificent in bed, a tawny, purring creature whose obvious hunger for him was tinged with genuine admiration. She made him feel not only like a man, but a man whose feet were solidly on the ground again after a long ordeal of loneliness he had not wanted to acknowledge even to himself.

They had seen each other every day after that. He learned all about Julie's past, her family in Minnesota, her married sister, her two brothers who worked in her father's contracting business, and the desire for adventure and excitement that had brought Julie to California.

What he did not learn until much later was that the night she met him she had been engaged to another man, an investment banker from Santa Barbara. She had broken off the engagement the morning after her first date with Tim.

Julie and Tim swam together, walked and sailed and fished and played golf and tennis together, and talked until the wee hours about themselves and the lives they had led. And they made love. Day in, day out, all night long they made love. The music of Julie's body, which she gave so freely, seduced Tim completely. What was more, her confidence in him and her openness were irresistible.

Within two months he had made the journey to frigid Minnesota with her for a quiet, traditional wedding ceremony in the living room of her parents' home. Tim hit it off right away with her father, a down-to-earth man who respected Tim's sense of responsibility and his handiness at physical work. The same went for Julie's brothers, with their plain-looking but friendly wives, as well as her sister Tracy and her mother.

Everybody took to Tim instantly. And Tim felt he belonged. After the wedding, when it was time to leave, his eyes were misty as he said goodbye to the family.

The honeymoon was a cruise down the coast of Mexico with stops at Puerto Vallarta and Acapulco. During those fourteen days Tim savored Julie's soft beauty, her incredible charms in bed, and above all her effortless honesty.

And for the first time in years he allowed himself to think of Laura. The comparison with Julie was a telling one. Julie was so fresh and healthy and open. In retrospect Laura seemed so inward, so complicated and opaque a creature that it was easy to see why he had been unable to find happiness with her.

Compared with Julie, the very thought of Laura was somehow unpleasant, almost disgusting, for it was a memory of painful separation, and of his complete inability to penetrate her inner world, a memory of loneliness and a sort of terror.

But with Julie there were no secrets, no private corridors down which he could not follow, no occult thoughts he could not share. She was not afraid to belong to him. And possessing her was such a pleasure. Indeed, she made Tim feel like a man again.

"All right, lazybones," Julie said as she kissed him a last time and jumped to her feet, the sight of her scantily clad brown limbs making him smile. "Get yourself together. I'm going to run into town to get some things for tonight. Will you be back for lunch?"

Tim thought for a moment. He had a meeting this morning in Ocean-side, forty-five minutes down the coast. It would be hard to get back for lunch. But he was in the habit of making love to his new wife at midday whenever possible. He resolved to make the trip back.

"Make it twelve-thirty," he said.

"It's a date," she smiled. "The coffee's ready. Your newspapers are on the table. See you later, handsome."

"Bye-bye," he said as she went out of sight.

He heard the outer door close, and then the heavy chunk of the Mercedes' door. The engine purred into life, and the wheels crunched on the gravel drive. He could almost feel the brilliant sunshine outside the curtained windows.

At last he got up. He could still smell Julie all over him. The traces of their intimacy were so sweet that he was loath to take a shower. But he forced himself, doing a fast seventy push-ups before turning on the water.

As he washed his body he lingered over thoughts of Julie. The essence of making love to her was togetherness. The natural warmth of her smile and her laughter transformed itself seamlessly into the heat of wanting and the joy of possession. In her arms he felt exactly as close to her as God had intended man to be with his mate, graced by the perfect balance of excitement and satisfaction.

With Laura it had never been like that. He had felt almost too close to Laura, too much under her spell, and yet never close enough, never in that sure and comfortable position of fitting and belonging, of mea-suring a woman's dimensions and knowing they matched his own, and thus being able to trust her with all his soul.

With Laura he had always felt he was on the brink of some sort of abyss which drew him downward into dark places where he could not breathe. He could never make that leap, take that fall which would have allowed him to penetrate her heart. So he had stood on the edge, con-fused and dizzy, feeling her slip away even at their closest moments.

Well, he did not like to think about it. Laura was in the past, where she belonged. He had made a mistake in marrying her, and had rectified it at considerable cost to himself. Today he was where he wanted to be, and with the woman he loved. Laura was a bad dream now happily laid to rest.

With that firm thought Tim turned off the shower, dried himself off, and padded to the kitchen. He drank a quick glass of orange juice and took a cup of black coffee to the deck overlooking the channel, his newspapers in the crook of his arm.

The first one he opened was *The New York Times*.

He did this as a habit. He knew, of course, that the Los Angeles and San Diego papers would tell him more about the local business news that interested him most. And for the market information he needed, *The Wall Street Journal* should come first. But nostalgia made him leaf through the *Times* every morning.

His sister was still back in New York, after all. And he enjoyed reading about the new Broadway openings, the dirty but somehow endearing politics of New York, the foul weather he never had to experience anymore, and the cultural and social events he remembered from his years there.

On the cover he noticed the latest story about Haydon Lancaster's troubles on the Democratic campaign trail for the Presidency. *Lancaster Hot Water at Boiling Point*, read the headline. Tim did not bother to read the article. Presidential politics did not interest him much. Whoever won would be all right with him, as long as the economy continued to be as strong as it was now.

He flipped through the various sections of the paper, looking languidly for a story that might interest him. When he reached the "Arts and Leisure" section his eye was caught by a headline.

TRIUMPH AT MOMA FOR PHOTOGRAPHER LAURA BLAKE

The headline was superimposed over a large black-and-white photograph of a little boy, which comprised the cover of the section. It was an arresting image. An extraordinarily precise lens had captured every pore, every contour of the child's fresh skin, as well as the affecting expression in his dark eyes.

There was a small caption at the bottom of the photograph: *Boy in the Afternoon—1963. Laura Blake.*

Intrigued, Tim pulled out the section and dropped the rest of the *Times* on the deck at his feet. His coffee sat forgotten on the table as he began to read the cover article.

The article was laid out around a montage of photographs, all of which were tight close-ups of people's faces. On the second page was a picture of Laura standing in the gallery where her exhibition was on display at the Museum of Modern Art.

Tim studied the picture. Laura looked a little older now, and was dressed in clothes he had never seen on her during their time together: a leather jacket, slacks, a sweater, and leather boots. There was a large Pentax camera around her neck. Though her hair was longer now, shoulder-length, she still had the same elfin charm as in the old days.

And her soft eyes, with their candid but complicated expression, were the same, if a bit more wise, more tempered by experience and by something else that was not immediately apparent to Tim.

He looked at the opening of the article.

FROM UNDERGROUND JEWEL TO NATIONAL TREASURE

The photographs of Laura Blake have been an open secret in the world of serious photography for several years now, as is her identity as the former sensation of American fashion design who abandoned her lucrative and famous career five years ago, at the height of her success.

Though Miss Blake—the name is an Americanization of her Czech maiden name—intentionally kept a low profile in her change of careers, her extraordinary talent as a photographer was not long in attracting the attention of the international critical community. She began winning awards even before graduating from the Parsons School of Design's prestigious photography program, and since turning professional has won prizes in seven countries and had her work exhibited with that of other promising photographers both here and in Europe.

But it took the one-woman show that opened at the Museum of Modern Art last week to stun the American photography establishment into singing its highest praises for an artist who is already being called the greatest American photographer since Steichen and the greatest female photographer ever to use a camera.

The *oeuvre* of Laura Blake is unique. Her haunting photos of old people, children, hospital patients, drifters, bag ladies, and others on the margins of society are so jarring that at first glance some hasty critics have called them exhibitionistic or overly sensational. But they have since been recognized as a poetic exploration of the human family unmatched in the history of photography. Comparisons to Rembrandt, Goya, Brueghel, and Van Gogh abound in critical appreciations of her work.

Tim looked at the selection of photographs accompanying the article. They rang a distant bell, for they showed the same inspiration that had been evident in Laura's early photographs, when she was still his wife.

But her vision had been sharpened by experience and growth, and it was so penetrating now that his first reaction to the faces in the pictures was to turn away. They seemed to reach out at him with a silent insistence that was disturbing.

One of the largest images was that of a circus clown. Laura's camera saw through his painted mask so quickly that it might not even have been there. She revealed the deeper mask formed by his eyes and the lines of his face, lines that seemed nevertheless to tell the whole life's story he was trying to hide. Laura had captured not only the rather pathetic subterfuge inherent in human flesh, but also its strange dignity.

Tim was no esthete. But he could feel the unity of these photographs, the distinctness of impact and meaning contained in them. He nodded his acknowledgment of what was obvious on the pages before him. Well, then, Laura had followed through on her obsession with the camera, and made herself into an artist. That was like her, that stubborn determination—and, of course, the deep vision, the ultra-sensitive eye and heart.

Laura was a famous artist. So be it, Tim thought. He was not loath to applaud her triumph, and to respect her for it. To judge from these photos, she deserved her newfound celebrity.

He noticed another picture of the little boy, quite different from the blown-up one on the cover of the section. It was a close-up, but caught in two large planes of glittering light that arrested the eye. The boy's expression was astonishing. It seemed to reveal something crucial about childhood, as well as something curiously specific about his own developing personality.

Fascinated by the difference between the pictures, Tim suddenly realized that the second one had been taken through a mirror. The boy's dark eyes were captured in a completely new perspective. And, in the background, outlined against a window behind which a blurred cityscape was visible, one could see the frail, dark silhouette of the photographer herself, bent forward with her camera at her eye.

The picture was entitled *Pandora's Box.*

Tim scanned the body of the article until a detail caught his eye.

The third room of the exhibition, and obviously its centerpiece, is devoted to a series of close-up studies of Laura's four-and-a-half-year-old son, Michael. For any but the most daring of artists such a gesture would have been called the rankest self-indulgence. Yet these pictures take Laura's art a step beyond even the more immediately shocking and spectacular images in the other two rooms.

At first glance these are merely photographs of a small, very beautiful boy, capturing his growth between the ages of one-and-a-half and four-and-a-half. But the more one looks at them, the more one realizes that they are documents of an almost supernatural intimacy between photographer and subject—an intimacy at once involved with and distinct from the love relationship between mother and child.

The title *Pandora's Box*, given to one of the most haunting images of the boy, is extended to cover the entire show. Though Laura claims not to know why the title suggested itself to her, it seems a perfect choice. For, like the Pandora's box of myth, the art of Laura Blake shows us something we perhaps feel we ought not to have seen, something that would have left us in peace had we never chanced to come upon it.

Her photographs are not easy to look at, for they liberate human feelings one would prefer not to confront face to face. Yet, as the myth says, the last item left in the fatal box when Pandora finally closed the lid was Hope. In the face of Laura Blake's little boy we indeed see hope: hope for the human race not as it would like to see itself, but perhaps as it will one day become, when the blindness and egoism of its masks have at last been stripped away.

Tim rubbed his eyes. He looked again at the pictures of the little boy. The dark eyes, the fine black hair, the composite expression were indeed fascinating.

Then he turned back to the text. *Four and a half years old* . . . The words stuck in his mind.

Tim read through the whole article slowly, oblivious to the sounds coming from the bay and the road beyond the drive. There was no mention of Laura's marital status, or of her marriage to Tim or her divorce. Simply the pictures of the little boy, and the mention of his age.

Four and a half years old . . .

Tim looked back at the picture of Laura. Now he saw that the walls behind her were covered by enormous images of the boy. And all at once he identified the mysterious ingredient in Laura's smiling eyes that had come neither from the passage of time, nor from her success as a photographer.

It was happiness—and love. Laura had the relaxed, fulfilled look of a proud mother whose devotion to her boy supercedes all other considerations in her mind and heart, and who is thrilled to give her best years to this child, even though, as the pictures proved so eloquently, he must soon grow up and pursue a life of his own.

No wonder she glowed so beautifully from that picture. No wonder, too, that her images of the boy were so seductive.

Something had stirred inside Tim as he read the article. It was more than a pang of chagrin over the fact that, years ago, he had cut the figure of an ogre who had tried to keep Laura from her photography.

And it was more than the mere sheepish discomfiture of a man who has been blind, whose pride has been hurt, a man who knows himself to be guilty of having played the fool.

Played the fool . . .

Tim stared at the two pictures of the boy. As he did so, face to face with the soft little features that were nevertheless so masculine, somewhere inside him a brittle rampart began to crumble, taking with it the foundations of his strength, his balance, all his careful plans, his cool indifference to the past, his newfound faith in the future.

Her son Michael . . . Four and a half years old . . .

There was not a word about the boy's paternity. Not a word about Laura's past, her marriage, her love life.

But Tim's mind was already back in the past, five years ago, when he was behind bars in Attica Prison, locked up like an animal for what had happened between him and Laura. Separated from her by granite walls and legions of lawyers, yes—but still married to her, for their divorce did not become final until a year later.

Behind bars, where the most brutal of injustices had put him, an injustice he had spent all these years trying to forget and live down as he rebuilt his life.

Behind bars, where he could not speak to Laura or touch her, or keep an eye on her, though she was still his wife. Locked up like an animal, by her own complaint and the legal system that was her accomplice—while she roamed free, had adventures, played the field.

Tim sat completely motionless. The past was coiled around him like a serpent. His fingers were frozen around the newspaper. His eyes were wide, riveted to the face of the child.

A son . . .

He looked back at the picture of Laura. Her smile glowed with the quiet satisfaction of motherhood. Tim thought of her childless years with him, of the agonies he had endured on her account, the miscarriage that had killed her only chance to give him a child, and the secret reason for it all, contained in the hospital chart.

Yet, during his imprisonment, she had found time and opportunity to make a baby.

With this thought, Tim was on his feet, striding quickly into the house with the newspaper still in his hand. In the kitchen he picked up the phone, hurriedly flipped through the yellow pages of the directory, and dialed a number.

"Hello," he said, when the phone was answered at the other end. "I'd like a reservation for New York, please. Right away, yes. Today."

He found a pencil and wrote down the flight number. After hanging up the phone he thought for a moment, and then walked purposefully into the bedroom to pack a bag.

Ten minutes later he was standing in the kitchen, a light leather jacket on his arm, his suitcase in one hand, the keys to the Ferrari in the other. He paused, picked up the "Arts and Leisure" section of the *Times*, and walked out without locking the door.

He did not leave a note for Julie.

He had forgotten her existence.

XIII

April 29, 1964

LESLIE CURRAN SAT in the leather visitors' chair in Amory Bose's New York State legislature office.

The oversized easy chair made her look like a little girl. She was gazing nervously across the desk at Bose. He had changed in the years since she saw him last. His complexion was redder, his hair whiter and more sparse. But the look in the small eyes was the same, as was the cigar smoke curling around his face.

Surprisingly, this office was rather more grand than his United States Senate office had been. The windows were higher, the portraits on the walls more venerable, the heavy walnut trim of the room more impressive. And somehow the look in Bose's eyes belied the fact that he had come down in the world politically. He seemed confident, almost triumphant as he puffed at his cigar and studied her.

Neither of them had said anything since the secretary let her in. Bose spoke first.

"Leslie," he said, "is there something you'd like to tell me?"

She looked at him. She had not been told why she was here. All she knew was that this morning his aide, Earl, had appeared at her door in New York and informed her unceremoniously that she was coming to

Albany to see Amory Bose. He had given her time to pack an overnight bag and driven her himself, not addressing a single word to her throughout the three-and-a-half-hour drive.

But she had had time to think, and to plan. And so she knew what to say now.

"Yes, there is something," she said. "Mrs. Lancaster came to see me. Haydon Lancaster's wife."

Bose raised an eyebrow. "Really?" he asked. "Pray, what did you talk about?"

Leslie measured her words. She wanted to sound nervous. This was not difficult, for the very fact of being at such close quarters with Amory Bose was alarming to say the least.

"She said that you were behind the rumors about her husband," she began. "Something about blackmail . . . she didn't explain. But she asked me to help her connect you to the Garrett Lindstrom scandal. She said she would make it worth my while. She was . . . she seemed frightened, and she tried to be persuasive."

"And what did you tell her?" Amory Bose asked.

She shrugged. "I turned her down," she said.

There was a long pause. Bose stared at her, a look of cold speculation in his eyes.

"And why did you not call me about this?" he asked.

This was the question she had been waiting for. She allowed the fear to show in her eyes.

"I was afraid," she said simply.

She hoped he would believe her. After all, truer words were never spoken.

Again Amory Bose paused, studying her slowly as the smoke from his cigar rose in billows to the ceiling.

"You look wonderful, Leslie," he said at length. "The years have been good to you."

She forced a small smile. She said nothing.

"Do you know who was sitting in that chair yesterday at this time?" he asked.

She shook her head.

"Mrs. Haydon Lancaster."

Leslie kept her silence. She could not know where he was leading. She only knew she would not be here unless the situation was serious.

Bose stirred in his chair. "Leslie," he began in a thoughtful tone, "things are getting a bit hot at the moment. I think it would be a good idea for you to drop out of sight for a while. Until this Lancaster business is behind us."

Leslie nodded obediently. "Where shall I go?"

"Wherever you like," he said. "Go on a visit. See a friend. Go to Niagara Falls. But don't go back to New York. I don't want you near that apartment for a while. Did Earl have you pack a few things?"

She gestured to her overnight bag on the floor beside her chair. "A few," she said. "I'll have to do some shopping."

"I'll see that you have plenty of money," Bose nodded. "Take a little vacation, Leslie. You look as though a rest would do you good. But let me know where you'll be. I'll need your number at all times. When it's safe I'll send word you can go back home."

She weighed his words carefully. Every cell in her body was alert, but she managed to keep up the pretense of simple trust and obedience.

"All right," she said.

"Good. I have a car for you," Bose said, producing a set of car keys from somewhere and pushing them across the desk top. "It belongs to a colleague of mine. It's very safe; it's registered in his wife's name. You can keep it as long as you need it. But the important thing is for you to leave tonight, right away. I don't want you spending the night in Albany."

She nodded, looking at the keys.

"Don't stop until you're an hour or two out of town," he said. "Once you're on the open road, make sure you're not followed. If you are followed, turn around and come back to me tonight. Is that clear?"

Again she nodded.

"Call your landlady long distance tomorrow," he said. "Tell her there is an illness in your family, and you won't be back for a while. You can have her take care of the milkman, collect your mail, and so on. It won't be long, I hope."

Leslie picked up the keys.

"The car is a blue Ford," he said, "The license number is on that keychain. The car is in the underground garage. Level C, Area 10. Can you remember that?"

"C-10," she repeated.

"Take care of yourself, my dear," he said. "And remember, don't tell anyone where you're going. Just call me when you get there. And stay away from your relatives. This is a solitary trip. Do you understand?"

Leslie stood before him, the keys in her hands. She was on tenterhooks. She did not expect to get out of this office before being asked for one more service.

He looked up into her eyes. He seemed to enjoy her obvious worry.

"I owe you a lot, Leslie," he said with a smile. "I always repay my debts. You'll be taken care of, no matter what. I can assure you of that."

"Thank you, sir."

He took a puff of his cigar. She saw his tongue lick at the chewed end, which was dripping with spittle.

"Goodbye, my dear," he said without getting up. "Be careful now. I'll look forward to your call."

Leslie stood motionless before him. She could not believe he was letting her go this way. It was not like him.

On an impulse she stepped forward and kissed his cheek. He patted her shoulder softly. His touch was full of subtle meaning that was not lost on her.

Then she left the office.

. . .

She found the sedan in the underground lot where he had said it would be. It was an unremarkable-looking Ford, a couple of years old, with New York plates and a broken tail light. It was parked between two other cars in a part of the garage that was neither remote nor central, neither well lit nor in darkness.

Leslie stood looking at the car from a distance. She listened to the silence of the lower level. She turned to look at the elevators behind her. The elevator was still at the C level, waiting behind the closed doors.

She walked slowly toward the car. When she was halfway there she turned around and moved briskly back to the elevator. She pushed the button.

The doors opened instantly, and she got in. She turned around and stood facing out at the silent lot.

She heard a car door open and close. Steps were coming toward her quickly.

She pushed the DOOR CLOSE button. Nothing happened. She felt her breath come short as she heard the steps coming closer.

At last the doors began to shut. A spasm of fear shot along Leslie's legs and up her spine. The purse and overnight bag in her hands shook. She gritted her teeth. The steps were very close as the old painted doors wheezed shut.

She took the elevator to the lobby level and walked quickly to the taxi area. She signaled to the driver at the head of the line, who opened the door of his cab for her.

"Go into traffic," she said when he was behind the wheel. "Make sure you're not followed."

They headed away from the Capitol building and through the unfamiliar streets of Albany. Leslie paid no attention to the sights outside the window. Nor did she turn around to see whether she was being followed.

She thought quickly. She knew Bose had brought her all the way from New York City because he was afraid of what she knew about him. He had found out about Bess Lancaster's visit the day before yesterday. That meant either that he had had Bess followed, or that Leslie's apartment had been bugged all these years.

One thing was sure. If she had followed Bose's instructions and got into that blue car in the underground garage, she would have been a dead woman. The issue at stake was too important, and her status too lowly, for her to think otherwise.

And if this was true, she was in danger at this moment.

"Are we clear?" she asked the driver.

"I think so, lady. In all this traffic I can't be sure."

"Go to the airport," Leslie said.

The cab took a brisk turn, hurtled through several city streets, and shot up a ramp to an expressway. Leslie said nothing more as the driver negotiated his way through relatively heavy evening traffic to Albany Airport.

When they arrived at the Departures area the driver brought the taxi to a halt and turned around to look at her.

"I want you to come inside with me," she said. "I'll pay you for your time."

The man stared at her suspiciously. She opened her purse and handed him a twenty-dollar bill. "Another twenty if you do as I say," she said.

With a sigh he got out of the cab and accompanied her into the airport.

With the driver at her side she got her bearings in the unfamiliar terminal and found her way to a night mail stand. She took a small package out of her purse, wrote an address on it, added the words SPECIAL DELIVERY, and put enough stamps on the package to cover the postage.

Then she took a small notepad out of her purse, tore off a page, and wrote on it.

Dear Mrs. Lancaster,
   Enclosed you will find the information you asked me for.
   Good luck to you.

She left the note unsigned and inserted it into the package, which contained the tape she had made of Amory Bose's voice six years earlier. She had not listened to it in all this time. This was a good thing, she reasoned now, since if Bose had had her home bugged ever since her arrival in New York, he might have overheard her had she listened to the tape.

She had used her wits this morning when Earl showed up at her door, his most threatening look on his face as he commanded her to pack an overnight bag and come with him. She had simply taken the tape from its place in her closet and put it in the bag under her clothes. She knew that Bose and his people would be concerned about what she might try to keep from him, and not about what she would pack to bring with her to his side.

The ruse had worked. Earl had not thought to search the overnight bag or her purse.

As she sealed the package Leslie heard Bess Lancaster's pleading words echo in her memory.

Six years ago you helped to destroy one good man. Save another one today. Wipe out your sin. Wipe the slate clean, Leslie. You'll never regret it.

Leslie dropped the package into the night mail box and turned to look at the nearest departures schedule. There were flights leaving soon for Los Angeles, Cleveland, Chicago.

She looked at the driver.

"I'll only need you another couple of minutes," she said. "Long enough to help me buy a ticket out of here."

XIV

New York
April 29, 1964

TIM STOOD in the silent living room of Laura's loft.

It was two o'clock in the afternoon. Laura was at her exhibition now. Her boy was at school. In another half hour or so she would leave the museum to pick him up. Not long after that they would return here.

Tim would be waiting for them.

He stood looking around him at the unfamiliar setting Laura had chosen for this phase of her life. It was very different from the lovely Central Park West co-op she had occupied with him before their separation. Here the rooms were cavernous, lit by the dirty skylight, rather dusty, and not at all as noiseproof as their former home. He could hear trucks rumbling by in the adjacent streets, and the sound of a musician practicing a piano a floor or two below.

The main room consisted of a studio full of lights, cameras, and backdrops, with the living room at one end, closed off by a couple of large standing partitions. The walls were covered with blown-up photographs, attached to cork supports by pushpins. Most were of people whose faces meant nothing to Tim. The remainder were of the boy. His dark eyes shone in the images with an innocence that made Tim look away. He could feel the waves of Laura's love for the boy and her preoccupation with him flow through the large room.

Tim reached into the pocket of his overalls and touched the gun he had brought. It was a .38 police special of high quality, purchased near Times Square this morning.

He had penetrated the loft a few moments ago, getting into the building by pushing all the buzzers at once, and using the tools he had brought to pick the Jensen lock on the door to the apartment. Obviously Laura was not seriously concerned about security.

He turned away from the living room and paced slowly through the apartment. The kitchen was built into a corner of the huge place, but had been made warm and cozy by the addition of brightly colored curtains and attractive wallpaper. Finger paintings done by the boy were tacked up everywhere. One of them showed Laura as a stick figure with a smile, and had the word MOMMY printed in childish block letters under it.

The kitchen table had three chairs, but only two place mats. On the counter was a small plastic cup for the boy to use, and a can of hot chocolate mix. In the cupboards, boxes of cereal and cookie mixes. In the refrigerator, along with bottles of milk and orange juice, Tim found a small vial of medicine. He read the prescription. It was an antibiotic for the boy, who had had an ear infection.

Tim went on into the bedrooms. There were four. Two of them were being used as storage areas for cameras, backdrops, props, tripods, and other photographic equipment. There were filing cabinets full of neatly organized file folders that contained negatives as well as records of shoots, with dates, film roll numbers and, sometimes, records of bills paid by customers. Laura was very precise about her new profession.

Then there was the darkroom, quite spacious and elaborate, with developing equipment for color as well as black-and-white pictures, and a very large printing set for the blown-up pictures that were all over the loft.

Tim looked into Laura's bedroom. There was a double bed with a simple frame and no headboard. An afghan and comforter were spread over the bed. There was a small, cheap chest of drawers, and a bookcase. And, as seemingly everywhere in the apartment, there was a filing cabinet.

Tim now moved into the boy's room. It had been lovingly wallpapered with images of characters from fairy tales. The small bed had a fluffy comforter of its own. Under the pillow Tim could see the edge of what must be the child's baby blanket, to which, at age four and a half, he was no doubt still firmly attached.

On the walls were paintings done by the boy. There was also a picture that showed Laura with the boy and a third small playmate, all done in expressionistic colors. The world ALFALFA was printed under the playmate. Tim could not tell whether the picture had been done by an adult in a deliberately childlike manner, or whether it had been done by an adult and a child in collaboration.

There was a toy chest, filled with little games and toys. There were stuffed animals. There was a small wood table with crayons and a sketch pad. Bright curtains hung at the window. The room was obviously furnished with love, as was the kitchen, to make the boy feel that the huge loft, so much a place of business, contained areas devoted only to domestic life with his mother.

As he turned to leave the room Tim noticed a curious night-light by the door, its glass globe painted in bright colors. He turned it on. Looking up at the ceiling, he could see the faint glow of a reflection of the figure on the globe. In the dark of night, he supposed, it must be an amusement for the boy.

Tim returned to the living room. There were two chairs and a couch, with a large coffee table on which he saw some photography magazines, a copy of *Newsweek*, and the "Arts and Leisure" section of the *Times* with the boy's face on the cover. There was a small television set opposite the couch. The rug was braided. There were a few hanging plants soaking up the light from the skylight.

The whole place had a rumpled, lived-in look, not far from downright messiness. It was obvious Laura lived so much for her work that she did not care at all about her personal surroundings. The place bespoke the life-style of a person whose mind is elsewhere.

Only the parts of the loft that were for the boy displayed a loving attention to detail, a warm feathering of the nest, which showed how deeply Laura cared for him. Her life was clearly divided between her commitment to her new career and her absorption with her son.

Tim sat down on the couch. He felt relaxed, detached. He was in no hurry. When they came home, what must be done would be done. What would happen from here on in was an impersonal matter, a matter of justice and of history. It was time to rectify his relationship with Laura, once and for all. Things had to be put right. He was sorry it had to turn out this way, but there was no choice.

Obviously, the *Times* article about the exhibition had crossed his path by fate. How perfect it was! It had shown him everything he needed to know about the extent of Laura's deception, the enormity of her crime. And it had shown him how to tie up all the loose ends at one stroke.

And all because Laura had had the pride, the stupidity, the egotism to publish those pictures of the boy for all the world to see! That was the key to everything. Tim wondered how a person as private as Laura could have fallen prey to such an impulse. It truly perplexed him.

He sat quietly, fingering the gun in the pocket of his overalls, and waiting.

Time passed. Once he heard steps on the landing outside, and leaped to his feet to hide behind the door. But the steps went away. A neighbor, no doubt. Tim went back and sat down.

At length he began to feel uncomfortable, sitting under the eye of the boy, who looked out from a dozen pictures with that disarming innocence of his. Tim got to his feet and wandered again through the rooms of the loft.

He paused at the doorway to Laura's room. He looked in at the double bed. Something about it attracted him.

He went into the room, bent down, touched at the mattress meaninglessly, felt the springs under his palm, and stood up again. He noticed a small bedside table littered with books and magazines. There were photography journals, and a copy of *The New Yorker*. One of the books was a novel, *To Kill a Mockingbird*. The other was Dr. Spock's *Baby and Child Care*. Tim bent to open it to the place marked with a bookmark. It was the section on earaches and other childhood infections.

The spartan simplicity of the room struck Tim. Apparently sleep was a thing that did not interest Laura much. She lived for work.

On the other hand, perhaps sometimes the boy, frightened by a nightmare, came in here to sleep with her. On such occasions the double bed would come in handy.

Then again, Tim mused, looking down at the bed, Laura had no facilities for guests in the other bedrooms, which were full of file cabinets and photographic paraphernalia. There was no place for a guest to sleep, except on the couch in the living room.

Well, perhaps she did not have guests here.

On the other hand, if someone stayed late, until after the boy was asleep, and then, after a glass of wine, decided to stay over, there was room in the double bed . . .

At this thought something dark came across Tim's vision, veiling the room, while only the bed stayed in perfect focus. He could see it all before his mind's eye: the loving mother tucking in her son and kissing him goodnight, before returning to the living room to curl up on the couch beside the guest, while quiet music played on the small stereo. Then the evening grew later, the building more silent, and Laura, in her jeans and sweater, took her guest by the hand, and led him quietly toward her bedroom, a smile on her lips . . .

Perhaps it was the boy's father. Perhaps he came here sometimes. Perhaps he was a regular visitor, almost a part of the family. Perhaps he slept often in that double bed.

Slowly Tim reached down, touched at the afghan, and pulled it with two fingers until it slipped off the bed with a soft rustling sound and fell to the floor. He looked at the comforter underneath it and pulled that off, too. Now he saw the sheets. He could almost feel Laura's naked body slipping between them, and hear her sigh, feel her frail arms pulling her lover closer to her as she smiled her welcome, her invitation.

Tim had reached into his pocket to take out the knife he had brought. Without realizing what he was doing he held the knife in one hand and slowly pushed the blade through the sheets and into the mattress.

He saw Laura's smile for her lover, over and over again, saw her arms reach out, her legs spread willingly, her tiny limbs all open and eager and warm with acquiescence. Again and again and again the image roared through the inside of his mind, like a train crashing through a dark tunnel. Her lips seemed to open for love inside his brain, her sigh of delight to echo through all his senses.

Tim could dimly feel the spasms shaking his body as he crouched on his knees atop the sheets. Then, somehow, he understood that he was wet between his legs. An ancient shame consumed him, and an equally ancient rage.

When he came to himself he saw that he had torn the bed to pieces with his knife. The sheets were in shreds, the stuffing of the mattress standing out in haggard tufts in the half-light from the curtained window.

Alarmed, he leaped off the bed and stood back, looking down at it. The bed looked as though the unseen fingers of a giant had clawed it in some maniacal anger. The naked, ripped mattress looked forlorn and pathetic in the sparsely furnished room.

Tim looked at his watch. Two forty-five. How long had he been lost in his fantasy? Could he have made sounds that might have alerted the neighbors to his presence here?

He stood listening, his breaths coming short. The building was still silent, except for the echoes of the piano down below. Tim was reassured.

He was about to go back to the living room when he noticed the file cabinet across from the bed. On an impulse he opened it.

The drawers were full of file folders, like the ones in the other cabinets spread around the loft. Each bore a date and notation on its tab.

Tim opened the four drawers one by one. In the bottom drawer something caught his eye.

It was a brown accordion file with a rubber loop holding it closed. Tim pulled it out, snapped off the loop, and opened it.

There were letters, photographs, and papers inside. Tim saw two diplomas, one from Laura's high school in Queens and the other from the Parsons School of Design. He also saw her awards from the American Fashion Critics, as well as assorted photography awards.

Among the papers was an old portrait photo of two people, a man and a woman, obviously taken long ago. Tim looked at the faces. He remembered this picture. Laura had shown it to him just after they were married. It was her parents' wedding picture, taken in the old country. The father looked bleakly into the camera, posing before the painted backdrop in his best suit. The mother had a mild, sweet air. Neither of them looked terribly like Laura.

Tim thought of his own parents, and put the picture back where he had found it.

Then he began to open the letters.

Several of them, he saw, were from himself. They had been written while he was on business trips, during his marriage to Laura. He did not bother to read them. He blushed to think of his clumsy endearments. But something about the fact that she had saved them struck him, and seemed to confirm him in his mission.

Among the other memorabilia he found a second packet of letters, with a rubber band around it. He tore off the band and opened the letters, one by one.

Their messages were brief. Hardly a word; just dates and times. Obviously, they were assignations.

Tim nodded. How right he was! How right he had always been!

A couple of the letters included sketches, done on fine-quality writing paper, of people and places. They were hasty drawings, but clever and full of energy. Tim thought he recognized two or three of the faces. They were political figures. Eisenhower, Nixon, and perhaps McCarthy.

And there was an additional sketch, drawn on a place mat from some sort of lunchroom or delicatessen. It was an image of Laura, done in bold pencil strokes. It was undated and unsigned.

Tim looked carefully at the letters and drawings. They were obviously done by the same hand as the large sketch on the place mat.

Tim felt something tingle inside himself. He realized that he had opened the back door into the most private place in Laura's heart.

He searched more eagerly through the remaining papers. Letters, certificates, an early example of alphabet practice by the boy. The ancient yellowed newspaper account of Laura's parents' deaths, and the item announcing her marriage to Tim.

There had to be something else. Tim could feel its presence at his fingertips, but it was still eluding him.

Then everything stopped as he noticed a large manila envelope separate from the other papers. He opened it.

The only thing that could have altered the inevitable course of this day, and of the entire future, was staring straight at Tim.

It was a photograph.

XV

April 29, 1964
6:45 P.M.

LAURA WAS SITTING at her kitchen table with Michael.

The boy was drinking a cup of hot chocolate and eating a cracker, his eyes on his mother. Laura did her best to smile.

In the loft there were four police officers. Two were in uniform, and two in plain clothes. They had arrived within a half hour of Laura's call this afternoon. One of the officers was dusting the studio and darkroom area for fingerprints. Another was taking pictures of the mess in the loft.

In the confusion of discovering what had happened, Laura had managed to keep Michael from seeing what had been done to her bed. He had only seen the overturned file cabinets throughout the house, and the scattered books, papers, and household objects. But it was obvious from the look in his dark eyes that this invasion of their home was a terrible experience for him. Laura had never seen him look so frightened. He was clinging to her for support. Even his childlike instinct for acceptance could not encompass an event that was purely hostile.

Laura had made a great point of seeing that all his toys and stuffed animals were safe. She had checked to see that Felix, the night-light figure, was unharmed, and had asked Michael to verify that Alfalfa, his imaginary friend, was well.

"There," she had said when he joined her in this ritual. "We're all fine. I'm going to sleep in your room tonight, so we'll all be together. The person who did this was very silly, and probably very frightened. If he was my son, I'd give him the spanking of his life. But don't you worry: everything will be just as it was, as soon as the officers and I have cleaned up."

She had concentrated on keeping him busy and amused while she helped the police determine what was missing.

But that was the rub. Nothing was missing. Nothing domestic or personal, at least.

"Whoever did this," said the detective in charge of the officers, "was either looking for something he didn't find here—and did the damage out of anger—or found something that you haven't missed yet." He shook his head as he looked at the closed bedroom door. "I don't like that bed, though," he said. "No second-story man would do that."

The officers had asked Laura all the usual questions about the neighborhood, the people in the building, her personal and professional life, and whether or not she knew someone who might have done this. She gave the usual answers.

Her own biggest worry was that all her photographic files had been overturned and scattered over the floors. It would take days, perhaps weeks, to put them back in order. Not even her meticulous system of marking each set of contact prints and negatives with an identification number could make this job less arduous. She would get started as soon as Michael was asleep.

So she sat with him at the table now, watching him drink his cocoa, and thinking about what had happened. Though she had lived in Manhattan since she was eighteen, she had never been burglarized before. Well, she reasoned, there was always a first time. But she did not like the tainted feeling of foreign hands touching her private things. And, like the detective, she was worried by what had been done to her bed.

"Miss Blake?"

She was startled from her reverie by a deep voice. She looked up to see a once-familiar face in the doorway.

"Dan Aguirre. Remember me?"

For a moment Laura was too confused by the distressing events of the afternoon to place him. Then his face emerged from the past with a striking clarity. The very sight of him seemed to turn the clock back.

He stepped into the kitchen and extended a hand. She shook it and smiled.

"Of course I remember," she said. "How are you?"

"Fine," he said. "Older, but otherwise the same."

To Laura, Dan Aguirre did not look older at all. He still had the same hard body, the matador's drooping mustache, the burnished skin, and the air of calm readiness that had so impressed her when she first met him. But he was a bit more smooth, more still in his manner than before. And his eyes were different. When she had first known him they had been policeman's eyes, absorbed in cool untrusting skepticism. Now they seemed wiser, perhaps more gentle. This made him, if anything, more strikingly handsome than he had been before.

"Are you with . . . I mean, did they . . . ?" Laura stammered, gesturing to the other officers.

"You mean is this my case?" He shook his head. "I'm on Homicide now, Miss Blake. But my colleagues told me what had happened, so I came over to see for myself. I hope you don't mind."

"Not at all," she said. "Would you like some coffee?"

"No, thanks," he replied. "I wonder, though, if you'd mind showing me around just a bit."

"All right." She turned to the boy. "Michael, I'd like you to meet Detective Aguirre. He's an old friend of mine. I'm just going into the next room to show him something."

The detective leaned down to speak to the boy.

"How do you do, Michael?" he asked. "Do you mind if I borrow your mommy for just a minute?"

Michael nodded with a half-smile, too bashful to answer.

When they had left the room Dan Aguirre said to Laura, "He's a beautiful boy. You must be very proud of him. I have two little girls, both a bit older than he is."

She showed him around the loft. He took note of the mess everywhere, and said a brief word to the other officers.

"Have you thought about the idea that what they were after had something to do with your photography?'' he asked Laura, gesturing to the prints and negatives strewn over the floors.

"Well, no,'' she said. "It never occurred to me. I can't imagine why.''

"Think about it,'' he said. "You see, nothing that an ordinary burglar would take seems to be missing. The TV, the stereo, the radio, the petty cash, your jewelry—it's all intact. And those overturned files don't make a lot of sense, unless the man was looking for something specific in them.''

"Well,'' Laura shrugged, "I can't think of what. None of my pictures are worth stealing. And I doubt that any of them would be an embarrassment to anyone.''

The detective noticed the "Arts and Leisure'' section of the *Times* on the coffee table and picked it up. "Congratulations on your success,'' he said. "I remember when you were just starting out as a photographer. You should be proud of what you've accomplished.'' He looked around him at the blown-up photographs on the walls.

"Thank you,'' Laura said.

He kept the newspaper in his hand as he gently steered her toward her bedroom door.

"Mind if I look?'' he asked.

Laura opened the door for him. They went in together. To her surprise, he closed the door behind them.

He bent down to look at the bed, with its flayed mattress. He noted the overturned file cabinet, and the file folders and bedclothes scattered over the floor.

Then he turned to Laura, and spoke in a low voice.

"Let me ask you something, Miss Blake,'' he said. "And please don't lie to me.''

"Why should I lie to you?'' Laura asked, genuinely surprised.

"Was anything taken that you haven't told the other officers about?'' he asked.

"Nothing,'' she said. "Nothing that I can find, anyway. The house is a mess, but everything seems to be here.''

"This was no burglary, Miss Blake,'' he said, a deadly serious look in his dark eyes.

Laura was taken aback.

"What do you mean?'' she asked.

"I made a call to California this afternoon,'' he said. "Your ex-husband, Mr. Riordan, left his home suddenly yesterday morning. His wife out there doesn't know where he is. Nor do the people he works with.''

Laura looked at the detective through wide eyes. She had not known

Tim was married. It had been years since she had allowed her thoughts to stray in his direction.

"A man answering your ex-husband's description bought a ticket to New York at the Los Angeles airport yesterday morning," Aguirre added. "I think he came here, Miss Blake."

Laura felt herself shudder. She looked into the detective's dark eyes in disbelief and growing alarm.

"Tim?" she asked. "But why? After all this time . . . Why?"

Dan Aguirre was holding up the newspaper in his hand. *"The New York Times* was one of the newspapers your ex-husband was reading yesterday morning when his wife left on an errand," he said. "I asked her to look through it about an hour ago. This section is missing."

He showed her the cover of the "Arts and Leisure" section, with little Michael's face gazing innocently at her.

Laura looked from the magazine to the officer's face, and to the slashed bed behind him.

"I can't believe it," she said, her voice quavering. "It's impossible."

The detective's eyes had hardened. Once again she saw that wary, hard-bitten look she had noticed in him when he had saved her from Tim five years ago.

"Nothing is impossible, Miss Blake," he said.

XVI

April 30, 1964
11 A.M.

TESS WAS SEATED before the camera in a TV studio in Washington, D.C. In two minutes she would join Hal on a remote hook-up for an interview with the NBC anchorman in New York.

Hal was in Detroit. Immediately after the interview he would get on a plane for Indiana, where he had to make an important speech to the Veterans of Foreign Wars. Tess herself, having made two appearances in Washington today, had to be in Philadelphia by this afternoon and in New York by tomorrow morning.

She had tried for the last hour to contact Hal by phone, but had failed. He had gone straight from his previous speaking engagement to the Detroit NBC studio. Earlier in the day she had made a dozen calls to his campaign people, but he had been on the airplane from Ohio at the time, and unavailable.

Tess cursed the incessant speaking commitments, airplane trips, and other obligations that had kept her out of phone contact with Hal throughout the campaign. She resolved that when this ordeal was over she would stay within six feet of Hal for at least a year, and not get on another airplane without him if her life depended on it.

But today, of all days, her frustration was at its peak. For she had crucial news, wonderful news to tell Hal, and so far she had found it impossible to get in touch with him.

At this moment, as the make-up girl was applying final touches of color to Tess's tired face, she could see Hal on the monitor. He was saying a word to someone off-camera, and looking at a typed page, which was probably a memo from Tom Rossman about the latest-breaking events in the campaign.

Tomorrow was primary day. Though Hal had done a magnificent job at playing down the storm of rumors about his candidacy, the polls showed that he would have a hard time winning tomorrow's primaries. His opponents had gained strength from the press's obsessive harping on the possibility of his imminent withdrawal, and close races were predicted in the four major primaries and the five party caucuses.

After tomorrow the campaign would be a horse race again. Hal's commanding lead would be a thing of the past. And with the convention approaching, a last-ditch strategy would have to be devised to secure the nomination after all.

If only Tess could speak to him! But all she could do was watch his face on the monitor and curse this remote hook-up that brought her so near to her husband while leaving her too far away for a private word with him.

She saw Hal smiling toward an invisible point off-camera. A boyish grin lit up his face.

"Peek-a-boo," came his voice through the speakers in the Washington studio. "I see you."

Tess blushed as she realized he was talking to her. He must be looking at her image on the monitor in the Detroit studio.

"Isn't she pretty?" he asked those around him, referring to Tess. "She looks a lot better than I do. That's not fair. She'll ruin my image."

Tess smiled at his humor and blew a kiss into the camera. She hardly felt pretty today. Even on the monitor her face looked pale and too thin. But she knew how lucky she and Hal were to have been invited to this interview. It gave them an opportunity to present a united front to the public on this last night before the primaries.

Though no one was saying so openly, there was an unspoken sexual implication to the rumors about Hal this past week. This was perhaps because Hal's image was so saturated with sexual undertones—his failed marriage to Diana Stallworth, his childlessness, the beauty of both Diana and Bess, Hal's enormous appeal to the female population, and finally the whispered stories about his great prowess as a lover.

Thus it was crucial that Hal and Bess appear happy and intimate in this joint appearance before the national public.

But all these considerations meant nothing compared to the news Tess had to tell Hal. The small package she had received from a Special Delivery messenger this morning contained precisely the weapon needed to end the threat to Hal once and for all. Though she could not reveal its contents to him, or tell him about the terrible secret that had been behind her ordeal of the last six days, she could at least tell him that the worst was over, the danger was past.

If only she could steal a private word with him!

The producer in the studio was counting down as the last seconds passed before the interview. The network anchorman's face appeared on the monitor. He introduced both Hal and Bess to the viewing audience, and asked the first question to Hal.

"Senator Lancaster, your campaign has suffered this past week from a persistent rumor that you're about to drop out of the primary race. Though you've denied the rumor, the polls have shown you slipping badly. Some observers are predicting you may lose all the major primaries tomorrow. Tell me, what will be your strategy if such a defeat occurs? How will you seek to restore the momentum of your campaign —assuming, that is, that it can be saved at all?"

It was a tough question, as Tess had feared it would be. She looked to the monitor to see Hal answer it.

"Well, David," Hal said, "at the risk of being impolite I'm going to say hello to my wife, whom I haven't seen for nine days and eight hours, before I answer your question. Hello, Bess. How are you?"

Tess felt a shock go through her as Hal's question resounded in the empty studio. How clever of him, and how considerate, to speak to her directly this way! She had to suppress the tears that came to her eyes as she felt his tenderness across the airwaves.

"I'm fine, Hal," she managed to say, stifling the *Darling* that was on the tip of her tongue. "I miss you."

"The feeling is mutual," Hal smiled. "I must say, David, that having a wife who is as good a campaigner as Bess is a mixed blessing. I love reading about her in the papers every day, and seeing her on television. But there's no one around here to help me tie my tie. It's a lonely feeling."

Tess was all admiration for her husband. Not only had he managed to greet her and send her his affection across the miles, while millions of viewers stood between them—but he also managed to send out precisely the right message to those viewers. He loved his wife and missed her and needed her, he was saying. This humanized him, and showed the public that his marriage was a happy one.

As Tess listened, he went on to parry the commentator's question with a stock answer about the falseness of the rumors about him. He explained that it was natural for the race to tighten at this time, and that he looked forward to an aggressive, hard-fought campaign that would land him the nomination on the first ballot at the convention in August.

"I'd like to pose my next question to Mrs. Lancaster," said the anchorman when Hal had finished. "Tell me, Mrs. Lancaster, what do you think your husband's campaign has to do to get out from under the mysterious cloud that has been over it for the past week?"

Tess mustered a smile despite the brew of secrets boiling up inside her.

"Well, David," she said, "I think the best thing Hal Lancaster can do in the weeks to come is to be himself. In my opinion, some person or persons who are afraid of Hal's popularity with the American people have thrown up a smoke screen as a desperate attempt to slow down his momentum. In other words, Hal is paying the price for being a front-runner. But the voters know what Hal stands for, and when all is said and done, it's their voice that counts. I have complete confidence in Hal, as millions of other Americans do. It will take more than a spate of groundless rumors to shake that faith."

"Thank you, Mrs. Lancaster," the commentator said. "I see that we're unfortunately out of time. Let me wish you both the best of luck tomorrow. Is there anything you'd like to say before we cut away?"

Tess looked at Hal's handsome face on the monitor. He was looking straight at her, an expression of affection and humor on his face.

She tried to think of something to say, but the right words would not come.

It's all right darling. You're safe now. We're out of danger.
I love you!

In that split second Tess felt the irony of being separated from Hal by the very medium over which she had exerted so much control all these years. Television had made it possible for her to almost reach out and touch him across a whole country. But there were millions of eavesdroppers who could hear every word she said. And it was for them that she must look her best and her most relaxed, even while she was bursting to tell Hal what was in her heart.

Seeing that she was tongue-tied, Hal broke the ice.

"Don't forget to vote tomorrow, sweetheart," he said. "And don't forget who to vote for."

"I won't," she finished weakly, trying to tell him with her smile how much she loved him and needed to talk to him.

The interview was over.

In the confusion of the studio Tess tried frantically to free herself long enough to call Hal. At last the producer took her to his own office and left her alone to use his phone. She called the Detroit NBC studio and asked for Senator Lancaster. It took her a long moment to convince the wary receptionist of who she was and why the Senator needed to speak to her right away. There was a further delay as the receptionist tried to relay the call to the studio personnel. Tess waited on tenterhooks.

"I'm sorry, Mrs. Lancaster," came the voice after a couple of minutes. "Your husband left right after the interview. I believe he had to catch a plane. Is there any message?"

"No," Tess sighed in frustration. "No message. Thank you anyway."

She hung up the phone. Once again the lines of communication between her and Hal seemed stubbornly closed.

She had to reach him as soon as possible. But there was another consideration that took precedence even over Hal in her plans.

She had to copy the tape she had received from Leslie Curran this morning and send it to its proper destination by tonight at the latest.

XVII

New York
2:15 P.M.

LAURA SAT CURLED UP in the corner of the sofa in her living room, feeling like a guilty child trying to delay the confession of a crime to its patiently waiting parents.

Detective Dan Aguirre was sitting in the armchair across from her, a newspaper on his knees. She knew perfectly well his eyes were on her, but she did not look up. The television set was turned on, but neither of them was paying any attention to it.

It was afternoon, Michael was at school. Soon Laura, accompanied by the detective, would go to pick him up.

Aguirre had spent the night catnapping on the couch and taking the occasional phone calls that came in from his fellow officers. Michael had been surprised to see the stranger in the loft when he came sleepily from his room this morning. But Dan Aguirre had managed to charm the boy and reassure him about his presence.

Indeed, by the time they left for the walk to school at eleven-thirty there was an odd confidence between the two, as though together they were responsible for protecting Laura. Michael was clearly impressed by the detective's calm friendliness. Aguirre, for his part, treated the boy with respect, but avoided patronizing him.

"I'd like you to meet my two daughters," Dan said simply to Michael over breakfast. "Denise is just a little older than you. Debbie is eight. Do you like picnics?"

The boy had looked up from his cornflakes, interested.

"I like peanut butter and jelly," he said.

The policeman nodded understandingly. "Denise does, too," he said, apparently unaware of how great a coup he had achieved in getting the shy boy to speak to him that way. "Debbie likes baloney," he added. "Have you ever been to the circus?"

"Mommy took me this winter," Michael added. "I liked the elephants."

Aguirre had mentioned, in answer to Laura's question, that he and his wife were divorced. The wife was living in New Jersey, where she had custody of the daughters, who spent weekends and holidays with their father.

Last night Laura had slept on a cot beside Michael's bed. She had cleaned up as much of the mess in the loft as possible, so that with the exception of several huge piles of photographic files, the place looked like its old self this morning.

It was only after they returned from taking the boy to school that Dan Aguirre had sat Laura down for a serious talk.

"I've spoken to the lab," he said. "There are no fingerprints. We've checked the local hotels and rooming houses; I pulled out your husband's mug shot from six years ago to show around. No luck so far. I called his wife again. She still hasn't heard from him. She's worried."

Laura said nothing. She thought of Tim's wife, so far away. What must that unfortunate woman be thinking this morning, after having received calls from the New York City police about her missing husband?

"To be on the safe side," Dan Aguirre said, "I think we have to assume he might come back here."

"I just don't understand it," Laura repeated. "After all these years . . . It doesn't make any sense."

The detective looked at her through dark eyes that communicated absolutely nothing of his own thoughts, but probed her own with an unsettling acuity.

"Have you thought of a reason?" he asked.

"No." Laura shook her head. "Honestly, I can't think of one. It's been so long. He has his own life, as you say. A wife . . . I just don't understand it."

Aguirre gave her the look of bland inquiry that was part of every policeman's equipment. It signified that he had heard what she said, but was far from being convinced by her protestations.

He pointed to the "Arts and Leisure" section of the *Times*, which was still on the coffee table.

"It was photography that came between you and your husband in the first place, wasn't it?" he asked.

Laura looked away. The sharpness of his memory had startled her.

His next question came from left field, and took her breath away.

"Who is the boy's father, Miss Blake?"

Laura turned pale. She shrank back into the couch. The detective's calm gaze never left her.

"Why do you ask that?" she said.

"I think it's important," he replied.

Laura shook her head. "It's not . . . relevant," she said, irritated by her own stilted language. "It has nothing to do with this. You must believe that. I can't tell you any more than that."

"I think you should," he prodded.

"It's none of your business!" she cried. "I mean . . ." She struggled to control herself. "It concerns only me. Please, I just don't want to talk about it."

Aguirre's expression softened. Laura was astonished at the depth of his tawny eyes. There was something world-weary about him, but also a peculiarly masculine sympathy.

"Laura," he said. "May I call you Laura, by the way?"

She nodded, forcing a half-smile as she looked at him.

He gestured to the blow-ups of Michael on the walls of the loft.

"This is about the boy, isn't it?" he asked, his words searing her like acid. "Everything that's happened . . . ?"

She closed her eyes. "I have nothing more to say," she said.

That was when the standoff began. Three hours had passed since then. Dan Aguirre had made small talk with Laura about Michael, about her exhibition, about everything from the Yankees to his daughters' chickenpox to the rate of inflation in Nassau County. But they both knew he was waiting for her to reconsider and answer his question. And all the while Laura recalled his frightening prediction that Tim might come back.

The phone rang every so often, and Aguirre answered it. Nearly all the calls were for him. At around one he returned from the phone with a piece of note paper and read Laura what he had written on it.

"Michael Stewart Blake," he said. "Born September 9, 1959, Doctors Hospital. Mother, Laura Bělohlávek. Father, Michael H. Stewart." He shook his head. "The father's Social Security number doesn't check out. He doesn't exist."

There was a pause.

"Laura," he said, "perhaps you think that in your silence you're protecting someone. I don't know who. But I do know that you may be endangering your son if you don't help me in every way you can."

Laura looked at him through fearful, stubborn eyes.

"I don't have anything more to say to you," she insisted.

Aguirre's gaze seemed to penetrate to her soul.

"All the questions that are going through my mind about your son," he said, "may also be in your ex-husband's mind at this moment. Maybe he already has some of the answers. Maybe that's what he found here. Please help me, Laura."

Laura took a deep breath. She saw the logic in his words.

"It was a long time ago," she said. "It wasn't a long-standing relationship. I suppose you could call it a . . . a one-night stand. The man never knew. I've never . . . I never saw him again. It was my responsibility. I won't tell you his name. He's outside of all this. Does that satisfy you?"

For an answer the detective gave her his neutral look of silent inquiry. She had no idea whether he believed her or not.

But she had said her last word on the subject. She had made up her mind on that.

Dan Aguirre thought about this mysterious woman and her unusual life. Everything about her was intriguing, from her two very different careers to her violent ex-husband to this little boy who had entered her life in the interval since Aguirre had seen her. He was fascinated by the combination of childlike pleading and ageless sadness in her eyes as she sat with him. Her obvious pain only confirmed his suspicion that she was concealing something essential from him.

The only thing in this scenario that was not mysterious to him was Tim Riordan.

He had come across the type before in his years of police work. And he had personally seen the look in Riordan's eyes five years ago as he had wrestled him to the ground and taken him to be booked while his wife looked on in horror.

It was the look of a fanatic. Dan Aguirre knew it well. A man like Riordan could go to the ends of the earth, become a missionary in Africa, a monk in Tibet, a mercenary in Brazil—and the sight of a picture of Laura, or the mention of her name at a weak moment, even after the passage of many years, could set him off, and he would come after her.

That sort of obsession never dies. The person who has it may make elaborate pretenses of starting a new life. But, like the thirst of a binge drinker who stays on the wagon for months or years until the moment he falls off, the pent-up possessiveness and rage inside a Tim Riordan must have their say sooner or later.

The reports from the police and prison authorities indicated quite clearly that Riordan had tried to forget Laura. He had been a model inmate at Attica, and had been paroled after only two years. He had become successful in the hotel and restaurant business in southern California. He had an attractive new wife, he drove a Mercedes and owned a sailboat and belonged to a prestigious country club. He had not made a false move in all this time.

But two days ago *The New York Times* had run a cover story on Laura's exhibition. Tim Riordan subscribed to the *Times*.

Yesterday Laura's apartment had been broken into, and her bed stabbed a hundred times by an unknown intruder.

Tim Riordan had disappeared from California.

Therefore Tim Riordan was the intruder. Until proved wrong, this was the theory Aguirre must follow.

But the theory left too many questions unanswered. Why hadn't Tim hurt Laura or the boy yesterday? Why did he leave the loft in this strange condition, with everything overturned and nothing taken? Where was he now? What was he planning?

On the other hand, had Tim taken something after all? And if so, did Laura know what it was?

Dan Aguirre had been a police officer for nineteen years, a detective for twelve. He had seen every variety of human passion and human violence that New York City had to offer. His experience had given him an instinct about cases like this one.

His instinct told him that the reason why Tim Riordan came here was the little boy.

Aguirre recalled only too clearly that the event that had precipitated Riordan's persecution and eventual abduction of his wife five years ago had been her miscarriage. It was her loss of his own child that had set him off, along with his suspicion that her love life had had something to do with the miscarriage. He could still remember the man's animal ravings. *You owe me a child.*

Now, five years later, Laura had a child. And, for some reason known only to herself, she had chosen to make the image of her little boy the centerpiece of her first one-woman show as a photographer.

And it was the boy's face, not Laura's, that had confronted Tim Riordan on the cover of the "Arts and Leisure" section of the *Times*.

Why had she done it? Aguirre could imagine the artistic reasons. They must be multiple, and complex. But the very fact that he was a cop, and not an artist, gave him an advantage now. He suspected that, whatever her esthetic thinking, Laura had been driven by something private, something secret to make that little boy's face public, to show it to the world.

Why? Out of love? Out of pride?

He had looked through the exhibition catalog on the coffee table in the loft. The odd title *Pandora's Box* had struck him. Taken from a single picture of the little boy, it had become the title of the whole show. Was Laura aware that in revealing the boy to the world she was tempting fate somehow, living dangerously?

The birth certificate showed that the boy was born four and a half years ago. That meant he was conceived after the husband's arrest and incarceration, but long before her divorce from him became final. Aguirre, a divorcé himself, saw the significance in this fact. No doubt Riordan had seen it, too.

Of one thing Dan Aguirre was absolutely sure. Laura was lying about her so-called "one-night stand" with a man whose identity was irrelevant to this case. Laura was not the type for one-night stands.

The identity of the father was central to this case. Aguirre could see it in the photos blown up all over these walls. And in speaking to the boy this morning he had felt it even more. Looking into that quiet little face was like looking into a sphinx's riddle. The images captured so obsessively by Laura's camera celebrated not only her love for the boy, and her physical bond with him, but also the unseen man to whom the boy was a living link.

Who was that man? Why had Laura taken such pains to cover him up all these years, only to display him indirectly to the world in her exhibition? Was she so sure that her private knowledge would remain hidden from others when she was showing it for all to see? Didn't she fear that, like the nakedness behind the emperor's new clothes, her secret would be discovered?

Aguirre needed to know these answers. But Laura was not going to tell him. He could see that.

And so, like a stubborn conscience weighing heavily on its victim, Dan Aguirre stayed close to Laura, matching his silence to her own, watching the hours pass and staring at the pictures of the boy while he waited for Tim Riordan to show his face again.

And the same question haunted his thoughts at every moment, so painfully that he almost felt like a jealous lover himself in repeating it over and over.

Who is he?

XVIII

Philadelphia
2:45 P.M.

TESS WAS AT her wits' end.

She had been calling Hal every time she had a free moment for the last twelve hours, and could not seem to make contact with him. His final desperate campaign speeches were devouring the last of his time and energies. When he wasn't making an appearance, he was on the way to one by car or plane. The best his campaign headquarters could do when she called was to estimate his probable location. Her calls were a fruitless pursuit of a man who had become a will o' the wisp thanks to the vagaries of this mad campaign.

Thus it was with surprise and relief that she answered a knock at her hotel room door to find a messenger bearing a dozen roses with a note from Hal that read

> MISS YOU BAD. LET'S GET OFF THIS MERRY-GO-ROUND. MEET ME AT HOME TONIGHT. WE'LL CHILL SOME CHAMPAGNE AND WAIT OUT THE VOTERS TOGETHER.

It was signed LOVE, HAL.

Tess sat on her hotel bed and clutched the roses to her breast.

"Hal," she murmured. "My love . . ."

So he had not forgotten her after all. She had been in his thoughts all this time. The smile she had seen on his face during the remote interview had been full of the same affection that was now betokened by these flowers.

She looked at her watch. In order to meet her in Washington he must be canceling his last appearances in Indianapolis and Columbus. She would do the same. If she hurried she could get home before he did and prepare the Georgetown house for an intimate dinner.

When they were alone together she would find words to tell him he was safe now, to tell him their ordeal was over, without revealing what had really been at stake or her own part in it all. It would not be easy, but she would handle it.

And tonight she would be in her husband's arms.

With that thought Tess reached for the phone to call her campaign secretary.

XIX

Albany
4:30 P.M.

"DOESN'T THAT TASTE GOOD? I know you girls love the taste . . .

"Is this what you did to Lindstrom? I'll bet you gave him a good time, didn't you? Tell me, Leslie: Where do you like it? Where do you like a man to come? Did Lindstrom give it to you where you like it most? Did you tell him where to stick it? Come on, now, tell Amory the truth. Don't be bashful.

"You'd cry if I didn't let you have it, wouldn't you? Wouldn't you cry great big crocodile tears? Just like poor Mrs. Lindstrom is crying tonight? Crying because you killed her husband . . ."

Amory Bose turned off the tape recorder and sat back in his office chair with a sigh.

So Leslie had outsmarted him after all.

He had known she was intelligent when he first hired her, all those years ago. She had been a bright student with a high IQ. Earl had told him that. However, they had both assumed that her small-town background and her natural innocence would make her no match for them in cunning or intimidation.

But she had fooled Amory Bose. She had worn a wire the night of Lindstrom's suicide. And, in taking his pleasure from her that night, Bose had said too much. Far too much. From the words on the tape one could determine his identity as well as hers, the date, the circumstances, and even the nature of her employment for him.

All because he liked to talk a little when he took his pleasure from women.

He could not allow this tape to become public. Since leaving the U.S. Senate he had come down in the world, but he still had a lot to lose. He still had a wife and daughter who loved him, respected him. He could not allow them to hear what he had just heard.

Oh, well, he mused. Win some, lose some. Bess Lancaster would get her wish. For this year, at least, her husband would be spared.

As for Amory Bose, he would live to fight again another day.

Suddenly the phone rang. Bose picked it up.

"Sir," came Earl's voice, "I think it's time to act. The time limit has run out. Tomorrow is voting day. If you want to get the story into the morning papers, we ought to make some calls now."

"No calls, Earl," Bose said. "Something has come up. We're not going to act on this matter. Not tonight."

The silence on the line bespoke Earl's surprise.

"Have you decided to wait?" Earl asked. "There's time before the convention, of course. You can act when you think best. But there are certain things I should see to in the meantime . . ."

"Not ever, Earl. Not on this one." Bose's voice was firm. "We have to back off. I'll explain later. Thank you for all your fine work on this project."

Again there was a pause.

"What about the girl?" Earl asked. "Shall I follow through on that?"

Bose smiled. Pretty Leslie. Finding her, hurting her, would only bring about his own destruction. She had outfoxed him royally. He would look back on her with new respect when he remembered this debacle. Thanks to Leslie, the course of history was changed today.

"No, Earl," he said. "Forget about her. Forget she ever existed."

Amory Bose hung up the phone. He sighed and reached for his cigar. Starting tonight he would take his own advice.

He would try his best to forget that Leslie Curran had ever existed.

It would not be an easy job.

XX

New York
7:45 P.M.

LAURA WAS ON her hands and knees, rooting through the piles of negatives and contact prints in the corner of her bedroom.

Behind her was the flayed double bed, still in its undisturbed state of raped innocence. The police had told her she was free to replace the mattress, now that they had completed their examination of it. But so far she had not had a moment to think about it. Perhaps she would find time tomorrow.

Detective Aguirre was in the living room with Michael, teaching him how to put together a model airplane. The boy had taken to the idea instantly. As he watched Aguirre arrange the wooden parts with patient fingers, there had been an expression in his little eyes that Laura had never seen there before.

She realized it was a boy's affection for a man as opposed to a woman. It made Laura uncomfortable, as did the model airplane, for she wondered if she had mothered Michael too much, and unwittingly kept him from contact with males as well as male hobbies.

So she had felt at once safe and uneasy as she retreated to the bedroom to try to put her files back together again. She could not help admiring Aguirre's way with Michael. The detective had an impressive calm that put the boy at ease, and an almost paternal warmth that opened him up despite his shyness. Laura was thankful for the sense of security that Aguirre gave her son at this difficult time. Nevertheless the intrusion of a new face, a new personality into her household after the attack from outside seemed to increase her nervousness.

So she was doing her best to calm herself by stacking and filing the contact prints, and matching them up with the scattered eight-by-tens that were still in sloppy piles on the floor.

As she did so she noticed the large accordion file that contained her personal papers and memorabilia. She had not gone through it yet, except to give it a quick look yesterday. It did not seem to have been disturbed, so she had left it aside and got on with the more urgent work.

Now, on an impulse, she sat back against the radiator and opened the folder. She saw her old bunches of letters in their rubber bands, her fashion and photography awards, the old cardboard portrait photo of her parents. She saw her diplomas from Martin Van Buren High School and the Parsons School.

Then her eye was caught by the manila envelope at the back of the folder. She reached a hand toward it, but hesitated to touch it.

Inside were the two photos of Hal that meant the most to her. The first was the picture she had taken of him by the swimming pool during their brief affair, before his marriage to Diana. The second was the eloquent snapshot she had taken of him the last night she ever saw him, here in New York.

She had not looked at it since the day she put it into this envelope five years ago. It was a close-up, taken in the quiet hotel room, showing Hal, shirtless, his war wounds as visible on his flesh as was the grief in his eyes over the goodbye that was about to separate him from Laura forever.

She had printed the picture as an eight-by-ten in order to commemorate that terrible, beautiful day, and thought of it a thousand times as she carried Michael through her pregnancy and then brought him up. But she had never dared to look at it again. Too much of her heart belonged to it. She had concentrated on Michael instead, and kept the picture hidden away.

But now she thought of Tim's entry into this loft, of his exploration of her private world—assuming, that is, that the intruder really was Tim, as Detective Aguirre believed. She must open this envelope, just to be sure the contents were safe.

No sooner had she touched the manila paper than she knew the envelope was empty. She tore it open, her hands shaking, and saw her fear confirmed.

A deathly chill came over Laura. She shuddered to think that this furtive purloining of the contents of one envelope was behind the huge mess in all her files, the thousands of photographs strewn all over the loft.

She searched through the private folder again. Everything was there —her few little notes from Hal, the place mat on which he had sketched her at Goldman's Delicatessen, her letters from Tim, the mementos of her whole life.

Everything but the two pictures.

Laura was on her feet almost before she realized what she was going to do. She padded out to the living room and looked down at Michael and the detective. The evening news was on, with the volume turned down low. Aguirre was listening to it with one ear as he played with the boy.

How comfortable they looked together, she thought. How natural.

But Aguirre had seen the look on her face and was standing up. He came to her side and spoke in a quiet voice.

"What's the matter?"

"I . . ." She was not sure what she intended to say to him. She had long since made up her mind never to tell him about Hal. But the significance of the stolen pictures was deepening inside her like a wound. She understood why Tim had left so abruptly, without seeing her or harming her. And, indeed, why he had made such a mess of all her files. He wanted to cover up the one thing he had taken.

And she knew why he had taken it. That, also, was clear now.

She was pale. Aguirre's hands were on her shoulders.

"What did you find?" His voice was low, but insistent. "Tell me."

"A picture," she said in a tiny voice. "Two pictures. Missing . . . They were in an envelope. It was in my private things. I didn't miss them at first . . ."

Aguirre looked over his shoulder into the living room. The boy could not hear their whispers.

"Who was it a picture of, Laura?" The hands were holding her firmly, their gentle pressure seeming to force the secret from her. "Was it the boy's father? Is that who it was?"

She hesitated for a last time, and then nodded.

Aguirre was looking into her eyes, a terrible urgency in his black irises.

"That's why he made the mess, then," he said. "To confuse us. To cover up what he had taken. That's why he didn't wait for you to come home. That's why he didn't try to harm you or the boy. He had found something that changed his plans."

Laura nodded mutely, helpless as a doll in his grasp.

"Who is it, Laura?" the detective asked. "Whose picture did he find? Tell me that, and I'll know where he's gone. Tell me that, and I'll stop him."

Laura was staring over his shoulder at the boy in the living room. Suddenly her whole body tensed. Her breath caught in her throat. Aguirre followed the direction of her gaze to the television screen. An image of Hal Lancaster was projected there, as the anchorman spoke of the primaries.

Aguirre looked long and hard at the screen, and at the boy crouched by the coffee table in front of it. Still holding Laura tightly by her shoulders, he glanced at the huge pictures of the boy on the walls of the loft, with their glinting shifts of meaning, their suggestions of Laura's features and those of a stranger.

He gestured to the television screen.

"Is it him?" he asked.

Laura, at the end of her rope, could not find breath to answer him. She felt like a prisoner being torn apart by forces gathered from her entire past. Hal's face was smiling at her from the television screen. Michael was looking up at her curiously from his game. Aguirre's eyes were boring into her. And in the empty envelope in her hands, as in the raped apartment around her, Tim was present, with his hatred and his obsession to get even with her.

"Tell me," Aguirre was saying, "and I'll save his life. Tell me, Laura!"

Like a terrified child she nodded, looking from the television to Aguirre.

"Lancaster," he said, to be sure.

She nodded again.

He released her and strode quickly to the phone. He dialed a number as she stood mutely watching, the empty envelope still in her hand.

"FBI?" he said. "This is Detective Dan Aguirre, New York City police. I have an emergency for you."

As he listened for a response his eyes rested on Laura, their depths filled with reproach, and with something akin to sympathy.

XXI

New Senate Office Building
8:00 P.M.

HAL SAT AT THE DESK in his Senate office.

He had been here for nearly an hour, savoring his solitude and ignoring the ringing telephone.

He knew Tom and his other aides wanted to talk to him about statements to the press, and above all about a statement for tomorrow evening in the event that he lost some or all of the primaries. There would be an avalanche of media attention, most of it centered on whether or not he would withdraw in the wake of tomorrow's results.

Hal needed to be alone now.

He had left the Georgetown house after writing a note for Bess informing her that he had some last-minute matters to tie up at the office before returning home for their evening together.

What he did not say in the note was that the last-minute business consisted of preparing what he would say to her tonight.

Hal was convinced by the polls that tomorrow would be a bad day for him. And he thought he knew the reason why.

The rumors in the press were not just a smoke screen. Someone was out to get him. And there could only be one piece of genuine ammunition behind the campaign against him this past week.

It had to be a woman.

Hal's sex life had been an open secret in Washington for many years, just as it had been a virtual legend in high society for years before he went into government. No one in public service was unaware that there were risks inherent in extramarital sexual activity. But it was so widespread that those guilty of it usually assumed that none of their opponents would dare to cast the first stone.

This logic was not unsound. Nevertheless, every few years someone in Congress or in the executive branch saw his career ruined by a sexual scandal. Such episodes occurred because the individual involved had an enemy who was determined enough to take the risk of making the attack public, and powerful enough to believe he could destroy his victim without himself being tainted by the backlash.

Hal had such enemies—not only on the Hill, but among the JCS, the National Security Council, and elsewhere. A lot of men in Washington had staked their professional careers on military confrontation in several international arenas, including above all Vietnam. Jack Kennedy had died with sixteen thousand Americans stationed in South Vietnam, and Lyndon Johnson was under heavy pressure from McNamara and the Joint Chiefs to escalate that figure to two hundred thousand within the next few months.

Johnson was holding off until the elections. A prudent man, he was delighted to be a lame-duck president where the hot spot of Vietnam was concerned. He wanted to leave the problem to his successor—as long as that successor was a Democrat.

Hal was the front-runner among Democrats, but he had made no bones about the fact that, if elected president, he would halt direct military support for the South Vietnamese regime—a leaderless government, since President Diem had been assassinated with the tacit approval of the United States—and leave that country to solve its own problems.

And now someone was after him—perhaps with ammunition powerful enough to embarrass him into withdrawal.

Hal thought back on his private life since he first entered politics. True, he had had affairs, but hardly more so than most of his peers. Yet Hal was introspective enough to wonder whether, in cheating on Diana so continually, he had been unconsciously tempting fate. Perhaps he had used infidelity as a way to express his reluctance about politics itself, and about the public life he had never really wanted in his heart of hearts. Perhaps he had wanted to be caught and punished all along, so that the sad truth about his marriage and his love life would would have its say at last—even if it cost him his career.

But now Diana was out of his life, and loyal, courageous Bess was at his side as the past came back to haunt him. That was why he had come back home to be with Bess tonight.

He intended to confide the whole truth in her, and to ask both her forgiveness and her advice. He suspected that his showing in the primaries tomorrow would indeed be poor. Perhaps this was a good time to call it quits after all. He had given so much of his life to politics . . . Perhaps this was his opportunity to take his hat out of the ring and try to make a private life for himself, with Bess. After all, she was his best friend in the world, and he would not trade her devotion to him for anything.

All he had to do was leave this cruel political circus behind him, go somewhere out of the limelight with Bess, and start living again. Perhaps he would find a new profession that suited him better. Perhaps, with the unrelenting tension of the political wars behind them both, Bess would succeed in conceiving a child. A whole new life could open to them.

It was something to think about. Something to lay before Bess, and ask her opinion about.

Hal turned these thoughts over in his mind as the phone continued to ring unheeded on his desk. He looked at his watch: eight-ten. Soon he would go home to Bess. He longed for the sight of her beautiful green eyes, the sound of her voice, and the feel of her soft body in his arms. He just needed a few moments more to gather his courage for what he had to tell her.

Suddenly he thought of the pool downstairs in the basement. A hard thirty or forty laps would help to wash the grime of the last week off his soul and prepare him for an intimate evening with his wife.

Hal got to his feet. Yes, he mused. That was it. A dip in the pool to clear his mind, to get him off dry land for a few minutes—and then home to Bess.

There was just time.

XXII

8:00 P.M.

TIM WALKED SLOWLY down the lower hall of the New Senate Office Building.

He looked the part of a bored Capitol maintenance man. He was wearing overalls, with a name badge pinned to his chest. A tool belt was about his waist. A large ring of keys jangled at his hip. He had let his beard grow for the last twenty-four hours in order to cover up his normally neat, elegant appearance. He wore old brown hiking boots. His hands were dirty and oily. A large rag was sticking out of his back pocket.

The .38 police special was tucked under his waistband. Inside the loose overalls it was completely invisible. The clip held eight shots. He knew he would not need that many.

Inside his shirt against his chest were the two pictures he had stolen from Laura's file. He wanted them next to his heart tonight.

He was amazed by his own calm. He had come from New York on a Greyhound bus, avoiding the risk of using his identification to rent a car or get on a plane. He realized there was a remote chance the police had come to suspect him by now, so he was being careful. He had not gone to a Washington hotel, but had simply changed clothes in the men's room at the bus station and come directly here.

No one would find him.

Not in time, that is.

He had called the Lancaster campaign and claimed to be a UPI desk man in search of confirmation of yet another story of Lancaster's imminent withdrawal from the campaign. From the involuntary hints of the girl on the other end of the phone he had easily gleaned that Lancaster was coming home to Washington to sit out the election results.

He had spent this afternoon casing the office building. The burglar's tool he had used on Laura's lock in New York would open the door he had in mind here.

Tim looked at his watch. Just after eight o'clock.

Lancaster was still upstairs in his office. He was off limits up there—too many security people on the floor. But his habits were well known. Tim had a good idea of what the man would do when his work in the office was finished.

Something was guiding Tim's steps, clarifying his thoughts, removing all haste, all doubt. What was to happen tonight would finish everything off, tie up the loose ends, and balance the scales of justice once and for all. There was no way to prevent it. Nothing could upset his calm steps, for fate itself was arming him to carry out its wishes.

The building was virtually deserted. He began to go down the stairs to the basement level.

"Just a minute, please."

Tim turned to face the voice from behind him.

It was a woman. She was young and attractive. She wore glasses, and a pastel suit with a chiffon tie. She had long blonde hair tied back with a ribbon.

She was standing in an office door.

"Can you help me with something, please?" she asked.

Tim felt the gun against his waist. He turned and walked back to her side.

"Yes, ma'am?"

She gestured into the office behind her. "I can't get that window open. I'm dying of the heat in here. I've asked John to fix it a dozen times, but he never does. I saw you passing, and I thought I'd ask you . . ." She peered at his name tag. "Dean."

Tim hesitated. There was a chance, just a chance, that she would make him late enough to miss his rendezvous.

Then he smiled.

"I'll have a look at it," he said, following her into the office. He could smell her perfume as she walked ahead of him. An expensive scent. He noticed she had a good figure.

He let the door close behind them.

She pointed to the window. He grasped the handles and pulled gently. It didn't budge. The pulley must be broken, and the slides jammed by rust.

He looked at the girl. She was standing with her weight on one leg, observing him appraisingly. "I haven't seen you here before, have I?" she asked.

Tim measured the distance between them. If he had to strangle her to stick to his schedule, he would.

"It's my first week, ma'am," he said. "I was at State until they moved me here."

"Call me Carolyn," she smiled. Her eyes ran over his handsome body. "I'm glad to have you with us . . . Dean."

He turned back to the window. As it happened, he had just the proper tools with him. Luckily for him, he was handy about fixing things.

"Shouldn't be too hard," he said.

"Aren't you hot under those overalls?" she asked, a smile in her voice.

"Doesn't bother me," he murmured as he took out a screwdriver.

XXIII

8:00 P.M.

EXHAUSTED AND RED-EYED after a long-delayed flight from Philadelphia, Tess entered the Georgetown house and turned on the lights.

There was no one downstairs. Her first thought was for Hal, but the house lacked that peculiar warmth it always possessed when he was inside it.

Without taking off her coat, Tess dialed the number of his office, thinking that he might have stopped there before coming home. There was no answer.

She hung her coat in the closet and called the housekeeper, Constance.

"Constance, I'm expecting a late supper with Hal," she said. "Could you make us up some caviar and perhaps a lobster tail?"

"Of course, ma'am. I'll do it right away."

Tess found a bottle of champagne and put it in a bucket of ice water to chill. Then she dialed Hal's office again. There was still no answer.

She wondered where he might be. Perhaps he was passing the time with one of his Senate colleagues in another office. Perhaps he had already left, and would be home soon.

She poured herself a glass of sherry and stood in the living room, wondering what to do. She could not have slept more than ten hours out of the last seventy-two. She needed a shower if she was to look her best for Hal. But first she must rest for a moment.

She wandered into the library, where she found her favorite swimming picture of Hal illuminated by its recessed light. She turned on the desk lamp. There was a note on the desk pad in Hal's handwriting.

Will be at office until eight-thirty. Last-minute headaches. See you for dinner—can't wait. Hal.

Tess smiled. So he had got here ahead of her.

She took a sip of her drink and sat down on the couch before the large photograph of Hal. She smiled up at the picture, her thoughts full of the good news she cherished inside herself. Of course, she knew she could only confide the tip of the iceberg to Hal when he got home. But she knew they would be happy tonight. And they would be together. . . .

She looked back on the enormity of the challenge she had met this past week. The worst was behind her. Hal would probably not do well in the primaries tomorrow, but when the smoke cleared he would rebound from his losses and win the nomination on the first ballot. The depth of his popular support among Democrats would ensure that.

The party would unite behind Hal. The convention would be a ringing explosion of solidarity. Hal would emerge as a choice so obvious to replace the assassinated Kennedy that the election itself would be a foregone conclusion.

Tess's nightmare of the past six days was over. The future was an open book.

With this thought in her mind, and the sherry bringing welcome calm to her nerves, she gazed up at the beautiful photograph of Hal looking down at her from his sweet youth, his smile sparkling through the droplets of water that were immobilized forever as they coursed down his unclothed skin.

To her surprise, the picture looked different tonight.

Of course, it still glowed with the familiar ambiguity that had made it a precious family possession. The curious amalgam of Hal's youthful optimism and the sadness of those tears of pool water coursing over him, like a negative grace note, had from the beginning captured something essential about Hal, something that captivated all those who loved him.

Hal's smile seemed to say, "I love life, and I accept everything it offers me, even if pain is part of its gift, even if I must be the victim of things larger than myself." He offered himself to the watery element with an almost mythical acquiescence that was part and parcel of his gentle, laughing personality. Hal was a lover, not a fighter.

But tonight Tess could see something new in the picture, something that had always been part of its magic, but which had never been visible to her before. It was the fact that Laura had been behind the camera the day it was taken. The smile on Hal's face was for Laura, and not for an impersonal lens.

Tess alone knew this. Tess alone had heard Laura's ill-disguised version of what had happened, and how that fateful picture changed the course of her destiny and started her toward a career as a photographer.

I don't know whether it was the camera, or just falling in love. . . .

Because of her knowledge Tess saw a new beauty in the picture, and a new sadness as well. For Laura had lost Hal to Diana. And she had loved Hal with all her heart, a love whose depth Tess had since come to realize.

But there was even more. For now, many years after the picture had been taken, the world outside it had changed so as to add a further dimension to it. The resemblance between the young Hal in the picture and the little boy in Laura's exhibition was unmistakable. Thus the picture was more than a document of the fleeting miracle of a young man's boundless confidence. It was also, in view of later events, a statement about his virility, his fecundity.

Of course, Hal did not know about the boy, so this secret dimension of the image was visible only to Tess.

To Tess, and to Laura, if she were here . . .

Laura, who had lost Hal before any of the others, but found him in a way none of them had . . .

An involuntary tear came to Tess's eye as she realized that the essence of Hal was love. No woman could resist him. That was why this odd, almost magical picture had traveled from one Lancaster home to the next, and haunted all the women in his life.

It was Sybil who had had the picture blown up, Sybil who loved Hal with such a private passion and trusted him alone among the people she had known in her short unhappy life. And Sybil had given the picture to Diana to copy, for she knew that the picture bespoke a love of which Diana could never be the beneficiary. Such was Sybil's cruelty and her sense of irony.

And then it had been under that very image that Sybil, her charred fingers oblivious to normal human pain, had pronounced her oracle and her curse to Tess—*except one*—the curse that was to follow Tess all these years, and to lead her finally, unexpectedly, to Laura, the woman who had taken the picture.

Ask the fellow in the pool. Of course! Laura had been three feet from Sybil and Tess at that awful moment of revelation, hidden behind the picture, her presence reflected in Hal's smile as her camera had captured it. And Sybil must have known that, because Hal must have confided some or all of the truth to her about Laura and what she had meant to him.

Yes, the picture had been the talisman that joined them all together in their love for Hal, a love that could never be requited, but a love that could not die. The picture was love in the flesh, and the cool dark brutality of fate that separated human beings not only from each other, but from themselves, condemning each person to walk a path in the world that led away from the happiness he or she would have given anything to possess.

It had taken Laura's budding talent as a photographer to express that terrible, beautiful complexity in one image. But they had all lived it, in their struggles for happiness and in their desperate pursuit of Hal.

These thoughts so overwhelmed Tess that she got up and impulsively telephoned Hal's office again. When there was no answer she picked up the phone book, found the number of the maintenance department at the New Senate Office Building, and dialed it.

There were many rings before the phone was answered.

"Custodian."

"Roy, is that you? This is Bess Lancaster."

"Nice to hear your voice, Mrs. Lancaster. I saw your husband this evening."

"That's why I'm calling," Tess said. "I've been trying Hal's office, but there's no answer. I don't suppose you could check the corridor for me . . ."

"Don't have to, ma'am. The Senator is taking a swim. I saw him go downstairs a few minutes ago. You know him—he likes his fifty laps when he wants to think."

"Thank you, Roy. Thank you very much."

Tess hung up the phone. Her glance came to rest on the picture of Hal once more. The droplets of water clinging to his bare skin looked more than ever like tears. Woman's tears. Tears of loss, of renunciation. Laura's tears, certainly, for even at that precious moment, so many years ago, she must have realized that Hal was slipping through her fingers despite the great power of her love.

And Sybil's tears, and Diana's, too. For every woman who had loved Hal had lost him . . .

This thought stopped Tess short. She looked at the picture. A final truth, infinitely more sinister than the others, seemed to leap from it. The liquid element surrounding Hal in the photograph spoke suddenly of loss, of doom. She saw Hal recede from her, his smile engulfed by the dark water as her own tears coursed haplessly over his wounded body.

She thought of this terrible week, and of the evil that had been coiled around Hal for so long, keeping him away from her, and even out of phone contact with her. She had used all her strength to fight off the fate that seemed in store for him, and she had succeeded.

Or had she?

Had her victory come too easily? Perhaps Leslie Curran's tape had not been the final weapon. Perhaps the worst was yet to come. Perhaps a disaster Tess had not taken into her calculations was bearing down upon Hal at this very moment.

The Senator is taking a swim.

A nameless horror opened Tess's eyes as she looked at the picture. All at once the spell it had cast over her heart all these years seemed to crystallize into one monstrous idea. Perhaps the picture was not about the past alone, but about the future. Not about life, but about death.

Ask the fellow in the pool.

Shaking in every limb, Tess hurried from the room. She gathered up her purse in the kitchen, pulled out her car keys, and rushed out into the night.

XXIV

8:15 P.M.

DAN AGUIRRE stood in the kitchen, the telephone in his hand, speaking softly to an unknown interlocutor.

Laura was on the couch, watching Michael read a book and trying to keep from hugging him at every instant with her frozen hands. She felt like clinging to him as though he were a tiny buoy atop a dark heaving ocean.

"That's right," Aguirre's voice drifted in from the kitchen. "About six-three, 215. Thirty-eight years old. Did you show her the picture?"

A moment later he hung up, came to the doorway, and signed to Laura to join him.

"Your ex-husband is being smart," he said. "He hasn't registered at any hotel in New York or Washington. He's stayed away from the airlines, and hasn't rented a car. We're doing our best to check the train and bus personnel, but that's always the hardest. They see too many faces in a day to remember."

"What about Hal?" Laura asked.

"There are about two hundred FBI men converging on his Georgetown house, his Senate office, and every outpost of his campaign," he said. "They're going to call me the minute they get to him. It can't take long."

He looked down at her ashen face. He could feel the intensity of her dread. She looked like a ghost.

"Will they—tell Hal?" she asked.

"Their orders are to get to him and take extreme precautions until this is over," he said. "That's all."

He could read her thoughts. She did not want any harm to come to Lancaster. Nor did she want him to find out about any of this—including above all her little boy. She wanted Lancaster alive, but free to live his own life.

He touched her arm. She was trembling. He knew she was blaming herself for everything.

"Don't do this to yourself," he said quietly. "Don't try to take it all on your own shoulders. We can't change what's past. Remember, you've got a little boy to think about."

She looked up at him through eyes so wide with understanding that he nearly looked away.

"Hang on," he said. "It's only a matter of time."

But he knew what she was thinking.

Perhaps it was already too late.

XXV

8:25 P.M.

THERE WAS NO ONE in the pool.

The only senator who ever used it late in the day was Flynn of Florida, an octogenarian whose doctors prescribed a daily swim for his heart. But he was apparently already gone. Hal would have the pool to himself.

He dived in and did a fast five laps, then five more. The tension and frustration of the past week combined to drive him to a great spurt of energy. He wanted the coursing water to cleanse him of all the hours of airplane immobility, the accumulated worry and sweat of the campaign, and above all the debilitating fear he had endured for the last six days and nights.

The power of his arms pulling through the water felt good, as did the working of his legs. Out of breath already—for he had slept little this past week—he slowed down, and began chugging back and forth, lap after lap, with smooth rhythmic strokes.

He had always found that a solitary swim cleared his mind better than anything else. But tonight he was doing more than trying to clear his mind. He was trying to wash away the whole stubborn taint of politics—the sham, the illusion, the ugly mask of public relations shrouding the reality of human beings and history.

He had given his adult life to the political world. But he had never really chosen it spontaneously and wholeheartedly, as other men choose their careers. Fate had arranged things so that this arena of cameras and handshakes and banners and speeches must be his lot. And he had accepted this, because from the day he lost Laura he knew that the door to the other world was closed.

Strangely enough, this was why he was an effective public servant. The core of himself was not engaged in politics, but the shell, the armor, was all for his country. He could be more dispassionate and perhaps wiser than other politicians, for the very reason that the secret heart of him was not in the public arena. He could be calmer, for the political prizes were not the answer to his dreams.

But did not this very separateness of his mission disqualify him from the game, in some strange sense?

For years he had tried to tell himself that the effort to do good, to be selfless in the service of his country, could not possibly be wrong. But somehow this past week, with its withering undercurrent of fear—a fear he hated above all things, for his manhood would not countenance it— had tarnished the dream, cracked his armor. He wondered whether the very sacrifices of the journey he had embarked on were blinding him to the fact that it was all leading to no good end.

As he churned through the water Hal struggled with his own doubt. He could not abandon the idealism that had sustained him for so many years, simply because one awful week had sapped his courage for the battle. Nor could he suppress his suspicion that something had been missing all along in his vocation or in the commitment he brought to it.

Well, he decided, he would put it all up to Bess tonight. He would share his worries with her, and ask her to help him understand himself as well as the obstacles he faced. She would share her wisdom generously, as always.

Hal clung to this thought as he traversed the quiet pool, lap after lap, at once refreshed and exhausted by his exertion. Soon he would be alone with his wife, whose warm arms and soothing voice were the closest thing he knew to a haven from the world's stubborn perils.

He was lingering over this feeling of anticipation when he saw a man standing at the deep end of the pool.

XXVI

8:25 P.M.

AT THIS TIME OF NIGHT the drive from Georgetown in to the Capitol was no more than ten minutes.

Tess made it in less, running every stoplight she dared and barely noticing the other traffic around her. She shot down Virginia Avenue to Constitution, oblivious to the White House, the Mall, and the Washington Monument hurtling past her windows.

She double-parked in front of the New Senate Office Building and left the car door open as she rushed up the steps. She heard an echo of complaining car horns behind her, but paid no attention to it.

When she burst into the lobby of the office building the security guard was taken aback by the look on her face.

"I'm Mrs. Lancaster," she said, "My husband is downstairs in the pool. I must see him. Please . . . Where is it?"

"Ma'am, that's a private area. The public isn't allowed . . ."

"It's an emergency. He needs me. Important news . . . Please, come with me . . ."

She was clutching at his arm and actually pulling him along with her, though she did not know the way. The look in her eyes alarmed him.

"Ma'am, I can't . . ."

"Come on!" she hissed with sudden violence. "Don't you know who I am? I've got to find my husband."

He started to take off his hat, to rub his brow. "Well, you take the north elevator down to the second basement," he said slowly. "But they won't let you in, ma'am . . ."

She had flown from his side before he could finish.

She hurried into the elevator, pushed the B2 button, and waited in agony as the doors slowly closed. She counted the seconds as the elevator crawled downward.

When the door opened she saw an unfamiliar corridor before her. There was no sign, no indication of where the pool was.

She turned left and raced down the corridor. She turned a corner and came up short at the door to a storage area.

Cursing her ill luck, she turned around to retrace her steps. A security guard, apparently attracted by the sound of her running feet, loomed up before her. He was a young black man, hardly older than twenty. He seemed amazed by the sight of her.

"Where's the swimming pool?" she asked.

He hesitated, looking at her skeptically.

"I'm Mrs. Lancaster," she said. "My husband is in there. Senator Lancaster. I've got to find him immediately. It's urgent. Please, come with me. Hurry!"

The guard turned slowly to his left. She pulled at his arm, half leading, half begging to be led. Infected by her terrible urgency, he began to walk fast down the corridor. She hurried alongside him, taking three steps to his two, her breath coming short, her hair awry. Something was telling her that what stood between her and Hal was more than mere space and time. It was danger, the worst possible danger.

Like an ungainly pair of comic dancers Tess and the security guard plunged down the corridor, deep in the bowels of the place where laws were made, locked absurdly together by an anxiety neither of them could fathom.

At last they turned a corner to another hall at the end of which was a sign that read LOCKER ROOM.

"Hurry," she said as the guard pulled out his key. She saw the gun at his belt.

"Ma'am, you can't go in there," he started to say.

"Then *you* go in! But hurry!" She looked at him through eyes so wild that he unlocked the door and pushed it open.

She watched him move forward. He had not closed the door, so she rushed in behind him.

The locker room was empty. As she ran through it she heard a noise, a subterranean echo almost mythical in its vagueness. A melancholy sound . . .

Tess clutched at her chest. The breath seemed to fly from her, her heart to stop beating. Too late she realized what she should have feared all this time.

The guard was disappearing into the pool area, his gun in his hand. Already feeling the world poised to engulf her, Tess plunged forward to Hal.

XXVII

TIM SAW LANCASTER pause in the middle of the deep end. Despite the water flattening his hair and coursing down his face, Lancaster was easy to recognize. His expression was one of indifferent curiosity. He did not know who Tim was, or what was about to happen, or why.

So Tim tried to put all that he felt and all that he was into the look in his eyes as he glared down at the man treading water in the pool. He needed a sign of acknowledgment, some sort of contact man to man, before he sent this stranger to his fate.

He raised the gun.

Lancaster looked shocked for an instant. But then, to Tim's surprise, a rather gentle expression came into his dark eyes, and he looked up almost trustingly, his hands moving back and forth under the blue water. There was an acceptance in that look, and it made Tim hesitate.

But no, he thought. This is the devil's work. I am looking at the man who ruined Laura, the man who wrecked my life, stole my child.

Tim steeled himself. He pointed the gun and looked straight into those soft dark eyes. For a split second it was almost like looking into Laura's eyes; and this, also, seemed to drain away his strength.

But then he realized that he was, after all, contacting his victim as man to man, with respect, with mutual understanding of what was happening, and why it had to happen. This was the way it had been in the war, when he and his proud enemy took aim at each other. They were joined by a fate that was not of their own choosing, but a fate that they could take on as two men of the same flesh, the same spirit.

Two men joined by the same woman, and destroyed by her.

He wondered whether Lancaster had loved her as he himself did. He had heard so many stories about Lancaster's charm and his many conquests. Nevertheless, Laura had chosen him. That could not be without importance.

And those dark eyes in the water were capable of love. Tim could see that. And, seeing it, he felt his strength return.

Tim fired.

Hal saw the gun leap, and felt the blow strike him before he heard the crash echoing off the walls. His arm went limp. He must have been hit in the shoulder. Korea, and the feeling of being wounded, came back to him all at once. The muted shock, without pain, without struggle; the earth's sudden retreat as the body closed upon itself to keep the life inside.

The second bullet hit him in the middle of his chest and turned him around in the water. The stranger's face was gone.

For a long moment Hal saw nothing. Then the blue expanse of the water reared up before him, and behind it a red wall came forward, marching upon him with an odd solemnity, higher and higher.

He thought he heard more noises. Another shot, a woman's cry. But all he could see was the ocean of blue and the red wave coming forward to take him in its arms, hurrying him away toward something at once mysterious and familiar, something from the furthest reaches of his memory and the remotest horizons of the future.

A great sigh of yielding came over Hal as he sank under the water. This, then, was where his steps had been leading him all these years. This was the heart of the labyrinth, the light at the end of the tunnel.

Hal smiled as Stewart came to take his hand, Stewart the sunlit god of youth.

Come on, Short Stuff. Mom wants you.

Stewart's grin glowed all the brighter for the fact that it no longer needed life to illuminate it. It was a smile full of peace and an odd good humor.

As though the bit of life they had known was a great, great joke on them all—and the light at the end of the tunnel was the meaning of the joke, a meaning that made everything happy at last, and not at all painful.

As the redness spread through the water and behind Hal's eyes, he felt the tiny blonde hand of Sybil creep into his own, and join Stewart in this azure pulling that was neither up nor down, but simply away, away.

And Sybil's eyes were smiling, too—not with that bitter sinister smile that had darkened her face before she was five and stayed with her for the rest of her earthly life, but with the sweet and candid smile of her earliest youth, the smile of mischief and of love that was even now sparkling in Stewie's eyes.

Say goodbye, Prince Hal . . .

The words were no longer an accusation, but a welcome, whispered like a password to take him to the place where he was going, where they were all going together.

He could still hear the shouts, the frantic female cries and echoes, as from a long way off. And he turned, his hands fluttering softly in the sweet blue water, to look up through the waves at the vague forms above him.

He thought he saw the urgent crying face of Bess gazing down at him, a piteous look of unbearable pain and loss in her eyes.

But no. He was wrong. The red wall under the water had colored everything, and fooled him. Bess was not here. The face he saw was Laura's. And she was not in pain—she was smiling, holding out her hands, welcoming him with her lovely dark eyes.

Come here, handsome.

The look on her face was warm, gentle, infinitely happy. It came from that secret moment when they had both dreamed that their love could open the door to another world that would be theirs alone. And now, as though to reward him for all the terrible years on his own, she was beckoning him to come through the door with her. For it had never really been there in the past, but in the future all along.

How shortsighted human beings are, Hal realized. They pine for what is gone without understanding that it is still waiting for them in a place just beyond human sight.

Now he knew he would be with her at last. And that alone mattered. Her eyes reached out to him, telling him how foolish he had been all these years, to have wasted his life, when she was his all along, and would always be his.

But that was the joke whose meaning was sending waves of laughter in blue and red throughout this room, and across the wide earth outside it. Life was the cruelest joke of all if one clung to it, but a gentle and caressing song of welcome when one let it go.

Come here, handsome . . .

Hal felt the water turn him to her, felt her hand touch his brow, the cool fingers soothing and curing. He tried to smile, but his lips would not move. Thank heaven, though, the wave bore him into her arms.

Come here . . .

He floated further down, and she was beneath him now, beckoning and smiling as the waves brought them together. She had never looked so beautiful, or so happy. Hal thanked his lucky stars, for he had never dreamed his long journey alone might bring him back to her at last.

Come . . .

That was the last word he heard, and her face the last thing he saw.

XXVIII

9:00 P.M.

THE VIGIL SEEMED ENDLESS.

The boy was in bed now. Laura had read him a bedtime story, some-how managing her normal, lulling tone of voice despite the knife twist-ing inside her heart.

Detective Aguirre was sitting on the couch, looking at Laura. The television set was on, the sound turned down to the barest whisper.

Her eyes met those of the detective. Their look said all there was to say. She clasped her hands in her lap. Laura was not a religious woman; but what was going through her mind, over and over again, was indis-tinguishable from a prayer.

Hal.

Oh, my Hal.

Please be safe.

Please!

The moments passed like hours. Aguirre spoke from time to time, but his words sounded like a foreign language to her. She looked at him uncomprehendingly.

She felt like the helpless victim of cataclysmic events that were be-yond her power to prevent or alter. If Detective Aguirre's suspicions were correct, Tim was in Washington, stalking Hal with a maniacal determination whose force Laura knew all too well.

And Hal knew nothing about it.

And, most horrible knowledge to bear, it was all because of Laura.

Because she had dared to show her photographs of Michael to the world. Because the media had published Michael's image, and chance had brought that image to Tim's eyes. Because Tim had looked at the boy's face and found the answer to his hatred in it. Because Tim had come here, broken into this house, and found his way through Laura's thousands of photographs to the single image that could link Michael to Hal.

But it went further back than that. What was happening tonight had its roots in her weaknesses as a woman and as a person. It was happening because she had allowed herself to fall in love with Hal, to give him her whole heart, when she knew he belonged to another woman. And it was happening because she had, in her grief over Hal, allowed herself to believe she loved Tim and could make him happy, when deep inside she knew her heart was no longer hers to give.

And, most of all, it was happening because fate had made her cross Hal's path that one last time, and because on that wintry night she had been weak enough, needful enough, selfish enough perhaps, to steal a child from him.

Laura looked back on her whole life to its very beginnings, wondering which of the many turns of her fate was the first cause behind this disaster, and what might have prevented it. If she had not decided to make her boy's pictures part of the exhibition . . . If she had not taken those fatal pictures of Hal in the first place . . . If, one day long ago, she had not delivered those dresses to Diana's house and met Hal there by chance . . . If, even longer ago, Tim Riordan had not mounted the stairs to her tenement apartment to pick up his sister's clothes . . .

The list was endless, and more painful the longer she lingered over it. A list of seemingly innocent first causes that brought unforeseen effects years and years later.

How wrong we are, Laura thought, to believe that time moves only forward, leaving actions and events in the past to be forgotten. The truth is that we bathe in an ocean in which the past and future swirl around us wildly, intermingling and altering each other at every turn, so that the tiniest decision, made and forgotten a lifetime ago, can suddenly take on a terrible, fateful significance.

With her hands clasped in the only imitation of a prayer that her body knew, Laura waited.

The phone rang at nine-thirty.

Dan Aguirre was on his feet instantly.

"Aguirre," he said into the receiver.

His face fell as he listened to the unseen caller. His fist clenched about the receiver.

"When was this exactly?" he asked in a low voice.

He paused, listening to the details.

"You're sure about . . . ?"

The question was unnecessary. The caller was sure.

Aguirre put the phone down. He turned around to look into the living room.

The program playing on television had been interrupted. The words SPECIAL REPORT were on the screen.

As he paced slowly toward the set Aguirre saw the smiling image of Haydon Lancaster appear. At the same instant he heard a strange muted cry unlike anything he had ever heard before. It was at once soft and piercing, delicate and fatal.

Laura was curled up on the couch. All the color had drained from her face. She was completely still. Aguirre had seen many dead people in his years as a policeman, but none had looked more lifeless than the tiny creature before him.

He touched her shoulder. She seemed as cold as the grave. She did not feel his touch. The single terrible cry had died on her lips, and she was silent.

"I'm sorry," he murmured.

She did not hear him. Her deathlike indifference so alarmed him that he dared to feel her pulse. To his relief her heart was still beating.

Suddenly he remembered the phone. He strode quickly across the room and picked it up.

"Are you still there?" he asked.

The caller had not hung up.

"You're sure that Riordan is dead, too?" he asked. "What about the wife? Where is she?"

He listened to the answers.

"All right," he said. "I'm coming there. I'll get a chopper. I'll see you in an hour."

He hung up the phone, thought for a moment, and dialed.

His own precinct answered.

"Give me the Chief of Detectives," he said. "This is Aguirre."

He could hear confusion in the background. When the chief answered, his voice betrayed that he had heard the news.

"Listen," Aguirre said. "I need to go to Washington right away. And I want someone to come over here, a policewoman, to stay with Miss Blake. I'll leave that to you. All right?"

He hung up the phone and turned to look at Laura. She was shriveled up on the couch, motionless. She seemed shrunk to half her own small size.

Part of the detective himself seemed to die at the sight of her. But there was no time to linger over his own emotion.

He had things to do.

XXIX

TESS LAY IN HER BED in the Georgetown house.

Her right hand reached out instinctively for Hal. Too late she recalled that he was not there, would never be there again.

She let her hand fall to the spread and closed her eyes.

She had been given a powerful sedative by the doctor who had been brought by the FBI. But the doctor did not know that over these difficult years Tess had accustomed herself to many drugs. She was wide awake and alert.

The horror inside her was too bottomless to confront now. But Tess's quick mind was working overtime.

She knew that, in all the essential ways, the thing that had happened tonight was the end of her. This knowledge gave her calm, and with it a new cunning.

It was time for her to undertake the final actions that would bring her spiritual life on the planet—if not her physical existence—to a close. She had to do the necessary things. Once they were done, she could retire to oblivion, to prison, to wherever, and know that the loose ends were all tied up.

She had heard the murmurs of the police and federal agents in the living room all this time. They were talking about the man in the pool, the man who had killed Hal, and at the same time deciding what to tell the press.

They thought they knew what had occurred in that swimming pool tonight.

But they did not know why, and they never would.

Tess alone knew the why of everything, now that it was too late to stop it.

And this knowledge armed her for what she must do now.

Tess got quietly to her feet. Daintily, cautiously, she padded to the closet and looked for something to wear.

She found a simple gray suit, put it on over her slip, and went into the bathroom. She made herself up hastily, returned to the bedroom, and got her biggest purse out of the closet.

Inside it, where she had left it several years ago, was a small gun. She took out the clip, made sure it was fully loaded, and put it back in the purse. Then, on an afterthought, she took two large bottles of pills from the medicine cabinet and put them in the purse as well.

She locked the bedroom door from the inside, turning the bolt silently. She checked her wallet for cash, put on a spring coat, and turned to the window.

Naturally there were reporters and policemen outside. But they were gathered at the front door, waiting for a statement.

The side alley between this house and the next one was dark. It was, after all, the middle of the night.

Tess carefully opened the window all the way. She slid through, the purse in her hand, and closed the window behind her.

Now she tiptoed down the alley. She knew that in another block she would reach Wisconsin Avenue, from which she could find her way easily to a cab stand.

Once safely inside a taxi, she was in the clear. Her mission was a delicate one, but she had no doubt she would carry it through.

She would get to New York before they could stop her.

XXX

3:45 A.M.

LAURA DID NOT KNOW what time it was.

The night was working its way slowly through its darkest hours. She had left the lights on in the living room, and the television, which was silent, for the volume was turned all the way down.

Laura was in her son's bedroom. Only the projection from the night-light illuminated the walls. The pixie face of Felix the elf colored the shadows on the ceiling, dim but triumphant, an image that could make any physical obstacle into part of itself.

She was on her knees beside the bed, watching Michael sleep. His breathing was gentle, almost inaudible. His mouth was slightly open, his hair tousled against the pillow. He wore pale blue pajamas. His baby blanket was in his arms.

Laura thought about his complete unawareness of the events that had happened tonight, events that formed a tangled web around his own existence, events she would do everything in her power to keep from him as long as she lived.

His father was dead, murdered by the man who had once been his mother's husband. A man who could not forgive Laura for having borne this boy, and who, had it not been for the chance intervention of two photographs, might well have turned the terrible force of his wrath on Michael himself.

Laura watched the sweet, natural rhythm of the young life in sleep. Ever since she was a girl she had been moving toward this moment and this opportunity—a mother's opportunity to protect her child, to keep him from the harm that can come from truths as well as people. Out of her own broken heart now flowed the determination to make sure that this boy had the benefit of all her love and all her strength from now on.

And he must never know. Never.

A curious sensation coursed through Laura as she watched her son. The cold center of her, scarred by the loss of Hal, was forcing itself to heal in order to love his son the better. Grief mingled wrenchingly with love inside her breast.

And a curious phrase, coming from the furthest reaches of her memory, echoed at the back of her mind.

Even beyond death, you will give him what he wants above all things. If you accept this pain . . .

Laura's whole past was gathered around her now, from her earliest rainy day thoughts, the thoughts that opened the door to a world beneath the world, all the way to the images that now hung in the Museum of Modern Art, and to the terrible news that had stared at her from the television screen tonight.

She could feel a confused unity in her life, a sort of nameless coherence, a sense that, if she were much wiser and possessed of a much deeper vision, she would understand that it could not have turned out any other way.

But her heart was not made for such cool wisdom, such detachment. She only knew that Hal was dead, and his child alive.

She was pondering this thought, rocking softly back and forth on her knees as she watched the boy—when she heard a knock at the apartment door.

She assumed it was the policewoman Detective Aguirre had called for before he left. Hours had passed since then. No doubt the police had been slow to follow through on Dan's request, in all the confusion of tonight's events.

Laura padded out of the room, closed the door quietly, and went to the front door.

She opened it a crack, and saw the face of Bess Lancaster. It bore a mask of grief, with an odd, urgent glitter in the beautiful green eyes.

Without a word Laura opened the door. The other woman came in and stood looking around the loft. The wildness in her eyes was over-laden by an enormous fatigue. She was obviously drained, and was operating on some instinct beyond human strength.

Laura wondered how she had got away from Washington and come all the way here. But she did not ask. This woman had lost her husband tonight, and Tim had killed him. It was up to Bess to say what she wanted.

She stood looking at the pictures of Michael on the walls. Then she turned to Laura.

"It was you all along, wasn't it?" she asked.

Laura could not think of an answer. She weighed the words, and saw the look in Bess's eyes. And she thought of Hal.

"Won't you come in and sit down?" she asked.

Like a sleepwalker Bess came to the couch where the forgotten TV was still on. Laura came to sit down opposite her.

Once again Tess felt the spell cast by Laura's small body and great dark eyes, the mystery of this tiny woman who had owned Hal's heart.

I am a novice at loving, Tess mused. Hal had introduced her to the cruel magic of love, after she had subsisted happily without it for a whole lifetime. But Laura's heart was as deep as the earth itself. That was plain to see in her photographs as well as her face.

And something else was also visible to Tess now. In looking at Laura she could actually see a shadow of Hal himself, of the soft melancholy look that sometimes danced at the back of Hal's eyes when his mood was caught between humor and wistfulness. Perhaps Laura was more than just the woman he had loved; perhaps she was the repository of that part of himself that had never belonged entirely to him, that had never found its home in his fate on earth.

For a moment Tess forgot her own agony, and her heart went out selflessly to Hal. How empty Hal must have felt all these years! Exile from Laura must have been like a slow-motion starvation to him. His wives, Diana first and Bess afterward, must have seemed like alien creatures beside whom he slept, shadows that could not warm his soul.

But Hal had done his best. He was a hero. And now Tess realized that this fragile creature, this Laura, was a hero, too. She possessed a special kind of strength, a kind that belonged only to women—the strength to endure the most terrible of losses and still be able to love.

Tess had never bothered to seek that strength within herself, and never known until much too late that she might need it one day.

She smiled.

"Did you know," she said, "that you and I were born on the same day?"

Laura shook her head. She said nothing.

"It was your husband who killed him," Tess said emptily.

"I know," Laura said.

"It was because of the boy, wasn't it?" Tess's voice was cool. It was more a statement than a question.

Laura nodded. Her eyes were cast down despairingly.

Tess turned to look at the photographs on the walls. Their eloquence brought her a strange calm.

"You know," she said without looking at Laura, "the world is such a riddle. I spent so much of my life fighting for things that weren't worth having. Things that were . . . nothing. Like those boys of ours who get themselves shot to pieces in Vietnam fighting for hills that are just numbers on a map, only to abandon them as soon as they've conquered them. It's all such a waste. A silly waste . . ."

She sighed. "Yet I believed in that fight all those years . . . Or did I? Maybe I guessed from the beginning what a mistake it all was. But I just didn't know what else to do with myself. So I made believe it was worthwhile, made believe it was leading somewhere . . ."

She gazed at the pictures, realizing that it had all led here to this room. She smiled to see herself surrounded by Laura's photos of human beings, each of whom, like Tess herself, plodded stubbornly down a road he deemed the only one for him, even if, underneath, he suspected that the mask he wore and the road he traveled could never lead to happiness, but could only take him farther and farther away from the only destination that might have brought him peace.

Laura, as no other artist, had managed to capture that mistake in the face of the human creature, and also the tragic dignity with which he pursued an elusive goal that receded a little more each day. In all Laura's faces one saw that fatigue, that endurance, and also the tiny ghost of a smile which proved that the human being divined, somewhere inside himself, that the joke was on him.

Wasn't that what it was all about? That ghost of a smile, which was never more eloquently incarnated than in Hal's face?

She turned to Laura, who had not moved.

"Tell me, please," Tess asked. "The little boy . . . When did you . . .?"

"It was a chance meeting," Laura said quietly. "Years after we had known each other. In the Park . . ." She saw the stricken look on Tess's face. "When I spoke to you at the exhibition, I wasn't really lying. I knew him for such a short time . . . It was before he married Diana. When he met you, I was all in the past. And I never came back. Do you believe that?"

Tess smiled. She knew Laura was trying to reassure her that she had been truly married to Hal, had been his woman. But Tess knew better, and had always known. There was no point in denying the obvious— that no woman but Laura herself had really possessed any part of Hal.

She shook her head. "I don't blame you," she said. "You didn't do anything wrong. How can love be wrong?"

She looked into the dark eyes, feeling more peaceful now. She knew she had to absolve Laura first. She must make Laura understand that jealousy was far from her mind tonight.

But now she looked down in surprise to see that the gun was in her hand. It was pointed at Laura's heart, just as the husband's gun, in the pool, had pointed at Hal's heart.

Laura saw it, too. She did not flinch. The changing images of the late movie on the TV cast vague shadows on Tess's face.

"It has to end somewhere," Tess said. "You can see that, can't you? It has to end somewhere. It can't just go on and on . . ."

Tess began to raise the gun. It seemed to move with a will of its own, as though held by a stranger. She felt marvelously removed from this scene. Only the cold steel of the trigger reminded her she was still on earth, still capable of making things happen.

Then, suddenly, a small voice rang out between the two women.

"Mommy?"

Laura's eyes turned to take in the boy. He was standing at the entrance to the living room, sleepy-eyed in his pajamas, his blanket in his hand.

Tess hid the gun in her lap.

"What's the matter?" Laura smiled, holding out her arms to the boy. "Did you have a bad dream?"

He nodded, coming forward to bury his face in his mother's breast without looking at her guest. He murmured a few words which Tess could not make out—the private admission of need that links a boy to his mother.

Laura kissed him and ran a hand through his hair. The hand came to rest on his hip as she whispered in his ear. Tess could see that his pajamas bore a pretty little appliqué, perhaps a bunny. His dark hair was like Laura's, and like Hal's.

"That's my brave boy," she heard Laura conclude. "I'll come and tuck you in. And remember: that monster is a lot more scared of you than you are of him. I know. That's why monsters look so mean. Because they're scared, and they can't show it."

He turned to draw her away with him. But suddenly, still protected in the crook of her arm, he looked through his sleepy eyes at Tess.

Tess gazed down at him in astonishment. How handsome he was! And what strength showed through behind those sensitive eyes. This tiny mild creature was the embryo of a man, the seed of that proud race that walked the earth with their eyes full of their quests and their burdens—while women desperate for their love pursued them with wiles almost clever enough to outwit fate. Women smart enough to fool them into anything but a love they did not feel.

Handsome, heedless race, Tess mused. Why had the capricious gods put them on earth to taunt women with hearts they could not own?

But now the grave little eyes were upon her, innocent and trusting even as they measured her foreignness.

"Michael," Laura said gently, "I want you to meet someone. This is Mrs. Lancaster. She's . . ." Laura hesitated, searching for her words. "She's my friend," she concluded.

The boy looked at Tess. She saw his oval chin, the fine brows and lips, and the eyes, dark and complicated, which would be his most salient feature. Eyes that seemed to join his mother and father across the years, weaving their separate fates together in one glimmering fabric of pure light.

How innocent he was! Innocent of all the people who had made him, of all the things that had happened, the dreams and plans and loves and losses that he would never know about.

He seemed to contain a whole race, this pretty little creature. The tributaries of the past flowed into his flesh, and thence toward a future he would make for himself, a future echoing with voices and faces and people yet to come, but all of them bearing the trace of the mystery that had made him.

And Tess saw, somewhere in that throng, herself. After all, none of them had loved this boy's father more desperately than she.

With that thought, all the pain and confusion in her mind moved backward a step, eclipsed by something nameless that approached.

"Would you like to shake her hand?" Laura asked the boy.

He came forward slowly, still holding the blanket, and held out a small hand. Tess let go of the gun in her lap and shook his hand.

She felt faint as his flesh touched hers. It seemed as though Hal was alive again in this soft miniature man's hand. As though what had happened tonight was not real after all, not real in the most final and important way. As though there was hope, hope for them all, hope for the world, because of this tender bit of human flesh that leapt from the lost past and led the way toward the future, borne by their collective hearts to something bigger even than death.

"Mrs. — ?" he said questioningly.

"My name is Elizabeth," she said with a sidelong glance at Laura. "But you can call me Tess if you like. I won't mind."

He smiled. "Tess," he said.

He held her hand for another second as he looked up into her eyes. Then he turned to his mother, eager for bed.

"Come on," Laura said as he came to her side. "I'll tuck you in."

Tess watched in silence, her hand on the gun, as they left the room. All at once an odd clarity had come to her thoughts. Laura was a fine, loving mother. The boy would be safe with her.

As for Hal, he was lying in the morgue tonight, being prepared for a burial in the cold earth among the heroes of the nation he had served so valiantly. But would he be at home among them? Had the world of men ever been his natural habitat?

He must not lie alone. That would be unfair to him, unfair to them all.

Of course, Tess thought. All her life she had belonged nowhere. But tonight, at last, she knew where her true place was.

In the bedroom the boy lay under his covers, very sleepy, but determined to savor his mother's presence before she left him.

Laura tucked him in and kissed his cheek.

"Who is that lady?" he asked.

Laura smiled. "One day I'll tell you all about her," she said. "She's very important to you. Sort of like an aunt—but closer than that. You see, she and I have traveled very different paths in life. But they crossed when you came along."

"Me?"

She sighed, running a finger along his brow. "In a way, yes," she said. "If I weren't your mother, she would be. There's no name for a relationship like that. But it's real, nevertheless."

"But you're my mother," he said, needing to be reassured.

"Oh, yes," Laura said, bending to hug him close. "Just me, handsome."

"Are the monsters gone?" he asked, changing the subject.

"Yes," she murmured. "And they won't come back for a long, long time. Not until you're a big strong man. And they won't scare you then. They'll be like children to you. You'll feel sorry for them, and pat them on the head to make them feel less afraid. Until then, though, I think they'll have to wait."

Mystified by her words, he looked up at her.

"I love you," he said.

"I love you, too," she said. "Have pleasant dreams."

His eyes fluttered closed. She looked at the long lashes, and saw sleep begin to cast its magic lantern over his features, just as the familiar face of Felix hovered on the ceiling. She let him slip away, musing that whatever might happen, he would be all right. There were too many people inside his tiny body to be extinguished by any danger that life could place in his path. They would see him through to the end.

She got up and moved to the door. She turned to look at him for a last time. She felt no more fear.

She heard the shot as she was reaching for the doorknob.

XXXI

*Arlington National Cemetery
May 3, 1964*

Our Father, we pray You to accept the soul of this hero who braved so many enemies in the service of his nation, and who gave his physical life as valiantly as he had given of his great intellect and loyalty, for the sake of his countrymen . . .

And we pray You to take as well the soul of his loving wife, Elizabeth, who chose to join him in death rather than to continue living in a world she could no longer share with him. We ask You to forgive her for the violence she did to herself in ending her life, and to reward her devotion with redemption and eternal peace. May she lie forever beside the man she loved.

THE SERVICE WAS OVER. The military color guard stood by the two caskets, each draped in an American flag, as the mourners were allowed to pass before them.

A hushed calm seemed to hang over the cemetery. The day was sunny and crisp, as though some governing power had decided to accept Bess and Hal into the hereafter with shining trumpets and angelic smiles. The Capitol building where Hal had toiled for over five years shimmered in the distance, along with the Washington Monument, the Lincoln Memorial, and the crowded old buildings in which the heart of democracy beat its youthful song.

Thousands of mourners were lined up, their ranks extending as far as the eye could see. They moved slowly past the coffins, dropping flowers, murmuring a word or two, many with tears in their eyes, others pale and stricken.

Laura was holding Michael by the hand. They both carried flowers. She wore a simple black dress she had made for the occasion. Michael was wearing a little suit and tie she had bought for him. His hair, combed carefully for the occasion, fluttered in the breeze coming off the Potomac.

Laura felt her knees go weak as she approached the coffins. She held hard to her son's hand and bit her lip to steady herself.

There was only a moment to pause, for thousands of people were behind them, moving slowly forward to pay their respects.

"Throw your flower with the others," Laura whispered to Michael.

He looked up at her, perplexed by the solemnity of the occasion.

"And say goodbye," Laura added. "These people were very close to you. Say goodbye, and try to remember this moment, forever and ever. Will you do that for me?"

She saw him throw the flower and watched his little lips form the farewell whose significance he would never know.

And she saw Hal in his face.

Now it was Laura's turn. She knew that time was short. Hal's earthly body was only inches from her hand. Beside it lay Tess, who had got her wish. She would lie beside him for eternity. Laura hoped that in this way Tess could regain what she had wanted so desperately of Hal, and not found in life.

Laura fixed her mind hard on the inert flesh inside this coffin, for she wanted to measure and accept the fact that Hal was gone forever. The earth would know his smile no more. His voice would come no more to soothe others' fears, to speak of sweet things and happy times. Laura would never again be able to muse in her solitude that somewhere in this world he was living his life, perhaps finding happiness, and carrying the memory of her in his heart.

In that brief second the tears came freely to her eyes, and she understood that this most fugitive of men, and most beautiful, had slipped through her fingers at last.

Yet, in the heart of her grief, she felt something else as well. The earthly corpse of the man whom she had loved with her whole heart could not serve as his sole memorial, for he had never wholly inhabited it as other men do. Hal was a being who was never at peace in the life he lived, whose spirit leapt and glimmered in a thousand fragments that escaped the narrow road he trod, each of them disappearing down forbidden and shadowed paths Hal himself was never able to follow to their end.

And Laura had known him in one of those secret places. Long ago she had accepted the fact that she could never have him in the everyday way a woman longs for a man. But only recently had she begun to understand that her belonging with him was on another level.

Some crossings, fugitive as shooting stars, are eternal. Was that not what the medium had told her so long ago, when Laura was a girl at Coney Island, blissfully unaware of what lay ahead of her?

Because of you, eternity will be his. If you accept this pain . . .

Laura understood now. Her love for Hal had never been a match for the separation that took him from her. But that was exactly the price for what she had of him. Her first photograph of him had proclaimed this harsh and beautiful truth, though she had not been able to comprehend it at the time.

So she looked at the two coffins, and was glad that they were together. She wanted to share him with Tess now, as the world had shared him with Laura herself.

"Goodbye," she murmured, sending her words into the imponderable ether where they would abide now, the place where past and future joined in a convergence that the human creature could never see or touch during his busy, driven lifetime, but which was nevertheless the light behind his searching eyes, and the only place capable of taking him to its breast when human time had run out.

So the tenderest of smiles touched her lips as she dropped the flower to send them both on their way.

Goodbye, my heart.

EPILOGUE

New York
May 3, 1964

THAT EVENING LAURA was back at home, having taken a crowded plane with Michael, many of the passengers being mourners who had journeyed to Arlington National Cemetery for the funeral.

Though drained by the day, Laura was keeping up a brave front for the boy, who was quite naturally confused about the significance of their journey and the emotion he had seen on so many faces in Washington, including Laura's own.

"Now," she said, "I think we both need cheering up. So let's make a pizza, and put on some music, and have a lovely little dinner, just the two of us, before we go to bed and get ready for tomorrow."

"Can Alfalfa help?" Michael asked.

"Alfalfa can help," she nodded. "Now, I'm going to roll the dough. And while I do that, you can set the table and get out the cheese."

He busied himself finding the napkins and silverware while Laura got out the dough.

The phone rang as she had the rolling pin in her hand.

"Hello?"

"This is Dan Aguirre."

There was a pause. Laura had not counted on contact from the outside world tonight. But the detective's voice was not unwelcome, for he alone knew everything, and understood what today meant to her.

"I'm just calling to see how you're doing," he said.

"Fine," she assured him. Hearing the hollow tone in her own voice, she laughed. "Really, we're fine. Thank you for asking."

"How is Michael?" She could hear genuine concern in Aguirre's voice.

"Wonderful," she said. "We're taking care of each other."

"I hope the funeral didn't upset him."

"I don't think so," she said with a glance at the boy. "He's made of strong stuff."

"Children have to be," Aguirre said. "If only we adults could borrow some of that . . ."

"Yes . . ." Laura held the phone in the crook of her shoulder while she looked in the refrigerator. But it was hard to concentrate. She forgot what she was looking for, at last closed the door, and leaned back against the counter.

"And you?" he asked.

There was a pause. The presence of that deep voice on the other end of the line seemed to sap the brittle courage that had been keeping Laura going these past days, and made her want to collapse into his own strength, to let him support her now as he had tried to do at her worst moment, three nights ago. But she reminded herself that she was on her own now, and this slim backbone was all she had to lean on.

"I'm okay," she said.

"Well," the voice resumed uncomfortably, as though sensing her resolve. "I just wanted to touch base with you. I . . ."

"Thank you," she said, a soft smile on her lips. "It was nice of you."

Again there was a silence. Somehow it did not embarrass her, for it joined her to him as well as words could.

"May I call you some time?" he asked. "Just to see how you're doing . . ."

The smile lingered about her lips.

"I'd like that," she said.

"Thank you, Laura. Goodbye, then."

"Goodbye, Dan."

She hung up the phone and went to the living room, where, on an impulse, she turned on the TV. It was news time. The faces of Hal and Bess were on the screen, for the funeral was the networks' top story.

Tears started out in Laura's eyes. She had thought the news report would comfort her somehow, but the image of Hal's face brought grief welling up unbearably inside her.

She would have given in to it had it not been for the little voice that sounded in her ear, eclipsing the murmur of the network commentator.

"Mommy, are you sad?"

It was Michael. He had seen her emotion, and it scared him. But there was something else in his dark eyes now. It was a man's determination to protect and comfort her.

"Yes, honey. I'm sad." She hugged him close, pain distorting her smile of gratitude that he was with her and would not leave her.

"Because of the man who died?" he asked. "And the lady?"

She nodded, kissing his forehead.

She felt him pat her shoulder, the small hand doing its best to reverse the roles and play parent long enough to soothe her anguish.

"I'll make you feel better," he said. "I'll cheer you up."

She held him out at arm's length. Behind his little face was Hal's image, projected on the TV screen. The smile that had captivated a nation was mirrored strangely in the soft black eyes fixed on her now.

"All right," she said. "But are you a good cheerer-upper? There are monsters inside of me. Can you make them go away?"

He nodded.

"They don't mean any harm," he said. "They want you to pat them on the head."

Laura nodded, tears glistening in her eyes.

"All right," she said. "We'll watch over them together, you and I. And we'll give them a happy house to live in, so they won't be scared anymore."

With Hal still projected behind him, Michael suddenly put both hands over his eyes and smiled at her.

"Who's that behind that mask?" she asked. "I can't see you."

"But I see you," he said.

She let her hands rest on his little hips and gave him a smile full of agony and relief. Yes, the words bore an odd comfort. She was not alone.

"Peek-a-boo," she heard his voice as Hal's face faded from the screen. "I see you."